Of Thorns and Curses

THE EALDSPELL CYCLE BOOK 3

JESIKAH SUNDIN

Dystopian Fantasy and Faerie Tales

Text and Cover Design/Illustration

Of Thorns and Curses
Copyright © 2022 Jesikah Sundin
All rights reserved.

ISBN-13: 978-1-954694-11-8
ISBN-10: 1-954694-11-3

Printed in the United States of America

Printed in the United States of America

Forest Tales Publishing
PO Box 84
Monroe, WA 98272
foresttalespublishing@gmail.com

All rights reserved. No part of this publication may be reproduced, stored in a retrieval system, or transmitted in any form or by any means – for example, electronic, mechanic, photocopy, recording or otherwise – without the prior written consent of the publisher. The only exception is brief quotations in printed reviews.

This book is a work of fiction. Names, characters, places, and incidents are the product of the author's imagination or are used fictitiously. Any resemblance to actual events, locales, or persons, living or dead, is coincidental.

Cover design by MoorBooks Designs
Interior design by Forest Tales Publishing

To all the women who march for social justice. And to all the men who empower our revolution

KINGDOM O

Erin Sea

Dreglind

Avenbury

Perla Tower

Merenna

Aurelie

Leaf

The Wilds

1. Burn Fields
2. Dwarven Mine
3. The Wilds
4. Caerenn Marsh
5. Astridian Coast
6. River Elvu
7. Bielyn River
8. Gabaston / Factory Row
9. The Remnants
10. The Pools of Perla Mist

EALDSPELL

Glenashlen

4

Spired Hills

5

Clifstan

2 Dwarven Mines

3

5

Erin Sea

Erin Sea

N
W E
S

WELCOME

KINGDOM OF EALDSPELL

Dear Reader,

Welcome to Ealdspell, a kingdom of standalone stories as old as time. A faerie kingdom hidden deep within a Druid's sacred oak tree, on a mere leaf. And welcome to OF THORNS AND CURSES, my *Beauty and the Beast* meets *Little Red Riding Hood* retelling set in a French Revolution inspired faerie tale world.

In case you were curious: the realms within Ealdspell each feature a completely different era in history with dystopian feels. They're also entirely influenced by Ireland, Scotland, Wales, England, Iceland, Norway, France, and Germany. The faerie tale lands of yore. And why some names and words may seem strange. I love Celtic, Anglo-Saxon, and Norse/Germanic names. *happy sighs*

While reading OF THORNS AND CURSES, if you're unsure of how to pronounce a word or what a word may mean, merrily skip to the end of the book and enjoy the:

Page 543. . . Cast of Characters with pronunciations
Page 549 . . . Glossary of Ealdspell Terms.

Though, here's a quick odd-pronunciation list for this story:

    Addien – Awe-dee-ehn
    Aurelienne – Oo-rell-ee-ehn

Benoit – Ben-wuah
Chateau Lumière Dorée – shah-toe / loom-ee-air / door-ee
Clifstán – Cliff-stawn
Dalbréath – Dal-bray-ith
Dúnælven – Dune-al-ven
Ealdspell – Awld-spell
Éireanna – Air-ran-uh
Fentienne – Fen-TEE-ehn
Mattieu – Matt-eww
Mon douce puce – Moan / doo-ss / pew-ss
Mon Père Michel – Moan / pear / me-shell
Mon petit caneton – Moan / pet-eet / can-ih-tun
Mon petit louveteau – Moan / pet-eet / lew-v-toe
Palais d'Aurélie – Pal-ay / dih / oo-rell-ee
Rhoslyn – Ross-lin

The rest should be easier to figure out. And, if not *gestures to cast of characters link above*

A few other goodies at the end of the book:

Page 524 . . . Historical Notes
Page 553 . . . More Books by Yours Truly
Page 555 . . . Etsy Shop (or use the QR code)

Grab your favorite drink and snack, put up your feet, and enjoy this gritty spin on the romantic tale of *Beauty and the Beast*. A story woven with faerie magic, pagan ritual, and French Revolution history . . .

Happy reading!

"He who makes a beast out of himself gets rid of the pain of being a man."

Dr. Suess

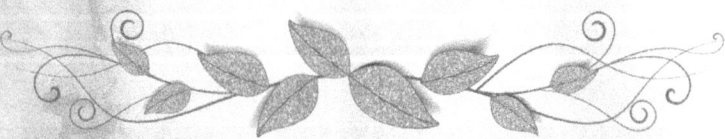

PROLOGUE

The Boy and the Wolf

The boy crept into the night-darkened woods, careful to mask every boot step until he was no longer within earshot of the barracks. Only another five yards or so and he would be in the clear. An owl hooted in a branch above him, and he eyed the bird's all-seeing gaze while quietly moving past.

The pack of food in the boy's hand jostled against his leg. The scent of sliced roast beef, apple carrot cake, oat bread, and boiled potatoes filled the night air around him. Thankfully, the aroma didn't alert the patrols. Slipping past those soldiers was always easy. Most spent their shift smoking cigarettes and chatting away the night with their patrol partner. A few even found dark corners to kiss their sweethearts who snuck onto the base at night—exactly what the boy had done during one of his shifts. Well, several shifts. There was no better cure for boredom than the adrenaline rush of clandestine kissing.

Especially because there was nothing really to guard except one's own reckless behavior.

No one had invaded Myrefell in his lifetime. No one had attempted to take the king's life either.

Every day was one boring day after another. Endless days filled with drills. Required obedience to one's uppers. Physical pain for failing expectations of military precision. Assignments to battlefields in Aurelienne soaked with so much blood the trenches gashed the land in a putrefying wound that would never heal. What exactly was there to live for save one's pursuits of pleasure? If not for fleeting moments of feeling something other than an abyss of apathy and animosity—the only two prided emotions at Myrefell—the boy would drown himself in drink. There was still time for that if the king continued to clip his angry wings.

Truly, there was an art form to striding through life in blasé disdain—caring for nothing to the point of despondency while caring so much that every word and thought sank their sharp teeth into one's carefully formed thick skin.

He peered over his shoulder, relieved when he could no longer see the barracks. Sneaking away from his platoon was much harder than the patrols. The cots creaked and footsteps, no matter how soft, echoed in the brick building. Even if a fellow soldier saw him leave, they wouldn't report him to a commanding officer. Or worse, the king—his father.

The boy had no delusions they kept silent out of any sense of loyalty, though. Tearing down one another for promotion and favor was a daily game at Myrefell. Even if one's target was a prince. But he made sure he was feared by all the young men while remaining an object of desire to all the young women. The latter being a continual thorn in his father's side.

The boy's free hand curled into a fist and he ground his teeth.

He would continue to be a thorn too.

Yesterday, his father had reprimanded him before an assembly with new rules: now that his third-born son was well within his sixteenth year, he was to refrain from dance halls or from speaking to any village girl who wandered onto Myrefell's military base.

Kissing wasn't speaking, he would point out if caught again. The poor girl was mortified when his commanding officer found them behind the trees while he was on duty. She would recover. He, however, never would.

His brothers had no such restrictions, not even his younger brother who was despised by his family. They each could do as they pleased with whomever they pleased. But *he* had been betrothed at the age of four to Maeline Kadelaryn Wyndham, the princess of the western realm of Avenbury.

To an elf.

A creature.

All to secure a trade agreement for cotton.

And to ensure the next King Consort of Avenbury remained a warrior, who would govern their military according to their laws.

As the third-born, he was expendable. A prince who would never become King of Clifstán. He was destined to either die in his father's war. Or die from the humiliation of being sold off as the crown's property to the

highest bidder.

Betrothals were archaic. Though his father's method was far more barbaric.

Queen Loriette Chalamet of Aurelienne, his mother, was stolen from her birthday celebration in the middle of the night. She was then forced into wedlock with the King of Clifstán as a power move to reclaim a throne that once belonged to his father's family—the House of Beausoleil. The once revered Realm of Gold's Sun Kings. Her younger brothers were killed right before her eyes, only her sister spared—to become a backup should the Queen of Aurelienne disappoint her new husband.

The king disgusted the boy.

Everything about this situation disgusted the boy.

An elf.

He was to *marry an elf*.

An inhuman race his realm loathed. A girl he wouldn't meet until their wedding day when he was twenty-two and she eighteen.

Even more infuriating, he was promised to a girl nobody had seen since she was two days old. The princess was hidden away after a faerie attempted to kill her as an honor price to satisfy a marriage law the Queen of Avenbury had willfully broken to marry a Dúnælven warrior in secret instead of wedding the human prince from a neighboring realm that Avenbury's high council had selected.

The same high council of elder faeries who had selected him for their princess.

How could his father ask him to produce heirs with a *creature*?

And hold him to a betrothal when one of the parties was basically missing?

The boy hated elves. He hated their cousins, the dwarves, even more. Really, he hated all faeries. They were conniving, soulless, self-serving beasts. If he was sold off to the fae like a prized bull for the cotton used in Clifstán's military uniforms, then he would enjoy as many girls as he wanted. He would keep as many mistresses as he wanted after the wedding too.

And he wanted *her*, the village girl he had met in the woods. The girl who made him feel things he had never experienced before, namely happiness. An aliveness he had craved for what felt like most of his life. They easily talked for hours, laughed too. There was something about the whimsical way she spoke that held his heart.

A small smile softened the edges of his mouth.

The moon silvered the rustling leaves above his head and lit the well-worn path toward a mock-battle site. But he would continue past the practice trenches toward Lake Hrólfr, the lake of wolves, to an old dock where he was to meet the village girl. Two months ago, she and her family had moved to Clifstán from Aurelienne. A brave move by her family to settle in enemy lands and so close to the fortress, though he had never met them. Or heard others talk about them. Strange, but he was too captivated by her to truly care.

Four weeks back, while wandering the woods on horseback on patrol to escape the barracks, he saw her and . . .

His heart had stopped.

Then beat with the sweetest desire, one he hadn't tasted until that moment.

She was, undoubtedly, the most beautiful young woman he had ever met. Long golden-brown hair fell to mid-back in gentle waves. Deep green eyes framed in dark lashes. A figure that haunted his dreams. Laughter that made him genuinely smile. A playful mind that disarmed him. An unspoken promise of a future, one where he wasn't a military prince and she wasn't his enemy. The simple, happy life she offered him had become an insatiable craving that hollowed out the rot in his chest.

He was no stranger to girls. But she kept him flirtatiously at arm's length—a siren's call to his ego. He enjoyed the hunt, the chase. The building tension. But, unlike most girls, she didn't throw herself at him for the thrill of being with a prince. Though, she didn't know he was a prince. Since she was Aurelienne, he kept that part secret.

The boy knew he was stupid. He not only stole rationed food from the mess hall this night, but secretly meeting with the enemy was an act of treason. A prince shouldn't chase after a possible Aurelienne spy. Genius really, to send a woman, if she were indeed a spy. Especially a young woman as unnaturally beautiful as she.

Still, fool that he was, tonight he would convince her to finally kiss him—

A low growl rumbled from the brush beside him. The boy stilled; the hairs on his arms stood on end. He slowly backed up a couple of steps, nearly

losing his balance when his boot rolled over a loose rock. Normally, he was armed with a rifle, a pistol, and several knives. But weapons were stored in locked closets every night by a squad leader. Wouldn't want soldiers killing each other under the cloak of darkness and in cold blood to advance one's career. Ridiculous. They were all going to die in the trenches anyway.

Yellow eyes reflected in a shaft of moonlight and locked onto his. The boy's pulse kicked into a gallop. He needed to run. Grab a stick. Anything other than stand frozen with his mouth agape. Only one monster roamed these woods—*Úlfar*. Wolves. And if there was one, there were more. The crunching sound of paws on winter-brittled leaves grew louder. And then a large gray wolf emerged from the underbrush. Its lips curled back in a snarl. But those yellow eyes were no longer fixed on him. An object behind the boy held the wolf's entire bristled attention.

The boy didn't move.

He wasn't sure if he were still breathing either.

What was behind him?

Perhaps this wolf wanted food.

Slowly, the boy lifted the pack and opened the tie. But before he could reach in and grab a slice of roast beef, the wolf lay at his feet and rested his head on one of his boots and whimpered.

Once again, the boy didn't move.

Was the wolf sick? It didn't seem to be.

Animals were attracted to his younger brother who had the Sight. They spoke to him too. The boy blew out a slow breath. Florian was the best thing that ever happened to him. But his little brother was an eternal source of embarrassment for their family with his feminine hobbies. But him? Not once in his sixteen years had an animal, especially a predatory animal, approached him. Nor submitted to him without provocation.

Well, that was not entirely true. On his twelfth birthday, he encountered a wild Aurelienne horse near the border. All muscle and feral and striking. The black stallion possessed an unfettered spirit he was desperate to know and also contain. A gorgeous horse that seemed made just for him. The guards captured the beast and he had worked every free moment he had with the war horse trainer to break in Loring, the name he gave the stallion. A name that meant "famous in battle" in Clifstánian. Until the girl, Loring was his only source of happiness.

Winter skies, to race across open fields on a wild horse was exhilarating. Motorbikes were fun too, but just not the same.

The wolf lifted its head to peer at him and the boy swallowed thickly. Taming a wolf was probably no different than taming a wild horse.

"There you are!" the girl's voice called out from the trees behind where he stood. "I thought you would not come."

The wolf jumped to its feet and snarled again.

"Fayette, *ne bouge pas! Il y a un loup*," he replied in Aurelienne—*Fayette, don't move. There's a wolf.* The girl didn't speak a lick of Clifstánian yet. She also didn't listen to his instructions.

"I'm not afraid of a big bad wolf," she said in that whimsical tone of hers, a humored tilt to her lips. A response directed at him, he realized. Was she teasing him?

The wolf's hackles spiked along its back and its growl deepened. Why did the wolf feel threatened by her but not him?

A rush of heat moved through the boy, a sudden woozy feeling he couldn't explain as his muscles tensed. The wolf locked eyes with him as he bared his teeth at the beast. The sound of his own snarling snapped him out of whatever trance he was just in. What was happening? He didn't remember moving in front of the girl either.

The wolf backed up and sat, its head down.

Fayette giggled while lowering the hood of her cloak. "She thinks you're her alpha."

"Hmm," the boy murmured, more in anxious thought than in reply. Then he fully looked at the young woman at his side, the hair on his arms rising once more. "Why are you not afraid of wolves?" If there were not a real wolf in their company and he had not snarled in warning, he would twist his words into something flirtatious. But his heart was pounding too hard to think straight. His hands were growing clammy too.

The boy's gaze darted around the woods. Placing one's entire attention onto a single wolf felt like a trap. Wolves hunted in packs.

The girl tilted her head. "Why should I fear when she recognizes her place before you, monsieur? *Non*, she will not attack unless you command her so."

"Her place?" The boy derisively laughed then. Fayette had lost her mind.

She twisted to face him, her green eyes intense in the silvered light. "*Oui*, boy named 'split crown.'"

The boy sucked in a quiet breath at her unwitting implications.

His full name translated to "little wolf of the split crown, the protector." Though, she didn't know his first or last name, only his middle—Fentienne. *Split crown*.

"In the Spired Hills," the girl continued, "there are golden-eyed mortals with no line of separation between man and wolf. Many who still roam the halls of Palais d'Aurélie."

The Golden Palace. He had seen it once during a campaign in the Spired Hills earlier this year.

"Démons, the locals call them," she continued. "Beasts."

The boy eyed the beast before him, his brows pushing together. Fayette had indeed lost her mind. Maybe. His family had descended from an imperial line in Dreglind—an ancient bloodline of dragon shifters. The dragon blood in his veins, however, was weak at best. He was human, nothing more. The idea of being something *other* curdled his stomach.

Still, perhaps wolf shifters existed once upon a time too.

Still, that didn't explain *this* situation.

"Don't believe me, monsieur?" she taunted with a huff. "Fine. Tell her to shoo."

Fayette laid a hand on his arm, smiling when the wolf sprang to her feet and growled. This beast really didn't like this girl and she really didn't care. She was a strange one, Fayette. But gods she was beautiful. The kind that made any good sense he possessed fall to his knees before her and beg for mercy. Remembering his *real* reason for being in the woods, he decided to give her advice a try.

"Go," the boy growled back. When the wolf didn't move, he risked being heard by the patrol and raised his voice, quietly shouting, "Go!"

The wolf's yellow eyes landed on him once more and held his intense stare for several erratic heartbeats. Then, to his surprise, the beast dipped her head before reluctantly loping back into the underbrush.

What the hell?

"Told you." The girl leaned her head on his shoulder and quietly laughed.

But the boy was too spooked to comment. "Come, Fenti," she said, using his nickname, and grabbed his hand. "We don't have all night."

No, they certainly did not.

"Did you bring me food?" she asked as they walked hand-in-hand toward the lake.

He eyed the brush along the trail to see if the wolf—or its pack—followed before meeting her waiting gaze. That strange rush of heat was still buzzing around his head.

"*Oui*," he answered simply. Lifting her hand to his lips, he softly kissed her knuckles. "For you and your family, if you choose to share."

Immigrants from Aurelienne would not have the same access to food as native-born families. They didn't deserve to eat his realm's food anyway. Let them starve. Less mouths to worry about in a land torn by war. But she was different. Since the moment he stumbled upon her by the lake a month prior, he couldn't get her out of his head. Not even kissing other girls satisfied the feverish longings pumping wildly through his heart.

The frayed, rough spun dress clung to her pleasing curves. An ankle length skirt with a fitted bodice in the peasant style of her homeland, which was distastefully old-fashioned compared to his own. Clifstán was years, perhaps centuries, ahead of Aurelienne—in dress, customs, and technology. They didn't even have radios or record players and used front loading muskets fitted with bayonets, unlike the bolt action or automatic rifles the boy used. They still used horse drawn carriages too. The boy couldn't imagine. While he loved horses, he was too enamored with the motorbikes and flying machines of Myrefell. Did the technology of his realm frighten her?

She never seemed frightened, though. Not even of wolves.

His brow furrowed once more.

Fayette unlaced their fingers and fell back against an oak tree to gaze at him beneath lowered lashes. "How is it you speak perfect Aurelienne, monsieur?"

"To woo Aurelienne girls, mademoiselle." He lifted a corner of his mouth in a devilish grin. "Is it working?"

"Say something romantic and I will let you know."

Casually, he dropped the pack of food to the forest floor and stepped toward her. Mesmerized by the way her chest rose and fell with every breath,

her porcelain complexion dusted in moonlight, how the breeze danced through strands of her long hair, he placed his hands on the trunk on either side of her face and slowly met her waiting gaze. "*Tu es plus belle que les étoiles dans le ciel.*" Her breath quietly hitched at his confession—*you are more beautiful than the stars in the sky*. Satisfied, he leaned in closer and whispered, "*Embrasse-moi.*"

"Kiss you?" She turned her head toward her shoulder, more of a flirtatious gesture than demure. "When your beautiful eyes look at me so, it is hard to resist your charms."

His eyes . . . a golden amber color courtesy of his mother. Eyes eerily like the wolf's.

The thrumming pulse behind his ribs accelerated once more. Was the wolf still nearby? Others in its pack?

"Fentienne," the girl whispered. "Why do you move away?"

His gaze skimmed through the trees, then he turned his attentions back to her with a lazy smile. "Better to see you with my beautiful eyes from this angle."

"If I am to kiss you, though, you must close those golden Aurelienne eyes of yours."

"So, my charms *are* working . . ."

Fayette giggled. "I have long waited for this moment, monsieur."

"Hmm." He lifted a single brow. "How long? Tell me."

She grinned. "If I kiss you, what will you give me in return?"

The boy returned his hands to the trunk beside her face and whispered in her ear, "I will perform any pleasure you desire."

"And if I want a pleasure owed in the future instead of now?"

"Yes," he whispered, leaning back to see her face.

"Any pleasure?"

He bit his bottom lip suggestively. "Anything."

"Say it, Fentienne," she whispered back. "I want to hear your promise to me."

"I promise, Fayette," he began, cupping her cheek. "If you kiss me, I will perform any pleasure you desire whenever you so choose in the future."

Her smile widened, a strangely wicked look. But it only added to her allure. Skies, she was beautiful in ways he never knew girls could be. He would invade his own realm in her name, if she asked him.

"Close your eyes, Adalwolf Fentienne Halivaard."

He obeyed, too besotted to notice that she had used his full name, one he had never introduced to her. Then her lips were on his and he was dying a thousand deaths at once. This was not a kiss of innocence either. She had clearly kissed other boys before. A moan escaped him with the soft feel of her body against his. Needing her even closer, his hand slid down her back to press every curved inch of her flush to every tortured inch of him—

A growl punctured the moonstruck stillness around him. Swearing, Adalwolf Fentienne broke away from the kiss and moved to cover Fayette with his body. Blood pumped in a frenzied rhythm through his veins. The gray wolf growled louder and the girl laughed. Adrenaline shot through the boy and his muscles braced for a fight.

Everything happened quickly.

The wolf's large body barreling into his and knocking him to the ground.

The girl's laughter growing more satisfied.

Adalwolf Fentienne grabbed the wolf around the neck and tried to roll the beast off him. But the wolf was quicker. Before the boy could jump to his feet, the wolf had pounced on Fayette.

She didn't even scream.

Instead, her laugh grew wilder.

Light flashed around her body and the wolf flew back, hit a tree, and landed with a whimpering roll.

"What in the . . ." The boy's eyes grew large and his mouth fell open. A misty light fogged around the girl in a swirl of leaves. Adalwolf's heart lodged in his throat and he stumbled back. "Fayette?"

The light faded into the night and an elf in a long midnight blue dress stood before him with pointed ears sticking out from her waist-length chestnut hair. Rose colored eyes settled on him and a wicked smile curved her mouth. The wolf remained in a heap on the forest floor, whimpering. The boy darted his gaze around the woods, to every moving shadow and shift of light.

"Prince," the elf said in a seductive tone.

"Where is Fayette?" he demanded.

She laughed. "Men are so easily fooled by a beautiful woman."

Horror tightened the muscles around his ribs. Then pain throbbed in his chest. A heavy ache that stole his breath followed by a hellfire of fury.

Fayette—"little girl faerie" in Aurelienne.

He was an idiot. How had he not considered the possibility? Though, he knew why. Fayette was a common name in Aurelienne for mortal girls his age, from when it was fashionable to mimic the elves in Gabaston. An easy ploy. And she had tricked him. For a promise owed at her choosing in the future. One that would bring her pleasure.

Disgust wormed in his gut.

But hatred...

Hatred unlike any other burned hot.

He was taught to hate the elves and dwarves. But this hate was different. This hate was *earned*.

"I risked accusations of treason for you," he seethed.

She blinked prettily at him. "You believed yourself in love? I am touched."

"You're *touched*?" Another panging ache ripped through him. "For Fayette, I would have been stripped of my crown, disowned by my family. Perhaps even executed."

"You *were* in love."

He dragged in a ragged breath. "Is Fayette even a real girl?"

"*Oui*, prince," the faerie replied in his mother's tongue and he felt the fury stoke hotter. "Until she died in Gabaston during one of Clifstán's attacks. The campaign your oldest brother was in, actually."

He flinched.

"Did you not realize girls like Fayette die in your war?" She tsked. "I made sure she didn't suffer much in the end."

"What is your real name?" the boy asked in a low growl.

She smiled a feline grin, her small canines glinting in the silvered light. "Addien, Your Highness."

Her name meant "beautiful" in runic, the Dúnælven faerie language. Of course, it did.

"Why me and not my older brothers who could grant you power and wealth?" he asked next. "What do I possibly have to offer you?"

"Revenge." She stepped toward him and he stepped back. "Centuries of unrequited love and rejection. A law broken must be paid. And since my queen hid away your betrothed, I have only you to play with. I bided my time while I watched you grow into manhood. You are a beautiful creature, *Fenti*. I did so enjoy making you fall in love with the enemy. I will still one day seduce you properly and *finally* make you mine." The boy fought back the bile creeping up his throat. "Do not look so forlorn, prince."

Adalwolf's fists clenched at his sides and his eyes narrowed into slits. "You will not address me. In fact, do not even look at me, you disgusting filth of existence."

"The next time I see you—"

"—if you even dare show your face to me again, I will—"

"What, prince?" She tilted her head in mock curiosity. "What could a mortal man possibly do to a faerie as old and powerful as I?"

He didn't have an answer for her. And not having an answer sent a fresh wave of rage to flame through his already white-hot pulse. A muscle jumped along his jaw. She had stolen his hope, his happiness. Not just stolen—poisoned it all. Addien wanted to treat him as though he were a plaything she could toy with and discard? All for her own twisted sense of honor and amusement? Then he could do the same.

The boy relaxed his body, his eyes slowly trailing up her body.

"What *I* could do?" His gaze flicked to hers. "I find much *pleasure* in suffering. The suffering of faeries most of all." This time he stepped toward her, each movement slow and predatory, an arrogant curl to his lips. "I would gladly create reasons for the crown to enslave *all* fae, not just the dwarves. Oh the things *I could do* to you as my slave." He ended with a bitter laugh. "For *revenge*, naturally. You understand how these things work."

"Who honestly loves you, Adalwolf Fentienne?" The pain of her words severed his breaking heart. Nobody loved him, especially now that Fayette was ripped from his life. "For who could love a beast?" The faerie stepped toward him, her movements sensual and equally as predatory. Desire burned in her rose-colored eyes as wavy, dark brown strands fluttered across his face in the breeze. "Marry me instead of the princess. I have always loved your monstrous ways, Fenti."

"I would rather die!" he spat.

"We could wield so much power together, beastling."

"*You* are the abomination, *creature*."

She laughed, entirely delighted by his fury. "Oh, prince. You have no

idea, do you?"

He stilled and the hair rose on his arms once again. "Leave."

"Yes, my love," she purred. "You owe me a pleasure of my choosing, Adalwolf Fentienne Halivaard. We will see each other again. And when we do, you will be mine."

Then the elf disappeared in a glittering fog of mist.

Holding in the scream scorching his gut, the boy kicked at the dead leaves, then hissed swear word after swear word, his entire body shaking with rage. Not even the silent darkness of the forest soothed his anger. A faerie trick, all of it. Even his swelling feelings for Fayette were manufactured. All his happiness . . .

He was now beholden to two elves.

Like hell he was.

Conniving, soulless, self-serving beasts. Every single one of them.

The boy faced Myrefell, his chest heaving furiously. The wolf beside him whimpered and his shoulders deflated a notch. He hesitated a few seconds, taking in the surrounding forest once more, then knelt beside the wolf on tremoring legs.

"Thank you," he said through clenched teeth. Besides Loring, animals held little meaning to him. But the wolf had tried to protect him. Why him? It made absolutely no sense. And still no pack arrived. "A lone wolf, are you?" he quietly asked. In many ways, he felt like one too. The only Halivaard prince of four who was promised.

What had he done to make his father marry him off to an elf?

Perhaps if he finally earned his father's favor, the king would dissolve the betrothal contract.

Unlikely. But the quickly snapping single thread of hope he still possessed wanted to believe there was an escape from this iron cage of misery. Something other than the blasé disdain lacing every breath in his suffocating existence.

The wolf whimpered once more, as if sensing his grief, his betrayal. Cautiously, the boy laid a trembling hand on the wolf's back and stroked her fur. Adalwolf expected the animal to lash out from its pain, all teeth and claws—like the wounded, trapped animal he was—but the beast only shuddered beneath his touch.

Beast.

The wolf pushed up to her feet. They studied one another; golden eyes locked in silent communication. Of what? The boy didn't know. But his carefully contained wildness, the feral anger deep in his chest, the maddening desire to run free felt a serene kinship. After several long heartbeats, the wolf dipped her head, like before, and then loped back into the woods.

The boy slowly rose and squared his shoulders. The woods closed in around him. He would leave the bag of food as payment to the wolf. Then he pivoted about face and began marching back toward the barracks, his heart growing more bitter and cruel with each step.

It would be six war-torn winters before he would see the unnaturally beautiful faerie again. Six long winters before he finally understood how a mortal man could become more beastly than the creatures he loathed.

She [the faerie] added that I [the prince] had only to abandon myself to the delight with which the certainty of becoming the husband of a powerful Fairy would naturally awaken. "Say, Prince," she said to me, "Do you not consent to give me your hand this moment?"

"No, Madame."

"Go wretch!" she said to me. "Boast that you have refused my heart and my hand. It is my pleasure that you will remain an object of horror to yourself and to all who behold you."

My occupation during the war, and the continual presence of my ancient ardorer, had prevented me from informing the Queen of what had occurred.

I [a good faerie] was about to take the child out of the cradle in order to breathe life into it, but I immediately conceived the idea of taking advantage of this melancholy event and substituted my niece for the dead child. I lost no time in making the exchange.

The merchant's family consisted of six boys and six girls.

Their house took fire; the account books, the notes, gold, and silver, were enveloped in this fatal conflagration. In short, he suddenly fell into the most abject poverty. The youngest girl, however, displayed greater perseverance and firmness in their common misfortune.

"La Belle et la Bête" by Madame de Villeneuve, published in *The Young American and Marine Tales*, 1743

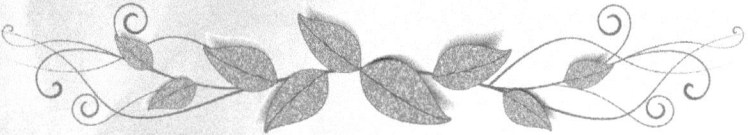

CHAPTER I

RHOSLYN

Rhoslyn wove through the crowd of factory workers along The Row toward the Saints District of Gabaston. Fear rivaled the anger simmering in her pulse. She had paid the priests for her nine-year-old brother's keep this month. Matthieu should have a roof over his head for at least another two weeks. The courier's note crumpled in her tightening fists.

Where would they live?

There were too many people in need of roofs over their heads after the attacks and not enough rooms to rent. Rooms given to mortals first. The only housing she could find on her salary was a tiny room she shared with three other grisettes—seamstresses who worked in the garment factories. A room with two beds. She shared a thin blanket and a single pillow with her dear friend, Amélie. Boys, regardless of age, were not allowed in the apartments. For well over a year, every spare coin went to her brother's care, where he would have three meals a day and medicine for his lungs. As long as he was cared for, she could survive penniless and hungry.

Rhoslyn shoved past the large wood doors into the foundling home for boys, the Underworld's fire in her belly. A young priest's gaze snapped to hers then slid to her brother, who sat on a bench by the door, shivering.

"You owe me for the two weeks room and board Matthieu will not have." She grabbed the young man's hand and slammed the courier's note into his palm.

"Mademoiselle, you would rob the saints of your tithes?"

She huffed a bitter laugh. "Rob the saints? Does their benevolent love not care for a sick boy who has done them no wrong?"

"Rhoslyn Gautier," a deep voice murmured from the doorway—Mon Père Michel. To the young man he said, "You are dismissed, Acolit." Deep scarlet silken robes swished along the ground as Mon Père moved toward her, his eyes cold, his smile colder. "You know we do not return tithes, fayette. Matthieu's bed will go to a boy with no kin. Would you *rob* an orphan of a home and meal?"

"A *mortal* boy with no kin," she gritted between clenched teeth. "By refusing me the unused funds that would help provide him a new home, you are tossing to the streets a sick boy with a lame leg who did not choose to be born an elf. I paid those tithes in good faith, Mon Pére."

"Your good faith will bless others and help protect your soul from the Beast of Gabaston."

"The temple is collecting tithes for protection?" Her mouth fell open.

"The saints be with you, fayette Rhoslyn."

Little girl faerie. How she loathed the infantile term used by mortal men for young unwed elven females. The same men who paid for common pavement nymphs in Factory Row.

The priest kissed the pads of his pointer and middle fingers, then turned them toward her in benediction. A satisfied smile curled his lips—a wolfish smile—and her heart fell to her sickening gut. Mon Père Michel held her furious gaze a beat longer, then turned and disappeared through the sanctuary's door in a flourish of silk robes.

A sob caught in her throat. Angry tears pooled in her narrowed eyes. But she would not cry in front of Matthieu.

Drawing in a slow, steady breath, Rhoslyn lowered herself beside her brother on the bench and tenderly moved an unruly lock of blond hair from his eyes. The soft empath magic moving through her grew heavy at the slow, grieving beat of her brother's pulse. "We will have an adventure this day."

"I do not mean to be a burden," Matthieu replied. The shame edging his voice was a knife to her heart.

She wrapped an arm around his frail shoulders and gently pulled his shivering body close to hers. "You are my joy, *mon petit caneton.*"

He sighed. "A little duckling can at least swim. I can barely walk."

"Then swim, *caneton.*" She knelt on the ground and gestured for him to climb onto her back. "The air will be your water."

Matthieu circled his arms around her neck, his small sack of belongings in his hand—a spare pair of stockings, small chapbook of scriptures, and a wooden game token he had fallen asleep holding the night of the fire. She reached behind her and scooped him up from under his knees. As she stood, her stockings began slipping down her leg. A constant problem since she sold her garter ribbons for half a bread loaf and a dozen coppers a month prior. It was either the ribbons or her hair. And now the temple owned her sacrifice.

There was no help for it now.

"Ready? I must hurry. Madame will ring the bell soon."

"*Oui*," her brother replied softly.

The streets of Saints District still held the stillness of morning. Factory Row, however, was thick with activity. She angled past street vendors already crying out their wares in song and verse. The smell of their foods mixed with the refuse in the streets and Rhoslyn nearly gagged. The hunger gnawing her stomach didn't help. A few nymphs, both human and elf, in nothing more than corsets and petticoats leaned against a small alley, their faces painted up like the aristocracy. All to service men before the official workday begun, and in unbearably cold weather. But most in the streets were factory workers like her, dashing to various buildings along The Row.

She slowed before *l'atelier de confection de robes*—the dress factory—of Gabaston.

"Do you feel safe sitting against the wall while I work?"

"You worry too much." Her brother's breath fluttered flyaway strands by her ear. "I will be fine."

"He can sit with me, *belle fleur*."

Rhoslyn turned toward the beggar man and nearly wept with relief. He was a gentle mortal of older years with a lame leg, an injury during the attacks. One of the reasons her brother struggled to walk too—an old injury from a wolf when age five made worse when Clifstán bombed Gabaston. An attack that also scarred his lungs from the fire that destroyed their family's home.

"Can I, Rosie?" her brother asked. "He can show me how to whittle again."

She gingerly lowered her brother, ignoring the discomfort of slouching stockings, and watched as he limped to the wall beside the scraggly dog curled up at his master's side. Matthieu partially buried his face into the dog's fur and smiled, a dimpled smile she could never resist.

"You are to speak to no one," Rhoslyn reminded quickly.

Matthieu rolled his eyes. "*Oui*."

"Love you to the sky and back, Matthieu Eric."

A tiny smile flitted across his lips. "I love you to the bottom of the sea and back, Rosie Mae."

She kissed his head and strode toward the door—and stopped.

Shouting from the streets drew her eye. A crowd of people were throwing trash and screaming insults at a carriage. People poured out from shops, ran to the commotion, and joined the unrest. Rhoslyn's gaze shot to where her brother sat. The numbers in the street swelled until the carriage had no choice but to stop.

"*Liberté, Egalité, Fraternité!*"

More joined in and the shouts echoed down The Row.

"*Liberté, Egalité, Fraternité!*"

Liberty. Equality. Fraternity—the cry of commoners all over Gabaston. Perhaps all Aurelienne.

The war didn't destroy Palais d'Aurélie. The invading soldiers never made it as far as the Golden Palace, or to any of the homes in Crowns Quarter. Shops and homes were burned from the cottages in the forests beside East Factory Row all the way to Saints District, like the chapbook printing press Rhoslyn's family once owned. Even merchants, once part of the bourgeoisie—the middle- and upper middle-class—now lived on the trash-filled streets of The Row.

Factory Row was still rebuilding after the Cold Winds twenty years ago too. A kingdom-wide apocalyptic event that froze livestock, buildings, and people to dust in a furious blizzard. The former realm to the east, Glenashlen, had dusted and blown away within two days. Every soul perished. Aurelienne lost significant trade income as a result.

Between the war and the Cold Winds, they were painfully destitute.

And *still* taxes continued to increase. Taxes for weevil-ridden flour. Taxes for living on one side of town and working in the other. Taxes for use of the town square well. Taxes on salt. Even taxes to tend the farms the aristocrats owned. The audacity. Truly. Those with more money than the coffers of Aurelienne could hold taxed *their* peasants to work *their* land. Peasants with hungry bellies who slaved to feed men and women growing fat on hubris and privilege.

The ruling House of Chalamet cared little for the suffering of common folk.

The House of Beausoleil before them too.

They dined on the finest unspoiled meats, drank aged wine that hadn't turned to vinegar, wore Merennan silks despite the trend toward Avenbury cottons. Their bread molded, their exotic fruits too, and *still* they could glutton to discomfort. *Non*, tucked away in their palace, behind gates made of pure gold, they were spared the lowly shame of considering rotten food found in the gutters as a legitimate meal.

Matthieu lifted his fist into the air and shouted, "*Liberté, Egalité, Fraternité!*" before doubling over in a coughing fit. The beggar man rubbed his back and murmured comforts. The pain around the older man's eyes deepened. His only child, a son, was buried in the Spired Hills somewhere with Clifstánian bullets in his chest. Like so many other men.

All to defend a throne that ignored their sacrifices and the suffering of those left behind.

Rhoslyn studied her little brother with both pride and concern. He was all she had left in this world.

The shouts grew more frenzied. Protesters dragged an elegantly dressed man with a powdered wig from the carriage and hauled him down the street. At this hour, he was most likely leaving a brothel where he had stayed the night. Cheers erupted around this end of The Row. The Guard would arrive shortly. But the unrest would stay on the street beside the carriage and not next to the garment factory alley.

With one last look at her little brother, she ran across the alley and into the dress factory, hung her grand-mére's burgundy cloak and grabbed her gray smock right as Madame rang the bell.

"Mademoiselle Gautier!"

Rhoslyn closed her eyes and blew out a slow breath, then turned to face the older woman. "*Pardonnez-moi*, Madame. There was unrest in the streets." She lowered into a curtsy and bowed her head. "I hurried as fast as I could."

Madame placed a finger beneath Rhoslyn's chin and lifted her face. "You will remain an hour after your shift and without pay."

"*Oui*, you are generous, Madame."

She laughed, a deep raspy, cruel sound. "Next time you will have to ask for Monsieur LeMont's pardon." Rhoslyn's gaze slid to where the disgusting man sat behind a desk—and shuddered. There was only one way he pardoned his grisettes.

"I understand, Madame."

The back of the older woman's hand cracked against Rhoslyn's cheek hard enough to jerk her head to the side. "Get to work, grisette."

Tears stung the back of Rhoslyn's eyes and she ground her teeth together. Fury rolled through her pulse, pounding in every heartbeat. Still, she lowered into another curtsy, then marched toward her workstation, her head held high. Fellow grisettes watched her pass beneath lowered lashes. A bruise was forming on her cheek, but she would not give anyone the satisfaction of seeing her cower or in pain.

However, if Madame attempted to touch her again, or Monsieur LeMont, she would start a riot in this very factory. She would also run into the streets and scream, "*Equality! Liberty! Fraternity!*" too. Her body may be forced to work prison hours for mere crumbs, but no one owned her. Not the aristocracy, not Factory Row. Not the priests who spoke for the saints. Not men given to their baser natures. Not women who cared not if she starved and slept in the cold, only that she sewed them pretty dresses.

The war destroyed her home and family. But not her. She would not be destroyed.

"Rosie," her dear friend Amélie whispered in horror as Rhoslyn lowered onto the bench beside her. The swelling handprint on Rhoslyn's cheek faced her friend. Amélie frowned, pity in her eyes. Pity Rhoslyn didn't want to see. "She's a monster."

Rhoslyn picked up the threaded needle and the bundle of muslin left for her to finish.

Stab. Fight the dulled needle point. Pull the thread. *Stab* again. Maneuver the dulled needle point through the delicate cotton. Yank the thread. *Stab*. She sighed. By the end of her now eleven-hour shift, the bruises on her fingertips would rival the one on her cheek. Why couldn't the saints just let her stab something repeatedly and effortlessly until her anger was properly sated?

Amélie leaned toward her. "Where is Matthieu?"

"Across the alley with the beggar man."

"Why is he—"

"*Mortal* boys who need beds."

"Oh, Rosie . . ."

Sharp pain pricked Rhoslyn's thumb. In her fury, she had been too forceful with the dulled needle. A tiny red dot bloomed on her fingertip and she sighed. Thimbles, decorative shoe buckles, and other odd-end metal sundries were confiscated and melted into parts for weapons and other military uses.

Perhaps she would tear a piece off her petticoat to wrap around her thumb like other grisettes. But this was her only dress and she had but one pitiful petticoat and no other undergarments. Very few with her starving income could afford the extravagance of underthings. And now she was without simple garter ribbons too.

Sans-culottes, the nobles called commoners—those "without silk breeches." Pointing out the obvious was, apparently, the depth of the aristocracy's creativity. One would think the education afforded them would produce an insult worthy of making.

L'habit ne fait pas le moine. The habit doesn't make the monk. The suit doesn't make the man.

Intelligence, unfortunately, wasn't as pretty as silk breeches to those frilly ornaments on the throne.

Rhoslyn quickly wiped the drop of blood onto her factory-issued gray smock, then once more pushed the needle point through the cotton gown in a monotonous motion she could pattern in her sleep. The yardage in her lap was the finest printed muslin she had ever worked with. A pity weaves with such beautiful, evenly spun warps and wefts were subjected to the violence of dull sheers and even duller needles. Or the destiny of clothing an overindulged peacock of the aristocracy.

Rhoslyn closed her eyes a moment to gather her wits. But it was no use.

"Mon Père Michel stole my tithes, Amélie." Her friend gasped. "I had secured another two weeks of room and board and he took my money to house a mortal boy."

Amélie reached for her hand under the table and squeezed Rhoslyn's fingers. "We can sneak Matthieu into our room until you find a place."

"*Non*, I could not risk you, Josie, and Anette joining me in the streets for breaking the rules."

"You cannot sleep in the streets, Rosie."

Rhoslyn's shoulders fell. "I will find an abandoned cottage for the night."

"But the démons—"

Démons . . .

A shudder trembled down her body. Outside of natural wolves, the people of Gabaston feared démons most. These mortal wolf shifters preyed on the wicked, the vulnerable, and virgins to build an army of souls for the Dark Saint of the Underworld. Mamans taught their children to leave tithes at the temple and to pray to the Nine Saints for protection, for black hearted mortals with rotting souls eventually lost their humanity and became possessed by the Dark Saint. Elves, thankfully, could not be turned into prowling démons of the Underworld.

"There are wolves in the streets too," Rhoslyn said quietly. "Not all roam on four legs."

"Does Matthieu know you will sleep near the démons?"

Rhoslyn worried a corner of her bottom lip. "I do not wish him to think of his fears all day while I work."

Her friend shifted to lean in and whisper, "But your nightmares . . ."

"They will haunt me," Rhoslyn murmured. "But more girls have gone missing, Amélie. Several are now nymphs. I would much rather face a démon and help Matthieu face one too than be owned for a male's quick alley pleasures."

Amélie sighed and nodded her head, making her wild copper curls bounce. It was a fear all orphaned young women knew.

"He also said my tithes would protect my soul against the Beast of Gabaston."

Her friend's gaze whipped up from the unfinished dress in her hand. "Protect an elf's soul? The temple is as greedy as Palais d'Aurélie."

"*Oui*." Rhoslyn returned to her work. "How much blood must they spill to satisfy their lust? I am so angry I could set the Underworld's fires on Saints District." Under her breath, she murmured, "Maybe Saint Cernunnos would accept my fae soul for his dark army then."

A couple of beats later Amélie squeezed Rhoslyn's hand again and said,

"I have a gift for you, *mon petit chou-fleur*."

The tiniest of smiles teased Rhoslyn's lips at her friend's endearment—my little cauliflower. "A gift?"

The shrill voice of Madame drowned out the factory noise, and Amélie winced. For the third day in a row, the older woman chastised the females who were responsible for cutting out various dress pieces from tattered patterns.

"She screeches like an owl," Rhoslyn whispered with a roll of her eyes. "Poor owls. I am embarrassed on their behalf."

Amélie bit back a laugh, lowering her head while slipping a hand into her apron pocket. Dusky light from a window glinted off her red hair. Rhoslyn was endlessly jealous of her friend's beautifully romantic auburn hair.

The clop of Madame's shoes echoed through the building.

When the sound faded, her friend gently elbowed Rhoslyn, then placed butcher's twine into her hand. "Silk garter ribbons for you, milady."

Rhoslyn's mouth parted and warmth spread across her chest. "Where did you find these?"

"The alley behind the butcher's shop. I scrubbed the twine yesterday."

Tears sprang to her eyes and the first genuine smile stretched across her face this day.

Amélie casually peered over Rhoslyn's shoulder. "Her back is to us on the other side of the factory."

With a grin, Rhoslyn pushed her skirt up one leg past her thigh and readjusted her stocking. The first string secured with a perfect fit. Lowering her skirt on one leg, she lifted her dress up the other leg and tied the twine around her thigh.

Her friend's lips twitched. "A proper aristocratic lady now."

"No need to be scandalized, monsieur silk breeches," Rhoslyn said with a flutter of her hand and Amélie quietly snorted.

A grisette across from them warned with her eyes to appear busy, how they communicated to one another if the screech owl was nearby.

The swelling handprint on Rhoslyn's cheek smarted anew. Pushing the needle through the half-finished dress in her hands, Rhoslyn sobered and concentrated on her work.

THE DAY WAS quickly falling into night. Rhoslyn looked up from her work only long enough to peer out the window and to glance at the candle on the table. One and one-half candlemarks remained before she could leave. Her fingers were cramping, her back ached. And she still needed to find a safe place to sleep. The cottages on the outskirts of the forest were more rubble than anything else. But with no doors and fallen walls, too many feared the wolves to claim a building for long. And for good reaso—

A male voice quietly spoke her name. A voice with a strange accent similar to the language of the saints—a blend of Dúnælven and Aurelienne.

Rhoslyn's head snapped up from the dress in her hands. Two elves in battle leathers stood beside her workstation. One with twin swords strapped to his back, his armor as black as the long hair pulled up into a knotted ponytail, and a raven perched on his shoulder. His violet-hued eyes remained still as she took him in. Divine Mother, he was beautiful. A terrifying type of beauty that stole her breath. For a flicker of candlelight, she nearly forgot all reason. The other elf, one with disheveled ear-length white hair and startling blue eyes, shifted on his feet as he studied her face, a muscle working along his jaw. Her brows pinched together. Hair and eye colorings aside, the white-haired elf looked eerily similar to her in many ways—and her heart stopped.

Why would Dúnælven elves seek her out, let alone know her name? Her gaze frantically darted around the factory. Madame busied with organizing swaths of fabric in the far corner. Monsieur LeMont scratched a quill across paper. Six other grisettes who were required to stay an extra hour like her busied with their work. Yet not a single person looked their way.

"The mortals are rune whispered for a candlemark," the black-haired elf said. "They do not see or hear us. Your employer believes she has sent you home."

She jumped to her feet and backed away from the elves. "Where is my brother?"

"He is safe with the mortal by the street," the same elf answered. The raven on his shoulder cocked its head; its two beady black eyes pinned on her.

The blood was quickly draining from her head.

"Peace, child of thorns." The black-haired elf stepped toward her. "For well over a year we have been searching for you and feared you perished with your family."

"What is your business with me?" Her voice began to shake. "I cannot settle any debts my father may owe—"

"I am Gedlen Fate Maker."

Rhoslyn sucked in a sharp breath.

The legendary warrior prince stood before her. The one all the storytellers revered for making the kings and queens of Ealdspell rise and fall. She gripped the edge of the table. Her lungs were gasping for air. Why would he wish to speak to *her*? A merchant's daughter without a home? Who couldn't even afford a loaf of bread?

The white-haired elf's throat bobbed, his eyes nervously meeting hers. Yet, despite the open concern, his gaze was soft—how she imagined she looked at her brother—until the elf spotted the bruise on her cheek. Then he stiffened, placed a hand on his sword, and turned to watch Monsieur LeMont, that muscle along the elf's jaw moving furiously.

Gedlen took another step toward her and Rhoslyn lifted a hand. "No closer, milord."

The white-haired elf eyed the bruise on her cheek once more. "Little thorn—"

"Who are you?" Rhoslyn demanded. *Little thorn?*

"Dalbréath Kadelaryn, second-in-command of the Dúnælven military." The white-haired elf's voice crackled with barely restrained anger despite the warm, protective way he looked at her. "And your—" He abruptly stopped when Gedlen faintly nodded his head. The heat in Dalbréath's blue eyes intensified as his voice lowered into a near growl. "Who harmed you?"

"It is done." Rhoslyn fluttered her hand in a dismissive gesture. "I cannot seek revenge for every person who harms me or wishes to. There would be no one left in Factory Row."

The corners of Gedlen's mouth curved in what she perceived was amusement. He was amused with her? Well, she was not amused with him or the way Dalbréath still gripped the pommel of his sword.

"Why are you here, Gedlen Fate Maker?"

The warrior prince grinned at his companion with her direct, unimpressed tone, his canines on full display. A look that made Dalbréath roll his eyes. But she was too stricken by Gedlen's beauty to care about their shared humor. Never had an elf appeared more terrifying to her—dark, dangerous, a lethal type of grace that painfully constricted the air in her lungs. She couldn't breathe. Her head was growing faint. Her eyes wanted to stare at him forever. The rapid pulse pounding in her ears shouted to bolt into the street, grab her brother, and disappear into the crowds. Instead, she squared her shoulders and stood tall, her chin lifted, her eyes narrowed.

No one owned her. Not even the famed, beautiful Gedlen Fate Maker.

The elf in question arched a single brow, his eyes once more intense. As if he could see her every thought, her every dream and nightmare. As if he could see *her*. A blush began creeping up her neck and she cleared her throat.

"My brother is waiting for me, milord."

Gedlen opened his hand. On his palm rested a dainty ring made of thorned rose vines in three different shades of gold—pink, green, and yellow. "You are wed by faerie blood," he began, "to a midnight beauty that is ugly and a sunrise ugliness that could become beautiful. But some wolves are too wild to tame. Some are too wounded to save. And some, like your mate, fight inner demons to break generational curses."

"Wolves?" Rhoslyn placed a trembling hand to her chest. "I am promised to a mortal démon? By faerie blood?"

"Married before the fae but betrothed before the humans until he claims you."

"I am married?" she shouted, too outraged to keep a civil tone.

Gedlen dipped his head so faintly, she almost missed it. "If—"

"If?" The fear icing her veins flamed the billowing fury in her thundering heart.

Her parents would never betroth her to a monster, especially the ones who haunt her nightmares. Gedlen spoke lies. He had to be. Tears stung her eyes once more. She knew he couldn't lie. But merchants didn't promise their children. Only royalty did so for political maneuvering.

She stepped toward him; her jaw clenched. "Why are you *really* here, Gedlen Fate Maker? I am not a queen nor were my parents part of the upper class. *If the stories are true, milord, you do not weave fates for poor grisettes.*"

"The stories are true."

She dragged in an angry breath. For a small sand of time, her heart stopped beating in her chest. Those Otherworldly light violet eyes of his darkened with answers he would not share. And she was done with the games of men and elves. Today was simply too much and there were still hours left.

"*Non*, milord," she spat at him. "You twist cruel words for riddles I will not solve for your entertainment." She spun on her heel to hang up her smock and fetch her cloak. But a hand gently grabbed hers.

Gedlen placed the ring on her palm and curled her fingers around the metal. "I cannot undo a contract made in faerie blood. You *are* married but not wedded to this future. Nor are you responsible for the choices of others, changeling child of thorns. Not those of your parents, of faeries, or of men who have become beasts. If at any point *after* meeting your mate this is a union you cannot abide, or one that is not safe, set the ring onto your bedside end table before sleep, place a drop of your blood inside the ring, and say, 'With my blood, I break these binds.' If you try before meeting your husband, the magic will not work, nor will it work when you do meet him. I could only place a limited spell on this ring. There will be repercussions, naturally, if the blood contract is dissolved. Fate is a delicate weave. But I will protect your decision, whatever it may be."

She wanted to ask why her loving, kind parents would promise her to a démon—binding this marriage with their blood. Why they never told her. And the name of the chosen half man, half beast she must meet. Instead, a bitter laugh left her too tight chest and she gritted out, "I do not have a bedside end table. I do not have a bed."

Rhoslyn grabbed her cloak and marched into the loud, dark streets of Factory Row. Tears burned her eyes. Fury daggered each step.

Changeling child of thorns . . .

The back of her hair rose on end.

Halting her steps, she peered over her shoulder. But only shadows remained where the elves had stood.

Chapter 2

Fentienne

Faces moved in and out of the black mist ribboning around his feet, their mouths open in silent screams. The battlefield writhed with dead souls and soldiers still living. Aurelienne cannons blasted the field in explosions of dirt and rocks and men. Clifstánian beetle mechs skittered the edge of the forests, the heavy artillery firing in deafening booms. The sounds of machines, of screams, the rat-tat-tat of automatic rifles echoed in his wildly beating heart. But all Adalwolf could hear was the pounding pulse in his ears.

His younger brother was on his knees, a gun pressed to his head. Florian consumed most of Adalwolf's vision. But he watched the king from the corner of his eye, not believing the man would truly kill his own son. Then the order. The cold, unfeeling order delivered as if just deciding he wanted cake instead of pie. A bored, mundane, one word command to his officer—"Major."

And the major—Aeldfrith, his oldest brother—pulled the trigger.

Florian's body jerked. A fleeting look of horror in his eyes. Then he fell boneless to the gravel.

The world slowed. Adalwolf's heart stopped beating.

This wasn't real. This couldn't be real.

His little brother dead, because Adalwolf had captured him in South Camp and brought him to Myrefell on the king's orders.

His little brother dead, because he didn't believe Florian in the underground train. Not about their father's and The Lady's plan to use Eirwen as a weapon of mass destruction. Or that Eirwen was The Lady's daughter, a princess the Kingdom of Ealdspell believed dead since infancy. Adalwolf didn't want to believe Florian. Didn't want to trade his anger for shame. Didn't want to treat Florian as an equal after years of being forced to see him as no different than the creatures Adalwolf hated.

The only friend he'd ever had and fed to the wolves—dead.

The kindest soul he had ever known and tore apart—gone.

"I hope Father orders your death. And I hope I'm the one who gets to torture you first."

Words he spat at Florian yesterday. But Adalwolf didn't mean them.

He wanted to vomit. He wanted to run to Florian and beg his lifeless body for forgiveness. But he couldn't move. Shock anchored him to the black souls slithering between his feet.

Fentienne . . . the dead whispered. Fentienne . . .

Take me, he whispered back. Bury me alive.

Eirwen hung by the wrists at the whipping post and screamed until the earth shook.

A keening so raw, a grief too painful to watch.

Then loud, delighted cackling drowned out Eirwen's heartbreaking cries. The Lady, an ancient fae queen, laughed at their pain.

And that's when he knew.

It was all a faerie trick . . .

"Say it, Fentienne," *a soft voice whispered in his ear.* "I want to hear your promise to me."

"I promise, Fayette."

"Say it."

A sob caught in Adalwolf's throat.

I promise.

I promise.

"I want to hear your promise to me."

"If you kiss me, I will perform any pleasure you desire whenever you so choose in the future."

"Close your eyes, Adalwolf Fentienne Halivaard."

Death kissed his lips and he was a starved man who hungered for the grave.

Take me, he pleaded the black souls. Bury me alive.

Barbed, tangled roots of hatred were burrowing deep into Adalwolf's heart with every tight breath. He craved the constant ache, the sickness in his soul, longed for the bleeding, festering wounds to fill him with a bottomless abyss of rage so he no longer felt impaled by loneliness. Or an empty lifetime of grooming to be cruel and feared for Father's approval.

Myrefell faded from his vision and a dark forested night swirled around him. Fayette laughed, a wicked sound. "There are golden-eyed mortals with no line of separation between man and wolf," she sang in his ear. "Many who still roam the halls of Palais d'Aurélie."

Fentienne . . .

Split crown.

"Third born." The forest disappeared and the battlefield flashed into focus. His eyes whipped to Eirwen who spoke to him in a voice that echoed the quaking arias of mountains, an entire ocean of crashing waves, and an endless sky crackling with lightning. "Adalwolf Fentienne Halivaard, I curse you to roam Aurelienne as a beast for your war crimes against the Kingdom of Ealdspell. By day you will be part man. By night you will be all monster." She dragged in a heavy, tear-choked breath. "Only when you learn to love selflessly will the curse be lifted and you'll once more return to a whole man for all the remaining days and nights of your life."

I curse you.

I curse you.

"Say it, Fentienne."

"I promise, Fayette."

Hot searing pain ripped through him. The bones in his body cracked. *There are golden-eyed mortals* . . . Claws tore through his fingers. He could feel his face stretch, his *incisors elongate* . . . *mortals with no line of separation between man and wolf.*

"Démon!" a woman screamed in the street.

The forested night glitched back into focus. Fayette, the girl he committed treason for, the girl he loved, traced a finger along his face. But it wasn't her. It was never her. "Marry me instead of the princess."

"I would rather die!" he spat.

"We could wield so much power together, beastling."

"You *are* the abomination, creature."

Electric lamps swung above him on the underground diesel train. Florian grimaced in pain and choked out, "Adalwolf, she will kill you. Father made a blood oath with a faerie."

"Why do you care if I live or die?"

"Because," Florian ground out. "All of nature and fae kind call you three beasts. But I hope there is goodness in one of my brothers. And, if I'm right, I hope it is you. I want it to be you."

Disgust curled Adalwolf's lips. "I hope Father orders your death. And I hope I'm the one who gets to torture you first."

The faerie's laughter grew louder. "Beastling."

His oldest brother pulled the trigger.

I curse you.

Blood pooled from the bullet hole in Florian's head. Vacant silver-gray eyes stared at him and blinked. "There is goodness in one of my brothers."

I promise.

A shiver flushed across Adalwolf's arms and torso. The trembling grew to convulsions and his teeth clacked together. He curled into himself for warmth beside his brother's corpse. Hoping, begging that someone would start throwing dirt on him too.

"Fentienne?"

Take me . . .

"Fentienne?"

His eyes squinted open to a blurry world. The muscles in his shoulders, his jaw, spasmed. His teeth chattered. The biting cold of marble flooring was burning his flushing skin. He blinked. Rolled to his back in writhing pain. Mold-stained walls and ceilings decorated with pure gold filigree and adornments moved into focus. He blinked again.

"Fentienne Chalamet!"

Groaning, Adalwolf pushed to a seat and wrapped sore arms around his knees, ignoring his mother. Tremors gripped his muscles while ripples of sharp, knifing pain bleated across his head. It was the same every sunrise. Wake up naked somewhere in the manor or outside in the gardens, in pain, fighting convulsions after reliving the same nightmare. The same one that had tormented him for the past year, even though Florian lived and was crowned Emperor of Dreglind with Eirwen at his side.

But Adalwolf's mind was trapped in a cycle of shame and terror and fury.

I curse you.

Where was the brandy? A foul, gamey taste coated his parched tongue. Adalwolf squinted his eyes open wider and groaned again. He was in the ballroom. The kitchens were downstairs. His clothes were upstairs.

The click of heeled shoes echoed in the room and he grimaced.

A sharp gasp. "What have you done, *mon fils*?"

Dried blood smeared the white marble where he sat and coated his semi-clawed hands. He didn't need to look down to know dried blood crusted on his chest and down his mouth too. He must have attacked another sheep.

Disgust daggered his gut.

Everything about him was disgusting.

"What I do best." His bleary gaze flicked to his mother's waiting golden amber eyes—eyes like his. Like a wolf's. A sneer curled Adalwolf's lips. "Kill."

The lines around his mother's eyes hardened. "You must lock yourself in at night."

A bored sigh, the most dignified response he had to the obvious advice. "Why are you here?"

"I brought you food."

"I only care about drink." A gruesome smile stretched across his mouth. "As you can see, I am capable of feeding myself."

His mother let out a low chuckle. "*Petit louveteau*, you are not a monster. Stop acting like one."

Little wolf cub. How he loathed her degrading childhood pet name for him.

No, he was every inch the monster she refused to see. To make the point, he licked the dried blood on one claw-tipped finger with a full canined grin, his eyes locked onto her in a predatory stare. Daring her to voice her delusions just one more time.

All five foot, two inches of Loriette Chalamet marched over in an entire garment factory of pastel blue and pink silks, a folded fan in her ring-adorned fingers, her face powdered, her lips painted into a heart. His mother was as ridiculously gaudy as the rest of the aristocracy. A far cry from the victory rolls, knee length dresses, heels, and red lipstick look of Clifstán she had worn for twenty-one of the twenty-two years he had walked this gods forsaken kingdom.

Voluminous skirts, dripping in bows and ruffles, poofed around her small frame as she bent over him. Adalwolf arched a single haughty brow, ready to tell her to leave and only return if she brought him barrels of whiskey and caskets of brandy. But she fisted his dark, unruly hair and yanked his head back, lowering her face to his until they were only inches apart.

"You think I do not know monsters?" Pain tingled his scalp with her grip and he gritted his teeth. "When you are violated in your own bed by a man who will continue to force himself on you, to bear him warrior sons who were bred to be super soldiers, sons who will kill for a throne his cursed family lost, then you learn what is man and what is beast. You, Adalwolf Fentienne Beausoleil Chalamet Halivaard, are *not* a monster. You are an angry, broken, confused boy." She released his hair and his gut sickened. A child conceived in hate. Groomed to hate. "The king is dead." His mother stepped back. "Do not keep destroying yourself to please a ghost, *petit louveteau*."

"I killed people, destroyed entire villages. Saw them as ants beneath my boots and savored the cruel satisfaction of doing my duty for the crown." Angry tears burned his eyes. He bared his teeth and growled, "Look at me!"

"*Oui*, I see you." She gestured at his naked body and he tightened the arms wrapped around his knees. "Every morning you are born anew. You are no longer a soldier in a war you never chose." She tilted her head.

A scoff was the only acceptable reply. Florian didn't choose war, like him. He didn't find enjoyment in overpowering and hurting others either. Adalwolf may not have chosen war, but he chose to make those around him suffer. Delighted in it, even.

She crouched before him in a swirl of silks and Adalwolf thought he might truly lose it. "Forgive yourself—"

"Courtiers are waiting to kiss your frilly slippered feet," he practically hissed, then dismissed her with a lazy wave of his hand.

Those heart-painted lips pressed into a thin line.

The former queen of Clifstán and Aurelienne didn't move a single muscle, her gaze locked onto his. And he swore he saw a faint light flash in her eyes. Shifters were either born or made, and the House of Chalamet were the only pureblood line of creatures. The aggressive way she stared at him . . . his breath caught. No, he would have known by now if she were a démon. She would have surely shared. Adalwolf blinked long and slow to keep himself from lowering his head at the intensity of her challenge. He would rather die than submit to anyone ever again. He gave the orders now.

"There is tale of a démon roaming the woods the locals call the Beast of Gabaston." She glanced at the dried blood on his skin. "A large wolf that is killing more than livestock. Whispers of a monster hunt are growing louder and the Monks of Glanis are now demanding a wolf cleansing."

"I know."

Loriette narrowed her eyes. "You still speak to the alphas?"

Adalwolf just held her hard gaze and remained silent.

"You're part of the Brotherhood." It was a statement not a question. Her eyes narrowed farther. "How many times have you visited the catacombs?" He continued to hold her gaze and said nothing. "You visit *Le Rêve Rouge* during the day?" She closed her eyes in a long blink and sighed, "How could you be so careless?"

She knew of the Brotherhood? And the catacomb entry in one of Factory Row's brothels? The twisted delight he would feel when she eventually discovered her *petit louveteau* sat among the twelve clan leaders as a guardian officer in the Brotherhood. Not that he answered to her, or anyone.

He narrowed his eyes back at her. "Get to the point."

"That beast is not you, *mon fils*." She pointed the fan in his face. "But you *will* lock yourself in at night."

Bile burned his throat and his muscles stiffened. "How do you know it isn't me?"

She rose to her feet and hit the folded fan in the palm of her hand while studying the dust-caked ballroom. "There is plenty of food to last you three to four weeks. Do not leave the chateau, Fentienne. The Row wants noble blood to paint their streets and a wolf to hang in the market square. The unrest is growing to dangerous levels." He already knew this too and heaved an irritated sigh. She returned her focus onto him. "And you are next in line to the Aurelienne throne."

Adalwolf laughed. "I am dead."

His mother's face remained grave and his bitter laughter faded into a horrified shudder.

"You told *her*?"

A corner of Loriette's mouth lifted in smug reply. "My sister needs an heir. Our cousin, who is next in line, is an imbecile. Le Duc Lucien Chalamet will destroy what is left of Aurelienne and plunge our bankrupt realm back into war."

"I am *not* your political pawn or hers." He bared his teeth. "You promised me."

I promise.

I promise.

"You were always destined to become the Aurelienne king."

All thought skidded to a sudden stop. *Always* destined? No, he was third-born prince. A piece of property sold to Avenbury's elven princess who wouldn't sit on the throne in his lifetime.

Aethelbert, second-born, was *always* destined for the Aurelienne throne—

The blood quickly drained from Adalwolf's head and he felt dizzy for a moment. His mother couldn't possibly be suggesting . . . but the knife twisting in his heart knew. Tears pricked the back of Adalwolf's eyes. That awful, sick bastard. His father was vicious, a truth he already knew but the depth of his cruelty he was seeing more and more every day since the Battle of the Black Winds. But gods. Unable to bear the building pain, Adalwolf rested his cheek on his knees and closed his eyes against the razor-sharp betrayal.

He was a Chalamet wolf. More Aurelienne than any of his brothers.

And Florian . . . his brother had the Sight since he could walk. The sign of who was chosen as Emperor of Dreglind in the Halivaard dragon bloodline—the most powerful mortal in the Kingdom of Ealdspell. But Adalwolf didn't understand this history until he was cursed and exiled a year ago. But his father knew. Knew and hated Florian—feared him. Only one mortal could overthrow King Aelfred of Clifstán. For years, Adalwolf believed it was because his brother preferred baking to soldiering, talked with animals instead of dominating them. But no . . . It all became so clear. So horribly, painfully clear. The king hated his youngest son for a birthright he had wanted himself and was denied—and denied by fae magic.

Florian tried to tell Adalwolf in the underground train.

And he led his little brother to a monster, desperate for that same monster's approval.

A rush of heat buzzed in Adalwolf's head and he could feel invisible hackles bristle down his spine. A low growl rumbled in his chest.

"Fenti." His mother said his nickname and his eyes snapped open.

"Get out!"

"Queen Adeline needed to know. How else do you think I sneak away with food?"

"I don't want your food!" He bared his teeth. "I don't want anything from you! *Especially* a throne." He sounded childish, but he didn't care. The pain blooming in his chest was seizing his every breath.

She peered around the chateau her father had bequeathed to her over forty years ago. "Then perhaps I should take away my manor, yes? Hand you over to Factory Row to pay for war crimes there too?" Her brow arched in that infuriating way of hers. "You came to me Fentienne Chalamet. I thought you dead, like your older brothers. But you found me, *petit louveteau*. Do not pretend I am now an inconvenience to your luxurious exiled lifestyle."

"I prefer Beausoleil," he gritted out.

"*Non*, that is your father's cursed line, *mon fils*. You are a Chalamet, a prince from the House of Golden Light. The Sun Kings are dead."

"*Oui*," he said to mock her. "A cursed name for a cursed *dead* man who will not become king."

His mother heaved a sigh. "Fentienne Beausoleil, *lock your doors*. I do not know when I will see you again." In a rustle of skirts, bows, and lace, Loriette marched toward the exit, the angry click of her heeled slippers echoing throughout the room.

Finally. Silence. He had enough accusing, demanding voices in his head.

His mother stopped at the door and twisted toward him, and he groaned. "The king granted me two hours each week to visit my sons and only under heavy supervision. I was not permitted to be your mother. But I love my boys. *Oui*, even your older brothers who were monsters like their father. To watch your sons lose all goodness . . . my heart will never stop aching." A tear slid down her painted cheek. "I did what I could to protect you and Florian, and I still do. But when you were children, I feared your father would see the depth of your Otherworldly natures. Warrior sons made from dragons and wolves." Another tear slid down her face. "You were safe when training and riding Loring, away from the barracks and war machines, and Florian was safe when in the kitchens. It was no accident Cook took Florian under her wing and no accident you found a wild Aurelienne horse."

The implications of her words punched the remaining air from his lungs.

"I know my boys." She pointed her folded fan at him. "But of you four, I understand you most, *mon petit louveteau*, Prince of Démons. *You* call yourself Beausoleil. Fine. But you *are* Chalamet." With her fan, she gestured at the moth-eaten coat of arms on the wall. A black wolf set against gold with white *fleur de lis*.

The door slammed behind her and Adalwolf grimaced against the sharp pounding in his head.

Warrior sons who were bred to be super soldiers.

Warrior sons made from dragons and wolves.

A fresh wave of fury shook the muscles in his body. Not that his anger mattered. Nothing mattered anymore. Perhaps nothing ever did. Slowing his breathing, he focused on the dark emptiness, the numbing loneliness to find him.

But he was never alone. This house was a haunted graveyard. The dead walked beside him down the hallways. They danced around him in the ballroom. They visited him in his sleep.

Adalwolf leaned onto his elbows and tilted his head back toward the windows. Sunlight caressed the chilled planes of his skin.

Take me, he begged the souls he killed, the souls his father killed. *Bury me alive.*

But they never did. Instead, he awoke each morning in a sunlit grave of gilded lies.

Chapter 3

Rhoslyn

Twilight wrapped around Rhoslyn in a chilly embrace. She pulled the hood of her mother's burgundy cloak farther over her head to shelter from the frigid pre-dawn air—a cloak that was once her grand-mére's. Only a few smatterings of stars still freckled the sky as the sun stretched its arms above the horizon with a lazy yawn. It was a reckless decision to be in the woods outside of Gabaston with only her brother. But she had little time to prepare flowers to sell after sewing for ten straight hours.

Ten hours with dull needles and pins. Her fingers wept at the thought.

Basket in hand, she plucked wildflowers beneath the waking trees with tender fingertips from yesterday's work. The stillness of dawn felt too eerily similar to when wolves stalked these woods. As if the entire forest were a deer in a hunter's sights—wide-eyed, not a single muscle twitch, just short, panting breaths of prayers for salvation.

Rhoslyn's gaze darted from shadow to shadow.

Predators were often asleep at this hour. It was the night they ruled.

But there were all kinds of monsters to fear as a female. Not all roamed on four legs, as she told Amélie. Thankfully, drunks and debauched alike were usually asleep at this hour too. Like the natural wolves and unnatural démons of Gabaston, they owned the night.

The morning dew dampened the frayed, dirt-stained hem of her skirt. The wet fabric lightly slapped against her legs as she moved through a small meadow on the edge of the forest trail. Rhoslyn bent and plucked a sprig of forget-me-nots and added them to the mossy basket she found in an abandoned cottage yesterday. A few yards away, Matthieu sat on the trail, partially hidden by the tall grass, and coiled the still-tight unfurling tops of fiddle head ferns around stems of flowers.

She couldn't afford ribbons or sneak one of the large spools of thread from the factory, though she did pocket sewing pins when Madame wasn't looking. Two days more until she could gather her weekly wages. But she had to somehow feed her brother, whose little belly had grumbled all night while she held him. This evening, the nobles gathered at the theater hall for a concert. She would sell corsages to the ladies for their gowns, the latest fashion trend in Gabaston.

If she didn't earn enough for a bowl of soup and slice of bread, she would sell her hair to peruke weavers for their powdered wigs.

For three nights, she and Matthieu had stayed in a rubbled cottage with no roof. Most of the walls had fallen too. But they had found a dry corner beneath two cob walls that leaned into each other beside strewn moss-covered timber posts. Matthieu slept peacefully while curled against her, beneath her woolen cloak. Rhoslyn, however, found no peace from nightmares.

Bloodthirsty blue eyes, large canined grin, sharp claws grabbing Rhoslyn's skirts while she climbed a tree for safety—these were the horrifying images from when just a girl of twelve.

Screaming, Rhoslyn blindly scraped above her head for a branch, digging her nails into the bark until the skin on her fingertips split. Another hard yank and she lost her grip right as a gunshot rang out. Air gusted wildly through her hair; the leaf-littered forest floor rushed up to meet her. Rhoslyn landed on top of the half-shifted démon—a woman—who had died before hitting the ground. A soldier tracking the beast had saved her. She sobbed into the shoulder of the young man as he carried her home.

That soldier had married her oldest sister a year later. And two years after they wedded, his body rotted in the Spired Hills next to hundreds of other fallen soldiers.

A familiar wave of grief rolled through Rhoslyn at the memory of her family. The pressure around her ribs stole her breath. But she kept moving. That's all she knew how to do—keep moving forward. To stop would mean she lost all hope and that was a piece of her heart she refused to part with, regardless of hardship.

"Rosie!" She twisted toward her brother and lifted her brows. "I need more fiddle head tops."

"I will gather some for you, *caneton*."

"*Non*, I see a patch by those trees not too far away." He pointed and she gnawed the inside of her lip. "I have my guardian with me."

The beggar man had carved a wolf from a birch limb with a fantastical tale of how it would protect Matthieu from wolves while he slept. Such a sweet, kind thing to do. Her brother rested in childlike belief that simple wood warded off evil. But what would happen if his guardian failed him?

"You really do worry too much, *ma sœur*. I'm practically a male grown now."

Her lips twitched. "You do make a persuasive argument. Well then, Monsieur Gautier, go ahead."

Matthieu's eyes brightened and a boyish, dimpled smile, one just for her, softened the hollowness of his cheeks.

"Do not stray from the trail."

That cherubic smile faded into a humored grin and he rolled his eyes. "*Oui*."

An ever-present ache in her chest grew tighter. She would do almost anything to make her brother smile. Still...

The cool morning air nipped at her nose and shivered across her skin. Rhoslyn pulled the hood of her cloak farther over her head and watched Matthieu limp toward the darkened wood. Her heart bolted into a gallop. Monsters were normally asleep at this hour, she reminded herself. Nonetheless, fear quaked down her limbs. Her brother had enough hardships without enduring an overbearing older sister who lived and breathed an unending cycle of what if's.

What if he got attacked and she couldn't reach him?

What if she couldn't earn enough coin to feed him?

What if his lungs sickened as the air turned colder?

What if, what if, *what if*...

The dark cloak Matthieu wore melted into the shadows. One that was adorably too large for his small frame. Yesterday, her friends Amélie, Josie, and Annette had brought him a cloak they had found on a passed out drunk in an alley. Another of Amélie's finds. Before armistice, her friend had pilfered fallen bodies on nearby battlefields for items of value to sell to traders. Her friend now scavenged alleys for treasures before and after work.

Rhoslyn lifted her skirts and strode toward the small cluster of prepared corsages and placed them in her basket. Then she moved toward a swath of wildflowers near where her brother harvested fiddle heads. Space she would give him, but not when he roamed out of sight. And, right now, she couldn't make out anything but trees and underbrush.

"Rosie!" her brother weakly called out, a sound too breathless, and a bolt of fear shot down her limbs.

"Matthieu, do not move!"

A cough rattled the stillness down the trail. Did his lungs wheeze for air he could not draw in? The last time he experienced a breathing attack, he had blacked out. The priests were able to open his air passageways with medicated vapors—an herbal steam. She didn't have herbs or a way to boil water.

Rhoslyn ran through the wildflowers and ferns, beneath tree limbs to the trail—but the trail was empty save the morning birds that were singing to the rising sun. Where was her brother? She spun around and scanned the trees and forest floor for his little body. The frantic rhythm of her pulse raced in dizzy circles in her head. *Mon petit caneton?* She tried to sound grounded, not wanting to frighten him and cause his lungs more stress.

"Can I peek around a tree to show you where I am?"

Her forehead wrinkled. "Of course."

A little head covered in a too-large hood popped out from behind a giant maple. "You told me not to move."

"Oh, Matthieu," she sighed on a laugh. Rhoslyn jogged down the trail and folded him into her arms, kissing his cloaked head. "You sweet, beautiful boy. I thought you couldn't breathe."

"Still worrying too much," he grumbled.

She kissed his head again. "What kind of sister would I be if I didn't worry about my little duckling?"

"You know I cannot raise my voice much, but you were too far away. The effort made me cough." He stared ruefully at the ground. "I do not mean to burden you."

Rhoslyn gently pushed him away and crouched until they were eye level. A tendril of her empath magic grew heavy when touching the shame in his beautiful heart. "You are *never* a burden to me, Matthieu Eric Gautier. Not even a little."

He nodded, as if not quite believing her, then turned toward the open forest. "Do you see it?" he quietly asked. "The castle?"

Rhoslyn slowly straightened and peered through the trees to a chateau abandoned in gothic splendor—a rusted gate on crooked hinges, a garden wild with weeds, stone walls, gargoyles, and spires covered in ivy.

"*Oui*," she answered her brother.

She knew of Chateau Lumière Dorée—House of Golden Light—and had wandered close before. When the fog rolled in, the country manor appeared veiled by the Otherworld. A place so haunted, not even those made homeless by attacks during the war sought its refuge. It was here the King of Clifstán had stolen the queen to make his bride and killed her five younger brothers. Naturally, their ghosts now roamed the manor until avenged. The specters of servants and guards too. Saints bless those poor souls. The king, however, spared Loriette's younger sister, Adeline, who boarded up Chateau Lumière Dorée and forbade the nobles from visiting the grounds.

An arrogant, unfeeling woman, Adeline. And the current sitting queen.

Loriette returned a year ago after armistice, widowed and grieving the loss of her three oldest sons. Only Emperor Florian Halivaard of Dreglind, former prince of Clifstán, survived the final battle at Myrefell. A kind and generous man, she was told by traveling merchants. His faerie bride, they also shared, was an elf who was raised as a hard-working peasant girl from the mountains, though nobility herself.

To serve a monarch who didn't flaunt their silk breeches while their people died of hunger and suffered in the factory slums? What an enchanting dream and Factory Row ate up every delicious lie. No Halivaard was capable of any form of kindness. The traveling merchants spun a cruel story for coin. That horrid family had destroyed Aurelienne. Killed her family in the attacks and burned down her home. *Non*, she could never live beneath the rule of a Halivaard and know peace. Especially one who also came from the House of Chalamet.

But the story of a powerful, kind man who fell in love with a poor elven girl—a fayette?

Changeling child of thorns.

Rhoslyn leaned against a tree and pressed trembling fingers to the bodice of her dress and felt for the ring Gedlen Fate Maker gave her. Saints, the Dúnælven prince was beyond beautiful. A blush warmed her cheeks at the memory of him and she blew out a slow breath to counteract the fluttering in her chest. An infuriating, arrogant male. He had angered her—deeply. But his dark, terrifying presence captivated her. Rhoslyn touched the ring one last time, then let her hand fall away. She had untied the butcher's twine from around one of her thighs to use as a necklace. A ring on her finger would invite trouble. Especially a ring so grand. The stocking on her left leg now slouched while the right leg stayed up. She would do away with stockings all together if it were warmer.

Perhaps she could make a new garter from fern stems.

Perhaps she should just trade the ring for coin and find another safe home for Matthieu.

Matthieu tugged on her cloak and pointed. "There are roses just inside of the gates. They could sell for more coin, *oui*?"

Rhoslyn squinted to better see the overrun garden in the dusky light. "Chateau Lumière Dorée is not safe."

Her brother's mouth fell open. *"This is the haunted chateau?"*

"Oui."

"Haunted roses would sell for even more coin."

"The manor has been boarded up for nearly forty years, *caneton*." She touched the ring beneath her bodice again. "There are reasons no one has squatted on these lands."

Matthieu lifted his chin. "I am more afraid of not eating than ghosts."

"A truer horror story, *oui*—"

A twig snapped behind them. Followed by the crunch of leaves.

Probably nothing but her imagination after discussing murder and cursed houses. Nevertheless, Rhoslyn pulled her brother against her and listened to the gentle sway of trees in a light breeze. No morning birdsong. The woods had suddenly grown unnaturally quiet. A predatory stillness that flushed across her skin and lifted the hair on her arms.

Something was stalking them. Or perhaps somethings.

Movement flashed across the corner of her vision. A dark streak now mere shadow.

Holding her breath steady, she twisted to peer into the widening maw of shifting shadows and dappled light. But the hood of her cloak obscured part of the view. Another black streak flashed through the underbrush. Rhoslyn stumbled back a step. Only one monster moved with such unnatural speed.

They needed to run.

"Ready to swim back to The Row?" she asked her brother while kneeling down, unable to hide the shake in her voice. Matthieu shrugged, unaware of the creature that was stalking them, then wrapped his arms around her neck. Anchoring her arms beneath his legs, she then awkwardly lifted her basket of flowers. "Hold tight."

Her legs trembled, but she stood and—her breath caught.

Inside the gated garden, by the roses Matthieu had pointed out, was a black wolf. A large beast that moved with a spellbinding grace, the motion of muscle too beautiful to be natural. She was about to step back onto the trail and run when it swung its head her way. Golden eyes locked onto her. Eyes that almost seemed . . . *human*. Rhoslyn wasn't sure if she were breathing anymore. The wolf held her gaze one more erratic beat of her heart, then loped toward the chateau and disappeared around the building.

A démon. She had locked eyes with a démon. And it had stalked them and never attacked.

"Why are we not moving?" Matthieu asked with childlike impatience, and she snapped out of her fear-stricken trance.

"Time to swim."

Rhoslyn gathered her skirts and sprinted down the trail toward the rubbled cottages and Factory Row, her brother's carved guardian digging into her back from his pocket.

Chapter 4

Fentienne

Warm water lapped around Adalwolf's hips and he moaned. Steam licked at his skin as he sank down another step, then one more until he was submerged to his chest. Closing his eyes, he leaned his head against the bath's stone lip, just one of several baths below the chateau. The natural hot spring still circulated water through copper pipes after all these years—thank the gods. His muscles ached to the point of grimacing. The pain each morning seemed to be growing worse too.

Other shifters didn't experience the same levels of pain he did. Most seamlessly shifted at will.

The magic binding this curse, however, only allowed him to become full beast at night and disallowed the return to fully human. And because he could not practice or master this magic, he suffered. The break of dawn and the setting of the sun were torment. Every. Single. Day. It frustrated his wolf to no end too.

His damn wolf.

The elves were an intricate part of nature. The environment was their spirit, their magic, and what enabled the fae to manipulate the world and minds around them. But démons? The magic of a wolf spirit lived inside of them. Shifters were both the animal and the human, but also two completely different entities—a symbiotic relationship that often blurred the lines of separation. An even blurrier line for him while half-shifted during the day. Elven familiars, such as birds, foxes, even bears, bonded with their fae outside of the faeries' bodies. But humans had familiars that bonded to them from within. Familiars that fully manifested when shifted. Adalwolf despised being controlled by another, including his wolf. And he and his wolf were constantly locked in a battle of wills.

Magic aside, most of last night his wolf had spent patrolling the woods in search of the monster who was terrorizing Gabaston. Two children and an older man were found dead yesterday near Saints District. Two young women, a child, and a man were slaughtered just outside of The Row two nights prior. No deaths yet reported from inside the gold gates, according to two shifters he knew in The Row. His mother's voice rang in his head to lock his doors. But he *needed* to know it wasn't him. Memories from when in his wolf form were fuzzy images bled through to his human mind, more impressions than full images. He preferred the nights when he recalled nothing—until recently.

This morning, though, he remembered everything.

Right as dawn was breaking, he found a natural wolf pack stalking a boy and girl ten yards from his home. Normally he didn't give a shit. They were idiots for wandering deep into the woods unprotected. But the boy seemed so frail. Even Adalwolf could scent his sickness. Easy pickings for a wolf. But not a fair fight, not a child. He did possess some semblance of morals, as few as they were. Kills so close to his home also invited trouble. The last thing he needed were pitchforks and muskets pointed at Chateau Lumière Dorée.

And the girl . . .

His chest heaved a long, slow breath.

She was *beautiful*. He had watched her pick flowers from the shadows, mesmerized by the long golden-brown hair draping in soft waves over the front of her cloak to her waist. Taken by the gentle tune she sang to herself. Even just watching her slender hand pluck a flower was captivating. The green eyes that held his wolf's were the darkest part of the forest on a drizzly day—glossy, deep, and Otherworldly. Every innocent feminine thing about her was utterly enthralling to him. He wanted to find her after shifting. The longing he felt was strange and unexpected. But the very idea sickened him. Nothing so lovely and pleasurable should touch something so ugly and defiled as him.

When watching the girl, though? He almost forgot he was a monster. Especially when she fidgeted with her stockings while draped in a dark burgundy cloak. The simple tease was alluring. One he far preferred to the games and seductions of nobility. Not gentlemanly thoughts, but he had never been one anyway.

Gods, he missed the simple clothing of Clifstán.

The excessive layers of fabric and accessories for people here were annoyingly frilly and garish.

But gartered stockings and corsets? . . . *that* he enjoyed. Immensely. Even his wolf found the view to his liking. Without question, those two female undergarments were the *only* things he liked about Aurelienne. That and the alcohol. Everything else could burn to ash and blow away.

Adalwolf opened his eyes and watched curling ribbons of steam dance across the water's surface.

Long golden-brown hair, dark green eyes, the way she sang and moved through the woods, a wool cloak and a dirty, fraying bodice dress . . . a familiar story repeating itself. He swore profusely at himself, then dunked his head beneath the water and raked claw-tipped fingers through his floating hair. Attraction to Aurelienne peasant girls he happened upon in the woods, no matter how passing, was something he could not—and would not—entertain. No one was allowed to own his heart or allegiance ever again.

Warrior sons who were bred to be super soldiers.

Warrior sons made from dragons and wolves.

Nausea swirled in his gut and anger stormed just beneath the surface of his skin.

Adalwolf was the name his father gave him. A name for the little wolf he had sired. The shifting power would have probably remained latent had Eirwen not cursed him. Beausoleil would become his new last name—the cursed Sun Kings from his father's line. The name Adalwolf, however, left a rotten taste in his mouth. He became the wolf his father had wanted, his super soldier. But he preferred the name Fentienne. Grief also stained this name. Not the stain of bloodshed, though. Not the stain of his father's violation.

Fentienne—*split crown*. He once thought this meant he was a prince from three powerful noble houses. Now he understood.

He was a man who always had been part mortal, part creature.

A man with a *broken* crown.

Third-born, Prince of Démons he may be, but today Adalwolf would die and Fentienne would be born. No one would ever have power over him again. Not the ghost of his father. Not the silk-wrapped husk of his mother. No mortal or beast. No faerie. And especially not beautiful, innocent peasant girls who created the illusion of normalcy and happiness right before ripping his barely beating, desperate heart from his chest. And gods, he was so desperate. So pathetically, foolishly desperate.

Water rippled around him as he broke the surface and stood. Dried mud, and who knows what else, no longer coated his body. His wolf entered and exited the chateau from a door he propped open to the hot springs. If he were lucky, he would shift back in the morning by the baths. Wiping the droplets from his face, he moved toward the stairs and stepped from the bath. Steam rose from his flushed skin and misted the large open bathing chamber. He slipped on a silk frock coat he used as a robe and poured whiskey into a cut crystal cup.

Lower class drunks drank straight from the bottle. He was nobility. A drunkard who sipped from a glass that would fund an entire month of fine meals for any commoner of Factory Row. *Haute noblesse*—a class as disgusting as him. He lifted his cup in salute to the peasants who wouldn't eat this day while his mother and her courtiers ate off dishes decorated in plated gold.

Fentienne walked through the chateau, up stairs after stairs, to the north tower room. Empty rooms, empty hallways, *empty, empty, empty* . . . loneliness had never worn a face so bleak. For the three years leading up to exile, he had shared quarters with five other officers. The ten years prior to that, he had slept in a room with twenty-five other men, all lined up in neat cots with chests at the end of their beds. Latrines in the open, the showers too. Only a small passageway connected the bunks of his platoon to the bunks of another, and those bunks to yet another. Like Florian, he had started out as an army scout but with combat expectations. Though, his younger brother belonged to a platoon that remained out of battle to serve exclusively as spies or to hunt down deserters. By Fentienne's eighteenth birthday, he was moved to a mech cavalry where he eventually captained three platoons of highly trained machine warfare soldiers.

And now he wandered a molding, moth-eaten abandoned chateau with only the occasional visit from his mother and, when not attending Brotherhood meetings, run-ins with fellow shifters in the woods, the ones who called him their prince. For only wolves from the House of Chalamet had golden amber eyes and he had arrived in a barely held together, torn Clifstán military uniform from shifting and with identification tags. They knew at once who he was and, from that moment, bowed to him as their alpha despite his military campaigns against Aurelienne. But he could feel *their* presence always inches from his back, the ones he had killed over the years. The ones his father killed in this chateau too. Hundreds of lives he had destroyed and for nothing—their beating heart he was trained to own and his duty to end.

A soldier since the age of eight. A military prince since the day he was born. It was all he ever knew. War was in his blood. Death coffined his pulse. The idea that a world without regimented routine, without any form or purpose, an isolated existence wasted on furious indulgence, was beyond imagination. And yet, here he was in a silk jacket after soaking in luxury baths. A bottle of aged whiskey worth the price of outfitting an entire platoon with automatic weapons was clutched in one hand and, in the other, a crystal tumbler that had only known the lips of nobles who had never labored a day in their deplorable life.

How did one not work? Every day he had been tasked with duties that reaped painful consequences if not performed exactly as ordered. And if not working, he was working out to keep his body in the fittest shape for battle. The nobles of Aurelienne were lazy, soft-handed morons who leached off the commoners to fund their excessive lifestyle. Though, he supposed in many ways, Clifstán was no different. Sons were tithed to the military for bread on the table. Even the sons of kings.

Fentienne laughed low, a resentful, bitter sound that echoed off the walls. A man who killed hundreds judging an aristocracy who starved hundreds? No, he would still judge and enjoy the sweet rush of feeling morally superior, even if he knew the high ground was a false floor. Intellectual dishonesty was a game he played well. Apathy was a delightful motivator for meaningless manipulations, even to oneself.

Once in his room, he let the black silk jacket fall from his shoulders to hang in his armoire. He should slip between the covers and find sleep after such a long night. But nightmares would find him too. From a bottom shelf, he fetched a pair of neatly folded knee-length linen breeches and pulled them up. He was in the middle of buttoning the waist when the hair on his arms stood on end and he froze. Animal instincts kicked in and he lifted his ear to the cold room. But he couldn't hear the soft shuffle of footsteps. Or panting breaths from climbing the tower stairs. His wolf, however, was growling. A low warning threat.

Fentienne pivoted about face and met a pair of rose-colored eyes.

Panic dropped a boulder into his already churning stomach and knocked the air from his lungs.

I promise.

I promise.

"Hello, beastling." A wicked smile curled Addien's lips as her gaze devoured the tensed muscles of his chest and upper arms, her eyes dipping lower and lower, down his abdomen to his bare feet before slowly traveling back up to meet the fury in his eyes. "What a beautiful abomination you are, prince."

Fentienne grabbed a thin, unlaced linen shirt from his armoire and threw it over his head. "You have five seconds to disappear before I tear into you."

"I am not afraid of a big bad wolf." She sauntered over to where he now stood by the end of his bed, each step slow.

He chuckled, an angry, devilish sound. "Four seconds."

"You owe me a pleasure of my choosing."

"Two seconds."

"Fenti—"

He didn't let her finish. Fentienne lunged, his claws out, his canines bared. Addien disappeared before he could grab her and, in a flash of light, glitched into focus across the room. *What in the hell?* He never understood how she could disappear or reappear. Other than The Lady at the Battle of the Black Winds, no other faerie he had met possessed this magic.

Pissed, he growled and stalked to where she stood with a taunting come-hither tilt to her lips. "Get. Out."

"You owe me, Fenti."

"I owed Fayette, not *you*."

Muscles bunched, he slashed clawed fingers at her, but she disappeared again. Another bolt of panic shot through him. Slowly turning, his eyes darted around the room.

Addien reappeared behind him, her gossamer dress floating over his neatly made bed. "The pleasure I ask of you—"

"I only offer you pain—"

"—is to be mine."

"I *still* would rather die!"

"We both know that is a lie."

Fentienne sneered at the female who still knelt on his bed. "You sicken me. Everything about you sickens me."

"You begged me to kiss you, prince." A feline smile taunted him. "You wanted me."

"I wanted *Fayette*."

"Yes," she purred. "I wonder how many fayettes you killed when invading Gabaston?"

Disgust wormed at his conscious. But he forced every feature to run cold. "Monsters don't keep a tally. But I would gladly count your death. Mmm, to hear you scream."

"I told you," she said low, almost breathless. "I am not afraid of wolves or monsters. I crave their company. I've always craved yours most of all."

"The image of you bleeding out is a delicious thought."

She waved him off. "I have news for you, Fentienne. The *fayette* you are betrothed to is believed dead."

He fully laughed at her now. Like he cared. Then his mind snagged on one word. "Believed?" he scoffed. "Dead, alive? I don't give a shit about your princess. I never did." He narrowed his eyes. "I'm no longer a Prince of Clifstán. Nor is a cotton trade agreement necessary without a military to outfit."

"You believe it was only about the cotton?" Addien tilted her head. "The betrothal was made in *your* and your father's blood, not your nobility status. You sealed your own fate, prince."

The hell?

Fuzzy memories scratched the corners of his mind, ones far too blurry to fully recall. But he remembered one emotion: *fear*. Fear of crying when the knife sliced his finger. Terrified of how his father would punish him if he did.

A tendon in his neck pulsed. "Barbaric to bind the promises of a four-year-old child in his own blood." Fentienne was about to shred the walls around him. "Conniving, soulless, self-serving beasts, all of you."

"Barbaric? I have never, with my own hands, killed a soul in all my years, *beastling*. Nor will I. Can you say the same?"

"Ordering a kill is still killing."

"Poor dear," the elf continued as if not hearing him. "Did you know that Maeline Kadelaryn Wyndham was hidden away as a merchant's daughter by the name of Rhoslyn Gautier? A changeling child. Rather clever of my queen. But can you imagine? A faerie princess raised in a working-class home. A poor one at that with six children." Addien lifted a slender shoulder in a delighted shrug. "The Gautier's home and shop burned down. All bodies confirmed dead save her and her youngest brother, unfortunately. Gedlen Fate Maker has been searching for her remains for over a year now."

Addien crawled across his bed to the edge and bit her lower lip. "Come prince," she said, curling her finger at him. "Become mine, body and soul. Marry me."

Body and soul? He shuddered.

"If I want a female, I will go to The Row. You?" he asked, curling his lip, "Are repulsive. I would much rather touch a diseased pavement nymph than crawl into your bed. And I'd run myself through before letting my soul be marked by yours."

"Your dark heart calls to mine, Adalwolf Fentienne Halivaard. The very sight of you intoxicates me." Her gaze made a slow trail over his body once more. "I created the blood contract between my queen and your king. Marry me and I will release your binds in this betrothal. We could wield so much power together."

Pain cracked across his chest. "You tricked me when I was only four. You tricked me when I was sixteen. Why do you toy with me now? This is more than revenge."

"You belong to me, Fenti. You have *always* belonged to me. Not *her*."

Disgust wormed in his gut.

She softly laughed. "Oh prince, who could love a beast?" Addien climbed off the bed and waltzed toward him. "You were one when Prince of Clifstán and you are still one, Prince of Démons." She tilted her head. "Tell me, who loves you? Who has ever loved you?"

The throbbing ache in his chest grew more intense, but he remained quiet.

No one loved him.

No one ever had.

The closest he came to knowing love was with Florian before Fentienne was conscripted at age eight. And . . . with Fayette. But it was all fake. A faerie trick. Every single godsdamn moment with her. But skies, those few weeks were the happiest of his life even though none of it was real. Made him an absolute fool. He was willing to give up his entire world for her. But never again would he be so foolish. No one deserved what remained of his torn heart, not even him.

Tears bit the back of his eyes, but he allowed rage to tie a noose around those feelings. He would not hang by the gallows of self-pity.

That meant *they* won.

That *they* still owned him.

And that's exactly what she wanted to do. Break him until he submitted to her grand designs for his life.

"Love is a beautiful lie to hide an ugly truth," he gritted between clenched teeth, then he took a calculated step toward her. "It doesn't exist. It has *never* existed. Everything the poets write? Every tear- and blood-stained word scribbled on the parchment of their breaking hearts? A fabricated feeling to escape the pain of one's shitty life. Strip away all the flowers and candies and diamond rings and you're left with another empty, miserable soul who, beneath all the overtures, hates their own life more than they hate others. We are born to die. So, we *trick* ourselves and others to feel happy first. What else is there to live for than the pursuit of our own delusions?" He leaned into her face and snarled, "How much more pleasurable the journey. How much more satisfying the destruction."

She reached out for his hand but he stepped back and relaxed his shoulders, pretending to take in the curve of her hips, her breasts. A wet strand of hair fell over his eye and heat warmed her gaze as she studied his face. Since he was four, she had chosen him for revenge. When a young man, she had wanted to know his love by pretending to be another. As if she were jealous of Maeline. But why? Addien truly desired him, of that he didn't question. The obsession was disturbing. Just another in his life who used and groomed him to satisfy their hate. Another who tried to own his life for their selfishness. She wanted his body? His heart? Wanted him to become her plaything? Good. More satisfying the destruction . . .

"Marry me, Fenti, and I will love your monstrous ways."

"Will you?" he asked, his voice rough. He circled around her, every step sensual, and she watched him from the corner of her eyes. Listening to her rapid breathing fed his lust for torment. Awareness of how her body vibrated in anticipation of his touch empowered his depravity. Oh the terrible things he could do to her. But the idea of intimacy with the monster who stole his life and poisoned his only happiness nauseated him too much, even if for revenge. Playing with her, though?

At her back, he brushed his nose along her neck, his lips close to her skin. "I could seduce you," he whispered in her ear. "*Te donner du plaisir.*"

Give you pleasure.

"Yes," she whispered back. Her chest rose and fell in a deep rhythm, and he knew she closed her eyes with the feel of him so near.

"I could make you believe I love you," he continued. "Real enough that you fall in love with me." He smiled against her skin and she shivered. "*Et tu m'aimerais.*"

And you would love me.

"I already do."

Bile coated his throat. "The ache for me, the longing? The ways I would toy with your heart?" He placed a soft kiss beneath her ear. "I would force you to kneel before me, delighting as you grow sick with desire while I destroy you slowly, snapping one emotional bone after another, until you wished you were already dead." She stilled and he grinned. Angling the rest of the way around her body, he faced her and murmured, "But you're not worth my time or energy. Already I'm bored of you."

Addien held his gaze for a beat, her face stricken with both disbelief and dawning understanding—she couldn't break his spirit to bend him to her will. There was nothing left inside of him to break.

"You promised me a pleasure of my choosing."

"You tricked me with a beautiful lie. My answer is the ugly truth." Fentienne turned toward the table, ignoring the sneer twisting her lips. "Now get out." He poured himself another hearty splash of whiskey. "Or I will literally rip the still beating heart from your chest."

"You *will* marry me!" she shouted at him. "Not her!"

"Hmm." The beginnings of a cruel smile flirted with the corners of his lips.

A shadow passed over her face. "You would break a promise to an ancient fae, beast?"

He lifted the cup in salute and arched a single brow.

Her eyes blackened; the prettiness of her face hardened into something utterly gruesome. "To refuse a favor owed is to invite a curse."

To hide the hackles of fear prickling down his spine, he took a nonchalant sip of whiskey.

"Say it, Fentienne," she hissed. "I want to hear your promise to die than be with me."

He smirked. "You thought yourself in love? I'm touched."

"Say it!"

He took another sip and held her darkening eyes. "I find your company as interesting as a rotting, maggot-filled fish." He leaned his hip against the table and humorously cocked his head. "For who could love a black-hearted, manipulative creature like you?"

"You declare yourself an oath breaker?"

"I promise to never marry you, Addien. Now, tomorrow, in a thousand lifetimes." Fentienne's voice hardened with barely contained contempt. "I promise to always think of you with revulsion. I promise to torture you if you dare approach me again. I promise to kill you after I'm done making you scream for mercy."

At first, he thought he saw true pain in her eyes followed by a jealousy so intense his predatory instincts went deathly still.

Then laughter began shaking her dainty frame. Her canines grew longer, sharper. Black veins webbed around her mostly pupiled rose-colored eyes, almost like tiny roots, and dark claws formed at the tips of her fingernails. Fentienne should feel terror at her sudden fiendish appearance, but he also wasn't afraid of wolves or monsters. And he was pissed. Fury held no candle to the rage gusting through him this moment.

She had tricked him—again.

Was Addien even her real name? Or another identity she stole?

The evil faerie locked eyes with him and her grin widened. "Adalwolf Fentienne Halivaard, prince from the dragons of House Halivaard and the wolves of House Chalamet, mortal with the black heart that owns mine, I curse the grounds and walls that shelter you."

I curse you.

His heart jumped to his throat and he clenched his teeth.

I curse you.

Images of his little brother flashed in his head. The look of horror in Florian's eyes right as the gun went off.

Eirwen hung from her wrist at the whipping post, screaming while the ground shook with her rage and her grief. A faerie laughed in the background, the cackling growing louder and louder. A sound that scraped knives down his spine.

A trick. It was all a faerie trick.

Black mist slithered between his feet, just like that final battle in Myrefell a year ago, and his eyes shot to Addien.

It was her laughter that filled this room, not The Lady's.

Her awful, hair-raising laughter.

"Your black heart will paint the walls," Addien continued. "Your black soul will haunt these halls. Since you would rather die than be with me, then you shall live in a grave of your own making alongside the ghosts buried in this chateau by your father."

The black mist rolled over the floor and up the walls and his mouth fell open. Whatever the mist touched turned black or to shades of a red or purple so dark, it was practically black. Even his clothing and linens. Candelabras, covered in cobwebs, lit around him and flickered eerie shadows across the floor. A fire roared to life in his hearth—a flame haloed in a slight green light. The Underworld's fires. The curtains next to him wildly fluttered in a dark breeze and he nearly jumped.

Bury me alive.

The nightmares that visited him each night began whispering in his mind.

Take me, he begged the souls he had killed, the souls his father had killed. *Bury me alive.*

Bury me alive . . .

Fentienne choked back the building sob in his chest.

"Adalwolf Fentienne Halivaard, I curse you in love," the faerie said, her sharp-toothed grin wide. "For who can love a beast? The ugly truth for an ugly man. You will know the horror of rejection, the terror of unrequited love. You will know the pain you've caused me before and now. The first female to wander through the broken gates will be trapped by your hate and bound to you for all her remaining days. She will fall in love with the whole man in her dreams and despise the monster when awake. Your true identity will never fall from your mate's lips or the lips of others when around her. She will have no choice but to call you beast."

Tears pricked the back of his eyes but he forced his face to remain cold, indifferent.

"She will be a rose and a thorn in your life. Beautiful beyond compare but painful to behold. And you will be her living nightmare. You may leave the property, but she will never be able to escape you. The walls, doors, windows, and gates will keep her locked inside the coffin of Chateau Lumière Dorée until she dies."

His lip curled, though he felt only hollowness. "Is that all?"

"You want more, prince?"

"Why not?" he tossed out as if bored. "Curse the air I breathe, curse the water, curse the food, curse me in death as well as in love." Fentienne lifted the crystal tumbler to his lips and savored a long sip of whiskey. "Curse me with nothing but alcohol to drink."

"I curse your roses."

"My... roses?" Fentienne threw his head back and laughed. "Please curse the violets and posies too. Nothing more terrifying to a beast than cursed flowers in a garden of weeds."

"Yes, Prince of Démons. I curse your roses. They will release a most profound perfume that will entice the Beautiful Rose of the Forest. Your rose and your thorn will wander through the gates of Chateau Lumière Dorée, enchanted by the garden, simply to smell the betrayal that awaits her. And then I will have cursed you both and my revenge in this lifetime will be complete."

Rhoslyn Gautier.

Beautiful Rose of the Forest.

A fuzzy image of the girl in the burgundy cloak faded into his mind. A cloak the color of the black roses his mother once tended that now climbed all over the chateau gardens. A girl picking flowers in the woods by his home beside a little boy with an injured leg.

"You didn't want her and now she won't want you." Addien laughed low. "Nobody will ever want you, beast. But I always have and always will."

"You will be wanting until I kill you."

Claws out, he lunged at her just as she disappeared. Fentienne growled and threw his tumbler of whiskey where she had once stood. Crystal shattered across his bedroom floor and whiskey splattered on his wall. He stared at the mess without seeing the glittering sharp pieces or the amber liquid. Muscles flexed and relaxed, his entire body on the edge of losing complete control. A few beats later, he charged down the stairs. He would dig up every damn rose in his mother's forgotten garden.

He [the father] entered the garden, where roses were exhaling the most delicious perfume . . . He picked one, and was about to gather enough to make a half-a-dozen bouquets, when a most frightful noise made him turn around.

"I warn you again," said the Beast, "to take care not to deceive her as to the sacrifice which you must exact from her or the danger she will incur. Paint to her my face such as it is. Let her know what she is about to do: above all, let her be firm in her resolution."

The Beast must be very hungry indeed," said Beauty half-jestingly [to her father], "to make such grand rejoicings at the arrival of his prey." However, in spite of her agitation at the approach of an event which—according to all appearance—was about to be fatal to her . . . that the preparations for her death were more brilliant than the bridal pomp of the greatest King in the world.

A lady whose majestic demeanor and surprising beauty . . . said to her, "Courage, Beauty; show yourself to be as wise as you are charming."

"La Belle et la Bête" by Madame de Villeneuve, published in *The Young American and Marine Tales*, 1743

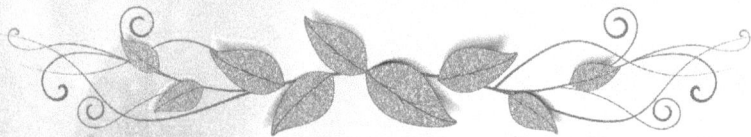

Chapter 5

Rhoslyn

"Flowers!" Rhoslyn sang out to the busy streets. She and Matthieu perched on the bottom step of the concert hall. "Flowers for your dress! Flowers for your lady!"

On the edge of town, where Factory Row met Saints District, the crowd was a mix of elegantly dressed aristocrats and middle-class revelers who angled between common drunkards. Oil lanterns, strung across the narrow cobblestone streets every twenty feet or so, flickered tall shadows across the buildings and taverns. A group of young men in silk breeches stumbled by, laughing loud while slapping each other on the back before disappearing inside one of the tolerant houses—a legal, registered brothel. Illegal nymphs across from her, in dirty, fraying corsets, thin skirts, and cheap makeup, enticed men with less coin into the dark alley.

One of the nymphs caught Rhoslyn's eyes and greeted her with a little finger wave. Rhoslyn dipped her head and smiled. The girls had brought Matthieu a small orange yesterday and fussed over him like he was their own little brother—they each had families at one point. Perhaps they still did. Bashful from all the attention, Matthieu showed off his carved wolf guardian and flashed them his dimpled smile, the one that would melt the scariest gargoyles from temple edifices. Her brother was so sweet. He understood their occupation. No child was innocent south of Saints District. But he talked to them as if they were dignified and worthy of respect, not soiled rubbish.

"Flowers!" Rhoslyn sang out once more. "Flowers for your dress! Flowers for your lady!"

Merchant stations packed Factory Row, their street cries a deafening musical. Each vendor had their own song, a signature sound to separate them from neighbors and competitors, and to be remembered. Songs for bread, songs for apples, jewelry, firewood, eggs, chairs, shoes . . . During the day it was harder to hear all the distinct vocal threads unless one was nearby. But at night, buskers crowded the pavement and added their musical instruments to the chorus of evening hawkers who sold ale, meat pies, coffee, sweets, and a variety of trinkets.

A finely dressed man climbed the steps to the hall and she walked beside him. "Monsieur, flowers for your lady?"

The look of disgust on his face stilled her footsteps. She would not apologize for being elf or poor. She was not ashamed of who she was or what she had to do to survive. Turning away from him, she locked eyes with a woman of middle years.

"Madame, flowers for your fine dress?"

The woman hesitated a moment but replied with a curt nod. "One corsage, *sans-culotte*."

One without silk breeches. Commoner. But she pushed away the ridiculous insult and selected the best petite floral bouquet in her basket and added a sewing pin. The noblewoman placed two coppers into Rhoslyn's outstretched hand.

"*Merci*, madame. Saints bless you." Rhoslyn lowered into a shallow curtsy, which hurt her soul to do. But she would lower herself a little to feed her brother. "Matthieu," she whispered and discreetly handed him the coins to hide inside his shoe . . . which they decided upon after inspecting for any holes.

This was the third evening she had peddled flowers. This morning the third she had gathered wildflowers in the woods. Strangely, she felt safer after her encounter with the black wolf démon. If it had wanted to harm them, it would have done so then. Still, the twilight of morning remained a gooseflesh breath on the nape of her neck. Every shifting shadow, every rustle of leaves. She felt eyes on her wherever she moved.

After collecting and arranging the bouquets and corsages, she would return to the rubbled cottages and place the cut flowers inside broken crockery, which she stored in the shallows of a nearby creek. Remnant pieces of pottery littered these fallen homes. The cool air blowing off the creek kept the flowers fresh while water swirled around the stems in the bottomless pots. After factory work, she had just enough time to run to the creek, fetch the flowers, and weave through the building revelry of Factory Row to her station by the concert hall—and all with Matthieu on her back.

Rhoslyn studied the remaining arrangements and smiled. Wood violets, wild roses, forget-me-nots, columbines in shades of red and orange, young ferns, and herbs she harvested from the weed-filled kitchen gardens belonging to the fallen homes. She fidgeted over the small bunches resting atop dampened moss and artfully rearranged them in her basket while humming a light tune to herself.

"I still think we should sell haunted roses."

"Hush, *caneton*." Rhoslyn eyed the passersby to see if they heard her brother. "We make enough for soup from the priests."

His little shoulders sagged. "*Oui*."

"Flowers!" Rhoslyn sang out again. "Flowers for your dress! Flowers for your lady!"

A sharply dressed, handsome young man slowed on the concert hall steps and eyed her curiously.

"Flowers for your lady, monsieur?" She added a thread of cheeriness to her tone while lifting her basket.

The young man didn't even glance at the wildflowers. "I would pay coin for other services, *sans-culotte*."

"*Non*, monsieur. I only peddle flowers." Warmth crept up her neck and she swallowed thickly.

A humored smile pulled at the corner of his lips. "A fayette as beautiful as you? Surely."

Rhoslyn turned her head toward her shoulder and clenched her jaw. "Move along, I have flowers to sell, monsieur." He stepped closer and her gaze snapped to his. She lowered her voice and gritted out, "I said, move along. I am *not* for sale."

The man grabbed her basket and threw it behind her. Rhoslyn flinched. Corsages and small bouquets bounced off the steps and tumbled to the street where the crowds crushed her flowers beneath their shoes as they passed by.

"Now what do you have to sell, fayette?" The young man placed a possessive hand on her arm and yanked her toward him.

"Guard!" her brother shouted and fell into a deep coughing fit. "Guard!"

He tried to shout again, but his lungs were wheezing.

The man chuckled at Matthieu's attempt to help her. Guards didn't care about poor girls. Nobody in authority cared about the guttered lives in The Row, only what they could take, what they could abuse, and steal under the law.

Matthieu continued to cough and Rhoslyn grimaced back the rising fear.

Fingers dug into her arm, a bruising grip, and the man tried to pull her off the step. Matthieu's eyes rounded in horror and he reached for her hand. Rhoslyn fought against the man's hold and shuddered when he tried to kiss her. But she turned her head away and his mouth crashed into her neck.

Fire licked at her veins and flamed every beat of her pounding pulse.

How dare he destroy her means of income.

How dare he decide to crush her like the flowers now strewn across the pavement.

The pompous, entitled, silk breech-wearing arsehole. Rhoslyn shoved him away from her body. Baring her teeth, to ensure he saw her small canines, she then stomped on his foot with the heel of her shoe. He released her arm and stepped back. Only for the briefest moment, though. Fury twisted the hard lines of his face and she knew she needed to run and disappear into the throng. But she couldn't leave her brother. Trembling, she rubbed her arms and looked around, hot tears gathering on her lashes. She wasn't sure of what to do.

The pain of hunger, the pain of always being afraid, the pain of defending her brother's worth to priests, the pain of being married to a démon . . . she was snapping inside.

Anger was quickly becoming an inferno that was demanding sacrifices. And she would start with *him*.

Rhoslyn wiped at a tear and flashed her canines at the man again. "*Liberté, Egalité, Fraternité!*" she screamed. "*Liberté, Egalité, Fraternité!*"

The man's eyes widened, then darted around Factory Row.

"*Liberté, Egalité, Fraternité!*" she screamed again.

Nearby vendors shouted back and began slowly surrounding the young noble when noting her broken basket and damaged flowers. She continued to scream "Liberty. Equality. Fraternity" at the top of her lungs. Even when the crowd thickened around them. Other female merchants settled beside her and screamed too. An older woman gathered Matthieu to her and rubbed his back.

Rhoslyn moved to reach for her brother, but a nymph who saw the attack wrapped an arm around her shoulder and gently wiped a tear from Rhoslyn's face. "He will be cared for. Take a moment to care for you, *belle fleur*." Nodding her head, Rhoslyn leaned into the girl's shoulder and began sobbing while cries for liberty, equality, and fraternity rang all around her.

This was their war cry. The monarchy had sacrificed the lower class to battle after battle, to eternally rest in the Spired Hills. The streets of Factory Row had run red with peasant blood for far too long. They were beyond hungry. They were working into the grave. They were drowning in taxes they couldn't possibly pay back in their lifetime. All the while the temples were spared from the cruelty of being extorted and allowed to extort those who depended on them for care.

The priests charged for soup.

They received tithes from the aristocracy *and* from the same impoverished people whom they then charged for a meager meal. Rhoslyn had swallowed her pride and asked Mon Père Michel to credit her the soup for not returning her unused tithes and he refused her, knowing her brother, once his ward, was sick and hungry. She paid the temple *more* of her hard-earned money to eat.

Tears continued to stream down her cheeks and rage quaked in her bones. Rhoslyn kissed the nymph's cheek, then straightened. She would fight. She would fight until her voice was hoarse and her bones could no longer bear the weight of injustice. She would fight until the last breath of air was forced from her burning lungs.

"*Liberté, Egalité, Fraternité!*" she screamed again and again and again.

Nobody owned her. Her life was hers and hers alone.

Matthieu grasped her hand and lifted his fist beside her.

Factory Row was a snarling dog ready to bite back those who had abused them all their lives. Aristocrats began running to the safety of their upper-class establishments. Angry dogs, however, do love a chase. And that's when the riot broke out.

Screams filled the dusky air around her. The young man who assaulted her was dragged into an alley by a group of factory workers. Perhaps she should feel shame for the beating that man would now receive. But she felt nothing but righteous fury. How many other females had he harmed or attempted to harm? Poor girls, like her, who worked from sunup to sundown to put bread in the hollowed bellies of their siblings and children they were too young to bear? Girls who had no protection from society or from the depravity of men?

A gun shot rang out and Rhoslyn shielded her brother with her body.

More screams and cries of alarm echoed in the night around them.

A crowd surged toward a wealthy dressed man who was running toward a carriage. Before hopping in, he pulled a pistol from his waist and fired. Men fell to the cobblestone. A puff of smoke obscured the aristocrat's face for a mere blink, then he disappeared inside the carriage and took off into Saints District. Blood stained the pavement and people screamed. Scooting up to a wall, a man in rough spun clothing coddled his leg. Those nearby scurried into action. A bystander removed his belt to cinch around the injury.

"What have I done?" Rhoslyn asked in both growing horror and wonder.

"What needed to be done, *belle fleur*," the nymph said next to her. "This is not your doing, *oui*? Let the nobles rot in their own fluids."

The angry mob charged up the steps into the concert hall and shoved through the doors.

Rhoslyn frantically looked at all the females who had gathered around her. Most had grime smudged across their faces. Hair lay limp, unwashed and barely styled. Many wore their hair down, like her, simply for lack of combs and ribbons. Other females from respectable middle-class homes had joined them as well, standing shoulder to shoulder with nymphs, legal prostitutes, and poor factory working girls. Each stood ready to fight, to rally. To shout into the night their grief.

They were not permitted to vote or hold land. But they were still required to pay taxes to the estate and tithes to the temples. They had little say in marriage and, in most cases, occupation. Unlike the males, if a female lost her job at a factory or became with child, she was unlikely to find replacement work—even if she had no family or husband. And why so many ended up in brothels.

The females around her may not be able to fight with fists, but they could still strike terror in other ways.

"To the gold gates of Palais d'Aurélie!" Rhoslyn cried out. "Let the queen and her courtiers hear our demands for bread! Our demands for lower taxes!"

Shouts roared around her and Matthieu grinned, his blue eyes large and full of pride.

For her brother, she would take on the entire realm. For her brother, she would take on Queen Adeline Chalamet.

Rhoslyn brushed an unruly lock of blond hair from Matthieu's eyes and cupped his cheek. Then she knelt and lifted his foot from the shoe hiding their coppers to pocket in her dress. Once their meager earnings were secured, she asked, "Ready to swim, *mon petit caneton?*" The crowd pushed them forward. But she pulled her brother to the side so he could climb onto her back.

"Time to swim!" he said into her hair.

As they marched, more and more females joined their rally. They banged on pots, rang bells, demanding to be heard. Their numbers swelled until the narrow streets of Factory Row could barely contain them. Still, they continued on, knocking on doors they passed. Shouting into taverns with a call to action. All around them, males lifted fists into the air and walked beside them.

And the empath magic swirling inside of her charged with renewed fury. Poverty wasn't laziness. The people around her didn't deserve hunger and unsafe living conditions as payment for hours and hours of hard labor, for sacrificing loved ones to Clifstán's bullets.

The edge of Factory Row and Saints District lay in rubble still. Rhoslyn studied the empty space that was once her home and family shop. Grief stabbed through her, a deep, sharp pain that mixed with the injustice fueling every step toward Palais d'Aurélie. Angry shouts crescendoed around her, but in the stilled center of her raging storm, she could hear her father's praise, her mother's voice as she sang in the kitchen, the laughter of her brothers and sisters. Matthieu kissed her head and she gripped the small hands wrapped around her neck. If she didn't have this boy still in her life . . .

"Rosie!"

Rhoslyn slowed and darted her gaze around the crowd.

"Rosie!"

She turned and Amélie fell into her arms and hugged both her and Matthieu. "I knew you would be in the crowd, *mon petit chou-fleur.*" Amélie gently grabbed her face and turned it side to side. "You have been crying."

"A silk breeches attacked her, Amélie." Matthieu's voice thundered with anger and he tightened his hold around her neck. "But Rosie fought back and started a revolution."

"*Non*, Matthieu." The corner of Rhoslyn's lip inched up. "Only a riot to serve justice to that despicable man. This protest has been building for weeks. We are dry tinder ready to flame at the mildest spark."

"Why have the guards not arrived?" Amélie peered around the agitated crowd. "Do you not think it odd?"

A chill trailed a finger down her spine.

"*Oui*," Rhoslyn said. "They will come. They always do."

She fell silent while following the march through Saints District to Quartier Étienne du Soleil—shortened to Crowns Quarter—named after King Étienne Beausoleil, the first in the Sun Kings line. In the center of Crowns Quarter was Palais d'Aurélie, a breathtaking palace on breathtaking grounds, originally built to be a hunting lodge for King Étienne.

But what good was a beautiful house if it only roofs ugly people? Appearances were deceiving. A part of her wanted The Golden Palace to burn down so the aristocracy could receive a taste of how the citizens of Aurelienne have suffered. Let their over-filled bellies scrape for food from the gutters.

"It is beautiful," her brother whispered.

The gold gates practically glowed beneath the streetlamps.

"Just the tip of one spire could feed so many," Rhoslyn said. "The opulence is beautifully grotesque."

The crowd of thousands paused just before the gates, shouting, hands fisted in the air. Those in the front began pushing against the gold bars. The angry shouts soon became a heave-ho chant as protesters rocked back and forth in ramming shoves. Gold was soft, though, and it didn't take long for the more decorative than practical gates to break off their hinges. The crowd lifted a cheer, then marched over the gold in their dirty, threadbare shoes. The imagery emboldened Rhoslyn and she began shouting "Liberty. Equality. Fraternity!" once again.

Palace guards, well over a hundred, outfitted with muskets with bayonets on the end, lined up in front of the march. More guards arrived and flanked the sides. This was why they hadn't stopped the protesters in the streets. The queen must have known they marched on Palais d'Aurélie. Those in the crowds had few weapons save the kitchen knives many of the females brought along, daggers some of the men carried, and pistols the middle-class merchants owned. A hundred-and-fifty to two hundred rifle men would overpower them. Or, at a minimum, cause far too many casualties.

The Row had already lost far too many men to the war and the women were already working far too much to care for their families in their absence. Rhoslyn hoped the protesters kept their wits about them despite the injustices demanding reparation.

Queen Adeline moved into view on the balcony and a hush rippled over the protesters. For many, this was the first time they had seen their queen. A woman holding a small dog in her arms settled beside Adeline on the balcony and, without introduction, Rhoslyn knew this must be Loriette Chalamet. The sisters both wore powdered wigs that set off the trademark golden amber eyes from House Chalamet, the House of Golden Light, the House of Wolves. The eldest wore a gown of peach silk while the crowned queen wore pale blue.

"Who demanded an audience with me?" Queen Adeline called out over the crowd.

The protesters looked to one another then began shouting.

The queen touched the side of her head and closed her eyes, clearly annoyed. "Silence! Or my guards will silence you." When the crowd quieted once more, she asked, "*Who* demanded an audience with me? I will speak with one, not the whole."

Once more, the protesters looked among one another. A few merchant class men began to move forward, but Rhoslyn didn't want males to speak for what the females started this evening. Or speak for elves who made up the larger population in the slums of Aurelienne. She was tired of never having a voice heard on anything.

"I will speak!" Rhoslyn shouted. "I speak for Factory Row!"

Amélie gasped. "What are you doing, Rosie?"

"I will represent the females of Factory Row. If a male wishes to speak after me, he may. But I will make demands first." She twisted to peer up at her brother over her shoulder. "Ready, *caneton*?"

"*Oui*."

Rhoslyn pushed through the people to the front of the march, Matthieu still on her back, her arms hooked beneath his knees. Gently, she lowered her brother to the ground and then straightened, lifting her chin. "Rhoslyn

Gautier, Your Majesty."

"You do not kneel, Mademoiselle Gautier?"

"*Non*, Your Majesty. I do not kneel before one who would starve her people."

The queen quietly laughed, a terrible, chilling sound. "If I starved my people, who would tend the farms? Weave fabrics and sew garments? Who would stack stone to build walls and homes?"

"And yet," Rhoslyn shouted up to the balcony, "your people cannot even afford a simple loaf of bread. How much bread did your courtiers enjoy this evening, Your Majesty? How many pastries? How many uneaten loaves are stale and molding from excess and gluttoned stomachs? You do not even spare your stale crumbs for your lowly citizens."

"Where do these wages go, Mademoiselle Gautier? Why am I made responsible for the drink factory workers drown themselves in? Or the coin spent for pleasures in the alleys and tolerant houses? If The Row saved their wages instead of spending their meals on drunkenness and debauchery, then perhaps a loaf of bread would not be so difficult to afford."

The people shouted insults at the queen.

"The Row is shamed for indulging in the same behavior as the aristocracy!" Rhoslyn yelled over the crowd. "A noble class who does not work long, laborious hours for their wages like common folk," Rhoslyn called out. "Your judgment is cruelly unfair, Your Majesty. We have few pleasures. I will not call out my sisters and brothers for how they choose to find happiness, even if for a few moments. Nor do people choose hunger. It is a painful way to die."

The crowd roared in agreement and Rhoslyn tilted her head in a smug, taunting gesture.

"How is a poor fayette able to speak and reason as if she can read and write?" She quietly laughed again. "Which upper bourgeoisie family do you hail from? I am not familiar with the name Gautier or know of any upper-class elves. You do Factory Row an injustice by claiming to represent common folk, especially mortal peasants."

"My parents were poor and owned a small chapbook printing press near Saints District before Clifstán destroyed our means of income and our home. Only my brother and I survived. We had four other siblings, Your Majesty.

Nieces and nephews too. Now I live on the streets and work in the factories and peddle flowers in the evening. I have no roof. I scrape by for food." Rhoslyn's gaze hardened. "My father taught us each to read, write, and speak the language of the saints so we could assist him in the shop. I am also well versed in arithmetic and logic. While I have not been afforded the privilege to paint or play the piano forte or eat mountains of breads and cakes," she spat in mockery, "my needle point would make the saints weep and poets cry." She paused in a dramatic beat. "Any other way you would wish to insult me, Your Majesty? Perhaps tell me and all others present here once more of how we are foolish with the wages we work ten hours and more a day to earn to barely feed and house those who survived the war and Cold Winds? And please keep in mind, madame, ten hours is only for one job. Many of us work two."

"You speak too freely, Rhoslyn Gautier." The queen rested her hands on the stone lip of the balcony. "I am not impressed with your insolence, or how you speak for a march who has vandalized my home, or how you demanded an audience with me, let alone one that interrupts my dinner party. Nor do I take kindly to the words of a poor fayette who believes her voice equal to mine while also refusing to bow before her queen." She leaned over the balcony. "You insult me then declare yourself the victim. I have heard enough." Queen Adeline turned to leave, but Rhoslyn wasn't finished yet.

"You are a wolf in spun silks!" she screamed, her lips curled and angry tears pooling in her eyes. "A wolf who wishes to convince the flocks of Aurelienne that you care for our wellbeing when you feed off us instead and leave us bleeding in the streets!" Rhoslyn clenched her fists at her sides. "The right to rule does not make you a queen worthy of your people. *Non*, a monarch is subject to their citizens and we demand bread! We demand lower taxes! We demand safer working conditions!"

The protesters became thunder with their shouts and stomping feet. Rhoslyn would gladly continue to strike as lightning.

"Perhaps the Beast of Gabaston," she continued, "the démon preying on the people of your fine city, is really *you*."

More cheers roared around her in support.

"Since you believe I feed you to the wolves, Mademoiselle Gautier," the queen said, each word measured and clipped. "Then feed you to the wolves I shall. Both you and your brother."

The former queen shot her younger sister a horrified look before speaking in a voice too low to hear below the balcony. Adeline replied in a harsh tone, and Loriette found Rhoslyn's eyes and frowned. Almost as if the former queen pitied her. Did she actually have an ally in Palais d'Aurélie? Rhoslyn narrowed her eyes, first at Loriette. Then she fixed the queen with a daggered glare, the lines of her face and muscles in her shoulders hardening. Let the woman see Rhoslyn's determination, the fury. Let her know that this poor fayette was unafraid. Let her see the promises that Rhoslyn would one day burn down the throne of House of Chalamet.

The bruise on her cheek, where Madame had slapped her, was nearly healed now. But Rhoslyn could still feel the sting of humiliation.

She didn't cower then; she wouldn't cower now. Even though every muscle in her body trembled at the idea of facing wolves and démons. Bile coated her throat. She and Matthieu would not live if the bold monster killing the people of Gabaston found them. Still . . .

"We have survived wolf attacks before," Rhoslyn shouted to the balcony. "We have survived much worse."

Queen Adeline pointed to a group of guards who broke from the line before the march and approached Rhoslyn and her brother. The queen expected her to fight or attempt to run. Instead, Rhoslyn remained rooted in place all the while keeping her eyes locked onto the predatory gold of Adeline's.

"I will carry my brother," Rhoslyn said to her. "Your guards will tie him to my back before roping my wrists."

The guards looked to the balcony for permission. And, to Rhoslyn's surprise, it was Loriette who spoke. "Do not separate the siblings and be gentle with the boy. He is an innocent."

Rhoslyn's gaze slid to the former queen's and she dipped her head in thanks.

Adeline's jaw visibly clenched but she didn't contradict her sister.

"I am only lowering for my brother to climb on," Rhoslyn said to the men who now surrounded her. "I *still* refuse to bow before your queen."

She didn't hear the protesters screaming behind her. Or see the angry wave of motion. She only had eyes for Matthieu, who wrapped his arms around her neck and waited for her to hook her arms beneath his knees. Slowly, she rose to her feet and offered her wrists. The guards wrapped the rope around her and Matthieu and finished with tying her hands. The lead guard yanked her forward and she lifted her head high.

Adeline's lips curled in a smug grin. "Leave them in the woods outside of Saints District, tied up. My gift to the Beast of Gabaston."

Tears appeared to gloss the former queen's eyes. As Rhoslyn was marched past her, Loriette called out, "Be brave, Mademoiselle Gautier. Do not stop being wise or courageous."

Matthieu tightened his arms around her neck and buried his face in her hair. Nearly fifty guards formed a barrier around them, bayonets out, guns loaded, as they were shoved through the protesters, who parted in a blur of angry chants and fisted hands lifted to the sky. Rhoslyn kept her chin up, fire burning every step with resolved conviction. She would take down the queen. She would liberate Factory Row from the life-choking taxes suffocating their ability to survive post-war poverty.

In less than three candlemarks, she and Matthieu were left in the night-darkened woods outside of Saints District.

CHAPTER 6

RHOSLYN

The dark forest swallowed their bodies in the moonlit night. Every owl hoot or breeze through the leaves chipped away at her resolve to remain strong for Matthieu. She was terrified. The adrenaline rush of fighting that awful man, the rally, and confronting the House of Chalamet in their own yard was wearing off and a new heat simmered in her trembling pulse—a different type of survival.

The guards, thankfully, took pity on them both, despite their queen's instructions.

"It is unforgivable to leave helpless girls and little boys to wolves," the guard had said. "My sister works in a factory. What you spoke is true." He reached for the dagger at his belt, cut the ropes, then placed the weapon in her hand to keep. "I am sincerely sorry, mademoiselle."

She and Matthieu had been alone in the woods for nearly a candlemark now. Torchlight had already faded in the distance. Since they had nowhere to store their possessions, they always wore their cloaks and Matthieu lugged around his small sack. Spending the night in the woods would be no colder or warmer than sleeping at the rubbled cottages. She kept her hood down, though, to ensure she had full view of the forest.

"You are weary, *ma sœur*," Matthieu whispered into her hair. The muscles in Rhoslyn's back and arms ached from carrying her brother around so much this day. Her legs shook from exhaustion and hunger. "I am useless against wolves. You need your strength. We can sleep in a tree, *oui*?"

"*Non*, I must find our way to East Row."

"Rosie—"

A howl punctured the slumbering stillness of the forest.

Her brother's breath fluttered in her hair. "Use the rope to hoist me into a tree."

"And leave you on the forest floor while I first climb up?" Rhoslyn's voice caught.

"I will never be able to work. You will be charged with caring for me all my days until I replace the beggar man on the corner."

"Matthieu, you will speak of no such thing." She ground her teeth together. "You are *not* a burden. I would gladly care for you all the days of my life. You are my heart and my joy. Do not rob me of the only good thing I have left."

Tears fell onto her head and he sniffed.

"Can you reach your guardian?" Her eyes darted around the woods when another wolf howled. Matthieu released an arm round her neck and dug into his pocket, before circling her neck once more, the carved wolf now in his hand. "Hold onto your guardian, *mon petit caneton*."

With the dagger out, she continued creeping through the underbrush. Where was the Beast? The one terrorizing Factory Row and Saints District? Every night, more people were found dead. Mostly females and children.

Another howl, this one closer and accompanied by other howls.

The pulse thundering in her chest was quickly draining the blood from her head.

"Remain still, Rhoslyn Gautier."

Rhoslyn spun toward the sound and lifted her dagger. A beautiful male elf in full battle leathers, with ear-length, white disheveled hair leaned against a tree. His sword was drawn and he peered out into the open forest, not at her.

"A Dúnælven elf . . ." her brother whispered in awe. "Rosie, how does he know your name?"

"Dalbréath?" she asked weakly.

Wings of fear lifted her feet, and—

"I would not run, little thorn," the elf said, his gaze still trained on the woods. "They hope you do."

They?

She could feel the démon's claws digging into her skin. Rhoslyn screamed, scratching frantically at the tree.

All thought left her body and those wings of fear took flight.

The arms wrapped around her neck tightened.

Trees raced by in a black lace curtain of raining leaves. Her breath came quick and sharp. The path back to Factory Row had to be here somewhere. She could hear *them* in the brush beside her. *Wolves.* A forming sob left her chest. She would not die this night. Nor would her brother. No, the only ones who would be fed to the wolves were the pigs dressed in silks behind the now broken gold gates.

A low growl rumbled beside her and vibrated through her body.

Rhoslyn's gaze shot to the underbrush. A foolish decision. She didn't see the tree root fingering across the trail and her boot caught. The forest pirouetted around her in a lush blur of dark greens, midnight blues, and shadows. The ground rose to embrace her in a carpet of moss. Matthieu flew a short distance from her back. Air punched from her lungs with the impact. Then pain quickly flared up her arm from where she broke her fall with her elbow, the dagger still firm in her hand.

A cough rattled up the trail not too far away from her.

"Matthieu?" she whispered on a terrified sob.

"I'm not hurt—" he coughed again and panic bolted through her.

Rhoslyn crawled over to him, but felt a tug of resistance, then the tear of fabric. Her skirt had caught on a branch. Digging her nails into the ground, she pushed toward Matthieu, the dagger loose in her hand. "Hurry," she whispered when reaching him, then rolled into a crouch for him to climb onto her back again.

They needed to keep moving. She needed to run. He coughed again and she blinked back more tears. Grimacing, she dragged in a ragged breath and scrambled to her feet once her brother was secure.

Two pairs of eyes, reflecting the moon, watched her from the shadows.

But it was not those wolves that attacked.

A different wolf emerged from the bushes in a growl—an enormous gray wolf. Rhoslyn shrieked. She swore the beast grinned, as if satisfied with her display of horror. But this was a natural wolf. Not a démon. The beast prowled toward her, its head low, its hackles raised.

Claws grasped her leg and yanked.

The skin on her fingers split, but she continued to scrape at the tree for a limb.

Tears streamed down her face. Unlike the last time, however, she now had a weapon. Hand shaking, Rhoslyn lifted the dagger and the wolf snarled.

"I will gut you," she growled back.

The gray wolf leapt at her, claws out, canines bared.

She tightened her hold on the dagger and stiffened her muscles. But it never touched her.

A rush of air caressed her cheek and fluttered her hair.

Then a collision of snarls and growls in the ferns beside her.

Rhoslyn's mouth parted in a sharp gasp. A striking midnight black wolf snapped at the gray wolf, viciously tearing into its shoulder. The other two wolves she had seen earlier leapt from the bushes, but the black wolf anticipated them and met both in the air. They tumbled to the ground in a swirl of claws and teeth. The gray wolf limped from the fight with a whimper. Once out of danger, he howled. A frightening sound that chilled the blood pumping wildly in her veins. Hearing the haunting cry, the black wolf stepped back and snarled. There was a grace about this wolf the others lacked. And it seemed to be . . . protecting her.

The black wolf released a loud growl and the three natural wolves tucked their tails and lowered their heads to the ground. As if bowing. Blood matted into their fur and their tongues lolled in heaving pants. Another fierce snarl from the black beast and the three departed in a loping run.

For several heartbeats, the black wolf remained still, watching the woods, its ears pricked.

But she could not remain still. Shock was trembling down her limbs. Her teeth began to chatter.

Slowly the dark démon turned and lifted golden amber eyes her way.

Beautiful eyes that were most definitely human.

Her heart fluttered a beat.

The wolf quietly snarled, baring its teeth. Then it was gone. A black streak among the trees.

"What . . . How?" her brother asked in a shaky whisper.

A soft breath left her lungs. She couldn't find the words to describe what had just happened—not quite yet.

Matthieu slowly opened his palm and adjusted the carved wolf in his hand. "My guardian summoned a démon who protected us."

She gently placed her brother on the ground and crushed him to her chest, kissing his head. "I should have never stood up to the queen."

Her brother coughed, a light breathy sound. "Someone needed to," he said into the layers of her dress.

She kissed his head again. "You're shaking, *mon petit caneton*."

"So are you."

"I was so very afraid. Did you think back on your wolf attack five years ago? How is your breathing? Are you hurt from our fall?"

"You *still* worry too much," he grumbled, his voice muffled.

"Worry?" Rhoslyn pushed her brother away just enough so he could see how outrageous he sounded. Then she crushed him back to her. "Nine Saints, we were attacked by wolves and saved by a démon! Of course, I am worrying!"

"The démon is our guardian," he muffled into her dress once more.

"*Oui*, I do believe you are right."

"Why did you move? The warrior elf told you to remain still, like you did me."

Her shoulders fell. "I panicked. All I could see was . . . never mind. It was a terrible mistake."

"Rhoslyn!" The white-haired elf dashed around the bend, his sword raised. Their eyes locked for the merest second. "Thank the gods," he said while studying the forest. "We were ambushed. Wolves attacked me before I could chase after you. Are you or Matthieu injured?"

"You know my name?" her brother asked, breathless.

Dalbréath ignored him. "Where did the wolves go? It's not like them to leave prey behind so suddenly."

"A dark démon protected us." Matthieu lifted his guardian and coughed into his sleeve. "I summoned him."

The warrior arched a brow, first at her, then at her brother. "A shifter?"

Rhoslyn ruffled her brother's hair, earning her an annoyed glare from Matthieu. "The démon protected us, milord."

The elf tilted his head. "Has this shifter protected you before, little thorn?"

"*Oui*, milord."

Matthieu turned round eyes her way. "He has?"

"He?" Rhoslyn asked. Her brother just shrugged. "By Chateau Lumière Dorée," she answered the elf. "The first morning we picked flowers to sell." Matthieu's eyes rounded even larger. "I did not wish to frighten you."

A muscle jumped along Dalbréath's jaw. "Have you seen this shifter's human form?"

"*Non*, milord."

The elf eyed her with a stillness that rose the hair on her arms. "The ri—"

"Yes." Rhoslyn tapped her bodice then gently touched the twine, and Dalbréath replied with a subtle nod. She didn't want her brother to know about the ring. He would ask questions she didn't know how to answer—or cared to.

"*Pardonnez-moi*, milord." Matthieu limped to stand in front of Rhoslyn.

Softly, Dalbréath interjected, "I am not nobility."

"Who are you, monsieur?" her brother continued. "Why do you ask my sister strange questions? And who is 'little thorn?'"

Dalbréath crouched before Matthieu and handed him the pommel of his sword with a soft smile. "You are a brave lad. And a brave lad should hold a sword when defending his sister."

Even though her brother's back was to her, Rhoslyn knew he was smiling that dimpled smile she loved so much.

"It is so heavy." Matthieu gripped the pommel with both hands, the point of the sword digging into the forest floor.

The white-haired elf grinned. "You will wield a fine sword like this one day, Matthieu Eric Gautier. Aye, I will see to it myself."

Matthieu twisted to peer up at her and her heart melted with the joy brightening his eyes.

Rhoslyn found Dalbréath's gaze on her, studying her every movement. The way he watched her was unsettling. "This démon was first by the House of Golden Light?"

"*Oui*."

He nodded and looked away, that muscle twitching along his jaw once more.

"Did you follow us from Palais d'Aurélie?" she asked him.

"No," Dalbréath answered. "I have orders to hunt the Beast of Gabaston."

"And to watch over me, *oui*?" Her question came out more forcefully than intended. "I am no fool, monsieur."

He considered her a moment. "Why are you in these woods unprotected at night?"

"Queen Adeline Chalamet." Rhoslyn lifted her chin.

"Rosie Mae confronted the queen before thousands at Palais d'Aurélie. We were arrested and thrown to the wolves as punishment."

Dalbréath's lips twitched, but pride shone in his blue eyes—blue eyes even bright in shadowed moonlight. "A warrior lass. You do your family a great honor. I only wish I could have heard your speech, little thorn."

"She defended Factory Row and demanded bread and lower taxes after a silk breeches destroyed her flower basket and attacked her."

Dalbréath's eyes shot to hers and fury visibly thundered across his face. Rhoslyn softly shook her head, a silent answer for a silent question—she was fine.

Matthieu looked up from the sword, unaware of the wordless conversation she and Dalbréath were having. "Do not hunt the dark démon, monsieur. He is not the Beast."

"He *is* a beast, I assure you," Dalbréath muttered, more to himself it seemed.

"He?" Matthieu's eyebrows inched up. "See, Rosie?" Her brother blinked at the elf and pushed his brows together. "Who are you, monsieur? And how is it that you know us?"

"My name is Dalbréath Kadelaryn." The elf gently moved Matthieu's fingers on the pommel to correct her brother's hold. "I met your sister a few days ago, at the dress factory."

"Why were you at the dress factory?"

Rhoslyn placed a hand on Matthieu's shoulder. "My brother asks a lot of questions, monsieur."

Dalbréath lifted another soft smile at Matthieu and helped him raise the sword. "Children are meant to ask questions. It is how they learn. Curiosity is a gift."

"Monsieur Kadel . . . Kaledy . . ." Matthieu huffed a frustrated breath.

"Monsieur Dalbrie, my sister needs to rest. She will not admit her exhaustion."

"Matthieu—"

"*Non*, Rosie," her brother interrupted her. "You take care of me every day. Allow me to care for you. Monsieur Dalbrie can help protect us, so you won't have to worry about me." He rolled his eyes at Dalbréath. "She is *always* worrying about me."

The elf stood and sheathed his sword. "Come, lad. You can sit on my shoulders." Dalbréath unstrapped a quiver of arrows from his back then handed both the arrows and his bow to her. "I will teach you how to shoot tomorrow, little thorn. All Kadelaryns are archers. We will have lessons on how to use that Aurelienne dagger too."

All Kadelaryns?

Changeling child of thorns . . .

"Can I also learn, Monsieur Dalbrie?"

Dalbréath grinned at her little brother. "You will be a quicker learner. I have trained hundreds of warriors and can tell these things." He winked at Matthieu, then hoisted him up and onto his shoulders. "Ready?"

"Time to swim!"

The white-haired elf arched a brow at her in a humorous sidelong glance and she quietly laughed. "He is my little duckling and swims through the air."

"A strong, brave duckling who faced a queen's wrath and summons guardian démons," Dalbréath added, twisting his head to peer up at Matthieu. "A true faerie boy." Her brother was beaming brighter than the moon under the praise. "Let us find shelter and then I will hunt for food. You both could use several warm meals."

"Matthieu and I have been staying in a fallen cottage on the outskirts of Gabaston. We could camp there."

"Too close to the city."

She stepped in his path to face him. "Let us come to an understanding before we take another step. I do not need your permission to return to wherever I call home."

"The queen arrested you before a protest of thousands." His eyes widened, like she was frothing mad. "Because you are dangerous. You spoke on behalf of Factory Row, correct?" She nodded. "She no doubt already has a bounty on your head on the small chance you survive the woods."

"*Faut pas pousser mémé dans les orties!*"

"Don't push grandmother . . . into the nettles?" Dalbréath translated the saying slowly in the language of the saints—a combination of Dúnælven and Aurelienne—and eyed her like she had grown a set of horns.

"It means, you go too far," she replied in Aurelienne.

"Right." That damn muscle in his jaw twitched again. "You most likely have a bounty on your head, but I go too far."

Rhoslyn drew in a shaky breath. "*Oui*, this is my fight to decide, not yours."

"Matthieu?" Dalbréath asked, peering up at her brother once more. "Cover your ears and hum your favorite song." Matthieu first looked to her, then obeyed. Once he started singing, Dalbréath lowered his voice to a whisper. "If she killed you before the masses, she would create a martyr and incite more riots. Allowing others to kill you instead at a handsome price makes them forget your real value."

She tilted her head. "And what is my *real* value, Dalbréath Kadelaryn?"

"First we sleep." He held her gaze steady. "Then we eat a warm meal."

She lowered her voice to a harsh whisper. "And after, monsieur? Will you then tell me how I cannot return to my friends or to those lives I have also put in danger with my words? *Non!* I am not a coward. I do not run away and hide."

"The defiance and fire in your blood is . . ." The words trailed off; his brows pushed together. "It is so much like your father's."

Gently, while balancing her brother on his shoulders, he took the leather strap for his quiver of arrows and loosely belted it over her cloak, across her shoulder to her hip. Loose enough that she could easily maneuver her arms but secured enough that she wouldn't have to awkwardly shoulder his weapon as they walked. Tapping her hand next, he guided her fingers around the longbow's grip, then stood back and smiled.

"You make your family proud, Rhoslyn Gautier." She opened her mouth to redirect him back to their earlier conversation, but he cut her off. "Shelter. Sleep. Eat. In those three orders. Everything else can wait."

"Can I uncover my ears now?" Matthieu asked.

"Yes, little warrior duckling," Dalbréath answered before she could. "Time to swim."

A wolf howled in the distance. Rhoslyn stiffened and frantically scanned the woods.

"They will not touch you," Dalbréath murmured while striding along the trail. "From what you have shared, the démon has staked his claim and desires to protect you. The pack wolves in this territory will not disobey his orders. He could have killed the ones that hunted you but let them go as a warning."

"I have done nothing to inspire his devotion." Rhoslyn absently felt for the ring tucked under her bodice. "Prowling démons are not known for their mercy."

"No," Dalbréath agreed. "They are not."

Not wanting to be exposed from behind, Rhoslyn quietly stepped forward on the trail in front of Dalbréath. Moonlight silvered through the trees and dimly lit the deer path they traversed. Shadows swayed in the light breeze. And wolves continued to howl. Fear skated across her skin. Her breaths came quick.

Then fluttered to a stop.

A pair of golden eyes watched her from the dark shadows beneath the trees. *His* eyes. They were beautiful and haunting and stole a beat of her heart for a single, quivering breath. Why did he wish for her to see him? Did he hear Dalbréath's words to her? Perhaps he really was her guardian. Rhoslyn dipped her head in his direction with a small smile and continued into the thicker forest, her fingers absently playing with the ring around her neck.

RHOSLYN YAWNED AND forced her eyes to remain open. She was on the verge of sleep walking. The air grew cooler and her teeth softly chattered. Dawn already crested the horizon, but shadows painted the forest in dusky twilight. She pulled the hood of her cloak farther over her head and sank into the momentary warmth, trying to ignore the large tear in her skirt. Where would she find a replacement? When they had paused for Dalbréath to readjust his hold on Matthieu, she also noticed rips in her stockings and that the hole in her shoe had widened. The toes of her right foot were chilled from the moisture that had seeped through. There was no help for it now.

They had been walking through the woods for what felt like hours, though she knew it was probably only around two. Wolves had watched them throughout the night, but none had attacked. Nor had they seen another shifter. But several natural wolves wanted to be seen and heard. And every time, her grip on the dagger tightened and her pulse kicked up into a gallop. But those incidences waned as the sun began to rise.

Matthieu was now asleep in Dalbréath's arms, his head curled up on his shoulder. Every so often, she would catch the warrior elf glancing down at her brother with affection.

"You are fond of children, monsieur," she said.

"Aye, I am," Dalbréath answered. "Faerie children are the purest form of magic."

"Are you a father?"

His smile fell and he drew in a slow breath. "I once had a daughter. She was so . . . beautiful, full of mischief, and my little arrow."

A familiar pang filled her chest. "I am sorry, monsieur. I had no right to ask you private questions."

"She died shortly after turning six, during a war. My mate, too, while protecting her." He visibly swallowed and Rhoslyn's lips trembled. Wars were crueler beasts than wolves. "My wee Brenna would be near two hundred years now, if she had lived. Still feels like yesterday, though. That pain is sharp and never leaves. The swell of love too."

Rhoslyn wiped away a tear and stared out into the woods. "Sometimes I cannot breathe, the pain is so terrible."

"Aye, it is."

"I just want him to have happiness."

"He is happy, little thorn." Dalbréath cut her a quick glance. "It is not easy to raise siblings. There is little rest for those in your situation."

She wiped away another tear. "Did you raise your siblings too?"

"I have helped raise dozens of foster siblings over the years, from infancy through adulthood." An impish smile tilted his lips. "But I am the youngest of seven in my family. All boys."

"Your poor maman."

"Dalbrenna is tougher than all of us, do not pity her. Pity us instead." That impish smile grew. "A Dúnælven warrior huntress. All of her sons are warriors." He held her gaze. "Her grandchildren too."

That unsettling feeling gnawed at her stomach again. Between that and her hunger, she wanted to curl up in the ferns and drift asleep to forget the ache. She was so hungry, her head grew light and her limbs became lead. Questions formed on the tip of her tongue, two she desperately wished to know—who were her parents and how was she related to Dalbréath? Was one of his six brothers her father? Most likely. Which would make this male her uncle. *Kadelaryn* . . . the name seemed so familiar, yet she couldn't place why. But as much as she wanted to know who her parents were, she dreaded the answer and was far too furious to ask. Grief and war already stole so much from her. Right now, she needed to believe that the Gautiers were her blood kin. That she was not, indeed, a changeling child with parentage high class enough to contract a marriage in their blood. That she was free to marry the male she fell in love with, not the monster forced on her.

"And your father, monsieur?" she asked instead. "Is he also a warrior?"

A breeze swirled around them and fluttered the elf's white hair. Almost as if the wind were comforting him. In fact, much of nature seemed to honor him as they walked. Even the trees. There were times the branches appeared to move of their own accord.

Tendrils of soft heaviness wrapped around her as her magic touched his heart. Since a small child, she had always been able to emotionally see the essence of another. This magic not only gave her insight, but also the words to speak directly to the root of another's heartache. No native-born elves of Gabaston had magic that she knew of, not even her family.

"I bring up too much pain for you," she rushed out after several heartbeats of silence. "Let us talk of more pleasant things."

"He was executed." His voice was so soft, she wasn't sure she heard him correctly. "A traitor to our kind."

Her lungs constricted. "Oh, monsieur, I should not have—"

"It is your right to know, little thorn. Ask me anything."

She cleared her throat and studied the forest trail. Rhoslyn knew what he was encouraging her to ask, what he was told not to share a few days ago with a single shake of Gedlen's head. As if the prince knew she wasn't ready to hear the truth. And he was right.

Gedlen . . .

"Where is Gedlen Fate Maker? I thought he traveled with you." A blush warmed her cheeks and she wanted to swear at herself for asking such a silly question. The warrior prince's words had infuriated her, but . . . his presence stole her breath and owned her reveries. A prince. She had never met a prince before. He was terrifying and—

"He returned to Leaf Curl shortly after we found you." Dalbréath turned his head and, noting her blush, started laughing. "Him? You find *him* attractive?" She couldn't lie and didn't know how to riddle her way around his question. Which only made Dalbréath laugh more and deepened her blush. "You like dark, broody, princely alphas. One of *those* girls."

Her jaw slackened. "I should feel no shame in whom or what I find attractive."

"No, you shouldn't." The humor slipped from Dalbréath's face and his brows pinched together. "But you tend to fall for dangerous, powerful males?"

"I have never fallen for anyone."

He nodded, that muscle pulsing in his jaw again, like when he asked her about the dark démon—like when Gedlen spoke of her contracted mate. Rhoslyn fidgeted with the vined wedding ring around her neck and loosed a trembling breath.

After a few heartbeats, a mischievous twinkle glinted in Dalbréath's eyes. "Never fallen for anyone except Gedlen."

She clenched her teeth. "I simply find him—"

"Sensual and dreamy." Dalbréath was grinning now and she narrowed her eyes to slits. "I suppose he's nice to look at," the elf beside her casually tossed out, "if you like dark elves who take the color black very, *very* seriously."

"He's beautiful," she confessed and blinked back the embarrassment. "And entirely too self-assured. His arrogance was unnecessary."

The corner of Dalbréath's mouth quirked. "Gedlen Faerondarl is many things, but arrogant is not one of them. That charm falls on me. I am arrogant enough for the both of us."

"You, monsieur?" Rhoslyn shook her head. "*Non*, you are bossy, but kind."

"I *am* kind." He winked at her. "Kind on the eyes. The *kind* of hero chronicled in songs. A military commander unparalleled in fae *kind*. Kind of an arse."

Rhoslyn spurted a laugh.

"His twin sister, Gellynor, is even more beautiful."

"If her brother is any indication, she must be stunning."

"That she is." He focused on the trail a few steps, a faraway look in his eyes. "Gelly is a pain in my arse."

Rhoslyn smiled to herself. "You remind me of my older brother, Renold. Only a year and a half separated us. He was . . ."

"Kind?" Dalbréath asked her, his lips twitching.

"*Oui*," she said on a laugh. "He was kind *and* waggish, just like you. I have missed our ridiculous conversations."

"We are rare diamonds. To think, you have known two such perfect males."

"Saints," she said, laughing even more. "You really are arrogant."

"Monsieur Dalbrie," Matthieu mumbled, his eyes half-lidded. "Is my sister crying?"

Dalbréath tenderly brushed an unruly lock of blond hair behind her brother's ear. "She is laughing."

"Good." He nuzzled into Dalbréath's shoulder again. "She frowns too much."

That one wild strand of hair flopped over Matthieu's closed eyes once more with his movements. A wolf howled in the distance and she flinched. There was an unusual amount of wolves out this night. Did the protest agitate them? Or something else? Her instinct was to look around, but she focused on her brother instead. Soft morning light touched his pale skin and she gnawed the inside corner of her lip. What had she done? Her brother would now know no peace because of her actions.

"We are near the House of Golden Light," Dalbréath said quietly.

Rhoslyn halted her steps. "We cannot possibly stay there."

Dalbréath stared off into the woods, to a cluster of shadowed trees. "We will camp outside of the manor. If your dark démon is your protector, he will not harm us." Did he sense natural wolves? Or worse? The elf studied the forest another couple of beats, then glanced her way. "He will not let anything else harm you either and you *need* that protection right now. Especially while I am out hunting."

"How can you be sure that he would protect me again?"

The corner of his mouth lifted in a taunting smirk.

"If you say it is because I fall for dark, dangerous males or that you are kind—"

"And deny me my bragging rights?" The corner of his mouth inched up higher. "Cruel."

Rhoslyn playfully fluttered her hand in the air. "*Oof!* I am not responsible for your ego."

"Your father is *the* biggest pain in my arse." Dalbréath arched a challenging brow in her direction.

Rhoslyn lifted her chin. "Are you calling me an arse?"

Dalbréath strode forward onto the trail and Rhoslyn remained where she stood, her hands now on her hips. After a few steps, Dalbréath peered over his shoulder, that goading, impish smile back in place, and she had to bite back yet another laugh. With a little shrug, a gesture indicating it was now her move, he continued onward once more.

"You have a concerning amount of pains in your lower half, *Monsieur Dalbrie*," she called after him.

Dalbréath snorted, as if she had stated the obvious. "The curse of being surrounded by those less perfect than you, *little thorn*."

Rhoslyn playfully groaned and stomped after him through the ferns—then slowed. Chateau Lumière Dorée moved into view through the trees and her heart almost forgot how to beat. Was *he* there? The démon who guarded her? Was his hair as dark as his wolf's coat? His eyes truly a beautiful golden amber? She wasn't sure of what terrified her more: the possibility of seeing his human form and her heart foolishly falling prey to his predatory beauty or that he was every inch the monster as all others like him and he was simply playing with his meal first?

Beasts were not merciful.

Démons didn't leave survivors.

Would her husband kill her soon after claiming her?

Some wolves are too wild to tame. Some are too wounded to save, Gedlen's words echoed through her. *And some, like your mate, fight inner demons to break generational curses* . . .

Then another thought even more terrifying clawed through her mind.

What if *he* was her husband and that is why he protected her? Could the magic of a blood contract bind him to her even if they had never met?

"Monsieur," Rhoslyn began, hoping the anger just rumbling beneath the surface remained calm enough to sound natural. "Were only the blood of my parents needed for the marriage contract?"

"No." He didn't look in her direction. "Your and your mate's blood were also added."

Dark clouds shadowed the sky beyond Chateau Lumière Dorée. Her fingers feverishly played with the ring, now untucked from the safety of her bodice. The blood pumping wildly in her chest grew lighter in her head.

"You do not ask me his name or who he is."

She glanced Dalbréath's way. "I do not want to know."

"You are not even curious?"

"I am curious, *oui*. But mostly furious. Saints, I'm so furious." Rhoslyn rubbed her arms and looked around the forest, desperately trying to grimace back the angry tears burning her eyes. "The moment I know his name, then he is real and so is the nightmare of being sold to a démon by parents who didn't even want to raise me." She threw her hands into the air. "Did they truly believe they could take me away from the only family I have known and pass me off to a complete stranger? A *monster*? It is unforgivable."

Dalbréath stopped walking. "Little thorn—"

"*Non*, do not defend them." The camaraderie she felt with him moments ago disappeared and she clenched her jaw once more. If Matthieu were not in his arms right now and if a warm meal were not so desperately needed, she would run. But she wouldn't get far. She was far too weak and exhausted.

And she had nowhere else to go. If a bounty were on her head, what would happen to her brother?

Chapter 7

Fentienne

Fentienne blew out the candle by his bedside and silently counted to three. The wick sparked back into flame—like all the cursed candles in this chateau. Mesmerized, he lowered until he could feel the warmth across his nose, his mouth. If he drew in air, the kiss of flame would blister his lips. Instead, he softly blew. Not to snuff, but to hear flame fight to remain lit. The flickering snap of resistance. The collision of fire and air, of hot and cold. The fluttering heartbeat of survival.

The sound of war.

He puffed his breath. The corner where he sat immediately dimmed. To distract his growing caginess, Fentienne touched the tip of his tongue to the curling smoke near the wick. *Three, two, one*—the wick popped and a tiny flame reappeared. He quickly darted his tongue back. But a part of him wanted to feel the sizzling burn. To feel a physical pain he chose.

Fentienne leaned back onto his bed, propped up by his elbows, and stared at the soot-hued crown molding along the ceiling. Playing with fire was horribly cliché and he wanted to kick the candle across the room. But the damn thing would relight, like they all had done. If the house burned down, would it flash back into existence at the count of three? Like the garden of roses he furiously dug up? Like the hearth fires he doused with water? Like the candles? Swearing under his breath, he relaxed his arms and flopped onto the bed. Claw-tipped fingers dragged through his hair and pulled onto the strands to hold in the building scream.

Three days ago, Addien had cursed the House of Golden Light to the grave. The walls, floors, linens, curtains . . . now all widow's weaves or colors dark enough to be considered black. All the clothing in the closets and furniture too. Cobwebs draped across corners and over candelabras. When he tried to clear them, they would flash back into place too. Trick candles dripped wax but never melted; hearth fires roared but never burned wood.

Such a ridiculous, over-the-top statement.

The ghosts, too.

Men and women in outdated Aurelienne gowns and suits danced in the ballroom, enjoying music and life, oblivious to Clifstán's military creeping in to attack. They cooked in the kitchen—spectral food for the feast his mother had planned. They brought clean linens to the baths—spectral items for the courtiers who prepared for the evening's festivities. But they didn't acknowledge him. Some cried. Some shouted. Most wore blank faces with tortured stares. Aelfred Halivaard's order had killed each of these restless souls.

The rotting walls and the flickering ghosts haunting this chateau were the least of his worries, though.

Dread pooled in his gut and he swallowed back the foul taste in his mouth.

Maeline Kadelaryn Wyndham was alive.

She was the girl in the burgundy cloak picking flowers by the chateau. The girl in the woods outside of Saints District before dawn broke this day. The girl the warrior elf called Rhoslyn Gautier right before she ran and the natural wolves gave chase.

Heaving a sigh, he pushed off the bed and strode to one of the large windows facing the forest. Sunlight crested the thick trees behind Chateau Lumière Dorée and he ground his teeth. Three candlemarks had passed since he shifted back to half-man, half-beast. Four candlemarks since he stopped trailing Maeline, her brother, and the warrior elf. Fentienne rested his forehead on the cool glass and closed his eyes. His heart was racing faster than a wild horse on a battlefield.

For years, he had believed she was tucked away somewhere in Avenbury, if not dead. The other side of the map wasn't distance enough for him. She could take a full masted ship from Merenna to explore worlds beyond Ealdspell and *still* not be far enough away.

She was the damned reason Addien chose him as a young child as an act of revenge.

The son of a monster who was born from a family of beasts. A super soldier bred to kill his own kin for a golden throne.

Making him fall in love with the enemy was only one of that fiend's many twisted layers. The sickest of them all? Maeline could be Fayette's identical twin sister, if the fuzzy-around-the-edges images his wolf shared with him were correct—his wolf who could think of little else but her. The uncanny resemblance made him want to vomit.

All this time, Addien *knew* Maeline was in Aurelienne—in Gabaston.

Her little speech was entirely for show.

Opening his eyes, he pivoted on his heel and marched from his room and skittered down the stairs toward the main floor.

"Is Fayette even a real girl?"

"Oui, prince. Until she died in Gabaston during one of Clifstán's attacks. The campaign your oldest brother was in, actually."

He flinched.

"Did you not realize girls like Fayette die in your war?" She tsked.

Anger growled low and deep in his chest. He marched past sitting parlors, the music room, toward the solarium. A spectral servant, carrying a basket of kitchen herbs, crossed his path and he walked through her, swiping his hand in the air as if swatting away a gnat. He swung open a back door and stepped out into the chill of morning. Trees and grass bent to the same wind whipping his dark hair around his face.

Addien didn't utter Fayette's name when she spoke of a girl who died.

The attacks had killed elves—girls *like* Fayette.

Maeline—*Rhoslyn* was twelve when he was sixteen. Old enough that Addien could guess what the princess would look like four years later ... And all to lure him into a lie and poison his happiness.

So he would hate the *real* Fayette.

And he did.

Gods, did he hate her.

But he hated himself more for daydreaming endlessly about Rhoslyn's beauty since the day his wolf found her picking flowers outside of the chateau. He hated himself even more when his wolf confirmed her pointed ears. But nothing compared to the physical pain he felt when she turned those dark green eyes his way this morning and thanked him with a dip of her head and soft smile. A pain that transcended man and wolf. It was like his blood caught fire and burned him from the inside out.

The gruesome weight on his chest was growing heavier by the minute. Fentienne unlaced his linen shirt, then wiped at the clammy sweat beading on his forehead with his sleeve. Skies, he couldn't breathe. Standing still only made it worse. He broke into a jog toward the woods. Needing to hide from his thoughts. Needing to run. She was heading toward the chateau.

She was heading toward him.

The Underworld's refuse fires—the ones used to eliminate souls—now burned throughout his family's chateau. Smoke writhed to the ceiling in pitiful prayer after prayer for his salvation. The foreshadowing would be hilarious if not for one detail: when Rhoslyn fell for Addien's trap and wandered onto his family's property, she would be doomed to live this horror alongside him until one of them died.

Each dawn and dusk, he survived bone-wracking pain. Each night, he traveled the shadowed planes of monsters. Each day, he drank himself into a stupor to forget he was ever born. To forget everything. But he wouldn't be able to forget her—her screams when seeing him, the revulsion when in his company, the grief of knowing his grave was now hers as well.

And there was nothing he could do.

Except let her die.

A part of him almost let the pack wolves kill her. It would be a mercy compared to the pain and misery she would endure trapped in his home. Cruel men like him didn't possess the kind of heart and soul girls like her fell in love with and willingly married. No, he was the dangerous, forbidden fun good girls sought for a night and nothing more. The kind of lover his comrades resented for intimately knowing their sweethearts first. No one had ever loved him. No one had wanted to. His mother confused her guilt as love for her son. It wasn't real.

Love was a beautiful lie to hide an ugly truth.

It didn't exist.

It had *never* existed.

But his wolf hungered for Rhoslyn, a completely different type of ravenous desire than the pack who licked their chops in anticipation of the feast they were about to enjoy. Not only did his wolf crave her touch, her nearness, her voice and scent—a betrayal to Fentienne himself—but his wolf would fight to the death for her too. And when the wolf owned its master, shifters went mad and lost all touch with reality. Those were the démons Aurelienne's feared—the wolves who slaughtered anything with a beating heart, like the Beast of Gabaston and other moon-addled creatures.

Fentienne ground his teeth.

One more entity that maneuvered to own him.

One more being willing to destroy him for their own selfishness.

One more creature grooming him to hate.

Barefoot, he barely felt the ground beneath him in his haste to escape his mind. Trees blurred by and ferns whacked his legs—

"Wolf Prince," a gravelly voice said nearby.

Fentienne slid to a halt, his clawed hands ready to strike. Lucas Fontine—a street vendor, alpha of Clan Palehide in Factory Row and fellow guardian officer in the Brotherhood—leaned his hip against a tree, his arms casually crossed over his chest. His blue eyes studied Fentienne with keen sharpness while flyaway strands of the long, dark blond hair tied back at his neck flew around his face. Tattered earthen brown linen knee-length breeches covered his lower half while a loose natural linen undershirt billowed around him in the slight breeze.

The young man pushed off the tree. "Your head would be ripped clear off your body by now, *mon ami*."

"Hmm."

"It is not like you to be distracted, milord." Lucas plucked the tip of a fern and rolled the bruising leaves between his fingers. But a mischievous smile curled the corners of his lips. "Who do you mourn?" He gestured at Fentienne's black breeches and linen shirt. "A good kill last night?"

"What do you want, lesser démon?"

Lucas ignored the insult for those turned wolf, or those born from a turned bloodline, and tossed the now slimy green clump into a huckleberry bush. "A female, then?" He peered over Fentienne's shoulder toward the chateau and arched a brow, that taunting smile still on his lips. "You did not run far to be so breathless. You pant as if starved for someone to warm your bed."

Fentienne ignored the man and stepped past him. But Lucas grabbed his arm and yanked him back.

"Touch me again and I will kill you, *sans-culotte*," Fentienne snarled in the man's face.

The man's smile grew even wider, more wolfish, but he dropped his arm. "All bark and no bite, silk breeches."

"No bite?" Fentienne stepped into the man's space, like he would a subordinate. "Peeling fingernails was my favorite method. Happy to provide a demonstration."

Lucas grinned. "*Oui*, definitely a female. Look at your hackles."

"You are—"

"Speaking of a female, there was a riot in The Row last night."

Fentienne blinked back his annoyance. "You came all this way to tell me about a riot *over a female?*"

"An aristocrat attacked a fayette peddling flowers outside of the concert hall. The Row became rabid."

Fentienne groaned a bored sigh and shoved past Lucas. "Go." He waved a dismissive hand. "Do not return or *I will* bite if you do." Inane street gossip was a waste of his precious, cursed time. He would rather pluck his eyebrows hair by hair than listen to a common occurrence in Factory Row. Riots were hardly news as well.

"Rhoslyn Gautier, the attacked fayette, led an angry blood march to Crowns Quarter," Lucas said to his back.

The hair on Fentienne's neck lifted.

"Ah, now I have your attention."

Lucas could hear the heart trying to beat from Fentienne's chest and scent the shift in emotion, so he didn't bother to argue. Instead, he relaxed his body and angled his head enough to deliver a message of haughty indifference.

"Do not worry, Wolf Prince. Your maman is safe." From the corner of his eye, Fentienne watched Lucas prowl his way, a satisfied curl to his lips. "But thousands of protesters, mostly female, did break down the gold gates and invaded Palais d'Aurélie to demand an audience with Queen Adeline." The shifter chuckled again and rounded to face Fentienne. Their eyes locked. "Mademoiselle Gautier refused to bow before your aunt and accused her of starving and overworking the lower class. Called her a wolf in spun silks. Then suggested the queen was the Beast of Gabaston."

Fentienne laughed, he couldn't help it. "Absurd."

"Is it, though?" Lucas cocked his head. "You and I both know the Beast is not from our packs. Not one death reported from Palais d'Aurélie or Crowns Quarter."

"Unless that is an intentional diversion to hide the Beast among the lower packs."

"Tell me, Wolf Prince. Who sits on the golden throne if our beloved Queen Adeline Chalamet is beheaded in the market square?"

Their eyes remained locked. "Are you asking if *I* am the Beast? To gain a throne?"

"*Non*, milord. You don't want the throne." Lucas smirked. "But it is in the clans' interests if you wear the crown. No other Chalamet roams the woods of Gabaston like one of us and you, our alpha."

Fentienne leaned into the shifter's face and sneered. "And a Halivaard who derived pleasure in killing Aureliennes. All of Ealdspell believes I am dead. Find another Chalamet wolf to politically manipulate."

"Adalwolf," the young man drawled.

"Fentienne Beausoleil."

Lucas considered him a moment. "Why the Sun Kings?"

"I am *not* your Chalamet puppet. Or the aristocracy's."

"But *our* golden wolf, Prince Fentienne Beausoleil," Lucas said with a mock bow, then continued. "Rhoslyn Gautier was left for the naturals and rabids as punishment. I was there. I heard Queen Adeline sentence her. Now four natural wolves are dead and three are injured. Guards will comb the woods later for her remains. And if not found, there will be a bounty on her head, which will send every hungry, desperate fool to these forests. We're already on the precipice of a full-fledged monster hunt because of the Beast. The Monks of Glanis cry for a wolf cleansing daily too." Lucas narrowed his eyes and Fentienne remained still, his face a marbled statue of bored contempt. "Why did you protect her this morning, *Fentienne Beausoleil*? Saints District isn't your territory."

"All of Aurelienne is *my* territory. I graciously allow you all to roam *my* woods." Fentienne shoved past Lucas, bumping into his shoulder, satisfied when the force knocked the alpha off balance. "No one is to touch Mademoiselle Gautier. Or harm her brother. Not even natural wolves. Understood?"

"What is Mademoiselle Gautier to you—" Lucas spun toward the trail behind them and lifted his ear. Dark blond stands, loosened from the tie at his neck, flew around his face in the breeze. Then dark blue eyes cut his way, his brows pushed together.

Footsteps and voices . . . Fentienne replied with a quick nod.

The scent hit him next.

"Shit," he seethed under his breath.

Lucas looked like he was ready to bark a laugh. "*Quand on parle du loup on voit sa queue. . .*" he whispered with a delighted wag of his eyebrows.

When you talk about the wolf, you see its tail.

The equivalent to "speak of the devil" in Clifstán. But his birth land didn't see wolves as the Dark Saint's démons. They were the symbol of mighty warriors. The only devil was an enemy who gained victory in war. And, right now, every bone in his body saw Rhoslyn as his enemy.

The trail leading to Factory Row was a few miles back. But if a bounty was indeed on her head as Lucas suggested . . . it would make sense that they would continue deeper into the woods toward Chateau Lumière Dorée. Pissed, he leaned back against a tree and closed his eyes. Muscles flexed and relaxed down his body; his hands curled into fists. Lucas crept to a different tree and crouched low behind the brush.

Only his wolf had seen her. She was mere memory and impression to him, and the air caught in his tightening throat.

"We are near the House of Golden Light," the male elf he recognized earlier said.

"We cannot possibly stay there."

Her voice . . . Gods, the weight on his chest became unbearable and he heaved for breath. With his back pressed to the tree, Fentienne craned his neck to peek around the trunk and met the waiting gaze of the warrior elf at her side. The male knew he was there. Knew exactly where he hid and every animal instinct bristled into an unnatural stillness. A slight curve inched up the elf's mouth—a challenge from one alpha to another. A soldier's taunt that made Fentienne quietly snort in derisive reply. The male spoiled for a fight? He would be happy to oblige.

"We will camp outside of the manor," the elf said to her but kept his eyes pinned to Fentienne's. "If your dark démon is your protector, he will not harm us."

The male's gaze slid to Lucas then flashed Fentienne a warning glare. Fentienne gritted his teeth but dipped his head. He wanted Rhoslyn dead, but he couldn't kill her. Didn't want anyone else to kill her either. His wolf would never submit to him if he did—and, if that happened, Fentienne would lose the last remnant of battle-fought agency he possessed.

Lucas crouched on all fours, ready to shift and lunge, if needed.

Satisfied with Fentienne's response and after one last look at Lucas, the elf focused on Rhoslyn while adjusting the frail boy in his arms. "He will not let anything else harm you either and you *need* that protection right now. Especially while I am out hunting."

Against his better judgment, Fentienne's eyes traveled to her cloaked form weaving beneath the ferns as she neared the tree he hid behind and—

Winter skies . . . she was . . . gods . . . all thought left him to emotionally bleed out.

He was a dying man.

A drowsy rush of heat hit him and his eyes closed in a long, languid blink. Her scent—the thrilling bite of a building summer storm and an earthiness he couldn't yet identify. She was . . . more beautiful than he remembered. Lovelier than his wolf's memories. Every feeling when sixteen, every ache he had known for the girl who made him laugh arrested his furiously beating heart.

Then, in a single flutter of his raging pulse, disgust began to curl in his gut.

A dark, writhing desire that seductively licked at the swelling hate cracking through the binds constricting his lungs.

Addien would pay. He would rip her apart, slowly, savoring every scream and plead for mercy. He wanted to watch her die with a blinding pain that would torment every decaying limb of her sanity, even in the Underworld.

He wanted her impaled on the blunt points of absolute agony—like him.

Lucas watched him closely, his eyes narrowed. Fentienne was struggling to keep his body under control. His wolf wanted to shift and drown in sensation—her scent, her voice, her everything—but the curse prevented him from being anything other than halfway to a wolf until nightfall.

"How can you be sure that he would protect me again?"

A smug grin playfully tugged at the corners of the white-haired elf's mouth and Rhoslyn scoffed.

They disappeared behind the trunk and Fentienne rolled his head in the other direction to watch their backs.

"If you say it is because I fall for dark, dangerous males or that you are kind—"

Fentienne could hear no more and covered his ears. Especially about how she fell for dark and dangerous males.

Everything inside of him chafed raw. He was quickly unraveling and looked anywhere but at Lucas.

The world above his eyes swayed in illuminated greens, golds, and blues. A breeze skipped by and carried traces of her intoxicating scent, and he swallowed painfully against the sharp knot in his throat. When he sensed they were farther up the trail, he lowered his hands. Another volatile rush of emotions crashed into him—a fight between man and wolf—a fight and flight that anchored his feet to the ground. The pressure inside of him was building, though, and he was a few seconds away from exploding.

"She's your mate, isn't she?" Lucas grunted a delighted laugh. "That is why you protected her."

Fentienne shadow sprinted with the unnatural speed of démons and slammed Lucas against a tree by his throat. "You go too far," he growled. "I am above you in rank and class. Whom I choose to protect and why is not for you to ask." He squeezed and Lucas clawed at Fentienne's tightening grasp. "Do you know how many creatures I have killed? How many I have tortured?" He tossed the man to the ground before the alpha could shift. "Do not challenge me again, *lesser* démon. I am *your* alpha."

Lucas rolled to all fours and coughed.

Fentienne grabbed his hair and yanked his head back. "Do you understand my orders?"

"*Oui,*" Lucas wheezed out.

"Yes, *what?*"

"*Oui,* Wolf Prince."

"Tell the other alphas and clan leaders. I'll address the Brotherhood at the next meeting." Fentienne released his hair and stepped back. "Dismissed."

Baring his teeth in a predatory snarl, Lucas shifted into a white wolf and ran off. Though he swore he saw the young man smile.

Muscles quaked down Fentienne's body. The territorial rage was new to him. Taming his wolf, who wanted to prowl after Rhoslyn, was proving difficult. Lucas *knew* better than to tease and question an alpha about their mate, even if Rhoslyn wasn't his. Perhaps he crossed that line with Fentienne to see for himself if it were true. Otherwise, the alphas could challenge Fentienne's protection order. But now . . .

Swear words hissed from his clenched teeth.

This didn't make sense. Why *her*?

Did Maeline's infant blood seal the contract too? If so, that primal part of him was drunk on the faerie magic binding them together. And Addien knew. That abomination knew he would literally lose all control and go mad if he refused the mate bonds.

I would rather die than be with you!

"Captain Halivaard," the warrior elf said a few paces from him—in Clifstánian.

Chapter 8

Fentienne

How long had Fentienne stood in this spot, lost to his spiraling thoughts?

He resisted his body's knee-jerk reaction to visibly startle at the elf's sudden presence. Instead, he turned enough to size-up the male, a brow arched—unimpressed—before turning away in disinterest. "I agreed to her protection. What more do you want, creature?" he replied in Aurelienne. When the elf didn't answer, Fentienne seethed, "Enjoying the hideous sight of my face? Let me know when you're ready for a closer look at my claws."

The male tilted his head. "Your brother asks about you whenever I pass through Dreglind."

Fentienne moved as a streak of shadow and stopped within inches of the elf's face and growled, "Tell him I'm dead."

"You hurt her, even a little, captain," the male whispered, almost a lover's whisper if not for the arrogant, canined grin begging Fentienne to swing first, "and I will ensure that message is true."

A dark chuckle rumbled from Fentienne's chest. "Threats do not work on me, elf."

"I do not need to play games. Did you hear me approach? Scent me?"

"Hmm." Fentienne leaned his hip and shoulder onto a tree beside the male and cocked his head. "If I had, that bow would be a useless prop, like you. But I rarely fault a weapon for target failure."

The elf full on laughed. "Since a wee lad, your wit has always been sharp and your heart even sharper."

The hell? A scowl formed between Fentienne's brows.

"Never could you keep your emotions in check, not even to please your father." The elf studied his eyes. "You feel so deeply, Adalwolf Halivaard," he added softly. "You care to the point of pain. A man with a bladed heart whose passion severs and liberates. The king didn't know how to break your wildness. But he knew an injured wolf would snap and bite and kill with little provocation. He knew a caged animal would do anything for the tiniest taste of freedom."

A man with a bladed heart?

Since a young lad? Who in the dark skies was this male?

Regardless, if the elf were here, that meant Rhoslyn was now at the chateau and his muscles flexed for control once more.

To hide the angry shivers racing through his veins, Fentienne sighed. "Threats and now a psych evaluation." He gestured to the bow. "Sloppy aim for someone who claims to know me since a boy. I don't fall prey to threats, sad stories, *or* pretty words."

"You want to ask who I am, but you won't." The elf's pointed grin widened. "This conversation unsettles you, but your pride—"

"My pride doesn't give a shit about social niceties. Or you."

"Dalbréath Kadelaryn, little wolf," the male said with a quick dip of his head. "Eirwen's foster brother and Maeline Wyndham's uncle."

Fentienne stilled at Eirwen's name and his muscles flexed again.

Kadelaryn . . . the right-hand officer to Gedlen Fate Maker. Commander of the Dúnælven military. And King Dallin of Avenbury's brother. Fentienne narrowed his eyes on the elf and curled his lip into a sneer—a warning to back off.

"How do you know Rhoslyn Gautier?" Dalbréath asked.

"I don't."

Dalbréath studied him for a beat—again. "How mortals lie."

"Every highly sentient being lies, *commander*." Fentienne leaned in and snarled, "Faeries cry victim to mortal lies at every chance to distract from the deceptions they compulsively weave for sport."

"There is that sharp wit again." Dalbréath tilted his head. "And that sharper heart."

Fentienne huffed a disgusted laugh. "Perhaps other mortals feel special with your praise, but I loathe self-serving, conniving creatures like you."

"Aye, there is much darkness in you, captain. But there is also a scared boy who aches for help. You rage to be set free from the barbed cage the king trapped you in and tear into anyone who tries to turn the lock."

"And yet you entrust your niece to me."

Dalbréath touched two fingers to Fentienne's arm and whispered words in runic before Fentienne could react. Fentienne jerked out of the way and bared his claws. He would rip into the male but killing the Dúnælven's second-in-command would invite too much trouble.

"Peace," the elf said. "I created a shield around us. Wolf ears are all over these woods."

Fentienne locked onto the elf's gaze, one alpha challenging the other. "Explain what the hell is going on."

Dalbréath dipped his head. "The future queen is not safe in Avenbury yet. The threat to her life remains as King Dallin's firstborn child."

"Why? Addien has known she was in Gabaston for at least six years now. She could have killed her at any time. So why hasn't she?"

Dalbréath leaned on his bow and rolled his eyes, teeth clenched. "Of course, Addien Wyndham would find Maeline and play coy."

"Wyndham." Fentienne closed his eyes in a long, angry blink. "Who is she to the queen?"

"Her cousin and head faerie on Avenbury's counsel as the next line to the throne if Maeline doesn't survive."

"No," Fentienne said, his voice low. "Who is she *really* to Queen Audra? Who puts a kill order on a baby for revenge over breaking a marriage decree by their ridiculous faerie counsel?"

"Fae curse infants to punish the parents. Innocent blood redeems the guilty. It's an old practice from Éireanna."

Éireanna? Florian had mentioned this place on the diesel train. And, like a monster, Fentienne hadn't believed him. "Barbaric."

"Aye." Dalbréath held his gaze for a beat. "The curse wasn't from breaking a marriage decree, lad. Addien was obsessed with my older brother after being rejected by a mortal man she obsessed over more, and Dallin chose his mate, Audra, over her. Just one more rejection, one more unrequited love in her long life. The marriage negotiations with Merenna were Addien's attempt to block Audra's and Dallin's union. But"—Dalbréath sighed—"They exchanged vows in secret. And unlike mortal vows, a promise by a faerie is bound by magic. Witnesses are not needed to wed because we cannot lie. A marriage contract made in blood is the same binding magic. You and Maeline are already married before the eyes of the fae. You were married as children. Humans see it as a betrothal until the man claims his faerie bride."

"I was the curse to punish her parents," Fentienne said more to himself in disbelief. He was a curse. A *curse*.

Dalbréath slowly nodded his head. "Your marriage to Maeline was Addien's curse, little wolf, presented to Clifstán as a cotton arrangement should the Wyndham heir be born female. For what father would wish for their daughter to wed a démon who was born to and raised by Aelfred Halivaard? Especially a father who knew that Addien's hands were bound in a curse by a lover she tried to kill a couple of centuries ago—"

"What happens if she gets blood on her hands?"

"I do not know, little wolf. But mostly likely die where she stands."

"Therefore," Fentienne said through clenched teeth, "finding a husband capable of killing Maeline was necessary."

The House of Thorns knew Fentienne was a Chalamet shifter by age four?

The elf's lips dipped into a sad smile. "Your marriage was sealed the very day Maeline was born," Dalbréath continued. "The alternative was her death."

Fentienne ground his teeth and peered out into the woods. Pieces of his heart started to break. Pieces he didn't know were whole enough to shatter. A child born of hate. Groomed to hate. Married as a curse because he was destined to hate.

"On Maeline's second day of life, Addien cursed her once more. A promise that the crowned princess would die once she had come of age, after you officially claimed her as your wife. Gellynor Death Talker was able to counter the curse that, in order for Addien to attempt Maeline's life, first Maeline had to fall in love with you and agree to remain married after being claimed. And, until then, Addien couldn't approach Maeline or speak to her."

"Then why make her into a changeling?" Fentienne's clawed hand curled into fists. "Unnecessarily dramatic, even for you meddling elves."

"No, lad. It wasn't because of Addien."

Of course, not. *He* was the curse. The depth of Addien's twisted cruelty struck him once more. The princess was hidden in Aurelienne with a poor merchant family because what Prince of Clifstán would claim a peasant girl from an enemy realm? Especially a dirty fayette from Factory Row?

Dalbréath frowned. "Your banishment to Aurelienne wasn't shown to Gedlen. Nor your ascension to the Aurelienne throne. He saw only your death. But Eirwen changed your fate."

"Die or die married to me." Fentienne leveled a heated gaze onto the male and growled, "Get her away from Chateau Lumière Dorée. It's cursed and she's not safe—"

"Queen Adeline will put a bounty on her head, if not already. Who better to protect her against your aunt than her heir? Maeline is *your mate. Your wife*. She has come of age and is yours to claim now, captain. I cannot stop this, even if I wanted to. And trust me, I want to with every breath in my body. I have since she was born. But not even Gedlen Fate Maker or the High Druid can break a contract made in faerie blood, especially by ancient bloodlines like my family's and the Wyndham's."

Fentienne opened his mouth but Dalbréath cut him off.

"Aye, we know the House of Golden Light is cursed to the grave. Gellynor Death Talker felt a large ripple of magic from the dead and spoke to the Well of Souls in the Land of Mist. Addien cannot attempt to end Maeline's life until my niece falls in love with you."

"So Maeline dies if she believes herself in love with me and remains my wife or dies if she or I break our blood bond." Fentienne darkly laughed and looked away, shaking his head. He wanted to raze this forest to the ground with teeth and claws.

"She won't die, not with you—"

"What the hell does that even mean? Not with me? Her death is entirely on my head! I was cursed to kill her from the time I was four!" Fentienne growled low, the blood pumping furiously in his veins. "Addien said she would break the betrothal contract if I agreed to marry her instead. Is this a faerie trick? One that would also put Maeline's life in danger?"

A muscle pulsed along Dalbréath's jaw. "Gedlen Fate Maker saw, in a vision, a bounty on Maeline's head two days ago and charged me to bring her to you for protection."

"He's a fucking idiot."

Dalbréath lifted his shoulder in a slight shrug. "Aye, sometimes. But I wouldn't be here if I disagreed with him. She is *my kin*. I lost a daughter to war, captain. My beating heart with her. I will not lose my niece too. I entrusted her to the Gautier family when only a few weeks old. Now I entrust her to you, *her husband*. Claim her before the packs. Make her officially your mate to witnesses, if nothing else than to protect her more from your aunt. You will not allow any harm to come to her or her brother, lad. I know you, Adalwolf Fentienne. You would put your life before hers. You already have."

"The Realm of Avenbury will not welcome a king consort to govern their military who has war crimes against the entire Kingdom of Ealdspell. Do not deny that it is true, elf." Fentienne bared his teeth. "I have killed hundreds of people. Entire families. Gone. Mothers and fathers lost their children, because of me. Husbands held their dead wives, because of me. I am more a moon-addled beast than any in these woods. But unlike them, I didn't have the excuse of a wolf gone mad."

"You were following orders, lad. None of those actions were ultimately your choice. You knew no other life until a year ago."

"Don't!" Fentienne stepped back. "Don't justify my war crimes, commander. I craved the pleasure in causing their deaths. I enjoyed every moment of violence."

"War turns even the kindest man into a killing machine. There is real pride and pleasure in fatally taking down the enemy." Dalbréath shifted on his feet. "Clifstán was the only realm with compulsory service beginning at age eight. All other realms are voluntary and require males to be a minimum of sixteen to eighteen years of age. That is eight years of indoctrination to see only enemies before one's first battle, captain. Eight years trained by Aelfred Halivaard to commit horrors and see them as justified. You were a child. A *child*. I do not justify the deaths or your pleasure in causing them. But I have played war for centuries and you can't even claim two decades as a trained soldier."

Dalbréath gently touched Fentienne's chest above his heart with two fingers. "You are not a curse, little wolf," the elf softly spoke and the words thundered through him. "I understand what has been done to you and why. And I know it takes a man who cares to the point of pain to break generational cycles of trauma and abuse. A man like *you*."

Fentienne knocked Dalbréath's hand off him and swallowed back the sob knotting in his tightening throat. "Do you think those families care about your psychology on the art of war? Florian was raised by the same hand of cruelty and chose differently. I had the same opportunity to be a better man, like him. But Addien Wyndham knew I wouldn't, didn't she?"

He stepped back and spat, "There *is* much darkness in me and nothing else. Do *not* make me into a pitied war victim for the girl I'm under blood oath to husband. I gave you my word that I will protect your niece even though she will be the reason I lose all control to my wolf and the fated reason she dies," he choked out and pointed at the bow. "Find different prey to manipulate with your pretty words. Or I will give the pack alphas what they want and leave Rhoslyn and her brother to the rabid démons to keep bounty hunters and the Monks of Glanis zealots out of these woods. I owe you *nothing*."

"You had just turned eight two days prior." Dalbréath crossed his arms over his chest. "Florian was building a house of sticks in the woods outside of the barracks while you gathered moss for the roof." The elf lifted a sad smile. "Captain Karlsen approached with two soldiers and your first instinct was to protect your brother. In three steps, you took your brother's hand in yours and maneuvered to stand in front of him as much as you could. Before the soldiers halted at the house of sticks, you whispered to Florian over your shoulder, 'I will protect you. Always.'"

"Do not speak another word," Fentienne growled.

"The soldiers had orders to take you to the junior barracks to begin your conscription. But you refused to leave your wee brother."

Angry tears pricked the back of Fentienne's eyes and he fell into the memory. Images flashed in his mind of laughing with Florian. They were always each other's secret happiness. And always forging adventures too. That day, they were pretending to survive being lost in the woods. First, they would build a shelter, then they would hunt for food.

How could Dalbréath possibly know this?

"You bit the hand of the first soldier who reached for you," Dalbréath continued and Fentienne's eyes snapped to his. "You kicked the other in the groin. The king knew you would fight, because you *always* fight."

"Stop."

"Your father, hidden to you, marched over to Florian..."

Fentienne couldn't move. He couldn't breathe. His entire body braced for what came next.

"...he hit him so hard, your little five-year-old brother doubled over in the dirt and choked for air."

A tear crawled down Fentienne's cheek.

"He ordered you to go with the soldiers but you ran for your brother instead. Captain Karlsen grabbed you and held you down while you screamed and kicked. Then your father..."

"I said stop!"

"...he whispered in your ear to scream at your brother, to tell Florian how you hated him before walking to the barracks with Captain Karlsen. From that point forward, you were to hate Florian and torment him. And, if you didn't, your father would break a finger on your brother's hand until you obeyed. Then the king violently yanked your little brother up to his feet. Florian was sobbing in pain. You were wild in Captain Karlsen's hold until the king grabbed your brother's hand."

Fentienne looked away as another tear slipped down his cheek.

"I saw the moment you understood that the king really would hurt Florian if you didn't obey him," Dalbréath continued, his voice soft once more. "I saw the moment your heart broke. And I heard the words. You screamed at Florian that you hated him. To protect him. Like you promised. Then you willingly followed the soldiers to the barracks."

The ache in Fentienne's chest was unbearable.

"Florian rarely fought back. But you, third-born prince... you had a spirit your father wanted to own and break. And he did. You and Florian did not have the same opportunity to choose differently. Because when you disobeyed your father, the king punished the one you promised to protect. You bullying Florian was the lesser of the two evils and that is how the king controlled you. But your sixteenth year? That was the year you truly broke and stopped caring, about anything. That was the year the king *finally* won and owned you."

The air rushed from Fentienne's lungs. "What did you just say?"

But the elf ignored him. "And that year, Captain Adalwolf Fentienne Halivaard, Prince of Clifstán and Aurelienne Prince of Démons, the bladed heart inside your chest sharpened to a deadly doubled edge." Dalbréath stepped close and lowered his voice. "The cage door is now open, yet you refuse to leave your prison. What are you afraid of, little wolf?" They stared intensely at each other, neither moving. Then Dalbréath leaned in even closer, tapped his bow, and whispered, "Bull's eye," and walked past him. And kept walking until he disappeared into the thicker woods.

Fentienne gasped for air. Cold sweat beaded on his forehead and his hands grew clammy once more.

That was the year the king finally won and owned you . . .

Flashbacks carouseled through his mind at breakneck speed. He couldn't breathe. Gods, he was suffocating. Fentienne leaned his forehead onto a tree and heaved for breath, gripping the front of his shirt above his heart. Closing his eyes, he thought of the small flame dancing on the candle's wick, the flickering snap of resistance. The collision of fire and air, of hot and cold. The fluttering heartbeat of survival.

The sound of war.

Sickened laughter squeezed past the sharp knot in his throat. Addien was the puff of foul air his father used to douse Fentienne's fire. And what little morsels of hope and kindness he possessed didn't relight after a count of three.

I hope Father orders your death. And I hope I'm the one who gets to torture you first.

Words he spat like a dog who licked its master's hand after being kicked. A betrayal to his brother.

He grimaced back the rising sob.

He was married to a girl who would die if she loved him.

The king had won his obedience through cruelty.

Addien craved a broken doll to play with—and *his throne*. The one he was *always* meant to inherit and they could rule together.

Split crown.

Man and monster.

Twisting toward the chateau, he furiously swiped at the angry tears on his cheeks and loosed a choked breath. Then he shadow sprinted toward the House of Golden Light to watch over the girl his wolf and Dalbréath charged him to protect, even if doing so killed her.

And him.

Each bitter breath fed the thorns tangling around his heart.

What are you afraid of, little wolf?

That he was born for destruction. That the gods cursed his soul before he was even conceived. That no one would ever want to protect him—and no one did. That, since his first breath, he was destined to become a villain so Florian, Chosen by Irminsul, Protector of Life, could play the hero beloved by all. That he would be why Maeline Kadelaryn Wyndham died and why the Kingdom of Ealdspell had yet another reason to hate him.

For who could love a beast?

Chapter 9

Rhoslyn

Cold, moss-covered stone dug into Rhoslyn's back. But she was simply too exhausted to care. Wind fluttered her hood as she studied the darkening landscape with heavy lids. Feeling her brother shiver, she wrapped her cloak tighter around Matthieu's sleeping form in her arms. A storm was coming in and fast. Dalbréath told them not to move but getting drenched was foolish in their transient state. They had no fire to warm their hands let alone dry their clothing. At least, no fire until Dalbréath returned.

A rain drop hit her cheek and she sighed.

Another breeze ruffled her cloak. Beside them, the wrought iron gates creaked and groaned on their crooked hinges. The heady scent of roses from behind the wall infused the thick air around her. Or haunted roses, as Matthieu called them. Their perfume wasn't as bold as the roses in Crowns Quarter. Rather, the fragrance was delicate and brought to mind the blushing innocence of a girl who stood before a handsome boy. As if the act of falling in love were woven into the very essence of each rose petal. Rhoslyn leaned her head back against the stone wall and closed her eyes for several beats of her fluttering pulse.

With the wind and misting rain picking up, she would find no sleep despite how her bones ached to do so. A proper shelter would be needed soon, anyway. Perhaps they could inch inside the gates to rest beneath the marble gazebo in the corner opposite of where they sat. Her brother had wanted to see the haunted roses for days now. Rhoslyn also desired to touch the petals and lift a flower to her nose. The draw was growing maddening. The scent more enticing with each breeze.

"Matthieu," she softly spoke. "Wake, *mon petit caneton*."

Her brother rolled deeper into her arms and pressed his face into her bodice, beneath her cloak, and coughed. "Too tired."

Rhoslyn uncovered her cloak from his little body. "It is starting to rain and we need cover."

Matthieu lifted his head and squinted at their surroundings with an adorable sleepy expression. "Where are we?"

"The House of Golden Light."

His blue eyes rounded. "The dark démon..."

"*Oui.*" She brushed that one persistent, unruly curl from his eyes. "Do you wish to see a haunted rose?"

"Truly?" He popped up from her lap and studied the gates.

"There is a gazebo just inside. The haunted thorns will protect us until Monsieur Dalbréath returns."

Changeling child of thorns...

Matthieu coughed into his arm, then flashed her a dimpled grin. "Haunted thorns are more interesting than haunted roses."

Rhoslyn pushed away the tinglings of fear nipping at the edges of her mind and, instead, took her brother's hand. Slowly, they moved toward the gates. Her brother's limp was more pronounced than usual. If she were hungry, he must be starved. Fatigue colored his face and lips in pale hues and shaded purple just beneath his eyes.

A sensation rushed up her spine, like the skittering legs of a thousand insects crawling over her. Casually, she peered over her shoulder toward the woods, but her hood blocked part of the view. Something was watching her and Matthieu. Did their guardian stalk them from the woods? Or a different démon? A low growl rumbled from the trees. Every muscle in her body tensed and her gaze darted between the shadows. Or was that thunder rumbling in the sky? If they stepped into the gates, they would be trapped in by the stone walls and easier prey for wolves.

Matthieu's soft intake of breath pulled her focus forward and her heart stopped.

The garden, wild and magical, wove around stone paths cut from gold-veined marble. Roses in an unusual dark shade of red, similar in color to her grand-mére's burgundy cloak, sprawled in every direction. The vined bushes climbed the walls, over the gazebo, snaked across the various paths, and covered stone statues of wolves in the courtyard's center beside a small water lily-dressed pool. Up close, the chateau was gothically romantic and Otherworldly. Gold paint chipped the outer walls with white decorative trim and stone capped windows. She tilted her head. Why were the windows unnaturally black? Her eyes drifted upward to the ivy-draped spires and balconies. Along the roof's edge, gargoyles in the shape of wolves guarded the property against the Dark Saint and his démons.

Matthieu glanced up at her, excitement twinkling in his blue eyes, then he stepped just past the gates and into the courtyard. "I hope I see a ghost."

"Are haunted thorns and roses not horror enough for you, *caneton*?"

"I hope I see *many* ghosts!"

Rhoslyn laughed and mussed his hair, earning her a playful glare. But her smile slipped the moment he turned away and limped farther into the garden. Raindrops grew fatter. Still, she remained on the dividing line between the woods and the chateau. Something didn't quite feel right. An electricity hummed in the air around them. Perhaps it was only the building storm.

Another low growl rumbled behind her and she twisted to peer into the woods, her heart in her throat.

The forest remained still save the roar of rustling leaves. Dark clouds moved above the bending treetops. Thunder then, nothing more.

She relaxed her shoulders and wiped a raindrop from her cheek. A chilly breeze swirled around her, like a gentle hand nudging her forward, and carried with it the pining sighs of rosy-cheeked maidens. Rhoslyn closed her eyes and breathed deeply, curious of what it felt like to fall in love. Was it as painful as the poets made it out to be? An exquisite agony? The static in the air grew louder. Her mind wanted to lose itself to the enchanting smell of haunted roses. Rhoslyn eyed the gazebo, then peered over her shoulder one last time before stepping past the gates into the courtyard.

"Rosie, smell this one!" her brother called out to her.

Sidling up to her brother, she leaned down and pressed her nose to the dark burgundy rose and smiled.

Thunder crashed above them and Rhoslyn grabbed her brother and jumped.

But it wasn't just thunder growling across the sky. There was a second rumble and her eyes whipped toward the gates. An enormous gray wolf, the largest she had ever seen, snarled at them from the courtyard entrance, its hackles raised, its head low. Rhoslyn pushed her brother behind her. They were still too close to the gates to reach the front door before the wolf reached them. Where was her dagger? She patted her skirts and bit back a whimper. Had she left it in the wild grass where they first rested? And why were there so many beasts out the past twenty-four hours? Her gaze shot back to the wolf.

The green-eyed démon prowled closer to the gates and lunged.

Scooping up her brother, Rhoslyn broke into a run toward the house.

She furiously scraped at the tree trunk, her fingertips slipping open as she dug in her nails. Claws pierced into the tender flesh of her calf and pulled.

Her legs shook and her breaths came too quick. Tears rolled down her cheeks. She was far too weak, but she would reach the door. She must for her brother's safety. The garden tilted with the sudden dizzy rush in her head.

A gun shot rang out and then she was falling, a scream scorching her throat.

"Dea Matrona!" her brother whispered in horror. *Divine Mother.*

The way she held her brother, he peered over her shoulder. "Do not look, Matthieu," she breathlessly choked out. "Close your eyes, *mon petit caneton.*"

"The démon can't get past the gates."

She heard his words, but they didn't register. Of course, the démon could get past the gates, as could anything.

"Rosie, stop!"

A loud yelp echoed behind her and she slid on unsteady feet to a halt on the stone, her head spinning.

"Look!"

Growling, the démon leveled its predatory eyes onto her and jumped. Rhoslyn's entire body froze up. She clutched Matthieu to her side and . . . what in the Nine Saints? The monster should have leapt through the empty space between the gates. Instead, it bounced, as if hitting an invisible wall. Before it hit the ground, a streak of shadow barreled into the beast.

"The dark démon," Matthieu whispered in awe.

Unlike the wolf, this démon remained half shifted. His back was to her, but she could make out that he was well-built for a man, tall too. Wavy, cheek length, earthen brown hair, glinting strands of gold in the light, wildly danced in the breeze. He wore black knee-length breeches and an untucked, loose fitting black linen shirt rolled up to his elbows, and nothing else. No stockings, no shoes. Not even a waistcoat and frock. The nearly undressed state would warm her cheeks if not for the fear ripping through her veins.

The wolf rose to its feet and their guardian swiped with claws out, tearing into the fur of the other démon's neck. Rhoslyn's eyes rounded and she backed up a step. The gray wolf reached the partially shifted man's chest, its paws easily as large as the man's head.

Their guardian leapt out of the wolf's reach and yelled, "Stand down! This is an order from your alpha!"

The wolf lunged, knocking the man to the ground. Sharp teeth snapped at his neck. But their guardian pressed his thumbs into the wolf's eyes right before head-butting the beast, then brought a knee to its gut. The wolf yelped and the man used his bare feet to shove the animal off his body.

"Submit now or I will kill you!" he shouted while jumping to a stand with an unnatural grace that rolled through Rhoslyn's stomach at the sight. Truly, the way he moved was beautiful and precise, as if he were trained to fight.

Matthieu reached into his pocket and pulled out his carved talisman and brought it to his lips. "Saint Cernunnos," her brother whispered, "God of animals and the Underworld, favor our dark démon." He kissed the wolf and then handed it to her. "Pray to the moon goddess."

"You prayed to the *Dark Saint*?"

"*Oui*. He is the saint of démons, no?" Matthieu peered at her as if she had lost her wits, as if two monsters were not truly fighting ten yards away. As if there were not a magical barrier between them and the beasts. "You really do worry too much, *ma sœur*."

Rhoslyn took Matthieu's carved talisman with shaking hands and swallowed against the pounding pulse in her chest. "Saint Arianrhod," she whispered over the birch wood. "Goddess of the moon and companion to wolves, protect our guardian." Like her brother, she kissed the wolf and then handed it back to him.

Matthieu wove his frigid fingers with hers and coughed into his elbow, his intake breath short and raspy. She peered up at the falling rain, then to the door behind where they stood. They would soon be drenched. Chateau Lumière Dorée was forbidden to enter, by decree of the queen, but Rhoslyn saw no other option to keep her little brother warm and dry. Nor did she care for the rulings of a soulless woman.

What would happen if the dark démon survived? Would he be in a battle frenzy and come after them next? Would he attack them for intruding on his territory? If the invisible wall kept that wolf out, would it keep her and Matthieu in? And if so, it was too late. Rhoslyn gnawed the inside of her lip as her thoughts spun. The forest was filled with far too many wolves since the queen's sentence. As if they knew. Did they?

And that was her deciding factor. Even the invisible wall allowed them to pass, their dark démon had yet to harm a hair on their heads. He may still, but his record was far preferred to those who possibly hunted her down for the queen.

"Come, let's sneak quietly to—"

Her mouth fell open and blood quickly drained from her head. Black soaked the hem of her brother's cloak and climbed upward. His breeches and undershirt coloring black too.

"Rosie Mae . . ." Matthieu whispered, his eyes owlish. Pointing at her clothing, he sucked in a sharp gasp.

Fingers of black inked the tattered threads of the ripped skirt hanging limply against her legs, followed by her stockings, shoes, and bodice. But not her cloak, which remained a dark burgundy hue as before. "What is happening?" Her head snapped up and her gaze shot to every shadow and corner of the garden. Nothing else was turning black, just their clothing. Slowly, her focus slid to the dark démon who swiped at the gray wolf and her brows furrowed. His clothing was entirely black too.

"Is it because I prayed to the Dark Saint?" Her brother's bottom lip quivered. "I didn't mean to sell our souls."

"Our souls are not claimed, *caneton*. He does not claim elves. This isn't rot. See?" She fingered her garment to show that it was still intact. "You have done nothing wrong." She pressed him into her side as tears squeezed from his eyes. "I think . . . it is the same magic that created an invisible wall between the gates."

"Ghosts?" his little voice asked.

"Non, an enchantment."

He lifted tear-stained eyes and her heart sank at how pale he truly was. "Why could we pass through the gates and not the démon?"

"I am not sure." Rain dripped down Matthieu's face and dampened his hair. "We cannot wait for Monsieur Dalbréath to find us first," she said and gestured to the House of Golden Light. "If the invisible wall fades, we are safest inside from wolves."

"Unless they shift." Matthieu faced the chateau and drew in a tight breath, then gave her a nod. "Oui, you are right. I . . . I do not feel well, Rosie."

She kissed his head and startled at the warmth of his skin despite his growing clamminess. "Come, let us find a hearth to light and some food."

Mustering what little strength she had, she picked up her brother and carried him to the front door five yards away, then settled him back on his feet. Behind her, a loud growl rumbled through the air followed by a whining yelp. She spun on her heel, every muscle tight. Their guardian stumbled back a couple of steps, his chest heaving. Was he injured? Her gaze darted to the gray wolf, who was now limping away toward the deeper woods with a bloody gash on its side. Nausea churned in her gut. She wanted to look away, but watched until the beast disappeared out of sight, then relaxed her shoulders.

A breeze gusted through the meadow outside the gate and her gaze traveled back to their dark démon. The once loose black shirt now clung to his wide shoulders and back and defined the muscles of his body. All thought faded into mist as she watched water droplets slide down the exposed skin of his calves and forearms. Sweet Springs of Glanis, he was mesmerizing. She started to turn away, but the man angled his head enough to peer over his shoulder, his earthen brown damp strands sticking to his face and hiding his features. They caught each other's eyes and . . .

. . . her heart stopped beating.

The garden fell away, the forest too.

The blushing scent of roses swirled around her and she breathed deeply the magic of a girl standing before a handsome boy, her pulse lost to daydreams of his kiss. Rhoslyn lifted trembling fingers to her lips, then he was mere smoke and shadow.

"The door opened," Matthieu said with chattering teeth.

Rhoslyn touched her cheeks, embarrassed at her immodest thoughts. Over a démon. A monster. What was wrong with her? He served the Dark Saint and perhaps killed many innocent lives, even if he did seem to protect her and Matthieu. He shredded the skin of the gray wolf with the claws of his hands. The very essence of his existence was steeped in violence. If indeed her mate, was she simply responding to the blood bind? She meant to ask Dalbréath if their blood was added separately or mixed together in the marriage contract. Perhaps they shouldn't enter his home—

"Rosie?"

"*Oui?*" Her gaze swung back toward her brother's wobbling posture, then took in the darkened entryway, a new panic hitting her pulse. She swept her brother up into her arms before he passed out and stepped into the chateau, kicking the door shut behind her with the heel of her shoe. Matthieu needed warmth and food and rest with a solid roof over his head. Sleeping outdoors these past few days, in the cold, while sitting outside all day, also in the cold, hurt his lungs. She would deal with their guardian, if he threatened them for entering his home uninvited.

"*Oh la vache . . .*" her brother said under his breath. *Oh damn.*

"Matthieu Eric Gautier!" He weakly grinned at her, his eyes glassy, and she melted when seeing those cherubic dimples. But she could not fault him his exclamation. Everything was black, even the tapered candles on the various candelabras. The floor, the walls, all the decorative molding, rugs, chairs—everything. "*Oh la vache,*" she whispered back and Matthieu softly giggled, then began coughing and his body shook in her arms. His eyes fluttered closed and she bit back tears. "Hold on, *mon petit caneton,*" she whispered into his hair.

Not too far down the hall, firelight flickered through the door. A hiccuped cry escaped her clenched jaw at the sight. A hearth was already roaring. She hurried past strange shadows made by the candles, resisting the urge to shudder, and shoved past the door and into a furnished parlor—a sitting room, by appearances. As she hoped, a large hearth roared on the opposite end of the room, beside a settee and two wingback chairs. Rhoslyn angled past end tables with vases and other odd-end items to the settee and gently laid her brother atop the dusty cushions.

His small frame was convulsing from shivers. She quickly untied his cloak and laid it on the floor near the fire. Then she pulled his thin shirt over his head. The threadbare stockings that disappeared up his breeches were soaked through. Soft but quick, she slipped them down his legs, not wanting them to tear, and hung them and his shirt off the arm of a wingback chair. Matthieu was so pale, her heart ached. To warm his skin, she began briskly rubbing her hands over his arms and chest, then his legs, and continued doing so in a pattern, until a rosier glow returned to his body. But she remained shivering, still in her cold, damp clothing.

Rhoslyn stood and untied her cloak with shaking fingers. Slowly, she slipped out of her dress to only her corset and thin petticoat, then covered her chest with her arms. The ring around her neck glinted in the firelight and she tucked it away quickly before Matthieu saw. Though eighteen, and raised with brothers, she had never been so undressed before a male before. Still, the last thing she needed was to catch her death too. Swallowing thickly, she turned her back to the door and hung her garments across the other wingback chair. Then she rolled her ripped stockings down her legs and draped them on the floor near the hearth.

They needed a blanket to trap in the warmth, and for her to preserve some semblance of modesty.

A quick glance around the room and she could not spot one, nor a chest where one might be stowed. Brow furrowed, she studied the room and settled onto the window drapes. A smile flitted across her lips. That would have to do. She yanked down a panel. Dust poofed into the air and she coughed, then sneezed. Snapping the fabric into the air, she turned her head away from the clouds of dust made with her movements. After one more snap for good measure, she returned to her brother and wrapped the black velvet around his small frame. Then she climbed onto the settee and pulled him in close to her body.

They needed food, but he needed to rest more. Perhaps in a few hours she could rouse him enough to find the kitchen with her. She would not leave him alone. Another cough wracked his body and she ran her fingers through his hair in soft, soothing motions.

What if his lungs had truly sickened?

What if she couldn't find a way to heal him?

What if the beast of this manor found them asleep and killed them while they were vulnerable?

What if she were stuck here until the queen forgot about her?

What if they were trapped if the invisible wall didn't let them pass?

What if their dark démon was the man her parents had chosen for her to marry?

What if she fell in love with him and he didn't love her in return?

What if . . .

The heavy weight of Rhoslyn's lids struggled to remain open. She stared at the fire without seeing a single flame, only her list of endless worries. Nuzzling her nose into Matthieu's hair, she finally allowed her eyes to close to leave one nightmare and begin another.

During her sleep, she dreamt... and lamented the misfortune that condemned her to pass her days in a place without hope of ever leaving it... A young man, beautiful as Cupid is painted, in a voice which touched her heart, then said... "Judge not by your own eyes and, above all, abandon me not, but release me from the terrible torment which I endure." Her sleep lasted more than five hours, during which time she saw the young man in a hundred different places, and under a hundred different circumstances."

... Probably this horrible Beast, who appears to command all here, keeps [the young man] in a prison. How can he be extracted? He repeated to me that I was not to be deceived by appearances. I understand nothing; but how foolish I am! I amuse myself by seeking for reasons to explain an illusion formed by sleep and, which my waking has destroyed.

"La Belle et la Bête" by Madame de Villeneuve, published in *The Young American and Marine Tales*, 1743

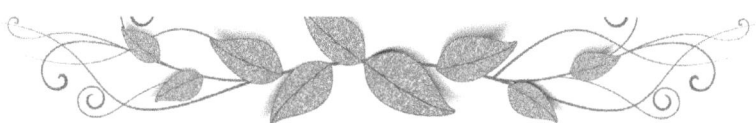

Chapter 10

Fentienne

Fentienne kicked open the locked back door and stumbled into the kitchens, his muscles shaking from pain and adrenaline. Blood soaked the sleeve of his ripped shirt and dripped from his bicep down his elbow, forearm, to the floor. Twisting to see the clawed slash on his side, he tensed. The wound was deeper than the one on his arm. But the injury he gave that wolf was fatal. The lesser démon would slowly bleed out. He could have ended her. A quick snap of her neck—a swift mercy kill—but he was too pissed to give a damn. Let her suffer for hunting on his property on behalf of the queen. For trying to take what he claimed as his. He hoped she writhed in blinding misery until her last breath.

More drops of blood splattered on the floor and he swore.

Aurelienne didn't have carbolic or boric acid, what soldiers used to treat wounds on the battlefields in Clifstán. But this saints forsaken realm had plenty of alcohol. The whiskey was nearly depleted. Not enough for his needs. He turned hand-blown glass bottles and flasks on the table until he found the one he wanted—cognac. The highest alcohol proof of brandy he had and far higher than wine. But gods, what a waste of fine drink. That lesser démon better take hours to die for this sacrifice.

He peeled the wet shirt from his body and eased it over his head, biting back a cry with the movements. Using his teeth and the hand of his uninjured arm to cut a small tear in the fabric, he then ripped the linen into strips using his foot and the same uninjured arm. The cloths and aprons in the kitchens were covered in dust. At least his shirt was clean-ish.

Sweat and drips of water and rain-drenched curls of hair dipped into his eyes. His breath came quick and hard.

Using his teeth once more, he uncorked the bottle of cognac, not wanting to cause more blood to weep from his injury on his bicep. He spat the cork onto the floor, then took a long swig of the drink. He fell against a wall and cinched shut his eyes several seconds to work himself up. This was going to hurt like a mother. Slowly, he poured the amber liquid over the gash on his side. White fire seared where alcohol hit blood and skin and muscle, and this time he couldn't hold back a cry. He sucked in air through his clenched teeth and drizzled cognac over his wound once more. The muscles of his stomach were violently flexing with each furious, tattered breath.

The bottle shook with his trembling hands as he placed it on the table. The brandy was going to leave a sticky mess on his skin. But better than an infection. Grabbing a long strip, he wrapped the wet fabric around his waist, wincing in pain with his injured arm's motions. Then he repeated the process with another torn strip from his shirt. When finished, he rested against the wall once more to catch his breath, his eyes closed. But he didn't allow himself long.

The amber glass he rested against his face cooled his flushed skin, then he pressed the bottle to his lips and tipped his head back. His belly warmed and pleasant heat swirled in his head. Fentienne enjoyed one more long swallow. Gritting his teeth, every muscle tense, he dribbled the cognac over the gash on his bicep. Fire billowed down his arm and he growled a string of swear words. Like before, he wrapped the strips of his shirt around his injury and tied off a knot with his fingers and teeth.

Only a few drops of drink left. He almost finished off the brandy but poured what remained over the linen strips around his side and arm, grimacing back the pain. He swiped at the drips of sweat and water rolling down his face with the palm of his hand and shook the water from his hair. All he wanted to do was fall face first into his bed. But he had one more task first.

In the larder, he grabbed two apples and dropped them onto a plate next to two small chunks of aged cheese, then filled a pitcher with water he pulled from the well last night before shifting. He tucked two wooden cups between his arm and uninjured side and dragged his legs up the stairs. They couldn't have gotten far. The boy looked like he was ready to pass out. The pallid hue of Rhoslyn's face and dry, cracked lips made his wolf growl in fury—the overprotective, demanding arse. To shut the beast up, he would leave them food and water. After this, they could fend for themselves. He wasn't a nursemaid or their servant in this trapped arrangement.

Quietly, he crept down the large hall off the main entry. Cool air brushed over the bare skin of his upper half. He peeked into the first parlor, the one with the giant hearth. His body trembled in pain; his head buzzed in blessed relief. Articles of clothing hung off the wingback chairs by the fire and the muscles of his stomach flipped. She was there. His wife. Undressed, from the looks of it. But he wouldn't glance her way. If he did, he wasn't sure what his wolf would do. It was hard enough to control those primal responses when she was covered in a cloak.

The electrifying, warm scent of a wild summer storm mixed with smoke filled the space around him. The scent of moss and ferns and unfurling spring leaves too. The breath was being pulled from his lungs and his chest rose and fell deeply. Fentienne placed the food and water on a table behind the sofa and gripped the edge. *Turn around, turn around.* From where he stood, he took in the threadbare, torn state of their clothing and a window missing a drapery panel. A ghost of a smile softened his lips. Clever.

He needed to leave. But this may be the only time he could steal a glance without her shuddering before him. And he needed to confirm. He needed to know it was really her. Straightening his shoulders, he stepped forward and images raced through his mind from when he was sixteen.

A girl who danced with him beneath the stars while the rest of the world slept.
Three steps.
A girl who beguiled his mind and made him laugh.
Two steps.
A girl who talked the night away and made him forget how empty he felt.
One step.
His eyes drifted to the sleeping forms on the sofa, skipping over her brother to drink in the way her dark lashes rested on her cheeks, the dusting of freckles across her nose—
Her cheek.
The fading mottled yellow of an older bruise lingered on the side of her face.

Every muscle stilled in his body. Fury growled hot in his chest, an instant flush of anger that heated his tightening skin. This wasn't from the wolf attack last night. Who had harmed her? Had they assaulted her in other ways too? His wolf snapped for revenge and Fentienne ground his teeth until pain spasmed along his jaw.

No.

This territorial response could *not* happen.

She was nothing to him.

The intensity of his attraction to her was already addling his mind enough.

Skies, she was the most beautiful girl he had ever beheld. A form of beauty that knifed through his chest and severed his heart in two—even though she was an inhuman creature. Long strands of golden-brown hair spilled around her head. Firelight limned the creamy length of her neck, shoulder, and arm, and—a soft moan left his parted lips. Sweet gods kill him now. She wore only her corset.

Fentienne stepped back—forcing his gaze to the ceiling—and swallowed thickly. A tremor of heat moved through his muscles, different from the fevered anger only a moment earlier. The claws of his hands curled and unfurled. His lungs drew in long breath after long breath. The bleating pain in his side bled into the deep ache carving out his heart.

"Say it, Fentienne. I want to hear your promise to me."

"I promise, Fayette." He cupped her cheek. "If you kiss me, I will perform any pleasure you desire whenever you so choose in the future."

"Close your eyes, Adalwolf Fentienne Halivaard."

The last fraying threads of his control snapped.

Fentienne pivoted on his heel and marched from the room, not caring if they heard him. In the hallway, he growled and dragged his claws across the wall as he strode toward the north stairs. Blistering pain fired from his injuries but he gritted through the burn.

Lies.

All *lies*.

He took two stairs at a time. At the top of the second floor, the ghost of a maid moved through the wall, her face frozen in terror. He walked through the apparition and kicked an end table holding a vase with the heel of his bare foot. An angry, bitter laugh squeezed past his roiling gut when the satisfying clink of shattering porcelain echoed throughout the large room.

Fentienne continued sprinting up more flights of stairs to the north tower.

She was truly here—his Fayette, his *wife*.

In his family's home.

This wasn't a faerie trick.

And gods did he despise her and Gedlen Fate Maker and Dalbréath Kadelaryn—*all* Kadelaryns—his wolf and the king and Eirwen and Addien and his mother and aunt and the entire godsdamn Kingdom of Ealdspell!

Who would protect him?

Who?!

His heart wouldn't survive another break.

He was barely surviving now.

A beast he would remain until he learned selfless love . . . and for what? Florian didn't give a shit if he lived or died. He hadn't sent scouts to see if Fentienne was well or needed help. His Imperial Highness, the Emperor of Dreglind, probably hoped his brother turned bully had died in the Spired Hills so he could finally be free of the family who tormented him.

Not one person had ever protected Fentienne—from *anything*.

No one had taken pain inside of themselves for him.

Not one soul had blackened so he may have light.

And yet *he* was the monster. The beast who needed to learn lessons on selfless love. Bullshit.

Fentienne practically flew into his room and slammed the door. He couldn't do this. He couldn't exist with the daggered reminder of Fayette chained to him until death ended this godsdamn curse. To constantly feel that swell of happiness, the desire to be wanted and needed, to be seen for who he was beneath the uniform and crown, only to have the reminder that it was all a faerie trick. A lie. Every moment together—manufactured. That he was fated to kill her.

Rhoslyn was here only because of Addien, Gedlen Fate Maker, and Dalbréath Kadelaryn. She wasn't here for him. She didn't choose him. And after she saw his face? Not that it mattered. Even if she wanted to be near him, he would never trust that anything between them was real and not the blood bonds of faerie magic. But even that didn't matter either.

She could *never* want to choose him.

He had to become a monster to protect her life.

Like he had with Florian.

And his heart would ache for her until his wolf went mad unless he agreed to marry Addien instead. Except he knew that was also a faerie trick. Everything with her was a trick. Addien wanted Rhoslyn to die and she wanted him to suffer.

Fentienne grimaced back the sob twisting painfully in his chest.

They still won.

They still owned him. Every hateful, manipulative person who used him for their pleasure.

"Fuck you!" he screamed at the walls. Again and again and again. Until his voice grew hoarse.

Blood dripped down his side and he let loose even more swear words. Marching over to his armoire, he threw open the doors, grabbed a clean sheet, and began ripping it into strips like he had his shirt. After he had a few long pieces, he wrapped the soft cotton around his waist and side as tightly as possible given his mobility limitations.

Drawing in cool air slowly through his nose, he exhaled a hot, panting breath.

Sleep. He just needed to shut off and recharge for the next battle in the hours to come. In case he slept until shifting, he slid a bolt into place on his door. His wolf would be pissed at being caged to this room. But his wolf could fuck off too.

Fentienne unbuttoned his rain-soaked breeches and stepped out of them. He kicked the garment toward the crackling fire still going strong in his hearth, not bothering to lay them out flat. The silk blanket and cotton sheets slid across his bare skin and he moaned as his head sank into a down pillow. He draped his uninjured arm over his eyes and forced air into his burning lungs. The way his mind raged and body screamed in pain, he thought it would take long to fade away. But in a few short breaths, black blissfully claimed him.

But not for long.

A WARM BREEZE skipped over his dew-chilled body. Fentienne squinted open his eyes to a bright blue sky and sunlight kissing his face. What the . . . ? He jolted upright and quickly scanned his surroundings. A sea of wildflowers surrounded him, framed in by a mixture of autumn-leafed trees in golds, reds, and oranges beside spring-blossomed trees in pinks and whites.

Pinching his brows together, he slowly stood and turned in a circle. The meadow danced in purples, blues, yellows, and reds in a myriad of textures and varying hues. The field's honeyed scent swirled around him on another gentle, warm breeze.

Where the hell was he?

A faerie realm? Did those even exist?

A nicker sounded behind him and his muscles stilled. Fentienne twisted to peer over his shoulder and the breath left his frantically thumping chest. Five yards away, in the shadows of a pink blossomed tree, stood a wild black Aurelienne stallion pawing at the ground. A saddle of fine black leather was secured to his back and a couple military braids decorated his mane.

Fighting back the excitement and the grief, Fentienne moved through the field of flowers toward the stallion. This couldn't be real. Loring was dead. He was forced to watch his oldest brother shoot Loring to punish Fentienne for disobeying a direct order during battle when nineteen—even though Fentienne had saved lives.

Slowing his steps, he paused before the stallion and ran a hand down his neck—and froze. *His hand.*

Fentienne gaped at his hands, flexing his fingers and turning them palm up and down to inspect each digit. No claws. His feet were fully human too. He touched his face and hair and hiccuped back a relieved sob. He hadn't known his body in over a year. The buzzing heat of his wolf was *finally* silenced too. The black he had worn the past few days was replaced by the softest linen— natural toned breeches and a simple undershirt, untucked with sleeves rolled up to just beneath his elbows. No stockings or shoes either. He liked the feel of earth beneath his feet and the elements on his skin.

A velvet nose snuffled the hair by his ear and Fentienne grinned. "Hey, boy," he whispered, then pressed his forehead to Loring's, a tear sliding down his cheek. "I don't know how you're here or where here is, but gods I've missed you. I'm . . . I'm so sorry . . ."

"*Pardonnez-moi*, monsieur, but have you seen a little elven boy with blond hair?"

His heart jumped to his throat.

Without turning around, he said, "No," not wanting to see *her*.

She tried to hide her sniffles with a soft, "If you see him—"

"I won't."

He could feel the heat of her eyes on his back.

"His left leg is lame, monsieur. His lungs are weak too. Injuries from the bombs in Gabaston." She loosed a shaky tear-stained breath. "He must be so frightened."

The thrumming pulse in his chest thundered against his ribs. And a dark wave of guilt flooded his mind. Were he and his men responsible for her brother's injuries? A year ago, he wouldn't have given a shit—a part of him still didn't. The enemy deserved death. But now? . . . he closed his eyes and leaned his head against Loring's once more, then he wiped away the tears and slowly turned to face the female who not only haunted his waking hours, but apparently now his dreams. Or whatever this cursed liminal space was between her mind and his.

She will fall in love with the whole man in her dreams.
And despise the monster when awake . . .

Clenching his jaw, quickly strategizing how to make her hate him, not only here but when awake, his gaze settled on her and—

"Skies," he breathed.

A cream-colored muslin dress draped over her body and fluttered in the breeze. Her hips were accentuated with small panniers and a bodice, embroidered in mauve roses and vined leaves, flattened her chest and pushed up her breasts. His eyes wandered upward and took in the dusty rose-hued ribbon tied around her neck as a choker and the long strands of her hair curled and fashioned beneath a wide-brimmed straw hat trimmed in white lace. Dark green eyes met his shyly and a blush colored her cheeks. But her lips . . . his breathing quickened. Her lips were red and flushed from crying. Lips he wanted to lose himself to. He softly blinked. Behind her, autumn leaves and pink petals tumbled through the air and he was completely, breathlessly mesmerized.

"His name is Matthieu," she whispered, her chest rising and falling as much as his as they continued to study each other. "He is all I have left of my family."

Did she not see that they were in an equinox world? The visual embodiment of life and death? Her brother, Matthieu, wasn't here. No one was here except them; he would bet money on it. This had Addien's fingerprint all over it.

Rhoslyn turned to peer out into the woods; a small wrinkle appeared between her brows. Beside her, a horse nickered. A different horse than Loring. His gaze lifted over her shoulder to a dove gray dappled Aurelienne stallion with a dark pewter-colored mane and tail. Faint white speckles coated the length of his body and down his rump. The stallion was also outfitted with a black saddle, similar to the one on Loring. She didn't ride side-saddle? Old gods help him, the imagery of her riding astride in that dress . . .

"Any assistance to search—"

"Leave me." He turned back to his horse, grinding his teeth, then brushed a hand down Loring's black mane. No rustle of fabric or the muffled clop of a moving horse. Fentienne glared at the sky to rein in his building anger. Guilt continued to lap against his conscience. But he gave his oath to protect her from those who threaten her life. He reminded himself that she didn't deserve his kindness. She didn't deserve his last remaining threads of sanity and control. She didn't deserve whatever illusions of happiness he dredged up to cope with the fractured monotony of his disgusting life. And that her blood was on his hands.

When she still made no move to leave, he curled his lip and gritted out over his shoulder, "You are dismissed," as if she were a mere servant. Or a soldier in his platoon.

"I am not yours to command," she shot back.

He bitterly chuckled and angled her direction. "Oh I think you *want* to be dominated, mademoiselle. Twice now you have disregarded my requests to leave me alone." Lowering his voice, he said, "Obeying me is not without its pleasures."

Rhoslyn's mouth fell open and a blush crept up her neck. "You are vile."

"*Oui*." His gaze held hers for a flicker of a heartbeat, a cruel, flirtatious tilt to his lips, then he wrapped Loring's reins around his hand.

"I feel pity for you that the depth of your creativity in insulting the opposite sex lies only in the shallows of depravity."

"Or perhaps it is you who lacks imagination. I never described what pleasures await in submission to my demands. Leaving my vile company is surely a pleasure you desire."

"*Non*, monsieur. Do not twist your own admission of guilt." She lifted her chin. "I will not give you the deluded pleasure of my compliance, nor will you degrade me further. I leave when I so choose. This meadow is not your property. You have no claim here."

"Hmm." He walked around Loring, his horse now between them, and began inspecting the blankets and saddle.

"That is your reply? *Hmm*?"

"Hmm."

Rhoslyn marched around his stallion and stopped within inches of Fentienne. The straw hat pinned to her hair reached just beneath his chin—her hands balled on her hips, her eyes a blazing wildfire—and his lips twitched. "Your dialect is aristocratic. You are clearly *haute noblesse*." He lifted a single, haughty brow. So? "I thought gentlemen didn't ignore a female's request for help. My brother may be in danger."

"Males are not little bells for females to ring whenever they want something. You lost your brother, mademoiselle. Go find him. He's not my problem."

"You would refuse to help a little boy?" Her lips parted and her gaze steeled. "You are a dog!"

A corner of his mouth inched up. "My darling, you have no idea."

"Your darling?" she scoffed. "Do not flatter yourself."

He lifted a shoulder in a slight shrug. "My nymph? My temptress? The one who pleasures me by obeying my commands? Which one do you prefer, if we are going to continue this pointless conversation?"

She bared her teeth and he almost snorted. "I am *not* a roadside pleasure."

"No, we are in a field."

Rhoslyn stilled, then took a step back. "A gentleman would never say such vulgar things to a female."

Oh yes, they would. Fentienne wanted to roll his eyes. Educated, "well-mannered" males spoke vulgar things to females all the time. Which, as a gutter rat of Factory Row, she already knew. Instead of arguing that point, or contemplating the slight shake in her voice, he leaned in slowly until his mouth rested near her ear and whispered, "*Je ne suis pas un gentilhomme.*"

Goosebumps shivered across her skin and his breath trembled. For an indulgent beat of his idiotic pulse, he closed his eyes and savored her nearness. He wasn't a gentleman, as he whispered in her ear. Polite society was a cage and he didn't need one more abuser. Fentienne straightened and the lines of his face hardened into bored contempt.

"Redundancy is not intelligent discourse." She took another step back and clenched her jaw. "Nor is pretending to enlighten me when I had already declared to you twice what you melodramatically confessed."

"You are delightful," he murmured, as if she were an annoying, praise-seeking child instead of grown and beautiful and his wife—bound to him by blood since children.

She was his. *His.* He owned her life and her death. The very idea was laughable. And sickening. She was fae. The point of her ears disgusted him and anger bristled just beneath the thin skin of his self-control.

In a lazy, dismissive gesture, he waved his hand and sneered, "My *darling*, as arousing as circular verbal foreplay is with clichéd, entitled females whose only weapon of argument is instructing men on how to behave, I find your moral lessons, after disregarding my requests to leave me alone, hypocritical. *Nothing* about you would ever please me anyway."

Everything about her was far too pleasing. Including her sharp wit and fire.

He was ready to rip his own heart out to end this misery and they hadn't even spent a full day and night with each other under the same roof yet.

"*Mon douce puce,*" she cooed sarcastically, "the feeling is mutual."

Her sweet flea, a strange endearment between lovers in Aurelienne, and he laughed under his breath. Clearly a jab at calling him a dog.

Ignoring the outrage in her eyes—the silent promises to cremate him alive—he mounted Loring, clicked his tongue, and gently nudged his stallion's flank into motion, unable to keep the shit-eating grin from his face. What he would have given to be at Palais d'Aurélie when she took on his aunt. Now for her to keep thinking of him with the same disdain.

"Go boy," he said to his stallion and promptly broke into a gallop toward the open meadow—and away from her.

Wind, sunshine, autumn leaves and spring petals . . . this dreamscape swirled around him as he cut through the air. Loring's hooves practically glided over the wildflowers and his body moved with the rocking gait. He missed this rush. Missed the unfettered power of a wild horse in his veins. Fentienne bent low on the saddle for less resistance and nudged Loring to go faster. Locks of Fentienne's dark brown hair whipped around his face and a summer wind bit at his skin.

They charged into the forest and a spray of petals exploded into the air behind him. Jewel-toned and pastel-clouded trees swallowed his vision. They swerved around mossy trunks and jumped over large, knotted roots. Fentienne smiled, a genuine contented smile. He hadn't felt this free, this happy in years. A lightness drizzled through him and he laughed.

A second clop of hooves sounded from behind and he twisted to peer over his shoulder and groaned. Shit, shit, *shit*. Rhoslyn galloped after him, the straw hat no longer on her head. Strands of golden-brown hair had fallen from their pins and fluttered wildly in the air. The muslin gown billowed around her legs, her voluminous skirts hiked up to ride astride.

Why did she chase him?

She was insane.

Cutting through a small clearing, Fentienne guided Loring out of the woods and startled when the landscape suddenly changed around him. Loring reared back and Fentienne tugged on the reins. "Whoa, boy. Steady." The duel-seasoned trees and warm summer breeze was replaced by a black-sand coastline and a rolling dark sea. The brilliant blue sky was now a cloud-dotted sunset dusk painted in vivid corals, golds, and lavenders. Clicking his tongue, Fentienne nudged Loring into a gallop once more, who gladly raced along the surf line, kicking up sprays of salt water.

Rhoslyn quickly caught up to him, barely sparing him a glance before gently snapping her reins. The dappled gray charged forward and Rhoslyn shot Fentienne a wicked grin over her shoulder.

What the hell?

Why was she here? *With him?* After how he treated her? Gods, how many times did he need to tell her to leave him alone?

Unless...

She figured it out. Her brother wasn't here. She wasn't dressed like her class in The Row. And they were the only ones who existed in this dream they shared.

Water splashed around her in coral- and lavender-lit sparkles. More hair tumbled behind her in the ocean breeze. He soaked up the image before nudging Loring to run even faster—and he did. Easily speeding past Rhoslyn and her gray stallion. While passing her by, he bit his bottom lip in a flirtatious taunt, too caught up in racing his horse to remember that he despised her and her kind. That she needed to hate him. She rolled her eyes before settling into a glare. He laughed, then pushed ahead.

The coastline was endless and they ran their horses through the shallow waves for what seemed like an eternity. He wasn't sure if horses wherever here was needed to rest, but he couldn't in good conscience keep pushing Loring as hard as he was. Gently pulling on the reins, he slowed to a stop and rubbed the sweaty coat of his stallion's neck while murmuring soothing words. Rhoslyn galloped past him but turned around and slowed her horse beside his. Chests heaving for breath, they stared out into the undulating ocean and to the sun that had yet to set, a smile on their lips.

"I thought nothing about me would ever please you."

Fentienne turned her way. "Whatever gave you the idea that my happiness is because of you?"

Her brow lifted. "Good. I wouldn't want to give you false hope, monsieur."

"False hope is the least of my worries, mademoiselle." His gaze swung back to the ocean.

"Though you are cruel and vulgar, I am more terrified of being alone in this surreal world than of you."

"Ah, you now see our predicament."

"My first instinct was to protect my brother," she said softly, "and I panicked. But he is not here and I . . . I could only see that he was missing and nothing else. He is my heart and the only good thing I have left in my life."

Fentienne simply nodded but continued to gaze out over the horizon. "We see only what we want to see, especially when angry and afraid." He casually peered her way from the periphery of his vision and studied how the sunset reflected in her eyes. "Night is no more evil than day. And yet, it is where we place all our nightmares. Appearances can be deceiving."

"*Oui.*" She visibly swallowed and drew in a shaky breath. "Why were you so heartless to me in my distress? Knowing that I was not fully aware of our situation?"

"Because I am a monster and do not behave differently."

"Perhaps." A faint wrinkle formed between her brows. "Perhaps not."

Their eyes locked and, up close, he wasn't entirely sure what to do with himself. Loring lightly danced on his feet and Fentienne tugged on the reins, his gaze never breaking from hers. Small waves crashed against their horses' legs and foamed over the black sand. A brine-laced breeze sweeping off the ocean cooled the rising flush of his skin. And her hair . . . no pins remained. Long, silky strands floated in the wind and he swallowed against the pounding pulse in throat.

"You do not apologize?" she softly asked, searching his eyes.

"Why should I when no one has ever apologized to me?"

Her eyes narrowed, as if studying him for the first time and unsure of what she was seeing. "Because," she said thoughtfully, "unlike them, you are not truly a monster."

"Oh but I am, my darling." His stare became predatory. "More so for I am self-aware enough to choose differently and don't."

Rhoslyn straightened in her saddle and pulled her gray stallion closer to Loring with a soft laugh, leveling a defiant look in reply. What the hell was wrong with her? She didn't know when to quit. Nor when to take him seriously.

"I am sincerely sorry, monsieur, for not giving you space when asked." Their legs touched and his heart stopped beating. "You were right to call me a hypocrite. *Oui*, if the roles were reversed, I would feel threatened and push back too."

Their eyes locked again and a collision of emotions tore through his chest.

Did she think that apologizing to him would bandage the wounds? Make him less of a beast? Girls were ridiculous in their romantic fantasies. Her act of kindness changed nothing. He didn't care that she was sorry for not leaving him alone when asked. That was not the apology he had wanted to hear all his life. But . . . he also couldn't ignore how her words warmed his body. Or how the muscles of his stomach tightened as her curious gaze openly roamed the curve of his jaw, the length of his neck, the way dark waves of his hair breezed across his eyes. The swelling intensity made him want to lean over his saddle and capture her lips with his. As if she were not a creature, an elf. As if her existence hadn't ruined his. As if his gut didn't also curdle at the thought.

Another wrinkle formed between her brows. "You look at me as though you are lost, monsieur."

"*Oui*." His gaze traveled over her face. "I will die when awake and resurrect while asleep. And, Rhoslyn Gautier, I do not know which one scares me more."

She never had a chance to reply. Black claimed him once more. And then his eyes flew open.

Chapter II

Rhoslyn

Rhoslyn startled awake, gasping for breath, her heart thundering in her chest. At first, she didn't move, unsure of what she was seeing. No longer did a coral sunset paint the sky of her mind. The haunting roar of the ocean didn't fill her ears either. Rather, black entombed her. Black walls, ceiling, drapes. Black tapers in the candelabras.

The chateau, then. Not a dream.

An unexpected emptiness filled her chest with that realization.

Blinking, she rolled from her back to her side, toward the hearth. The fire still roared strong. Had the démon kept the fire for them? Rhoslyn pulled the velvet drape up to her chin as a blush crept up her neck. If so, he would have undoubtedly seen her undressed. She sat up, careful to not disturb Matthieu. Light peered in from the window with the missing drape.

Candles near the settee gave her pause and she squinted her eyes. She didn't know how long she had slept, didn't know if it were even the same day, but the tallow should have melted at least a little. Did their guardian replace all the tapers in this room as well as tended the fire? And why was the House of Golden Light decorated and furnished in darkness? She had heard tales that the molding and other decorative pieces were made from pure gold, similar to Palais d'Aurélie. Her eyes wandered to her garments—still black.

The house was under an enchantment. There was no other logical explanation. Perhaps the stories were true and ghosts haunted these walls until avenged. Shivers trailed down her skin.

Inching from the settee, Rhoslyn stood and covered her chest with her arms. Her petticoat and overskirt were both dry, her bodice too. Quickly, she dressed. The tear in her skirt was much larger than she remembered, the tears in her stockings too. The muslin she wore in the dream, a finely stitched gown with panniers and petticoats, edged in delicate lace . . . it was the most beautiful dress to have ever touched her skin. Skin that was washed and smelled faintly of the forest. Her hair had been clean and fashioned prettily too. What she would give for a bath with soap and laundered clothing.

Worrying her bottom lip, she considered her brother. Matthieu's blond hair haloed around him as he slept. The pallor of his complexion was still sickly. Gently, she tucked the blanket around him and brushed the hair from his eyes. They should find Dalbréath, but she would let her brother rest a little longer. Dalbréath hopefully figured out they had taken cover in the rainstorm and, if she were correct, had camped outside of the chateau to await them.

Rhoslyn started to turn toward the fireplace when an apple caught her eye on the table behind the sofa. Two apples. Her gaze flitted around the room for movement. When she didn't suspect anything in the room, she strode over to the plate and licked her dry lips. There was a pitcher of water and two cups. She could weep. She didn't realize how thirsty she was until this moment. Or how scratchy her throat was from screaming her grief into the night. Pouring herself a glass, she downed the contents within seconds, then poured herself another. The liquid hit her empty stomach with a twinge of nausea. She should have drunk slower. But she was too thirsty and hungry to care. Beside the apples rested two chunks of aged cheese and tears sprang to her eyes.

Cheese.

She hadn't had cheese since her home burned down. And even then, only when they had the spare income. Pottage, vegetable stew, and baked bread were their home's staples. Simple fare, but still a richer meal than most.

Where did this food and water come from?

Another part of the house's enchantment or the dark démon? But she knew the answer and covered her chest with her arms once more and swallowed. If he had indeed seen her undressed, she might die of mortification. But she was also immeasurably grateful for the food.

Rhoslyn palmed the cheese and apple and collapsed into one of the wingback chairs and stared into the fire, mesmerized by the dancing flames. The hollowness in her gut sickened at the thought of eating and also at the thought of not eating. Taking a small bite of the cheese, she moaned and closed her eyes for a spellbinding moment. Saints, that was divine. She enjoyed another bite and pulled her legs up onto the chair. Not a ladylike position, but she was sitting in a comfortable chair, before a crackling fire, a solid roof over her head, eating cheese. The indulgence was too rich to share with decorum.

Were her friends safe? Did they have food this day? Guilt swirled with the nausea as she swallowed the last bite of cheese. Logic told her to regain strength so she and Matthieu could return to Factory Row and rejoin the fight. Logic also told her that perhaps Dalbréath was right and it was best for her to lay low for a while, not only for her safety, but the safety of her brother too.

Losing herself to the hypnotic flames once more, she bit into the apple and sighed.

She needed a better strategy than marching up to the gates and demanding change. Those in power wouldn't give up their entitlement without a stronger fight. How did one unseat a queen? Or radicalize the class system?

A pair of honeyed amber eyes flitted unbidden to her mind. Not the eyes of their guardian, but of another. He was unusually tall and well-built, as if he came more from the north, like Dreglind, though his eyes suggested he was Chalamet. The Row held the lowlies of several realms. Men of his frame, often from Dreglind, were put to work in the iron factories, extracting iron from ore and forging, en masse, parts for steam engines, carriages, pipes, and other items blacksmiths could not produce in high quantities.

Saints, he was the most beautiful man she had ever seen.

An arrogant, unfeeling man. A darkness surrounded him that she found equally as alluring as repulsive. Her magic, however, was drawn to his heart. A good heart despite his behavior and a broken heart that felt keenly familiar. The latter being impossible. They had not met until last night. But *mon Dieu*. He made the fluttering beat of *her heart* sigh with each glance.

His smile, while racing their horses, stole her breath—sensual yet unabashed. Boyish, even. Almost as if he had forgotten to keep up that ruthless, cold-hearted mask he wore so effortlessly. And his hair . . . not typical fashion for the men of Aurelienne, especially the aristocratic men, who preferred shoulder length or longer hair to tie at the nape of their neck. Though, men from Dreglind had long hair too. But he wasn't Dreglindish. Of that she was certain, despite his size. Butterfly wings fluttered through her blushing pulse at a memory. Him on his wild stallion, the sunset and sea in the background, the wavy, chin-length silky strands of his dark earthen hair dancing in the breeze. She took another bite of the apple and, as she chewed, a wrinkle formed between her brows.

Who was he?

He knew her name. Her *full* name.

That dream was no mere dream. It was an Otherworldly reality where only they existed. Was this yet another part of the house's enchantments? Did that mean he lived here too?

The way he moved was graceful yet precise, like every step and tilt of his head were calculated. It reminded her of soldiers who marched down Saints District in a parade—each step synchronized, bodies stiff, muskets held in a uniform fashion. Had he fought in the Spired Hills? But, strangely, his body was simultaneously relaxed, carrying a dismissive posture of indifference she had only seen exhibited in men of power. The strange culmination of a rigid bearing and aloof nonchalance beguiled her. His accent carried the bored, murmuring lilt of the aristocracy, as if the very act of speaking were beneath him. He verbally sparred as a well-educated man too. Nobility didn't send their sons to war. To die on a battlefield was peasant work. A flush warmed her cheeks when remembering his casually undressed state. In simple homespun linen, no waistcoat, nor shoes, he didn't dress like the upper class either. But the haughty arch of his brow, the arrogant tilt of his lips, the contemptuous intensity of his eyes? He was mercilessly handsome, darkly elegant, and beautifully cruel all at once.

Until he smiled at her while racing his horse through the shallows. Then, he was . . . *devastating.*

"Rosie." She turned at the sound of her brother's weak voice—a slight wheeze in just one single word. The velvet drape fell from his shoulders, and she bit back the anger at how his ribcage poked out and at the boniness of his arms. "Have you seen him?"

"Monsieur Dalbréath?" She shook her head. "Once you dress and eat, we will leave and search for him."

"*Non,* the dark démon."

"Oh." Rhoslyn's studied the apple core in her hand. "Our guardian left apples, cheese, and water on the table behind the settee while we slept."

Matthieu's mouth fell open. "Haunted cheese?"

"*Oui,*" she said on a laugh. "Ghostly apples too. The water is especially ghoulish."

The dimpled grin brightening his pale face tightened her chest. It was full but sluggish and deepened the purple circles beneath his sky-blue eyes.

Rhoslyn eased from the chair and brought a cup of water and plate of food to her brother. "Eat and drink slowly. You might sicken after going so long without a meal."

He nibbled on the cheese like a little mouse, his glassy eyes closing after a few bites. At first, she thought it was in pleasure. The haunted cheese was truly divine. But he swayed and she caught the plate before it toppled from his hand. Placing the food onto the chair, she knelt before him.

"My sweet, beautiful boy," she whispered into his hair, then kissed his forehead. Rhoslyn reared back. His skin was too clammy. The slight bluish tinge of his lips clenched the muscles of her stomach, the shallow breaths stilling her own. Lifting the cup of water to his lips, she said, "Drink, *mon petit caneton*." He took a couple small sips, then leaned his head onto her chest and coughed—a tight, wheezy sound. She ran her fingers through the soft curls of his hair, grimacing back the tears.

She didn't want to let go. Holding him in her arms kept the fraying seams of her heart from falling apart. But she needed to find herbs to boil for her brother to breathe in. "I love you to the top of the sky and back, Matthieu Gautier," she murmured against his clammy skin while rocking back and forth with his body pressed to hers. "Keep fighting, my strong warrior duckling." Gently, she lowered him to the settee and tucked the velvet drape over his shoulders.

In the pocket of Matthieu's breeches, she pulled out the beggar man's talisman and curled her brother's fingers around the carved wolf. Then she grabbed a single candle holder and strode toward the hallway. The kitchens had to be downstairs. She moved through the door, not looking over her shoulder, afraid she would run back to her brother if she did.

The black was dizzying. Were all wolf shifter dens this sinister and creepy? Shadows moved across the walls and she swore some of them looked human. Kissing the back of her thumb, she whispered, "Saint Annea Clivana, protect Matthieu from malevolent spirits. Saint Belenus, please take pity on a sweet little boy and heal his lungs." Shadows continued to move around her. The sudden cold touch on her skin was startling, but she pushed through the sensation. Her brother depended on her to make medicated vapors.

At the far end of main floor, she found a flight of stairs to the lower floors. Candles on the wall flickered. She probably didn't need the candle in her hand; the entire chateau was apparently lit. Was this also part of the enchantment?

Down she hastened over the cobblestone steps. The stairs paused on a landing that split into another descending set of stairs and a door frame leading into a hallway. She ventured through the door and dashed toward the first arched opening. Tables, workstations, and cast irons ovens spread over the room. A fire burned bright in a giant hearth with a large cast iron pole in the rock from one end to the other to hang pots. Several dust-coated windows lined one wall and let in dusky light.

Rhoslyn set her candle on a table and moved through the maze of workstations, baskets, pots and pans. But no buckets. She needed a bucket to fetch water from the well, which she figured was just outside of the kitchen. Glass bottles littered one table. She lifted one and sniffed the uncorked opening and grimaced. Soured wine. Slowly, she lowered the bottle while taking in the room once more and gasped. On the stone wall directly across from her was a smeared handprint. She crept closer, nearly shrieking when finding a trail of drops of what looked like blood over the floor beside the shredded remains of a black shirt.

The blood had dried but didn't appear old. The linen shirt either.

Nausea bubbled in her gut and her head grew light. She had never fared well at the sight of blood.

Either their dark démon had brought in a kill to finish eating or he was injured. Rhoslyn settled on the latter, mostly to calm the fear prickling every nerve ending in her body.

Pressing a hand to her stomach, she moved past the blood to a small room with a cellar door—a larder. Aging meat hung from rafter hooks. Wheels of cheese, baskets of eggs, crocks of lard and jam, plus a variety of fresh vegetables and fruit lined the shelves. Bags of flour, sugar, and salt too. Dried garlic hung on the walls, as well as dried parsley, sage, and rosemary. But no other herbs as far as she could see. Not the ones she needed, at least.

Who was this man that he could afford such rich food for only himself? With eyes of gold, he must be from the House of Chalamet—same as the man in her dreams. She could not reason how he could live inside these cursed walls otherwise. Saints, the Chalamet family were like rats—they climbed from the sewers of Palais d'Aurélie in unfathomable numbers. What was it like to have so many relations? The political infighting must be intense.

Ready to move on in her search for a bucket, she nearly passed one by. Inside the larder, in the corner, were two buckets already filled with water. She found a wooden spoon and dipped it into one and tentatively sipped, relieved when the water was fresh and even somewhat sweet. Grabbing a small cast iron pot, she ladled in water, then used a hooked pole to hang the pot above the fire.

A few yards away, a wooden door hung on broken hinges. She looped a basket through her arm, then pulled on the iron ring and studied the splintered wood where a boot must have kicked in the door. Or a bare foot, if indeed it was their guardian following his fight with the gray wolf démon.

Spooked, her gaze swept across the overgrown kitchen garden. In the far corner was a well, as she suspected. On a second inspection, her shoulders relaxed. Unmanicured herbs covered the grounds. She tip-toed down the path and hunted for mint, afraid any noise might alert a monster over the stone wall. Several large bushes grew behind a moss-covered stone bench. She plucked a few sprigs and placed them in her basket. Not too far away was mullein, another herb known for its breathing properties. Stepping carefully through the various greens, she sighed in relief when finding horehound and placed a clump in the basket, then hurried back into the kitchen.

Rhoslyn tore and bruised the aromatic, medicinal leaves before placing a large quantity into a brass kettle hanging above a cast iron stove. Slowly, she ladled boiling water into the kettle and closed the lid. The metal was growing too hot for her hands, though. Not finding an apron or towel at a quick glance, she gathered up her ripped overskirt and bunched it over the handle, then began her ascent to the main entry.

Her body still felt weak and she wanted to pass out after climbing the many stairs. But she would crawl on hands and knees if necessary to reach her brother. Careful not to spill a scalding drop of the therapeutic tea, she hurried down the hallway and nearly into a dark, moving shadow. Rhoslyn clapped a hand over mouth with a small, terrified cry. A tremble began wending its way down her spine.

Claws grabbed her leg as her fingers dug into the bark.

She backed up and forced herself to meet his eyes.

The démon yanked and she screamed, falling through the air to her death.

The man's golden gaze held hers with a cruel intensity that stilled the air in her lungs. But she could see little of him between the flickering shadows and his clothing. A black oil cloth duster covered his broad back, large arms, and reached his knees with a highwayman collar popped up to cover his mouth and nose. Saints, he was tall. Black military breeches tightened around his legs and disappeared into large boots. Wavy, dark earthen hair fell unbound around his face, covered by a black tricorn hat that sat low on his brow. Was this her mate? *Saints.*

"Milord." Rhoslyn lowered into a curtsy on shaking legs. "*Merci*, for protecting me and my brother yesterday."

"I didn't do it for you."

The gravelly sound of his voice quaked in her bones. "And for the food and water. You are most generous, milord."

"Nothing I have done is for *you.*" He studied her exposed petticoat and the kettle in her hand.

"My brother is asthmatic." She blinked nervously, confused by his words. "Forgive my rudeness, but I must see to his care." He stepped into her path and she squared her shoulders and lifted her chin despite the heart trying to beat from her chest. "Matthieu is struggling to breathe, milord. Please let me pass by."

"You will only have access to the kitchens with my permission. Steal my food again—"

"No different than my life in Factory Row," she spat, too exhausted to bite back her anger, even if she riled a monster. Truly, the audacity! "You aristocrats control all the food, always. Go ahead, throw me in chains for stealing herbs and water for my brother."

"Females in my company are to be silent," he snarled. "You will *only* speak when I ask for your comment. I do not care for the witless chatter of lower-class uneducated females."

A bitter laugh spilled from Rhoslyn's mouth. "*Non*, milord. No male will quiet me. Not you, not anyone. Once my brother is well, we shall depart. Unless you wish to punish a sick boy for my opinionated tongue and toss us out into the cold and rain?" They held each other's heated gaze. Divine Mother, this man better not be her husband. The very thought sent fresh waves of rage crashing into her already galloping pulse. And yet, her magic felt a strong, kind heart. A good heart. No, it was her exhaustion speaking. She moved to angle past him and he gently pushed her into the wall. "My brother, milord," she ground out. "He is innocent in this exchange."

His body leaned into hers, his face lowering until they were eye to eye, and she clenched her jaw and continued to stare back as furiously as he regarded her. "The very sight of you disgusts me, Rhoslyn Gautier," he growled, but his voice was also strangely breathless. An emotion that didn't quite line up with his words. The soft, pained look in his eyes was startling too. But she had to be imagining everything in her exhaustion. Within a wink, the hardness returned in his gaze. And the next words he bit out reignited her anger. "Do not steal my food, roam my house, and do not speak to me. Abide those three rules and I will let you live."

"Do not demean me, *beast*, and perhaps I might let you live too."

He chuckled, a dark sound that shivered across her skin. "Adorable." Then he shoved off the wall and strode down the hallway and disappeared around the corner.

Adorable?

Adorable?!

If Matthieu didn't need these medicated vapors so badly, she would have thrown the searing hot water onto that beast of a man and laughed at his screams, which she was sure were absolutely *adorable*.

What did he mean that his protection as well as the food and water weren't for her? Loosing an angry breath, she marched into the sitting room and paused before her brother. His breaths came quick and shallow. The fire pumping in her veins quickly iced and familiar fear gripped her once more. She couldn't imagine a world without her baby brother.

She reached out to gently shake his shoulder and stopped. A soft down blanket covered his body instead of velvet drapery. She looked behind her and noticed the drapery back up over the window. He could have harmed her brother, could have intentionally terrorized him too. But he brought him a blanket and . . . a new pillow rested beneath Matthieu's head. On the wingback chair next to the fire was a folded woolen blanket and another pillow—for her.

Was his brutishness all for show?

Gnawing the inside of her lip, she focused on her brother once more. "Matthieu, wake up." She rubbed his back in a jostling motion. "I need you to breathe in medicated vapors."

His eyes fluttered open. "I saw him." The words were weak, wheezy.

She sat on the settee and gently pulled Matthieu onto her lap, his side pressed to her front, pulled the blanket over their heads, then removed the lid from the kettle and lifted it close to his nose and mouth, using the down blanket to also protect him from the heated brass. "Breathe, *caneton*. The herbs will help your lungs."

Matthieu leaned forward over the vapor and held his carved wolf close to his heart. "I saw him, Rosie. He was kind to me."

"Just breathe while the water steams," she soothed into his hair. "We will talk later."

Her brother relaxed and began to finally breathe in the herbs. But Rhoslyn's mind began spinning. Was the dark démon's protection and food all for Matthieu? Why him? She had never heard of a démon protecting a child before. Perhaps this man once had a fair-haired, blue-eyed little brother that he missed, one that looked similar to Matthieu.

There were many lessons she had learned from living on Factory Row. But the one easiest to forget was how everyone had a family once. For many a family they loved and missed—the most hardened drunk, conniving thief, and painted nymph. Parents, brothers and sisters, even mates. And most would do anything to provide for the young children left in their care, including suffer darkness to keep their loved ones safe. Had their guardian given his soul to the Dark Saint to protect a brother? Rhoslyn knew she would do so to protect Matthieu, in a heartbeat.

Though, her brother could melt a beastly heart with just one dimpled smile too.

Perhaps this was the goodness her magic sensed.

Well, as long as the démon was kind to her brother and continued to be his guardian, she couldn't care less how he treated her. Thank the Nine Saints he wasn't her mate. Regardless, she refused to be silent—the absolute arrogance!—and would steal food in this cursed chateau until her brother's ribs no longer poked out from malnourishment and his lungs no longer wheezed from weakness. At least, until they reconnected with Dalbréath and left. That aristocratic man wouldn't kill her despite his snarls, or he would have done so already.

Adorable.

Oof, he would pay for that belittling remark.

Matthieu coughed, but the sound was looser and, from the faint light bleeding through the crack in the blanket over their heads, she could see color returning to his lips and face. Rhoslyn buried her face into his soft curls and bit back happy tears.

"He wouldn't tell me his name," Matthieu said quietly. "But he knew mine."

Rhoslyn stilled, remembering her exchange with that soulless man.

He knew her name too. Her *full* name.

"You were not scared?" she asked Matthieu.

"Why do you always worry so much, *ma sœur?*"

Rhoslyn softly laughed and kissed her brother's head. How she loved this little boy.

Chapter 12

Fentienne

The smell of sewage and factory waste assaulted Fentienne's nose and he swallowed back the rising bile. Holding his breath, he stepped over rotting garbage and dead rodents. A drunkard passed out in his own piss slouched against one of the two-to-three story cob and stone factories and apartments framing the cobblestone paved street. In every direction, vendors cried out their wares in verse. He grimaced at the discordant sounds. Sensitive smell, sensitive hearing... why he didn't visit the slums of Gabaston often. How other shifters bore this pain, daily, was beyond him.

But shame kept him from the slums too. Everywhere he looked held evidence of the attack from a year and a half ago. Pieces of buildings still missing. Large divots in the cobble street. Charred fire marks running up the side of bricks and stones and cob. The bedraggled, skeletal shells of homeless people. The children with bloated bellies from hunger. The memory of Clifstán's invasion—the pleasure in destroying the homes and businesses of his enemies, the same pleasure he had when demolishing the dwarven towns and mining camps—swirled with a guilt so intense he hated himself more than he hated his family and the entirety of the Kingdom of Ealdspell.

He breathed in through his mouth to diminish the sharp stench and slowly exhaled through his nose.

Factory Row bustled with activity for mid-afternoon, but the air was tight. A current moving around him carried the hushed whispers of fear. Carts and stalls strung the entire length of the street, on both sides, with guards posted every few yards. The slums were on a form of lockdown? Not surprising. His gaze roamed around the scene before him, tucking away details. Middle-class males inspected knives, ordered tools, and paid for small casks of ale—their heads down, their voices lower than usual. Females haggled for eggs, milk, and vegetables while their snotty-nosed kids chased chickens or threw rocks at passersby. Children who were far too skinny. Younger mothers grabbed their children by the arms when he passed by and darted looks toward the guards. Did they worry another riot with an aristocrat in their presence?

He angled past grisettes washing bolts of cotton in an alley. The young girls watched him with fear in their downcast eyes. They couldn't see his face and his hands were in gloves. But men of means came to The Row for two reasons and two reasons only—custom orders from the factories or vendors, and to pay for pleasures their innocent, aristocratic wives failed to perform satisfactorily, or at all. The same was true in Clifstán. Many soldiers preferred call girls over their wives or sweethearts.

Two men in coarse brown robes, their beards and nails grotesquely long, flicked holy water from buckets onto those who passed by the execution block. "Bathe in the truth of Saint Glanis," the taller one cried out. "Drown the Dark Saint's whispered lies from your souls and gain the Sight to see wolves among sheep."

Fresh blood painted the ground near the guillotine. Had they executed another wolf this morning? A headless body rotted above the execution block in a gibbet cage and fury pulsed down Fentienne's limbs.

The monks flicked more water onto those ambling past. "A cleansing is coming! A cleansing is upon us!"

A small crowd of people stopped, their hands lifted in supplication. For a copper, the self-proclaimed monks dribbled a ladle of holy water over their heads. Every Friday, for five coins, they performed ritual bathings in the Springs of Glanis for the faithful to worship the God of Healing Springs. The hot springs beneath the chateau were in dedication to Saint Glanis as well. Clearly the holy water didn't drown the Dark Saint from the souls of men. First, the Dark Saint would need to be real—any of the saints—rather than a religious hoax to control the people of Aurelienne into political submission.

But these men were allowed far too much power. The temple loathed their existence, claiming them a cult. For all the power the temple had in Gabaston, controlling the Monks of Glanis was not one they possessed. The guards seemed to protect them too.

The shorter monk target locked onto Fentienne and narrowed his eyes.

A chill ran down his spine. Was the Beast of Gabaston perhaps a zealot? Or hired by the monks to create panic? And who was turning in wolves? Before the religious charlatan could draw attention to Fentienne, he picked up his pace and focused on sounds other than the prophetic cries of these disturbed men.

From the street, he could hear a woman screaming at her grisettes from inside Gabaston's premiere dress factory. The way she tore into the girls, the deafening tone of her voice reminded him of drill sergeants at Myrefell. Fentienne stole a glance inside the shop as he strode by and gritted his teeth. Listening to a man shout all day was one thing. The shrill screeching of this woman's voice grated on the fraying edges of his sanity. Gods, he would snap. He was already on the verge of snapping.

Resisting the urge to cover his ears, he increased his steps and forced his fists to uncurl.

"Tithes for the saints' protection!" a young man shouted into the bustling crowd, ringing a bell. "Cleanse your heart and the Beast will not harm you!"

Fentienne slowed his steps and eyed an acolit who clutched a basket of scrolls in one hand and a brass bell in another. First the greedy, delusional Monks of Glanis, and now another holy man snaking money from the desperate poor. A fresh wave of anger rippled through him, but he reined in his emotions and approached the young man.

"You sell confessions?" Fentienne asked him, contempt edging his voice.

"*Oui*, milord." The acolit bowed. "The Beast does not attack the pure of heart."

Mon Père Michel had a wicked sense of ironic humor and Fentienne resisted the urge to scoff. "Tell me, how exactly does the Beast know who has paid for absolved sins?"

"The knotted sign of Saint Annea Clivana, protector goddess, will appear on the foreheads of those pure of heart, and the moon sign of Saint Arianrhod, the virgin goddess, if confessor is a maid. The mark is invisible to all save the Beast. The cleansed receive a sealed absolution from the temple too." The acolit touched a scroll and dipped his head in groomed humility. "Do you seek to protect your soul from the Dark Saint and the Beast, milord?"

"Hilarious."

"You do not mean it, milord."

"Would you recognize an agent of the Dark Saint, even if they prayed before you and lit a candle at your altar?"

The acolit's mouth fell open and the blood visibly drained from his head. "A démon's flesh would burn within the walls of the temple."

Fentienne snorted.

Tipping his hat lower on his brow, to further hide his eyes, he turned back toward the main market. Another aristocrat passed him on the street that moment, his face hidden beneath a large cloak. The man's garment was too fine a quality for him to be anything but *haute noblesse*. They studied each other for the merest second, the man's gaze narrowing when noting the golden color of Fentienne's eyes, but neither acknowledged the other. Many aristocrats wore masks and cloaks to hide their identities in the slums. Especially those who visited the tolerant houses during daylight. But there was no hiding that Fentienne was a Chalamet noble.

A body bumped into his side, then two little boys, brothers from their similarities, squeezed past him toward the small crowd up ahead. He watched them weave through the distracted people, slyly picking pockets as they did. All his belongings were beneath his duster and tied to his belt; he knew the run-in wasn't accidental. The older boy, hidden from the guards, lifted a meat pie from a cart while the baker busied with a middle-class merchant woman, then a sealed absolution from the acolit who didn't hear the rustle over the clanging ring of his bell. Fentienne couldn't resist the ghost of a smile tugging on his lips. But the smile quickly returned to a frown.

How did Matthieu survive on these streets? The little boy in his parlor could barely open his eyes when he brought clean blankets and pillows earlier this day. Guilt pricked at his conscience. The young blond-haired, blue-eyed elf reminded him of Florian in a few ways—the fair colorings, gentle spirit, and the uncanny way he noticed the smallest details around him. While speaking to him, Fentienne could see the boy's ability to read between words and actions. The latter traits made his brother exceptionally skilled at tracking and spying.

Fentienne drew in a shaky breath and pushed away the shame.

Rhoslyn's brother was never meant to be a part of his curse. But there was nothing he could do about that now.

He watched the brothers until they disappeared in the crowd, then turned away.

Where did Matthieu go when Rhoslyn worked? Fentienne assumed Rhoslyn had a factory job. In truth, he didn't know anything of her life before Chateau Lumière Dorée other than she picked flowers to sell—a seasonal job—and her family once owned a press and chapbook shop near Saints District.

Rhoslyn Gautier.

Just her name in his thoughts made him want to punch a wall. She was the most infuriating female he had ever met. The elf didn't know when to back down from a fight or take danger seriously, not in that strange dreamscape or in reality. He wouldn't hurt her. But she didn't know that. Skies, the fire in her dark green eyes, the stubborn lift of her chin, how her hand fluttered in the air when pissed, the threatening grit of her voice when pushing back . . . the Princess of Avenbury stole his breath and branded every beat of his heart with her defiance. His wolf went panting mad when in her presence.

Her fury was . . . *breathtaking.*

But it wasn't real.

Every disgusting, out-of-character feeling he experienced was manufactured—a faerie trick.

Just the blood of children on a contract.

And he needed her to hate him. Even though her eventual death would destroy his wolf and, thus, him. But nobody cared about how he would suffer. Not a godsdamn person. Only that she survived Addien's curse. Per usual, he was a means to the end.

A freshly powdered up pavement nymph dressed in a dirty corset and petticoat grabbed his arm and leaned into him with a coy smile, attempting to pull him into an alley.

"Not interested."

"You are a large man, monsieur."

Fentienne loosened her grip and kept walking without bothering to look back. Her comment made him grunt a laugh under his breath. All descendants from Dreglind were large, part of their northern hereditary and his imperial line. A different nymph trailed her fingers down his arm, but he didn't acknowledge her and continued to angle through vendors and street girls. Apparently, the guards were not interested in arresting illegal prostitutes.

Paying for pleasures was a trade as old as time, but pavement nymphs were either far too young or forced into prostitution. Females had to choose this profession for him to enjoy their services, legally licensed too, which meant they had come of age. Since living in Aurelienne, he had enjoyed the company of Claudette a dozen times or so, a lesser démon and the Madame at Le Rêve Rouge, a popular tolerant house on The Row. The brothel with the hidden entrance to the catacombs. Fentienne could moan just thinking about Claudette's soft curves and how he had plenty of tension to work out. But, right now, he was visiting her for other needs before attending the Brotherhood.

"A pretty orange, milord." A man thrust a fruit into Fentienne's face. "Sweetens the breath and a man's blood."

Fentienne practically rolled his eyes and turned to Lucas Fontine. The young alpha wiggled the orange with a suggestive smile. Oranges were a treasured aphrodisiac in this saints cursed realm. Utterly ridiculous. Still, he knew the drill and asked, "How much, *sans-culotte*?"

"Three coppers." Lucas leaned in. "Five coppers and I'll give you a fruit from under the table. Extra juicy ones that are guaranteed to increase a man's performance in bed."

A corner of Fentienne's mouth lifted. "Stamina is not something I lack."

"Twice now you passed by me while lost to your female troubles." Humor glinted in Lucas's blue eyes. "I would be insulted, *mon ami*. But clearly you need something to help your performance and I can satisfy your present needs."

Fentienne stepped closer and, in a lover's whisper, said, "You wish, lesser démon."

"We all have our price, milord." Lucas rested his hip onto his cart with a smug grin.

The double meaning wasn't lost on him. He glanced around The Row, plucked the orange from Lucas's hand, and pretended to inspect the fruit. "Is there a bounty?"

"*Oui*, a large one." Lucas drew in closer. "Ten gold pieces."

"Shit." A muscle ticked along his jaw. "Did you relay my message to the pack alphas?"

"Not all agree, the clan leaders need more convincing of your reasons. But the packs will leave mademoiselle alone for now. Ten gold pieces, though—"

"I will pay for the carcasses of wolves who refuse my orders."

Lucas stepped back; his brows cinched low. "You want to turn wolf on wolf?"

"I don't want wolves on my property to hunt what is mine." Fentienne lowered his voice and gritted out, "And *she is mine*."

The young man narrowed his eyes and studied Fentienne a moment. "You are serious."

"A large female attacked me before the gates of Chateau Lumière Dorée to kill for my aunt, even if she had to kill me first."

Lucas's eyes hardened and he growled, "Who?"

"Gray wolf. Refused to submit to her prince and alpha. Never learned her name or pack before shredding her intestines. Not a rabid, though."

A vendor eyed both him and Lucas, and Fentienne turned a cold, predatory gaze onto the eavesdropping old man peddling cabbages.

"*Non*, this fruit will not shred your intestines, milord," Lucas said loudly, his lips twitching in a barely contained smile.

Fentienne tossed the orange up into the air and caught it to keep himself from punching the alpha's arrogant grin. "How exactly are your oranges juicy, *sans-culotte*? I would not think you a man capable of exciting anything, let alone fruit."

Lucas laughed under his breath, then replied, "Exciting enough to sweeten your lady's valuable blood. You forget, we both live on Factory Row. She did not suddenly materialize for you."

The muscles in Fentienne's back and arms flexed. Lucas smirked, knowing he had irritated his wolf's territorial response and there was nothing Fentienne could do about it in such a public place. The man was lying, though; he could scent it. Rhoslyn didn't come across as a girl who would submit to a male's designs on her, honorable or not. Still, his wolf didn't care.

"Arsehole," he snarled and Lucas's grin grew wolfish.

The cabbage vendor turned to help a customer. Not wasting a second, Lucas leaned in close and whispered, "Five more dead. That count will go up daily the more idiots enter the woods in search of *what is yours*."

"Still no deaths behind the gold gates?"

Lucas shook his head.

"A monster hunt still in discussion?"

"*Oui.*"

"Did the monks execute démons this morning?"

Fear darkened Lucas's eyes. "Three. From Factory Row."

Fentienne's heart kicked up into a gallop and he suddenly became aware of wolf ears around them. Someone had to be selling out names to the monks.

"And," the man paused a beat, "wolf attack survivors are reporting a rabid lone wolf in the forest. A *black* wolf."

The blood drained from Fentienne's head. Was he the Beast? A new, dark pain bloomed in his chest. To appear natural, hoping the lesser démon didn't hear the shift in his pulse, he passed Lucas a bored side glance and pressed a silver into his palm. The lesser démon's eyes snapped up to his. He didn't pay for information normally, especially with a fellow guardian officer in the Brotherhood, but Lucas had proved invaluable lately. And he wasn't above buying loyalty, especially with coin from a substantial abandoned treasury he discovered in the en suite chambers of Chateau Lumière Dorée.

"For your troubles in hefting an orange from under the table," he murmured.

"*Merci*, milord," Lucas said, loud enough to draw attention from other would-be customers. With his trademark taunting smirk, he added, "Tell Claudette I said hello."

Invisible hackles bristled down Fentienne's spine. No doubt Lucas could smell his wounds. Like Fentienne, the alpha was one of twelve guardian officers in the Brotherhood. Initiate meetings happened every month on this day. Still, he couldn't shake that there was more behind his parting words. As if Lucas was tipping him off that he was watching him.

Unnerved, Fentienne stepped closer once more and lowered his voice to a warning growl. "Cross me and I will shred your intestines too, officer or no."

Lucas lifted his shoulder in a shrug. "All bark and no bite, silk breeches."

"Who do you spy for?"

"What makes you think—"

"A trained army scout can spot another."

Lucas slowly nodded his head. "I spy for no one but myself, to protect my clan and Factory Row."

"We all have a price, monsieur," he said, throwing Lucas's own words back at him. "Sell me out and I don't care if we're fellow officers. I will force you to watch as I torture each wolf in your pack. I don't show mercy." The alpha returned the challenge in his gaze with one of his own, but Fentienne was satisfied when the man's skin paled a little. "If you're a scout with any skill, then you already know I don't bark, only bite."

"*Oui*, I know all about you." Lucas leaned in close and whispered, "Go ahead, bite, Wolf Prince. I might enjoy it." Then he turned his back in a dismissive move to greet customers.

The claws in Fentienne's hands strained against his leather gloves. The hot blood pumping through his veins begged to shift so his wolf could rip out the alpha's throat for insubordination. He didn't take orders or threats from lesser démons. He didn't take orders or threats from anyone. But the man had him cornered, publicly, and Fentienne needed to see the Brotherhood, not face The Row's wrath for a half-shifted démon in their market. Or face the Monks of Glanis. He needed a spy on his side too. Lucas eyed him over his shoulder, his mouth tilted in a smug grin before puckering his lips into a mocking kiss.

"Dark Saint's Bastard," Fentienne said under his breath, knowing the démon would hear, then pivoted about face and marched toward *Le Rêve Rouge*. Soft laughter followed him a few steps and he clenched his jaw. Oh how he would make that man pay when he no longer served Fentienne's purpose.

The sun in the sky was still high, at least three or four more hours of daylight. Enough time to finish his tasks and return to the chateau. Crossing the market square, he angled by a woman carrying a basket of flowers on her head—cultured flowers, not forest meadow pickings.

As he approached the brothel's red door, it sprang open and a man exited with two girls hanging on his arms to steal one last kiss before he strode away. Loud laughter and music traveled outside from the opening. One of the girls raked her eyes up and down Fentienne's body while touching his arm with a flirtatious giggle. He ignored her, and the blonde-haired girl at her side, and ducked inside.

Dark red walls swallowed his vision. *Le Rêve Rouge*—The Red Dream. Everything was decorated in sanguine shades of scarlet and crimson—the walls, the silk curtains, the beds. Most of the pleasure rooms were behind the tavern. But a few were left open with only sheer black and white panels as doors for those who desired to watch.

Tobacco and opium smoke clouded the front tavern. Behind the bar was another room, a Gentlemen's Club for those of means while lesser classes crowded this front room. Men lounged in chairs and drank while fae, human, and unshifted démon females in white and black corsets, their petticoats bunched up to show their silk gartered stockings, wandered around the tavern, seducing the men into drinking more, smoking more, and to follow them into a back room. None of the patrons noted his presence, too lost in their own indulgent escapisms. Fentienne maneuvered around the various activities at each table and sidled up to the bar.

"Drink, monsieur?" a bartender asked without glancing up.

"*La Fée Verte*. Premium reserve."

The man nodded and grabbed a green cut crystal bottle to make Fentienne a "Green Faerie," as it was called in Gabaston. Absinthe splashed into a mouth-blown glass with a small reservoir at the stem to accurately measure the spirits. The bartender then plopped a cube of sugar atop a slotted spoon and placed the solution beneath a decanter fountain and turned the valve for a slow water drip. The louche was immediate, what the locals called it when the wormwood, anise, and fennel spirits turned green and cloudy as the sugar water dripped into the cup. Fentienne tossed a few coins onto the bar, stirred his drink to ensure the sugar dissolved, then wandered back toward the entry, careful to keep his drink from spilling. He didn't care for opium, so he would need every drop of absinthe to dull the pain of what was to come.

"*Pardonnez-moi*, milord," a girl purred, emphasizing his nobility status.

The Aurelienne gold eyes of House Chalamet annoyingly gave him away wherever he went. Thank the old gods they were *many* Chalamet nobles.

Keeping his back straight, his expression bored, Fentienne slid his gaze to a girl who was perhaps two to three years younger than him. Russet hair fell over her shoulders in curls, her face powdered with a penciled black heart mole on her cheek and with lips painted red. The barely covered creamy curves of her body brushed his arm as she coyly peered up at him.

"What is your pleasure?"

"I seek Claudette."

"*Oui*, milord. Follow me." She slinked by him toward the voyeur hallways, a slight sway to her hips.

He ducked beneath an ebony wood archway and trailed after her, keeping his eyes straight ahead. And only because he needed his head to focus only on business and nothing more, and gods was that an effort. Girls with coquettish smiles waltzed past, inviting him to choose one of them with flirtatious lip bites, soft laughter, demurely lowered eyes, and while touching his chest, hips, and arms in light, provocative caresses. But he ignored each one, barely sparing a glance their way. Corsets and gartered stockings reduced him to utter stupidity. Amber candlelight limned bodies too. Whenever his mind would slip, he would think of Rhoslyn—how the very sight of her sickened him, how he loathed faeries, how her extraordinary beauty was deceptive.

How he would flay the skin from Addien Wyndham's body one day and feed her remains to the flea-ridden stray dogs of Factory Row.

His guide paused before large ebony wood double doors and knocked.

"Enter," a familiar, smoky voice answered.

Fentienne pushed open the door and walked in, sliding the bolt to lock him inside, then slowly turned toward the twenty-five-year-old lesser démon Madame with light gray eyes and silky black hair, fashioned partly up with a couple of loose curls falling over a dainty shoulder.

"Your Highness," she purred and arched out of a blood-red settee, a small smile on her rouge-tinted lips, and he bit the inside of his cheek to stay level-headed. She sashayed toward him in a black corset and flimsy black sheer petticoat, both decorated in red rosettes, a black ribbon choker, and thigh-high white stockings with blood-red garter ribbons tied into bows. "What a delightful surprise. It has been some time since a prince warmed my bed."

He set his untouched drink onto a side table, the orange from his pocket too, then removed his hat. "I am not here for pleasure."

"Oh?" She began unbuttoning his duster and highwayman collar while peering up at him through lowered lashes, unafraid of his face. But Fentienne still fought back the shame. "If it is pain you seek, I can send for Marielle."

A corner of his mouth inched up slightly. He knew she could scent his injuries. "I have a request for you, *ma chérie*. Actually, two requests."

"Whatever you ask of me, Your Highness." She slid the coat off his shoulders and tossed it to the floor with a graceful flourish, a sensual slant to her lips. "Oops."

"Mmm, tease me all you like. Bend over, touch me, but I *still* will not warm your bed in the way you wish this day."

"Then your coat can remain where it lays." She placed her hands on her silk-clad hips with a pretty pout. "Finish undressing yourself, prince."

Fentienne chuckled, holding her playful stare as he removed his frock coat, then unbuttoned his waistcoat and tossed both garments atop the duster. Drawing in a fortifying breath, he pulled his shirt over his head with a grimace. Claudette's eyes widened at the poorly wrapped injuries on his upper arm and side, now stained with blood.

She gently touched his side and whispered, "Adalwolf, what happened?"

He was going to correct her on his preferred name and to not be so informal with him but, instead, he grabbed his drink, taking a hefty sip of the licorice flavored spirits, then strode over to the large four poster bed draped in swaths of red silk curtains.

"Another she-wolf got her claws on me to earn coin," he deadpanned. Lowering onto the edge of the mattress, he met Claudette's beautiful gray eyes and swallowed back the rising desire. Skies, he was suffering. To give his hands something to do, he drowned the rest of his absinthe, then opened the end table drawer, moved the snuff box aside, pulled out a cigarette, then lit up with a nearby candle. Fentienne closed his eyes and leaned back on the mountain of pillows, sucking in a long drag and slowly exhaling. "I killed her."

"The alphas talk of nothing but that grisette . . ."

Grisette?

". . . the one rumored you claimed to protect."

He heaved a bored sigh. "Your tongue serves two purposes, Claudette, and I am only interested in one of those skills this afternoon. Discussing Mademoiselle Gautier is *not* it. But I do wish to discuss another matter."

She tilted her head and nibbled a corner of her bottom lip. "I could employ both skills."

He grunted a laugh, staring at the ceiling, then puffed on the cigarette once more.

"Is *she* why you do not seek my pleasure this day?"

"Gods no." Fentienne rolled his head in her direction. "I need my wounds stitched up. Of course, I will compensate you for your troubles and for your silence."

"And my tongue?"

"Court gossip."

"About?"

"How many nobles have you serviced these past two to three weeks?"

She sauntered over to an armoire opposite the bed and opened the doors. "Several, including your second cousin, le duc."

Duke Lucien Chalamet, his mother's first cousin. A pompous upper thirty-year-old man, the last born and surviving heir to a legacy fortune belonging to his mother's aunt, the former king's sister. And the next in line to the golden throne if Fentienne didn't miraculously resurrect from the grave—Nine Saints be praised—which he wouldn't. Lucien could have the crown and sink with the ship that was once the prosperous Realm of Gold. His mother was delusional to believe that Aurelienne would welcome a Halivaard and Beausoleil to rule as their king. Not to mention, if his aunt died tomorrow, as a half-man, half-beast king he wouldn't last even one full day before losing his head in the market square.

The bootlegged Clifstánian cigarette dangled loosely from his mouth as he sank lower onto the pillows with a sigh. Hopefully, the Brotherhood listened to his request to dissolve any notion of their Wolf Prince becoming their Wolf King as well as his command to focus all attention onto the Beast and not Rhoslyn.

Claudette shut the cabinet doors and returned with a surgery kit and fresh strips of cotton. "Your thoughts are heavy, Your Highness."

"Do any of the nobles speak of Gabaston's Beast?"

The surgery kit rolled out beside his thigh and he puffed on the cigarette again to rein in his mounting anxiety. Stitching his swollen, angry flesh together was going to level him. And he couldn't lose control in front of Claudette.

She waited for him to notice her arched brow. "Do you really think nobles come all the way to The Row to discuss the Beast of Gabaston with prostitutes?"

"Only to the ones who enjoys discussing beasts for pillow talk." He flashed her a slight, one-sided smile. "Do they know your secret? Or do they seek you because they, too, can be beasts in your company?"

"Do not bait me to stroke your intelligence, prince. My skill lies in stroking something far lower."

He leaned up on his elbows and blew a stream of smoke from his lips. "Those men? Pathetic wastes of human lives without a brain cell between them. But I know your value to the Brotherhood."

"Ah." She grabbed his belt and tugged him into a full sitting position. Their gazes locked and she softly blinked, making him hyper aware, once more, of her touch, of how he would rather spend the afternoon in her arms than traverse the catacombs to meet with old men in cloaks. Those same old men who placed her, the daughter of an alpha, in this brothel to study The Red Door's varied aristocratic clientele, especially fellow démons. Mostly to spy, but also to assassinate as needed. And to mend injured wolves, like him. Wolves who did not heal quickly, also like him. With nimble fingers, she began untying and unwrapping the linen bandages.

"And what does my value to the Brotherhood mean to *you*," she spoke, her smoky voice like velvet, "besides stitching up dogs who get into fights?"

"See?" Fentienne winked. "It is arousing to have one's intelligence stroked."

She plucked the cigarette from his fingers and enjoyed a short drag before returning it to him. "Intelligent girls are not pleasurable to men."

"Their loss. My gain."

"*Oui*, the many girls you've bedded were each the height of intelligence."

Fentienne barked a laugh. "Only one, *ma chérie*."

She softly prodded the inflamed skin and he flinched. "Do you need a belt to bite down on?"

"No."

Claudette peered up at him through lowered lashes for the merest second before threading a needle. "Whiskey?"

He shook his head, one that was slightly floaty from the absinthe.

"The wounds do not appear infected." The prick of needle on his skin shuddered through him. The first pierce made every muscle in his body scream. "There is talk of the Beast," she said in soothing tones and he knew it was to distract him. Fentienne exhaled through clenched teeth and braced for the next stitch. "Le duc speaks of a wolf cleansing to prevent the rise of another serial killing moon-addled beast."

Sweat beaded on his forehead from the flaming wall of fire burning his skin with each poke and tug of the needle and thread. Her words pushed through the pain and his brow furrowed. "The duke isn't a wolf?"

"*Non*, and he is desperate to become king." Her eyes fluttered to his.

"He works with the Monks of Glanis, then?"

"There are rumors that the third-born prince of Clifstán lives and will claim the golden throne. Stories say he is a Chalamet wolf to be feared. The suspected Beast."

His heart leapt to his throat. News he was alive was bound to reach the wrong ears eventually, that he expected, especially after his mother's loose tongue. But the Beast . . . was he? He still couldn't find evidence that he wasn't. Killing was in his blood.

"Do you believe I am the Beast?" he choked out as she pierced his flesh once more. With shaking hands, he placed the near butt of his cigarette between his lips and inhaled, then rubbed it out on a small dish beside the bed. He should have ordered two absinthes to better dull the pain.

Claudette stopped stitching and sat up straight to meet his gaze. "Possibly."

"You are not afraid?"

"I am afraid of a wolf cleansing not the half-beast before me." She scooted closer and caressed his cheek. "You are not the Beast, Prince Adalwolf Fentienne. Such a monster wouldn't care if he were. But you care." A wrinkle formed between her brows and her fingers trailed down his neck to explore the muscles of his chest. "For a man with a long list of war atrocities, why do you worry if you are? You have not shown mercy to the people of Aurelienne until the wolves of this land found you."

He grabbed her wrist. "I'm still a soldier in a war. The Brotherhood's secret weapon. Why do you think I still live?"

She yanked her hand from his grip and returned to his wound. "The alphas bow to you because they are incapable of denying your power. A primal, magic entrenched response from their wolf spirits."

"What are you saying?" he snarled.

"Your war crimes against Aurelienne are not even a consideration. The laws and magic of wolves couldn't care less about a land's politics, only their own." Her eyes snapped to his. "And do not let the Brotherhood tell you any different, prince."

He blinked back the surprise of her words. "What is it you want? I'm not an idiot to think for one second that you offer me this advice from the kindness of your heart."

"You are now an expert of my heart, Your Highness?" She lowered the needle and crawled up over his body and lightly kissed his lips. The soft breasts spilling from her corset caressed his chest and he nearly moaned, wanting to grab her around the waist and move her body closer to his. His wolf began growling warnings to him under her touch, the arsehole. Claudette kissed his jaw and continued down his neck. "Perhaps I like you," she whispered into his skin.

Fentienne gently pushed her back. "My wounds, *ma chérie*."

"Has my tongue pleased you?"

"*Oui*," he whispered into the space between them. "I only have a couple of hours before nightfall, Claudette."

Her gaze swept over his face before searching his eyes and he fought the urge to look away with her sudden intensity. This was her value to the Brotherhood beyond medical treatment, spying, and assassinations. She could see a shifter's wolf spirit and its aura.

"Your wolf is in love with her. This is beyond protection orders or mate claiming." Her head tilted curiously and her eyes flashed then narrowed. "How does your wolf spirit know her so completely when you have just met? Or have you?"

Fentienne shifted to open the end table drawer and pulled out a fresh cigarette, forcing his face into bored arrogance. "How much do you want for your medical care and silence?"

"Prince—"

"I no longer have use for your tongue," he growled in warning. "Only your healing."

She coolly arched a brow and smiled demurely. "Whatever pleases you, Your Highness."

He closed his eyes and puffed on the cigarette, grimacing against the pain while she finished, then looked anywhere but at her when she wrapped his torso and bicep in fresh bandages. The words she spoke too freely unsettled him—deeply. How could his wolf be in love with Maeline Wyndham? It was all fake. Every. Single. Emotion. The gutter rat didn't even know her real identity, though she walked with the authority of a female who already wore a crown.

What drove an elf in tattered rags with a sickly brother, who reeked of Factory Row, to break down a gate and face off with a powerful queen? What was she thinking? His aunt could have publicly executed her in the market square and left her brother to the wolves without any form of protection. Skies, Rhoslyn Gautier was infuriating. And his wolf salivated each time she fought back, pissing Fentienne off even more.

Ten gold pieces.

Ten saints cursed gold pieces.

Did his aunt know who she really was? If so, what was the political advantage to killing the crowned Princess of Avenbury? Only war would come from Maeline's death. Either his aunt didn't know Rhoslyn's identity or Addien had tempted her to do her bidding, despite the threat of war with Avenbury, in exchange for something that Adeline wanted. And Fentienne would bet his life on the latter.

Claudette rose from the bed and sauntered to his heap of clothing, slowly bending down to ensure he received a good view. A coquettish smile softened her lips as she slinked back to him. He reached for his garments, but she pulled them out of reach and shook her head. Sighing, he raised a haughty brow her way. She wanted to dress him? Fine. And he let her, holding her bold gaze the entire time.

"You should fully heal within a couple of days, my prince."

Unlike other wolves who had full control of their magic.

"*Merci*," he murmured and rubbed out the butt of his cigarette on a small dish. Reaching into the coin purse on his belt, he pulled out five silver pieces and tossed them onto the bed. A flirty smile teased his mouth up on one side. "Your tongue is quite skilled. Your hands too."

Claudette leaned into him and licked his bottom lip. Every muscle in his body groaned. But his wolf growled again, an angry threat, and Fentienne almost hissed a few choice swear words. Pulling away—misreading his struggle—she flashed him an invitation beneath lowered lashes.

"The catacombs, *ma chérie*," he drawled.

Gesturing with her finger to follow, she waltzed over to a door hidden behind a dressing screen and silk curtains, just one of two entries into the catacombs inside *Le Rêve Rouge*. The other door belonged to her father, Jules Aris, the owner of this establishment, and a guardian officer in the Brotherhood.

"Come back and I will make you forget all about her."

Fentienne studied the gray of Claudette's eyes for a few unsteady

heartbeats. There was no escaping his contracted wife. Or his wolf's obsession with the girl he was fated to kill. Still, he dipped his head then ducked into the catacombs, wishing he had drunk the whole bottle of absinthe and the bottle of whiskey Claudette offered him too.

Chapter 13

Fentienne

Cold, musty air enveloped him. The dirt and stone tunnel swallowed him in darkness, but his enhanced sight didn't struggle without torchlight. The brittled bones of royals and upper-class merchants lined the walls in dugouts. Rat- and moth-eaten funeral garments hung from the open tombs and fluttered in the natural air current.

Fentienne maneuvered around marble coffins dotting the center of various tunnels. Many belonging to the Beausoleil monarchy, easily recognizable from the intricately carved suns on the lids. The Chalamet coffins were more ornate, decorated in wolf gargoyles. One day, would his remains rest beneath the cobbled streets of Factory Row and Saints District? Or would his head be severed by a guillotine, his body quartered then burned at the stake for "serving" the Dark Saint? For being the treasonous Prince of Clifstán who dared claim a throne the peasants of Aurelienne were sacrificed for, one after the other, to protect their land from the return of the cursed Beausoleil-Halivaards?

The ceiling lowered and he bent to the side, leaning his head slightly toward his shoulder. A few of the shifters were of larger stature because of their wolves. But the men here were sometimes nearly a full head shorter than him. He would stand out more in The Row if not for the Dreglindish iron factory workers. But a Chalamet noble? Winter skies, he wished there were ways to disguise his eyes.

Cool air caressed his skin as the tunnel opened to the ossuary, a large, rounded room called the hall of thrones, and he straightened. Torches rested in holders on walls made entirely of human skulls and bones. In the archway, a rat squeezed through a black, empty eye and climbed through the open jaw, disappearing back into wall. Twelve stone thrones bathed in amber light and shadows faced each other in a circle, with rows of benches behind the dais separated by columns made from skulls, each one positioned in a cardinal direction. Voices hushed at the sound of his approaching boots. Guards appeared from hidden spots and pointed bayonets at his chest. But when recognizing him, they moved back into position.

"Prince," a familiar voice crooned. Mon Père Michel pushed the hood of his cloak back from his face. The older man, who acted as the head alpha regent until Fentienne arrived, lifted a tight smile. "Kind of you to join initiation this fine day." The priest gestured for Fentienne to join him. Behind Mon Père Michel were eight iron gibbet cages, each one filled with a man or woman—sentenced criminals. A rabid démon was chained to the wall beside them, snarling and snapping at those who stood too close. "Bring His Highness a cloak," the priest said over his shoulder and a young man, probably age fifteen, bowed and disappeared into an adjoining room.

Fentienne strode toward the sentenced criminals, settled before the priest and, with a sneer, asked, "Selling indulgences?"

Mon Père Michel smiled. "All to benefit the people, naturally."

"I can scent your lies and you reek."

"Careful to not offend the saints, Wolf Prince"

Fentienne huffed a laugh. "What kind of Dark Saint is so easily offended by priests who prey on the poor for the aristocracy's gluttony? Imagine the outrage when the common folk discover they fear a softhearted Lord of Démons."

The older man's smile remained, a kindness that never reached his brown eyes. "Not gluttony, Your Highness. Aurelienne is on the precipice of economic collapse because a cruel, warmongering family's greed waged war on our realm for three generations."

"Hmm." Fentienne leaned in close, grimacing back the sharp pain in his side with the motion despite the absinthe-induced lightness in his head. "I helped destroy the beating heart of your land but you destroy her soul. We are both proper predators, priest. Dark Saint be praised." He reached into his coin purse and pulled out a gold piece and dropped it into the older man's hand. "Now absolve me."

They locked eyes and the priest's smile turned wolfish.

The boy returned at that moment, oblivious to the charged air between Fentienne and Mon Père Michel, and offered a black cloak reserved for the twelve guardian clan officers of the Brotherhood, of which he was one.

"Dress," Mon Père Michel crooned. "We will await you."

Fentienne removed his hat and duster, giving both to the boy, who placed them onto a bench. Walking toward the group of officers and lower members, Fentienne threw the cloak across his shoulders, wincing with the pain in his stitched-up bicep, tied the laces, then lifted the hood over his head until his face shadowed. As much as he despised keeping company with most people, he drew comfort in not being a face of horror among démons. Many half-shifted when they wanted to be fully aware with their human mind but draw on the supernatural strengths of their wolf spirit.

"Prince," the fellow officers said with bows. Only seven clan leaders present today.

"Proceed with initiation," Fentienne replied back. "I wish to discuss matters of import afterward."

Several Brotherhood officers moved toward the rabid wolf. Drool dripped from his mouth and a pinprick of red dotted the center of his dilating pupils. Brown fur was matted and snarled in patches. And sharp claws had grown longer and clicked at the stone floor while straining against the chains dungeoning him to the wall.

Who was this unfortunate soul?

A few weeks ago, Fentienne wouldn't have given a shit. People departed their miserable lives every day. Many went mad from grief, hunger, and other various hardships too. Only a fool believed they could save every wayward mortal soul. Let the weak destroy themselves. Good riddance. But now? Fentienne watched the moon-addled wolf with grotesque curiosity. This could be him—would be him—in a matter of weeks.

"Terrifying," a bored, lilting voice murmured beside him. Fentienne's gaze slid to his distant cousin, Alain Chalamet, one of three leaders in the Goldfang clan and an officer. "Never ceases to unsettle me."

Fentienne remained silent as Bastien Chapelle—captain of Factory Row's guard, alpha of the Nightwalker clan, and another guardian officer in the Brotherhood—marched down the line of gibbet cages. Alain shifted on his feet, disgust curling his lip. The man's dismissive disdain humored Fentienne, but only because it was entirely *tres haute noblesse* in every clichéd way. And how Fentienne behaved to play the part of entitled prince for an even more entitled aristocracy. At least Fentienne knew he was a villain and why. These monsters fainted when a twelve-course meal arrived three minutes later than expected and cried victim when a lice-infested commoner complained of hunger.

In his mid-forties, tall and lean, graying brown hair, the famed family golden eyes, and draped in the finest pale blue silk . . . his relation had cozied up to Fentienne the moment they were introduced months back. Despite the obvious attempt to gain favor, his fourth cousin thrice removed on his mother's father's sister's branch of their rotting family tree—or however they were related—had never treated him with any contempt or superiority. Hadn't once challenged him in any way either. And, to Fentienne, that was a more glaring red flag than open hostility.

Alain chuckled under his breath. "Our dear beloved queen snaps as ferociously these days."

"She's delusional to believe The Row will starve quietly."

"Or accept more taxes. There are times I almost pity the filthy fleas."

More taxes? Skies, Gabaston frothed at the mouth for a stale crumb of bread. Fentienne twisted toward his cousin and dropped his voice to a near whisper, knowing the wolf ears in this room would still pick up their conversation. "Allies calling in debts?"

"*Oui.*" Alain finally met his eyes.

Not sure what he expected, especially of his brother, but rebuilding a realm required money. And, right now, three realms were in new construction after the war. Dreglind had supplied weapons to Aurelienne's military plus iron ore and coal to the manufacturing factories. His ancestral home especially had a vested interest in defending their neighbors to the east. But Avenbury's involvement had surprised him most, especially given his marriage contract with their crowned princess. Why had his father allowed their supposed ally to supply cotton and wool, as well as grain, flour, beans, cured meats, and other nonperishables to enemy soldiers? Something wasn't adding up properly.

"Rothlín and Merenna too?" he asked Alain.

"Rothlín had a treaty with Clifstán, no?"

Fentienne softly snorted. "Contracts between realms are as cheap as a pavement nymph's perfume."

Alain grunted in agreement and returned his attention to Bastien who, with the help of Armand, a fellow guard, wrangled the rabid wolf to face the criminal in the narrow human birdcage-like contraptions. Or what the Brotherhood referred to as human dog crates. Gibbet cages were a torture device favorite here, used to expose a dying body to the elements and hung from execution blocks until the bones were picked clean. A horrifying reminder to not commit certain crimes. Fentienne wasn't convinced the publicly caged dying and deceased actually dissuaded those greater crimes. The only ones disturbed by the visual were the law abiding morally uncorrupted.

"His Imperial Highness is investing in Clifstán's economic infrastructure for King Lufric Blackvein," his cousin casually tossed out. "Dreglind does not seem to suffer for any debts owed them. The Halivaard litter runt has no sense of loyalty to his mother's ravaged land."

A swell of anger rushed through Fentienne at the mention of Florian and Eirwen's dwarven foster brother now King. The dwarf was tearing down Myrefell brick-by-brick, removing any history of the military base and fortress. The fae male knew Fentienne lived and, if Gedlen Fate Maker meddled in affairs, per usual, then Lufric probably also knew Fentienne was heir to the Aurelienne throne. What if Fentienne decided to invade Clifstán to regain yet another throne lost to his family? As the oldest surviving prince, he could reclaim the Halivaard seat of power—and rule both realms as the rightful heir.

Lufric Blackvein appointed as the King of Clifstán was not only laughable, but an insult to the entire war. Dwarves couldn't defend themselves against a northern army before, let alone fight the soldiers of their own stars blasted realm. Without a strong military presence, any campaign against those pathetic maggots would be swift, like swatting an annoying gnat. And it will happen if raven stone—the rare resource of the Seven Jeweled Hills—remained unprotected. The power those gemstones harnessed for weapons were unparalleled.

Demilitarizing Clifstán brought an additional worry to Fentienne besides unprotected raven stone too: a new war to claim the Cold Winds dusted realm of Glenashlen to the east of Aurelienne and Clifstán, just over the Spired Hills along the Ærin Sea. The salt mines in Glenashlen would line

pockets heavily with gold. The logical strategy would be to invade by sea—and it would eventually happen. There was no question since the strongest, most modern military in the eight realms no longer existed and Aurelienne, who made up the largest land border, couldn't afford to pay war debts let alone outfit another campaign.

Unless he invaded Clifstán and reestablished the military.

To think, his father's dream for the House of Halivaard to rule the eastern block of Ealdspell could be realized, if Fentienne wasn't cursed to roam only Aurelienne.

Warrior sons who were bred to be super soldiers.

Warrior sons made from dragons and wolves.

A dark, bitter laugh rumbled from his chest. He would sooner run himself through with a dull, rusty spoon than give his father any form of victory, even in death. He owed that demon of a man nothing. Not the throne of Clifstán or the throne of Aurelienne.

Alain leaned in. "Pity his Imperial Highness's older brother hadn't survived the war to negotiate debts on behalf of Queen Adeline."

"Absolute shame, that," he murmured in reply. Though humored, he kept his voice bland and added, "Perhaps our hero Le Duc Lucien will finally become useful and lose his head after failing to broker a fair repayment plan."

Hearing his comment from three to four yards away, Benoit Faivre angled his head enough to catch Fentienne's attention beneath the shadows of his cloak and slid him a playful smile, almost flirtatious. The notorious twenty-nine-year-old playboy had excessively powdered his face, which he accented boldly with makeup, and sported a gray periwig, one with a ridiculous *pouffe* and rolled pigeon wing curls above his ears—the height of Aurelienne couture for men in their late teens through thirties. One Fentienne loathed. Every pastel silk suit and lace edged cuff, the bows and ribbons men put in their hair and donned on their shoe buckles, the powder, rouge, and even lipstick . . . it was an affront to his modern military upbringing. The shady things he would do for a motorcycle, cigarettes, and a record player some days. And to pilot a mech through the forest, to feel a machine roar beneath him as metal and circuitry tore up earth and trees. And flying machines, gods. This backwards realm had to be a dimension of the Underworld on the mortal plane.

But Benoit was revered among social circles as a prime example of masculinity—which Fentienne would never in a million lifetimes understand. Not that he needed to. The aristocrat's family owned almost half of Factory Row. Money and social status he did understand. After Benoit's father suffered a stroke, which he survived, the Brotherhood ignored Benoit's drunken exploits and appointed him one of the twelve guardian clan officers. The upper merchant class wielded power—and cleverly—in ways nobles couldn't begin to conceive, the lazy arses.

The aristocrat winked. "Royal executions are a riot."

Everything stilled inside of Fentienne. A primal response. Was that a threat? But he couldn't dwell long on the man's unexpected words. His stomach lurched as sharp images suddenly sliced through his mind.

His little brother, on his knees, a gun pressed to his head. Then the order. Just one word. A look of horror pained Florian's silver eyes right before he collapsed to the gravel. Fentienne wanted to vomit. He wanted to scream. But his mind couldn't make sense of what he had just seen. His feet refused to run to Florian—

A shriek yanked Fentienne from the nightmare in his head and the catacombs faded into focus. Swallowing back the thudding pulse in his tightened throat, he forced his face into insouciant arrogance and ignored the clammy beads of sweat dewing on his forehead. Florian lived. He was alive and rebuilding Dreglind and Clifstán. His little brother's death was an illusion, a faerie trick. Their oldest brother, who was glamoured to look like Florian, was the one who was executed, the vile, gods awful man. Yet, no matter how many times Fentienne relived those moments, even knowing the truth, it was if for the first time all over again.

"Mon Dieu," Alain quietly said beside him, as if they shared the same horrified reactions. "Disgusting."

Fentienne hardened his features. Damn preternatural senses. The grief and panic were probably rippling off him like a pile of shit baking in the sun. The sight of blood did nothing to Fentienne. Watching people suffer and die also did nothing to him. Or hearing the terrified cries of those in pain. He was trained to turn off all feeling during torture, to appear turned on by it instead, to see the objective not the soul. But when it came to his little brother . . .

Armand gripped the arm of a middle-aged man covered in dungeon grime and yanked it from the iron bars of the gibbet cage. The rabid wolf lunged and sank his teeth into the sentenced man's flesh. A low scream slipped the criminal's trembling lips, growing louder when the wolf began thrashing his head in attempt to rip off the arm. Bastien gently knocked the rabid démon on the head with an iron poker and the wolf released the man's arm. Before the criminal could retreat and cradle his wound, another guard turned him around and held his back flush to the bars. Armand approached with a brand he had heated in a torch and seared the clan symbol for Ironbite onto the nape of his neck. Maximilien Barras, owner of a couple iron factories, Brotherhood officer and leader of the Ironbite clan, stepped forward and dripped blood from his hand into the criminal's torn flesh—claiming him.

One by one, Armand and Bastien turned the humans to wolves and branded each man and woman in the human dog crates, where they would remain until the possession's fever frenzy passed and they responded to simple commands of obedience. Then they would join their new packs as indentured slaves.

Before armistice, male criminals were turned into démons for the military. The unnatural strength and speed, as well as quick healing abilities, kept Aurelienne from utter decimation in the Spired Hills, a war strategy Fentienne fully appreciated though he had lost men to these shifters. And to ogres. Soldiers were picked off by those nasty creatures, too, especially the injured. Thankfully, not many ogres survived the constant barrage of bullets and cannon fire—if any.

"Welcome, initiates," Mon Père Michel intoned over the weeping, bleeding mortals. He lifted his pointer and middle finger in a benediction and waved it over the cages, saying, "Saints bless you." When finished, he turned to Armand and a few other guards. "Wheel them into the Tombs of the Forgotten."

Bastien yanked on the rabid démon and forced him into the center of the twelve thrones.

Fentienne followed the other officers and stood before his assigned throne as the others took their position. The lower members—various pack alphas and their betas—gathered on the benches behind them.

Mon Père Michel pulled a ceremonial silver dagger and gold chalice from his cloak and approached the moon-addled shifter. "You have done a great service for the nine clans. We honor you in life and in death, brother. Join the saints and intercede on our behalf as we toil for Aurelienne." In the speed of shadows, the silver blade slit the former man's throat in a swift kill. The priest then gathered drops of spilled blood into the chalice and held it above his head. "Roam the night."

The room chanted back, "Roam the night." Except Fentienne. He never bothered with funereal sentiments.

The priest dipped his fingers into the blood and left a red handprint onto the matted brown fur of the sacrificed—their symbol for a redeemed curse. With the same stained fingers, he approached each officer and smeared a fresh blood-dipped finger from their forehead down between their eyes. A barbaric ritual.

Torchlight flickered shadows across the walls made from skulls and the many dugouts throughout the room, each one containing the bones and black weaves of guardian clan officers who had roamed the night for one to two hundred years now. Officers from this century rested in a separate room until their flesh decayed and only bones remained. Royalty, however, were still buried in marble and alabaster coffins.

He wouldn't be buried in Clifstán with his family.

Or be buried in Dreglind with his ancestors.

He probably wouldn't be buried in Aurelienne with this family either. Not in the catacombs, at least.

A sickening feeling twisted in his gut as he stared at the sacrificed démon. This was his future. His blood would paint the faces of his brothers and anoint the throne dais after turning criminals into slaves.

Because he was a curse. Third-born prince who would not become king. A split crown. A monster. A broken man never to be made whole. Addien knew it. Maeline's family knew it. His father knew it. Gedlen, Dalbréath, Florian, Eirwen... they knew it.

For who could love a beast?

Tears pricked the back of his eyes and he clenched his teeth so hard he feared they might break.

"Wolf Prince," a voice crooned.

His eyes snapped up to meet the smiling, predatory gaze of Mon Père Michel. The older man's finger trailed down Fentienne's forehead, nose, and over his lips. Not the simple line between the brows like the other officers. No, the priest had ceremonially marked Fentienne as their head alpha, their Prince of Démons.

The alphas bow to you because they are incapable of denying your power.

War drums beat in Fentienne's pulse. The mark of ownership burned his skin.

Their chosen head alpha: the son from a line of kings who waged war on their lands for well over five decades. The great grandson of the Aurelienne prince and king consort of Dreglind's empress who became cursed by the High Druid after he slaughtered his own family in both realms to become Emperor of Dreglind and King of Aurelienne. The great grandson of the same man who unseated and killed the dwarven sorcerer king and claimed Clifstán's crown.

Their chosen Prince of Démons: the man before them who didn't even know he was a wolf until a little over a year ago after he earned a curse of his own for his war crimes against the Kingdom of Ealdspell. A man cursed like his father, grandfather, and great grandfather.

The laws and magic of wolves couldn't care less about a land's politics, only their own.

Every muscle in Fentienne's body flamed with rage. His claws itched to grab the silver dagger at the priest's hip and make the older man's blood spill next. He refused to be their secret weapon in a war for a throne he had been bred in a violating act of hate to overturn. A throne his father had *always* destined for Fentienne to rule. Nobody owned him. *Nobody.* But his wolf howled from a dark, cavernous place in his chest, the sound echoing in the marrow of his bones. A territorial cry claiming Fentienne's place at the top of the clans and packs. A sound he knew every wolf spirit in this room heard and obeyed.

And do not let the Brotherhood tell you any different, prince.

The priest smiled, leaning in close, and whispered, "You're absolved."

Mon Père Michel turned in a flourish of red silk robes beneath the black wool officer's cloak.

Fentienne was shaking. He wasn't sure if it was because his wolf strained to shift in the surge of power fevering his blood. Or if his rage had tripped a minefield of explosive feelings ready to level this entire room to dust and bones.

"The Brotherhood is in session," Jules Aris—alpha of Red Bane clan, one of the twelve guardian officers, and owner of *Le Rêve Rouge*—said over the quieting crowd. "*Frères de la forêt. Loups liés par le sang.*"

Voices joined together and repeated the pledge. *Brothers of the forest. Wolves bound in blood.*

"*Protégez les clans*"

The men chanted in reply. *Protect the clans.*

"*Gardez les meutes.*"

Once more the men intoned back their vows. *Guard the packs.*

"*Guerriers. Défenseurs. Frères dans la vie et dans la mort.*"

Fentienne bit out the ending pledge along with the rest while holding back an eye roll. "Warriors. Defenders. Brothers in life and in death." Most in this room were going through the motions as well. Wolves were too territorial to give a damn about other clans and packs. One of the main reasons the Brotherhood didn't mark the entire population of Aurelienne as future démons. The infighting would be apoplectic and make the war look like children playing with tin soldiers. Better to initiate slaves than more comrades.

Your war crimes against Aurelienne are not even a consideration.

Claudette's words cycled in his thoughts and a new panic gripped his heart. Each man in this room resented him. The distrust and simmering anger permeated every stone and skull in the catacombs with their stench. He was the villain who had waltzed in packless, a lone wolf who had never submitted to a clan alpha—nor would he. Starved after weeks of roaming the Spired Hills and the woods of Gabaston. Confused by what was happening to him while fighting agonizing pain from the shifter magic he couldn't control. Their enemy, the man who had invaded and bombed their city. Killed their loved ones. And now their wolves demanded they bow before him as their top dog.

It was just as Claudette had said—and every argument he had prepared ashened on his tongue.

If he didn't protect Rhoslyn, his wolf would turn on him.

If he made Rhoslyn hate him, his wolf would turn on him.

But if she fell for him, she would die and then his wolf would turn on him.

If he didn't protect the Brotherhood, his wolf would turn on him.

If he refused to become their king, his wolf would turn on him.

Fentienne studied the sacrificed man in wolf form, his blood drying on Fentienne's skin, and gritted back the fear and betrayal.

And fresh anger. He didn't want this throne, or any throne. Nausea churned violently in his festering gut. Furious tears burned the back of his eyes. Not that how he felt about anything mattered. Eirwen's curse was permanent. He wasn't capable of selfless love—whatever that meant. Love didn't exist. Regardless of what he did or didn't do, it was a death sentence. For him and for Rhoslyn.

"Your Highness"—Aris turned to him and bowed—"The floor is yours."

The first order of business was a moot point now—he wouldn't be able to convince them to pick another head alpha. His wolf and theirs made that decision for them. Nor did he sense that convincing the Brotherhood to pick a different Chalamet to become their Wolf King would go over well in this session, even if Fentienne agreed to remain their appointed Prince of Démons alpha. So, he settled on starting off with the second discussion point.

Fentienne moved to the center of the dais beside the sacrificed démon while all in attendance lowered to their seats. For a few electrified seconds, he met the eyes of the seven elders present, staring them down. A few looked down in submission. A few held his challenge, but he could see their internal fight.

"Warriors. Defenders. Brothers in life and in death," Fentienne said to the room. "Yet some are selling out wolves to the Monks of Glanis and one among us is the Beast of Gabaston." He gestured to the sacrificed man at his feet. "These treasonous acts aren't the work of a rabid."

"*Oui*," Ambroise de Rosier said, a vintner, distiller, and fellow clan officer. "Our scouts haven't found any new rabids in the woods this past week. Our kennels are full. No reports of turning moon-addled wolves from pack leaders either."

Though not said, every man here knew it was impossible for a rabid to remain hidden within the city walls.

Benoit lounged back on his throne with a devilish smile directed entirely at Fentienne. "His Highness came all the way from Chateau Lumière Dorée to discuss the Beast? I do not think so."

"Fascinating. I never took you for a man who knew how to think, Faivre." Fentienne lifted a smug smile of his own when a wave of laughter rumbled around them. "S'il vous plaît, monsieur, enlighten us with your newfound skill. What am I here to discuss if not the Beast?"

That gaudy aristocrat—one of three pack leaders of Clan Goldfang, the same clan as House Chalamet—chuckled and shifted in his throne to lean forward, stupidly taking the bait. He was an idiot. Also, whoever named the clans was an absolute child. They were horrendously abhorrent. So was this trussed up, porcelain doll of a man. What females saw in him—he stopped himself. No, never mind. He knew. Those parasites only saw his wealth and socio-political power. Fentienne understood this better than most in this room. He also understood that he and Benoit were the youngest officers in the aristocracy by nearly two decades.

Waving his hand for Benoit to continue, banking on the man to not think through his next action, Fentienne lifted a bored, impatient brow. Let the pissing contest commence. The arse could attempt to mark his territory all he wanted. He wasn't the saints cursed Prince of Démons.

"How is it Mademoiselle Gautier—"

Fentienne moved with the unnatural speed of démons before Benoit could finish. Wolves didn't challenge an alpha about their mates. The bond was untouchable upon penalty of death. Resting his hands on the arms of the aristocrat's throne, Fentienne lowered to Benoit's face and growled, "Her name will *not* cross your venereal-diseased lips."

Benoit slid him a lazy smile. "Then, by all means, prince, be my guest. Tell us about your fayette. Why do you protect her from your aunt at the cost of your brethren?" The man caressed Fentienne's cheek in an act of domination, like the death-wish eating imbecile he was. There was no attraction. Every open flirtation was an attempt at humiliation from one young alpha to another. Different realm, same tactic. The soldiers in Myrefell employed a similar chess move.

But unlike Benoit, who grew up with silks, family portrait sessions, and feasts, Fentienne had crawled through blood-stained mud with bullets whizzing by him, pressed weights daily to stay in top shape, and captained highly trained machine warfare soldiers. There was only one way to motivate territorial arrogance into submission. A move drilled into him since he was old enough to walk.

Fentienne straightened. His gaze prowled behind Benoit's throne until he found the man's beta. The room immediately silenced to a predatory stillness. Without breaking eye contact with the unfortunate older beta, he quietly said to Benoit, "Bow at my feet and he lives. If you refuse, I will pick off your pack one at a time, starting with those in attendance."

"Your Highness—"

"—I will not offer you this mercy again."

Benoit slipped from the throne, the shame reddening his cheeks, despite the mounds of powder, and lay prostrate on the ground. Not what Fentienne had asked, but he appreciated the opportunity. He placed the heel of his boot on the back of Benoit's head and pressed down until the aristocrat's mouth kissed the dirt and he began coughing from inhaling rock and bone dust.

"Any other questions about Mademoiselle Gautier?" he asked the room. Every alpha in attendance, including within the twelve, plus the lower members, dipped their heads and averted their eyes in submission. "Excellent. Then you understand that she is my mate. *Mine*. I claim her. Any wolf who attempts to collect on her bounty or harm her brother will eat dirt like Monsieur Faivre . . . after being buried alive. I will pay for the carcasses of traitors too."

Seconds ticked by and Fentienne reveled in the racing heartbeats he could hear around the room.

When satisfied that most present feared him, he removed his boot from Benoit's head and shouted, "On your feet!" like he would to one of his soldiers. The ridiculous man scrambled to stand, but kept his eyes squarely on the ground, trying to hold in the urge to keep from coughing. A muscle ticked along Benoit's jaw and Fentienne grinned. He moved into the aristocrat's space, as a commanding officer to a disorderly private, and peered down his nose at him. "Like I said, I never took you for a man who knew how to think and you didn't disappoint." He grabbed the aristocrat's arm and, with a sharp twist, dislocated Benoit's shoulder and broke his arm. The cry echoing in the chamber was a beautiful aria to Fentienne's ears. "Stop your sniveling or I'll break your knee next," Fentienne hissed in his face. "You'll heal in a couple of hours. I could do this over and over again." Gently, with the back of his finger, he caressed the man's cheek. "Mmm, what fun you and I could have together."

"*Oui*, Your Highness," Benoit choked out in a quivering voice.

"Attempt to dominate me again, Faivre, upstage my investigation, or use my mate to discredit my authority and it won't be just your beta who loses his life." He bent and whispered in the man's ear, "Executions are a riot."

He pushed Benoit back into the stone throne behind him, then returned to the center of the room. "I am aware that the sudden nature of my relationship with Mademoiselle Gautier puts wolves in danger. Nor will I accept claims of intentionally endangering my brethren when you would behave no differently with your own mate." He slowly circled around the sacrificed démon. "We are men of power and means. Ten gold pieces is nothing between us. We could do far better than the bankrupt monarchy behind the now broken gold gates."

Mon Père Michel folded his hands in his lap and leaned back against his throne. "What do you suggest, Your Highness?"

"A monster hunt of our own." A wicked smile curled the corners of Fentienne's mouth. "Offer up a bounty among démons to capture the wolves selling us out to the Monks of Glanis and another for the aristocrats orchestrating this war on our kind. These traitors are to remain alive for questioning. We will perform our own wolf cleansing."

The older man dipped his head. "Anything else, prince?"

"*Oui.* Offer up a separate bounty on behalf of the business owners of Factory Row to Aureliennes who capture the Beast of Gabaston. A price far higher than the one for Mademoiselle Gautier. If the Beast is delivered dead, the bounty is forfeit." Fentienne met the eyes of each clan officer present. "I want the Beast alive to torture for information, but mostly for the monks to lose favor among the people. Each wolf they execute is another meal stolen from the hungry." He paused to let his words sink in. "And we all know what happens when Factory Row is denied bread."

The officers and attendees placed a fist over their chest and howled.

Fentienne's gaze drifted over to Benoit, who howled despite the fury writhing in his dark brown eyes, and Fentienne's wicked smile grew wider.

Chapter 14

Rhoslyn

The roar of the parlor's fireplace misted into the background. A soft lulling trickle of water sang in her ears instead. Rhoslyn opened her eyes to a sea of twinkling green leaves above her head. Hundreds of shades of green. As if each leaf were hand painted by the Divine Mother herself. Lifting her fingers, she traced the smudged edges of several wispy clouds in the robin egg blue sky just beyond the lacy trees. The cloud right above her head held the shape of a cow with wings and she softly giggled.

A blissful sigh left her lips. The arm she extended toward the sky fell above her head while the other draped across her middle. Ferns danced in the breeze around where she lay. Rolling her head to the side, she watched a vibrant blue butterfly prettily flutter overhead until it disappeared from sight. And that humming melody of water, the one merrily trickling behind her, filled her chest with wondrous awe. She didn't need to look to know it would be magical. How long had it been since she spent a lazy afternoon watching the clouds drift by? But she was too curious to see if *he* was here to lie wistfully content beneath the trees and ferns.

Rhoslyn rose to her feet and tucked a flyaway curl behind her ear and paused. Her long, golden-brown hair was fashioned around her head in curls and rolls, tucked beneath a *bergère* hat, a straw shepherdess style hat positioned at a downward angle over her face and tied beneath her chin, one decorated in silk rosettes and bows, from what she could feel. She bit her lip in a pleased grin when noting the rest of her garments next—*robe à la polonaise*. A beautiful silk pastoral-styled gown with an ivory petticoat that reached just above her ankles, decorated in dusty blue and rose pin stripes. A cornflower blue overskirt bunched up in three poofed swags around her hips and backside and a low-cut, dark rose corset bodice with three-quarter sleeves adorned with ivory and pale blue flowers and bows, all paired with an ivory pair of heeled shoes. Polonaise pastoral gowns were considered somewhat scandalous for exposing so much of a female's leg and décolletage. But Rhoslyn loved the heavy feel of the silks draped over her body, the flounce of her skirts from the rump roll and voluminous swags as she slowly turned in a circle, the touch of grass and ferns on her silk-stocking clad ankles. This dress was an absolute dream . . . which made sense given her present state.

To sew such a gown! She would luxuriate in the soft, cool touch of the silk with each stitch.

Though, she knew, in reality she would despise each poke and tug of the needle. This dress could feed dozens of families. Children would go to bed with full bellies. Parents and siblings wouldn't need to work as many hours to provide for those in their care. But, since this was a dream, she would enjoy the indulgence without guilt. There was nothing wrong with enjoying fine things in life, in reality or in fantasies. Just not at the cost of another's ability to live.

Lifting up her petticoat, she grinned once more. Her stockings didn't slouch from lack of proper ties. The light rose-colored ribbons around her thighs were beautiful. Saints, between her torn, fraying dress and the strand of butcher's twine to hold up one ripped stocking, her cheeks began to warm. How she must have looked to that beast when he cornered her in the hallway. She lowered her skirts and sighed. Perhaps the chateau had dresses she could refurbish to replace her tattered garment and to cut and sew pieces to replace Matthieu's clothing too—if she could locate a sewing kit. That démon would undoubtedly throw a tantrum over how she disobeyed his pompous orders. Good. He could behave childishly. She might even find it adorable.

Speaking of infuriating men . . . Rhoslyn spun toward the sound of the tinkling, babbling water and her mouth fell open. He *was* there. The man she raced horses with along the black sand beach. He faced away from her with hands clasped behind his back, similar to a soldier. His build was unmistakable. But that was not what stilled the breath in her lungs. Actually, that wasn't true. He was one of two reasons for her lightheadedness this moment.

Small streams of water fell from a cluster of moss- and wood violet-covered boulders into a pond. The perfectly still dark emerald surface of the water reflected the surrounding trees and sky. More wood violets, blooming beside toadstools, poked out from beneath ferns and crowded around rambling tree roots dotted in soft patches of moss and ruffled lichen. Rhoslyn ducked beneath a branch while stepping toward the enchanting scene, gasping when catching sight of blue glowing faerie wisps skipping just above the inky water and weaving between the ferns. The man angled his head just enough to barely acknowledge her over his shoulder before returning his focus to the faerie pond.

A flock of those vibrant blue butterflies fluttered dizzily in her stomach. Unlike their last encounter, he was fully dressed in a silk dusty blue three-piece suit. Though, the frock coat draped neatly over a rock beside him, a black tricorn hat too. The silhouette of his back and legs in the trim waistcoat, breeches, and stockings, contrasted with how the sleeves of his shirt billowed in the breeze, drizzled the most delicious sensation down her body. Like last time, his hair fell to just above his chin in dark, earthen waves with golden highlights beneath the sun. He was so . . . striking.

Pressing a hand to her midsection to settle her nerves, she stopped beside him on the banks and watched the playful wisps.

And said nothing.

Nor did he.

They remained in a silence strung tight enough to snap. Rumbling thunderclouds surrounded him, a melancholy fury that was palpable. She was tempted to speak first, to ask if he was well, but the intensity of his focus, how he seemed to stare right through the illusion of this dream, held her back. Nine Saints, she had so many questions, though.

Rhoslyn attempted a nonchalant glance his way beneath lowered lashes, struck once more by his dark elegance. Back stiff, head straight, he appeared ready to strike, to fight. A small scowl wrinkled the space between his brows, a slight frown lined his full lips while a muscle angrily ticked along his jaw, and those Otherworldly honeyed amber eyes framed in by dark lashes—

"There's a basket of food and wine." He gestured to a rock beside his coat and hat with a curt, blasé wave of his hand—like an aristocrat. Still, he did not look her way. "When you're done appreciating my profile, mademoiselle. Take your time."

Ignoring his arrogance, she asked, "Will you join me?"

"No, my darling." The endearment came out biting. "And before you demand I speak civilly, my feelings toward you have not changed."

"*Mon douce puce*, I have no desire to instruct a grown man on how to behave. Especially one who, quite melodramatically, declared he was not a gentleman."

A tiny smile flitted across his mouth.

"But I must tell you," she continued. "My nine-year-old brother has far better manners than you."

"Clearly, mademoiselle, the boy fears your overbearing entitlement to perpetuate male social oppression."

Rhoslyn stilled, too outraged by his words. Then the Underworld's refuse fires rolled through her veins and she bared her teeth, placing one hand on her hip while the other flew into the air. "*Oui*, males lack every advantage in society. How tyrannical of me to exercise female dominance on the fairer sex."

That tiny smile grew wider.

Oh. That . . .

Rhoslyn huffed.

That smug, infuriating arse was baiting her. On purpose.

Lifting her chin, she angled past him to the picnic basket and plucked out the open bottle of wine. Alcohol was needed if they were to continue any form of discourse or be forced to tolerate each other's presence whenever they apparently both slept. But there were no glasses. Why were there no glasses? Well, at least he was spared social decorum. She wore a scandalous dress—which she loved—and would further scandalize the situation by drinking straight from the bottle. With her head still held high, she returned to his side, placed the bottle to her lips, and enjoyed a long sip. Longer than was acceptable, but she had to uphold a standard of female dominance now. It was the polite thing to do. The man still didn't peer in her direction, but his lips twitched with an obvious effort to keep from laughing.

She handed him the bottle and said, "To male oppression."

He lifted the bottle in solute and murmured, "To oppression," then drank.

Silence heavily dewed the air they breathed, though their inner thoughts were loud and riotous. The kind of silence where there were far too many things to say and, yet, not enough. A strange understanding had settled between them. Not quite a cease fire, but an appreciation for the other's sharp wit. And, she could be wrong, but he seemed lighter than when she first found him. Not by much, though.

Only two dreams shared, with minimal conversation, and already she had learned the nuances of his emotional tells.

But not his name.

"Milord..."

He turned to her that moment and her pulse... Sweet Springs of Glanis, her pulse quivered at the lightning storm of emotions raging in his eyes. A more sensible girl would be frightened by the dark wildness clawing just beneath his surface. One, that if unleashed, would level everyone and everything around him. She, however, found herself willingly swept away by his barely restrained fury. He was beyond lovely, a cruel, dangerous form of beauty that rewrote every sonnet and verse her soul carried.

"*Oui*, mademoiselle?" he asked, a bit breathless—not correcting her address. The sound, in one heady, pleasurable rush, settled low in her belly. There was no malice or challenge in his voice. No vulgar retort or verbal attack. The tone was entirely soft and... vulnerable.

She couldn't answer him, not when he peered at her as if she were also the most beautiful creature he had ever beheld. Was she? But then she remembered his words, that he wasn't sure if he were more afraid to be awake or asleep.

A wrinkle formed between her brows. "You know my name."

The uncharacteristic softness winked out and disdain, once more, etched every handsome line of his face. "*Everyone* knows your name now. Don't pretend to be so naive."

"But how did you know—"

He quietly laughed and the hairs on her arms stood on end.

"Then you are real."

"Hmm."

"I cannot reason how we share this dreamscape save an enchantment over Chateau Lumière Dorée."

"Then spare us both and no longer attempt to reason." His gaze slowly trailed down her body and back up to rest on her mouth. "You are far prettier when silent."

Rhoslyn rolled her eyes. "So are you."

The barest hint of amusement touched his lips.

"Then you are on the property."

"The man you see before you is trapped." The derision seeped out of every word. "Except in his dreams."

"That beast holds you prisoner?"

A shadow crossed over his face. "He torments me, yes."

Her mouth fell open. "How long has he held you captive?"

"All my life."

The unapologetic heartlessness and tremoring rage he worked hard to restrain... it all made sense now. He truly was afraid and lashed out to survive. If that awful beast who cornered her in the hallway believed she would be quiet after learning this, he was sorely mistaken. Even if he was Matthieu's guardian, and her magic believed his heart was good, the very thought that this man had suffered all his life so cruelly set her pulse on fire.

"Do not let appearances deceive you, mademoiselle." The man held her eyes with a predatory stillness that shivered down her spine. "I'm the real monster."

"*Non*," she said, shaking her head. "He is a cursed démon, claimed by the Dark Saint."

"And what of those born cursed?" he spat, lowering his face to hers in what she knew was an intimidation tactic.

The sudden hostility startled her. Were these the emotions snapping sharp teeth to be set free?

"Those who celebrate when their family die," he seethed and her back stiffened, "even though they will never be free of their ghosts and will forever feel the injustice and shame of the violence shown them every fucking heartbeat of their godsdamn life?" He drew in a tremoring breath that pulsed against her skin. "Do you declare those souls whose lives were robbed from their first breath to be claimed by the Dark Saint too? Are they also worthy of society's scorn for a life they never chose?"

The blood quickly drained from her head and angry tears gathered along her lashes—furious over what he was insinuating. A tendril of magic touched his heart, one that felt eerily similar to the beast's. But this heart also felt wilder, more passionate, and ready to declare war.

"I would offer you my compassion," she said quietly, "but I know that is not what you want even if it is what you need."

"You know *nothing* about me. Don't insult us both by believing you do."

She refused to look away from his daggered glare. "Tell me, milord, why not choose to behave differently if you know you cause others the same pain inflicted upon you?"

"The démon curse, *my darling*, is that you become what grooms you." He stepped back and attempted to hide his anguish beneath a haughty smile. "Some monsters are made from birth and cursed to live without hope or redemption."

The misery darkening his eyes tore at her heart. How did one reply to such an enormity of pain? Factory Row was rife with empty, suffering souls. But this felt more personal between them, though she didn't understand why. Was it? It was abundantly clear that he resented her and for reasons she couldn't comprehend. Even more perplexing, horror was growing across his face and he blinked, drawing in a sharp breath, with a look bordering on both guilt and disgust. The words he retched, they were never meant for her, she realized. The shock was evident. He looked truly sick to his stomach. Before she could reply, he sharply turned on his heel and marched away, growling a guttural, furious scream while throwing the wine bottle at a tree while passing it by. Rhoslyn flinched at the loud shatter of glass.

Then he was gone. Lost to the forest's shadows.

She couldn't move, too overcome by the rawness of his confession. But she also couldn't let him go far. Not like this. What if this was the last dream they shared? The way he stormed off . . . those were the retreating steps of a confused, broken, terrified man.

What had happened to him since last night?

Did something happen to him earlier today?

Rhoslyn's disdain for that beast back in reality grew even more.

But she didn't know what to do. Saints, the agonized look on the man's face would haunt her.

Memories of her two older brothers fluttered to her mind. Her eldest displayed a temper whenever he felt cornered or failed his own expectations of perfection. Truly, he was a man possessed at times. Though never cruel. Those hot, burning emotions didn't dissolve with hearing logic or truth either, not while worked up at least, but by redirection into something more productive. This man in her dreams, the one held prisoner by the beast of Chateau Lumière Dorée, needed a purpose outside of emotionally surviving by lashing out.

And a dunk in cold water to cool his fire.

She smiled when remembering when she threw a bucket of water in her brother's face during one of his famous outbursts. He had gaped at her as if she had gone mad, then he started laughing—laughed until he wiped away tears—and pulled her into a hug to ensure she got wet too, laughing even more when she squealed.

A familiar ache throbbed heavy in her chest. She loved her two older brothers, her two older sisters too. The mischief they caused each other and their parents was never-ending. But so were the laughter and warm embraces. Pain gripped her heart until she wanted to double over and water the earth with her grief. But she set aside her tears to focus on another's.

Rhoslyn chased after the man, grateful for a shorter skirt that wouldn't drag on the ground or snag as easily onto sticks and thorns. The blue faerie wisps whirled around her while she ducked beneath branches and stepped over roots and rocks. She seemed to have walked for ages and still no sight of him. Had he woken up? Disappointment tightened the air in her chest at that thought. Disappointment and sorrow. But she pressed on. The crude trail meandered back to the pond and . . . her heart fluttered a wild beat. Then relief flooded her body with a myriad of dizzying emotions.

He stood on an old, mossy dock, his shirt sleeves now rolled up to his forearms. The breeze played with strands of his dark hair as he watched the wisps skip over the water. Then his body stiffened. Golden amber eyes snapped to hers and his lips parted.

He sensed her presence?

"Gods, you never back down, do you?"

Rhoslyn arched a brow and approached the dock. "*Non*, milord. We were not finished with our conversation."

"Mademoiselle, when a man leaves a conversation, he is done. We are not vapid, attention-seeking females who walk away solely to watch males grovel after us with apologies to compensate for a shallow sense of self-worth—"

She rested her finger on his lips and his entire body stilled. "Shhh. I was talking."

The inferno in his eyes, the hard, livid press of his lips beneath her finger screamed warnings for her to run—the first time she had ever felt real danger in his presence. Would he actually harm her? He blinked, long and languid, an attempt at calm. Then a slow, devilish smile flirted across his lips.

He grabbed her wrist and, before she could react, he sucked her offending finger into his mouth. Breath rushed from her lungs and he grinned, satisfied with her wide-eyed gasp. "Mmm," he moaned while gently biting down the tip of her finger. The low, gravelly sound shuddered down her body. A male had never kissed her before, especially not like this, and her heart thundered in her chest. Whispered reminders that she was married scratched at the back of her mind. He needed to stop. She needed to pull away. But she couldn't, not while his lips trailed down her hand, kissing her palm, then her wrist.

"What were you saying, my darling?" His eyes flitted to hers and he smiled against the skin of her arm.

Saints, she couldn't think when he looked at her like a man starved and she the meal he yearned to savor one slow, torturous bite at a time. But the dark glint in his gaze snapped her out of her lust-induced haze.

He was mocking her.

Every kiss, every smile.

After another whisper-soft kiss across her skin, however, she decided that, in the name of female dominance over the fairer sex and archaic arranged marriages, it was only courteous that she used him back to indulge in this pleasure. The sinful rush of him was too glorious not to.

"If you were anyone else, Rhoslyn Gautier," he said while softly taking her finger into his mouth once more and . . . Saints. Divine Mother. Slowly, so deliciously, achingly slow, he guided her hand across his lips, down his neck, murmuring, "I would have bitten off their finger."

Now she could be mad. Monsieur silk breeches was done with his demonstration.

Mustering up the most convincing scandalized scowl she could do, she yanked her arm from his hold. The satisfied smirk he shot her way only added to her delight. It was *darling* how clueless he was while attempting to frighten her. Flashing him a smug half-grin of her own, she placed her hands on his lower chest . . . and shoved. Hard.

Surprisingly, her petite frame was capable of unbalancing such a large man.

The whites of his eyes rounded right before he fell backward into the pond. The splash from impact sprayed water droplets over her dress. But she couldn't stop laughing long enough to truly care. The man shot up from the inky surface, shaking water from his hair, his face hard and eyes steeled.

And Rhoslyn was gutted in the absolute best way. "You look like a wet dog, *mon douce puce!*" she managed after several failed attempts from laughing so hard. "If you were anyone else, milord," she half-snorted, laughing too hard while trying to sound like him, "I would have—"

Her scream cut off her words.

Rhoslyn's body hit the water stiff, then folded as the air punched from her body. Panic coiled around her veins and she frantically clawed at the ribbon around her neck, holding down her hat. Releasing the tie, the choking pressure around her throat was instantly relieved. Blindly she reached out. Her hand found his arm as he pulled her up and she sputtered water onto his chest. The pretty ivory heeled shoes were lost to the pond along with her straw hat and she wrinkled her nose when her stockinged feet sank into the squishy sediment. Her dress. Her dreamy silk *polonaise* gown. Rhoslyn locked eyes with the man, ground her teeth, then splashed water in his face.

A grin was his reply—a wicked, delighted grin. He was so viciously beautiful. And that mouth, the one captivating her this very moment knew the taste of her skin. She was ready to float away across the water. But first she had to win whatever war this was. She didn't back down from challenges. Especially his.

He started to move toward the bank and she fisted his waistcoat and tried, terribly, to push him back under. He was too large and gravity was no longer on her side. That impish, boyish grin of his widened just as his hand dunked her head beneath the surface. She kicked him in the shins and he released her with a laugh. It wasn't a hard kick. Pathetic, really. Growling, she stalked after him in her sodden dress and jumped onto his back near the bank, in knee-deep water. Perhaps it was the weight of all the soggy layers of silk, or not expecting her to be so aggressive, but he toppled over. They both landed in the water, on their arses.

The sound of his genuine laughter rumbled through her chest. Deep, lush. Dark as a moonless winter night but also the pleasant playfulness of a warm summer breeze. And she had the humbling impression that he didn't openly laugh often or often enough in front of others. He rolled over onto his side, circling an arm around her waist, and propped his head up by his elbow, smiling. Water lapped against his body and dripped down his face.

"You are unbelievable," he said softly.

She was leaning back on her elbows, her chest desperately heaving for air as her skirts floated around them. "I do not know how many dreams we will share. But . . ." she reached out and caressed a wet strand of his hair in the water beside her, not helping her effort to catch her breath. "I will fight for you in each one, milord. To prove you are not a monster." The relaxed happiness disappeared into one of his familiar stern expressions, his brow now deeply furrowed and eyes guarded. To lighten the mood, she gave him a teasing smile. "*Oof*, or fight with you," she said with a flutter of a hand she poked up from the water. "Which we will probably do anyway."

Tightening his hold around her waist, he pushed up and leaned over her and, in such a way, she was forced to lower more onto her elbows and tilt her head back to meet his eyes. Dark strands of his hair fell in damp waves over her face. Beside them, faerie wisps danced around their partially submerged bodies and . . . she didn't want this heady magic building between them to end—marriage contracts be cursed! For if this man were even a fraction as passionate in love as he was in his anger, she would never want for anything else ever again.

His gaze caressed her face, drinking her in with every slow, appreciative sweep of his eyes. "Why?"

"This is how redemption begins."

"My darling," he whispered so softly her heart cracked. "Do *not* try to save me. You won't."

"I will find you," she rushed out. "When I wake, I will search for you and demand that horrible beast to release you from his prison."

"No." He gently shook his head. "Let me deal with him."

"But—"

"No." He swallowed and tried to smile. "Give me the pleasure of your obedience just this once."

The way he peered at her right now, in both dazed wonder and escalating fear, she could deny him nothing. Arching a brow, she lifted on her elbows to draw closer and whispered across his lips, "What is your name?"

But he never had a chance to answer.

Her eyes fluttered open and a sob tightened in her chest. The trickling, melodic falling water singing in her ears misted away to the roar of a hearth fire. The tip of her trembling finger pressed to her lips. The one he kissed.

Rhoslyn rolled to her back and stared at the black ceiling just as Matthieu snuggled deeper into her arms. She buried her face into his soft curls and kissed his head. Then the tears fell.

For the siblings lost to the bombs and fire.

For the parents who loved her as their own though she wasn't their kin.

For the man in her dreams who, if her magic was correct, experienced another fight for him for the first time in his life. And she would. She would fight for him and all others held prisoner by the many beasts of Gabaston.

. . . An awful roaring announced his arrival. Terror took possession of Beauty. But recovering herself in a moment, she suppressed her agitation. Seeing the Beast approach—whom she could not behold without a shudder—she advanced with a firm step.

"Yes, I protest to you . . . you and I are the only breathing creatures in this place." The Beast said no more, and departed more abruptly than usual . . . That charming youth existed only in her imaginations, she now looked upon this palace as a prison which would one day be her tomb.

Shortly afterward, she began to wander through the numerous apartments of the palace. She was enchanted with them, having never seen anything so beautiful. The first that she entered was a large cabinet of mirrors. She saw herself reflected on all sides. At length a bracelet, suspended to an ornate candlestick, caught her sight. With joyful haste, she put the bracelet on her arm, without reflecting whether this action was correct.

"La Belle et la Bête" by Madame de Villeneuve, published in *The Young American and Marine Tales*, 1743

CHAPTER 15

RHOSLYN

"But i don't want to leave." Matthieu plunked down on the settee and refused to take his cloak from her hand.

Rhoslyn sighed. "Monsieur Dalbréath is hopefully still waiting for us outside of the gates, *caneton*."

Matthieu crossed his arms over his chest and squinted his eyes. "Invite Monsieur Dalbrie inside, *ma sœur*. I will wait."

"Are you giving me orders?"

"*Oui*. I'm practically a grown male now." His lips pressed into a tight line. "And I have made the very important decision that we are staying."

Rhoslyn tossed his cloak onto the wingback chair and began pacing back and forth before the hearth fire. Flyaway strands had fallen from her unbound braid, tickling her cheek, and she blew the hair from her face before whirling toward her brother. "First, a male is not entitled to make decisions for a female simply because of her sex or his."

"You make decisions for me."

She closed her eyes and sighed—again. But all she could hear was the man in her dreams tease about male social oppression at the hands of clichéd, entitled females. And she wanted to push him into the pond at least two more times. Maybe ten. But her heart fluttered violently at the image of his wet clothing clinging to his body and how the damp strands of his hair had curtained around her face while leaning over her. Nine Saints, he was sinful. Perhaps she would push him in twenty more times, then—minimum.

Snapping her eyes open and back to reality, she quietly stepped over to

Matthieu and lowered onto her knees so they could be eye level. Those same strands of flyaway hair tickled her cheek once more with the movement and she resisted the urge to yank them out. Stars, this was turning out to be a long morning.

Softly, she drew in a fortifying breath and said, "You are nine and I am eighteen."

"Almost ten."

"Almost ten," she conceded. "But still not old enough to make *this* decision for us both. I *need* to speak with Monsieur Dalbréath. If he could access the chateau, he would have by now. And *you are* coming with me."

Anger darkened his face. The look was so unlike her sweet, mild-mannered brother, she stilled. "We have a roof and heat!" he shouted. "I have medicine!" A coughing spasm hit him from the excited volume of his voice. She reached for him but he dodged her hand and glared. "You don't have to work two jobs so I can eat! We don't have to run from wolves!" A tear squeezed past his eyes and slipped down his flushed cheek. "You won't have to worry about me so much," he said through more tears. "And . . . and, you can finally be happy."

"Oh, Matthieu . . ." She tried to tug him to her but he pushed her away and shoved his carved wolf talisman into her face.

"If you make me leave, I will summon our guardian."

She paused a beat. "You believe I want to leave the chateau permanently?"

His eyes narrowed farther and he wiped a tear from his cheek.

"*Non, mon petit caneton*. I do not wish to leave the chateau yet. We need new clothes and regular meals. We need rest." He slowly lowered the wolf in her face. "But we do need to *leave the chateau* to speak with Dalbréath and I will not *leave* you alone in this cursed house."

"The dark démon was kind to me, *ma sœur*."

"We cannot trust that he will be so again. Would you be comfortable if I were alone with him and you were not near to help me?"

She pushed back her brother's ever-present unruly blond lock from his eyes to keep from balling her hands into fists. How many others did that beast keep prisoner? Were she and Matthieu his next victims? If he had held the man in her dreams prisoner all his life, then that démon had no qualms with dungeoning children for his amusement. But they really did need new clothes and a few more meals in their bellies. They wouldn't last long in the wildness around Gabaston otherwise. It was just as dangerous, if not more so, to return to Factory Row, even though she longed to embrace Amélie, Josie, and Anette and ensure they were safe.

A selfish part of her also wanted to see the man in her dreams at least one more time too. If she were to endure the horror of marriage to a démon, she would indulge in every heart-blushing moment drowning in that mysterious man's wicked smiles, haunting golden amber eyes, and sharp wit.

"I'm sorry, Rosie." Matthieu's small shoulders drooped and he lowered his head.

"Matthieu Eric Gautier, do not ever apologize for standing up for yourself or demanding to be heard." She kissed his cheek. "Your needs and wants are valid too." A teasing smile inched up the corners of her mouth. "You will be a formidable opponent once Monsieur Dalbréath teaches you how to use a sword."

A twinkle brightened her brother's blue eyes and he flashed her a dimpled smile. "*Oui*, then I will go to Merenna."

"Oh?" she asked, playing along. "And what awaits you in Merenna?"

"Pirates." He slashed through the air with a pretend sword and Rhoslyn softly laughed.

"I will miss you terribly if you become a company man."

"Rosie," he said with an eye roll. "You are coming with me. How else will I be able to take care of you?"

Her heart melted into a pool of beautiful tears. A few days ago, he saw himself only as a lifelong burden. She would never be able to repay Dalbréath's kindness for making her brother believe he could one day protect her with a sword in hand. "Then," she said, kissing his other cheek, "I can continue to worry beside you instead of from afar."

He wiped away the kiss, but grinned. "See? We both win."

"*Oui*." She grinned back, blowing those saints cursed strands of hair from her face.

Perhaps the chateau had a brush and combs to hold her hair back too. Rhoslyn reached up to push back those irritating flyaway strands—*again*—and met resistance. *Divine Mother, what now?* Gently yanking at the wisps of hair, she felt the butcher's twine tug free from her bodice. A ring she had tucked into her corset and away from little blue eyes. Trying to appear natural, hoping her brother wouldn't notice, she continued untangling her hair from the butcher's twine, trying to palm the ring while doing so. She didn't want to explain anything to Matthieu, not yet. But she could see the various golds shine in the firelight.

Matthieu's gaze slipped down to the front of her dress and a wrinkle formed between his brows. "Where did you get that ring?"

The blood in her veins froze. Then bile coated her throat. She didn't know how to answer him. Outside, she had planned to give Matthieu a job, far enough away from the gate that he wouldn't hear her discuss these details with Dalbréath... But he would eventually hear. Either accidentally from her or from another. The cruelty wrapped around the weeping organ pounding painfully against her ribs, cruelty that she would break his heart over losing one more thing he held dear—blood kin. He truly had none.

Swallowing against the sharp knot in her throat, she whispered, "The ring is from Gedlen Fate Maker."

"Gedlen Fate Maker wants to marry you? He's real?" Her brother's eyes rounded. "Is this why Monsieur Dalbrie visited you at the dress factory?" A cough wheezed from his chest and Rhoslyn rubbed his back, frowning.

Normally the mention of that dark elf spun her pulse into a dizzying speed. But the nausea bubbling in her stomach was intensifying with every breath. "*Non*, the ring is not Prince Gedlen's promise. But another's."

His eyes rounded even more. "You are to be married? *To a prince?*"

"I am not sure of his class or title." The ache in her chest tightened even more. "Matthieu... Monsieur Dalbréath is my uncle."

"We have family..." The words were barely a whisper and Rhoslyn wanted to build walls around her brother to protect him from the hope burning in his eyes. "A warrior family in Dúnælven." His brows pinched together. "Why did Père and Maman never talk about Uncle Dalbrie?"

She tried to draw in air, but the burning pain in her constricting lungs was too much. "I... I don't know how to share this with you."

Matthieu took one of her hands in his and rubbed her back with his other, like how she had comforted him during his breathing spell moments earlier. "I am nearly a male grown," he said with childlike confidence. "We are strong together, Rhoslyn Mae Gautier."

Tears sprang to her eyes. He rarely used her full given name. This child. This dear, sweet boy. The hearth fire reflected in his eyes and shadows from flickering candlelight danced across his face. And, for a moment, she glimpsed the male grown he would become—unwaveringly loyal, compassionate, tender but unbreakable, sensitive enough to feel the coming storms and strong enough to weather them all. One whose heart loved deeper than the Ærin Sea.

"I survived a wolf attack a few years ago and you survived a démon," he continued, his voice strained as he tried to hold back another wheezy cough. "We survived the war, the fire, losing our family, and Factory Row. We survived Queen Adeline." He leaned in and kissed her cheek as she had him. "My leg is weak. My lungs too. But I am stronger than you think, *ma sœur*. Even if I never make it to Merenna and instead sit by the alleys like the beggar man." He paused to catch his breath, then softly added, "You can tell me anything."

Tears rolled down her cheeks. "I love you to the top of the sky and back, Matthieu Eric."

"I love you to the bottom of the sea and back, Rosie Mae." His dimpled smile was nearly her undoing.

She drew in a trembling breath and sniffed back more tears, then squeezed his hand. "Prince Gedlen said I was a . . . a changeling child."

Matthieu's mouth fell open and his eyes, once more, grew owlish. "Like a faerie story?"

"He called me changeling child of thorns."

"Because your name means beautiful rose?"

"And," she continued before she lost her nerve, "that my birth parents, whoever they may be, wedded me to a démon when I was an infant and . . . and sealed our marriage contract in their faerie blood, as well as with mine and my husband's. Gedlen Fate Maker gave me this ring with the warning that I would meet him soon and that he couldn't prevent this future."

The blood visibly drained from Matthieu's face, but not from fear. The anger in his eyes was startling. "They married you *to a démon?*"

"This is what I wish to talk to Monsieur Dalbréath about."

Matthieu nodded his head, as if he had a few words he wished to speak to Dalbréath about too. "Then let us go, so I can begin my sword lessons to protect you."

"You . . . you are not upset that we are not blood kin?"

A bittersweet smile softened his lips, one that simultaneously broke her heart and pieced it back together. "You *still* worry too much, *ma sœur*."

My sister. Those two words branded her soul and a sad smile of her own pushed through the tears.

Before she could properly reply, fury returned to his sweet, boyish face. "I will find a way to take care of you so you don't have to remain married to a démon."

Rhoslyn grabbed her brother and crushed him to her. "You are my heart and joy," she whispered into his hair. "Nothing will ever change that. No matter what we learn today, remember this. You forever belong to me and I to you."

"To the bottom of the sea and back."

"To the top of the sky and back."

Matthieu leaned away and took her hand. "Let's go find Uncle Dalbrie."

The hallway swallowed their slow-moving forms, allowing her to truly study the chateau for the first time. Wallpaper of trees with birds framed in by, what was once, undoubtedly, elaborate gilded trim lined the walls. The print was faint in black, but still lovely in the amber candlelight. Above their heads, elegant crown molding lined the ceilings in delicate filigree designed flower vases and leaf scrolls.

A strange tear in the beautiful paper, beginning where they now walked, caught her eye. Three tears parallel to each other, as if from claws. The rips appeared to continue to the grand entry. Rhoslyn peered in the other direction and noticed the same set of tears on the opposite wall. Was the beast given to outburst often? A shudder wended down her spine.

It took them a few minutes to reach the chandelier lit entry. Every five or so yards her brother needed to rest—his lungs were still weak. But he was determined to walk out of the House of the Golden Light himself.

After living in darkness for nearly two days, the brightness of the garden and gray clouds burned her vision. She sank into the shadows of her hood and shielded her eyes with a hand to hunt for any moving objects. When all seemed quiet, she crouched low, kneeling one knee onto the gold-veined marble entry. Matthieu climbed onto her back and she scooped him up from under his knees, then made her way through the brambling dark burgundy roses.

And, with every step forward, fear gripped her heart.

What if a démon prowled over the stone walls?

What if bounty hunters had camped outside of the gates?

What if Dalbréath no longer waited for them?

What if that invisible wall was still in place and no one else could enter?

What if the enchantment of Chateau Lumière Dorée prevented them from leaving?

The what-ifs were endless, per usual. But it was the last one that had continued to simmer in the back of her mind and now demanded her fullest attention. And the answer terrified her, because she knew. If the man in her dreams was trapped by the beast, then the Dark Saint's magic enchanting the house worked entirely for that démon and did his bidding.

"Fire," Matthieu whispered in horror.

Rhoslyn turned toward Gabaston. Black smoke curled over the forest in the direction of Factory Row. Were they under attack? Clifstán had demilitarized, so she had last heard. Did another realm attack them while they were still weak? Without another thought, she dashed toward the gates. She needed to reach her friends. Had to know if they were safe—alive.

Familiar images tormented her mind.

Beams and walls of fire crumbled before her parents as they shouted her name. The uppermost floor where her siblings and their families slept had already crashed to the other living quarters below. Renold, the brother just one and half years older than her, she and Matthieu had made it outside with coats, cloaks, and shoes. All round them, the world burned and families cried out the names of their loved ones while running for cover. Terrifying machines in the shape of spiders and beetles, that could walk and shoot bullets, moved down Factory Row and shot at the panicking bystanders. Renold, in his grief, ran back into the shop to help any family he could find before the building collapsed. And then it did. In a burst of twinkling embers and whoosh of flames. Leaving her and Matthieu alone. Screams keened from the marrow of her bones, from a severing in her soul. Screams that burned her lungs and scorched her throat.

Rhoslyn wanted to curl up in the street and sob and scream until she passed out. But they needed to hide from the machines and invading soldiers. She had run all the way to Crowns Quarter, her little brother on her back, and hid them in a gated garden attached to a large home of an aristocrat, where they remained for several days. Falling in and out of consciousness from inhaling too much smoke. When awake, she chewed up leaves and herbs in the garden for the burns on her brother's leg and held him while he wheezed for air and writhed from pain. Three days later, they returned to Factory Row, to the ash remains of their home and family.

And Rhoslyn knew two things in that moment: she refused to become the victim of a tyrannical crown ever again and she would ensure her brother's every happiness.

The images finally released her mind and she gulped for much-needed air.

Was this her fault? Was it because she stood up to Queen Adeline?

A form moved into view and she nearly cried out in relief. Dalbréath's blue eyes were wild as he took her in, wilder than the disheveled white hair fluttering in the breeze. Another storm was approaching—and fast. Hopefully, the rains would douse the fires.

"Are you hurt? Has he harmed you?" The words ended on a growl and every muscle in his face and neck flexed in rage. "The magic refuses me entry. I swear to the gods I will bring down the sky and shove it up her arse if you can't leave."

She halted before the opened wrought iron gates and tried to pass through but met the invisible wall.

No, no, no!

Touching her head where she met solid air, she choked out, "The fire..."

Dalbréath peered over his shoulder then back to her.

Terror crawled beneath her skin. They were trapped. Factory Row was on fire and she couldn't save her friends, just like she couldn't save her family. And more images returned to haunt her mind.

After hours of laughing, she, Matthieu, and Renold had fallen asleep by the shop's fireplace while playing jeu de l'oie—game of the goose—a board game Père surprised their family with after a week of steady chapbook orders. Matthieu should have been tucked away in his bed, but he had curled up in Renold's lap and fallen asleep, holding onto a game piece. A little snuggle bug from the moment he was born and Renold his favorite pair of arms. For hours she and her older brother had rolled dice and moved their marker around the spiral in a race to the final square. They hadn't smelled the smoke at first or heard the crackling flames having fallen asleep beside the fireplace. Not until their names formed screams and they awoke to blistering walls of fire.

The gutted fear in Dalbréath's eyes pulled her back from the horror replaying in her mind. The white-hot fury in the clench of his jaw matched her own, she was sure of it. Rhoslyn slid her brother to the ground, then grimaced back the sob crushing her lungs. If she lost another she loved, especially to fire . . .

"My friends," she pleaded. "Amélie!"

"I will check on your friends," Dalbréath said softly. "And ensure they are safe."

Matthieu pressed his face into her dress and circled his arms around her waist. Squeezing him to her with one arm, she wiped at the hot tears on her cheeks and asked, "Are we under attack?"

"No," Dalbréath replied simply. "I didn't want to leave to investigate in case you left the chateau. But Aurelienne is not under attack."

"It's my fault," she cried out. "People will die this day because of me!"

"Little thorn . . ." Dalbréath sighed, long and slow. "We don't know what is going on. But *nothing* about this is your fault. Queen Adeline declared war on Factory Row by denying affordable access to food and then, yesterday, demanding higher taxes."

The blushing scent of roses wrapped around her in the breeze and she hiccuped back more tears. The hood of her cloak fluttered in the wind and she pulled the burgundy wool tighter around her. "Why can't we leave?"

"I knew Chateau Lumière Dorée was cursed to the grave, but not this," Dalbréath answered. "The souls didn't share this with Gellynor."

"You knew the chateau was cursed?" she shot back. "And you didn't think to warn us first?"

"The instructions were shelter. Sleep. Eat. In that order. Everything else could wait." His voice settled into an angry calm that only stoked the simmering rage in her nauseated gut even more. "Gods, Rhoslyn, you were so weak from hunger and physical exhaustion; I thought I was going to have to carry both you and Matthieu Never crossed my mind that you would go inside the gates. Or that you had the strength to. Or that you would be trapped inside if you did. I didn't want to leave you either. But you needed to eat."

Rhoslyn threw her hands into the air. "It was raining—"

Matthieu interrupted her. "Our guardian protected us, Uncle Dalbrie."

The elf's eyes slid to Matthieu and stilled. "Little warrior duckling," he said softly while lowering to kneel before her brother. Dalbréath noticeably swallowed, then lifted a smile so tender it made her heart clench. "He protected you, nephew?"

Nephew . . .

Their eyes touched over Matthieu's head and an entire ocean of emotions swam in Dalbréath's gaze. This was her uncle. The very first blood kin she had ever known. Had he really been searching for her since the attack on Gabaston? Betrayal knifed her chest over and over and over again every time she thought of his family. But she knew with every beat of her heart that he truly would bring down the sky for her and her brother.

"It was raining and we were going to take shelter in the gazebo." Matthieu pointed to the very one behind us, his finger barely visible beneath the droopy folds of his large cloak. "A démon came from the woods over there"—he pointed to the right of the gates with a small cough—"and tried to attack us. Rosie picked me up and ran toward the door. But the wolf couldn't get past this wall"—he flattened his hand onto the invisible magic—"Our guardian fought and protected us."

Dalbréath pressed his hand to the invisible wall before Matthieu's. "Are you afraid?"

"*Non*, Uncle Dalbrie." Matthieu looked up at Rhoslyn for a fleeting moment—blond curls adorably poking out from his hood—then back to Dalbréath. "The dark démon is kind. He told me he was sorry that I must suffer the curse too and put a pillow under my head when I was too weak to sit up."

Rhoslyn furrowed her brow.

She forgot to ask her brother about his conversation with the beast. Why would the démon apologize if he wanted them trapped? The man in the hallway was anything but kind. Perhaps he was playing with his prey first. But her brother spoke true about the blankets and pillows. Nor was he in distress about meeting the démon when she had returned. And her magic insisted his heart was good. Saints, he was confusing.

"Rosie was making me medicated vapors," Matthieu added. "We have medicine here, Uncle Dalbrie. We didn't when living in the rubbled cottages."

"Still, I will break you free," Dalbréath said to her brother, but she knew the words were really for her. "After I check on Rhoslyn's friends, I must go to Leaf Curl and speak to Gellynor Death Talker."

Matthieu let out an excited gasp. "She can talk to ghosts?"

Dalbréath tilted his head, a humored smile inching his mouth up on one side. "Aye, she is a rune walker. You'll have to ask her to share ghost stories when you meet her."

Her brother peered up, his blue eyes sparkling with excitement, and she couldn't help but smile back despite the fear still gripping her every breath and tremoring down her limbs.

"Rhoslyn," Dalbréath said while standing back up. "Find a hand mirror and keep it by your side."

She arched a brow. "Do you plan to explain why or is that an instruction I must await, *Uncle Dalbrie?*"

"The mirror, *little thorn*, is for Gellynor to reach you. As a rune walker, she can move through dimensions, such as mirror worlds."

"Mirror worlds . . ." Her brother's eyes lit up again. But only for a blink of an eye. That dimpled smile of his dipped into a frown. "Is it true that Rosie Mae is married to a démon?"

Dalbréath's gaze shot to hers, and when she nodded, he softly answered, "Aye, it's true."

"She's married against her will." Anger sparked in her brother's eyes, and he took her hand in his and squeezed. "Teach me to use a sword. I will protect my sister."

"I will, warrior duckling. When I return." That tender smile softened his mouth once more. "You will be a remarkable swordsman when we are through."

"Who is he?" Rhoslyn blurted. "Who is my husband?"

"Are you sure you are ready to know now?"

Rhoslyn ground her teeth. "If I am trapped here, then I want to know who my démon husband is. The beast of Chateau Lumière Dorée may know him. He might release me, if he does."

That muscle along Dalbréath's jaw jumped again and he peered into the forest, seeming to struggle. Then, he drew in a slow breath and faced her, fear pooling in his bright blue eyes. "Rhoslyn, he *is*—" Dalbréath's entire body froze. His throat worked, then his teeth ground together. "The magic," he gritted out in a low growl, "has silenced me."

The chateau wished to hide the identity of her husband? To test her fear, she asked, "Is he nobility?"

Once more, Dalbréath tried to answer, his entire body unnaturally still, but words wouldn't come.

Rhoslyn blanched. "Is . . . is it the beast of Chateau Lumière Dorée?"

Her uncle attempted to answer once more and, yet again, he was prevented from replying. And she had the horrifying realization that he couldn't even nod his head, indicate an answer with facial expressions or hand gestures.

That wildness in his eyes, the one she saw when first approaching, returned. "She will not survive me."

Rhoslyn blinked back the confusion. *She?* This was not the doing of the chateau's beast?

New fingers of fear wrapped around her tightening throat. She pressed her forehead to the magic wall and whispered, "Dalbréath, who am I?"

Their eyes locked. Anger was rolling off him in thunderous waves. "There are wolf ears all over these woods. I was foolish to talk so freely with you the night of the march. I can't risk putting you in more danger."

"Can't you whisper a space around us like at the dress factory?"

"No," Dalbréath sighed and leaned on his longbow. "I would need to physically touch people to do that and you are not within my reach. Gellynor or Gedlen could create a shield without physical connection. But I don't have that level of spell weaving skills."

"Tell me something. Please."

The tension in his shoulders slumped, then nodded. "I held you in my arms for weeks." Sorrow pulled at his lips as he rested his forehead to the invisible wall opposite of her. "Whenever you cried, my heart cried too." Grief strained his voice. "You, Rhoslyn, were my little thorn—"

His head snapped toward the overgrown path leading to Factory Row, eyes narrowed. Then, in lightning quick movements, he slid an arrow from the quiver at his hip and spun toward a part of the wall she couldn't see, his longbow poised to shoot. The unexpected, graceful choreography of his body in sharp motion startled her back a step. "Reveal yourself, slowly."

Chapter 16

Rhoslyn

"I mean no harm, monsieur."

"Who are you?" Dalbréath demanded, every muscle in his body taut, his eyes sharp.

"Lucas Fontine, a lowly street vendor."

"And what brings a lowly street vendor to the House of Golden Light?"

The man in question moved into view, his strides like the soft, lazy ripples across a still lake, and caught Rhoslyn's eye. He was young, perhaps in his early- to mid-twenties, with long blond hair pulled back at the nape of his neck, a few loose strands framing his face, rough spun clothing, and mesmerizing dark blue eyes. Lucas slowed before Dalbréath, allowing the point of the arrow to dig into his chest, his hands up at head level.

The man, still holding her gaze, offered a handsome smile and dipped his head. "I wish to speak with *le rebelle sans-culotte* Rhoslyn Gautier."

The commoner's rebel?

"Do not try anything clever, démon." Dalbréath's voice was quiet but the threat was loud.

"Alpha of Clan Palehide in Factory Row and guardian officer in the Brotherhood, elf. Not just any démon."

"You know her protector then, lowly street vendor?"

"*Oui*," the man answered with a charming smile. "I do not fear his bite. Or your arrow."

"Démon?" Rhoslyn took a step back, her eyes wide.

"Mademoiselle, it is a great honor to stand in your presence." He lowered his head again in a bow. "Factory Row—"

"You are a démon?"

Dark blue eyes searched her face for a rapid beat of her pulse. "We are not all the monsters found in children's bedtime stories. Those tales are about the rabid moon-addled wolves. You have lived among démons your whole life."

Matthieu stepped closer to the wall and Rhoslyn resisted the urge to yank him back. "You look just like a normal man."

Lucas laughed. "I am a normal man." His gaze slid back to Rhoslyn, that charming smile teasing her once more. "With enhancements."

Dalbréath rolled his eyes on a loud, dramatic groan. "Let me shoot him, little thorn."

Lucas's grin turned wolfish and the hairs on Rhoslyn's arms stood on end.

"But how could you be normal if you serve Saint Cernunnos?" Matthieu frowned, then coughed into his sleeve.

Divine Mother, this child never stopped asking questions. He stood before an alpha démon. A démon who spoke to them with intelligence and human emotion. How much more dangerous could these monsters get? Yet her brother didn't seem afraid. Unlike Rhoslyn, whose pulse thundered in her ears, drowning out the rattle of leaves in the wind and the light plop of raindrops on marble. Lucas watched her closely, too closely, as if stalking her in the woods.

"I was born a wolf, from a long line of alphas." Thunder rumbled overhead, but Lucas held her eyes, not a muscle moving in his body. "Most wolves are born, not made."

Matthieu nodded his head as if that made complete sense. It made absolutely no sense to Rhoslyn. Another wheezy cough sounded from her brother's little body. The strain of standing and walking was beginning to pinch his expression too.

"Let me help you sit, *caneton*." He didn't argue when she helped him lower before her, to use her legs to lean against. "If you need to go inside, do not be silent. I already spoke with Uncle Dalbrie." Matthieu smiled weakly at her, but he didn't say anything further and she knew he was too fascinated by the démon. And ghosts and anything haunted or monstrous. Were all little boys like this? Or just her ever curious brother?

Rhoslyn's gaze flicked to the black smoke above the tree line, then back to Lucas. "Speak, Monsieur Fontine. Do you come with news of the fire?"

"*Oui*. Factory Row needs you, Mademoiselle Gautier." Those dark blue eyes of his traveled over the ripped, black clothing peeking out from her cloak, then Matthieu's. "Palace guards line the streets since the march and have attacked innocents in regular displays of dominance. The tension finally snapped this morning after a guard beat an eleven-year-old boy. People rioted, turning over vendor carts and stealing the food under the protection of Palais d'Aurélie. Guards shot people running in the streets—"

"Saints," she gasped. "Did the guards set fire to a building or the rioters?"

Lucas dipped his head and lowered his eyes. "The guards set fire to the dress factory you worked at."

Rhoslyn clapped a hand over her mouth as furious tears burned behind her eyes. "Amélie..."

"Amélie is safe, mademoiselle. I knew she was important to you and ensured her safety first."

"How... do you know Amélie is my friend?"

"There is little that passes my notice on Factory Row."

"You watched me?"

"I have noticed you, *oui*." He tilted his head. "You do not carry the same scent as other lowly elves nor the scent of your family." His gaze first touched on Matthieu then cut to Dalbréath. "It is similar to his, though. A Dúnælven warrior."

Rhoslyn squared her shoulders and lifted her chin. "A dog following a scent trail, for what exactly, monsieur?"

That charming smile returned. "Perhaps I simply enjoy yours."

"Please, little thorn," Dalbréath said on another loud, dramatic groan, "I really want to shoot him."

She ignored her uncle. "The other grisettes?"

"All safe and the fire is contained. The only casualty is Monsieur LeMont." Lucas's smile crept wider. "My men could not save him."

At first, she felt relief. He was truly a despicable, depraved man. And then a thought hit her. "Was he a wolf?"

"A son of a bitch from West Pack." He lifted a shoulder in a nonchalant shrug.

Rhoslyn peered over his head to the smoke once more and anger vibrated in every part of her body. A smattering of raindrops plopped onto her cloak and she lifted her face to feel the light shower on her skin, but nothing would ever cool the fury burning in her except justice.

"Those girls now have no income and will be turned out to the streets," she gritted out. And everyone knew what happened to girls with no jobs. The hands at her sides curled into fists and she bared her teeth. "Is she punishing females for interrupting her feast to demand bread?" She sucked in a sharp breath. "*Non*, she is punishing me."

"I very much think she was hoping to smoke you out of hiding. And punish you, *oui*."

Her mouth fell open. "Are you saying the palace guards planned to light the dress factory on fire this day? Even without a riot?"

"They were prepared and organized, mademoiselle. It would seem so. The Factory Row guards appeared surprised by their actions."

The ties of her cloak had loosened in the breeze and she suddenly felt indecently exposed despite her many layers. Lucas studied her face with predatory stillness before resting on the butcher string around her neck and tucked into her bodice. Charm still tilted his lips, but it seemed a cover. Almost as if he were using an appearance of flirtation to catalogue details. And he was very handsome. Shifting on his feet, his gaze flitted back to hers.

"Are you willing to stand up to Queen Adeline for Factory Row again?" he asked her.

Rhoslyn shook her head. "Chateau Lumière Dorée is cursed."

"I noticed." He gestured to her clothing. "But not your cloak. Why is that, do you think?" When she didn't answer him, Lucas opened his mouth to speak and stilled. Like Dalbréath, she could see his throat work, but no words emerged. "I cannot say his name," he said in a shocked whisper. "Or title." That penetrating dark blue gaze studied the House of Golden Light. "But I could in the woods just beyond the property and also on The Row when he, too, wore only black." He swung his attention back to her. "You do not know who the master of Chateau Lumière Dorée is, do you?"

"*Non*, he did not introduce himself. But I know by his eyes that he is Chalamet."

"But you have spoken?"

"*Oui*, only for him to remind me that my place is to beg for food, remain silent, and to stay out of his way."

Dalbréath's face darkened with fury but Lucas burst into laughter. "Please tell me, mademoiselle, that you gave him the same treatment as our gracious Queen Adeline."

"No one will silence me or tell me my worth. Or prevent me from protecting and caring for my brother. *Especially* a Chalamet."

"*Bien.*" Lucas nodded. "And this is why Factory Row chooses you"—he eyed Dalbréath, a smug smile on his lips, and added—"little thorn."

"Rhoslyn," Dalbréath gritted out, raising his bow an inch higher. "I haven't wanted to shoot someone this badly since this morning . . ."

"*Uncle Dalbrie,*" Rhoslyn tossed out with a wave of her hand. "Be *kind*. Lower your bow. I am sure you will find another you want to shoot even more so this afternoon."

Dalbréath lowered his bow but not without a goading grin directed at Lucas, one that invited him to strike first. Then, sliding his gaze her way, he muttered, "This adds to the pains in my lower half, *Rosie.*"

Matthieu's face scrunched up. "You have pains in your lower half? Are you injured?"

Despite the monster before her and the fury boiling her blood, Rhoslyn threw her head back and laughed. The hood of her cloak slipped off her head, but she didn't care. The light sprinkles felt refreshing. Dalbréath's eyes twinkled with mischief and, when Matthieu turned to peer up at her, he shot her a rude gesture, making her laugh even more.

"I am well, lad," he eventually said to Matthieu. "Only a joke between me and your sister."

When she eventually calmed, she turned back to Lucas who eyed her with the same charming smile, his gaze roaming over her hair and fully exposed face. "You are a rare beauty, Mademoiselle Gautier, well-spoken and intelligent. He would be a fool not to have claimed you."

Claimed her? A blush warmed her cheeks under his compliments and she turned her head toward the garden to gather herself. But she couldn't shake what he insinuated and curled her fingers into fists once more.

"I am not *his property* to claim," she spat with a slitted glare at the démon. "He is kind to my brother but not me. And if he so much as growls my way again, I will make good on my promise to end him."

Lucas's eyebrows shot up and that charming smile he pretended to have transformed into a delighted smirk. "I am sure he would enjoy for you to try, mademoiselle."

She ignored him. "Nor can I help Factory Row. I am stuck behind these walls, Monsieur Fontine." Her hand fluttered angrily in the air. "Part of the curse."

"Perfect."

Her mouth fell open. "You are pleased that I am a prisoner of Chateau Lumière Dorée? Of that horrible beast who dares claim me?"

"No one can touch you." He lowered his voice. "You are safe to lead the people of Factory Row. They will not need to fear that their leader will fall to the guillotine. And with you safe behind these walls, your horrible beast can focus on other duties for the clans. He will not have time to growl in your direction."

"Factory Row's leader?"

"*Oui.*" He dipped his head and lowered to one knee. "Queen of The Row."

"A queen..." Matthieu whispered in awe.

"You are mistaken, Monsieur Fontine." She shook her head. "I am the daughter of a poor merchant and a grisette. My grief took over the night of the protest—"

"Rhoslyn Gautier, your instinct is to fight for and protect the people, to stand up for the underdogs. What we wolves call a den mother." Lucas rose to his feet and stepped closer to the wall. "I was there that night, in complete awe of your courage and strength. You stood before Aurelienne's queen with a crown on your head. One you do not see, but we do."

"I am sorry, Monsieur Fontine—"

"And you are educated, a rarity on Factory Row, especially among females," he said in the language of the saints.

Matthieu peered up at her, pride in his blue eyes. "Père taught us many subjects. Rosie loved to learn," he replied in Aurelienne's second tongue. "She was teaching me and two other boys in the foundling home to read in both languages whenever she visited."

"*Oui*, a den mother." Lucas's gaze grew intense, a strange glint in his eyes. "A queen among common folk."

Dalbréath's body went rigid. Then his hand casually rested on the pommel of his sword. But he refused to peer in her direction, even though she knew he felt her eyes on him. That telling muscle along his jaw pulsed and fresh wings of fear beat in her stomach. Did Lucas know she was a changeling child? That her birth parents were aristocrats? Noting her intensity, the démon's gaze nonchalantly floated over to Dalbréath, a soft crease between his brows, then snapped his enthralling eyes back to hers.

You do not carry the same scent as other lowly elves nor the scent of your family. It is similar to his, though. A Dúnælven warrior.

The sprinkling rain let up, but another loud clap of thunder rumbled overhead. A gust of wind fluttered her cloak and, once more, wrapped the delicate scent of roses around her. The sweet but heady rush of a girl standing before a handsome boy. Absently, her fingers found the ring tucked beneath her bodice and she drew in a shaky breath. Who was her husband? Was he from the House of Chalamet? She peered at Chateau Lumière Dorée over her shoulder, an unsettling feeling racing through her veins.

You are wed by faerie blood to a midnight beauty that is ugly and a sunrise ugliness that could become beautiful. But some wolves are too wild to tame. Some are too wounded to save. And some, like your mate, fight inner demons to break generational curses.

Rhoslyn twisted back to face the invisible wall. "What are you saying, Monsieur Fontine? Speak plainly."

"The right to rule does not make you a queen worthy of your people. *Non*, a monarch is subject to her citizens." Lucas's smile grew wolfish once more as he took another step toward the wall. "Is that not what you said to Queen Adeline, mademoiselle? Factory Row heard your words and has chosen their queen."

Rhoslyn slowly turned to Dalbréath, who worked hard to keep his face neutral. But he didn't have to say a single word. She knew. Gedlen Fate Maker didn't weave fates for poor grisettes.

"Does the beast know you seek my help?" she asked the démon, surprised she was able to hide the shake in her voice.

"*Non*, it is better if he doesn't." Lucas winked. "For now."

Dampening flyaway strands of hair blew across her face. "Will not telling him we spoke endanger our lives?"

"He will assert his dominance over me. A bite I can handle, mademoiselle.

Do not worry. For you, your beast is all bark," Lucas said, that flirtatious smile directed at her again. "If he bites you, it won't be for anger."

Heat flamed across her cheeks at the mention of being marked in a mate claiming.

Matthieu peered up at her, his eyes large. "Why else would he bite you, *ma sœur?*"

A snort sputtered from Dalbréath, who turned around to hide his amusement. She shot a glare in his direction, which made him laugh more.

Rhoslyn huffed. "*Oof!* You may shoot him now, Uncle Dalbrie."

A pleased laugh rumbled from Lucas, a sound that erupted goosebumps across her skin.

"Rosie?" Matthieu pressed his lips together, anger sparking in his blue eyes. "Will he bite you?"

"*Non, caneton.* He will not lay a single paw on me if he wants to live."

To further hide her embarrassment, she leveled a cool glare at the démon and redirected the conversation. "Protect the girls who lost their jobs today, Monsieur Fontine. Do not let men take advantage of their hardship. Find families to take them in and, if you have sway, new jobs."

Lucas dipped his head. "I will do my best, but that is a large request. Anything else, Queen of The Row?"

"*Oui,*" Rhoslyn said, an idea forming through the fury lacing every breath. "If Queen Adeline is willing to destroy an entire factory to punish a single grisette, then let us remind her that she and all other silk breeches do not control industry. We do."

"What do you have in mind?"

"A strike."

His eyebrows shot up. "For how long?"

She bared her canines. "We paid in blood to protect a Chalamet throne. We will not sacrifice more lives for a Chalamet queen who abandons her people. If The Row agrees, then no more food will be delivered to Palais d'Aurélie. No one will work until she sells her golden throne to pay her own debts. And," she spat in her building fury, "let Factory Row eat like the aristocracy while the nobles starve. I want her to beg for bread."

"You are declaring war on the entire House of Chalamet," Dalbréath interjected.

Lucas dipped his head at Dalbréath. "Your Uncle Dalbrie is right. We will need time to plan a defense for a people with weakened bodies and few weapons."

"Aye, palace guards *will* attack," Dalbréath continued. "She might even gather former soldiers sympathetic to her crown. Are you prepared to deal with losses, little thorn? People *will* die."

Those last three words cooled her rage and she pressed a hand to her sickening stomach. What else could they do, though? Queen Adeline already proved that she would not give up her throne without war, same as her father and her grandfather. And she mocked those dying of hunger and blamed common folk for their poverty. The people may pay in blood again, but this time they would be fighting for themselves and their families . . . instead of hers.

"*We* would be declaring war, not I," she corrected. "*Non*, I will not force this decision on Factory Row. It is theirs to make and make alone. And our collective losses to bear together." Dalbréath opened his mouth but she lifted a hand. "People are already dying of hunger. If they choose to fight, let them die empowered and with dignity instead of being used and cast aside."

"I envy your horrible beast," Lucas said softly, no false charm present. "May he appreciate what he believes belongs to him." A mischievous glimmer returned to his dark blue gaze. "If he does not, I will comfort mademoiselle."

Rhoslyn rolled her eyes. "You are shameless, Monsieur Fontine."

"*Oui*." His smile widened. With a dip of his head, he turned to Dalbréath and held out his hand. "We both serve the same queen, monsieur. Let us shake hands in understanding. You will not shoot me with your arrow and I will not rip your throat out with my teeth."

Dalbréath chuckled, a friendly sound, and grabbed Lucas's hand. Then he yanked the démon to him. Lucas growled, his eyes flashing as he pushed away, his hands now claws, but Dalbréath was quicker. In a single blink, blue light crackled from his fingertips onto the temple of Lucas's head as he whispered into the man's ear. Flashing a fanged grin, one dripping in smug, male satisfaction, Dalbréath released Lucas and stepped away.

"Now go," he commanded. "Hunters are in the forest."

Lucas replied with a loud, bleating sound, before bounding away in long leaps toward Gabaston. What in the Nine Saints was wrong with that man?

The toe of his shoe would touch the ground only long enough to soar over the grass and wildflowers to land on the other.

"Run faster!" Dalbréath swiped an arrow from his quiver, lifted his bow, and shot at the soil by Lucas's feet.

The démon stilled, eyes wide. Then he was off, gracefully vaulting into the woods in airy steps.

"I feel a little happier now," Dalbréath said on a wistful sigh.

Merde, her heart was in her throat. That man began to shift! The sight of his sudden claws, the angry way his eyes flashed, how his canines elongated and snapped at Dalbréath . . . Rhoslyn was on the verge of fainting. For a spell, she had forgotten that beneath all his charm, handsome smiles, and hypnotic dark blue eyes was a real monster. How did she forget? Was that part of his predatory nature? To make girls forget he was a creature of nightmares?

"What did you do?" Matthieu asked.

"Rune whispered his mind to believe he was a deer for a candlemark."

Matthieu's mouth fell open. "You can glamour minds?"

"As I told your sister," he replied with a canined grin, "I am not only *kind* on the eyes, but the *kind* of hero chronicled in songs. A military commander unparalleled in fae *kind*—"

"*Kind* of an arse," Rhoslyn said, biting back a laugh.

"Especially that last one."

The rain picked up, large drops that splattered audibly onto the marble. "We must return before Matthieu gets soaked." Rhoslyn pulled her hood back over her head. "He is still not fully well."

Dalbréath nodded his head and knelt before her brother once more. "Take care of your sister for me until I return, warrior duckling."

"I will protect the Queen of The Row."

"Aye, I know you will, lad. She needs you." Rising to his feet, his eyes found hers. Once more, an entire ocean of emotions stormed in his gaze. "Find a hand mirror and keep it with you as reasonably possible. Do not let the beast of Chateau Lumière Dorée push you around. And do not speak to Lucas Fontine alone, if it can be helped. I will return in two to three weeks with Gellynor. Possibly Gedlen too." He pressed a hand to his chest, his mouth softening into the sweetest smile—one tinged with grief. "My heart still cries when you do, my wee thorn."

She returned the bittersweet smile. "Safe travels, Uncle."

They held each other's gaze another beat, then he turned and moved toward the woods, bow in hand.

Rhoslyn wanted to watch until he disappeared, but she didn't want to be soaked through again. "Ready, *mon petit caneton?*"

Kneeling down, Matthieu climbed onto her back and shouted, "Time to swim!"

She wasted no time and jogged to the entry door, kicking it shut behind them with her shoe.

BLACK COFFINED THEM, despite the candelabras, and she paused to let her eyes adjust. The heaviness of this house joined the weariness in her bones. A brittle feeling she could touch, as if the next breath may shatter what little support structure she kept rebuilding in her soul.

Factory Row heard your words and has chosen their queen.

A queen among common folk.

"Matthieu," she whispered over her shoulder, into the darkness. "Do not share *anything* discussed outside with the beast of this chateau, understood? Or how that démon visited us, *oui?*"

He sighed, as if the obvious pained him. "*Ma sœur*, will you never stop worrying?"

"Never," she replied back with a giggle. "Let us go to the kitchens and make breakfast."

With her brother still on her back, she trudged across the grand entry, her eyes darting from one shadow to another. A cold chill touched her skin and passed. Rhoslyn shivered but kept moving. In the back of the chateau, she found the servant's stairs and traveled down the stone steps to the next floor's landing. Was the beast awake? She left shortly after sunrise, hoping her captor was asleep after a long night of doing whatever it was he did in the woods after the sun went down. Could démons remain human at night? She actually didn't know. Lucas was the first wolf in a fully human form that she had ever conversed with. At least one she knew was a démon.

She lowered Matthieu onto the edge of a kitchen worktable and peered around the duskily lit space. If the windows were washed, this room would be bathed in sunlight. Maybe she would clean up the kitchens to rebuild strength and for something to do.

"Is it wrong to want bread when our friends won't have any?" Matthieu frowned.

The same guilt gnawed on the starved edges of her gut too. "Everyone, including us, must do what they can to survive." She lowered the floppy hood of his cloak. "Denying ourselves available food we cannot share will not feed others. We are both still weak from hunger and need to eat. But I share the same sadness. It means we care, *caneton*. That we have empathy. We don't want others to suffer like we have, *oui*?"

The oversized brown wool cloak puddled around his body and, with his pointed ears peeking through his mop of gold curls and the freckles on his nose, she had to keep from smiling, despite the frown between his eyes and the sorrow in his eyes. Matthieu chewed the corner of his lip, then nodded his head.

"While I make us something to eat, I will prepare a bath for you."

"A bath?" He grinned and those dimples immediately lightened her mood.

She touched his nose with the tip of her finger and, with a smile, spun away with a flutter of her hand. "*Oui*, I am your Bath Faerie, almost male grown, Monsieur Gautier."

Her brother laughed, one she hadn't heard in so long, and the magical sound filled her with the brightest, sparkling joy.

A candlemark later, she had filled a copper washtub she found in a dusty corner with water heated over the large hearth fire plus cold well water she retrieved two bucketfuls at a time. While outside, she had plucked mint, mullein, and horehound to seep in the pot of boiling water first. Her brother could bathe and breathe in medicated vapors simultaneously.

She helped him strip down to his breeches, which he insisted on wearing, then lowered him into the water by the fireplace. The happiness on her brother's face stole her breath. He loved the water, always had. Picnics by the swimming creek were his favorite outings. Their mother called him her little water sprite, which made him giggle.

With Matthieu settled and after scrubbing a worktable, she went into the larder and pulled out ingredients to make chewy sweet biscuits, her brother's favorite cookie. Not finding any yeast to make bread, she first mixed flour and water together and set it aside to ferment with a waxed linen cloth cover, which she found buried in a work basket. In four to five days, she would have the beginnings of a sourdough starter. She poured flour onto the table, made a well in the center, then added a spoonful of lard. Once she had made little crumbles with her fingers, she added an egg and a large spoonful of sugar to stir in with her hand. Listening to the splashes of water while kneading unleavened dough filled her with a normalcy she had craved for well over a year. She could almost hear her mother and sisters singing and couldn't resist a favorite counting song for when kneading bread, even dough for chewy biscuits.

"*One silver ring to Marie,*" she sang out. "*Two silver rings to Marie.*"

"*Three queens in a palace,*" Matthieu joined in.

She grinned. "*Possessing the three sons of Étienne. Playing, humming each with her silver ring.*"

"*Four acolits singing praises,*" Matthieu added with an unexpected clarion voice despite his lungs.

"*Five very black crows, crossing a peat-bog.*"

They both sang, "*Six brothers and six sisters. Seven days and seven months.*"

Matthieu started coughing, but he waved his hand for her to continue.

"*Eight little threshers on the barn floor, threshing peas, threshing pods.*" Rhoslyn thumped the ball of dough on the floured table. A turn of kneading for each count. "*Nine sons in arms returning from war, their broken swords, their bloody shirts*"—she turned the dough with another thump—"*The most terrible son who holds his head high—*"

"I made it clear you were *not* to access the kitchens without my permission."

The deep growly voice trembled through her body and her head snapped up just as her heart fell into the quickly filling well of fear in her gut. In the doorway stood a giant of a man dressed in black silk finery, and . . . her knees began to shake as sudden lightheadedness threatened to topple her over. Golden eyes pinned her in place with a still fury that commanded submission. Where fingers should be were sharp claws. But his face. Saints, his face sent a violent shudder down her body. It was longer than a normal man's. The skin around his nose and upper mouth was dark compared to his otherwise fair complexion and protruded as if the beginning of a snout. A mouth that boasted sharp teeth. Dark hair fell around his face in soft waves and the beginnings of a beard covered his cheeks and upper neck. Did he remain half-shifted to frighten her? After meeting Lucas, she now knew démons could retain their human form.

He stepped into the kitchen and she dropped the ball of dough and made to move toward her brother, who gaped with the first hint of fear she had seen on his face since entering Chateau Lumière Dorée.

"Do not touch him, démon." Her voice shook. "Do not harm my brother."

The beast kept his intense gaze trained on her. "It is not him who broke my rules."

The fury in his eyes sparked the still simmering rage in her and she straightened. "Then throw us out, milord." He paused across the table from her but said nothing. "Ah, you cannot." She bared her teeth. "Because we are trapped with you!"

The click of his claws on the table shivered down her spine and she swallowed when he slowly leaned toward her, his body coiled and ready to lunge. "You trespassed onto Chateau Lumière Dorée," he snarled. "You are *not* my guests. My rules are not for you to question but *obey*."

Rhoslyn scoffed. "I will *not* starve my brother to please your hubris."

He chuckled, a soft, dark sound that rumbled in the space between them. "I am the head alpha of the clans. And you are a filthy elf from Factory Row." He leaned in even closer. "Men of power bow before me, *fayette*," he growled. "And so will you."

Rhoslyn placed her hands onto the table and leaned toward him, refusing to be cowed by his arrogance despite the dizzying terror pounding in her pulse. "I may be a filthy fayette from Factory Row, but you know who I am. And you know what I did. I will not tolerate mortal lies from a man who is barely house trained." His mouth curled into a sneer and she rolled her eyes to hide her rising fear. Then, before she could think better of it, she reached out with a trembling hand and scratched behind his ear and cooed, "You are *adorable* when trying to be scary, beast."

Quickly, she removed her hand and grabbed the ball of dough and pounded it onto the table. Dipping her fingers into flour, she sprinkled a dusting over the table, then flicked her fingers at him. The look of surprise on his flour-dusted face nearly doubled her over in laughter.

"You're in my kitchen, démon," she added with a dismissive flourish of her hand. Stars, she was on the verge of fainting, despite her humor. "If you're nice to me," she added with more courage than she felt, "I might share these chewy sweet biscuits with you."

He slammed a clawed-hand onto the table and she jumped back with a squeak.

"If you wish to fight, Rhoslyn Gautier," he said in a low growl, "Then learn to do so with a weapon other than your sharp tongue."

Placing a hand on her hip, she lifted an eyebrow at him. "*Non*—"

"Tomorrow morning at ten," he said while walking backward toward the door, "I will meet you in the ballroom on the second floor."

She sucked in an angry breath. "Are you challenging me to a duel?"

He just grinned, what would have been a horrifyingly wicked grin if his face wasn't dusted in flour. Rhoslyn started laughing, a sputter at first. The delight, however, quickly grew into a full laugh from her belly. Those predatory golden eyes darkened right before he pivoted on his heel and marched into the hall leading to the stairway. But she didn't miss his tiny smile, as if amused, before disappearing into the candlelit shadows.

Yet, despite how she fought back and laughed in his horrific face, or how he might have been somewhat amused by her attempts to push back, she couldn't stop the repulsed shudder quaking down her body once more.

A splash of water brought her back to the present and she turned toward her brother, who peered at her as if she were a mythical creature of legend. "You are not afraid of anyone," he said in a small voice. "Not even monsters."

"I am terrified of him, *caneton*." She knelt by the copper tub. "I was terrified when standing before Queen Adeline too."

Be brave, Mademoiselle Gautier. Do not stop being wise or courageous.

The former queen's encouragement floated back to her memory and pleasurably warmed her chest.

"You don't seem afraid," he replied quietly.

We see only what we want to see, especially when angry and afraid. Night is no more evil than day. And yet, it is where we place all our nightmares. Appearances can be deceiving.

These words, by the man in her dreams, moved through her in a rush of heat—the kind of fire that refined instead of destroys.

"A monster on a throne tricked me into believing I was powerless," she said softly. "And I was afraid. I am *still* afraid of what she can do to me. But she is more afraid of what I can do to her." She paused to wipe a smudge of dirt from Matthieu's cheek. "Monsters, like her, only have power because I was trained from birth to give it to them. A power that belongs to me. And you. And the nymph in the alley, the grisette in the factory, the vendor selling produce, and the iron worker who pounds metal into steel."

She leaned back on her heels and smiled at her brother. "*Oui*, I am afraid. But then I remember . . . I have all the power and monsters must terrify me to feel like they have any."

Chapter 17

Fentienne

Fentienne was dead on his feet. Since the last dream he and Rhoslyn shared, he refused to sleep. Which meant he had been awake for over twenty-four hours to reset his schedule. The exhaustion was a pounding pressure behind his eyes. After weapons training, he would find rest for a few hours then remain awake until she rose the next morning.

He almost kissed her.

Worse, he *wanted* to kiss her and damn the consequences.

An elf.

A creature.

Rhoslyn's beauty had always made him feel foolishly reckless. He longed to know her lips when younger. He longed to know her lips now, despite his disgust toward her kind. But the attraction, the lust wasn't the thorn digging into his self-control these past twenty-four hours.

Nor was this almost kiss to satisfy boredom or endless angst. Or to appease his anger and drive to dominate.

No, he longed to taste worthiness. Ached to sample the tears of redemption on her lips.

Gods, she infuriated him. A writhing hatred the poets confused as love. Already, she was stealing his sanity.

When she pushed him into the pond, he knew with absolute clarity that he was in a losing battle. And when she jumped onto his back and toppled them both back into the water, skies . . . he had never been so turned on in his life. Or as happy in years. Then yesterday morning, scratching behind his ear and flicking flour in his face—the face of a snarling monster.

Rhoslyn Gautier was more of a fearless soldier than most he had captained. Fearless but idiotic. A warrior queen unaware of her true political power—a fatal problem and one that needed to be rectified and soon. She marched into situations fueled by a righteous fury willing to fight by any means possible, a need for justice that demanded she never back down—regardless of who stood opposite her or if she were equipped to survive long enough to win.

He wanted to shake her, lock her in a room, growl and snarl and rage until she came to her senses. Challenging a queen without thought to the repercussions was a dangerous game, one she almost misplayed. And he wasn't the kind of man girls like her should try and save. *Especially* her. Once she learned his identity, this twisted faerie tale would end in violence.

Yet, as his body hit the pond, he started falling.

Falling through the water.

Falling through the dream.

Falling through the mortal plane to the Underworld's fires where he burned to nothing but a desperately beating, terrified heart—for her.

Then she fell with him and he was undone.

It didn't matter if the feelings were manufactured by a blood bond, everything he felt was horrifyingly real. The logical war strategy was to let her fall in love with the whole man in her dreams to ensure she continued to hate the monster when awake.

But it hurt too much. And he was ill-equipped to manage this kind of tearing pain.

A flush warmed his face for a few thundering beats of his pulse. The revulsion on her face yesterday, the way she had shuddered in disgust, then laughed at him—he had shutdown, a marble tomb of dust and bones. Training kicked in to become the dark prince his father had engineered. Cold, indifferent, seductively cruel. Finding pleasure in pain. The shame was too great, though. His admiration for her warrior spirit too. He *wanted* to feel every cut. Deserved to be gutted and left to bleed out for all he had done. Begged for the ghosts slain by his hand to bury him alive until the guilt constricting his lungs suffocated with him.

He had done many unspeakable things in his life. But letting her kiss him, to fall for him . . . would make him worse than the abomination who tricked him into falling in love with the enemy. Because, unlike Addien who acted in revenge, his only motive was loneliness. It didn't matter how much he loathed her existence either. He couldn't destroy Rhoslyn, his wife, his mate, any more than he already had just to feel whole for a few blessed moments in his wretched life.

His mate.

His, his, his. Only his.

This possessive passion building inside of him was fracturing his mind. Already his wolf was taking control. The more Fentienne resisted her, the stronger his wolf became.

Just as he finished that last thought, the ballroom came alive with spectral dancers in absurdly large dresses and over-the-top frilly three-piece suits. The men wore more bows here than the little girls in Clifstán. The ghosts stepped a minuet to invisible music while other attendees crowded the edges of the room and watched.

He twisted back toward the doors and ground his teeth together, ignoring the dead. Where was she? A large part of him hoped she showed more reason than attempting to fight a monster, as she believed was happening this morning. Marching into the parlor to endure a round of verbal back and forth until she joined him in the ballroom wasn't how he wanted to spend this day though.

Skies, he needed to sleep.

Antsy, he fidgeted with the various weapons he had laid out onto a table he dragged into the ballroom right after shifting this morning. If she wanted to fight, he would teach her how and teach her when to pick her battles. Protecting her indefinitely was never in the playbooks. He wouldn't live long. He promised to protect her and, to him and his demanding arse wolf, that extended after his death.

The door cracked open and he straightened.

Fearless but idiotic.

She believed he was challenging her to a duel and, here she was, without any proper knowledge on how to use a pistol or sword, to prove that she wouldn't back down from a fight and with her brother as witness to her fatal stupidity.

"*Bonjour*, beast," she clipped out, chin lifted, as she lowered Matthieu to the ground about three to four yards from where Fentienne stood. Dancers whooshed through her and Rhoslyn shivered, her gaze darting around nervously. Her eyes slowly slid to the weapons and then she swallowed. "You brutishly demanded my presence?"

The boy met his eyes, his face pinched with anger. How old was Matthieu? Eight? Nine? Fentienne had entered the barracks at his age. For Rhoslyn to fight without distraction, her brother would need to grow stronger too. Otherwise, his codependency would be her downfall. A smart enemy would use him as leverage against her, and she was surrounded by smart enemies. Fentienne returned focus onto Rhoslyn with the beginnings of a smug smile. He would teach Matthieu first just to rile her up as lesson number one—know your enemy, followed by lesson two—react smart and not be led blindly by passion.

"Boy," he said and gestured for him to approach.

Rhoslyn put her hand on Matthieu's shoulder. "*Non*, this is between you and me."

Fentienne chuckled, low and dark. So predictable. "This is between me and him."

Matthieu's face blanched. "What did I do to offend you, milord?"

"I'm not offended with you." He crouched to be more eye level, then pointed at the weapons. "Which one interests you most?"

Rhoslyn's mouth fell open. "You would duel with a little boy?"

"Would I?" Annoyed, he marched over to where she stood. Leaning into her face, he snarled, "First lesson in strategic fighting, *know your enemy*."

"I know enough about you, beast."

"Are you willing to bet your life on it? On his?" When she didn't answer, he softly chuckled again and began prowling around her. The bodice of her dress rose and fell quickly; a vein near her temple wildly pulsed. "You *assumed* I would duel with you and then your brother. Why go through all the effort? I could kill you at any moment I please." She stiffened when he rounded to her back, an animal stillness before a predator. "What, exactly, do you know about me? Should you keep me in your line of sights at all times?" With that warning, she twisted to glare over her shoulder and he smiled before continuing his rotation to face her once more. "My motives? My weapon of choice? My strengths and weaknesses?"

"I know you are head alpha of all the clans."

"And, therefore, I challenge little boys with damaged legs to duels. A natural conclusion."

She clenched her jaw. "One does not become the head of all démons without cruelty."

"*Oui*," he said with a wolfish grin. "I am, undoubtedly, the cruelest man you have ever met." The scent of a building thunderstorm mixed with the pleasant earthiness of moss and ferns wrapped around him and his wolf panted feverishly, and Fentienne craved the feel of his lips on hers. The drowsy intoxication of breathing her in was messing with his mind. Unable to help himself, he lowered until his mouth touched her ear. She was barely breathing and the pounding rhythm of her pulse filled his ears. "What do you actually know about me, Rhoslyn Gautier?" he husked, unable to keep the longing from his voice. "Who am I?"

Her breath hitched, then she shuddered, and he smiled, knowing she could feel his satisfaction at her reaction. But, really, he felt a tiny fissure crack in his heart. Pulling away, he stepped back, forcing the shame away. The spectral dances continued to spin around them. Rhoslyn turned her head toward the balcony glass doors and glared, her chest now heaving with mounting fury.

"You are a disgusting, entitled Chalamet!" she spat.

He waited a couple of beats, then lowered his voice. "Who am I?"

"A black-hearted, cursed man!"

He waited another couple of beats, then asked the same question. "Who am I?"

"I don't know!" she screamed.

Fentienne laughed at her frustration. "But you *knew* I would challenge a little boy with a lame leg to a duel, for I am a cruel man. Still betting your life on it? On his?" He shook his head slowly when her lips pressed into an angry line. "Mademoiselle, every answer you gave were ones I already told you or an observation anyone with working eyes could make." She bared her teeth in a frustrated growl, so he bared his in reply, snarling, "Know. Your. Enemy."

"You do not have any authority over me—"

"—Who am I, Rhoslyn Gautier?"

"To demand my obedience—"

"—Who am I?"

"Stop asking me that infuriating question!"

"No."

She growled at him. "I know you keep people imprisoned at the chateau." Her hands curled into fists and her face sparked with fury. "Some since they were small children."

She was . . .

An idiot.

"What prisoners?" He cocked his head. "And how does telling me I have prisoners, which I would already know if I did, help you in this fight?"

She stilled. "You do not have prisoners?"

"Mademoiselle, we are the only living souls who reside at Chateau Lumière Dorée." She blinked back the shock of his words. "Wherever did you get that notion that I held prisoners, including children?" He knew, but he wanted to see how she played her cards out. She never agreed to his request before they awoke.

"But—"

She drew herself up to full height, which reached him mid-chest, and he fought back an amused smile. Instead, Fentienne marched forward until he stood right in front of her once more, to keep her on guard and riled up—how soldiers were trained in Myrefell. Learning how to strategize while inflamed and intimidated, instead of constantly reacting, was a critical skill she sorely needed.

"You just handed me the advantage. While you scrambled to recalculate new battle plans, I'm already on you. Because. You. Don't. Know. Your. Enemy."

Slowly, she lifted her head to meet his eyes and bit back another shudder at his nearness. "What if I had surprised you instead?"

"Cruel men are not surprised by others knowing of their cruelty." The hint of an arrogant smile played across his lips. "You didn't surprise me and you had no backup plan."

"What are you doing?" she asked, her voice just barely above a whisper.

Fentienne held her stare longer than necessary, just to assert his dominance, and it worked. She looked away and blinked. "You have a sharp tongue and a sharp mind—"

"I thought you didn't tolerate the witless chatter of uneducated lower-class females?"

"Keep talking and, when you do, actually listen to yourself."

Gods, the outrage sparkling in her green eyes, the one promising him a slow, painful death, made him delirious. The scent of her swirling anger, her need to fight pulsed hot in his veins, and he was on the verge of pushing her against a wall and kissing her until her every breath submitted to him. Until her body submitted to the contours of his. But her stubborn anger also infuriated every bone in his saints cursed body. If she were one of his soldiers, he would be all over her arse for insubordination and for willfully endangering his men by refusing to learn.

He wasn't a gentle man by nature and she was trying his patience. Lack of sleep wasn't helping.

And thank the winter gods the ghosts of the fallen finally rested for a period. The ballroom was now empty save them.

"Answer me without riddles, démon." She tilted her head. "Why do you appear only half-shifted?"

"Ah, now we are inquiring instead of assuming. Progress." Fentienne causally strode back to the weapons and tapped his clawed fingers on the table. "I am under a curse, mademoiselle, and do not have complete possession of my magic. Half man during the day, full wolf at night. There is no cure for my condition."

"I see." Her skin paled a little and she blinked a few times. Daintily clearing her throat, she asked, "Why *did you* demand my presence this morning?"

"If I am to tolerate your defiance, as well as the rest of Gabaston, then learn how to defend yourself to ease that burden you place on everyone else." Her mouth fell open and he could see her winding up again. "You were lucky Queen Adeline didn't publicly execute you on the spot or the next day in the market square. Your brother is lucky he wasn't used to torture you first before execution or made an orphan after witnessing his sister's death in what would have been a horrific manner. And, in his present state, he wouldn't survive Factory Row without you."

Splotches of red appeared on her cheeks and he was relieved she *finally* understood the gravity of her situation, even if she had contemplated the fallout of her choices before now. Rhoslyn was an intelligent creature. Idiotic.

Fearless. But smart.

"There is a large bounty on your head," he continued. "Not only are starving men looking for you to feed their families and relieve their own suffering, but démons too. Should the invisible barrier around Chateau Lumière Dorée fall, how would you protect yourself? Protect Matthieu?" She drew in a sharp breath and grimaced back tears. "Your fire and cunning wit are truly admirable, mademoiselle, your rebellion and demands for change too. But you are reckless."

She was quiet a few seconds. "Is that why you claimed me before the clans? To protect me from wolves?"

Fentienne narrowed his eyes. Who told her that? Invisible hackles rushed down his spine. "Only one of several reasons why."

"I am not property to be owned!" she spat.

"Nor am I and yet that is the barbaric way of things for people like us."

Her eyes widened. "You know who I am?" her question came out soft and breathless.

Fentienne stepped closer and placed a clawed finger beneath her chin and forced her to hold his gaze, making her pale. "*Oui.* I know measurably more about you than you do me. *I know my enemies.*"

Her breath came quick and she swallowed. "Who am I?"

He laughed, unable to stop himself, and she balled her hands into fists when realizing she had parroted his words from earlier. There was nothing to hold him back from revealing her identity. Her thin frame, the weakness in her muscles ... This knowledge would demand action. And she wasn't ready for the burden of knowing she was next in line to rule an entire realm. Skies, he barely was and he was raised at court. He and Rhoslyn would have this conversation eventually, but now wasn't the right moment.

"I will tell you," he practically purred to rile her up even more, to deflect and buy time, "after you learn how to shoot a pistol or reasonably use a smallsword."

"You honestly believe I will fall in line after how you treat me?"

"No, I know you won't." Pivoting about face, he returned to the table and rested his clawed fingers onto the edge. "Boy, what weapon interests you most?"

Matthieu perked up and craned his neck to see.

Fentienne gestured for him to approach.

"His leg and lungs are weak, démon," she spat, her fire still blazing hot. "His body from malnutrition too, though you would make him beg for food from your well-stocked larder. Now, you ask him to walk three yards, then fight with a weapon he can barely lift?"

Fentienne ignored her. "Come, Matthieu. Choose any weapon."

The boy limped forward a step and Rhoslyn sucked in a sharp breath. "Matthieu," she warned in a low growl.

Her brother also ignored her and limped forward another few steps. Pausing to rest his leg and catch his breath, he asked, "If I make it to the table, milord"—he drew in a wheezy breath—"give my sister a piece of her identity?"

"Name the piece before I agree."

"Mathieu!" The color drained farther from Rhoslyn's face. "What are you doing? *Non, mon petit caneton*. This is not your fight."

Matthieu straightened his shoulders and leveled him a bold but curiously thoughtful look. "The name of her husband."

Fentienne's heart fell to his stomach. "That is information I'm unable to share. The magic of the chateau prevents me."

"Matthieu Eric Gautier!"

The little boy nodded his head at his answer. "Then her parents. She wants to know of her parents."

Fentienne held his hands behind his back and cocked his head. "If you make it to the table, Matthieu Gautier, and select a weapon, I will tell your sister where her parents live and no other information for now. But she must earn the rest of the information herself." Even though Matthieu was young, he was still a faerie and making promises to him were equally as binding as to grown elves. Every detail had to be spelled out. "Are we in agreement?"

"*Oui*, milord." The boy nodded his head once more. "I agree."

"How dare you use my brother against me!" Rhoslyn started to march toward Matthieu.

"Halt!" he roared and she stopped her steps with a squeak, her eyes wide as his voice echoed over the room. "Before you take another step forward, Rhoslyn Gautier, ponder your own words." His fury was snapping and he no longer cared if he was too frightening. "Then use that sharp wit of yours to contemplate what I am generously offering your brother and why." Her face fell and she whipped her gaze toward the balcony doors, her bottom lip trembling. "Will you challenge me again?"

She barely shook her head no just as an angry tear slipped through her closed eyes and crawled down her cheek.

Matthieu seemed to struggle, watching his sister. But then he turned determined eyes Fentienne's way and dragged his leg forward another step. Fentienne detested children. Outright refused to train junior soldiers. They were needy, too emotional, and required far too much coddling. But Matthieu reminded him of Florian—the fair looks, a quieter, curious personality, and an agile mind. The wheels were constantly turning in that little boy's eyes—an ability to take in a large amount of detail while not revealing all his observations. Even to his sister, which Fentienne respected. But mostly it was the iron wall of strength beneath the outward perception of weakness.

Fentienne could live a million lifetimes and would still never forgive himself for what he had done, for the vile words he spewed at Florian all those years and for not protecting him when he had the chance. He could have let Florian go and counted him as a casualty during the fall of South Camp when reporting back to Myrefell. But Fentienne chose his father over the brother he vowed to *always* protect, like the good little monster his father had designed, the super soldier, the wolf bred to kill and dominate.

A father who would kill his own son to convince a girl to sacrifice her heart to power a weapon.

Rhoslyn's shoulders were shaking and more tears fell down her paled cheeks and his wolf growled, pissed that Fentienne had hurt her. The pain in his chest was deepening with every tight breath. Clammy sweat was beading on his forehead. He needed her to hate him, to protect her, but not so much she no longer desired to remain married to him. Gods, he was bitterly tired of being the villain to protect and empower the *real* villain.

He knew Addien. He knew his enemy. Regardless of if he pushed Rhoslyn away or lived civilly with her, the end result would be the same: his wife would hate him once she learned his identity and break their blood bond. And Addien would still make an attempt on Rhoslyn's life even if, in Rhoslyn's inevitable hate for him, she chose to remain in this arranged marriage. Since Maeline's birth, Addien's entire agenda has been his mate's death.

There was no doubt in his mind that Addien Wyndham was whispering into the ear of Queen Adeline. The identity of his wife would be a valuable weapon for his aunt to use to further her political and economic gain.

And, without question, Addien and Queen Adeline *will* use Matthieu to break Rhoslyn first.

Fentienne studied the little boy. The good leg dragged too. He couldn't lift it too high otherwise he would lose balance. The shoes on his feet were barely holding together. Better support would help his balance. A cane too. Fentienne's gaze roamed over the little boy's threadbare clothing. Short, shallow breaths wheezed from Matthieu's lungs. The space between his brows creased with concentration. He was perhaps six paces away now.

"Mademoiselle," he said when Matthieu rested again. "Gather herbs for his medicated vapors. And prepare him another bath, to ease the overtaxed muscles in his legs."

"This moment?" Her gaze darted to her brother and back to him.

"This moment," he repeated. "I won't harm him. You have my word."

"The word of a monster?"

He blinked back the irritation. "The word of a man."

"*Oof!* That is supposed to be better?" One hand fluttered in the air while the other rested on her hip.

He sighed and closed his eyes a beat to will patience. "If you wish for him to wait longer for relief, so be it."

Once more, her shoulders fell. "You know that isn't true."

"Then go," he snapped as he waved his hand dismissively. "I will bring him to you after he chooses a weapon."

Rhoslyn held his gaze and he arched a haughty brow. "Matthieu," she said without looking away from Fentienne. "Do you feel safe with this démon of a man?"

"*Oui*, he is always kind to me."

Fentienne froze at his words. No one had ever called him kind. Was this little boy's life so hard that any form of attention, even from monsters, was seen as kindness? A rush of unexpected emotions hit him and he broke away from Rhoslyn's intense glare and pretended to look around, bored, while waiting for her consent. Though, in Fentienne's opinion, it was Matthieu's choice. But he was used to boys his age having autonomy from their guardians.

The Underworld's fires roared in Rhoslyn's eyes as she marched over to Fentienne. "If you so much as scratch my brother," she seethed, halting just inches from him, her voice low. "I will destroy you by any means possible."

"Rhoslyn," he whispered roughly, his gaze lowering to her flushed lips, "you're already destroying me."

Her eyes widened, then narrowed. The raw, vulnerable beauty in how she looked at him clenched the muscles in his stomach—soft, confused, as if she would stop fighting with him to fight for him. His wife couldn't resist a wounded soul to champion, he was learning. The scent of her fury, the beating wildness of her warrior heart, the way she carried herself with an authority most females in her class wouldn't dare exhibit to someone of his office . . . it pissed him off. It made him weak.

And he was falling once more.

Falling through the cursed roses and thorns.

Falling past logic and reasoning.

Falling headfirst into dangerous waters he didn't know how to navigate.

Rhoslyn turned on her heel, kissed her brother on the top of his head, and furiously strode through the large doors toward the kitchen.

Fentienne's pulse pounded painfully against his ribs. Skies, he couldn't breathe. Why did he confess those words to her? Words whispered as if he longed to claim her lips with his—because he did. He furiously clawed at the cravat around his throat and threw it onto the table. Then he unbuttoned his waistcoat and unlaced his linen undershirt. The bastard wolf inside of him relaxed his bristling hackles and warning growls. Fentienne, however, stabbed his sharp nails through is hair with a low, guttural growl of his own. The air was growing warmer, tighter. He bent to lean his head on the table and cinched his eyes closed. Tears burned behind his eyes and he heaved in a sharp breath.

He didn't want to be the reason Addien killed her.

He didn't want to be why Matthieu was orphaned.

He didn't want to fall for Rhoslyn.

He didn't want his wolf to take over because he refused the mate bonds.

"Is what you spoke true?" The furiously flexing muscles in his body stiffened and he slowly turned his head toward Matthieu who had made it to the table. *Shit!* In his escalating panic, he had completely forgotten about her brother. He didn't hear or scent his approach either. "My sister is destroying you?"

Fentienne straightened and clenched his jaw. The breath in his lungs constricted tighter and his hands were shaking.

"Come here, milord." Matthieu offered him a sad smile.

Fentienne eyed him several beats, an entire battlefield of emotions raging in him. The little boy pointed to the space before him. Fentienne wasn't sure why he obeyed, but he did and knelt on one knee before Matthieu, too humiliated to meet his eyes. An alpha, submitting to an elven child!

The boy placed a hand on his back and began rubbing in a soothing circle. "This helps me breathe easier."

Fentienne closed his eyes and fought back the tears. He wasn't sure when he was truly comforted last, if ever. And a child . . . Gods a faerie child . . .

"I know who you are, milord," Matthieu said quietly, then coughed into his arm. "I figured it out when you circled my sister and whispered in her ear. I saw the love on your face when it was hidden from hers."

Love? Fentienne's head snapped up. "Matthieu, whatever you think you saw—"

"You're her husband, aren't you?"

The little shit. That's why he challenged him. Bile coated Fentienne's throat and rolled in his stomach. He wasn't sure what flooded him first, the intensity of shame or the overwhelming fear. Already he struggled to breathe, but now he was suffocating. Fentienne looked over his shoulder, clammy sweat flushing across his face, and tried to scent if she were hiding behind the doors listening. But he couldn't smell her storm or her earthiness.

Peering back at Matthieu, he said in a low, threatening voice, "What weapon do you choose?"

"You said 'people like us.'" Matthieu tilted his head. "You were married to her against your will too. You claimed her because you have to, *oui*? But you actually love her."

"I do not—" Fentienne stopped and swore under his breath, unable to say "love" aloud to Rhoslyn's brother. His heart was beating so fast. The need for air burned hot in his lungs. Matthieu continued to rub circles on his back and Fentienne was shattering. "That knowledge will put her in greater danger," he choked out. "She can't like me, Matthieu. That, too, will put her in danger. Just know that everything I do, even my mistreatment, is for her protection."

The boy's eyes widened. "That's why you're mean to her but not me," he said more to himself, the puzzle pieces coming together in those observant eyes of his. "Please do not harm her, milord."

"I couldn't even if I wanted to." His godsdamn wolf would seize control before Fentienne could truly physically cause injury. But Mathieu didn't need to know that.

"She was attacked by a démon when twelve, milord. My sister still has nightmares."

Heat buzzed in Fentienne's head, down his muscles, and he had to control the urge to shadow sprint into the forest and attack the first démon he encountered as retribution for the moon-addled démon who wanted to kill her. "The wolves know she is off limits. Natural wolves too."

His mouth parted and he asked, breathlessly, "You can command natural wolves?"

"Promise me that you will not say anything to her," he continued in his panic. "And before you agree, remember that you are making a deal with me that will be sealed by the magic that governs your kind."

He studied Fentienne for several seconds, taking his warning and request seriously. Those wheels were spinning fast in his eyes. Then he nodded his head. "I will not tell her, milord, unless she's in danger and it will save her life. Or if she is too tormented by not knowing." He coughed into his arm again, a deep wheezing cough. "You can't ask me to willingly hurt my sister."

Fentienne drew in a trembling breath. "Matthieu Gautier, you surprise me and very little surprises me."

He grinned. "That's because I'm not your enemy."

He couldn't help it and quietly laughed. "What am I to do with you?"

The boy threw his arms around Fentienne's neck, startling him, and leaned in. "I have a brother again."

Every thought stopped. His pulse, his breath. The world flipped upside down beneath Fentienne's feet and he shuddered back the sob knotting in his throat.

Captain Karlsen held Adalwolf's gaze as he and two soldiers approached. Florian dropped the sticks in his hands and blinked back tears. *They were going to take Adalwolf away from his brother. They would put a gun in his hand and teach him to kill boys with little brothers like him. Teach those little brothers to kill too.* Fire burned hot in his belly. His father's men would have to fight him first. Adalwolf moved in front of Florian, taking his hand. Peering over his shoulder, he tried to smile. "I will protect you. Always."

Gently, Fentienne placed his clawed hand onto Matthieu's back and selfishly indulged in the false worthiness while pieces of himself were obliterating.

"One day you will be grateful I'm not your brother," he whispered into his hair. "The magic of Chateau Lumière Dorée prevents me from sharing who I am. But I'm not a good man. There is no redemption from the wicked things I have done and will still do." Matthieu pulled away and frowned; Fentienne tried to keep the anguish from his eyes, but he knew he couldn't. "Your sister is sensible and knows what she deserves. And you, Matthieu Gautier, deserve an older brother who knows how to be one."

He placed a small hand on Fentienne's shoulder. "Are you sorry?"

The ache in Fentienne's heart almost doubled him over. "For many things, I am sorry. For many things, I'm not. Sometimes . . ." He paused to gather his thoughts. "Sometimes it's difficult to judge what is right and wrong when you've been groomed since birth to see the world and your place in it through a narrow, cruel lens."

Matthieu eyed him for several seconds then nodded his head while dropping his hand. Whatever he was thinking, he kept to himself. The little boy was wheezing. Fentienne met his eyes for another beat of his crumbling heart, then stood and wiped the sweat from his forehead with the sleeve of his linen shirt.

"We will start weapons training slowly," he said quietly. "You need to regain more strength first."

"*Oui*," Matthieu replied softly. Then he placed his hand on a pistol. "I choose this weapon."

They would put a gun in his hand and teach him to kill boys with little brothers like him.

Teach those little brothers to kill too.

Fentienne felt his lungs constrict for air again and his hands started to shake. "Very well. And while you're learning to care for and load a pistol, you will also learn basic fencing techniques using a switch until you regain enough strength for a wooden sword."

Matthieu grinned. "Uncle Dalbrie is going to teach me sword fighting too. Then I can go to Merenna and fight pirates!"

"Come," Fentienne said, holding out his hand. "I'll put you on my shoulders until we reach the servant's stairs."

He didn't know how to reply to Matthieu about his boyhood fantasies to fight pirates. Interacting with children made him nervous, actually. And the conversation he just had with Matthieu still tumbled sharply in his chest. Every breath hurt. Rhoslyn's brother took his hand and Fentienne stilled. His hand was so small compared to his own. It wouldn't take much to crush this little boy. And yet, this little boy wasn't afraid of him.

Gently, he scooped Matthieu up and placed the boy on his shoulders. Matthieu was grinning and Fentienne let out an annoyed sigh. It was hard enough to handle one Gautier who was unafraid and foolish. Dealing with two was unbearable.

"Time to swim!"

Fentienne's brow furrowed. The hell?

Too tired to ask what that meant, or care further, Fentienne marched out of the ballroom. They moved through the halls and down to the first floor. Every so often, Matthieu would reach out a hand to trail along the wall or to try and touch a chandelier overhead. To rebalance, he would clutch Fentienne's hair as if a horse's mane, making Fentienne gritted his teeth. But Matthieu didn't ask questions. Only the occasional cough. Either he, too, was far too exhausted to care or his head was filled with too many heavy thoughts.

At the servant's stairs, he lowered Matthieu to the ground long enough for him to crawl onto his back, like he so often did with his sister. Once secure, Fentienne descended the stone steps, careful to duck in low ceiling spots to ensure Matthieu didn't hit his head.

At the landing, her scent hit him first, a sparking sensation that ignited his blood. Followed by a soft earthy smell, one he wished was from pressing her into the moss, their bodies hidden beneath the ferns.

NO.

That imagery, that *want* couldn't exist. No matter how much his wolf panted for her, he didn't. Intimacy with an elf disgusted him.

But he knew that wasn't how he truly felt. Not anymore. Those dark emotions were quickly fading into something equally as intense. The torture of trying to untangle what was real and what was faerie magic was unspooling his mind—rapidly.

You care to the point of pain.

A man with a bladed heart.

Dalbréath was right. Fentienne's mind and heart were always wrapped in sharp blades. In childhood and now. Every thought, every feeling consumed him until he craved the cruel, detached pain of caring for nothing.

He lowered Matthieu by the prepared copper tub, refusing to meet Rhoslyn's eyes. Not doing so would give her dominance over him, though. He hissed swear words at his wolf, then flicked his angry gaze to hers.

Gods.

She had unwoven the braid falling down her back earlier. Golden brown strands rippled to her waist in waves. An image of her racing a horse along the coast moved through his mind's eye. How her hair had danced in the wild wind and floated around her face in the laughing breeze. The sunset's purples and corals reflecting in her dark green gaze. And those lips. Skies, how those lips tempted him when she sat before him on horseback, while they sat in the pond, droplets glistening on her cheeks, and now, while she stood behind a table covered in herbs she bundled to dry.

Rhoslyn tilted her head as she peered at him, her fingers tapping furiously on her hip. The pulse fluttering in her veins told him a different story, the acrid scent reaching his nose. She was terrified of him.

"After his bath," Fentienne said, clearing his throat. "Work the muscles of his damaged leg."

"You will need to be more specific, beast."

He turned to Matthieu. "May I show your sister what I mean? I will need to touch your leg."

"*Oui*, milord."

Fentienne picked up Matthieu and laid him on a table. Then, as softly as possible with his claws, cradled the boy's calf and attempted to massage the scarred skin and tissue. "Get the blood flowing here and loosen the knotted muscles." Taking Matthieu's ankle, he gently turned it in a circle. "Work the ligaments and muscles in his ankles and feet too."

Matthieu's face pinched in discomfort. Fentienne lowered his leg and stepped aside.

"How do you know so much about the care of a lamed leg?" Rhoslyn asked, eyebrow raised.

"I wanted to stay alive on the battlefield. And I wanted my men to survive too." Fentienne pivoted on his heel. If he stayed, he would see the pity in her eyes, the desire to heal the mass of twisted scars and muscle of his heart. And he knew his enemy. Knew this vile, cruel monster of a man would indulge in every undeserved kind touch and word until he gave into madness. To ensure she didn't grow soft toward him, he turned at the door and snarled, "Bathe next, mademoiselle. Only Matthieu will be welcome to lessons tomorrow if you don't. The chateau houses natural hot spring pools on the bottom floor. Use them."

Then he left.

The fire in her eyes would now be begging to burn him to ash. A look that always sent blood rushing.

Another could flay his skin, pull out his teeth one-by-one, crush his bones, leave him in near-freezing conditions without clothes . . . and still *nothing* would torture him more than this marriage contract and the enormity of self-control he exercised to emotionally and physically keep his distance. Night and day, he was tormented by not trusting if anything between them was real or only the result of faerie magic.

Perhaps he wasn't chosen to be Maeline's curse, as all others believed.

Perhaps Rhoslyn was chosen to be his—from her first breath until his last.

Chapter 18

Rhoslyn

Tall, dark ceilings stretched above Rhoslyn. But with the curtains pushed back along a row of large windows, the space seemed almost airy. Little feminine touches appealed to her as well. A delicate porcelain bowl and pitcher by an intricately carved vanity and mirror framed in by sconces in the shape of opening roses. Leaf scroll molding with falling wooden trim wildflowers running down the walls in intervals across the room. Were those trim pieces once gold plated?

She lowered Matthieu onto a damask upholstered chair, ignoring the light poof of dust. Every room was covered in layers of dust. Some more than others. This room, however, was fairly clean compared to most. Did the beast first choose this room? Or had another stayed here for a spell?

The small heels of her shoes clacked across the black marble floors until reaching an enormous rug. In the center of the room, pushed against a wall decorated in ornate tree, sun, and flower wallpaper, was a canopied bed. The four posts twisted in carved tree trunks and leaves and branched out with small, leafed limbs from one post to another. She ran a hand along the coverlets, appreciating the repeating floral design in the silk. In the corner stood a large armoire. The previous rooms didn't have any clothing. But she had a feeling this one might.

The armoire doors creaked as they opened and, to her delight, there was an entire closet full of skirts, petticoats, bodices, and chemises. All black, but she didn't care. She peered over her shoulder to Matthieu whose eyes sparkled while those darling dimples flashed her way. They had searched five rooms. No hand mirror. No brush, combs, or hair pins. No clothing.

Rhoslyn turned the silk coverlet upside down to ensure a clean surface, then pulled out dress piece after dress piece and draped them onto the bed, admiring the lace trim, ribbons, rosettes, and the fine boning in the bodices. These garments were at least forty years old if not older. And, surprisingly, very little moth damage. A few holes here and there, but not as many as she would expect. Panniers of different sizes hung beside the skirts. She pulled out a rump roll from the closet's base to puff the skirts around her waist rather than bother with widened hips while learning how to use weapons. Rhoslyn knelt to better see in the shelves beneath the dresses and gasped. Corsets! At least three and . . . she could faint. Real silk garter ribbons and silk stockings.

"There are several cotton chemises. Enough that I can sew you two new shirts." She turned to her brother. "I can sew you a frock coat, waistcoat, and breeches from the dress yardage too."

"I will look like a silk breeches." He wrinkled his nose.

Rhoslyn laughed. "*Oui*, but you'll be properly dressed and warm when outside too." Her fingers trailed along a bodice with embroidered roses down the face, decorated in silk rosettes along the hem and bows that ran down the center of the front. "Cover your eyes, *mon petit caneton*."

Matthieu turned in his chair to face the windows. "Is this good enough?"

Loosening the ties on the side of her bodice, she struggled to contain her grin. "*Oui*."

She slipped out of her petticoat next, then removed her corset and camisole. Quickly, she threw one of the full-length chemises over her naked form, pushing out a tight breath to calm her anxiety. The cotton had a slight musty smell. But her skin smelled of lavender and roses, courtesy of the soaps she found in the baths below the chateau. Saints, she had never experienced anything quite so luxurious. Nor had her hair shone so beautifully in an age. She fetched a corset and laced the front until her breasts pushed up. Next, she rolled the stockings up her legs and giggled when tying the silk ribbons around her thighs. Amélie would squeal.

Rhoslyn peered around the room to the vanity and had an idea. "Matthieu, I need to pin up my hair before adding the bodice and skirts. Do you mind? Should not take long."

"*Non*, I do not mind. I want you to be happy."

"*Merci*, you sweet, beautiful boy."

She practically danced to the vanity and opened a drawer. Her hands flew to her mouth in delight. A hand mirror, hair combs, a brush, and several pins. In a separate drawer were several pairs of small dangling earrings, a choker made from three strands of pearls, and two dainty gold bracelets. She pulled out each object, one set of earrings, and quickly went to work, pinning her hair in a terrible fashion. But with practice, she would master this art. Satisfied with her first attempt to wear her hair like a female grown instead of a girl who had yet to come of age, she flew on tiptoes back to the bed.

Attaching the rump roll was fairly easy. Pulling first the petticoat over her head and then the silk skirts proved difficult. But she managed them both after a few frustrating attempts. In the future, she would pin her hair after donning skirts. The bodice, thankfully, was simple. Overall, the clothing hung large on her. She was far too thin. With better meals she would fill out these garments without much alteration.

"You may turn around, *caneton*."

Matthieu's mouth fell open, then he closed it. "Saints. You *look* like a princess."

A blush warmed her face with his praise. She felt like a princess. Besides the dresses in her dreams, she had never touched anything so fine in reality let alone wore a garment near as rich. Unable to resist, she spun in a circle to watch the skirts flare. When she stopped to face Matthieu again, another figure stood in the doorway and she startled back a step.

Those wolfish eyes trailed up her body, blinking softly. His lips parted. When he didn't speak right away, Rhoslyn feared she had angered him too much. But then he swallowed, hesitantly meeting her waiting gaze, and another blush, this one deeper, stained her cheeks. Rhoslyn caught a glimpse of herself in the vanity mirror and drew in a quiet breath. She was truly transformed, as Matthieu said.

Swinging her gaze back to the beast, she squared her jaw and straightened her spine. "We need new clothes."

"*Oui*," was his only reply and in a voice uncharacteristically breathless for him.

She angled her head toward her shoulder and lowered her lashes. The rough, affected sound did strange things to her pulse, despite the monster before her. One who terrified her. However, a male had never spoken to her as if she were too beautiful for him to even form words.

"I plan to use dress yardage to sew new clothing for Matthieu."

"Good."

Her head snapped up. "You are not outraged that I explored the chateau without your grand permission? Or that I took liberties to wear clothing that belongs to you?"

A tiny smile flirted across his lips despite the cold stare aimed her way. "I prefer my females to be quiet ornaments for my viewing pleasure."

She rolled her eyes. "Of course you do, démon."

He stepped into the room and continued toward her. The muscles in her stomach clenched and she took a step back, looking behind her shoulder. The fluttering pulse in her chest beat so hard she had to concentrate on breathing. There were moments he didn't frighten her as much, such as when she flicked flour onto his face in the kitchens. But right now? She already felt vulnerable wearing jewels and so fine a dress before a man who treated her as if she was nothing more than Factory Row rubbish. A dress and baubles fit for a queen.

His large, imposing form paused before her. "You bathed."

"You walked all the way here to discuss my toilette?" A scowl formed between her brows and a hand fluttered in the air angrily. "*Oof!* Are insults no longer as sharp from the doorway?"

A single clawed finger reached out and touched the black pearls dangling from her earlobe, then caressed a loose curl of hair against her neck. Rhoslyn shivered and her skin erupted into goosebumps. The hair fell back to her skin and her muscles stiffened. He could rip open her throat with a quick flick of his wrist. The tip of his claw slipped beneath the butcher's twine and he tugged the ring free from her corset. The gold band of thorns and roses in his palm shone in the afternoon light. Fear billowed down her body and swam dizzy circles in her head. His gaze lifted from the ring and roamed down her face, her neck, to her breasts. He swallowed again. Then his own body stilled, as if snapping out of a trance, and his face donned the cruel mask she was used to seeing. Those Chalamet eyes flashed and locked onto hers with predatory focus.

"How is it that a poor fayette has a ring worth coin bags full of gold?"

The blood was quickly draining from her head. Was this ring truly worth so much? "It was a gift, from Gedlen Fate Maker."

"Hmm."

Rhoslyn's brow creased. The way he hummed a bored, dismissive response reminded her of the man in her dreams and her eyes narrowed. "Since you know who I am," she said quietly, cautiously, "you know why Prince Gedlen gave me this ring, *oui*?"

He stepped back and the ring plunked against her bodice, an arrogant, bored slant to his mouth.

She lifted her chin. "You never told me where my parents lived as agreed with my brother."

Matthieu's eyes were large as he looked between them, but a small smile brightened his face. Why was her brother smiling?

The dark démon prowled around her and she didn't move. She wasn't sure if her lungs still drew in air. Remembering his warning that she should keep him in her sights at all times, Rhoslyn turned her head to peer over her shoulder. Their gazes touched and a cruel smile curled his lips.

Then he leaned forward until his breath warmed the back of her neck, beneath her ear, and whispered, "Avenbury."

Her world tipped upside down. "Changeling child of thorns," she said to herself.

The dark démon circled back to her front, his head cocked to the side, watching her closely as he lazily ambled toward the door in backward steps. Too closely. As if she were prey in the forest he stalked for his amusement. Giving that prey space so he could hunt longer. But the flood of thoughts racing through her mind captured her attention too much to be frightened by his presence.

"House of Thorns," she said, her voice wobbly. "I'm from the House of Thorns."

She picked up the ring dangling from her neck and studied the thorned design. Curious, she slipped a finger through the band despite the twine and flicked her gaze to the beast's. His chest rose and fell deeply, his attention fixed on her fingers. Arrogance hardened his features but those eyes . . . those eyes reflected an entirely different emotion—longing.

Wolves weren't the only predators of Gabaston. Men who lusted for females were more dangerous and a new fear shuddered down her. She had no protection from him, in any form.

Rhoslyn removed her finger from the band and took another step back. "Matthieu and I are relocating to this room. Throw a tantrum like a spoiled, entitled Chalamet. I care not. This *will* be my room." At least this space had a bolted lock on the door. Though she knew he could easily tear down any door if he wanted.

"I don't force myself on females, especially elves I find disgusting, like you." His voice burned with contempt.

Her eyes widened in horror.

A monstrous grin taunted her. "I can scent emotions and hear your pulse."

Rhoslyn was going to be sick and wrapped an arm around her middle.

"You are terrified of me. I repulse you."

She swallowed thickly, feeling faint. "I know my enemy enough to be afraid."

"No, mademoiselle," he said on a low growl. "You don't even begin to know the reasons of why you should be afraid."

"Are you threatening me?"

He laughed, a soft but dark sound that scraped down her spine. He found her fear amusing? The cold touch of terror vanished as the heat of anger flushed her skin once more. She curled her hands into fists and bared her teeth at the démon who found pleasure in playing with his prey.

"I detest you!" she spat. "You are an abhorrent man!"

A grin was his first reply, all fangs and sharp teeth. "How fickle a female's heart. You didn't find me abhorrent when I protected you in the woods and before Chateau Lumière Dorée."

Fickle? Indignation twisted tighter in her chest. "If you find me so disgusting, *beast*, why did you protect me?"

A shadow streaked toward her and abruptly stopped. She sucked in a sharp, startled gasp. Towering over her, the broad shoulders and width of his back blocked the light from the window. Dark hair fell forward as he lowered to within inches of her face, then he snarled in a deep guttural voice, "Because you are mine, Rhoslyn Gautier. *Mine*. And I don't share."

Bile coated her throat and she stumbled back toward the bed on shaking legs, clutching a post for support. The possessive warning in the curl of his lip, the monstrous growl in his voice, the blazing hunger in his eyes trembled down her body. But the dominating anger winked out within a few shared rapid breaths. A look of shock blanched the cruel angles of his face, as if he couldn't believe what he had just confessed. The pale, clammy skin quickly turned a sickly pallor. Before she could scream at him to leave, he pivoted on his feet and marched from the room, slamming the door behind him.

Rhoslyn clung to the post for a few minutes, not trusting her legs to stay upright. She was his prisoner. Despite his insistence that he didn't keep prisoners, including children. But he had possessively trapped her inside the stone walls of Chateau Lumière Dorée.

What did he want with her?

Was this a political hostage situation?

Or was he depraved and desired to break her before taking his pleasure?

Though she didn't think the latter were true. He genuinely looked sickened by his own confession. The nausea in her stomach roiled at the reminder of his claims and she bolted to the porcelain bowl at the vanity and threw up. A shudder wended down her spine and settled in her churning gut and she retched again. Closing her eyes a few seconds, she attempted to settle her breathing. She wiped her mouth with the back of her hand and straightened.

How dare he make her his property!

How dare anyone use her so hatefully for their own greedy agenda!

Betrayal sickened her gut further. Her family, the ones from the House of Thorns, the ones from Dúnælven, had tossed her aside. They chose for her to grow up realms away with a family she loved but was not her own. A family she would be ripped from in marriage to a monster.

The ring glinted from the candlelight above the vanity. Prince Gedlen provided her a way out of the marriage contract, but only after she met her husband. She hissed a swear word under her breath. In the forests of Gabaston, she denied herself the opportunity when Dalbréath offered answers. Now no one could utter his name, class, or title. Not Dalbréath. Not Lucas Fontine. Not the dark démon who prowled these halls. All claiming the curse blackening the House of Golden Light prevented them.

But...

Nausea swirled in her stomach once more.

She was starting to suspect her husband was the very master of this coffined home. The hair on her arms stood on end. The flush of anger drained from her face and she pressed a hand to her middle. And she was tired of her magic telling her he had a good heart despite his uncouth behavior. Until she knew for certain if he were her husband or not, she wouldn't place a drop of her blood into the band. She could only do so once. And what if her husband was another and far crueler?

Rhoslyn grabbed the hand mirror and studied the green of her eyes, the light dusting of freckles across her nose, the sweep of golden-brown hair pinned into loose, falling curls atop her head. Raised poor but born an aristocrat. From the House of Thorns in Avenbury, not from the upper class or Chalamets of Aurelienne.

The beast didn't own her.

The Kadelaryns didn't own her.

The House of Thorns didn't own her.

Factory Row and Queen Adeline didn't own her.

She belonged to herself. And to her brother.

Straightening her shoulders, she turned to Matthieu, the hand mirror clutched in her fingers. "We must wash the linens and garments and beat the mattress."

"I can help wash." Her little brother was frowning, a strange look on his face.

Rhoslyn nodded. "*Oui*, I will need your help, *caneton*." She peered around the room and drew in a shaky breath.

"*Ma sœur*—"

"Turn around while I change back into my old dress."

He nodded and did as instructed, his shoulders slumped.

Within a candlemark, she had resumed her tattered dress and underthings. Tears edged close to release. She wouldn't give her family or that démon the satisfaction of making her cry. Instead, she scooped up the chemises, stockings, and silk garters in her hands, then lowered for Matthieu to climb onto her back. She would leave him in the kitchen after filling the copper tub with cold well water, to soak and agitate the silks. The cottons she'd set aside to boil. Once he was busy, she would return to the rooms and drag down the coverlets, blankets, pillowcases, and mattress cover. Clean the vanity bowl too. Eventually she would wash the drapes and beat the rug. But for now, she just needed clean linens and clothing for them both.

The busyness would keep her mind occupied and give her anger and grief an outlet.

Grinding her teeth, she stomped down the stairwell toward the main floor.

THE NEXT MORNING, she returned for weapons lessons. If she became adept enough in using a smallsword or pistol, she could liberate her and Matthieu from the démon's vile presence. Know your enemy, bah! He was a monster. There was nothing else to know.

But he didn't show to the ballroom. On the table was a long, dainty gold chain, one she knew was meant to replace the twine around her neck. Her traitorous heart fluttered at the thoughtfulness, even though the apology still wasn't enough.

He didn't appear the day after. Nor did she see or hear him in the chateau.

He didn't show for an entire week. And when he finally graced her with his haughty presence, his words and mannerisms were stiff and clipped. Eight days had passed since his return. And each day, detached instruction and nothing more fell from his lips for their two- to three-hour training session. Those wolfish eyes would glance at the gold chain around her neck, a strange expression in his gaze, then he would disappear again until a meal was ready, if he were home. He ate mostly in silence too.

The darkly elegant man in her dreams had yet to return too and she feared their connection was permanently severed.

Had the démon silenced the man in his jealous possessiveness?

Or was this man simply a figment of her imagination?

Perhaps the charms of this cursed house were playing with her mind.

Even if so, her thoughts were consumed by him—by the cruel, elegant planes of his face, the murmuring roughness of his cultured voice, those hauntingly beautiful honey-amber eyes, the way his dark, earthen wavy strands glinted with strands of gold in the light, how the sharp angles of his intelligence delighted in cutting across hers. Mostly, she thought about his pain, the way his voice broke with the shattering grief he had shared. Had no one ever fought for him before? Told him he was worthy of happiness and goodness and . . . love?

Saints, he really was sinful. Just thinking about his broad build and the sensual way he smiled made her heart sigh for a few dizzying, heavy-breathing beats. Without him, her dreams turned into nightmares and Chateau Lumière Dorée became a dark, lifeless prison.

Rhoslyn pushed back the growing despair.

Sitting in her now scrubbed and airy room, Matthieu tucked into bed fast asleep beside her, she lifted the hand mirror and waited. Hopefully Dalbréath and Gellynor Death Talker would contact her soon. She desperately needed a drop of hope before she lost herself to the mountain of grief rumbling for release since the fires.

The House of Golden Light would *not* become her grave—metaphorically or literally.

Chapter 19

Fentienne

Factory row was strangely quiet for early morning. The gray of dawn had burned away to blue, cloudless skies. A welcomed sight after a week of rainstorms. Fentienne had shifted only an hour earlier. With the season stretching closer to summer, the dawn came far sooner, thankfully. Exhaustion pounded behind his eyes. The ache in his bones and joints still flamed and winced, especially after shadow sprinting most of the way to Gabaston. He was a man on a mission. Time was far too limited to coddle physical pain—but dark skies, how he craved alcohol to dull his body, mind, and heart.

These past three weeks.

These godsdamn three weeks.

He wanted to break windows, shatter furniture, shred walls.

Just the simplest, fleeting thought of Rhoslyn shoved him closer to insanity. Made his muscles and blood pump with hyper-level alpha aggression. Made him do stupid things like confessing to Rhoslyn that she belonged to him and no one else—as if an obsessive animal.

He was becoming more animal about their mate bond too.

His wolf wanted her. All of her.

But... so did he.

A repulsive truth that nauseated his gut and gleefully flung every hateful thought about the fae back in his face. A wicked, cruel reality destroying him breath by breath.

He couldn't fall for Fayette again.

He refused to let Addien win.

Lifelong faerie curses these confusing, infuriating feelings may be, but skies. He wanted to die in Rhoslyn's arms. The excruciating torture of aching for her was pushing him dangerously closer to revealing all his secrets. Once she knew, all threads tethering them together would be severed. His wolf would own him. Then he would join his brothers and father in the Underworld.

There were ways to show her his identity. Myrefell's military tags were tucked inside a chest in his chambers. The remnants of his uniform too, which he couldn't bring himself to burn. Handing those over would be the same as gifting her a hammer and nails to his coffin. Removing the leash from his wolf's collar.

He didn't for two reasons.

Until she was capable of better protecting herself in his absence, he couldn't physically die.

But Fentienne hungered to die from the pleasure of his body exploring every dip and rise of hers; thirsted to memorize the rhythm of her excited breaths and heady beats of her heart.

She was his.

His, his, his.

His mate. His wife.

His.

And he was going mad.

A few vendors wandered to their stations, pulling him from his intoxicating thoughts. Small pockets of workers scurried to the factories, the early shifts to restoke forge fires and refill boilers in steam engines. But an oppressive weight laid heavily over Gabaston's slums. The stench of death and rot, sewage and sickness mixed with the acrid, wispy remnants of smoke, curdled the contents of Fentienne's gut. The dress factory lay in ash, save for the twisted clumps of metal that had yet to be scrapped.

Fury simmered hot in his blood. His aunt punished Rhoslyn for her defiance by punishing others. Fentienne was well acquainted with this tactic. He was no saint, having leveled entire dwarven villages and mining camps on the brink of winter. And this week, thanks to his benevolent, kindhearted family, close to sixty girls had lost their safe, dependable source of income. Many, he knew, were already prostituting themselves in the alleys simply to survive, if not forced to by the men who kidnapped unprotected females.

He didn't know what to do, but a broken piece of him felt responsible. A crack in the arrogant, apathetic façade he used as a shield against the enormity of emotions he didn't know how to contain or process—or understand.

Had he not helped lead an attack on Gabaston while Florian tracked the Black Witch through the Seven Jeweled Hills, would a high percentage of commoners in Factory Row still resemble gaunt, half-dead bodies that staggered from one miserable moment to the next? Would the bellies of children be rounded from ample food instead of swollen from hunger? Would young females, some not even old enough to legally marry, be forced to sell their bodies in the alleys to feed their families and survive?

Poverty was a plague that would always pox every realm.

The suffering of lower classes was unavoidable.

Still, his family allowed sewage to run down these street gutters; did nothing to clean up the dead, diseased rats littering the cobbled streets; laughed at those who lived a daily wake of their buried dignity while dining on golden plates in a palace surrounded by a golden fence.

Still, Fentienne also just couldn't be bothered to care.

People were born to die. What was the point? Good life? Bad life? The end result was the same. The time between birth and death was a desperate attempt to find a meaning in one's existence that didn't exist while convincing oneself that it did. Happiness was a fool's game. For him, it existed only in moments that were never meant to be.

Still, the bladed heart in his chest was bleeding him out. He wanted to double over in horror at what his family had done—both in Clifstán and Aurelienne—and how he had reveled in the suffering of others. *Groomed* to find happiness only in another's pain.

The empty eyes in Gabaston haunted him.

The defeated shambles of his former enemy still brought him measures of satisfaction.

People were selfish, greedy, self-serving arseholes, and he was more so than most.

Palace guards lined the streets, their eyes tracking his movements. He paid them little heed.

A glass bottle clinked in his duster's pocket. An empty corked bottle. Bringing back Rhoslyn's family was impossible. But he could still bring back part of her home to keep. First, he wished to pay a certain backstabbing wolf a visit. One he wanted to kill but needed alive. One he gravely distrusted but also trusted with his life.

Fentienne paused before a rundown cob building and pushed through the door. The stench of sickness and unwashed bodies hit him first. He tried to take shallow breaths through his mouth, even while jogging up the stairs to the third floor. The rotting wood creaked and groaned beneath his weight. Wallpaper peeled from the walls stained with mold. At the end of the hall, he knocked on apartment number 312.

The door scraped open, and before the man could greet him, Fentienne clutched the wolf by the throat and shoved him against a wall, kicking the door behind him.

Lucas bared his canines and growled but stopped his shifting when Fentienne squeezed. There was no fight. His wolf knew to submit to Fentienne's.

"I want to kill you," he snarled through his highwayman collar in the lesser démon's face. "I want to rip the beating heart from your chest and force it down your throat."

"The people . . . chose her, Wolf . . . Prince," Lucas rasped and Fentienne squeezed even harder.

"You did not have *my permission* to speak to her. She. Is. *Mine* to protect. My mate, Lucas. You know the penalty of touching let alone conspiring with an alpha's mate."

"She was . . . already . . . outside. With her . . . uncle."

Fentienne's hand and arm were shaking from holding himself back. Infuriated, he growled in Lucas's face and released his throat. The man slumped against the wall, coughing, and Fentienne changed his mind. This couldn't go without punishment. He was the alpha over all the clans, the Prince of Démons. Lucas had challenged his authority the moment he went behind Fentienne's back. But it was far more than that. Rhoslyn wasn't just any fayette of Factory Row.

Claws out, he slashed across the lesser démon's chest. Red bloomed the shredded night shirt. Lucas inhaled a heavy breath and bared his teeth but didn't fight back.

Still not satisfied, Fentienne took the démon's arm and twisted at the elbow until the bones of his forearm snapped. The man cried out and, finally, Fentienne smiled. Lucas would heal within hours. Within fifteen to twenty minutes, he would feel no pain while healing. But that satisfying snap followed by the sounds of agony would echo prettily in Fentienne's mind for days. Grabbing Lucas by the hair, he dragged him into the main living quarters and threw him onto the floor. Fentienne removed the highwayman collar around his face and dominantly stared down at the quivering man.

"I'm sparing your life," he spat at the alpha. "But *only* because Factory Row needs you. As do I."

"*Merci*, Prince Fentienne." The man's raspy voice trembled in pain as he cradled his arm against his bleeding chest.

Fentienne crouched down, an arrogant curl to his lips. "I want to break your other arm. I want to break both of your legs."

Lucas blinked back the rising anger. Alphas didn't like being taken down. Especially by other alphas. But he also scented pleasure. The sick bastard liked pain. Or he enjoyed seeing Fentienne so possessively pissed. Probably the latter.

Annoyed, he growled, "Queen of The Row."

"*Ou . . . Oui.*"

"An organized strike."

Lucas nodded his head, his eyes still submissively focused on the floor. Eyes that burned with fury. The man's pride pained him more than his injuries.

"My mate is an excellent strategist. I support her plans. But you will *never* go behind my back again if you want to live. I will take your family out with you too."

The lesser démon attempted to roll to a better position and grimaced.

Fentienne cocked his head. "Did you really believe I wouldn't hear?"

"*Non*, milord." Lucas drew in a shaking breath, still averting his gaze, and gritted out, "I knew you would."

"But you didn't think I would know you spoke to my mate, who is under *my* protection?"

A muscle feathered along Lucas's jaw. "Of course you would."

"Ask me how I found out."

"Tell me," the man said in an obviously placating tone. "How did you find out?"

"She asked why I had claimed her. I never told her that I had." Fentienne grabbed Lucas's broken arm and yanked. The man cried out again, making Fentienne grin. "I paid a visit to Mon Père Michel who shared that *you* represented the Queen of The Row, believing I already knew because she is my mate!"

Lucas paled, breath hissing through his teeth in his pain. "Apologies, milord. I dishonored your authority as head of the clans."

Fentienne laughed darkly. "The least of my godsdamn worries."

The lesser démon's sharp eyes snapped to his.

"Wolf neighbors?"

Lucas pointed to the floor with his good hand. The apartment below? They wouldn't hear their whispers then.

Fentienne crept closer to Lucas, who brazenly held his gaze. "I need to share a well-guarded secret with you," he whispered to the lesser démon. "Because you hold the ear of Factory Row. Also," he continued, "despite your recent actions, I need to trust someone who will protect my mate when I am dead and I foolishly trust you."

"Dead?" Lucas's eyes rounded. "I am truly loyal to you and you alone. *All* that is yours."

"I don't give a shit about pretty words, *sans-culotte*. Or groveling."

"It is not flattery or groveling, Wolf Prince. I am willing to seal my words in blood."

"Yet you went behind my back."

"The wolves circle you, milord," Lucas said between pained breaths. "They want a seat at your golden table."

"Not you?" Fentienne bitterly laughed. "You're not using me for your political gain too?"

Lucas grunted an ill-humored laugh in reply. "What seat, milord? When are peasants allowed to dine with kings? *Non*, this *sans-culotte* is not so delusional."

Fentienne heaved an irritated sigh. "Get to the point, lesser démon."

"That is part of the point."

"You're loyal to me because I won't acknowledge you as equal among royals?" Fentienne arched an impatient brow. "I'm seconds away from no longer restraining myself—"

"Over forty years ago," Lucas cut in, "a young queen cared about the poor. My grand-mére shared how Queen Loriette gave toys to children and her old cotton dresses to women in rags. She shared her food that would spoil uneaten. Factory Row loved her." Lucas paused and his gaze darkened. "But the aristocracy believes commoners are responsible for their poverty. We are lazy, uneducated, dirty, and the Dark Saint's curse. Why else would all we touch rot? Why else would the other saints turn their backs on us, no?

"Loriette Chalamet was a den mother," Lucas continued. "An alpha over all the clans who protected her subjects. Females are not alphas in our world, *oui*? But wolves bowed to her like our wolves bow to you."

Fentienne's heart dropped to his stomach.

Gods, his mother was an actual wolf shifter. Even though he already suspected, hearing it confirmed still surprised him. But a female alpha? His mother? Lucas studied him, predatory eyes target locked onto his every movement. The man could scent Fentienne's rising emotions, could hear the rapid beat of his heart. But Fentienne was too enraged to care. Details suddenly clicked into place.

You think I do not know monsters?

You, Adalwolf Fentienne Beausoleil Chalamet Halivaard, are not a monster. You are an angry, broken, confused boy.

He was conceived in hate. Trained to hate. But his mother . . . gods, his mother.

I know my boys. But of you four, I understand you most, mon petit louveteau, Prince of Démons.

None of his brothers had a nickname. Only him. Her little wolf.

And this was the power his father had wanted. It wasn't just about regaining the golden throne of Aurelienne but dominating the wolves to turn them into supernatural soldiers.

Betrayal sank its sharp teeth into Fentienne's heart. Clenching the muscles of his jaw, he whispered harshly, "The Aurelienne aristocracy sold Loriette Chalamet to Aelfred Halivaard."

"The price, Wolf Prince—"

"The death of her younger brothers. King Aelfred wanted a guarantee that his own son would claim the throne and rule the wolves."

"*Oui.*"

His father slaughtered the nobles who gave him their queen. All but Adeline Chalamet. He could have claimed Adeline when Loriette failed to provide him heirs for years—but didn't. Because Adeline wasn't an alpha or held any rank among the wolves. When invading Gabaston a year and a half ago, they received explicit instructions to attack Factory Row only and to not cross the line into Saints District.

Invisible hackles bristled down Fentienne's back as thundering rage rumbled in the marrow of his bones. What had Adeline done? What sort of alliance had she struck that cost the lives of both realms but none of Aurelienne's aristocracy beyond the slaughter at Chateau Lumière Dorée?

He turned his knife-edged gaze back onto Lucas. "How do you know this?"

"I protect what is mine just like you protect what is yours. And Factory Row is mine." Lucas dipped his head, adjusting the arm he cradled. "Prince Fentienne Beausoleil, my Wolf Prince and future King of Aurelienne, son of beloved Loriette Chalamet, I give you my word, as a man, the alpha of Clan Palehide, fellow guardian officer in the Brotherhood, and . . . as your friend." The last two words were spoken softly. "I will protect your secrets and your mate to my grave."

"I don't keep friends, lesser démon."

"I know, *mon ami.*" Lucas's lips twisted in humor.

Skies, he didn't have the patience for this. His heart was now preparing for battle. Already his pulse beat war drums. Gods, his mother . . . But for Rhoslyn's sake, he needed to remain levelheaded. Ignoring the man, Fentienne crept closer and leaned in toward Lucas.

"Rhoslyn Gautier is a changeling child," he began. "A girl I was married to before the fae when age four and she a newborn. A girl I am now married to according to human laws after claiming her before the Brotherhood and clans."

Lucas stilled, not a single muscle moving. "She is Princess Maeline Wyndham from the House of Thorns?"

"Ah," Fentienne sneered. "You know my court politics."

"*Merde.*" Real fear slipped into the man's gaze for the first time. "I suspected she was a changeling. Her scent is far different than her brother's, than her parents too." He paused to cough and clear his rasping throat again. "I couldn't place the aristocratic family who hid their child until I scented her Dúnælven uncle. He is a Kadelaryn, no?"

"*Oui*, Gedlen Fate Maker's military commander," Fentienne growled in a low voice. "Maeline Kadelaryn Wyndham is my legal *royal* wife, bound in faerie blood. The changeling Rhoslyn Gautier doesn't know her identity yet, or mine, or that I'm her husband let alone my wolf mate, but I am certain Queen Adeline now does. Maeline and I have a common enemy whom I would bet my life on is currently working with my aunt, if not before the blood march." The lesser démon's brows drew together. Fentienne could see the questions burning in his blue eyes, but the man remained quiet. "Think, Lucas. Think like a war strategist. An army scout. What will Queen Adeline do with the Crowned Princess of Avenbury?"

"Use her as a hostage to negotiate debts owed."

They held the intensity of each other's imploring stare for a long beat. "And risk war with Avenbury and Dúnælven? Aurelienne wouldn't survive."

Lucas drew in another trembling breath and winced. "*Non*, you are right—" His eyes grew large again. "Marry her to Le Duc Lucien Chalamet, since you are dead. To dissolve debts."

Fentienne slowly nodded his head. "My cousin isn't particularly kind to females, if rumors are to be believed."

"The rumors are true, milord. His mistresses go missing and are never found again."

Heat buzzed in Fentienne's head. He would kill that man if he so much as looked at his wife. Reining himself in, once again, he continued. "As king consort to the Queen of Avenbury, when she ascends to the throne," he whispered, "what privileges does that grant le duc according to their elven laws?"

"*Pardonnez-moi*, milord, I do not know their laws intimately."

Fentienne bared his teeth and another flush of anger swept through him. "The King Consort governs their military. The Queens of Avenbury have a long history of marrying warriors for this reason."

"Saints," Lucas whispered. "He would use Avenbury to invade Dreglind on behalf of Queen Adeline."

"My brother is rebuilding Dreglind's military," Fentienne whispered back, "but they are in soldiering infancy and would not withstand an attack from both Avenbury and Aurelienne."

"And Clifstán is now demilitarized."

Fentienne growled, "Queen Adeline will have dissolved debts at the cost of the two nations she owes and while sacrificing more of Factory Row to the battlefields." They were quiet for several rapid heartbeats. "Beyond wolf laws and politics, do you now understand why I go to such lengths to protect what is mine?"

Lucas swallowed thickly. "Chateau Lumière Dorée is under a dark magic. Is this by your and your mate's common enemy?"

Fentienne dipped his head in a single, curt nod. "Addien Wyndham, first cousin to Queen Audra and next in line to the throne after Maeline. Be on your guard as the Queen of The Row's voice. Addien is a rune shifter and finds pleasure in destroying men."

"*Merde* . . ." Lucas swore again under his breath. A crease appeared between the lesser démon's brows. "I could not say your name or title before the gates."

"Addien doesn't want Rhoslyn to know who I am." Lucas opened his mouth and Fentienne quickly added, "The details of this curse are between me and Rhoslyn only."

Lucas remained quiet another couple of beats, then asked, "Why is Madame Beausoleil not aware of her identity?"

The breath tightened in Fentienne's chest. *Madame Beausoleil.* His wife. A drowsy, pleasurable sensation waltzed down his body. But he hardened his face to bored arrogance and blandly murmured, "It's the carrot I dangle to force her into combat and weapons training."

The lesser démon barked a laugh. "It is no doubt necessary. She is—"

"Headstrong and reckless."

Lucas offered a tiny smile. "Passionate and cunning, Wolf Prince. I envy you." Fentienne started to growl and Lucas lifted his uninjured hand in surrender. "I do not encroach on your territory. I admire madame for what she tried to do for Factory Row. What she continues to try and do. The people see a crown on her head, as they should."

Fentienne lowered himself to sit on the floor instead of crouch. "Tell me, lesser démon, what else has the Queen of The Row planned that I should know about?"

Lucas boldly met his eyes again. "Madame asked, as Factory Row's clan alpha, that I help find families to take in the grisettes as well as safe employment."

Warmth filled Fentienne's chest, a foreign soft feeling. "And have you?"

"For twenty grisettes, *oui*. The youngest and unprotected first. I am still working, though." Lucas loosed a heavy sigh. "The alpha from West Pack will not assist me."

Clan Palehide was divided into two packs, East and West. The dress factory was in West Pack's territory. Fentienne's lip curled. "Is Bertrand Sibille loyal to the queen or fears retribution?"

Lucas's frown inched up into something smug and he shrugged with his uninjured arm. "I replaced West Pack's fallen officer two years ago. The Brotherhood chose me as the next clan alpha in Palehide instead of an alpha from West Pack and Bertrand still licks his wounds."

"Ego, then. He will submit to his clan alpha. I'll see to it."

"*Merci.* You will no doubt be more persuasive than me."

"More executions?" Fentienne asked.

"Four more. A total of twenty-three as of this morning." Lucas's face grew grave. "And more reports of a rabid black wolf in the woods. More deaths too. Factory Row is crying for justice from the Monks of Glanis."

Fentienne's heart dropped to his stomach. But he needed to keep his pulse and emotions under control. "Those bastards will eventually pay in blood for the blood they've spilled."

"*Oui*," Lucas agreed.

Pretending to be thinking to regain control of the fear pumping through him, Fentienne peered around the sparse room. But this space was unthinkable. How did people live with so little? A table with one chair stood in the corner. Opposite of the table was a disheveled cot with two thin blankets. Mold dotted the ceiling and dust coated the outer windows. Beside the table was a cabinet, what Fentienne knew was a small larder. A stove backed the corner behind them. And that was all.

"You are curious why a clan alpha lives in poverty." Lucas adjusted his position on the floor. Fentienne's gaze slid back to the wolf. "What kind of alpha feeds off those who cannot feed themselves? *Non*, I do not take their coin for myself as the clan alpha of Factory Row like my father before me." Sweat beaded on his forehead from pain, his pallor pale and clammy—though his arm was already healing. But Lucas's familiar taunting smile returned to his pinched features. "I have never worn silk breeches."

"You would look hideous in silk breeches," Fentienne murmured. "Everyone does."

Lucas laughed. "We are frilly men compared to Clifstán, no?"

"Only two garments exist in Aurelienne I appreciate, even more so than any article of clothing in Clifstán." A smile ghosted Fentienne's lips, a truce offering. "Corsets and gartered stockings."

A grin stretched across Lucas's face. "Brings a man to his knees. His wolf too."

Fentienne huffed a quiet laugh, then pushed to his feet. The lesser démon struggled to stand and Fentienne shoved him back down with his boot. "You enjoy this pain?"

Lucas's eyes glinted with mischief. "I warned that I might enjoy your bite."

"We are *not* friends, lesser démon."

"*Oui, mon ami.*"

"Do not hope to become lovers either."

"I prefer redheads." Lucas openly grinned at him now. "The softness of breasts too."

Fentienne closed his eyes in a long blink, willing patience—again. "Nor am I sorry for your arm or chest. I won't apologize for my anger or threats either. They were deserved and gracious, considering."

"You worry about my feelings, prince?" Lucas flashed him another taunting smile and waved his uninjured hand in a playfully dismissive gesture. "Wolf business, *mon ami*. I have done the same. And you were most gracious, *merci*."

Friend. Lucas kept calling him his friend. Did the man have a death wish?

Resisting the urge to roll his eyes, Fentienne pivoted on his heel toward the door.

"Bring Amélie Demarr to visit madame at the chateau gates," the lesser démon whispered. "Or allow me to deliver madame a note from Amélie."

He spun back toward Lucas.

"Everyone needs *friends*, milord," the man challenged. "Your mate was beside herself with grief when learning of the dress factory. She feared she had lost her Amélie."

Fentienne studied him a few seconds. Keeping Rhoslyn isolated would break her spirit over time. Addien wanted to torture her, not him. "A note only and you may wait for madame's reply. No visitations from anyone but you while Chateau Lumière Dorée is cursed and Rhoslyn's life remains in danger." He pivoted toward the door and—

"One more moment, prince."

Fentienne groaned a sigh and snapped, "What?"

"Be warned about madame's Uncle Dalbrie." A wolfish smile darkened Lucas's face, then he snarled, "The elf is a rune whisperer."

Fentienne arched a brow. That he didn't know—a very dangerous magic.

"And," Lucas continued, a wicked smile on his face, "ask madame where her brother lived until a few weeks ago and why he was thrown to the streets."

The boy hadn't always lived with Rhoslyn? "Anything else?"

"*Non*, milord."

"Bring a letter from Mademoiselle Demarr to Chateau Lumière Dorée in two days, no later than nine in the morning." He reached into his coin purse and tossed a silver at Lucas. "For stationary and ink, and for her secrecy. She is to burn *Mademoiselle Gautier's* letters immediately after reading them and you will watch her do so. If she so much as shares the smallest detail of Rhoslyn's life to others, I will personally kill her."

The lesser démon's eyes rounded. "Prince—"

"Good men sacrifice their desire to protect what is theirs for the so-called betterment of society. One that will just fall into the next corrupt cycle of life. But I would sacrifice every living being that walks the Kingdom of Ealdspell to keep Rhoslyn safe." His eyes narrowed at Lucas. "Even kill Amélie Demarr if she puts her *friend* in danger. Make sure she understands the risks before writing my wife."

"Mademoiselle Demarr is resourceful and well liked among working girls. She could prove valuable in organizing the strike."

"Then she'll know to keep her mouth shut and eyes wide open."

And with that, he put his highwayman collar into place and marched from the apartment on a warpath toward the main factories. The alpha of West Pack needed a reminder that he submitted to his clan leader and bowed before his prince and to now also bow before the Queen of The Row.

A corner of Fentienne's mouth ticked up. Two alphas to bloody in one morning. He wouldn't be as kind to West Pack as he was to Lucas, though. That wolf doomed girls to a life of violation. Girls from his territory. The only prostitution Fentienne permitted among the clans was the legal, registered work females personally chose.

Fentienne picked up his pace, eager to get this over with.

The glass bottle clinked in his pocket and he tensed against the rising battle pounding in his chest. He meant what he said to Lucas. To keep Rhoslyn safe, he would destroy anyone who threatened her. Hell, he was destroying himself for her safety. But unlike in the past, that declaration now came with a permanent blood stain of shame and a hefty dose of paranoid guilt from the blurred moral lines constantly warring in his head.

Not that shame over his actions would change anything.

Heroes were overrated good-doers who were, ultimately, self-centered. Remaining morally upright was a game of chance. All fights required sacrifices from all who played. Their refusal to bend ethics in the name of righteousness forced others to do so for them. Villains, however, didn't care about being good. Fentienne would cross moral lines as many times as necessary to protect those in his care. He didn't give a damn about polite society, either. All those rules to control and oppress people were meaningless in the end. And oh how he understood that more than most as the son of a warmongering villain who delusionally believed he was Ealdspell's hero.

Fentienne pushed out a heavy breath and focused on his next few tasks before he gave into the intense fury whipping through him.

After dealing with West Pack, he needed to pick up the cane he had made for Matthieu and shoes he had custom ordered for both Gautiers. His mate's shoes were barely holding together and Matthieu's were worse. The little boy would be stronger and more independent with better balance. The glass bottle in his pocket clinked again. He would also bring a piece of her home and family back with him, a silent apology for how he helped destroy all she held dear. And how he would continue to ruin her life.

The clopping sound of his boots on the cobbled street echoed in his ears. He lowered his head to avoid curious stares and nearly stumbled back a step. A rivulet of watered-down blood trickled between the stones. His head whipped over to the execution block. Two girls threw buckets of water over the guillotine and surrounding ground to clean while a Monk of Glanis watched. Fentienne pushed into the thickening crowd of factory workers before the monk could stop him.

She began to doubt whether she ought to prefer the imaginary devotion of a phantom to the real affection of the Beast. The very dream in which the Unknown appeared to her was invariably accompanied by warnings not to trust her sight.

She now knew that her love for the Unknown was not incompatible with her affection she entertained for the Beast, seeing that they were one and the same person.

The Beast replied, "I promise you never to have any wife but you."

"Then," rejoined Beauty, "I accept you as my husband and swear to be a fond and faithful wife to you."

"La Belle et la Bête" by Madame de Villeneuve, published in *The Young American and Marine Tales*, 1743

Chapter 20

Fentienne

Lowering his hat farther over his eyes, Fentienne angled around a tree leaning into the wooded path and picked up his pace. Per usual, he took a forest trail leading to Crowns Quarter for any watchful eyes, then would sprint home once out of sight. Guards knew he was *haute noblesse* with a simple sweep of his gaze, so they left him alone. His larger size intimidated *sans-culottes* from threatening "Liberté, Egalité, Fraternité!" in his aristocratic face. But Factory Row was a bomb with a lit fuse. Just a single drop of unrest and boom.

I know my boys. But of you four, I understand you most, mon petit louveteau, Prince of Démons.

A long, hot breath pushed from Fentienne's burning lungs. He was also seconds from exploding. Forcing West Pack's alpha into submission did little to cool his fury either. Lucas's story about his mother, a former queen of two realms, became a jagged thorn shoved deep into an already festering, putrefying wound. A white-hot rage was violently re-landscaping his reality—of himself and of the role he was born to play.

I understand you most, mon petit louveteau . . .

Did the démons sell her out to the King of Clifstán too?

A female alpha was unheard of, let alone as the head of the Brotherhood.

Until declared the head of the clans himself, the Prince of Démons, Fentienne didn't possess any real authority. Since his first cry of existence, there was always someone above him who dictated his moves. Not anymore. He no longer served those who held power over him and he refused to become the subject of another who could.

If Fentienne sat on the golden throne of Palais d'Aurélie and became the king consort to the future Queen of Avenbury, he would eventually control the military of the two realms on either side of Dreglind. This advantage allowed him to protect Florian while also protecting his mate from being eaten alive by court politics.

A sickening knowing in his gut screamed that Addien plotted one possible death for Maeline by arranging a marriage to Le Duc Lucien Chalamet on behalf of Avenbury. He didn't have proof yet, but he knew his enemy.

Addien wanted him—wanted him to emotionally die and wanted him physically as hers. Wanted his throne and his power.

And she wanted Maeline to suffer love scorned leading up to her promised death.

Regardless of if his mate bond was real or manufactured, regardless of how much he loathed faeries, Rhoslyn Gautier was his. *Only* his. The Beast of Gabaston would look like a mangy alley dog compared to Fentienne's moon-addled rampage if Rhoslyn were given to Lucien as a bride.

I will fight for you in each dream, milord. To prove you are not a monster.

When I wake, I will search for you and demand that horrible beast to release you from his prison.

He still didn't understand selfless love. To love, however that was defined, *was* a selfish act. Whatever. Breaking Eirwen's curse couldn't be central to claiming his birthright—or any decision, really. Ealdspell would riot no matter what. His Imperial Highness, former Clifstánian prince, held the eight realms in the palm of his Irminsul-blessed palm. Forgiveness only stretched so far, though. Absolving one Halivaard didn't cleanse Fentienne of his crimes. Florian was born saint anointed. But Fentienne . . . he was démon cursed. A so-called child of the Dark Saint. Already he could envision the poison dripping from the frothing mouths of the faithful as Fentienne's half-shifted head rested beneath the blade—

A growl rumbled behind him.

Fentienne spun on his heel, an ear turned to the wind. Nothing moved in the forest, still his eyes jumped from shadow to shadow. Then he saw it. A large black wolf démon hidden behind a huckleberry bush. Female, if the scent was correct. No, not female. But not male either. A scent he hadn't picked up in another shifter before.

Yellow eyes tracked him from a head postured low to the ground, their lips curled back to reveal sharp teeth. The démon growled louder as they prowled more into the open. Blood tinged the fur around their snout with splotches down their neck.

"Shift," Fentienne commanded.

The démon appeared to laugh and prowled closer.

"Shift, démon," Fentienne growled back, his golden eyes locked onto the golden eyes attempting to dominate him in return. "This is a command from your alpha."

A black wolf, just like him. He had yet to encounter another in the woods, though he knew others must exist. Perhaps black was a Chalamet trait? He had only seen a handful of Chalamet démons in wolf form and all were grays.

"Last warning." Fentienne lowered the shoebox and cane, removed his duster followed by his gloves, not once taking his eyes off the démon. "I will kill you for insubordination. Shift and I'll show mercy."

The wolf lunged. Fentienne leaned hard left, out of the démon's trajectory, and slammed his elbow in the wolf's ribs as they sailed past. The démon yelped, rolling to a stop on the ground. Claws out, Fentienne shadow sprinted to where the wolf struggled to their feet. He slashed, but his sharpened nails met only air. The démon had winked out and reappeared three yards away to his right, on all fours and snarling a laugh.

"Shit," he hissed under his breath. Was this a faerie rune shifter?

If he chased after the creature, they would only teleport out of the way. Fentienne narrowed his eyes. How did faeries teleport? Démons defied the physics of the natural world when shadow sprinting. They were, after all, a form of magic too. But he only knew two faeries who blinked in and out of visibility and one was dead.

"Addien Wyndham," he said, a cruel twist to his mouth. "I know your secrets."

She winked out again. Fentienne's heart leapt to his throat. The faerie would reappear in the midst of an attack. Tensing his muscles, Fentienne braced for impact, not knowing what direction it would come from. As expected, she reappeared—jumping onto his side.

Sharp teeth sank into his arm. The arm mostly healed from his injury over a week ago. Fentienne roared in pain to distract her from his counterattack.

The teeth bit down harder. Using his closest leg, he swept Addien off her feet. Flesh, muscle, and linen tore down his arm. Not giving the creature a chance to react, he spun and, using his other leg, stomped onto her unprotected ribcage.

Bones crunched beneath his boot and her shifted wolf form yelped.

Fentienne darkly laughed through the blinding fire hitting his nerve endings. Blood dripped down his arm. But he pushed all sensation away save rage.

Once more she winked out. A half-heartbeat later, she reappeared right before him mid-air. The impact staggered him back a couple of steps. Sharp teeth snapped at his throat. The muscles in Fentienne's uninjured arm shook as he pushed against Addien. She bit at his shoulder instead, cutting through fabric and skin.

Fentienne let the fiend have access to his shoulder as he pretended to lose his balance and fall backward. The moment he hit the ground, her jaw released him. He grabbed the black wolf by the head and twisted—hard. The snap was immediate. The body going limp too. He shoved the creature off him with his feet and exhaled an angry growl.

For a moment, he could only focus on the blue, gold, and green moving above him as trees swayed in the breeze. Sweat dripped into Fentienne's eye and he blinked. Burning pain screamed down his arm and across his shoulder.

He killed Addien.

Sweet mountain gods.

She was dead. *Finally* dead.

A light feeling floated through him—an airy sensation he wanted to desperately lean into. Was this relief? Did this mean he and Chateau Lumière Dorée were now free? He didn't know if he wanted to cry or laugh and was on the verge of both. Pain bleated down his right side with every movement. Nevertheless, he slowly turned his head. The black wolf form started to fade and Fentienne grinned, unable to contain his delight at seeing her vacant stare—

"Oh gods..."

The hair rose on the back of his neck.

He had to be hallucinating. This couldn't be real.

A male elf lay beside him on the forest floor. An elf with golden blond hair.

Fentienne shot up to a seat, gritting back the sharp, undulating waves of pain, and quickly swept a panicking gaze around the forest. Goosebumps flushed down his torso. Nothing about this situation made sense. His body felt the ripping pain of teeth and claws but his mind denied what he was looking at. Yet a niggling fear clenched the muscles of his stomach—this male probably wasn't the only elven rune shifter to masquerade as a wolf.

Was he the Beast of Gabaston?

Were several faeries the Beast?

And, if so, did they all look like his wolf—large, black fur, golden eyes?

Moving onto his knees, Fentienne bit back a cry of pain, crawled over to the male, and then rolled him over. Brown eyes stared vacant at the trees overhead. The elf wore dark blue Dúnælven battle leathers. But the rancid scent of Factory Row was all over him. And he smelled distinctly male now too. Fentienne picked up the elf's hand and inspected his nails. Coal and oxidized ore dust—he worked in the iron factories.

Elves in Gabaston had magic?

If so, why not negotiate and glamour to earn regular coin? Factory Row housed more elves than humans. It would be so easy for them to gain favor and, eventually, replace the aristocracy with their own kind.

But they didn't. They suffered beside all other races on The Row. More so, actually.

Was their magic latent like his own had been?

Blood dripped from Fentienne's arm onto the ground. *Shit!* If a démon passed by, they would know it was him who killed this elf. Already, his open injuries were probably drawing wolves to him. Walking back into Factory Row to find help with the body and for Claudette to stitch him up would be a suicide mission with the amount of blood on his clothing. The guards would notice. The monks too.

What had the rune shifting elf attacked before him? Blood had stained his snout.

Fentienne found his feet and stumbled over to the huckleberry bush. Three natural wolves lay dead. A tiny whimper caught his ear. His eyes cut to a hole in a log and narrowed—a wolf cub. Slowly it crept from its hiding spot toward Fentienne and whimpered again. A female cub. She didn't appear or smell injured.

"Go back to the log," Fentienne ordered. He needed to move her parents and sibling to the elf, to cover his blood and to make it appear like a natural attack. The little cub obeyed and toddled back into the log and laid down.

Fentienne removed his waistcoat with a grimace. Then pulled his linen shirt over his head, unable to hold back a small cry. Like before, he ripped his shirt into strips and tied off the injury on his arm, then wrapped up his shoulder, thankfully the same side, as best as he could.

A few minutes later, the elf was surrounded by the natural wolves. One he cut into to spill blood over his own.

Dizziness spun through him. Fentienne's head was growing far too light. He needed to shadow sprint back to the chateau before he lacked the magic to do so from the blood loss.

He stuffed his waistcoat and what remained of his shirt into a pocket of his duster, then slid the coat over his bare torso. The shoebox, cane, and gloves were where he had left them. He started to reach for them when he remembered the cub. She was too little to leave behind. And he didn't have the strength to find her pack. It was against the Brotherhood to leave orphaned cubs behind—natural or shifter.

"Come," he called out to the pup. A few seconds later, she wobbled through the brush and ferns toward him. Light gray fur haloed around her in the sunlight. She blinked up at him with sky blue eyes and let out a tiny howl.

Fentienne placed her into a large pocket inside his duster. She wiggled around while he awkwardly buttoned his coat with the claws of one hand. Annoyed, he placed his tricorn hat back onto his head then picked up the shoebox, cane, and gloves before streaking through the woods toward Chateau Lumière Dorée.

BY THE TIME he reached the kitchen in the lower gardens, he could barely stand on his feet. The world blurred in and out of focus. In his injured state, using magic gravely depleted his energy stores. The roiling fury didn't help either. If not wounded, he would raze the forest to the ground.

How many elves in Gabaston now practiced magic?

How many elves had Addien convinced to impersonate him?

He needed to warn the Brotherhood, not only of the rune shifters, but that he wasn't the Beast. Hopefully, Lucas visited in two days because he wasn't sure if he'd be awake to travel tomorrow. Using his good shoulder, Fentienne pushed open the door and staggered inside.

Rhoslyn looked up from kneading bread and gasped. Her green eyes traveled over his face downward to the spots of blood staining his coat. After how he had treated her, he expected Rhoslyn to celebrate his injured state. Delight in his misery. But his mate couldn't resist the wounded, even if they were cruel and arrogant toward her apparently. She dropped the dough in her hands and rushed over. Gently she took the shoebox and cane from his good arm, saying, "Let me help you," while guiding him to a bench against the wall.

Before he could thank her, she placed the objects onto a worktable and ran toward the larder. A few seconds later, she returned with a bucket of water, ladle, and wooden cup. She poured him a drink and brought it to his lips.

He rolled his eyes, refusing to be babied, and took the cup of water with his good hand. "Spirits," he said between quick breaths. "Spirits to disinfect. Wine to dull pain."

Rhoslyn nodded and dashed toward the larder once more.

A little bark sounded from his pocket. He had almost forgotten about the cub. Fentienne downed the water then set the cup on the bench seat beside him. Awkwardly, he unbuttoned the duster. His clawed nails usually required both hands for this feat. But, somehow, he managed in the woods and again in the kitchen. Gently, he slid his hand into the large inside pocket and pulled the cub out by the nape of her neck.

"A puppy!" a boy's voiced called out. Matthieu, he realized through the haze of his acute exhaustion.

Fentienne put the cub onto the floor. "Go to the boy by the fire." She barked at him, wagging her tail while biting onto his boot. "Do as I say, she cub," he said with more force. "The little boy. Go." She whined but turned away a second later.

He watched her toddle on young legs toward Matthieu, to ensure she obeyed his commands. But the pure joy on that little boy's face held all Fentienne's attention. Matthieu was practically glowing. Was that how he had looked when seeing Loring the first time? Dark skies, he missed his stallion.

He caught Rhoslyn's gaze over Matthieu's head. A small smile flitted across her lips and gratitude brightened her green eyes. It was only a fraction of a second. He wasn't even sure if what he saw was real, he was so tired.

The wound on his arm throbbed and he could feel more blood dribble to his wrist. Grimacing, Fentienne pulled his good arm from the coat. A cold sweat broke across his forehead and he paused to catch his breath. Rhoslyn set three bottles of alcohol onto the table across from him, then reached for the sleeve of his injured arm. He swallowed thickly then gave a go-ahead nod. Gently, inch by inch, she slid the sleeve down his arm, her face growing paler and paler until she appeared sick enough to vomit. The linen strips made from his shirt were completely soaked through.

"Dare I ask, démon?" she whispered.

His eyes flitted to Matthieu then back to her. "Help me to the top of the third floor after my wounds are treated."

"To your room?" Her mouth fell open and a touch of color returned to her face as she took in his shirtless state. If he wasn't on the verge of passing out, he would be amused.

"No, mademoiselle. Just to the top of the stairs. To talk in private."

"How do I know—"

"I can barely remove my coat!" he gritted out furiously. Closing his eyes in a long blink, he added more quietly, "I don't have energy for another fight. Let alone any *other* activities."

She placed a hand on her hip and tilted her head. "*Oof!* If we do not fight, how will I know if you are still alive?"

He smiled, leaning his head back onto the stone wall. Clever, creature. But she wouldn't bait him into arguing about arguing. A starburst of pain shot down his arm and his exhausted smile turned into a sharp hiss. Unlike Lucas and the alpha from West Pack, who would heal in one to two hours with pain relief within twenty minutes tops, Fentienne wouldn't heal for at least a week and with minimal relief. Not having full control of his magic was aggravating, especially when fighting fellow monsters. His eyes shuttered half-closed while focusing on steadying his breathing.

He almost forgot about his wife before him as he fought through the persistent, stabbing ache. But she was taking him in—the flexing roll of each heaving muscle, the blood smeared over his body, the tousled, finger raked state of his hair—before turning her head to watch Matthieu on the floor with the she cub.

"I need stitching up, grisette," he murmured.

Rhoslyn blanched again. For a couple seconds, he thought she might faint. Was she queasy at the sight of blood? Straightening her shoulders, she placed a near full bottle of wine into his good hand and said, "Drink, beast. I will return shortly with a sewing kit."

"*Merci*," he whispered, grimacing against another wave of fire pulsing down his arm.

He pressed the bottle to his lips, guzzled quickly—and coughed. His face twisted in a shudder. This wine was horrid. Did she bring him souring wine on purpose? Probably—the brat. Bracing for the slight vinegar aftertaste, he forced himself to drink until the last remaining drops. Leaning forward, he reached for the next bottle of wine and began downing the half-full contents.

Gods, he was ridiculous.

The man who mocked the pain of others could barely handle his own. Fentienne started to laugh under his breath. Over a year ago, he wouldn't have contemplated the comparison. Outside of shifting back into half-man each morning, he hadn't sustained injuries of this magnitude until these past two weeks. Not one major war injury or broken bone. Only surface level cuts and bruises. Disciplinary lashings didn't tear deeply through muscle either, not like these bite wounds. Skies, he was a mess. Even Lucas taunted Fentienne for considering his feelings after Fentienne had clawed his chest and broke his forearm.

He was growing soft. It was disgusting.

Or just too tired to keep up pretenses.

Probably both.

"What is her name, milord?"

He slid his blurry focus toward the hearth fire. Matthieu giggled when the cub licked at his face.

"No name," the she cub barked.

Fentienne sighed. "She wasn't named yet. You choose."

"Yet? When are wolf pups given names?"

"Each pack is different. Some cubs are named at birth, some when earned."

"She should choose." Matthieu nuzzled his face into the wolf pup's fur. "What would you like to be called, *ma petite louveteau?*"

I know my boys. But of you four, I understand you most, mon petit louveteau, Prince of Démons.

Tears bit the back of Fentienne's eyes. The little wolf barked and he swallowed against the grief knotting in his throat at her choice. "Drurie."

A wolf name that meant *one who is greatly loved.*

Drurie barked wolf pup gibberish and licked at Matthieu's face again. "Do we get to keep Drurie?"

"She belongs with her pack." Fentienne slowly blew out a shaky breath. "Don't get too attached."

"Did her parents attack you?"

"No."

"Why did you take her from her pack?"

"Her parents were dead when I found her."

"Who killed—"

"Matthieu," Fentienne said through gritted teeth. "No more questions."

The little boy studied him again, nodded his head a few seconds later. Drurie playfully tugged on Matthieu's breeches, making the boy grin.

Sleep called to Fentienne, but he didn't want to answer endless questions about Drurie and her kin to remain awake. Especially questions that would lead to answers only Rhoslyn should hear. Still, his eyes struggled to remain open. Drurie barked again and a fresh wave of fury hit him.

How did Addien control the male elf's mind to do her bidding? Could she rune whisper, like Dalbréath? Or did she seize control through means more archaic, like a potion? And why did the elf attack natural wolves? Or had the wolves attacked the elf, sensing an impostor? To protect Fentienne as alpha over all wolves?

Gods, every time his mind contemplated one question, thirty more cropped up.

When his mind wasn't so soupy, he would ask the she cub questions.

Which reminded him . . . Lucas told him to ask Rhoslyn a question about Matthieu's housing arrangements. But he wanted to hear the answer from her brother instead.

"Boy," Fentienne began, swiveling his head toward Matthieu, "Where did you live while Rhoslyn worked?"

Matthieu glanced up and frowned. "In the foundling home for boys until three weeks ago, milord." He coughed, drew in a breath, and continued. "Mon Père Michel gave my bed to a human boy. I still had two weeks left on the tithes Rhoslyn paid. But Mon Père Michel refused to return Rhoslyn's tithes."

"He stole her money?"

"*Oui*. Rhoslyn had to leave her apartment. They don't allow males." Matthieu frowned again. "We lived in the rubbled cottages and she worked two jobs to feed me." Matthieu coughed into his arm. "The temple still charged us for soup and stale bread, milord. I didn't have medicine again until living here at the chateau."

Matthieu was forced to go without medicine? And Rhoslyn had to leave a solid roof over her head and live on the streets?

A howl of rage rumbled in his chest.

"He is a wolf in sheep's clothing," Fentienne growled low.

Matthieu's mouth fell open. "Is he really a démon?"

Fentienne was too pissed to answer. Instead, he closed his eyes in an attempt to calm his pumping blood. Every urge in his body demanded he go to the temple this moment and rip that man to shreds for hurting his mate and her brother. Despite his injuries, his present pain, anger rippled from his wolf in violent waves and pulsed out to each flexing limb.

Slowly he drew in a breath and slowly he exhaled.

Nothing could be done right now. He wasn't strong enough to fight an elder démon. Plus, he needed a better strategy than alpha aggression. Mon Père Michel was an integral part of Gabaston's community and the Brotherhood.

Footsteps softly echoed closer and he forced his eyes open, grateful for the distraction from his spiraling thoughts. Rhoslyn set a porcelain bowl, linens, scissors, and a sewing kit onto the bench, then picked up his large duster off the floor. A clink of glass reminded him of his gift and he loosed a nervous breath, his anger nearly dissolving. He had never given gifts to anyone before. Warmth crept up his neck and face, but he pushed away the fear. Just to see her happy before he passed out . . .

"Rhoslyn," he said quietly, trying to focus on her face. The magic drain fuzzed his vision, the heady buzz of alcohol too. "The front pocket of my coat."

She dug through the garment. Curiously, she lifted a blue, cut crystal vial no bigger than his hand. A wrinkle formed between her brows as she inspected the corked contents. "Where do you want me to place this?"

"It's for you." His eyes fluttered closed, but he forced them back open. "Ashes from your home."

"My home . . ." The slackened, disbelieving shock on her face daggered his heart. She gaped at the remains of a life his family had destroyed. A bittersweet smile trembled prettily on her lips, followed by a short laugh tinged with forming tears. Pressing the vial to her chest, she shyly met his gaze and whispered, "*Merci*," then drew in a soft, hiccuped breath. He couldn't speak. He couldn't do anything but stare at the constellation of tears on her lashes. "You confuse me, démon." Reverently, she caressed a thumb over the glass surface. "For over three weeks, you have growled threats in my face. You even threatened my life once. And now you give me a piece of my heart?"

"You'll need the comfort," he murmured, hoping to hide the ache in his voice. "Court life is an Underworld of torment."

"Court life?"

"The cane is custom made for Matthieu," Fentienne rasped, ignoring her question. "To help him balance better and become more independent."

She ran a finger down the carved ebony wood and sniffed. Matthieu played with Drurie, unaware of their conversation and, for a few thumping beats of his heart, Fentienne was glad to share only this moment with Rhoslyn.

"The box," he said next. "Open it."

Rhoslyn gently placed the ashes on the table and slowly lifted the wooden lid on the small box and stilled, her eyes wide and mouth parted. "Milord?" she breathed in shock.

"If they do not fit, I'll have them refitted for you."

She pulled out a pair of black silk heeled shoes adorned with bows and softly giggled—a girlish sound that settled warmly in his chest. The tears gathering on her lashes finally slipped down her cheek and she sniffed again. Fentienne's wolf vibrated with pleasure at her response. But Fentienne was falling through a dark sky toward a turbulent ocean of razor-edged emotions—fear, regret, desire, shame, want, longing, anger. A rapid, terrifying sensation. She was a princess in rags. Winter skies, a new pair of shoes reduced her to humbled tears. Unaware of his struggle, Rhoslyn next lifted a pair of boy's shoes from the box and another tear fell from her lashes.

"Your kindness—"

"It's not kindness," he murmured and his heavy lids shut once more. "As I've said, I desire females to be quiet ornaments for my viewing pleasure."

A body sat beside his on the bench. "I desire males to not bloody up my kitchen."

He grunted a laugh, squinting open his eyes. "The pain you'll cause me while suturing my wounds will make up for enduring my pleasant personality and bloody scrapes."

"*Oui*, it is a start," she teased back, but her voice shook as she studied his injuries, the blood smeared over his body. The pallor of Rhoslyn's skin bordered on green, her lips pale too. "I do not do well around blood . . ."

The alcohol was swirling fast in his head—any easy hit in his depleted state—and the room tilted. He blinked and tried to focus on his wife's face. "My darling," he whispered, "I already repulse you. Don't act squeamish now."

Green eyes snapped to his and narrowed. Once more, she was taking him in, every sweep of her intense gaze studying his face. He wasn't sure what he had said to unnerve her so. Fentienne pushed out another shaky breath and closed her eyes. Right now, he didn't want to think about her, or how the rhythm of her pulse shifted from the rapid beats of fear to confusion and . . . excitement? No, he was clearly too delirious. Fentienne leaned his head back more against the wall and swallowed.

A light touch tugged on the linens and he clenched his jaw. Gingerly, she removed the soaked strips. He kept his eyes closed, trying to breathe without breathing her in. What he would give for a cigarette this moment.

"Was this from the gray wolf?" A finger trailed over the previous injury on his arm.

"Yes," he said, his voice faint. Gods, her touch on his bare skin . . .

"Are you often injured?"

"No."

The light splash of water filled the tightening space between them, followed by the plink of droplets. A cool rag dabbed around the torn flesh of his arm and he sucked in a sharp breath. In the background, he could hear Matthieu and Drurie play before the fire. A sad smile softened the edges of his tightened mouth at the sound of laughter and happy barks. This was how all boys should feel at Matthieu's age. Not the sharp whip of a commanding officer for not following directions or the fear of pulling a trigger for the first time, knowing one day those bullets would rip through flesh and not paper and straw.

Rhoslyn continued to wash the skin around his injuries and his mind slipped into a twilight, not quite asleep, not quite awake. The tender pain began to dull behind the alcohol. Everything began to dull. The only time he knew rest was when drunk.

"You were a soldier?" Rhoslyn quietly asked him.

His heavy-lidded eyes squinted open. "Until the Battle of the Black Winds."

"But you were not injured often?" She picked up the scissors and began cutting strips from the bed linens.

"Nothing so dire as this." He swallowed and stared absently at the dried blood on his claws.

"I did not realize nobles fought in the war. Soldiering is peasant work."

"The aristocracy didn't send their sons to war like the lower classes. But those sons could still join."

Gently, she angled the cloth over her lap as her shears slid across the linen. "Your family must then be grateful you survived."

Fentienne bitterly chuckled. "Did your brothers fight?"

"My brother-in-law." Those green eyes darted to him, then back to the linen strip.

"Let me guess, his family threw a large dinner the night before he was deployed," he slurred in barely restrained contempt. "He endured pleas to return home alive. Your sister gave him a lock of her hair and a love letter to keep pressed to his heart from inside his coat pocket. His mother and possibly yours tenderly packed him extra food and woolen stockings for his pack, coated in their tears." Fentienne stared up at the ceiling to push back the anger. The room was spinning, but all he could see was the cruel curl of his father's lip and his cold, soulless Eyes of Ice glaring as Fentienne marched off with his next orders to succeed or face punishment. At the train station, no one saw him off and no one waited for his return. Rhoslyn had stopped cutting bandage strips and studied his face. Fentienne rolled his head away from her. "Did he survive?"

"*Non*, milord."

Fentienne squeezed his eyes shut. "The ones with the most to lose are always the ones who fall first. The rest of us?" He bitterly chuckled again and slurred, "We leave for war empty and return even more hollow."

"A living death," she said barely above a whisper. "Grief is a grave robber."

"There are things done in war," he replied quietly, "that will haunt a man even in death. Monsters are made on the battlefield."

A heavy silence settled between them and Fentienne focused on the sound of water sloshing into a bowl and not the storm in his chest. Why did he confess so much to her? His mind was moving in and out of focus. Gods, he just wanted to lay down and fall into an oblivion.

A gentle touch on his hand pulled him back to reality. "Time to disinfect," Rhoslyn softly said at his side.

His eyes fluttered open. The world around him spun fast and he blinked against the disorientation. A flush of heat dewed his skin in sweat. That godsdamn wolf was trying to take over to heal faster. He had only experienced a shifter fever one other time. Normally what a démon experienced after initiation, when critically injured or sick, or while inching closer to becoming moon-addled.

"Will you attack me in your pain?"

His bleary gaze settled on her face. "My threats were all to make you hate me, nothing more."

Her mouth fell open. "You wish for me to hate you?"

"Rhoslyn . . . I will *never* hurt you."

"How can I be sure? You confuse me, beast."

"I've bled for you before, my darling. I'll always bleed for you."

A slight blush warmed her cheeks and she focused on the bottle of spirits in her hands. "Anything you need before . . . before . . ."

Lifting his good hand, he caressed her cheek with the back of a clawed finger. "You are all I have ever desired, Rhoslyn Gautier, and . . . and I'll never deserve your heart," he choked out. "I'm . . . I'm so sorry about your brother-in-law and family. I'm unforgivable."

"Milord," she warned, taking his hand and placing it back on his lap. "You are drunk and fevering from the pain."

"Skies, you are beautiful."

The blush staining her cheeks deepened and he grinned, leaning his head against the wall once more with a quiet laugh. An exquisite, reckless feeling spurred his pulse into a breathless gallop, like racing across a field on a wild horse before enemy lines in open fire. The danger, the rush was irresistible. There was only one other time he had felt this way. And like when he was sixteen, he was marching toward his own destruction.

A drop of liquid fire hit the puncture wounds on his shoulder and all humor fled. A growl passed his lips and he gripped the edge of the bench with his good hand. More alcohol spilled onto his skin and he sucked in air through his teeth. Convulsions quaked down his body. Bolt after bolt of pain struck the nerve endings of his arm. But a sudden breeze soothed the burn. Then he smelled her, the sparking bite of a summer thunderstorm and the earthiness of velvet moss and lacy ferns. Rhoslyn leaned over and softly blew onto his shoulder and Fentienne quietly moaned with the feel of her breath on his bare skin.

"Torture me," he murmured against her cheek. "Make me hurt."

Slowly, she leaned back and lifted the bottle of spirits toward his arm. It took everything in him to not pull her onto his lap. But holy hell, the bleating pain. It came rushing back. His muscles stiffened and he dragged in a raspy lungful of air—then he stopped breathing all together. She dribbled alcohol over the injury on his arm and a strangled cry passed through his clamped jaw. Fire writhed through the torn muscles of his bicep and stars, that hurt like a mother. Black framed his vision and he gripped the bench seat to keep from passing out.

Just as he started to relax, another rush of heat pulsed through him—the hot flush of alcohol, pain, and his bastard wolf. Sweat dripped down his forehead, down his cheek. Gods, he was burning up. But was it from his wolf's attempt to heal? Or was he turning moon-addled from refusing the mate bonds? One thing he knew: he was irrevocably mad for her.

Fentienne rolled his head against the wall toward Rhoslyn, nearly moaning at the feel of cold stone against his warm skin, and watched as she threaded a needle. The kitchen warbled and blurred and spun. But he could still make out the waves of long, golden-brown hair tumbling down her back. The rosy hue of her lips. The tears flickering firelight on her cheeks.

She was crying?

Black smudged the edges of his vision. All thoughts dissolved. The magic drain demanded oblivion, his wolf too. And before he could ask why she was crying or felt the first prick of a needle piercing his skin, he passed out.

Chapter 21

Rhoslyn

She rung out a cloth in a fresh bowl of vinegar water. The man blacked out two candlemarks earlier, allowing her to stitch his wounds without him writhing in agony. The heartbroken confession and enormity of pain twisting his face brought tears to her eyes. She couldn't help it, despite how he had treated her up until this day. Her magic was overwhelmed by the cutting pain in his heart. Twice she had to run to the garden to empty her roiling stomach. Sewing together his torn muscle and flesh removed layers of repugnance toward him. He was a beast, yes, but also a haunted, vulnerable man.

You are all I have ever desired . . .

Warmth pooled low in her belly at the memory of his drunken, fevered confession, a horribly confusing feeling. The ache in his voice was real. The anguish in his eyes too. The fayette of Factory Row he had known for a little over three weeks and found disgusting was the object of his desire? She rifled through her memories at all their exchanges these past few weeks and there was something strangely familiar about him. The way he watched her cherish the bottle of ashes and the lovely custom-made shoes reminded her of the shy wonder the man in her dreams held when leaning over her in the pond. A blush even colored his skin while directing her toward his gifts. Their dark démon, a monster, *blushed.*

Why did he want her to hate him? Did he fear affection, even among friends?

And what had attacked him?

There was so much blood. Saints, she still needed to clean up the kitchen around them.

Her gaze rested on the cane and shoebox. In all his misery, he desired to see her reaction to his gifts, then proceeded to jest with her. A frown tugged on her lips. Both the cane and shoes he must have ordered two weeks ago for them to be ready this day. She studied the man before her once more. Was he perhaps related to the man in her dreams? The similarities were unsettling at times—their movements, body language, how they spoke. The way her magic responded to his heart. She would believe them the same save the beast of Chateau Lumière Dorée was cursed to be half or fully shifted only. Did he perchance have a twin? A younger or older brother?

Blowing a sticky strand of hair from her face, Rhoslyn concentrated on her task instead of his strange contradictory behavior. She softly dragged the cloth down his chest below his shoulder wound. The muscles beneath her fingertips were so defined her breath fluttered at the sight. He was . . . beautiful. Heat bloomed on her cheeks—again. She had never stood before an undressed man. Not even her older brothers walked around shirtless to maintain propriety. Were most men sculpted like him? Ridged lines of hard muscle and soft, warm skin? Rhoslyn was fairly certain she could appreciate the sight of him for hours and her moonlight-dusted pulse would continue to sigh days after. But she tried not to stare much, to preserve his dignity—and hers. After she finished bathing him to prevent infection, she would cover him with a blanket and finish cleaning the kitchen.

Trying to think of anything but him, she wiped the cloth down his stomach and along his sides. She had already cleaned his injured arm and both hands. Divine Mother, it was difficult not to watch the rag's trail of drips slide down his skin, though.

A little whimper sounded from behind. She peered over her shoulder toward the fire, where Matthieu and Drurie had curled up together. The sleeping pup's paws ran in a dream next to Matthieu, who was currently nose deep in a folktale book she knew the beast had left for him to find—like all the other books Matthieu had discovered the past couple of weeks.

Rhoslyn smiled when cub's paws started moving again.

What a little gift Drurie had been. A lovely name for a puppy too. Without her adorable antics, she feared how Matthieu would have handled the past hour. But the wolf cub's presence created even more questions in her mind.

She considered the man before her. Was he attacked by natural wolves? Did he not command natural wolves? A memory floated on the surface—when he protected her from the gray wolves, ones that had bowed to him before loping off injured with tails tucked between their legs.

Faint firelight flickered over the démon's body in the dusky late morning. He was mostly clean now, save a few spots on his face and neck. And saints, his skin was hot to the touch. Was he ill?

Swirls of red dotted the rag in her hand and a dizzy spell lightened her head. His blood still crusted beneath her nails. The tips of her fingers had pruned, yet her nails remained dirty. After scrubbing the stone floors and the bench, she would take a vegetable brush to her hands.

Nausea bubbled anew in her gut.

How could a man bleed so much?

Oof! If he wasn't kind to her after the horror of this morning, she might rip open the stitches and make him sew up his own wounds and clean up the mess too—the arrogant brute.

Rhoslyn drew in a tired breath. She wanted to pass out like both wolves in this room. But there was still too much left to do.

Slowly, she rose to her feet, the bowl at her hip, and walked into the garden where she tossed the contents. Back inside, she ladled cool water into the ceramic bowl she had fetched from her room, then added a measure of vinegar to keep the skin clean from infection. Rhoslyn grabbed a fresh cloth from a supply she had washed yesterday, and thank goodness. She had also cut up a recently washed bedsheet to wrap around the sutured wounds. Stitches she had covered in honey—to expedite the healing and protect further against infections—and mint leaves she pasted with a pestle and mortar—to cool the pain.

Dipping a rag into the new vinegar solution, she lightly squeezed out the excess and brushed a dampened edge across the soft lines of his jaw. Dark lashes rested along his flushed cheeks. His full lips parted slightly in sleep. In this relaxed, vulnerable state, he looked so young. How old was he? Originally, she thought him twenty-six or older. But now she wasn't so sure. Rhoslyn wiped along his forehead, brow, and down his cheeks in slow caresses. She feared any moment he would wake and lash out in confusion. Phantom pains in the tips of her fingers swelled to the surface as her mind flickered with images of the démon who attacked her when twelve. Still, she continued lower to clean his neck, especially on his injured side. Another appreciative breath fluttered from her chest. Even his neck was beautiful.

You are all I have ever desired . . .

She quietly dropped the rag back into the bowl and then, with trembling fingers, gently tucked a few chin-length strands of dark wavy hair behind his ear—and paused. Black lines caught her eye. What was on his scalp? A scar? Dried blood? Placing the bowl onto the bench, she stood and leaned closer, ever so softly moving his hair. A design was drawn onto his skin. Her eyes darted to his face. When he gave no sign of rousing, she continued to move more of his hair until an image took shape. A skull and crossbones. Shivers clawed down her spine and erupted goosebumps over her arms. Were more images inked onto his scalp? She moved quickly along that side of his head and then the other and discerned several more designs, a few she couldn't make out, a few she could: mountain peaks, a dragon, runic symbols from a language she didn't know but suspected was Dreglindish.

Aureliennes didn't ink their skin. At least, she didn't think they did. But she had seen images on men from Dreglind before, on their necks and hands. A few from Merenna too. Though, none on their scalps. One's head would need to be shaved. No designs decorated the top of this man's head either, only the sides. Why ink one's scalp only to grow out one's hair? Is this why his hair was shorter than most Aurelienne males?

Two weeks ago, he confessed to serving in the military and commanding men too. As head over all démons, was he required to fight in the Spired Hills? And ink his skin? Did the House of Chalamet employ démons to attack Clifstánian soldiers? Another chill iced the blood in her veins.

Chalamet—the House of Wolves.

Were they a line of démons or was this simply a house symbol? The latter thought spurred even more questions, more so after meeting Lucas.

Rhoslyn gritted her teeth. Nothing about this man or this situation made sense to her.

"Who are you?" she whispered, eyes narrowed.

But she knew. Even as she spoke her last question a terrible knowing twisted in her stomach.

You are wed by faerie blood to a midnight beauty that is ugly and a sunrise ugliness that could become beautiful.

I am under a curse, mademoiselle. Half man during the day, full wolf at night.

This démon was her husband.

Rhoslyn softly blinked and took a few steps back. He terrified her. And he was right, he repulsed her too. The haughty temper, the hideousness of his growling wolfish face, the entitled, apathetic aristocratic view of commoners, elves in particular, and how he spoke to females. While she couldn't shake the way he had wanted her to feel afraid and small in most of their encounters, her heart still beat wildly at the timid gentleness he hid beneath all those monstrous overtures. A fragility he worked hard to protect. A heart and soul that was good.

My threats were all to make you hate me, nothing more.

Was this the real man? He truly cared about her and Matthieu, a fact she couldn't deny. He wanted her brother to feel capable and independent. And he wanted her, a female, to use a sword and pistol like a male, to bring down his family without falling with them. How strange that he didn't defend his family too.

Blue glinted in the periphery of her vision and she stepped farther away from the beast and approached the worktable. Those ashes . . . her breath quivered as her thumb caressed the ornately cut-glass bottle. It was one of the most beautiful gifts anyone had ever given her. This foolish man risked being caught by the Monks of Glanis and Factory Row's guards to return to her a lost piece of her heart. He bled, so she may draw comfort from a family and home that had loved her.

Was he married to her against his will too? Rhoslyn's brow furrowed. Of course he was. He was a small child when she was born.

Why did he have Dreglindish markings but Chalamet eyes?

The only aristocratic family she knew of who were both Aurelienne and Dreglindish was the House of Halivaard. But there were more Chalamets crawling the streets of Gabaston than the diseased rats of Factory Row. And the only Halivaard prince still alive was his Imperial Highness. But why would a Chalamet noble ink his scalp?

Rhoslyn played with the ring dangling from her neck, eyeing the démon before her fearfully, then covered a yawn with the back of her hand. The adrenaline of this past hour waned. She needed to scrub the floors, set the rags to soak in a baking soda solution, care for their stained garments, and try to revive the bread she was kneading until that aggravating, confusing man practically fell through the kitchen door. But three of the four tasks would require multiple trips to the well. Already she had pushed herself this week to clean her new room and kitchen while training to use a pistole and smallsword.

She would need to go slow and take many breaks. She also needed to change into a clean dress too. This one needed to soak.

For the next few hours, she scrubbed and washed and prepared food. Matthieu helped her chop vegetables for a stew and played with Drurie. Several times, he limped outside, using his new cane and wearing his new shoes, for Drurie to go potty and play among the herbs. She came in smelling of sage and rosemary and mint.

Rhoslyn was not able to fully revive the loaf bread, but she was able to turn the dough into flat bread to dip in the stew. And as the stew cooked, Rhoslyn strung rope near the hearth fire, between two wooden posts, and hung to dry the man's now cleaned duster, her once bloodstained dress, and all the cloths used to clean him and the kitchen.

All the while, the démon slept, his skin flushed and beaded in sweat.

Despite her bone-weary body, she forced herself, after an early dinner, to practice the fencing moves the beast had taught her while wearing her new shoes. The foot and arm work only, no switch or smallsword in her hands. Matthieu watched while Drurie tugged on a cloth Rhoslyn had knotted into a toy for her.

Still, the démon slept and didn't move a muscle.

The sun was now starting to lower, though still a good hour or so before sunset. Matthieu had fallen asleep on the rug beside Drurie, both curled up together. A soft warmth filled her chest at the sight. Rhoslyn hadn't seen her brother smile so much in an age, but saints was she exhausted.

Slumping onto the bench next to the fevering man, she leaned back onto the wall, like him, and studied the cobwebs along the ceiling. Maybe she could rest until Drurie woke her, which shouldn't be long. Rhoslyn turned to peer at the démon beside her. She feared he might fall over and tear open his wounds, though he had yet to move. Since he passed out, she had planned to sleep sitting up next to him if he didn't wake by nightfall, though the idea frightened her.

You are all I have ever desired . . .

Those words continued to violently swirl about in her heart like tumbling leaves in a storming wind. Moving closer, so the side of his uninjured body pressed to hers, she allowed her eyes to fall shut. If he moved, she would feel it and wake. A few minutes later, the kitchen and démon faded and the overworked muscles in her body finally relaxed.

A CLOUDLESS, STARRY night stretched above her. In the distance, a string quartet serenaded the frolicking summer breeze rustling her hair and skirts. Rhoslyn twisted on the wrought iron bench to peer over her shoulder and gasped. A pleasure garden!

Lantern lights flickered before the mirrors of a merry-go-round just a few paces away through an avenue of trees. Behind the carousel was a tall windmill tucked into the center of a labyrinth made from rose bushes framed in by lavender. Across from the labyrinth, a large columned and domed gazebo towered over the park.

For a moment, she nearly forgot herself—forgot about the beast, his injuries, and the kitchen once coated in his blood. Forgot about the dread gnawing in her gut and the confusion muddling her head. Forgot that she was in an enchanted dream tethered to a man she still didn't know by name or had seen in two weeks. *Non*, her head could not make sense of the sights and sounds around her. Why was she in a pleasure garden? But when she stood, and felt the weight of silks, she floated back into awareness.

Nine Saints, what in the temple edifices was she wearing? The square-cut bodice hugging her torso dipped low across her breasts and without a sheer scarf for modesty—the lowest cut bodice she had ever worn. Rhoslyn crossed her arms over her chest and frantically looked around to see if anyone else walked the gardens or if she were alone.

Unlike in previous dreams, with strands intricately fashioned up, her hair was left in soft ironed curls and waves down her back, with sides and front pinned up and, from what she could feel, decorated in bows and florets—a style befitting young aristocratic females of marriageable age who were stepping out into society for the first time.

And the color of her gown . . . a rich burgundy with a gold petticoat. The skirts flounced from a large rump roll and slightly dragged behind her in a small train. Lowering her arms, she couldn't help a small, delighted giggle. The dresses in these fantastical dreams were beyond beautiful, though growing more scandalous in turn.

Too curious to see the attractions, Rhoslyn practically skipped toward the stone and wrought iron arched entrance.

Père once printed chapbooks commissioned by Palais d'Aurélie for nobles to showcase the delights found in the royal park's newly built pleasure garden. Rhoslyn, then age thirteen, had snuck a biscuit from under Maman's nose, dashed up to the room she shared with her unwed sister, and studied the block art printed on various pages before they were saddle stitched together.

A chord of grief plucked at the fraying strings of her heart. She softly tucked away the memory for a different time. Right now, she wished to indulge in this brief pocket of happiness.

The scent of baked confections twining with the dark, rich notes of freshly brewed café infused the air. The orchestral music grew louder the farther she ventured into the park. Silk lanterns of various colors hung from the limbs of various flowering fruit trees. Small glass lanterns in the shape of stars dotted the trees too. The magic wrapped around her and she laughed.

Not too far up ahead, the merry-go-round called to her. Was being pushed at spinning speeds as dizzying as being pushed high on a tree swing? She could almost feel the wind blowing her hair back, her grin wide as up and up she went. A few seconds suspended in the tree and sky beside the birds. Her hair dancing before her face as she plummeted back toward earth. She often wondered if falling in love was like swinging up to touch the clouds before the kiss of gravity's pendulum released her heart, mind, and soul to blindly rush her toward a new high.

But she would probably never know.

Rhoslyn approached the merry-go-round and slowed before an intricately carved sea serpent. The tips of her fingers brushed over the green-painted scales in wonder. The next seat was a silver-eyed scarlet dragon with its long, bat-like wings tucked in. She moved toward the next creature of myth, another sea serpent, when a shadow filled her vision. Startling back a step, she pressed a hand to her mouth.

The silhouette of a male moved into view while pacing at an agitated rhythm. Gritting out a frustrated groan, he dragged a hand through his hair, his arm falling back to his side a heartbeat later. He pivoted to walk the opposite direction on his path, took a step, and stiffened, as if suddenly sensing her presence, though his back was turned to her. A preternatural stillness fell over his body. Then, slowly, he swiveled his head to casually peer over his shoulder and Rhoslyn stopped breathing.

Familiar honeyed-amber eyes locked onto her, his face half in shadow, the other half warmed in lantern light. He was alive. The beast had not harmed him. Why had he hidden from her the past two weeks?

A cool night wind fluttered a few strands of wavy hair over his mouth, a dark, dangerous look that thundered down the length of her. Those full lips, the ones she wanted to kiss in their last dream, parted at the sight of her. And, as he turned, the open awestruck reverence softening the mercilessly handsome lines of his face settled low in her belly. A curling, delicious heat that glittered in her dancing pulse. He seemed paralyzed in a similar state as his gaze roamed down her body.

"Gods," he croaked in a reedy whisper. "Shoot me now."

A burgundy waistcoat hugged the broad lines of his chest and back. The matching frock coat lay in a heap a mere hand toss away and, much to her distraction, the sleeves of his linen undershirt were rolled up to his elbows. The toned muscles of his forearms captivated her. A teasing exhibit of masculinity she didn't know would be so scintillating until him.

"Milord," she offered in reply, unsure of how to respond to his bewildered admiration.

Modesty demanded that she avert her eyes, but a hot, sparking current of awareness immobilized all thought and reason. Only feeling pushed her up and up to touch the sky and, with the next rapid beat of her pounding heart, she began to fall.

And saints, the rush.

He was the most beautiful male her eyes had ever beheld. Darkly elegant, cruelly striking. But it was more than that. An unspoken understanding existed between them, a familiarity she couldn't quite place or describe but her heart instantly recognized. More so, beyond even that strange connection, she knew his pain. He had made himself vulnerable before her and she promised to warrior his heart until he saw only the man and not the monster.

As if reading her thoughts, his chest heaved a deep, tremulous breath. A sound full of longing *and* rising panic. Then he spun on his heel and marched into the shadows of the merry-go-round, toward the entrance.

Rhoslyn stood dazed in place, but only for a single disbelieving moment. He left. He stared at her as if she were the very rising sun and he a wilting, frost-tipped leaf basking in her radiance. Then he left. Clenching her skirts in her fists, she jogged after him, muttering a few choice words under her breath.

He groaned when hearing her footsteps and whirled back toward her, his contemptuous mask snapped firmly back into place. "Desperation isn't a pretty face and you, mademoiselle, are—"

"Desperation?" she scoffed. "I am not the one who runs away when feeling an emotion other than anger and dominance."

He laughed low, a seductively dark sound. A wicked smile flirted the slanted edges of his lips as he prowled a slow, sensual step in her direction. "You give chase to be dominated by me?"

"Do not twist my words to pet your conceit."

That devilish grin widened. Rhoslyn lifted her chin as he approached, refusing to look away from the fury thundering in his gaze. Gently, he wrapped his hand around her throat and softly squeezed, the tip of his pointer finger on her thrumming pulse while his thumb caressed the skin beneath the opposite ear. Terror zipped through her first, followed by a heady wave of excitement. The last time he tried to physically unnerve her, she was left awakened by pleasure, followed by vindicated delight when she shoved his oversized ego into the pond.

"Are you afraid yet?"

Rhoslyn lifted her chin higher, giving him more access to her throat. "*Non*, you are a scared man who must threaten me to feel important." The muscles along his jaw feathered, the heat in his eyes dimming a shade. Satisfied, her steeled gaze fell to his lips. "But *you* fear me."

"Hmm."

"Use your words, *mon douce puce*," she admonished as if he were a small child. "Or does my clichéd entitled female presence frighten your poor socially oppressed male's ability to speak? This is why you run away with your tail tucked between your legs, *oui*?"

Relaxing the grip on her throat, he watched dispassionately as his hand slid down her neck. A tactic meant to intimidate her, but she saw only the caginess he struggled to contain. Believing himself still in charge, which she allowed, the tips of his fingers outlined the soft swell of her breast in provocative caresses. Rhoslyn had to force the quivering night sky in her veins to behave, but Divine Mother, he was sinful. His touch burned her skin in the most delicious, tantalizing way. She was a couple of heartbeats away from tangling her fingers in his hair and kissing him until she forgot how to breathe—arranged marriage be damned!

"Obeying me is not without its pleasures . . ." The words he spoke to her three weeks ago trailed off in a rough whisper.

"You will *not* dominate me," she bit back.

The man's eyes flicked to hers, a livid pool of dark molten honey. "*My darling*, I already have."

"You are adorable," she cooed.

He stepped in closer and lowered his voice. "No other male has touched you but me."

She laughed. "You attempt to mark me? Saints, your ego is ridiculous."

"Mademoiselle," he practically purred, his hand trailing to her waist, "I could have you moaning my name in a matter of seconds."

Rhoslyn arched a humored brow to hide her blush. "I would first need to know your name."

The man's entire body stiffened, a wall of fear darkening his eyes for a mere blink. "The Chateau—"

"You are not a prisoner at Chateau Lumière Dorée."

"When did I mention a *literal* prison?"

"No more lies. You confirmed you lived at the chateau, for how else could we share these dreams?" She stepped back and his hand fell from her waist. "Only the beast, Matthieu, and I live on the property. No one can enter and I cannot leave. *Oui*, I would have seen you by now, if you lived at the chateau. How are you, then, trapped by that démon?"

"Lies? Mademoiselle, your assumptions speak to your character not mine. Burden another with your self-righteous lectures and accusations."

"Answer my question," she ground out, "How has that démon trapped you since childhood?"

"There are many ways to imprison another." Rancor dripped from each word. "And not all require physical restraints and iron bars."

She paused, unable to keep the grief from her face. "You allowed me to believe you were physically dungeoned. I ached to demand your release. My heart hurt for you so." She balled her fists into her skirts. "All you do is mock me, milord."

"Stop acting so scandalized." His eyes were cold, but his Adam's apple bobbed in obvious distress. "You know what I am. 'Vile' and 'a dog' I believe were your exact words."

"Choose different behavior, milord. I have seen glimpses of the real man and he is beautiful, gentle, and contains a wildness that was meant to be free." She gestured at the length of him and choked out, "Not this angry caged animal."

"I left." He pointed back to where she found him by the merry-go-round, his voice cracking. "I chose to not engage with you and you, once more, forced yourself on me."

"You *ran*. You have been running from me for two weeks!" She was seething at this point. "You bared your grief and now you fear me."

The man stepped toward her until their bodies nearly touched and bitterly laughed. "You know *nothing*. Drop this notion to fight for me. It embarrasses us both, especially *you*."

"Saints, use *this anger* to fight for yourself, milord. Take that furious injustice and revolutionize your life. Break the curse of being born to monsters to spite them. Because the man I saw is worthy of redemption." She poked at his chest. "I will not use your pain against you. Unlike those who raised you, I am not a monster. And neither are you. Behave better than *them*."

"My name can't even pass your lips, but you are so sure I'm not a monster," he derided, but his voice was strained with grief. "Believe whatever delusions you wish, mademoiselle. My identity will not be hidden from you forever."

"I was with the man who raced a horse and smiled as if he had touched freedom for the first time. The look of joy on your face, milord. It was heartbreaking in its beauty. I wanted to capture that joy for you to have and remember." Her voice softened. "You were meant to run with the wind, carefree."

It was like a furious storm was punched from his tattered sails, the way his body seemed to slump inward with her words. And panic, true panic, blazed in his eyes. Why did seeing what brought him joy scare him so dramatically? She tilted her head and softened her voice even more.

"I was with the man who genuinely laughed when I toppled him back into the water after pushing him into the pond. A sound that left me breathless for I knew it was rare. You were meant to laugh, milord. You are meant to be unfettered and happy."

Red suffused his face and neck. Was he blushing? The man who thought he could dominate her with seductions was blushing? He tore his gaze from hers and clenched his jaw, but not in anger she realized. In grief. In frantic confusion. Rhoslyn sat back on her heels and took in the man she rendered bashful. An unexpected boyishness softened the hard edges of his face, an almost sweet expression she wanted to hold in her hands and softly kiss. Instead, she remained on topic point.

"Perhaps I am not the one who is delusional."

"I have done nothing to deserve your kindness." The ache in his quiet words tightened in her chest.

This was the gentleness she knew existed. The beautiful heart he refused to let others see but her magic touched.

"You exist." She wove her fingers with his. "Your beating heart shares my dreams. That is enough."

"Remember, my darling, we see only what we want to see, especially when angry or afraid." He studied their entwined hands, his brows pushed together. "Night is no more evil than day, yet that is where we place all our nightmares." Dark golden eyes slid to hers and stilled. "Appearances can be deceiving."

The hair on her arms rose. She wanted to ask how he was related to the beast or if that démon was her husband, but he was already spooked. *Non*, this man needed to touch happiness again. He needed to laugh and feel young. Caged animals familiar only with cruelty distrusted that the new hand feeding them wasn't the same one that had abused them. And he was, without question, a trapped animal. His imprisonment now made complete sense.

"Well then," she said, tugging on the fingers entwined with hers while marching toward the merry-go-round. "Let us play until reality returns. This is a pleasure garden, no?"

Chapter 22

Fentienne

An unsettling sensation pooled in Fentienne's gut.

Did these dreams enchant her mind to fight for him regardless of how he treated her? His wife had made it clear before half of Gabaston on her feelings toward the aristocracy and House Chalamet. And yet, she defended the Chalamet noble before her to see himself as something more than the cruel man who had raised him. Almost as if she were blinded by notions of love.

She will fall in love with the whole man in her dreams and despise the monster when awake . . .

Not she *could*. But she *will*.

You will know the horror of rejection, the terror of unrequited love.

For who could love a beast?

Fentienne pushed back the growl rumbling in his chest.

Every second he remained in this strange liminal space, he became more convinced that he needed to change his battle strategy. But he didn't understand faerie magic enough to know if Eirwen's curse would override Addien's in the event he somehow, miraculously, performed an act of selfless love. Which he was starting to think was according to Eirwen's definition rather than a generalized one or even his own warped ideas of what that meant. And if he returned to a whole man in reality, would Rhoslyn still defend the monster, a Halivaard one at that? Maybe he should take Eirwen's curse more seriously. Maybe nothing mattered and he should just let the curses take their natural course.

But it wasn't in his nature to just roll over and let sleeping dogs lie. He was a man of action.

And he knew his enemy—Fayette. The peasant girl he met in the woods was saccharin sweet, girlishly playful, not a confrontational bone in her body. The moment he met her while on patrol, Fentienne was completely taken with her beauty and innocence, but fell in love with her happiness. He committed treason for her laughter, for midnight waltzes beneath the stars and nights spent talking under the moon. Life with her was uncomplicated and such a departure from his world, he was enraptured by the escape she offered him.

But with Rhoslyn? Other than believing neither knew of his title and crown, very little resembled Fayette save outward appearances. His wife was enthrallingly feminine and in ways that weakened him. But unlike the submissive personality Addien gave Fayette, his Rhoslyn was fierce. The type of beauty she possessed was unparalleled to any other, and not just in face and form. The peasant girl he first saw picking flowers in the meadow was a warrior queen. And gods, she disarmed him with ease. It was pissing him off and turning him on simultaneously. With each interaction, his emotions were left scrambling for a new battle strategy. But it was a losing war. He was held hostage by her indomitable spirit. A prisoner to her wit and compassion and . . . competitive nature.

A smile touched his lips at the memory of her scratching behind his ear and flicking flour in his face. At the outrage in her sparking gaze when he dunked her under the water after she tried to unbalance him. And then she did, and they both fell back into the pond. Skies, he had laughed so hard. Genuinely laughed from his gut. That tiny girl had brought him down.

She was still unbalancing him.

Life with Fayette would have lacked the challenges and danger he craved. Life with Rhoslyn was a terrifying adrenaline rush—like leaping from a zeppelin with a malfunctioning parachute on his back. It was certain death. Execution by guillotine, by a firing squad, falling in battle . . . anything was preferable to the horrifying reality that she could crush him with little effort.

And she will.

The long, curled strands of his wife's hair bounced with her determined steps. She peered over her shoulder with a fleeting glance, flashing him a large smile. His eyes caressed the curve of her cheek, the lines of her jaw, the point of her ear. Dear winter gods, he had traced along the swell of her breast and she had let him. Just to win this push-pull verbal game they played. If his wolf had control of him in this dreamscape, the intensity of every touch, glance, and familiar scent would drive him to madness—especially *those* touches. And, yet, he was deliriously addled without his wolf.

She just drove him mad. Period. Made him furious and made him crazy for her.

Rhoslyn slowed before the merry-go-round but didn't release his hand. "What creature should I choose?"

Fentienne answered without hesitation. "Dragon."

At the carved wooden beast, she trailed her fingertips over its scarlet wings and paused before the silver crystal eyes—Eyes of Ice. The eyes of his father. The eyes of his brother. And his ancestors: the dragon shifter sky and sea warriors of Dreglind.

Sky and sea warriors.

Fentienne studied the dragons and sea serpent once more and quietly swore under his breath. Of course, Addien would remind him of his grief in a place meant to create happiness.

Rhoslyn grabbed the tip of the dragon's tucked in wing and pulled herself up onto the platform. Once settled, she peered around at the contraption. He counted four dragon and four sea serpent seats bolted to the roof by a pole that lanced through each mount. The ride consisted of two planked-covered cogs. The lower wheel remained stationary around a tiled mirror column housing an axle. A column meant to look like a large tree trunk, the mirrors the bark, the roof of the merry-go-round its leafy canopy. Two tree branches limbed from the column and, at such a height, they formed levers. Irminsul, he realized. The Tree of Life his family's dragon blood spun around, the one that chose Florian as its Protector of Life.

Fentienne ground his teeth together.

Rhoslyn twirled toward him, her hands before her mouth in excitement. "Will you push, milord?"

He tore his gaze from the merry-go-round and arched a brow. "If you can manage to climb onto that dragon without assistance, I will push."

"In this dress? There are no stirrups!"

He lifted his shoulder in a nonchalant shrug, working hard to remain blasé at the incredulous look on her face. "That is my offer."

"*En voilà des manières!*" she huffed.

A tiny smile slipped through his defenses. "I'm not a gentleman, mademoiselle. If you desire someone who is mannered, then be my guest." He gestured to the empty park.

Those forest green eyes narrowed and her jaw clenched, as he expected. But he knew it was all show. She liked to fight as much as he did. And, so, if she wanted to play, then he wanted to flirt with her competitive spirit—he could compromise when it suited him. Watching her angrily attempt to mount that dragon was fair payment for asking him to operate this ride. And she didn't disappoint.

Rhoslyn gripped the pole and jumped, but not quite high enough. Another attempt, this time with a loud grunt. She inspected the dragon, her focus settling onto the tail. Gripping the tips of the bat-like wings, she sought to climb the tail as if a tree, but she slipped on her skirt and slid back to the platform. Fentienne snorted a laugh; he couldn't help it. Her eyes snapped to his, fury shooting daggers his way. That very feistiness was a drug to his system. And he craved another hit to satisfy his addiction.

He didn't have a chance.

A smug smile edged the sharpening slant of her mouth. A dangerous look that shivered heat down his body. Her blazing eyes fixed onto his, she slowly started to inch up her skirts. Up and up, the white silk stockings hugging her calves and knees bright against the lantern lit night. She tucked the bottom hem of her overskirt and petticoat into her waist, a swath of fabric now resting against her knees instead of her ankles. Then—her gaze still murdering him, her boldness staining her cheeks scarlet despite her confident glare—she stepped out of her shoes, reached beneath her skirt, and ... pulled until a black ribbon dangled from her fingertips.

Skies, his chest heaved a ragged breath. And he knew the haughty mask he wore had melted completely into a look of unadulterated want. His lessons on knowing one's enemy were paying off—he was completely disarmed. If she desired to dominate him in this way, he wouldn't stop her. Hell, his mind was already two steps ahead in forming other challenges to invoke this battle strategy of hers.

Another tiny smile brushed along his lips. Had suggestively taking her finger into his mouth at the pond awakened this minx?

He was in so much trouble.

Seemingly satisfied with his response, Rhoslyn faced the dragon and roped the garter ribbon around the wooden pole. The length wasn't long enough for what he knew she was going to attempt, but never had he enjoyed the process of trial and error so much.

Holding onto the ends of the ribbon, she leapt onto the tail.

She *leapt*.

Far higher than he would have expected given her height and the amount of silks draping over her lithe body. But the length of the ribbon left her little choice.

Sweet gods, who was this girl?

Was she normally this agile when not weakened from malnutrition? She raced horses in an absurd amount of skirts, tackled large men in ponds, and now sprang onto a sinuous incline in a balancing act.

The silk stockings made it difficult for her to find traction. Nevertheless, she angled the arches of her feet and toes into the valleyed dips of the dragon's tail. Fentienne struggled with whether he should move closer should she fall—he didn't know if he could shadow sprint in this plane. Rhoslyn would only grow angrier, though, and he didn't want to create a distraction. In just a few carefully planned steps, she made it to the dragon's back, gripped the pole, and eased herself down to ride the beast astride.

Fentienne suppressed a moan. Holy hell, that move. He was . . . undone. The shady, corrupt things he would do to be that dragon beneath her this moment *and* a few moments ago.

Rhoslyn threw him a victorious grin, unaware of his suffering or how her innocent slide onto the dragon's back was anything but innocent. "I fulfilled my end of the bargain," she said in a self-assured sing-song voice.

Articulating an intelligent verbal reply wasn't going to happen for another second or two. So, instead, he plucked the silk ribbon from her fingers and draped it around his neck, his eyes cemented on hers to reassert his dominance in this game they played.

"This is now mine."

Her eyes rounded. "You cannot keep that around your neck," she whispered harshly, as if others might overhear or see.

"Mmm, I think I can." He stepped out of reach toward a lever, flashing her a wicked grin while tucking the ribbon ends into his waistcoat. "You want it back? Come and get it, my darling."

She growled. "After you push me, *mon douce puce.*"

"Am I not pushing you enough?" Fentienne arched a brow in a checkmate look, knowing it would piss her off even more. And he was right.

"Do not riddle yourself out of your agreement."

Another taunting corner of his mouth ticked up as he pivoted away from her and took up position in front of a tree branch lever. Rhoslyn clutched the pole in anticipation. The first push counter-clockwise from Rhoslyn strained his muscles. This was a job meant for two men. The axle moved easier as it gained momentum and the merry-go-round platform began rotating clockwise.

A squeal whooshed by him. Rhoslyn's head tipped back in laughter. Her skirts and hair fluttered wildly behind her. Each time she passed him another piece of his dented-up armor fell away. The symbols of his family surrounded Fentienne. And Rhoslyn—his faerie bride—spun around him unaware of the ride she was *truly* on. Or that he *truly* operated the world spinning around her. But, for a few moments, he lost himself to her bliss.

The unabashed happiness on her face hypnotized him.

The girlish rhapsody of her laughter a siren's call leading him into deeper waters.

He ached to touch her carefree joy.

Fentienne pushed against the lever while jogging, timing when Rhoslyn blurred past in peals of laughter. Another rotation and, when she came into view, he counted then jumped onto the platform, grabbing the pole attached to her dragon mount. Rhoslyn squealed, first in alarm. Delight, however, quickly transformed her face and his heart stuttered at the beautiful smile directed entirely at him.

Round and round they went.

Round and round his mind spun.

Dark hair whipped around his face as the wind rushed against his back. He was free falling toward his heart's center of gravity.

Falling through this dream to a reality he yearned to know.

Falling into a fire that would destroy him.

Falling into a future he no longer wanted to run from.

The garden continued to carousel by them. The flickering lanterns twinkled in the tiled mirrors they spun past; a starry night created just for them. Alarms blared in the back of his mind. This was exactly what Addien had engineered to happen. That fiend wanted him to watch Rhoslyn fall for him the way he had fallen for Fayette. A romance built on lies and betrayal. But he shoved that voice away to indulge in the headiness of Rhoslyn's happiness. All he wanted was happiness . . . and to make another happy.

Blood bonds, faerie curses, and marriage contracts be damned.

Reverently, he played with a lock of her hair as the merry-go-round slowed. The intense draw to touch her, kiss her, allow her to see parts of him no one else did both thrilled and sickened him. Nothing so lovely and pleasurable should touch something so ugly and defiled as him. But he was selfish. Utterly, cruelly selfish. His gaze rested on her lips for a heavy, erratic beat of his heart. Fentienne blinked and peered over her head to a café, a large gazebo, and a windmill. Anything but directly at her.

Kissing her wrist and fingers or touching her body wasn't the same as intimately knowing her breath, her tongue, or the feel of her mouth dancing with his. He was the boy who stole kisses to feel anything other than the apathy of his existence. The man who enjoyed women to forget his loneliness and give the intensity of his grief a false sense of belonging. Seductions were dangerous games they played. Kissing though? Kissing was his weakness, had been since his first one. He hungered to taste Rhoslyn's lips. But kissing her would change the game rules.

And he wouldn't seal her curse with a kiss the way Addien had sealed his.

To mask his distress, he threw her a smug smile, then hopped off the platform and walked backward, holding her narrowing gaze. She got onto the dragon. She could get herself off it too. Though, really, he just needed a few minutes of separation to gather his wits before he completely lost his mind.

She opened her mouth, no doubt to chastise him for not offering his assistance, then clamped it shut. To rile her up even more, he heaved a loud, bored sigh, the sound of his long suffering while waiting—and she growled back. She was stuck and he was an arse. In that dress without stirrups and with the seat being about chest level on her, there was only one feasible way for her to dismount, and his blood ignited in anticipation.

Checkmate.

Swearing under her breath, Rhoslyn arched back while holding onto the pole with one hand. Curled strands puddled over the dragon. And her breasts, sweet gods, her breasts pushed out more the farther she leaned back. He was bad, so very, very bad to put her in this predicament. But he wasn't sorry. Zero remorse. Biting her lower lip in a focused look, she lifted the leg facing him to move past the pole in a balancing act to sit side saddle. The already hiked up skirts of her dress slipped down her leg, past the silk ribbon tied into a perfect bow around her thigh. A groan rumbled low in his throat at the sight.

The image of her sliding down the pole to straddle the dragon in that low-cut dress and now this arched back, graceful show of leg would keep him up at night—forever.

Rhoslyn lowered onto the platform and adjusted her skirts, then stepped back into her shoes.

She was going to explode.

And like the reckless, thrill-seeking fool he was, he pulled her garter ribbon from around his neck and dangled it out as bait. The wrinkled nose, pursed lips pinched look of fury on her dainty face did him in. He lost it. Laughing louder when she marched over in clipped stomps and pushed him. When he didn't so much as sway, she growled, teeth bared. And he laughed even more. Rhoslyn swiped her hand up to snatch the ribbon and missed. Refusing to give up, she jumped, then jumped again. Incrementally, he lifted it higher and higher out of her reach.

"You are an arse!" she shouted.

"Hmm," he replied, knowing this dismissive response would piss her off again—and it did.

She jumped one more time and, as she landed, Fentienne looped the ribbon behind her neck, pulled her in closer, then dipped down to whisper in her ear, "My darling ... I win."

He didn't wait to see if she would make another attempt at the ribbon. Darkly chuckling into her neck, he then stepped away, taking the ribbon with him. Walking backwards again. Biting his bottom lip in a goading grin.

"I am going to destroy you!"

He unlaced his cravat just enough to stuff the ribbon down his shirt. "If you want your ribbon back ..."

Her mouth fell open. "You believe I will ... undress you for a garter ribbon? *Non, vous vous comportez comme un libertin!*"

"*Oui.*" Giving her his most rakish smile, he dropped his voice and reminded her, again, "*Je ne suis pas un gentilhomme.*"

He wasn't a gentleman. He would never be one. Calling him a libertine wasn't an insult or a threat. Good society could choke on their pearls. He didn't give a shit.

And neither did she.

Rhoslyn planted her hands on her waist and tilted her head. The set of her jaw, the tension in her shoulders, the fingers tapping her hips both irritated and amused him. All this scandalized bluster was for show. She enjoyed every moment of seducing him in return. Calling out her hypocrisy was on the tip of his tongue. But she could think herself above these games . . . for a little while longer.

Though, maybe he should say something just to move past this standoff.

They were locked in an aggravating staring contest, a battle of wills. He arched a bored, aristocratic brow. She narrowed her eyes. He crossed his arms over his chest. She lifted her chin. He peered down his nose at her. She scoffed . . . and his lips twitched in annoyance. Over a decade in training to lock up his emotions before an enemy and he was cracking.

This was ridiculous.

He was twenty-two, not twelve. Fentienne rolled his eyes and looked away, shaking his head. Laughter burst past her compressed lips, believing herself the victor. Whatever. He'll surrender this battle and use her newly gained confidence against her in the next round.

"Come!" She grabbed his hand, yanking him from his irritated thoughts, and dragged him toward the next feature—an enormous stone gazebo. As they strode down the avenue of flowering trees, he studied their entwined hands and furrowed his brow. "Do you visit Factory Row?" Rhoslyn peered at him briefly over her shoulder and his gaze jumped to hers and narrowed.

The unexpected question raised his hackles. Was she ferreting out if he were at the chateau or trapped in a home like her? "*Oui*, I visit Factory Row."

"Do you know Lucas Fontine?"

The muscles down his body flexed. Hearing that lesser démon's name on her lips, especially in *their* dream, stabbed him with intense jealousy. His wife could speak the name of another alpha, but not his . . . as she so smugly reminded him earlier. Except, the first time she uttered the words "Adalwolf

Halivaard" to his face would be in disgust and horror.

The man I saw is worthy of redemption.

The muscles in his stomach clenched.

"Milord—"

Fentienne tugged on her hand at a pâtisserie and café and halted his steps before an outdoor tea cart loaded in mounds of fresh pastries. Those intelligent green eyes landed on him and held a hundred different questions. The puzzle pieces in her mind were attempting to assemble a clear image. Clever creature that she was, the clues would add up and quickly. Right now, though, she still saw only what she wanted to see: the beast as someone incapable of being a whole man while seeing the whole man as someone incapable of being a monster. For that reason, among many, they could discuss Lucas when he was the beast.

This dream wasn't supposed to happen.

And a shared dream would never happen again.

Hoping to distract her, he gestured to the tea cart. "Dessert, mademoiselle?"

Those imploring eyes drifted away from him and widened when *finally* seeing the confections. "Saints!" Rhoslyn gasped. "Has anything ever smelled so divine?" She leaned over the cart, her eyes bright. "Macarons and madeleines! My maman made madeleines topped with whipped cream and strawberries for our birthdays." Her smile dimmed. "I am not familiar with the other pastries."

"Pick one."

Rhoslyn straightened and fidgeted with a rosette on her bodice. "If this were not a dream, I would be furious over the extravagance while so many starved for simple bread." Her hand fell away and pressed to her stomach. "The guilt is sometimes difficult to ignore even in my fantasy. Even the guilt over wearing such extravagant gowns."

"Court life is a constant cat and mouse game of indulgence and guilt," he replied quietly. "We are expected to exhibit the power of our station because that imagery is what creates compliance among power hungry aristocrats, prevents civil war, and holds alliances together. Living in entitled extravagance is part of that illusion of power."

"*Non*, do not defend a monarchy—"

"I am defending the way of things in nobility, mademoiselle. Not the queen's abuse of power. The necessity of court politics both makes and breaks those born under the right to rule." He placed a finger beneath her chin and lifted her face toward his. "Do not *ever* let it break you, Queen of The Row."

A breeze stirred her hair and rustled her skirts as she peered up at him shyly. "I feel as though I am already breaking. The pain around me is too much to bear." Her skin warmed under his touch and his brow furrowed again. "The former queen, Loriette Chalamet, defended me that night."

Fentienne's heart dropped to his stomach and he lowered his hand. Fresh anger boiled in his blood at the reminder of the woman who bore him and his brothers against her will. But he remained quiet, too afraid he would snap. His mother understood more than most the brutality of court life. She may not have starved like Factory Row, but she endured the cruelty of two corrupted monarchs.

"When the palace guards led me by roped hands toward the forest, she told me to be brave," Rhoslyn continued. "And to not stop being wise or courageous."

A twinge of betrayal jabbed at his festering wounds. All his life, he had yearned to hear a kind word from one of his parents. Still, he couldn't be upset at his mother. Not anymore. A mother he once thought despised him. Just one of many lies he believed uttered from that despicable man's mouth.

Use this anger to fight for yourself, milord. Take that furious injustice and revolutionize your life. Break the curse of being born to monsters to spite them.

Wa that what his mother did?

"Loriette Chalamet," he murmured to hide the enormity of emotion swirling through him, "is a fine example of one born with the right to rule who didn't break under torture. Or court politics." Memories of Loring flitted through his mind. How that stallion brought him joy and his mother knew he would.

Needing to change the subject, he gestured at the tea cart again. "The former queen would want you to indulge in this dream."

"You know Loriette Chalamet intimately?" Her eyes widened.

"Queen of The Row," he said slowly, emphatically, "choose a pastry."

She eyed him curiously for a second, then pointed to a beignet. "What is this, milord?"

"Pâte à choux." He picked up the powdered sugar dusted puff pastry she indicated and offered it to her. "A custard filled beignet, specifically." He chose the same type—his favorite. But he wouldn't share that. Lifting up the pastry, he said, "To oppression."

She lifted hers and said, "To male social oppression," as they had jested at the pond.

Fentienne brought the pastry to his mouth but waited until she took a bite.

Moaning, her head fell back onto her shoulders and her eyes fluttered shut. "Divine Mother, this is the taste of transcendence." She took another bite and moaned even louder. "You have ruined me, milord."

Gods, he would feed her hundreds of beignets to ruin her again and again and again. The ecstasy softening every feature of her face accompanied by those intense sounds of pleasure were killing him.

Tearing his eyes from her, he took a large bite then strode inside the quaint coffee shop. A moment later, he returned with a tray carrying two cafés, a small pitcher of cream and bowl of sugar, and placed them onto a table for two.

Rhoslyn doctored her coffee and enjoyed a sip. "*Merci beacoup.*"

Fentienne replied with a single, curt nod.

"Do you have siblings, milord?"

The coffee and beignet turned to ash on his tongue. Irritation bubbled to the surface. He loathed small talk about one's families and discussing his mother already put him on edge. "I once had three brothers," he gritted out as politely as possible. "Only my younger one lives."

She lowered the demitasse cup from her mouth and frowned. "Do you still see your younger brother?"

"No." Fentienne ran a hand through his dark strands and sighed. "Not in over a year." And because he knew what she would ask next, he added, "He moved to Dreglind."

Her eyes widened. "Are you Dreglindish?"

Fentienne clenched his teeth and stared out into the avenue of flowering trees. "My father was Dreglindish and Aurelienne and my mother is Aurelienne."

"Milord, perhaps you know then," she began, gnawing on her lower lip in thought. "Do Dreglindish men mark their scalps?"

The ground fell from beneath his feet. How in the hell did she know this? Had she... inspected him while passed out? Shit. Would she hunt his room while he was incapacitated too? He had planned to show her his military uniform, but when awake and healed. Right now, he was entirely at her mercy while blacked out from a shifter fever.

"Have you heard of sky and sea warriors?" he asked, hoping his voice remained unruffled. She shook her head no and sipped her coffee. "They are the ancestral dragon shifters of Dreglind. Men who carry Dreglindish dragon blood tattoo their scalps for each front line battle they fight in and survive, like the sky and sea warriors before them. It was a custom that fell out of fashion a century ago but still honored in some noble families."

Rhoslyn blanched. "Can a mortal man be both a dragon and wolf shifter?"

"Unlikely." Fentienne cleared his throat. "Dragon blood is but a trace now in mortals, unlike wolf magic."

Rhoslyn played with a crumb on the table and quietly asked, "Was your bro—"

"Tell me your darkest fantasy." Angry mountain gods, he couldn't take another question about his brother or family. Already, his nerves were frayed. She had inspected his *scalp?!*

Rhoslyn snorted. "You believe I will divulge such a secret to you?"

Fentienne arched a bored brow. "You might earn your garter ribbon back."

"Oh no, milord. Please keep the ribbon as a trophy of your arrogance."

A tiny smile brushed his lips. "My fantasy," he said low, holding her eyes, "while not dark, is for my wife to wear only her corset around the house. The ones with silk ribbons tied into bows at the shoulder, with matching garter ribbons. Strands of pearl necklaces gracing her neck too."

Rhoslyn pulled a face of disgust. "Arrogant and vulgar. Women do not exist expressly for a man's pleasure."

"I would worship her," he said just above a husky whisper, still holding her eyes. "A queen who would want for nothing." Fentienne ended with a slight shrug and arched a brow again. "But *only* if she wears her corset and other underpinnings around the house for my viewing pleasure."

She rolled her eyes and scoffed. Then sipped on her coffee.

After another sip, Rhoslyn flounced back to the tea cart with a plate while humming a melody he knew but couldn't immediately place. "If only I could, in a dream," she quietly sang to herself while peering at all the desserts and bouncing on her toes. "Hold her heart under a spell. . ." The folk song *Les Trendres Souhaits*, he realized—*Loving Wishes*. A strange warmth filled Fentienne's chest. "If only I could make that delusion become reality," she sang as she selected more pastries, this time jam filled crullers, more beignets, mille-feuille cakes, and glazed pâte à choux.

The last line, "I would like to be everything her eyes delight in," Rhoslyn didn't sing but hummed right as she lightly tapped the tip of her finger onto the top of a pastry still on the cart, like whimsically touching a nose—and he paused. Had she sung from the pastry's point-of-view? A pining for her to select one of them?

She was continually . . . unexpected.

To hide his laugh, he took another sip of coffee as she returned.

This girl.

In a gleeful flourish of skirts, she set the plate on the table and lowered into the chair right beside him. He reached for another beignet and she swatted his hand. "*Non!* Go fetch your own, milord. I am not your servant."

"This is your gratitude after I serve you coffee?"

"*Merci.*" She bit into a rounded puff. "Now shoo." She dismissed him with a wave of her hand in the direction of the tea cart. "*Oof!* Do not give me that disgruntled look. You believing that I would wait on you is perhaps the most fantastical part of any dream we've shared yet."

"From guilt to indulgence," he tsked. "Only one pastry and already you are now a proper aristocrat."

A mille-feuille cake paused halfway to her mouth. Yes, he was an arse. But so was she.

Flashing her eyes at him, she lowered her voice to sound like him and said, "Desperation isn't a pretty face and you, monsieur silk breeches, are—"

"Perfection," he interrupted. "The most handsome man you have ever had the good fortune to look upon." Smiling over his cup, he leaned back in his seat and took a sip, arched a brow, and murmured, "And you, mademoiselle, are infuriating, stubborn, reckless, and—"

He didn't get to finish. Rhoslyn smooshed a jam filled cruller in his face.

The cup of coffee in his hand spilled over the rim onto the saucer.

"You were saying, *mon douce puce?*" Rhoslyn bit into her cake and blinked with mock innocence. "Infuriating, stubborn, reckless, and?"

Fentienne set his café down and twisted in his seat with the grace of a predator, his eyes hard. The hell? Pissed, he cocked his head, a scowl wrinkling his brow, his mouth set in a firm line. His wife continued to nibble on the cake, thoroughly pleased with herself.

"*My darling,*" he said, punctuating each word. A drop of jam fell from his chin and she snickered. "You enjoy cake?" His voice was a dark, slithering threat. "Allow me to feed you."

She squealed and sprang from her chair, throwing what remained of her cake at him. Fentienne ducked, then clutched her wrist with lightning speed. Grabbing the other small multi-layered cake with his free hand, he returned the favor and squished it on her face.

Rhoslyn sucked in an angry breath, then lifted a wicked grin of her own. "You like beignets, *oui?*" She plucked the puff pastry from the plate and attempted to attack him again, but he caught her arm.

"This means war, Rhoslyn Gautier."

She laughed while trying to wriggle out of his grasp. "Surrender now. This will not end well."

"I take no prisoners."

Fentienne, being much stronger, redirected her hand back toward her and she screamed as he pushed the dessert into her face. The pink frosting- and cream custard-drenched fury she shot his way was the cutest thing he had ever seen, and he threw his head back with a loud laugh. He was laughing so hard, he didn't see her grab a fistful of pâte à choux and hurl them his way like snowballs. The little puffs bounced off him and rolled onto the ground. He shielded himself then jumped from his chair. But Rhoslyn beat him to the tea cart, being closer.

"Waive the white flag," she said in a syrupy voice, "or I will have no choice but to sacrifice these decadent sweets to your demise."

"Hmm."

"Hmm," she threw back with an indignant toss of her hair, but her eyes were laughing.

Grabbing her by the waist, he lifted her up and plopped her on the ground behind him. And didn't let go. She tried to charge him, but he held her in place with little effort. An arrogant smile flirted across his lips, widening into a wicked grin when her competitive spirit billowed with rage.

"Yield," he commanded her.

"Never!" she shouted back.

"Then I have no choice."

"No choice—"

Fentienne leaned down toward her face and she stopped moving, her chest heaving at his sudden nearness. His eyes flicked to hers for only a single, haughty heartbeat. "You really shouldn't have declared war on me," he whispered along her jaw, his voice rough. Nuzzling into her neck, he grazed his nose down her throat, and she gasped. The familiar scents of a crackling summer storm, moss, and ferns, dusted in sugar and vanilla, wrapped around him. "I take no prisoners, but you're . . . *mine*." Goosebumps erupted across her arms. Fentienne darted out his tongue and licked at the frosting on her lower cheek. "Mmm, the sweet taste of victory."

"Did you just . . . *lick me?*"

He grinned against her skin. "Victory is"—he licked at the frosting again—"*Mine*."

"Gross!"

She shoved him away with a playful growl and he let go of her waist, laughing at the wrinkled disgust on her confection-covered face. The annoyance pinching her elven features, however, quickly faded into a look he didn't quite understand—eyes soft, mouth slightly parted, but not from lust or arousal—and his amusement quieted.

Reaching up, Rhoslyn caressed his bottom lip with the tip of her fingers and his entire body stiffened. "Your smile," she said breathlessly. "Your laugh . . . never has a man worn them so handsomely as you."

A flush heated his skin, but he was too stricken by her words to look away. No one, not once, had genuinely gazed at him as if he were the golden sun warming their winter sky and the silver moon cooling their summer night. Fentienne was a nightmare, not a pleasant dream. A weapon engineered to bring death and win wars. An intentionally bred monster. His smiles, even when seducing another, were sharp knives meant to slice away at their confidence—his laughter an intimidation tactic to dominate.

Being used, using in return . . . those were relationship exchanges that made sense to him. But admiring his stolen moment of happiness simply because it brought her pleasure to see him so? He had no reference for these terrifying emotions.

"There is a wildness in you that fights to be set free." Her fingers left his mouth and pressed to his chest. "A beautiful darkness."

Fentienne drew in a tight breath and blinked back the confusion. "There is darkness in me and little else."

"There is rascally laughter, boyish smiles, charm and wit, unrelenting passion and conviction, and . . . a heart deserving of unfettered happiness." His wife stretched on her tiptoes, kissed his cheek, and whispered, "Night is no more evil than day. Fight for yourself, milord. Revolutionize your life. You are worth it."

Tears burned the back of his eyes. "Rhoslyn—"

"Come!" She grabbed his hand and tugged him toward the tree-lined avenue. "We are still in a pleasure garden, *oui*? Let us play."

Shame curled around his fevering pulse; he was struggling to breathe. Nausea churned heavily in his gut and he swallowed back the bile coating his throat.

No more lies. All you do is mock me.

Every urge told him to push her away, make her hate him, mistreat her in the name of protecting her life. It would be so easy to make her think he was simply dominating her right now. But by hurting her, he played right into Addien's designs for Fentienne to break his wife in the same way that monster had broken him. And he couldn't hurt another person he cared about in the name of protection.

No more lies.

She would know the truth of their relationship eventually.

She would hate him enough.

No more lies.

By confessing now, Rhoslyn could think under fire when Addien made her next move rather than be blindsided.

By confessing now, he gained back an element of control.

One less entity that maneuvered to own him.

One less being willing to destroy him for their own selfishness.

One less creature grooming him to hate.

No more lies.

He followed his wife beneath the flowering cherry trees and silk lanterns toward the stone gazebo. And, once there, he would share everything the curse allowed him to speak aloud.

Chapter 23

Fentienne

The pleasure garden around Fentienne faded into the black of his mind. Panic grabbed his pulse by the throat and squeezed, suffocating each beat. His thoughts tripped with every step toward a solid plan. Maybe he should just stop thinking all together and just begin spilling all the lies between them.

Rhoslyn let out a little gasp, the sound shoving him back into awareness. Assessing for danger, his gaze darted around the park while remaining aloof.

"We are clean!" she announced.

Fentienne halted his steps. *Clean?* Sure enough, jam and frosting no longer coated his fingers. All evidence of their food war had also disappeared from her face and dress. Throwing him a delighted smile, she yanked on his hand again and continued on toward the stone gazebo.

Palais d'Aurélie had a similar structure, though not anywhere near as ornate. Dark red climbing roses covered parts of the ridged columns and draped along the wrought iron lace-worked roofline. The dome was made from hammered copper and covered in thin wrought iron connected swirls.

Music grew louder the closer they approached—a small orchestra—and Fentienne realized, with growing horror, that it was an outdoor ballroom. The inner-ceiling of the dome twinkled with hundreds of star-shaped lanterns affixed at different lengths.

With the merry-go-round, the symbolism was a clear personal attack. But now he knew, without question, that the entire park was meant to torment him.

The last girl he danced with beneath the stars was Fayette.

Rhoslyn slowed before the gazebo and breathlessly whispered, "Magical

. . ."

The twinkling lanterns reflected warmly in her verdant eyes. It was magical, she wasn't wrong, and he swallowed against the knot forming in his tightening throat. He needed to confess to her. She needed to know everything. But she grabbed both of his hands and led him to the entry between two columns before the words fell from his mouth. And then the confession dissolved to ash on his tongue.

His muscles started to lock up.

Memories gusted though his mind, of Fayette humming a pretty tune as he led their steps, and he swallowed thickly again.

"Will you dance with me, milord?"

Fentienne closed his eyes for a second, willing his mind to stop racing, but the images kept coming. The hopeful glee on Rhoslyn's face, however, was his undoing. He really was growing soft, a nauseating observation. Resigned to give his wife pleasure from his pain, he gestured with his head to follow, then released her hands and reluctantly marched onto the dance floor, guilt twisting in his stomach.

The open room pressed in on him immediately. Music from a hidden orchestra echoed in his pounding ears. Fentienne gritted his teeth and dragged his gaze back to the main entry and . . . he sucked in a soft breath. The vision of Rhoslyn in burgundy and gold silks framed in by red roses, before a dark blue sky and beneath hundreds of candlelit stars, was the most beautiful form of magic that existed in all Ealdspell. And he was instantly under her spell, thoughts of Fayette and Addien and confessions nearly all but forgotten. Grinning, Rhoslyn practically floated over to him in her excitement and his chest constricted.

Looking around, she nervously nibbled on the corner of her bottom lip. "I mostly know *contredanses*."

He didn't how to respond or what to do, so he just gave a curt nod. Though he was familiar with the pretentious choreography favored here, even country dances as she mentioned, he only engaged in customs from Clifstán. Half-shifted monsters weren't exactly welcomed at court, not that he would participate in their preening.

"How about the *minuet*?" Her fingers fidgeted with a rosette on her bodice. "This is the only court dance in my *sans-culotte* repertoire."

"The *minuet* is horrendous," he murmured, his lip curling in disgust. "I don't prance, for any reason. Especially for a ballet to express a mating ritual at court. Gods."

Rhoslyn tried to smother her giggles but failed miserably. "Oh, but now I must see you prance, *mon douce puce*," she spurted in-between laughter.

"My darling, that will never happen. I would fall on my own sword before stepping a *Pas Bouré* or *pirouetting* to my dance partner."

"The *minuet* is a fine expression of masculinity."

"No."

"An example of athleticism and male virility, the dance books say."

"Absolutely not."

Though still humored, her shoulders deflated. "Do you know a *contredanse*?"

Sighing, Fentienne proffered his hand and she eyed it curiously, but didn't take it.

"Country dances are still prancing." He gently clasped her fingers and pulled her to him. Keeping his face bland, he positioned one of her hands on his chest and held the other between them while wrapping an arm around her waist.

Her eyes rounded. "The Forbidden Dance?"

"*Oui.*"

"*Non*, milord. My father printed chapbooks for the physicians who chronicled the effects of waltzing. The dance is"—she glanced around the park—"lewd and requires improper proximity."

Words spoken like a saints-raised lady, yet she didn't push out of his embrace. Nor did the idea of lewdness bother her earlier when she intentionally seduced him in a game of dominance. He almost pointed out her inconsistent opinions but he was too amused. And slightly confused too. Why *would* it bother her now?

A blush crept up her face, clear to the tips of her pointed ears, and she whispered feverishly, "Females succumb to madness and uncontrollable urges."

"Rhoslyn," he drawled, "how else will you get your ribbon back?"

The horror on her face was worth losing their previous war of wills at the merry-go-round and being covered in sticky jam. And he couldn't stop the laughter rolling out of him. Skies, he couldn't have planned a better trap if he tried. She was actually rendered speechless, even as the wide-eyed shock faded into slitted vexation.

"Tell me," he punctuated humorously, "who is in charge of your body, you or a dance? And since when does the girl who challenges queens before thousands and dominates arseholes like me through seductions need a pompous charlatan to tell her how she feels or should feel *this* moment? You are a far cleverer creature than this, Rhoslyn Gautier."

Rhoslyn huffed a bitter laugh. "If only I could disregard morals and social mores whenever I pleased. Males are not affected by waltzing."

Fentienne rolled his eyes. "Morals and social mores according to whom? To the gods you've never seen? The aristocrats of Palais d'Aurélie who enslave Factory Row? To a society that would force you to sell yourself in the alleys than keep you employed in a dignified job because of their prudish rules?" He paused before her. "Please, mademoiselle, enlighten me. Who made the rules of conduct you defend here in this place?"

An angry blush crept up her neck while her hand fluttered in the air. "*Oof!* You are impossible."

"I believe in consent between adults. Everything else is rubbish. What else is there to disregard? There is no reason for me to feel shame or guilt over a silly dance, nor should you. Who would see us?"

"You speak of a *laissez-faire* life privileged enough to disregard rules, but you are an aristocrat and a man," Rhoslyn spat. "What do you know of being female in a world that owns you, let alone poor with few options for employment? Those prudish rules allow me to care for my brother in the absence of male kin. Nothing else does."

"It is wholly unjust," he agreed. "I do not argue those facts. We live in a corrupt system."

Her eyes narrowed farther. "Are you mocking me?"

Fentienne loosed an irritated sigh. "No, mademoiselle. The opposite. I admire your strength and perseverance . . . " His voice trailed off as a thought hit him. "Are you afraid if you succumb to waltzmania here in this dream it will transcend to reality?"

She blinked back her embarrassment.

When she didn't answer, he continued. "*You* control your body, not a Clifstánian dance. Not backward uneducated charlatans who have the audacity to call themselves physicians. Waltzmania is propaganda. Whatever dance we share in these dreams together will not affect your ability to care for your brother in reality."

Rhoslyn's face warmed. Clearing her voice, she quietly asked, "Why is the waltz banned, if not for its compromising effect on females?"

Fentienne snorted. "And allow Clifstánian customs to become fashionable in Aurelienne courts? Blaming females for a realm's morale degradation is textbook control tactics. Moral degradation defined by jealous, weak-minded males who treat females as nothing more than chattel while they indulge however they please. Is this not what you were just telling me?" Fentienne paused a beat to let his words sink in. "A war was to be won, mademoiselle. Where do loyalties lie when the new wave of soldiers and nobles born are half Aurelienne and half Clifstánian?"

"They belittled my sex for . . . *war propaganda?*" Understanding dawned furiously in her eyes. "All because they feared Clifstánian men will be seen as desirable if their customs are?"

Fentienne pulled her body tighter against his and lowered his voice. "For what better way to enjoy the waltz than with an enemy soldier."

A soft breath left her body. "A treasonous romance."

For a moment, Rhoslyn disappeared and Fayette was once more in arms. His throat bobbed. "Your sex really does hold power over mine."

Green eyes snapped to his. "I will *not* retrieve my ribbon, milord."

Wasn't his angle, but he slid a barely there, raffish smile her way to lean into her misconception. Then, to the room he said, "Waltz," and the invisible orchestra changed from a slow three-quarter *minuet* ballet to a slightly faster, less theatrical three-quarter beat waltz.

Without further preamble, he pressed his leg to hers. "The steps are simple. I will lead with my left foot first and you step back with your right. I then step to the right with my right foot, you with your left, while I slightly rotate us clockwise. Feet come together like first position in a minuet. Then I will lead us backward in a step similar to the first, another to the right, slightly rotating us in a circle once more. Always clockwise."

"Similar to sashaying."

Fentienne groaned. "No prancing. Follow my lead."

Rhoslyn tilted her head with a teasing side-smile. "Let *you* dominate me?"

"You want to dance?" he countered. Her teasing grin remained, just to spite him. To combat her playful defiance, he bent down until his cheek grazed hers and whispered, "As I've said, obeying me is not without its pleasures. You won't suffer." Goosebumps raced along her skin and her breath fluttered. But he could also practically hear her eye roll. Not giving her a chance to riposte with her rapier tongue and wit, he stepped forward to the beat.

Her eyes flew to his and blinked back the surprise. In the next beat, he turned them while stepping to the right. Fingers tightened in his. His hand splayed across her lower back. Drawing in a nervous breath, he guided her backwards a step toward him. Again they slowly spun while stepping to the side. A grin brightened her face as he led them forward a step once more, like at the beginning . . . and he was unraveling in her arms.

Skies, she was breathtaking.

Amber starlight caressed strands of her golden-brown hair and limned the enticing lines of her face, neck, and soft curves. Silk skirts swished around his legs in a tantalizing rhythm. This close, her earthy scent enveloped him and heat spilled into his pulse. An ache that set his soul on fire.

Another small turn and their gazes locked. It was then the music swirling around them grew louder. A haunting melody their bodies seemed to know by heart. It was common to trip over each other's feet when first learning the give-and-take steps. Yet they moved as one, their bodies in perfect rhythm, as if they had been dancing together all their lives. And perhaps, in a way, they had been.

Step forward, push her away.
Rotate around a future that neither can control.
Step backward, chase after him.
Rotate around a dream their reality will never own.
Step forward, chase after her.
Rotate around a past that can't be changed.
Step forward, push him away.

The hand on his chest slid up to wrap around the back of his neck and tangled into the strands of his dark hair. All thought was vanishing beneath her unexpected touch. The red roses, the midnight sky, everything blurred into the background but her. They moved around the marble floor, their bodies pressing tighter and tighter together. His heart was racing and he could feel her own heart beating wildly against his chest. Another half turn and her thumb grazed down his neck, pulling a hot, languid breath from his chest. Lantern light flickered in Rhoslyn's gaze as they held his, then those green star-flecked eyes fell to his lips.

Gods, his defenses were crumbling—and fast.

No more lies. All you do is mock me.

The music continued to swell louder and louder, but their steps slowed. She peered up at him through dark lashes, the permission clear in her eyes. He was still the boy who stole kisses to feel something meaningful. Still the man who enjoyed a female to fix his loneliness.

The girl in his arms, however, held his breaking heart.

Fentienne took a step back to squelch the pain blooming behind his ribs. The hopeful look on her face crumbled and she angled away to hide the disappointment. Hot, angry tears burned the back of his eyes and his teeth clenched until his jaw ached.

No more lies.

A cold sweat broke across his brow. A shake began in his hands. Pushing through the panic, he opened his mouth to begin his confession, but the words died on a strangled breath.

White hot fire cracked down his bones. Muscles, skin, fingers, and toes contorted and reshaped. A growl thundered in his chest.

He was shifting in reality.

Drurie toddled up to him and barked, "Wake up, alpha."

How was Drurie in their dream?

The cub chewed on his shoe, barking once more to wake up, and he gently nudged her aside. But the motion, even in this liminal space, screamed in every corner of his being, and Fentienne grimaced back the urge to cry out.

Rhoslyn didn't notice his distress, thankfully. Instead, her gaze fixed entirely onto the she cub at his feet, and frowned.

Then he woke with a start—as his wolf.

SCENTING HER BROUGHT out the moon in their veins. This elf girl intoxicated them. Made their blood pound and heart howl. She was their wolfsbane and their roaming night.

Wolf gently licked her hand while she still slept.

Human fool refused their bond. Would rather die than possess her love. They needed her love to become strong. Invincible. Wolf growled low. Human was not allowed to harm their mate. Human denied devotion and care.

Their mate stirred.

Wolf whimpered to feel her hands stroking his fur, longed to lick her cheek and nuzzle into her neck. Wanted to lay his head in her lap. She needed to know their affection to strengthen the bond. But Wolf needed to leave before she awoke. Scaring their mate would push her away and make Human alpha happy. Human was skittish around elf girl, even though Human panted for their mate.

She cub nipped at his paws. Growling low once again, Wolf stared down little she cub until she stilled and lowered her eyes. Wolf used his teeth to pick up the orphan and place her on the bench next to their mate. She cub licked the elf girl's hand and jumped onto her arm and barked for food.

Wolf loped to the landing. With one last look over Wolf's shoulder at their mate, he continued down the stairs, past the hot pools, and loped out the door to prowl the night. To protect their mate, Wolf would find démons hunting elf girl and kill them.

Chapter 24

Rhoslyn

A tiny bark sounded in her ear. Something was jumping on her arm. Rhoslyn's eyes fluttered open to Drurie, tugging on her dress sleeve. Little blue eyes met hers and she softly smiled.

"Come here, *ma petite louveteau*." Rhoslyn gathered the wriggly pup into her arms—and gasped.

The bench seat beside her was empty. A pair of black military breeches pooled on the floor beside a pair of boots at her feet. Did the démon's wolf watch her? The hearth fire lit-kitchen came into sharp focus. Shadows flickered on the walls and across the floors. But no other shadow moved. She didn't spot reflecting golden eyes, either. Her brows wrinkled. The bench was too high up for Drurie to climb.

Drurie.

Rhoslyn softly stroked the cub between her ears and strode toward the kitchen door. Cool night air brushed along her cheek. An owl hooted in the forest. The hair on the back of her neck rose, but still she set the cub among the herbs. Drurie toddled around the kitchen garden a couple of feet away, sniffing the ground. The scent of sage and thyme infused the air with her movements. Rhoslyn plucked a sprig of lavender and twirled it between her fingers, anything to calm her rattled nerves. Her mind, however, continued to race.

How had the pup entered her dream? And if the little wolf cub could, why didn't Matthieu?

Rhoslyn peered over her shoulder into the blackened forest over the stone wall and rubbed at her arms with shaking hands. Saints, the démon had shifted right beside her. No shield separating them like when Lucas started to shift beside Dalbréath. A woozy sensation floated around her head, the dizziness growing stronger with every second she remained outside.

What had attacked the beast? He didn't have a chance to tell her before passing out.

Rhoslyn scooped up Drurie after she finished her business and dashed back inside and shut the crooked-hinged, splintered door. Her skin was crawling. The dark walls around her only added to the galloping pulse in her chest. She peered around the kitchens and swallowed against the sharp, rising panic. Matthieu was still curled up on a rug before the hearth, his cheeks rosy from sleep, the wolf talisman clutched in his fingers and his new cane beside where he lay.

Drurie gnawed on her finger and Rhoslyn sighed.

"You are going to chew holes into everything, aren't you?"

Setting the cub onto the floor, she then fetched a wooden bowl and ladled in a small scoop of cooled vegetable stew for her. Drurie practically tripped over her paws to reach the bowl. The poor little thing. She tried to feed her earlier, but the pup was too excited and stressed.

A shadow passed along the wall, one that appeared human, and Rhoslyn froze. A chill flushed over her skin. This happened often in the chateau. The ballroom let in ample natural light during the day, but a cold touch would still pass through her body while she practiced her fencing footwork. She didn't want to think long about what they were, but she had a suspicion they were restless spirits—those slaughtered by Aelfred Halivaard who waited to be avenged. Not one ghost had been malevolent, thankfully. If they were ghosts and not her imaginations, that is.

To distract herself, Rhoslyn wandered over to the worktable and ran her fingers over the blue glass bottle of ashes then over the shoebox. The little heels fit perfectly. She wore them only while practicing her fencing, not wanting to dirty them while fussing around the kitchen afterward. They were so beautiful, she couldn't help opening the lid and caressing the tiny silk bows, just for the sheer thrill of knowing these were hers. Not ones that would fade with a dream or moth-eaten forty-year-old shoes found in an abandoned armoire. The last pair of shoes she owned, the ones now in tatters, were her sister's. She had worn her older sisters' castoffs all her life. Even now, she wore a gown and underthings that once belonged to another. But today, she owned brand new shoes—her first brand new anything.

Rhoslyn pulled a black silk heel from the box and hugged it to her, biting back a smile. How did the dark démon know the size and shape of her feet? And the simple, but elegant embellishments she would like? Even more strange . . . why did he care?

Gently, as if lowering a newborn babe into a bassinet, she tucked the shoe beneath the protective linens and closed the box lid.

That infuriating man confused her to no end, seeking out her company only to push her away. Showing his care with little gestures and unexpected gifts but his contempt with his snarling words. The longing in his eyes frightened her sometimes, the hatred too. But the intensity of his raw, vulnerable emotions, the ones he tried to hide behind the territorial, aggressive, controlling alpha male tendencies, drew her in . . . when not vexed by his brutish presence. He disgusted her often, but he also had her compassion.

And now her deep gratitude.

The bottle was cool against her warm hands as she lifted it to her mouth and gently kissed the glass. A tear slipped down her cheek and plopped onto the table. For a man who couldn't make up his mind on how to behave around her, this was an enormously thoughtful gesture. If not for this gift specifically, she would think he was lying about wanting to make her hate him. But why? Was it because she was a dirty fayette from Factory Row and he a noble? *Non*, he knew she was a noble from the House of Thorns and had known from the onset. An ache panged in her tightening chest. She hugged her home and family close to her heart, then set the bottle back onto the table.

Drurie finished her small meal and yawned. Rhoslyn took her outside once more. The entire time, Rhoslyn's gaze darted around the yard, over the stone wall, and back toward the opened fire-lit doorway. When in his wolf form a few weeks back, the dark démon hadn't attacked her in the woods. And his wolf was beautiful—dark midnight fur and spellbinding in the graceful way he moved. But she couldn't shake the spooked feeling shivering in her veins.

He was her husband, her mate. He had to be.

Dalbréath led her right to him—because he knew. Rhoslyn was so furious over this realization, she was ready to tear down the sky and shove it up her uncle's arse.

And the man in her dreams . . . it was just too uncanny. Why would

Drurie approach him? The only possible conclusion was that those who could share dreams must also share the same cursed roof. But that wasn't true for Matthieu.

"Ma petite louveteau," Rhoslyn spoke quietly. Drurie toddled over to her and Rhoslyn clicked her tongue for the cub to follow her back into the kitchen. Once inside, she closed the door as best she could. Slivers of the night still peeked in at her, though, and Rhoslyn shivered again.

Drurie snuggled up close to Matthieu and closed her eyes. Rhoslyn watched them both for a few seconds with a soft smile. Then her shoulders sagged. Spending the night in the kitchens with a door that didn't lock wasn't a pleasant thought. She resigned herself to this discomfort for the beast's sake. But he wasn't here. While treating his wounds, she had forgotten that he would shift into a wolf at night. Drurie, however, might need to go outside once more before dawn.

Rhoslyn folded a freshly laundered sheet and placed it beneath Matthieu's head. The hearth was warm enough that he wouldn't need a blanket. She tied her dark red cloak around her shoulders and lifted the hood to keep her ears warm. Fetching the hand mirror from the work basket she kept beside the table, she settled onto the bench.

In the firelight, her eyes appeared nearly black. The freckles across her nose faded into the dusky shadows. Her lips, however, appeared tinged with dark rouge.

The man in her dreams thought her pretty. He had not spoken so directly to her, but the confession was written in the way his eyes softened when he thought she wasn't looking; how his lips would slightly part as a breeze danced through her hair; the deep, measured breaths when she smiled his way—and, saints, the gentle wonder on his face when she laughed and smiled! As if he couldn't believe he made another happy. He was terrible at hiding his emotions, despite his attempts to appear aloof and disgruntled. Perhaps he fooled others, but her empathetic abilities saw the scared boy beneath all the masks he wore. Saw the man who hungered to be loved and to give his love in return.

And to be loved by such a man . . .

For three weeks now, she had been pining for a man not her husband, one of the most darkly beautiful males she had ever seen. Divine Mother, he was every forbidden fantasy to sensible girls like her. Sinful was too weak a word for the way he possessed her fevering pulse. His passionate nature set her ablaze and she wanted to burn for him until nothing of her remained. His intelligence and sharp wit made her mind sigh and heart quiver. The rascally but dangerously sensual way he played captivated her heart. And his smile. *Mon Dieu*, his smile was *devastating*—somehow both boyish and elegantly cruel.

The majority of males she knew were intimidated by her confidence. He, however, seemed to enjoy her intensity just as much as she enjoyed his. The foolish man seized every opportunity to provoke her too. And she knew it, rising to the occasion to make him believe he was in control. But only because his armor fell off piece by piece when he could control their flirtations. Though, the slack-jawed look on his face when she seduced him in return. . . a blush warmed her skin. Not a trace of haughtiness or anger on his handsome face. Only desire. A powerful man like him *desired* her, a girl he believed whose station was no higher than the streets of Gabaston.

Rhoslyn pressed a hand to her stomach to quiet the riot of butterflies in her fluttering pulse.

Butterfly wings that picked up speed when she remembered his laughter after he smeared cake across her face—loud, unabashed, his head thrown back, thoroughly delighted by her frosting-covered ire. Followed by the soft feel of his nose trailing down her neck, his hot breath pulsing on her throat, and . . . his tongue on her lower cheek as he licked at that same frosting to goad his victory in their confection war.

Had his mouth brushed across hers . . . a pleasurable shudder wended down her body in a delicious rush at the very thought.

Would he kiss her in their next shared dream? Was she bold enough to kiss him first? Were his lips softer than silk? Would knowing the cadence of his affection so intimately ruin her for any other male?

She *wanted* to be ruined by him too.

Rhoslyn's fingers curled into her skirts and the hand gripping the mirror's handle clenched tighter. Her eyes drifted back to the blue glass bottle and a different flock of butterflies released in her veins. The man in her dreams was a wicked indulgence, like sugar-dusted pastries after just begging for bread. The monstrous man in her reality knew she needed her family, especially right now as her world was tipping upside down.

"You'll need the comfort. Court life is an Underworld of torment." The words of the beast.

"The necessity of court politics both makes and breaks those born under the right to rule." The man in her dreams had said, placing a finger beneath her chin and lifting her face toward his. "Do not ever let it break you, Queen of The Row."

Her heart stopped beating.

Those born under the right to rule . . .

Did the man in her dreams also know her true identity?

Anger rippled down her limbs and her fingers curled tighter until her knuckles whitened. She was tired of males determining her future and holding her life hostage to their whims. If The Row wanted her as their queen, she would not only fight for the affordability of basic staples, like bread, but for females to be regarded as equals in society.

Lowering the mirror, Rhoslyn peered around the night-darkened kitchen. She couldn't remain hidden behind cursed walls while Factory Row spilled more of their blood to protect their families and livelihood against a tyrannical monarch and aristocracy. What kind of queen allowed her people to suffer while she fattened on safety and comfort?

The only hesitancy in her convictions was the safety of her brother. Who would care for him should she die in her fight to give the common people back their power?

"Rhoslyn Gautier?"

A squeak yelped past her clenched teeth. The mirror fell from her hands and clattered to the floor, landing face-down. Swearing under her breath, Rhoslyn scrambled to her knees. A soft, bluish light glowed from beneath the metal edges and colored her black, silk gown a midnight blue where the light touched. Slowly, she turned over the mirror and sucked in a sharp breath. A female elf illuminated from the surface with ruffly black, chin-length hair and soulful marigold eyes.

"*Demad*, Your Highness," Rhoslyn said in the language of the saints. *Hello.* "You are Princess Gellynor Death Talker, *oui*?"

The female snorted. "Just Gellynor. No milady or Your Highness." The elf turned her head. "Clearly, I like her more than you." Gellynor rolled her eyes and returned to the mirror. "Tyllie is affronted that she had to call me princess for nearly a century before I told her to stop." The elf humorously shook her head and muttered, "Owls."

Owls?

Did she regularly carry on conversations with owls in mirror worlds?

Gellynor sobered and met Rhoslyn's wary gaze.

Blinking back the shyness, Rhoslyn couldn't help but notice the similarities to Gedlen—the graceful, pointed arch of her brows, the sophisticated sweep of her cheekbones, the handsome lines of her full lips, black satin hair, bright Otherworldly eyes—and Rhoslyn's heart fluttered a moment while thinking of the prince.

Dalbréath was right. Gellynor was extraordinarily beautiful.

"Is he treating you well?"

Gellynor's question pulled her back to the present and she almost laughed. The "he" in question snarled and growled at everything, lacking all good manners and any sense of hospitality. But . . .

My threats were all to make you hate me, nothing more.

Rhoslyn glanced at the gifts on the table across from her. He did exhibit thoughtfulness and often: the apples, cheese, and water the first day in the chateau; the blankets and pillows; his apology to Matthieu on also being stuck in this curse; the gold necklace; wanting her to make herself and Matthieu better clothing; teaching her and Matthieu how to fight and strategize; leaving her brother fables and adventure books to read; noting when Matthieu was pushing himself too hard, then helping to carry him down to the kitchens while Rhoslyn ran ahead to start a warm soak for her brother's overtaxed leg and lungs. She even caught him placing an extra ginger biscuit on Matthieu's plate when her brother had bent over to pick the talisman he dropped on the floor. And now these gifts.

There was such goodness in him.

Still. He was a vexing, self-centered, arrogant man.

She opened her mouth with every intention of sharing how he was unpredictable and constantly snappish. "He had shoes custom made for me and is teaching me sword fighting techniques," tumbled from her mouth instead.

Gellynor tilted her head. "He bought you . . . *shoes*? That cursed man went *shoe shopping*?" She burst into laughter. "Gods, the picture I have in my head." She turned to the owl again, one Rhoslyn couldn't see. "Tyllie wants to know if he has good fashion taste?"

Rhoslyn grinned. "They are pretty little things, practical yet elegant, and fit my feet perfectly, though my feet were never measured."

"Huh." Gellynor's brows wrinkled.

"Hoot!"

"No, I'm not meddling in their romance," the elf said to the owl.

"Hoot!"

"Really?" Gellynor scoffed. "Don't mind her," she said to Rhoslyn. "Tyllie is a gossip—well, you are. Don't give me that look. Anyway," Gellynor said, returning her attention back onto Rhoslyn. "You feel safe, then?"

"He promised that he would never harm me."

The wrinkle in Gellynor's brow deepened. "And you believe him?"

"Should I not?"

The elf's lips flattened into a thin line. "His father was horrifyingly violent toward females." Rhoslyn's eyes rounded. "Use that same fire to stand up to him like you stood up to the queen. Kill him if he hurts you. He doesn't get to use his position of power or strength over you, understand?"

Rhoslyn nodded her head. "*Oui*, no one owns me. I have stood up to him several times already, though not for physical violence."

"If he has yet to physically harm you—"

"He hasn't touched me except . . ." Rhoslyn's pulse fluttered a beat and her face heated. "Except to caress tendrils of my hair on occasion. Or to correct my positions during pistol and smallsword training. His touches are surprisingly gentle despite his growly personality."

The elf frowned. "I'm doing everything I can to shatter the shielding wall around the chateau. The souls didn't know about the wall or roses when I first spoke to them. Dog Breath has been beside himself."

"Dog Breath?"

Gellynor snickered. "Dalbréath. King Félip's nickname for him."

"Uncle Dog Breath," Rhoslyn said with a laugh. The idea that the Dúnælven Faerie King called him this made it even funnier. "Matthieu calls him Uncle Dalbrie."

"Well, your Uncle Dalbrie is a pain in my arse right now." The smile on Gellynor's face turned into a tired sigh. "When that male is worked up, I can't keep him busy enough. And my loving, ever attentive brother conveniently departed on a patrol mission and left his second-in-command behind for me to deal with."

Rhoslyn bit back another laugh. "Tell Uncle Dalbrie that his niece said to be *kind*."

A soft look settled in Gellynor's marigold eyes. "You are every inch a Kadelaryn. I now see why my brother was humored by you."

The air in Rhoslyn's lungs choked. Saints, the prince spoke about her to his sister?!

"So," Gellynor drawled out, redirecting the conversation, "The chateau is under a powerful curse, one woven in the old runic language of Éireanna. Curses involving the dead are always difficult to untangle and break. Their existence is temporary or forgotten. Eventually most are reborn. Ancient curses lose their potency after a while for this reason. Curses involving love are by far the most difficult. For love is eternal. What binds two souls together could trace back to the first breaths of time. Or it could be so new there is still not language to describe its possession."

"Cursed in . . . *love*?" Rhoslyn's mouth fell open. The dark démon was cursed to never know love? A tiny piece of her heart cracked.

The mirror flashed, went dark, then faded back to Gellynor.

"Need to make this quick. Mirrors each have their own personality. One reason why it's important not to stare too long into one. They like to project. And your mirror isn't fond of—" Gellynor silently spelled out L-O-V-E in the language of the saints. "Unfortunately, everything to do with you and him and your curse and his curse and the curse over the House of Golden Light has to do with exactly *that*."

"My curse?"

The mirror flashed again.

"Gellynor, is he . . . my husband?"

The elf froze, her face relaxed, but her eyes widened. Not in fear, more like annoyance. "The curse—"

"*Oui*, the curse." Rhoslyn fluttered a hand into the air and muttered, "I am to know nothing about the man I am trapped with."

"Ask him, Thorn—"

The mirror flashed again before returning to Gedlen's twin. "I need you to do two things," Gellynor rushed out, scowling at the space around her.

"Ask that dark, dangerous man if he has seen Addien Wyndham recently, but riddle your words to appear as though Dalbréath mentioned her. The souls are agitated by her draw of magic beyond the chateau being cursed to the grave."

"Hoot!"

Gellynor slid her gaze to the owl and smirked. "I thought you would like my broody descriptions."

"Hoot!"

"Tyllie adds 'angsty.'" She leaned in and lowered her voice. "She's addicted to romance novels ever since meeting Eirwen. I swear the queen did it on purpose just to irritate me. Sends Tyllie a new romance book every month that I'm forced to read aloud so this spotted chicken can coo."

Romance novels? Did such a thing exist? Sweet waters of Glanis, Rhoslyn would cease to exist if ever she read a full novel-length story about falling in love. Perhaps Tyllie could live with her, instead. She would gladly read pages and pages of swoony stories to this owl.

Rhoslyn blinked. The dark elf said *Eirwen*.

"You speak of his Imperial Highness's mate?"

"Yes," Gellynor said in a strange voice, her marigold eyes narrowing. "Has the cursed man spoken of Florian Halivaard?"

"*Non*," Rhoslyn said with a little shake of her head. "Not once."

"Mentioned Queen Eirw—"

The mirror flashed again. The surface blackened and Rhoslyn panicked when Gellynor didn't return a few seconds later.

"Please, mirror," she begged.

No light, not even a little wink.

Rhoslyn pushed up from the ground and perched on the end of the bench.

"I will give you a good polish." There. A soft light flickered. "Would you like me to prop you up near a window so you may reflect upon nature? I imagine being in a drawer for decades would be dreadful." The soft light flickered again, flashed to black, and then Gellynor's face returned.

"Thank the gods!" Gellynor closed her eyes a brief moment. "I thought I would need to find another mirror. Okay, quickly . . . ask if he has seen Addien recently and if he knows of what she may be doing. And burn two roses each day into one of the Underworld fires. The souls can slowly consume the curse in the roses. That may hasten things along to drop the shields around the chateau while I hack my way through all this runic spell code."

"The roses are cursed?"

"Continue to keep this mirror by your side. I'll contact you at night. Dalbréath and I will travel to you in another week or so. I don't want to alert the chateau's cursed man of my presence too soon—"

The soft blue glow winked out. Rhoslyn slumped against the wall with a sigh. "Thank you," she whispered to the mirror and caressed the ornate metal design behind the surface. Per her promise, she propped the mirror up on a shelf that faced the cleanest window. "Enjoy the sunrise," she said, then returned to the bench.

Pulling her cloak tighter around her body, she leaned onto a cabinet and closed her eyes. Tonight would be rough. Her mind was spinning faster than a country dance. Her heart was equally as dizzy. It took her far longer than usual to fall asleep, still too spooked to fully relax. It was sometime after midnight when she finally succumbed to sleep.

RHOSLYN WOKE WITH a start and found Drurie sitting on the floor at her feet, little blue eyes fixed on her. The cub whined. But that wasn't the sound that startled her awake. A strangled cry muffled through the kitchen door. Was someone hurt? Shooting to her feet, Rhoslyn crept to the door and, as quietly as possible, nudged it open enough to peek out.

Drurie whined at her feet again, distracting Rhoslyn with her insistent whimper. The little wolf was in clear distress, which only added to her anxious pulse. Matthieu yawned and rolled over toward the hearth, curling up once more. After one last glance at her brother, she nudged the opening wider.

The sky out the door blazed golds, corals, and pinks over the forest. Various greens in the garden trembled in the smallest of breezes. Rhoslyn started to open the door even farther when a quiet grimacing cry of pain shattered the new morning's illusion of peace.

Her heart jumped to her throat.

Slipping through the door, Rhoslyn jogged into the herbs, her eyes furiously darting around the overgrown path and along the wall. A flash of skin caught her eyes and she paused only long enough to register the body five yards away before she took off in a run.

She slid to a stop with a sharp breath, not prepared for the sight. The man, now half-shifted, writhed on the ground near the stairs leading to the bathing pools. Agony twisted his face and . . . Saints! He was completely naked! The hottest blush of her life painted her skin almost instantly. But she didn't dwell long on gaping at the male form before her. Instead, Rhoslyn quickly untied her cloak and draped it over his middle, then fell to her knees beside him.

"Shhh," she soothed, too afraid to touch him in this state. Afraid he might lash out while confused and in pain.

The hard, defined muscle down his chest, stomach, and arms flexed and relaxed. His eyes cinched shut, his teeth bared as he heaved in tight breaths. Dark hair tangled around his face in messy waves.

"I'm so sorry," he choked out. "I promised," he said on a half-sob next. "I promised you."

A tear slipped down Rhoslyn's cheek. Her magic shuddered at the violent grief gripping his heart.

"Shhh," she soothed again. "You are safe."

"I didn't mean it," he cried so quietly she almost didn't hear him. "Gods, I didn't mean it."

The man curled into himself and covered his face with his claw-tipped hands. The muscles down his body continued to tremor and ripple, and his teeth began to chatter. Rhoslyn's gaze trailed over his injuries. The wraps were gone and dirt stuck to the honey salve in spots. But the sutures still appeared intact, thankfully.

Drurie climbed over Rhoslyn's skirts and snuggled up against the beast's chest, whimpering again. Did this man suffer each morning when he partially shifted back? The unnatural transformation had to be enormously painful.

"Bury me," he whispered into his hands. "Bury me."

The little cub lifted her head and peered at the man, then licked his fingers. She was such a little sweetheart. Rhoslyn gently stroked the fur of her back, then pushed to her feet. The beast would be humiliated if he found Rhoslyn hovering over him in this state. And while he had attempted to humiliate her at the beginning of their forced living arrangements, she would not torment an already tormented man. Quietly, Rhoslyn scooped up Drurie and tip-toed back to the kitchen.

Once inside, she leaned against a wall and sniffed. Tears rolled down her cheeks. Why he pushed her away, why he wanted her to hate him, started to make some form of sense given the trauma haunting his dreams. It made his gifts far more precious too. If his father was horrifically violent toward females, how was he toward his own son?

Rhoslyn brushed at the tears and straightened her shoulders. She would make him egg-dipped bread and molasses for breakfast, a meal he seemed to enjoy last week. Already he would know that she saw him when he discovered her cloak draped across him. Seeing her blotchy, tear-stained face would only add to the embarrassment he would certainly feel.

Males like him couldn't appear weak. He was the head alpha. Men of power knelt before him.

But males like him also needed to know there were safe places where they could break and still remain whole. And when he was ready to wrap his wounds, she would be there.

CHAPTER 25

FENTIENNE

The ballroom doors loomed ahead and Fentienne swallowed against the sharp knot in his throat. He had hoped to find her in the kitchens first, when returning her cloak after bathing and dressing. A plate of egg-dipped toast, molasses, and stewed apples were set on the closest table beside fresh linen strips, but she, Matthieu, and Drurie had already left. The meal flushed a different kind of warmth in his chest than the shame of knowing she had seen him fighting his nightmares right after shifting—possibly even seen him shift. He ate in silence, trying to contain the chaos of emotions tumbling through his unraveling heart and mind.

He didn't know what he would say to her then.

He didn't know what he would say to her now.

But he knew one thing: he needed to confess everything. It was the only way to fully arm her against whatever Addien had planned next and to survive after he died. Everything he was, everything he would be belonged to her future anyway. She was bound to a monster. And he was becoming more moon-addled every day.

His Myrefell identification tags clinked in his coat pocket with each step and he gritted his teeth. War was coming to Gabaston. The people's war. Whatever Rhoslyn needed in support of Factory Row, he would lend her.

Pausing before the ballroom, Fentienne closed his eyes and willed the pulse pounding in his ears to quiet. Yesterday morning, once reaching the chateau, was a blur. He remembered bits and pieces. The bittersweet smile when Rhoslyn held the ashes of her prior life. The tears when opening the shoebox. Their conversation about her brother-in-law. His conversation with Matthieu. Beyond that? Nothing.

But their dream . . . he couldn't recall a single moment in his life when he had genuinely laughed so much. Not even with Fayette. Gods, when he licked the frosting off Rhoslyn's cheek, he had to will himself to behave. If she had turned her head, they would have kissed. A desperate, foolish part of him wanted her to create that accidental brush of lips too.

A sudden hot flush heated his body—his godsdamn wolf. An urge to rage pulsed through him but he stood firm, growling back his own threat. Yesterday, his wolf tasted the power of possessing his will, making Fentienne's fever one step closer toward becoming rabid. After the sun set, his wolf also tasted the pleasure of standing before Rhoslyn without Fentienne's mortal body coming between them. This morning, however, his wolf frothed over breaking her heart, snapping and clawing and snarling. But his wolf didn't own him. His wolf didn't own Rhoslyn either. His wolf knew shit and only acted on primal instinct—not on carefully planned out strategies of war.

Opening his eyes, Fentienne drew in a tight breath.

His stomach clenched in nauseating spasms.

Then he pushed open the doors and entered.

Rhoslyn lowered the smallsword in her hand and turned toward him. Their eyes gently locked and the muscles in his stomach clenched harder. Those Otherworldly green eyes lowered to the burgundy cloak in his hands and a soft blush warmed her cheeks.

When she found him, he was completely bare. Skies, imagining the desire and appreciation on her face made every cell in his body moan. The alpha in him bristled at even considering that another had introduced her to the carnal delights of the male form. She was *his* to pleasure. Only his. Being naked before her, even without his consent, didn't bother him either. After living in shared quarters almost all his life, showering and toileting in the open next to an entire military base of men, he didn't possess a sense of modesty.

"Rosie, why does he have grand-mére's cloak?"

Matthieu's question immediately yanked Fentienne from his spiraling fantasies and anchored him back into reality.

Rhoslyn smiled sweetly at her brother. "I must have left it in the garden when taking Drurie out this morning, *caneton*."

At the mention of her name, Drurie perked her ears and peered up at Rhoslyn. But when spotting Fentienne, she scampered over to walk beside him, barely keeping up with his long strides.

Matthieu's brows pinched together. "Why would you take your cloak off so early in the gardens?"

"Return to the boy," Fentienne commanded the she cub. "Stay by his side."

Rhoslyn hesitantly found his eyes once more. "Please set my cloak on the table, milord," she said, adding, "*Merci*," over her shoulder as she turned around and moved back into a garde position followed by an attack.

Drurie whined at his feet. "She cub, go to the boy."

"Do you not like puppies, milord?" Matthieu asked him.

Good. The boy no longer had his hawk-eyed mind trained on his sister.

Fentienne watched Drurie to ensure she obeyed his commands, then met Matthieu's curious gaze. "She is young and wants to imprint on a guardian. I'm the only other wolf at the chateau and her alpha."

"And she needs to return to her pack," Matthieu finished for him, his voice uncharacteristically sad.

Fentienne nodded. "I'm not a suitable guardian for her. She needs her blood kin."

Matthieu pulled Drurie onto his lap and buried his face into her fur. "What if she no longer has blood kin?"

A charged silence fell over the room with his question, one laced with so many emotions Fentienne's mind didn't know where to settle. The little boy lifted glossy blue eyes his way and a terrible thought struck Fentienne in that moment. Did Matthieu no longer have blood kin? The scent of heartbreak moved around Rhoslyn's brother in answer and Fentienne felt pieces of his own heart fracture in reply.

"I'm sorry," he said softly. "For everything."

"I understand, milord," Matthieu quietly replied, not understanding at all. "I will love her while I can."

Fentienne's gaze slowly drifted back to Rhoslyn with Matthieu's ending words. Another pretty blush warmed her skin and she shyly blinked. Love was a construct, an illusion, but the desire to provide for and protect his mate was quickly becoming more essential than the air he breathed. He still didn't know if his affection was born of a faerie blood contract or authentic. He didn't care anymore, though. Whatever words were used to paint his feelings, the final picture was the same—he was hers. All of him. Either by his choice or against his will, it made no difference.

Ealdspell could take his life for all the monstrous things he and his family had done. But it was hers to take first. He owed her that much.

"I didn't think you would be well enough to train today, milord."

He set her cloak onto the weapons table and clenched his teeth. "I shouldn't be."

"Do démons really heal so fast?"

The tip of his claw picked at a chip of paint peeling from the table while he tried to hold in his fury over yesterday's possession. "Démons heal extraordinarily fast. Most major injuries within an hour, maybe two at the most. Minor injuries within minutes. But not me," he quietly spat, his gaze snapping to hers. "I don't have full control of my magic despite being head alpha."

"Because of your curse?"

He replied with a single, curt nod. "I have strength and speed, but not regeneration."

"Perhaps it is not the curse." Rhoslyn stepped toward him.

A low, dark chuckle rumbled from his chest and he looked away, shaking his head. "Everything, mademoiselle, leads back to my many curses. Being stripped of control and forced to feel pain is part of that punishment."

"Perhaps, milord, you simply do not know how to heal." A stillness fell over Fentienne's body with her words. An animal awareness. "How can you call on a skill you don't understand how to use? As a soldier, you already understand how to wield strength and speed. You . . ." Her voice trailed off as she settled before him. "You carry many battle scars, milord. And many wounds still bleed. Perhaps all you needed was a kind hand to stitch you up and a heart who asked for nothing else in return other than your happy recovery."

Fentienne's chest rose and fell deeply with her words. "Rhoslyn," he whispered and stopped, dragging in a painful breath. The pity in her eyes tore up his confession and blew the ripped shreds into the wind. He couldn't think straight when she looked at him like he was worthy. Because, gods, he wanted that look to actually mean something. But it didn't.

A bitter laugh begged for release.

His wife couldn't resist a wounded creature to champion. Or a monster to fight. And he was both.

"Ready to begin today's lessons?" she asked him, lifting her sword.

Fentienne nodded and stepped away, grateful for the change in topic. Combat he knew. Shifting through fight positions and sparring was a language he spoke fluently. Sword fighting was archaic, flintlock pistols and muzzle loaded muskets too. But he was trained extensively in Aurelienne fencing techniques for when undercover as one of their soldiers to spy for Myrefell.

Grabbing a smallsword with his uninjured arm, he ordered, "Parry two." With the tip of his blade, he pointed at her feet, which were just peeking out beneath the volumes of silk draping from her waist. "Remember, heels positioned along the lines of a small square. Bring your left foot in more and make sure your knees are slightly bent. Yes, precisely. Now keep the sword tight to your body. Low point toward your front foot."

"Parry four." He inspected her position. "Parry one." Walking around her, he studied her form. "Parry seven." Round and round he went through the various garde positions, increasing the speed of his commands. The dainty elven features of her face pinched as her arm began to shake. Still he pushed her, faster and faster.

"Parry five. Hold." Fentienne stopped behind her, satisfied with the straight line of her back. Touching the palm of his hand to her elbow, he encouraged her to raise her arm a few inches higher. "Do you wish to attack your enemy or your head, mademoiselle?" he asked over her shoulder.

She heaved a sigh. "I am struggling to keep the sword aloft."

He leaned in close and murmured in her ear, "Fight your body."

Flyaway strands along her neck fluttered with his breath and she shivered. Closing his eyes, he drowned in the biting summer storm scent furiously swirling around her. A drowsy heat kindled into flame down his body, curling into a desire so hot, for a flicker of a heartbeat he could think of only the feel of his face buried into the sugared shadows of her neck. The soft feel of her skin as his fingers slid down her throat to trace around the swell of her breast. Another rapid beat of his heart and the flickering heat dropped to the pit of his churning gut. He swallowed back the rising bile.

He didn't know how to tell her. Each minute stretched him deeper into fight or flight responses too. And pissed his wolf off even more.

Stepping back, his voice strained, he added, "You'll have no choice when facing an opponent."

"*Oui*," she huffed. But the sound was far too breathless for irritation.

"Outfit yourself for better arm movement, too." Slowly, he sauntered around to her front. "Do you have a strapless corset?"

Her mouth fell open. "That is none of your business—"

"Attack!"

She arced down and thrust the point of her blade at him, but with a wobbly arm instead of conditioned grace. He easily parried, then cut the tip of his blade back toward her unprotected hand and lightly nicked the pad of her thumb. A small line of blood welled on her skin.

The look of disbelieving shock quickly faded into bared canines, the promise to murder him in his sleep if he did that again. Gods, that look. He craved this fire. Fentienne grinned, a dark, arrogant smile he knew would stoke that combative nature of hers. But the smile hurt. A persistent ache continued to tighten his chest and sicken his gut.

"In open positions," Matthieu said to his sister from the sidelines, "bring your action hand closer to your chest."

Fentienne considered her little brother. "And in closed positions?"

"Arm and hand behind you when angled away from your opponent," he recited from previous lessons. "Less surface for attack." Matthieu turned toward his sister and smiled, a lock of blond hair flopping over his blue eyes.

Rhoslyn sighed and faced Fentienne again.

"Parry two." Fentienne arched a brow and settled into fourth position. His eyes quickly trailed over her form, then shouted, "Attack!"

Rhoslyn thrust toward his right hip and he parried.

"Guard."

She brought the sword back toward her a quarter of the way and halted.

"Attack!"

Once more she thrust toward him.

"Guard! Retreat."

Pulling the blade toward her a fraction, she stepped backward while he advanced with slow attacks she could parry in second and seventh position. He loved this. Loved the fierce set of her eyes, the deep groove between her brows as she concentrated, the pressed lines of her lips. Loved the thrill of sparring her with actual weapons. If life were kind, he would want for nothing more than to spend his remaining days with Rhoslyn and Matthieu, playing house. But he was born for destruction.

"Advance. Third position." Fentienne retreated as she moved forward.

"She's in sixth position," Matthieu corrected from the sidelines once more. "Turn your wrist, *ma sœur*."

Fentienne acknowledged Matthieu with a dip of his head. "Good eye, boy." To her, he said, "Parry three is a true edge. You're in sixth position, as Matthieu pointed out. False edge. Turn your wrist so your knuckles face you." She corrected and he slowly attacked, still retreating. "Now lunge."

Fentienne tilted his head to study her form. "Hold." In a few steps he sidled up to her. She was leaning too far forward. Gently, he placed his hands on her shoulders and straightened her posture. "Your thumb should be up. Yes, like that. Lift your arm just a little more until it is slightly above your shoulder." He slowly circled around her. "I can't see your feet and leg positions in all those skirts when dipping low, so look at my example and correct yourself." Fentienne faced her and lunged. "Notice how my front foot is in-line with my leg, which is perpendicular to the floor. Back leg is fully extended. The heel is flat."

Rhoslyn started to adjust her position and winced. "My legs are shaking too much."

"Do you think your enemy will give you quarters?"

"And a fine cup of tea." She rolled her eyes. "Any other obvious questions, milord?"

Ignoring her, Fentienne rose and lowered the tip of his sword to the marble floor. "Resist me," he instructed and nudged her arm. As expected, she fell over in a poof of skirts and petticoats. Green eyes slitted sharper than the blade in her hand and slashed his way. "If your footwork was correct, you would have had better balance, even with shaking legs." A goading smile walked up a side of his mouth at her groan. "On your feet!"

She pushed to a stand with a low growl. "I loathe drills."

"Hmm." That dismissive reply always pissed her off and he had to keep from laughing at the sudden fire darkening her eyes. "Drills are what—"

"Make competent fighters, I know," she groaned.

"I could shout commands at you, in your face, loud enough to shake the glass, if you need more excitement." The baiting smile he threw her way billowed the searing flames in her gaze. "Don't tempt me, mademoiselle. I would enjoy every second commanding your submission."

"Obeying drills is *not* the same as obeying *you*," she riposted.

The air rushed from his lungs and the muscles in Fentienne's stomach knotted painfully once more. This was his opening. A line he knew she would recognize immediately. One that would seal his fate and hers. But Rhoslyn deserved the whole truth. He was tired of being Addien's weapon of revenge. Tired of hurting those he cared about in the false name of protection.

"Obeying me," he said barely above a whisper, imagining his blade running through Addien's heart with each word instead of his own, "is not without its pleasures."

The sword in Rhoslyn's grip loosened. Her free hand clapped over her mouth. A tiny drip of blood slid down her wrist, the first of many wounds he would give her this day.

Fentienne leaned in close and she stiffened. "Stomp from the room," he whispered. "Shout whatever you like at me, but we have an audience. What I have to share is for your ears only."

Her eyes shot to Matthieu, who thankfully was distracted by Drurie and didn't notice their exchange. A deep, quivering breath shook her frame before her wounded gaze cut back to him.

"I will meet you in the hallway," he added.

Straightening her shoulders, angry tears pooling in her eyes, she stepped backward. Then she marched from the ballroom, the smallsword still clutched in her hands.

Fentienne watched until the door slammed shut. A tremor started up in his hands. Gods, he couldn't breathe. Gasping for air, he twisted toward the weapon's table and gritted his teeth. A flush rushed down his body and his mind spun for a frantic heartbeat. His damn wolf was attempting possession again. The fever simmered dangerously in his mind. The muscles in his arms and torso flexed. The need for aggression snapped at his heels.

"NO!" he growled low at his wolf.

If he didn't chase after Rhoslyn now, Addien would win. His father would win. Every fucking person in his life who used him and taught him to hate would win.

Skies, he wanted to vomit.

"Matthieu," he choked out, fighting back the undulating anger. "Stay here until your sister fetches you."

The little boy didn't ask questions—for once. The distress was written into every tense line of his face. "Do not be afraid," Matthieu encouraged.

Fentienne drew in a tight breath and, without another glance Matthieu's way, pivoted on his heel and marched from the ballroom.

He found her at the end of the hall, her back to him as she stared out the window over the vast forests. The tremble in his hands increased. His vision blurred for a moment and his head grew light. In all the battles he had faced, not one terrified him like the one he was walking into. The thin threads of rabid aggression faintly pulsing through him didn't help.

Hearing his footsteps, she spun toward him. Tears glistened on her long lashes. Her normally rosy complexion paled to moonlight—cold, haunting, Otherworldly. The deep, soulful green of her eyes held his, then roamed over his face in sweeps of slow recognition and fear-laced caresses.

"Appearances can be deceiving . . ." The shake in her voice quaked in his bones.

"Night is no more evil than day, my darling."

Her bottom lip trembled. "And yet that is where we place all our nightmares."

Fentienne blinked back the stinging tears and roughly confessed, "I am your nightmare and your dream, Rhoslyn Gautier."

"My heart . . ." She blanched further, rubbing a hand over her chest, and choked out, "I defended you and—"

"There is no redemption for cursed men like me. I'm unforgivable." He clenched his jaw and growled low, "I was born a monster. Raised by a monster. I will be one even in the Underworld. I told you multiple times."

"*Non*, milord." She squared her shoulders. "You are *not* a monster. You simply choose to behave like one. But your heart is good."

Fentienne groaned, stabbing his hair with his clawed fingers. "Rhoslyn—"

"You heard me, *mon douce puce.*" She lifted her chin. "Unlike you, I cannot lie, nor do I twist my words. My magic?" She stepped closer to him. "I am an empath. You confuse me. You have *always* confused me. But I see past all this—" A tiny drop of blood splashed onto the marble floor as she gestured at the length of him. "—to the man beneath."

Frustrated, he leaned into her face and snarled, "You still know nothing. Stop defending me!"

"I know you deceived me," she hissed back with equal force. "And while I'm furious and I want to pound you into the ground for endlessly mocking my trust and vulnerability, I also know there is reason, beyond humiliation, that you didn't want to reveal until now that the man in my dreams and the démon before me were the same. Though, I did have my suspicions." She softened her voice. "You are unforgettable, milord, in both spaces."

A muscle pulsed along his jaw. "The people who hurt us *are* unforgettable. Do not confuse abuse for attraction, or chase dreams meant to break us—"

"I know you are my husband."

His entire body deflated and he looked away.

"I know you care deeply for Matthieu."

Tears burned his eyes.

"I know you care deeply for me."

"Rhoslyn . . ." His voice cracked. "Let go of your girlish romantic notions. You can't save me and it doesn't matter if I care . . . about *anything*. Our story will *not* end in happiness."

"Your feelings clearly matter, *husband*, without consideration for mine," she punctuated sharply. "Your belittling, at times terrifying threats were only to make me hate you, per your drunken confessions yesterday."

Gods, hearing her call him husband was a hundred bullets hitting him all at once.

"You also confessed that I was all you ever desired and would never deserve." Rhoslyn's face twisted in sorrow. "Why would you willingly hurt the one you desire? You could have chosen friendship and instead chose cruelty. And don't you dare use the excuse that you are a monster. You are far too intelligent and so am I for nonsense answers." She pointed a finger in his face. "A monster wouldn't care but you are a raging sea of conflicted emotion. Saints, you feel so intensely the torment cuts the beating heart from your chest to bleed out onto every sharp-edged word you speak."

"Because," he ground out, "we are two souls cursed from birth for a fated romance built on betrayal. I tried—" He peered up at the ceiling, blinking back his furious grief. Another fevered rush of heat flushed his body. His damn wolf snapped at him. But he understood the message. Leveling his gaze back onto Rhoslyn, he said softly, "I promised to protect you, knowing it would cost me my life."

A tear slipped down her cheek. "Why would you promise your life for mine and desire my disdain as gratitude?"

"Fayette, I fell for you when I was sixteen. I thought myself so in love, I committed treason just to see you smile at me, hear your laugh, and to feel genuinely wanted—"

"Milord, we didn't meet until—"

"—With you, I felt seen for the first time in my empty, despicable life. You couldn't desire me for my title or my power because you didn't know who I really was."

Rhoslyn fidgeted with the wedding band around her neck. "I still don't know who you are."

He pressed on. "You weren't the girl my father forced me to marry at age four in exchange for a cotton trade alliance either. I *chose* you. I *needed* you. And—" he curled his claws into fists and furiously growled, "And you destroyed the little happiness I possessed. Manipulated my loneliness and desperation, then sealed your betrayal with a kiss. Except . . . it wasn't *you*."

Large eyes, glistening with unshed tears, locked onto his, her pulse fluttering faster than a war horse charging a battlefield.

"From my first breath," he choked out, his skin crawling with shame, "I was taught to hate fae kind, Rhoslyn. Not just hate but kill them. I'm a highly trained killer and have taken the lives of hundreds of fae, mostly dwarves."

The blood visibly drained from her face, but she didn't look away.

"And the rune shifter who posed as you knew this," he growled low. "She came to me as a human girl. One who looked identical to *you*. Delighting that one day I was required to claim you as my mate and it would break me when I saw the face of the elven girl I was bound to in faerie blood. Break me and make me hate your kind even more." He drew in a shuddering breath. "Because if I truly hated you, I wouldn't prevent your death, whether at my hands or another's. And I did, Rhoslyn. I hated you for years."

She still didn't look away, but the grief on her face tore at him. The knuckles fisting tight around the smallsword's pommel whitened.

"But that hate... I couldn't hate *you*. Even when I wanted to." Fentienne took a small step toward her. "My heart knew yours the moment I saw you walking with Dalbréath toward my family's chateau after daybreak. Whether from a faerie blood marriage, a wolf mate bond, or my inability to not fall for you, then or now, my heart is yours. And Rhoslyn Gautier, my wife," he said breathlessly, "I hated myself far more than I ever hated you in that moment. But I hate Addien Wyndham the most." He bared his teeth and snarled, "She wants to kill you to punish your parents. And why Dalbréath asked me to protect you by claiming you before the clans and declaring you my mate, because he knew I take promises of protection to my grave and that my wolf would never let me harm you. And I couldn't say no, even though looking at you brought me both immense pleasure and shattering pain."

A thousand questions burned in her eyes. A thousand different emotions too. The hand fidgeting with the wedding band around her neck stilled. Tears, however, continued to roll down her cheeks. He knew what question she would ask next. He knew because it would be the one he would ask too.

Dropping the ring, she lifted her chin and met the intensity of his gaze with her own. "Who am I, milord?"

Fentienne didn't hesitate. "Princess Maeline Kadelaryn Wyndham, next faerie queen from the House of Thorns, you were cursed at birth to die because of scorned love. And I was chosen as your husband so you knew cruelty instead of love before your death."

Chapter 26

Rhoslyn

A princess.

She was a *princess*.

Rhoslyn pressed her back to the window and stared at him wide-eyed, the smallsword clutched in her hand. Her chest heaved and she swallowed. The fear pounding in her pulse was growing louder with each galloping beat of her heart. The torment in his eyes, the grief and shame pinching his flushing face... he was telling the truth.

This man had killed hundreds of fae. As a soldier? Did he still hate her kind even though he no longer hated her or Matthieu? Why did Aurelienne order the deaths of dwarves while taking many in as refugees? Despite the horror shaking the marrow of her bones at his confession, her magic was drawn to the good heart that was furiously fighting against a barbed cage. And, once more, he confused her.

How could a man be both good and evil? A villain and a hero? Beautiful and ugly?

The snapping, brittle heartbreak he protected slivered tiny thorns deeper into his wounds. A persistent cutting pain he had grown to live with and didn't know how to live without. No wonder he didn't know how to heal.

The muscles in her body tightened. That faerie, the one who had destroyed his trust and happiness, lit a raging fire in her veins. How dare Addien Wyndham use her to crush this man! To twist and mangle his beautiful darkness into something horrific. Into a monstrous lie that he believed with every razor-edged breath in his body—love wasn't a weapon to punish him or a curse. Rhoslyn wouldn't use his pain against him, no matter how he had treated her. Addien was the real monster.

All for loved scorned, which Rhoslyn gathered had something to do with her father and this faerie.

She was a *princess*.

The next faerie queen of Avenbury. Queen Audra Wyndham and King Dallin Kadelaryn were her parents and Prince Henri was her younger brother. Saints, she had no idea what to do with that information. Though she had wanted to know for a few weeks, she was grateful she didn't know until now. There had been far too many life-altering changes already and this reveal radically changed everything.

"My thoughts do not know where to settle," she said finally, breaking the tense silence. "I have heard of Addien Wyndham only recently, milord, but with little detail. Who is she?"

His dark brows pulled together. "Your mother's cousin and the head of Avenbury's faerie counsel as next in line after you. The throne is only passed down to queens." He continued to explain the politics of Addien's obsession with Dallin Kadelaryn and her fury over unrequited love. "Your curse," he said and paused, "was that she could order your death after you came of age and I claimed you officially before my own race."

Rhoslyn gasped. "But you claimed me—"

"Yes, but not for this reason." His golden eyes searched her face. "Gellynor Death Talker amended the curse that Addien couldn't kill you unless you fell in love with me and agreed to remain my wife."

"And so you wanted me to hate you..."

"Rhoslyn—" His chest heaved and he gritted back the tears pooling in his eyes. "And you will. I'm not a good man. I will *never* be a good man. Addien knew you would refuse our bonds because of who my father is and how I was raised. She knew it would torment your parents to wed you to a démon. But they did it because the alternative was to bury their infant." Lowering his voice, he choked out, "To not be married to me will bring your death. To love me will bring your death. Hate me but remain married to me and she can't act on her curse. But then you are also trapped in this chateau, married to a man you despise until one of us dies."

She brushed at the wetness on her cheeks. "You are afraid of being loved."

He groaned, then shouted, "You are so stubborn and reckless! Out of all the things you should be feeling right now... this is absurd. *You* are absurd."

"I don't know how to feel about everything else!" she shouted back. "There are far too many things to process. All I know is the man grieving beside me and my heart grieving with him. Everything else is inconsequential for now."

"Are you mad?" He paced away from her, stabbing his clawed fingers through his hair, growling as he paced back. "You are cursed, and if you don't survive, she will be the next queen of Avenbury."

"*Mon Dieu*, you speak as if I am certain to die," Rhoslyn shot back. "Will I be struck down immediately? Because if so, I would no longer be alive to have this argument with you."

His mouth fell open and his body slumped in disbelief. Then tears welled in his bloodshot eyes once more. "Do *not* fall for me, Rhoslyn Gautier."

"Your heart can know mine but mine can't know yours?" Rhoslyn hooked her index finger around his and caressed his knuckles. "I can fall for whomever I want and no one, not even death himself, will control my heart but me."

Their chests heaved furiously, their breaths trembling. His face was gruesome—sharp teeth, wolfish eyes, unnatural features. But also one of the most beautiful faces she knew—cruelly elegant yet boyishly sweet—with a dark, dangerous heart filled with a soft, gentle light he tried to hide from others. How could she not fall for this man?

"By faerie blood and our own," he said in a rough whisper, staring at their joined fingers, "we are bound. You can't trust your judgment and I can't trust mine. Our marriage is just another faerie trick."

"Ridiculous," she spat. "All my life males have told me what I feel, how to behave, what my life's value is." She tugged him closer and lowered her voice, "I know my heart and my own mind. Stop trying to dominate me with your fears."

His Adam's apple bobbed. "She will fall in love with the whole man in her dreams," he quietly spat in reply, "and despise the monster when awake." He stepped even closer to her until she was forced to tip her head back to see his blazing eyes. "Addien cursed me in love before you ever stepped foot onto Chateau Lumière Dorée."

"Then why don't I despise you now?"'

A dark, bitter laugh rumbled from his chest. "You have a fatal flaw, my darling. You can't resist a wounded soul to protect and nurture, even when it will get you killed. You put your life on the line for Factory Row. Now you are putting your life and your throne on the line over a man you don't even know by name."

"But it is perfectly reasonable for you to trade your life for mine in the name of protection?" she gritted back. "Regardless of how I feel on the matter? The absolute arrogance."

A vein throbbed on the side of his forehead, the gold stillness of his eyes now predatory. Another flush warmed his skin and the muscles and tendons in his neck flexed. "You don't despise me only because you now know I am the whole man in your dreams. And you perhaps despised me less and less the more you believed I was possibly him as well. But you *did* despise the monster and for far longer than you have not." He leaned into her face and snarled, "You can't trust your judgment."

"*Non*, husband. You *wanted* me to hate you and used your half-shifted form to terrify and dominate me. Addien had nothing to do with making me despise the snarling, angry beast when awake or fall for the infuriatingly divine man in my dreams." She tilted her head. "We see only what we want to see, especially when angry and afraid, *oui*? Your words, *mon douce puce*. And you strategically designed what I should and should not see."

He loosed an angry breath and peered out the window over her shoulder. A muscle ticked along his jawline.

"But awake or in my dreams, you are the same person," she added. "Only your behavior toward me when awake has changed."

"In our dreams," he said just barely above a whisper, "my wolf doesn't control me nor am I bound to this curse. I am *not* the same man."

Rhoslyn let go of his finger to cradle his cheek and he went deathly still. "I cannot pretend to know what it is like to live a life without happiness," she whispered. Her thumb caressed his soft skin, her eyes furiously searching his. "Or a life where the idea of being loved terrified me. But that doesn't mean my judgment is wrong. Your trust issues and mine are not the same."

"My darling . . ." He closed his eyes and leaned into her touch with a shudder. A single tear rolled down his cheek. "I want to be worthy of you," he whispered in reply. "I want us to be more than a cursed boy and a cursed girl, trapped in a cursed house and fated in a cursed romance. I want," he said, his breath choking on a quiet sob, "I want *you*. My wife. But that is all a beautiful dream. You still don't fully understand the nightmare."

Gently, he stepped away from her touch to stand beside her sword arm. "I wish I were never born," he whispered. Carefully, he lifted her arm up until the point of the blade was positioned into an attack.

"What are you doing?"

"I wish I had died on a battlefield years ago." He wrapped his hand on the blade to ensure she didn't move, then stepped in front, leaning in until the tip pierced through his waistcoat just above his heart, and choked out, "I wish I never existed so you didn't have to know this pain. To know what I have done and still be forced into a relationship with me to live." She started to pull away, frantic, but his hand shot out and gripped the blade again. A small cry left her lips.

Locked sharply onto her gaze, he reached into his coat pocket and pulled out a necklace, offering it to her. "I give you permission to run me through without guilt. I deserve nothing less."

Rhoslyn accepted the identification tags, tears streaming down her face. "You are Clifstánian? I don't understand."

"Born in Myrefell, but I am Dreglindish and Aurelienne as I shared in our last dream."

"But you fought for Clifstán?"

He nodded. "I commanded machine warfare soldiers and was one of six torturers, all personally trained by my father."

Torture? The hair on her neck stood on end and goosebumps fleshed down her arms. The sword began to shake in her hand, but his grip tightened around the blade holding it steady. This poor man. If his father trained torturers, he probably had little choice but to comply.

Rhoslyn gnawed the inside of her lip. A conversation with him over coffee, as the whole man in her dreams, floated back to the forefront of her mind. Dreglindish sky and sea warriors marked their scalps—noble men with dragon blood. And there was only one family with titles in Clifstán, a royal Dreglindish family from the House of Dragons. A noble bloodline that also belonged to House Beausoleil and Chalamet of Aurelienne. With a connection to his Imperial Highness, as Gellynor hinted at. A younger brother who still lived, as the man had also shared in their dream.

The identification tags cut into the palm of her hand, but she didn't need to look. Based on age alone, she knew who this man was.

Prince Adalwolf Halivaard.

A shudder wended down her spine and a wave of revulsion crashed through her. Her parents had wedded her into the Halivaard family and believed that was better than death. How had Adalwolf survived? Disgust curdled in her gut, but not at him. He couldn't help who his father was no more than she. Nor could he help how he was raised.

Divine Mother, her heart beat furiously over this man—angry at him, hurt by him, full of love and full of compassion.

Some wolves are too wild to tame. Some are too wounded to save. And some, like your mate, fight inner demons to break generational curses.

Gedlen's words now made sense. Rhoslyn didn't want to tame his wildness. His passionate, rebellious spirit was meant to entwine with hers. Nor was he beyond salvation. He just needed to know how to heal his wounds. Saints, to be raised by such a horrid man. Rhoslyn shuddered; she couldn't help it.

"I will not harm you," he said so softly her heart ached at the sound.

Rhoslyn took in a hiccuped, tear-stained breath. "*Oui*, I know." And she did, but from the anguish in his eyes, he must have harmed someone she loved. Curling her fingers around the metal tags, she boldly met his eyes. "Were you part of the attacks on Gabaston?"

His entire countenance shattered. "Yes."

Just one word, but it spoke an entire library's worth of tomes. The guilt on his face twisted a cold, jagged dagger into the raging organ thundering in her chest. This was why he brought her the ashes of her home and family. It wasn't just for her to carry a piece of her heart when forced into court politics, but also as an act of atonement.

The Underworld's fires burned hot in her belly.

Images flashed rapidly in her mind. The screams. Bullets whizzing through the air and horrific machines skittering down Factory Row. Buildings on fire and collapsing. Her family now ash. Her little brother's leg damaged. How he writhed in pain for days, weeks.

And her husband commanded some of those machines.

Her bottom lip trembled and face grimaced with restrained grief. She heaved back a sob. Those gold eyes never wavered from hers, soaking up every angry, disgusted emotion. He didn't offer any excuses for himself or apologies. Nothing he said would bring her family back or her home. Nothing would erase the horror of caring for her brother on a meager income and hollow gut this past year, terrified that she would be forced to service males in the alleys just to live.

"We had orders from the king." His lip curled at the mention of Clifstán's former monarch—his father. "My younger brother was sent on a tracking mission to find the Black Witch in the Seven Jeweled Hills. The day after he left, I was deployed to the Spired Hills, then to Gabaston. I don't know why the king attacked Factory Row, but I suspect he had an arrangement with Queen Adeline. We were ordered not to move into Saints District or Crowns Quarter, especially not on Palais d'Aurélie."

She released her grip onto the smallsword and let it clatter to the marble floor and furiously ground out, "If she allowed Clifstán to attack—"

"I'm fairly certain she did."

"Why would she destroy Aurelienne's industry and means of income?"

Adalwolf shook his head slightly. "Coercion. It could have been the lesser of two evils. Or just one psychopath having fun with another."

Rhoslyn wrapped an arm around her sickening stomach. She didn't know what a psychopath was, nor heard the term before, but that didn't matter. "Other than losing Matthieu, there is no greater pain or betrayal than how my family brutally perished." She sucked in a ragged breath. "Their screams, milord. I still hear their screams and my mother calling my name behind a wall of fire. I lost my older brother who was my best friend," she cried out. "And Matthieu . . ." Her words trailed off as another wave of nausea passed through her. "How he suffered. There was little relief I could give him."

Adalwolf's eyes fell shut and he stiffened, muscles flexed, another tear carving down his flushing cheek. This man found happiness in her brother. The smiles he thought he hid when Matthieu spoke, the softness in his gaze when her brother pushed himself and grinned that cherubic, dimpled smile she could never resist. How he would sneak sweets and extra food onto his plate.

"I still see my little brother's eyes right as the gun went off against his head." Adalwolf's eyes snapped open.

Her lungs drew in a quiet gasp. Florian was executed? Then who was emperor? She thought Adalwolf said his younger brother lived. The persistent nausea in her middle roiled again. The horror of seeing one's sibling shot in the head at close range...

"He was ordered to die by our father right in front of the elven girl my brother loved, to punish the girl. My oldest brother pulled the trigger." Rhoslyn clapped her hands over her mouth. "Her soul-severing screams haunt me every night. The sky and ground grieved with her. Do you know why it is called the Battle of the Black Winds?" Rhoslyn shook her head. She had heard tales, but they sounded far too outrageous to be true. "When this elven girl keened, she awakened the dead and released the black souls of the Underworld onto the battlefield in a sudden gust of wind. A black wind."

The heat drained from Rhoslyn's head and she swallowed back the bile creeping up her throat.

"My brother's corpse reanimated right in front of me. Blood still dripped from his head wound. And... he killed our father. Stabbed him." Her husband shuddered. "My body had locked up. My mind said run but my feet refused to go. Fear and a pain unlike any I had ever experienced ripped through me like shrapnel. My heart..." He dragged in a tight breath and choked out, "My heart was obliterating. This man I thought was invincible, that I had been terrified of my whole life? Who had tormented me since age eight to bully my younger brother? The man who made me watch as that brother was tied to a post several times over the years and whipped for my disobedience? Who forced me to learn torture techniques starting at the age of twelve? He just fell. A weak, disgusting heap at the elven girl's feet.

"But my little brother." Adalwolf clutched his waistcoat above his heart and inhaled another breath wrung with grief. "Gods, my brother, he was the only good thing I had left in my life and he was executed right across from where I stood and I did nothing, Rhoslyn. I did *nothing*. The day prior I had taunted him that I hoped Father killed him and that I hoped I was the one who got to torture him first. Empty, hateful words I didn't mean but groomed to say. I didn't believe once that my father would actually order his death, because I saw only what I wanted to see in my fear and anger." Adalwolf started darkly laughing through his tears. "And it wasn't him."

His eyes cut back to hers and he growled, "The elven girl's mother was a powerful faerie and had glamoured my oldest brother to look like the youngest and an elven male to appear like my oldest. Our father had executed the oldest. It was a trick. The obliterating pain in my chest was because of a faerie trick. Another godsdamn faerie trick!"

Rhoslyn lowered her hands, eyes wide. "Your little brother lives?"

"My little brother lives." He paused a beat, then continued. "The elven girl gained control of her magic and sent the black souls back to the Underworld and the dead back to their graves. And commanded that the black souls take my father, oldest brother, and her still-living mother with them. Then she cursed me to be half-man by daylight, full beast at nightfall for my and my family's crimes against the Kingdom of Ealdspell."

A chill scraped down her spine.

"It was my fault, Rhoslyn. None of that would have happened if I wasn't such a coward." He swiped at the tears on his face. "I obeyed orders from the king to bring my brother back to Myrefell to be stripped of rank, not tried for treason. I destroyed dwarven villages on the brink of winter to force my brother out of hiding and to capture the Black Witch." The man was sobbing now. "All to please a man who hated me except for the glory I could bring him as an intentionally bred super soldier. Gods, he raped my mother repeatedly for sons. And I obeyed *that* man."

The claws of his hands curled into fists and he clenched his jaw, baring his sharp teeth.

"I killed my brother," he wept. "Tormented the girl he loved. I attacked Gabaston and may have even fired on your family's home and shop. All the homeless, hungry people on Factory Row. And Matthieu—" He dragged in a choking breath. "I'm unforgivable. Do you now understand why there is no redemption for me? Why you can't fall for me? You will die! I would be responsible for the death of another I care about and I . . . I can't, Rhoslyn. Just hate me. Please, just hate me."

The glittering pieces of glass that were once his heart and hers clattered to the marble around them, each harsh breath grinding the broken pieces into dust.

"Adalwolf—"

"—I will continue to do terrible things," he snarled through his tears, not even registering that she used his first name. "I was raised by a cruel man to be cruel. It was all I knew for twenty-one years. And I still sometimes find pleasure in another's pain."

She started to open her mouth to speak and he cut her off.

"I know you, Rhoslyn Gautier, Princess of Avenbury, Queen of The Row. You want to defend me and make me see reason according to your world of hope and goodness and redemption. But I am head alpha of all the clans. That role is aggressive and dominant. It falls on me as top dog to punish alphas who defy orders or overreach their positions through torture tactics to humiliate them into obedience. Even kill them or members of their pack, if necessary. And I won't even think twice about it. I might even enjoy it. Wolves are territorial. Démons are even worse. Drastic measures are needed to keep other alphas in line." He leaned into her face and ground out, "I was born for destruction and will *never* be a good man."

"I don't want a *good* man," she gritted back. "I want a prince who is a *better* man for facing the trauma of his childhood to own the pain he has caused others. I want a *beautiful* man with a beautiful soul who would rather cut out his own heart than hurt another he loves. I want a *passionate* man with a wild spirit who was meant to run with the wind. I want a *dangerous* man who knows his power over others but is learning to not abuse that position for his own pleasure. I want enough *darkness* in a man that he is sinful in ways that ruin me completely. And, saints help me, I want an *intelligent* man who intentionally provokes me for the thrill of the fight."

Bashful wonder blushed across his face, but fear continued to darken his gaze. Rhoslyn tucked his identification tags back into his coat pocket, then slid her hands up the hard planes of his chest to cup his face, and his breath quietly hitched.

"This world and the world beyond are full of good men who do noble things," she whispered across his lips flushed from tears. "I am angry with you and hurt. There are trenches of grief and betrayal between us that will take time to mend. But you, Adalwolf Halivaard . . . you are the beautiful, passionate, dangerous, dark, intelligent man I want."

The muscles down his body stiffened when hearing his name. Dark brows creased together and those golden eyes, still glossed from crying, stilled. She could almost imagine hackles bristling down his back.

"You are not responsible for Addien's curse over me," she stressed. "We are stronger together. Pushing me away only hurts us more—"

"Say my name again."

"Oh." Rhoslyn arched a brow. "Prince Adalwolf Halivaard."

"You didn't look at my tags. When . . ."

"Shortly after you handed them to me." She lowered her hand from his face to rest on his chest. "There is only one Dreglindish and Aurelienne family from Clifstán with power."

"You are far too clever a creature."

"Hmm."

A slow smile spread across his face, entirely sweet, boyish, but still with enough sharp edges that his cruel beauty struck her once more—as it always did. And, strangely, she didn't see the démon smiling at her right now, but the whole man from her dreams.

"Adalwolf is no more," he said quietly. "He belonged to my father. A few weeks ago, I changed to my middle name, Fentienne . . . Fentienne Beausoleil."

She smiled in reply. "I want *you*, Prince Fentienne Beausoleil." Rhoslyn tucked a strand of wild, dark wavy hair behind his ear.

He quietly moaned and turned his head to press a kiss into her palm and murmured, "I will never tire of hearing my name on your lips." Fentienne then grabbed her hand and kissed her fingers before reaching a claw toward the necklace around her neck, lifting her wedding band from her bodice. "I'm afraid," he whispered, "that there is far too much between us to reach for one another in trust. And I'm terrified that what we feel is glamoured. But what a beautiful lie, if so."

"We are *not* a faerie trick."

"I'm still not convinced."

"This marriage may have been arranged as a curse." Rhoslyn unclasped the necklace behind her neck and slid the ring free onto her hand. "But *you are* my husband, Fentienne Beausoleil. *Not* a curse. Let me be your wife."

He closed his eyes for a second and swallowed thickly. "And let Addien—"

"*Oui*, let Addien try and claim my curse. Love is not a weapon to punish you."

His gaze traveled over the vining thorns of the ring. "You are asking me to willingly trigger your curse. I . . . I can't lose you or Matthieu."

His affection for her brother emboldened Rhoslyn even more. "I already triggered it the moment I declared that you were the man I wanted. None of this is your fault, Fentienne. Choosing you, loving you is *not* a curse."

Fentienne continued to study the ring, a muscle pulsing along his jaw. Blowing out a slow breath, he found her eyes and softly blinked. "I can deny you nothing, Rhoslyn Gautier. My mate." His gaze grew intense and possessive as he breathlessly adding, "My wife." Gently, with the tip of a claw, he picked the ring from her palm and placed the band onto the tip of her finger. "Even if this marriage is a trick, even if you never forgive me, I would burn the entire Kingdom of Ealdspell to the ground to protect you." His gaze caressed her face. "You are mine, Rhoslyn. You have always been *mine*."

The joy bursting inside of her was more radiant than the sun. Rhoslyn pushed the ring the rest of the way up her finger and grinned. But the smile dimmed when seeing the confusion in his eyes. He still didn't believe himself worthy.

"Fentienne . . ." She slid her newly ring-adorned hand up his chest. "I forgive you."

"Not now." He grimaced back another swell of emotion. "I'm not ready to accept one more unbelievable truth. Be angry and hurt with me for a while."

"Forgiveness isn't the absence of grief. I can both love you and be angry with you. I can be hurt and still show you affection." She stood on tiptoes and kissed his cheek. "Let us get through these coming weeks. We have an entire lifetime to rebuild what was stolen from us, *oui?*"

The vulnerability in his tender gaze surrounded her. Saints, she wanted to be wholly consumed by him, and rail against him until her heart fell against his in acceptance. Unable to resist touching him, she cradled his cheek. "You are so beautiful beneath your armor."

"Rhoslyn . . ."

Another blush warmed his cheeks and she bit back the urge to melt before his feet. Making this dark, dangerous man blush while rendering him speechless was going to become her new favorite thing. Also making him smile and laugh. Divine Mother, he better seduce her in their next shared dream too.

Her racing mind came to an abrupt halt. His last name was unexpected.

Fentienne's sharp eyes narrowed intensely onto hers with the shift in her thoughts.

She forgot he could scent her emotions and hear her pulse, a disturbing ability. "I'm curious why, out of all your noble bloodlines, you chose the Sun Kings."

The crease between his brows deepened but his shoulders relaxed. "My great-grandfather, second-born Prince Renon Beausoleil and king consort to Astrid Halivaard, the Empress of Dreglind, started the war between Clifstán and Aurelienne. The High Druid cursed him. I shouldn't exist. The family line was to end with my father." He sneered, "The things my father did for warrior sons are vile."

Rhoslyn couldn't imagine the terror and revulsion Loriette Chalamet endured.

Fentienne nuzzled into her hand and closed his eyes in a long beat, swallowing thickly. "I'm next in line to the golden throne, a Chalamet Wolf King and the first Beausoleil to return to power in four generations. But I am a cursed dead man, my darling. There is no future for me."

This was what he meant by men of power knelt before him. Not just pack and clan alphas, but the aristocracy. Saints, she was married to a cursed prince, a future king! And she was a cursed princess, a future faerie queen. Matthieu would never stop asking questions . . .

Fentienne's last words echoed back in her mind and her magic ignited.

"*Non*, we have a future together. We are curse breakers now, no? One no longer exists in this chateau, *Fentienne*, because we took back control and began healing pieces of our grief. And we will break them all, you and I. Nobody owns us, especially *her*." Rhoslyn fluttered a hand in the air and lifted her chin. "One day, when morning dawns, you will be a whole man before the rising sun, a king who is uncursed and alive. *Oui*, I approve of your name."

"Your fire is an addiction." A hot breath shook from his chest. "Gods, it would destroy me if she killed you."

"I am too stubborn and reckless to die." She tilted her head and lifted a brow, placing a hand on her hip. "And if I died, who would be here to socially oppress you, Wolf King?"

A quiet laugh rumbled from him, but it was full of dark promises—Addien would not survive them. Queen Adeline too.

Rhoslyn raised on tiptoes and kissed her husband's cheek once more. "Come, *mon douce puce*. Prepare yourself, Matthieu will have a thousand questions for us." She grabbed his clawed hand and yanked him back toward the ballroom—and froze.

Matthieu stood outside the ballroom door, leaning on his cane, Drurie sleeping in his arms, and a giant dimpled grin on his face. "Finally!"

Rhoslyn's mouth fell open. "How long have you been standing there, *caneton*? And what do you mean 'finally?'"

"You *still* worry too much, Rosie Mae." Matthieu gave a little shrug, a sly twinkle in his blue eyes. "You finally know he is your husband."

She slowly rotated back toward Fentienne who waited for her wildfire of fury with the barest hint of a smile on his arrogant lips. "Do not start lectures on what amounts to how your brother is more observant than you. You should apply yourself more, my darling."

"More observant?!"

Fentienne arched a haughty brow and sauntered past her with all the blasé ease of a taunting yawn. "Here," he said to Matthieu, taking Drurie from him. Twisting back toward Rhoslyn, he then placed the little sleeping pup into her hands and murmured, "Be useful, *wife*. I will allow you, this once, to be more than just an ornament for my viewing pleasure."

She rolled her eyes. "You think a wolf pup will keep me from destroying you, prince silk breeches?"

"No," he answered, carefully lifting Matthieu onto his shoulders. "He will."

"She called you her sweet flea." Matthieu giggled as Fentienne descended the large marble stairway toward the entry. "Is that because you're a démon?"

And the thousand questions began . . .

Rhoslyn trailed behind them, stroking Drurie's soft fur. "I would never use you as a weapon against that horrible beast," she quietly cooed at the pup, knowing Fentienne could hear her. "You are much cuter than him. Far sweeter too."

At the landing, Fentienne angled to glance at her around Matthieu's leg, a challenging arch to his dark brow and a ghost of a humored smile still on his lips. She smiled mock innocence in return and made a show of kissing Drurie on the head. Divine Mother, he better join her in a dream tonight. Their hearts had unfinished business to discuss.

Beauty exclaimed almost angrily, "Know that I would lay down my life to save his, and that this Beast, who is only one in form, has a heart so humane, that he should not be persecuted for a deformity which he refrains from rendering more hideous by his actions."

She saw the lady who had appeared to her some nights before, and who said to her, "You are taking the true path to happiness. You will be blessed, provided you are not led by deceitful appearances."

"You came, charming Princess, and the first sight of you produced upon me [the prince] a diametrically opposite effect to that which my monstrous appearance must have done upon you. To see you was instantly to love you."

"La Belle et la Bête" by Madame de Villeneuve, published in *The Young American and Marine Tales*, 1743

Chapter 27

Rhoslyn

A familiar scent roused Rhoslyn—fresh paper, printing ink, and leather. The smells of home and family. Fluttering open her eyes, she took in the room around her and bit back a bittersweet grin. Books. Mounds and mounds of books stacked onto tables and in piles around the floor. Surrounding her were wall-to-wall shelves complete with rolling ladders too.

Rhoslyn sat in one of two large wingback chairs beside a gentle fire. A fresh cup of tea and a steaming pot were positioned beside her on a slightly dusty end table. Her smile widened at the light dust. It was nearly impossible to keep rooms of books dust free. Just opening the pages sent the tiniest paper particles into the air.

Across from her, a lattice window left ajar allowed the atmospheric night in. The tinny pitter-patter dance of raindrops echoed throughout this vaulted ceilinged room. How she loved reading on stormy days. Rhoslyn reached for the cup of tea and wandered over to the window, savoring a rich, comforting sip. Midnight blue drapes and the pages of open books fluttered around her in a gust of warm wind, the air static with electricity.

"This is your scent," Fentienne said softly from behind her. "A biting summer storm."

Rhoslyn peered over her shoulder and the very sight of him stole her breath. His dark earthen hair fell around his face in messy waves. The natural, soft gold highlights threading his lightly mussed strands glinted in the candlelight. And those eyes, the way they slowly roamed over her body sent a jolt of pleasure clear to her toes.

A champagne-colored silk waistcoat and frock hugged the broad lines of his frame. Silk breeches in matching tones fitted tightly to his thighs and . . .

Saints, she couldn't breathe. Fentienne possessed a ruthless beauty in anything he wore, but in wedding finery? He was elegant in a way that only heightened his commanding masculinity.

Rhoslyn turned away from the window and demurely stepped toward him, placing her cup of tea onto a stack of books. A terrible decision. But she had a feeling this night would be full of many bad decisions, none of which she would regret.

Like him, she was swathed in silks, though lighter in hue and decorated in ivory embroidery. Swirls of champaign-colored ruffled trim traveled down the center of her low-cut bodice and edged the open panels of her window-paned overskirt. Around the skirt were more ornate ruffled trim designs, tastefully dotted with ivory rosettes of various sizes. The hip lines of her dress were accented by small panniers, and ivory silk heels peeked out from the hem of her heavy skirts. She could feel a velvet choker around her neck, but draping down the bare skin of her chest, past her bodice line, were strands of pearls in various lengths. She could only imagine how intricate her hair must be. Only a few strands curled down her shoulder.

Now standing before him, she couldn't think as well as breathe. Rhoslyn peered up at him through lowered lashes, hoping the blush staining her cheeks appeared more like rouge and not shyness. "A summer storm?"

"I lose my mind whenever the thundering sky on your skin surrounds me." The thready roughness in his voice shivered across her body. Taking her hand, he gently kissed her fingers, then slid his lips down her palm. "You are a dangerous temptation, wife," he whispered against her wrist, "and I desperately crave the thrill of you."

Blessed saints, he was sinful.

"But—" he released her hand at her waist and stepped behind a table. "—if I give into these desires, it will compromise my judgment and—"

"Do not run away," she ordered. "You know I will chase after you."

Fentienne trailed a lazy finger over a stack of books, the furrow between his brows deepening. Slowly, he created more distance between them, each step with the graceful precision of a predator. And all she could think about was the soft, reverent feel of that same finger tracing the swell of her breast.

"The wolf mate bond is aggressively territorial and possessive. A form of moon-addled madness. It would consume me." His gaze flicked to hers. "*You* would consume me and skies, I would never wish to leave your bed."

An image of his defined muscles beneath her fingertips as she bathed his body faded into memory. The way those same muscles flexed when she found him naked in the garden too.

He cleared his throat and studied a book. "Not having you is literally driving me to madness. That primal urge to mark you as mine is overwhelming. Especially as head alpha." Fentienne blew out a ragged breath and closed his eyes for a long blink. "I tell you this because I will be forever undeserving of you. And also because I become more and more moon-addled every day I resist you, not because, as my wife, I believe you owe me any part of yourself. You don't. You never will."

Tenderness swept through her at his declaration. He didn't want to be like his father who forced himself on his mother out of perverted entitlement.

But she did understand the primal madness of mate claiming. Fae marked their mates too. Already she felt similar stirrings, though not anywhere near to the same degree as him. He was led by a more violent form of magic than elves. The marriage contract bound them before her kind. He had claimed her as his mate before the clans. But that wasn't the same as marking. That was a different magical binding.

Ownership of another left a bitter taste in her mouth, though.

Nobody owned her. Not even him.

Still, despite her heavy feelings on the subject, she stepped toward him and he casually prowled behind another table. "Then do not leave my bed, prince. Do not resist me," she said, surprised by her own boldness. "Let us find comfort in one another and heal the divides between us."

"Rhoslyn . . ." he hissed in warning. Fentienne's chest heaved and he groaned, both with desire and in frustration. "Just the thought of you makes parts of me rabid. And I *need* to remain focused on wolf politics until we discover the traitor selling us out to the Monks of Glanis. You, Queen of The Row, *need* to focus on the strike as well as claiming your birthright. We *need* to watch our backs too. Addien is coming for us both and she is a rune shifter."

The haze in her mind instantly cleared and she abruptly halted her chase. "A démon is turning in their brethren to the monks?"

"Or démons, yes."

"How many executions these past three weeks?"

Fentienne tapped his fingers atop a book in an angry rhythm, his gaze fixed on the rain falling outside the open window. "Twenty-three as of the day before yesterday, if my count is correct. The streets were bleeding when I left Factory Row." His Adam's apple bobbed as his fingers stopped tapping to curl around a book until his knuckles whitened.

Rhoslyn's body deflated in horrified shock. In all her eighteen years, never had there been so many beheadings in one year let alone three weeks. "Are they also put on . . . public display?"

"A few are rotting in gibbet cages."

"Are any your friends?" she asked softly.

Fentienne met her eyes. "I don't keep friends, my darling. Makes messy politics even messier. I prefer to think of everyone as my enemy. Most are anyway."

Rhoslyn tilted her head. "No wonder you are lonely."

Her husband returned his attention back onto the stacks of books, a muscle ticking along his jaw. "Le Duc Lucien Chalamet supports this wolf cleansing," he continued, ignoring her and resuming his prowl around this library of sorts, "and he's using the Beast of Gabaston as a motivator. And before you ask, no, we don't know who the Beast is, though I now have a strong lead."

Rhoslyn's eyes widened. "The Beast attacked you."

"A male elf from Factory Row in Dúnælven leathers," Fentienne answered, poison dripping from each word, "glamoured to appear like a black wolf with gold eyes and to behave like a rabid." His gaze cut back to her. "For all I know, the Beast attacks have been a different glamoured elf every time, all made to look like me."

"Please don't blame the elves of Gabaston, milord," she said, unable to hide the catch in her voice. "I do not believe they are volunteering for this cruel trick nor condone the murder of innocent females and children."

"Many people find cruelty against others entertaining, especially against females and children. Growing up on Factory Row, this shouldn't surprise you." He was right and Rhoslyn bit back the growing dread in the pit of her stomach. Fentienne peered out the open window once more and murmured, "You claim to have magic. What of other elves in The Row?"

"I am Dúnælven and a Kadelaryn," she gently reminded him. "Until recently, I didn't know why I had a light form of magic and not others, not even my family."

He raked his fingers through his hair on a loud, irritated sigh. "I just don't know what to think," he said more to himself than to her.

She took a tentative step toward him. "Does le duc know you live?"

His arm dropped back to his side and those newly tousled strands fell to his chin and caressed the tantalizing curves of his jaw. "A few weeks back, my mother informed me that, behind closed doors, I was named my aunt's successor and the official Crown Prince of Aurelienne. Which could have happened months ago. Mother's visits are sporadic." Fentienne let out a mirthless laugh. "Le duc undoubtedly knows I'm alive since he was next in line after Florian abdicated."

"Revenge, then."

Fentienne dipped his head in a curt nod.

"And Addien is most assuredly helping him."

The muscles along Fentienne's jaw and down his neck tensed. "We triggered that disgusting creature's ability to claim your death. And like an addled, lonely fool, I placed that ring on your finger . . . Rhoslyn," he said her name on a shaky breath, "if she kills you, I *will* level Ealdspell to dust. Nothing would remain, not even me."

Those golden eyes holding hers turned to dark, molten honey. Delicious, curling heat poured into her pulse and settled low in her belly. She would eventually talk him off his path of destruction, but not right now. This moment, she desired with every beat of her fainting heart to savor his intensity or *she might die.*

Saints, to be loved by such a passionate man . . .

"My enemies *will* use you to break me," he said softly. "Anything we share will only make it that much easier for them."

"Perhaps." She lifted her chin slightly. "But you are also afraid of being loved. You have feared me from the very beginning."

He rolled his eyes and resumed trailing his fingers over a table of books. "Love doesn't exist," he derided. "It's a beautiful lie to hide an ugly truth. How can I, therefore, be afraid of what is nothing more than the fiction of poets?" His gaze slid to hers. "Or the romantic notions of girls who are raised from infancy to believe they exist only for marriage?"

Rhoslyn scoffed. "The fiction of poets?" Grabbing a book, she pressed it to her chest and recited, "I lose my mind whenever the thundering sky on your skin surrounds me."

The scantest hint of amusement touched his lips despite the brooding lines between his dark brows. "That isn't love, my darling." Leaning onto the table, as if he owned this entire dreamscape, he added, "That is lust, which *does* exist."

Rhoslyn slammed the book in her hands onto the table and dust poofed into the air. "You *do* love me."

"Hmm."

That minuscule smile transformed into something altogether sensual. A smile made entirely of moonlight. And, for a flicker of candlelight, she forgot she was supposed to be annoyed by his dismissive response.

But she knew him and knew he would try to dominate her as a form of deflection—he was seduction incarnate and enjoyed fevering her pulse to distraction.

"Tell me you don't love me, Fentienne."

"And ruin your girlish fantasies? While in a wedding dress?"

Gritting her teeth, she threw a book at him. "You are such an arrogant arse!"

Fentienne dodged the book and dodged the next one she hurdled his way as well.

The sensual curve of his lips widened into smug satisfaction. "Destroy me, wife," he said in a low, goading purr. "Just try."

"I am trying!"

"It's adorable—"

"—What in the eight realms did you just call my fury?"

He threw his head back and laughed at the scowl burning every muscle on her face.

"Not all girls believe they are born only for marriage! Not even girls married at birth to a complete arse!"

"Noted, but love is still the fiction of poets, no matter—" he ducked again "—how many books you throw at me."

Out of breath, Rhoslyn lowered an especially large tome in her hand to rest on the table before her. "If Addien kills me, you would turn Ealdspell to dust... because you *lust* after me?"

A light flashed in his gold eyes and he growled low, "Because you are *mine*, not *hers*."

"So I am a toy you own, *oui*?" Outrage, unlike any other, boiled in her veins. "If Addien breaks your toy, you will throw a tantrum."

Fentienne clenched his jaw. "You are not a toy."

"Because you love me!"

"Whatever you need to tell yourself!" he shouted back.

Rhoslyn bared her teeth and growled in return, then grabbed another book and threw it at him. Fentienne caught the small, leather bound with a triumphant grin.

"A book of poetry," he said, opening to a random page. "Perfect."

Rhoslyn hurled another book at him and he jumped out of the way and began to read aloud.

"*Your love smudges fingerprints of moon dust on the soot-stained wing'ed moth of my affection.*" He threw her a look of mild disgust. "Moon dust?"

"Read the first two words again, *mon douce puce*."

"Why? So I can reiterate that the poets confuse love for lust?" Fentienne returned to the page and said in a dramatic voice, "*It is ichor tears wept onto yesterday's broken muscle, the candlelit beads of salt dewing the skin of my obsession.*" He peered over the book's rim at her. "Lusting for her to an obsession. Yes, true love, indeed."

Rhoslyn rolled her eyes. "A broken heart sounds like lust to you? *Non*, he pines for a forbidden love he flew into the flames for and the mere thought of her loving him in return heals the wounds from his willing sacrifice."

"*War drums thunder in my chest for your surrender.*" She arched a brow at him and his lips twitched in humor. "*But I am already made hostage to the fatal wounds of desire for you. Every violent beat of my dying heart remains fortressed behind bone, impenetrable save for one word.*" Fentienne blinked softly at her and whispered, "*Yes.*"

The energy between them shifted with just that one, powerful word.

"Yes," he whispered again, then continued roughly, "*my trembling breath may kiss the starry sky of our forbidden midnight pulse.*"

He stepped around the table toward her. "*Yes, the parched deserts of my hands may drink heavily the oases of your wild, unexplored landscape.*"

The embered fire in his voice heated her tightening skin.

"Yes, my name may be the worshiped deity at the altar of our passions—" his eyes locked onto hers "—*the name you cry out to for salvation.*"

Saints . . .

"*Yes.*" He slowed before her, his voice breathy. "*Yes*" Fentienne set the book onto a table, then leaned in until he hovered over her lips and whispered, "*Yes.*"

Her head grew listless at his nearness.

"You lust for me," he husked. "I lust for you. That entire damn poem is about a man obsessively lusting after a woman he is forbidden to touch to the point of his carnal release."

A blush furiously warmed her face with what he insinuated. Undeterred, Rhoslyn's thumb caressed the corner of his lips as she pressed her forehead to his, and his entire body tensed up. But he didn't pull away.

"I lust for you *and* love you," she said softly. "I can feel both simultaneously and so can you and so can that poet. The consummation of love isn't the same as paying for a pavement nymph in a back alley or an indulgence of forbidden passion. Nor is it mate claiming or attraction alone. It is the *desire* to be one heart, one pulse. To make one the lives of two. To feel whole in another."

"Why in the dark skies would you want to feel whole in one whose family brought the violent death of yours?" His angry breath trembled across her skin. "This has Addien's designs all over it."

The tips of her fingers traced the sensual lines of his jaw.

"You brought me the ashes of my home and family because the thought of breaking my heart broke yours." Rhoslyn's hand trailed down his neck to his chest. A gentle roll of thunder rumbled outside. "Whoever told you that you weren't lovable is the real beast. You are a beautiful man, Fentienne Beausoleil. How could I not fall in love with you?"

"Rhoslyn . . ." Her name was said like a strangled, desperate plea.

"This is *not* a faerie trick," she whispered, her pulse in rhythm with the pouring rain. "You have always been a protector and a provider. And I am humbled you would deem me worthy of your closely guarded affection after all you have suffered because of me." She pressed her hand to his heart as lightning flashed across the sky. "You *love* me."

A gust of summer wind blew through the open window and rustled the pages of open books. Candles flickered, limning his face in dancing shadows as the drapes snapped and fluttered behind them.

"You *love* me," she whispered again, this time more emphatically.

Electricity charged the space between their bodies as he continued to fight her wild storm, and she no longer had patience for his push-pull behavior.

"Fentienne," she growled, "if you don't kiss me right now—"

"Gods," he swore right before his mouth collided with hers.

And Holy Mother Divine . . . the all-consuming feel of him.

His lips were the softest caress, but his kiss was dark, bruising—a storming night sky of sensation. A lightning strike of pent-up anger and grief. Every possessive stroke of lips and tongue confessed what he refused to say aloud while railing against the lies still whispering to the broken pieces of his heart.

He did love her. He loved her so much he was still trying to protect her from himself. But she craved his black, moonless nights, the sharp teeth and claws of his wildness and defiance.

Rhoslyn tangled her fingers into his hair, holding him tight to her, and this princely, dangerous alpha practically went limp in her arms with a quiet moan. A sound that invited the furious wind and marching rain to dance in her pulse.

That aggravating man would not run away from her in the name of faerie tricks. The former Prince of Clifstán and future King of Aurelienne would know that she *chose* him, not an arranged marriage, not blood bonds made by their parents, not a curse designed to punish a warrior who made a queen his bride instead of the queen's cousin.

Leaving his lips, she kissed along his jaw, down his throat, and his head fell back, granting her more access. But he was too clothed and so was she— her breath fluttered in excitement. All her life, she thought she would be mortified to undress a male, or undress in front of one. To know every curve of her husband's body was far too much a temptation to care about modesty, though.

Slowly, she unwound strands of his hair to untie the cravat around his neck. Fentienne's chest heaved, then his mouth crashed onto hers once more in a searing kiss. Tossing the cravat to the floor, she slipped the frock coat down his shoulders. He shrugged off the silk jacket, never breaking their kiss, while she unbuttoned his waistcoat to toss to the floor next.

Fentienne pulled away only enough to take a small step back. They didn't speak, far too worked up. But desire inked poetry across his swollen lips and flushed cheeks. Words of love and lust. Biting his lower lip in a flirty smile, those predatory eyes of gold locked onto hers, he reached behind his back and slowly pulled his shirt over his head. Muscles flexed down his torso and rolled across his chest and arms with the movements.

And she was dying.

Saints, he was the most beautiful man to have ever existed.

"The hell with wars and faerie curses," he murmured, tossing his shirt to the floor. Wavy hair, disheveled from her fingers, swept down his cheekbones. "I'm physically falling apart resisting you."

"Then do not hide from me, husband. I want to know all of you."

"No you don't," he said on a dark, quiet chuckle. "To know all of me would require your obedience."

Rhoslyn arched a brow. "Maybe in the bedroom, I *might* yield to you. Out of the bedroom, you surrender to me."

"Mmm, to taste your submission."

"Whatever delusions please you, milord." Rhoslyn smirked; she couldn't help herself.

The unchaste tilt of his lips spilled sun drenched heat into her wildly beating heart. At this moment, with the hungry way he stared at her, she thought she might truly submit to him, simply to sample the pleasures he promised if she did so. Fentienne stepped toward her and Rhoslyn backed up to lean against a table. The motion toppled a stack of books and her teacup from earlier shattered on the wooden floor. A sound that mirrored her shattering self-control—and his.

Right as the last clatter of porcelain silenced, the library around her spun into an entirely new landscape.

A slumbering forest embraced them. Fireflies danced through soft, silver beams of moonlight slivering through the trees. Fentienne peered over her shoulder, brows wrinkled, and she turned. Small lanterns hung in low branches beside a faerie bridal bower made of moss, ferns, and flowers. Gauzy sheer fabric dipped across the bower from one tree to another, the excess swirling onto the forest floor like pools of rippling water. The mossy bed was covered in furs and jewel-toned pillows.

Warning jolted in Rhoslyn's chest. "Did Addi—"

"No," Fentienne said, interrupting. "I asked the dream for a bed, but this . . ." His voice trailed off as his gaze settled on her in a long, languid blink. "Skies, you're so beautiful."

Cool night air brushed along the bare skin of her arms and chilled around her legs. Rhoslyn's eyes grew wide. A thin, ivory cotton petticoat fluttered against her stockinged legs. And around her torso was the most ornately embroidered, front-lacing corset she had ever seen. Two-inch shoulder straps fastened together in ivory silk bows just above her pushed-up breasts. The pearls she wore with the wedding gown still draped her chest in various lengths. But her hair now tumbled down her back in silken waves.

Taking her hand, he kissed her fingers and murmured, "Tell me stop at any point and I will."

Rhoslyn loved him even more for this. "Make me yours, Fentienne Beausoleil, body and soul."

"How I crave you." The heat of her husband's body surrounded her. A wicked light glinted in his eyes, a sinful slant to his lips. An angry, scared, broken-hearted boy had kissed her first. But this démon of a man before her now edged for control beyond their previous seductive games for dominance. This was the alpha who wanted to mark his mate.

"Do not move," he softly commanded, then prowled around her body with preternatural grace. The calloused pads of his fingers caressed over the front of her corset, the barest touch of him brushing over the pearls of her necklaces and along exposed tops of her breasts. Rhoslyn's chest rose and fell in a furious rhythm, wanting more of his skin to map more of hers, but she remained in place. "Good girl."

Rhoslyn snapped her eyes to his and glared. And he grinned, knowing exactly how that taunting smile after his belittling praise would piss her off further, as if she were his pet. Good girl, her arse. If he tried that again, she would scratch behind his ear and tell him, "Good boy." Stoking more of her fire to tame was his game, she knew. For now, though, she would let prince silk breeches think he was in control.

Catching her eyes for the briefest flutter of her sighing pulse, Fentienne moved her long hair aside, then kissed up the back of her shoulder, up her neck in breathless moans, then licked the tip of her ear.

Oh...

"I want you completely unraveled," he whispered into the crook of her neck. Goosebumps shivered down her arms. "I want you sated with pleasure." A satisfied smile kissed her skin. "I want you to beg me for more."

Using a hand to turn her face, he captured her lips over her shoulder. Then his hand slid down to softly curl around her throat and the muscles in her legs grew weak. The fingers of his other hand splayed over her hip and pressed the soft curves of her body into the hard lines of his.

This kiss was slow, torturous. The sweetness of honey mead but the headiness of too much wine. She wanted to drink from his cup forever, to be endlessly drunk on him. Fentienne softly tugged on her lower lip with his teeth. Another arrogant smile tilted his lips. Then he was lifting her up into his arms and carrying her into the bower.

"You are *mine*," he growled low against her mouth, reverently resting her atop a fur blanket covered in flower petals.

"My bride."

In achingly slow movements, he crawled up her body in a trail of kisses, and her eyes fluttered shut at the feel of him.

"My wife."

His lips brushed along her jaw, down her throat, his tongue carving his name into her skin, until his teeth rested on the place where her neck met her shoulder.

"My mate."

Then he bit down and she cried out. Not in terror or in pain, but from an explosion of sensation—writhing, delicious heat, a possessive lick of moonlit fire, a melding of souls. The tip of his tongue darted out to soothe the marking, gently pressing his lips to the sensitive skin. He murmured on another soft growl, "Mine."

Rhoslyn's eyes opened on a ragged sigh. Lantern light warmed the contours of Fentienne's arms and shoulders as he straddled her hips. To worship this man's beauty... his body was both divine and fallen from grace all at once. Her hands rested on the curves of his biceps and a drowsy hit of pleasure moved through her at the aroused flush of his lips. Another lush, excited breath and her fingers began roaming, unable to drink in the feel of his bare skin fast enough. The muscles of his chest tightened beneath her admiring touch. The ridges of his stomach tantalized her. The sensual lines of his hips leading beneath the soft linen breeches hanging low on his torso even more so.

Moaning her name, Fentienne wrapped his fingers around a couple strands of pearls dangling across her breasts and pulled her by the necklaces toward him. Her back arched; her chest heaved with a thousand sighs. Dark hair curtained around her face, his breath hot on her flushing skin.

"My darling," he teased against her lips, "the things I want to do to you . . ."

Then his body was in motion. Lowering her back to the crushed flowers, he captured her mouth with his. There was nothing sweet about this kiss. Every hungry caress of his lips spelled danger, each erotic sweep of his tongue a promise to make her suffer in countless forbidden ways. His hand traveled beneath her petticoat and up her leg, higher and higher, until his fingers rested on the silk garter ribbon around her thigh. In a gentle tug, the bow loosened and he grinned a rakish smile into their kiss.

The defiant part of her wanted to push back at his possessiveness. But, saints, she wanted to be ruined by him. Desired to be owned by his heart, his body, by his darkness to the point of unraveling madness. The passion he stirred in her was deliriously celestial.

In a breathy kiss along her jaw, he grabbed her hands and pinned them above her head.

"I give you my crown," he whispered into the kisses he pressed to her throat. His fingers slipped the ribbon beneath her wrists. "I give you my throne." The ribbon tightened and she drew in a trembling breath. "Want me, hate me." The fingers of one hand curled around the knotted silk while the other pushed up, displaying a defined dance of muscle across his shoulders and chest. "Desire me, despise me," he said low, their eyes locked, breaths heavy. "All that I am, all that I have is yours, Rhoslyn Beausoleil."

Her heart fainted.

Holding onto the garter ribbon around her wrists, he devoured her lips, the swell of her breasts, her neck. Kissed her in ways she never knew existed. Deep, scandalous, all-consuming. Kissed her until his name became a whispered prayer on her lips. When she thought she might draw her last breath beneath him, his body . . . Sweet Mother, his beautifully wicked body began moving against hers in slow, sensual confessions of a fragile romance that together they made unbreakable. Gentle but commanding. Dominating but with a heart entirely submissive to hers. Devilish yet with an innocence she could touch.

To be loved by Fentienne Beausoleil was exquisitely beautiful and sinfully divine.

And Rhoslyn was officially ruined.

Chapter 28

Fentienne

The catacomb walls pressed in tight with each panicking breath. Fentienne blinked back the blinding fury crawling just beneath his skin. Only a few steps inside the tunnels and already the faint scent of alpha males made him want to tear through the dugouts and bury them all alive. Gods, he was a lit fuse ready to blow. Didn't help that the heady perfumes and opium smoke of *Le Rêve Rouge* still clung to his clothing.

Fentienne leaned into a wall and slowly inhaled the cold musty scent of clay and bones to redirect his racing mind. But he was still too worked up. The ghosted feel of hands touching his chest, arms, and hips shuddered disgust down his body once more. Nothing compared to last night, the most beautiful, intimate experience of his life.

Since a young man, he thought making love was just a softer way of describing a more carnal act. But skies, Rhoslyn tore his heart open to bleed emotion into every kiss and touch until there was nothing left of him but breath and body.

Every anguishing inch of him screamed to return to the chateau. This separation was absolute torment. Normally males disappeared for two weeks to honeymoon away their territorial aggression until the possessiveness calmed. Mate bonds didn't give a shit about head alpha duties or a city on the brink of war. And now, because he was a besotted, desperate idiot, his wolf had gone mad for new reasons.

The muscles down his body flexed for control.

"Wolf Prince," a familiar voice crooned.

In a shadow sprint, Fentienne pushed off the wall and pivoted on his heel toward Lucas, claws out and canines bared.

"Always female problems with you, *mon ami*." Lucas chuckled.

"What do you want, lesser démon?"

The catacomb tunnels were drenched in thick shadows. Torchlight only graced the hall of thrones. Fentienne, however, could make out every detail of Lucas in the dark. The young man practically floated on preternatural steps toward him, the hem of his cloak slithering through the dirt.

Slowing before Fentienne, he lifted a wax sealed envelope. "For the Queen of The Row."

Shit. Between his injury and confessions, he forgot to mention Lucas's planned visit for this morning. But he would have torn into Lucas the moment he looked at Rhoslyn. Dark skies, this territorial aggression was aggravating. Arching a haughty brow, he attempted to appear aloof despite the rage trembling beneath his skin. He plucked the letter from Lucas's fingertip and slipped it inside his frock coat's pocket. Not sparing the man another look, he pivoted toward the hall of thrones.

"You are injured and—"

Fentienne spun and slammed Lucas against a wall. "I don't answer to you, *sans-culotte*."

A suggestive smile quirked the sides of Lucas's mouth. "—and you reek of mate claiming."

His wolf growled low in warning, hackles raised, and Fentienne bared his teeth, trying to breathe slowly to calm the rage. Just one truthful observation from Lucas and already he was spinning for a fight. She was in his blood. The magic from marking her soul to his saturated every possessive part of his being.

"You *need* a beta," Lucas said carefully, lowering his eyes in submission. "Your wolf is too dangerous rogue."

Fentienne dragged his clawed hand through the wall beside Lucas's head instead of ripping out the man's throat, his other hand curling into a fist. Chunks of dirt and ground up bone crumbled to the path. "Your obvious, desperate attempt for power is pathetic."

"We are not meant to be lone wolves, milord," Luca continued, eyes downcast. "A pack, even a small one, will naturally siphon off some of that territorial aggression to strengthen pack bonds. That is the burden of an alpha." He paused a beat. "You bear that burden alone by refusing to blood bind yourself to the clan leaders or any guardian officer."

"Men in my position only have enemies," he snarled. "Men not in my position want to be me." Fentienne bared his canines again and seethed, "I am the oldest heir from two of *the most* powerful families in the Kingdom of Ealdspell—"

A sudden thought shot through the war in his head and the storm in his body stilled for a fleeting second. How the hell did he not manifest until cursed and exiled?

Adalwolf . . . Father knew he was a wolf from birth by name alone.

Fentienne . . . Mother knew he was destined to become head alpha from his first breaths too.

Split crown.

The prince of two realms. The future king of two realms.

Man and monster.

There's no way he was latent if his parents knew from birth, as well as the realm of Avenbury. But this territorial aggression, the wildness running in his spirit, even from a small child he protected what was his. And his father knew and twisted that natural instinct to protect him instead of any other.

Betrayal pounded in his ears, a bleating pain that ached down to his toes.

Lucas cocked his head, predatory eyes studying him from a submissive position. "What will you do when you see the elder démon who once housed Matthieu."

A bomb of fury exploded in his already raging pulse. Fentienne pushed off the wall and stalked away five steps before he killed Lucas. Muscles strained against layers of clothing. Fire breathed from his lungs. His eyes flashed, the dominant wolf in him battling for control. Mon Père Michel deserved to suffer for hurting his mate and her brother. Fentienne would set his still beating heart on fire—

"This is why you need a beta." Lucas gestured to Fentienne's barely restrained moon-addled manifestation.

Fentienne charged Lucas. The lesser démon shadow sprinted out of reach. Fentienne anticipated his move and feinted left knowing Lucas would go right. One of the first lessons in Myrefell: in fight or flight, people go right considerably more than left. Bet on those odds.

He and Lucas collided in a thunderclap of claws, snarls, and teeth. Dust clouded the air around them with the force of their bodies hitting the ground. All Fentienne could see was red. He wanted blood. Thirsted for blood. In a growl, he slashed at Lucas, who rolled out of the way. Fentienne grabbed his foot and yanked. Lucas twisted from his hold. Fentienne grinned at him, a sinister smile promising only slow, torturous pain. The man shoved to a sit position with a smirk, then barreled into Fentienne with the speed of démons. Fentienne caught Lucas by the throat and slammed him into the ground beneath him. The brittle bones from a dugout fell over their bodies. But neither moved.

Breathing heavily, Lucas gritted out, "Where is the man who strategizes? The one who puts his mate first? This isn't you, *mon ami*."

"Power stealing from the head alpha," he sneered in Lucas's face, their faces close enough to kiss, "is every man's wet dream in that room."

"*Oui*," Lucas rasped. "And every alpha in that room understands they are dangerous without a pack. *You* are a liability right now, Wolf Prince." The young man pushed against Fentienne's hand on his throat to get closer to his face and harshly whispered, "Think of *her*."

The wind punched from his lungs.

Sweat dripped into Fentienne's eyes and he blinked back the salty sting. The muscles in his arms were shaking. A fever flushed his skin. The man in him knew to let go and walk away. The monster in him wanted blood. Wanted to snap the lesser démon's neck for just breathing in his space.

You are not a monster. You simply choose to behave like one.

Lucas stretched his head to the side, exposing more of his throat, the lesser démon's body relaxing beneath his in submission. Fentienne yanked his arm back and rolled off Lucas to lie on his back beside the man, heaving in angry breath after angry breath. If he lost complete control and went on a territorial rampage, the Brotherhood would put a silver bullet in his chest. Claim he was the Beast of Gabaston and execute him. No roaming the night. No painting the faces of his brothers in his blood.

Worse, his death would leave Rhoslyn and Matthieu completely unprotected. Then he will have failed his promise to both.

The lesser démon was right.

Gods, he shouldn't have bonded with Rhoslyn last night. He had seen what it had done to less powerful men. But she chased him. She always chased him. And he wanted to be chased. The feel of her hungry lips worshiping his body shuddered down him in a rush so hot he had to bite back an audible moan.

And . . . Addien had counted on him to cave to loneliness and the ache to be wanted for the whole man—not his crown, his power. To be wanted, sins and all. Now he appeared in every way believable as the Beast of Gabaston. Skies, he knew better. Knew better and failed to protect his mate and her kin.

"Do not regret your choice." Lucas turned his head to peer at Fentienne. Another urge to slash that lesser démon to shreds for mentioning his mate tightened in his muscles. "I know what you are thinking right now."

"You can scent what I'm thinking," Fentienne snarled.

"That too." Lucas scooted back to lean against a crumbling wall and crossed his arms over his chest. "I was there in the woods the day you saw her for the first time, no? I have seen other mate connections, but nothing soul gripping like yours. You were . . . *enraptured*. Your wolf already loved."

Your wolf is in love with her. This is beyond protection orders or mate claiming.

Claudette's aura reading echoed past the firing squad in his mind. The sharp claws of his furiously pacing wolf treaded over what his heart refused to accept but also knew with every pounding beat—they were a fated fatal attraction.

Fentienne pushed up to a seat and pulled his knees to his chest.

Nothing made sense.

Nothing ever made sense.

"You are true mates," Lucas continued. "A powerful bond. Do not regret her, milord. It will only make you more moon-addled."

"True mates," Fentienne derided on a bitter laugh, "is a faerie tale."

"*Oui*, yours." Lucas rolled his eyes. "You have mated with your fayette before in a previous lifetime. She is your faerie bride once more in this one."

His fayette . . .

A prickling awareness settled in his shoulders and scraped down his spine. Fentienne stilled, unable to move, unable to run as a thousand thoughts hit him all at once. The catacomb walls pressed in tighter. The cravat around his throat was too tight.

You belong to me, Fenti. Addien materialized in his mind. *You have always belonged to me. Not her.*

His fayette . . .

Claudette's voice tumbled back into focus. *How does your wolf spirit know* her so completely when you have just met? Or have you?

Addien was obsessed with my older brother after being rejected by a mortal man she obsessed over more.

"Oh gods," he choked out.

Betrayal blew on the barely lit candle in the windowsill of his soul. Closing his eyes a few seconds, he thought of the small flame dancing on the candle's wick, the flickering snap of resistance. The collision of fire and air, of hot and cold. The fluttering heartbeat of survival.

The sound of war.

Dallin Kadelaryn wasn't her loved scorned.

A dark, slithering laugh rumbled from Fentienne's chest.

He was.

In a previous lifetime. Maybe many lifetimes. Dallin was the setup for her to curse Maeline to punish Fentienne, to force him to hate the one his soul desired more than any other.

That meant . . . Addien Wyndham was not only a rune shifter but also a rune walker.

She waited for his soul to be reborn. Waited for Maeline's. And *knew* when they would be.

And how she was able to curse the House of Golden Light to the grave.

Fentienne closed his eyes and bit back the burning tears. The muscles down his body flexed while his wolf snapped and clawed. And the thorns of Addien's obsession constricted tighter around his heart. How many times had he rejected her for Maeline Wyndham? How many reincarnations of this curse had he taken to the grave only to be reborn to carry once more in an endless cycle of hate?

For who could love a beast?

Whoever told you that you weren't lovable is the real beast.

"Love is a beautiful lie to hide an ugly truth," he said aloud, laying his cheek onto his knees. Bile coated his throat. He wanted to curl up. He wanted to retch.

Lucas's eyes narrowed, but Fentienne ignored him.

Addien—a name that meant "beautiful" in runic—glamoured herself as Maeline to know his love. Knew he would recognize his mate the moment he saw her face. And didn't just glamour herself to experience his love or to trick him into marriage, but to make him hers body and soul. A mate claiming, to remove Maeline's mark for her own.

And he rejected her—*again*.

But why him? Out of all the mortals in Ealdspell, out of all the nobles to gain a throne, why would Addien fight so hard to mark his soul? More and more questions cut across his mind.

Your wolf already loved.

Until Lucas revealed his mother was once head alpha, Fentienne hadn't given much thought to head wolf succession. Like most things in his disgusting life, he was just born into power. Nothing was truly earned. Captaincy was a guarantee eventually. Becoming a Major next. But alpha succession? The King of Aurelienne before his mother wasn't head alpha. His maternal great uncle had been, Fentienne's great-great grandfather before him.

Who were the head alphas really? If Fentienne's soul had been reborn into this position, the head alphas before him must have been too. And there was only one conclusion he could perceive.

The Dark Saint was real and the head alphas were his children.

He would think this was ridiculous, garbage fed to desperate people to control, but Florian was the Soul of Ealdspell. His brother was reborn with the soul of the First Dragon, the Protector of Life. Fentienne always knew he was born for destruction. The dark to Florian's light.

A literal child of the Dark Saint. A Prince of Démons.

Lucas continued to study him, brows wrinkled, eyes sharper than a blade. With hands up at chest level to show he was no threat, he slowly, cautiously scooted toward Fentienne on his knees, as if Fentienne were a rabid beast. Perhaps he was. Pain was ripping through his chest and burned the air in his lungs. The wild rush of a full moon spilled into his fevering blood to the tempo of paws running through the forest.

The simplest thought of Rhoslyn—the intoxicating feel of her skin, the soft breaths of pleasure, the way his soul caught fire when he marked her as his—roared a possessive fury that thundered in the marrow of his bones. In the very fabric of who he was.

She was his. *His.*

His wife.

His mate.

Power pulsed down his limbs, fire blazed in his eyes. Eyes that locked onto the lesser démon nearing where he sat. Fentienne bared his teeth and growled. And, to his surprise, Lucas started to shift, bared his canines and growled back, his eyes flashing in warning.

"Your wolf howls at your aggression for control," the lesser démon rumbled so softly, Fentienne barely heard Lucas over his hot, angry breaths and screaming thoughts. "The alphas in that room," he gestured behind Fentienne with a clawed finger, "were taught from boyhood to control their wolf. You, prince, have no mentor, still a young démon in many ways, and wield a dangerous alpha magic that is under a curse. And you're losing control fast like a feral, lone wolf trapped in a cage." He stilled before Fentienne, eyes downcast. "I do not want to steal your power, *mon ami*. I want you to *live* for her sake." A corner of his mouth tipped up. "And for my sake too."

"A poor street clan alpha wanting power from a prince before war breaks out on The Row?" Fentienne snarled. "And I am to believe it is only from the kindness of your heart?"

"Go ahead—" Lucas waved a hand toward the hall of thrones. "Walk in there unprotected and territorially rabid."

Fentienne bristled, the pounding of paws running in the forest growing louder in his ears. Another flush trembled down his body and his muscles tremored for release. A bleating pain tore at his head.

"She is my queen and I am her Factory Row alpha," Lucas growled low, eyes still lowered in submission. "I am protecting her as you charged me. Do not be stupid."

Fentienne dragged in a terrified, angry breath. Everything in him felt cornered by Lucas's words. A persistent voice in his head shouted that Lucas needed to submit or die. And Fentienne's crawling blood itched to make another bleed. To watch their muscle, intestines, the organ beating in their chest bow before his dominance. But the door to his barbed cage since birth was wide open. A more persistent voice told him to burrow deeper into his prison.

A sad smile tipped Lucas's lips. "*Mon ami*, you are a skittish animal who draws comfort in snapping his teeth."

What are you afraid of, little wolf?

"There is zero reason to bind yourself to me other than political privileges."

"I like you." Lucas lifted a familiar smirk. "Beneath this power and dominance—" eyes focused on the floor, he gestured nonchalantly at the length of Fentienne's body "—is an honest man with a sharp wit and sarcastic sense of humor. There is no pretense with you. What you see is what you get. I can trust a man with open emotions, even the ugly, aggressive ones." Lucas leaned in and lowered his voice, still in a posture of submission. "You play the game without gaming those around you, and I highly respect that in an alpha, an aristocrat, *and* in a friend."

Fentienne grimaced back the escalating panic. "How do I know you do not work for Addien Wyndham?"

"You don't." Lucas's gaze snapped to his. "And nothing I say will convince you either."

"If you are tricking me," Fentienne growled, "I will kill everyone you love in front of you. I will make them suffer so horribly you will die a thousand times with them. I will destroy your entire pack and not even blink an eye at the carnage."

Lucas snorted. "I would expect no less of you, Wolf Prince. And as a clan alpha and fellow officer, I would do no less either."

They stared intensely at each other for several blaring siren beats of Fentienne's heart, long enough for Fentienne to search the truth behind Lucas's words, before Lucas lowered his eyes in submission. His heart was in his throat. Another flush of clammy sweat broke out over his flushing skin.

"Promise me—" Fentienne's voice cracked. Nausea sickened him with every tight breath. "Promise to perform a favor I desire whenever I so choose in the future."

The predatory blue of Lucas's eyes narrowed on him and flashed. It was a strange request among démons, but it was the only way Fentienne could test if he spoke to Lucas not Addien right now. Or if Lucas was being influenced by that fiend.

"I promise."

Fentienne blinked hard, a fight or flight response. The fear slithering beneath his skin writhed for release. "Say it, Lucas," he commanded, repeating Addien's words to him six years ago. "I want to hear your promise to me."

The lesser démon tilted his head, his lips pressed thin. "I promise my head alpha a favor of his choosing at a time he appoints."

Relief flooded Fentienne, though the aggression still nipped mercilessly at his heels. Hand shaking, Fentienne extended it toward Lucas and sliced across his palm with a sharp claw. "Swear your fealty as my beta, Lucas Fontine, alpha of Clan Palehide in Factory Row and guardian officer of the Brotherhood."

Lucas straightened his shoulders, his jaw set in a firm line, but warmth softened his averted eyes. "I promise I will be a brother to you, Wolf Prince. I will protect you not because you are my alpha, but because I am now your wolf kin." Lucas bared his palm and sliced it open with a claw and wove his finger's with Fentienne's. "I swear my fealty to you as your beta, Adalwolf Fentienne Beausoleil Chalamet Halivaard, Prince of Démons, future Wolf King of Aurelienne, once my enemy, now my friend and brother."

"I accept your fealty and brotherhood," Fentienne replied, and started to pull his hand back, but Lucas's grip tightened.

"I am your beta in kinship only," the lesser démon continued, "Not for pack succession."

Fentienne's mouth fell open. What was Lucas doing? This wasn't part of the ceremony.

"I seal my abdication in blood." Lucas's gaze locked onto his, this time as one alpha to another. "I will never replace you or desire to as your beta or fellow alpha. I swear never to siphon more power from you than necessary to balance yours. *Oui*, I am nothing more than a poor man with no political connections for your throne. I have nothing to offer you but my life and my friendship. And I give it freely to protect my Queen of The Row, my prince, and your heirs, future démon princes, my future alphas, and the future kings and queens of Ealdspell."

A spark ignited in Fentienne's chest and bolted down his arm to the hand he clasped with Lucas. Images filled his mind. Ferns bending in the night-darkened woods. The forest floor cool beneath his paws. Running beside him was a white wolf, his fur bright in the moonlight. They leaped over a moss-draped log to run in the shallows of a river. Along the water's edge, he pricked his ears for any danger while surveying the shifting shadows. The white wolf loped up to his side, considered him only for a swish of a tail before he pounced on him playfully into the water, then raced off. He could almost hear the wolf yip a snickering laugh.

Fentienne was pulled from the vision to find Lucas watching him with a humored twist to his lips.

"You needed to cool off, brother."

Fentienne didn't know if he wanted to assert his dominance or laugh.

Their hands still clasped, Lucas asked, "Do you feel more in control of your wolf?"

He did. The mate bond aggression still thundered down his body, but it was more a storm on the horizon now. "You went beyond swearing fealty," Fentienne murmured, a mock bored arch to his brow to hide the swirl of emotion warming his chest.

Lucas squeezed his hand. "*Oui*. Now you know I am not your enemy."

A ghost of a smile touched Fentienne's lips. "My ally, but *not* my friend, *sans-culotte*."

"Far worse, silk breeches. We are blood brothers." Lucas quirked a corner of his mouth with a little shrug. "*Merde*, I am now stuck with you and your female problems."

Fentienne softly snorted and untangled his clawed fingers from his—and froze. Where a slash should cross his palm was now knitted skin smeared in blood.

"That was you, *mon ami*."

He touched the stitches on his shoulder and arm and felt . . . nothing. No pain, not even a slight wince of tenderness. Maybe Rhoslyn was right and he had just lacked the knowledge on how to heal himself. But he didn't remember actively choosing to heal.

Between his confessions yesterday, making love to Rhoslyn, and now his pack bond with Lucas, he must have stepped out of the cage designed by his father to keep Fentienne's dominance in submission.

Skies, he healed himself.

This changed *everything*.

Another prickle of awareness lifted the hair on the back of his head. He angled his ear toward the open tunnel. Did a démon hear their conversation? The hall of thrones was at least a half mile down a maze of corridors, but their rumble was possibly loud enough to attract a hidden audience.

"Earlier," Lucas said, pulling his attention back to his beta, "I lost you to a trauma memory."

Fentienne's lip curled at the reminder of Addien.

They needed to hurry to the hall of thrones. The elders were waiting on him to interrogate possible traitors. But first he needed to share with Lucas what had happened two days ago when leaving his apartment. Grabbing the man by the arm, he tugged Lucas close, pressed his mouth to the lesser démon's ear, and whispered under his breath his encounter with the elf and what he knew of Addien Wyndham, including his revelation moments earlier, while clawing into the wall to further mask his voice.

The muscles down his beta's body flexed in a low growl.

Lucas pulled away and locked eyes with Fentienne, a snarling wolfish grin stealing his face—all teeth and malice. "Saint Cernunnos and his Underworld will fear us when we are done with her."

"And those who allied with her revenge too," Fentienne added, a wolfish smile of his own.

With that, Lucas pushed to his feet and stepped toward the tunnels leading to the hall of thrones. Peering over his shoulder, the threatening grin softened to his trademark smirk. "Come, brother."

Brother . . .

Such a loaded word, but one that filled Fentienne with both pride and humility. Pushing to his feet, he trailed after Lucas, his beta, blood brother, and the only man in all Ealdspell he trusted outside of Florian.

Chapter 29

Rhoslyn

The candle in her hand fluttered and snapped in the light morning breeze. Rhoslyn peered around the rose garden. Since waking, every noise set her on high alert. She didn't see Fentienne this morning before he left for the Brotherhood. But he cautioned her in their shared dream to be wary of everything and to carry a weapon on her wherever she went. And when she entered the kitchens this morning, a dagger and sword belt were left for her beside his military identification tags.

Tags she tucked into her corset to carry close to her heart.

For a spell in their dream, they laid face to face, their legs entangled and noses touching, their fingers unable to stop caressing the other. They playfully fought, shared their fears and heartaches and longings, stealing kisses until those kisses turned into so much more. But their time together ended by discussing war strategies for the days to come.

She bit back a smile. He had called her his warrior queen.

This man made her feel so powerful and beautiful.

Rhoslyn studied the woods beyond the stone wall. Three weeks had passed since she and Matthieu had walked through the creaking wrought iron gates. Four weeks since she learned she was a changeling child and married to a demon. Horror and betrayal had sickened her gut and stabbed her heart.

Now it was her love story.

You are wed by faerie blood to a midnight beauty that is ugly and a sunrise ugliness that could become beautiful.

The Sun Kings were dead. But a new king was rising over the dark night of his family's reign of terror. Nine Saints, Fentienne Beausoleil was breathtaking beneath all his armor. A Chalamet wolf whose wildness should never have been tamed. A broken man who was learning to heal his battle wounds. A child of the Dark Saint who warred to break the tyranny of generational curses plaguing his family. And she would help him break every single one until the golden radiance of a revolutionized, whole man rose with the morning sun.

Cupping her hand around the flame, she set the candle against a rose in the front garden. The petals wilted and singed. Blinking embered eyes trailed across the flower as a strange mix of soft green and gray smoke curled into the air.

Three mornings ago, right after speaking with Gellynor, she clipped a rose to bring inside. But it flickered from her fingers and reappeared onto the bush uncut. After two more attempts, Rhoslyn quickly gathered the roses were no different than any other enchanted object in the chateau. The candle she brought outside snuffed with any finger of wind but sparked back into existence a few heartbeats later. Setting the candle to the rose, though? That worked. The rose didn't reappear.

The surrounding air filled her nose with the garden's soft, heady scent, one that blushed in her mind. She was the girl who stood before a handsome boy. A boy who loved so deeply, he was afraid of his own heart. And she held that very heart close to hers while dreaming.

Saints, she wanted to drift away all day on a river of fluttering butterfly-winged sighs.

The candle in her hand faded into the lantern light painting her husband's hard, defined muscles in warm light and cool shadows. Amber light that caressed the dark, silken hair framing her face as he kissed her heavy, pleasure-laden breaths. She could still feel his fingers possessively trail the length of her body, hear the thready, rough way he whispered words of desire into her neck, her shoulder, her—

"That's two haunted roses, *ma sœur*."

Rhoslyn blinked back the feverish reverie visiting her since waking. The candle had caught another rose on fire. Surely a third rose wouldn't hurt anything. She lifted a smile for her brother who limped toward her with the help of his cane. Between new shoes and a cane, it was incredible how much his balance had improved in just three days. Without all the strain, his breathing had improved too.

Yesterday, she and Fentienne answered endless question after endless question. Well, she mostly answered questions. But Matthieu knew a great deal now—her and Fentienne's true identities, their curses, to hide if Addien shows. Her brother fought that last instruction, wanting to protect her. But Fentienne explained how Addien does not kill with her own hands. She could take him, though, and use him to torture Rhoslyn.

And then he knelt before her brother, eyes lowered, confessed his role in the attacks on Factory Row and apologized for all the pain he and his family had caused him. The head alpha of all the clans, a man who was taught to kill the fae, the future king of Aurelienne submitted to a nine-year-old elven boy. And that sweet, beautiful little faerie boy said one of the most profound things Rhoslyn had ever heard and to one of the most powerful mortals in the Kingdom of Ealdspell. She watched the rose burn while her mind spun back to yesterday.

Matthieu's bottom lip trembled and a tear slipped down his cheek. "A year ago, I was a different boy. I had a large family and friends. I could walk. A year ago, you took that away from me." Fentienne's eyes closed and he drew in a choked breath. "But you were a different man. You didn't have a family or any friends. You didn't have anything to lose, so how could you care about what you took from others, oui?" Her brother placed a hand on Fentienne's shoulder. "Now you have family, mon frère. Now you have something to lose and you're sorry because you care so much it hurts. That's how my heart hurt too."

"My heart hurts so much, I can't breathe."

Her brother threw his arms around Fentienne's neck and whispered, "Our hearts can hurt together, mon frère. That's what family does. It hurts and laughs together."

They held each other for several minutes. Then her husband pulled back and cupped Matthieu's small face with clawed fingers. "I promise to protect you, Matthieu Eric Gautier Beausoleil." He blinked back tears and whispered hoarsely, "Always."

Matthieu's mouth fell open. "You gave me the name of kings . . ."

"You are a prince now." Fentienne's hands dropped to rest on his upright knee. "A Kadelaryn and a Beausoleil. Take both names if you want. But you will always have mine. You and Rhoslyn are mine."

"Does this mean I'm in a wolf pack?" Matthieu's eyes grew wider.

Fentienne's lips twitched. This little boy cared more about being in a wolf pack than being a prince and she had to keep herself from laughing too. "You bear the head alpha's name, right?"

Her brother turned to Rhoslyn with the biggest dimpled smile and she swore the storming oceans stilled and the sun shone brighter.

It was that moment when Rhoslyn knew two things with absolute certainty: her brother possessed a rare unwavering kind of love and strength that made all other magic pale in comparison. And a monster was capable of possessing more humanity than most men.

Matthieu took confident steps toward her. Drurie trailed after him, her tail wagging furiously, her tongue out in happy pants. The rosy roundness of her brother's cheeks threatened tears to spring to her eyes. He looked so much healthier. Healthier and stronger. Happier too. Even his unruly mop of blond hair had taken on an adorable type of fluffiness from regular bathing. Perhaps some curses were blessings in disguise.

"Why is Fenti not here?" Matthieu asked when settling beside her. "He hasn't missed a lesson in over a week."

"Fenti?" She arched an eyebrow.

"*Oui*, Fenti." Matthieu playfully rolled his eyes. "Your husband. Do you forget him so quickly?"

Rhoslyn rolled her eyes back. "I knew who you spoke of, *caneton*."

A cherubic, dimpled smile warmed his face. "'Fenti' is what his maman calls him."

That was sweet, actually.

"*Fenti* had business in Gabaston." She brushed by her brother toward the kitchen gardens and waited for him to catch up. "What else did that irritating man tell you yesterday?"

"That I was a better fencing student than you." At this, Matthieu's grin grew large right before he laughed in delight at the mock outrage on her face. A laugh that wasn't accompanied by wheezy coughs for once. They took another few steps. "Rosie Mae, I do not understand how you mix up second and seventh positions almost every time. Third and sixth too. It is not *that* hard."

Drurie romped ahead of them a few steps to chase a grasshopper and tripped on her paws. This cub and her shared a similar lack of grace, it seemed.

"Alas, I will not have a career fighting pirates."

Matthieu paused to catch his breath. After a few beats, he added, "*Mon frère* said he was too much of a distraction for you."

Ignoring her quickly melting heart whenever Matthieu called Fentienne his brother, Rhoslyn placed her hands on her hips and faced the little boy with the twinkling mischief in his blue eyes. "*Oui*," Rhoslyn huffed, "I want to stab that arrogant smile off his aristocratic face and can think of nothing else."

"He said that too. Well, his arrogance, not his smile." Matthieu turned toward her, his brows creased. "Did you really call him an arse to his face?"

Her mouth fell open. Oh, *Fenti* wanted to play that way, did he? She was going to throw a thousand large books at that man's head. Push him into a pond a hundred times too. Then eat platefuls of beignets in front of him and slap his hand if he even tried to taste sprinkled sugar on the plate.

"That is the last time I'm leaving you two alone while I make dinner."

Matthieu giggled. How she loved that sound.

They were near the door leading to the kitchens and her brother hadn't needed assistance. A slight wheeze was rattling his quick breaths, though. She was about to ask him if he wanted help inside when Drurie crouched low, her rear and tail up in a let's play position, her nose next to the grasshopper.

Matthieu shook his head. "Leave the grasshopper alone, *ma petite louveteau*."

The little cub pounced before the last word left Matthieu's mouth, both the pup and grasshopper in the air. Rhoslyn and Matthieu started laughing. But her brother's laughter quickly turned into a coughing fit. She rubbed his back gently, then wrapped an arm around his shoulder and pulled him in close.

"Do you want me to carry you inside?"

"*Non*," he said with a weak smile. "It is only a few steps." Clicking his tongue, he called after Drurie and slowly limped to the door, coughing into his arm once more.

"Rest by the fire, *caneton*. I will make medicated vapors for you after I gather herbs."

He nodded his head as he disappeared inside the door, Drurie on his heels.

Rhoslyn drew in a tight breath, her eyes fixed on the flickering shadows of the kitchen. Her brother was stronger, but not strong enough for what was coming ahead. And she didn't know what to do. Fentienne now knew she had talked to Gellynor Death Talker and why. Fear had shuttered his gaze. He wasn't upset, though. Being trapped meant Addien had more control over them all. Disabling the shields, however, meant others had opportunity to harm her—for Addien or the queen.

Which was why they needed to hit hard and move fast. Create chaos to pull attention from her bounty, the wolf cleansing, and the Beast of Gabaston. The only way to create that level of upheaval on Factory Row was to shut down industry and go on strike, starting today.

And they had a plan.

She suggested women start another blood march to raid the armory outside of Saints District. He suggested the Brotherhood protect Factory Row as partially shifted démons to make heroes from villains. Soldiers who healed fast with supernatural speed and strength were an asset that shouldn't be wasted.

Saints, the look on that man's face when she mentioned raiding the armory. It was if he was seeing her for the first time. Then he kissed her thoroughly, breathlessly, a kiss with so much heat, every sweep of his lips singed hers. That was when he called her his warrior queen. A foolish, reckless, stubborn, intelligent, compassionate, beautiful den mother of a warrior queen.

Rhoslyn had to push him back for him to focus, making him groan. But after heaving a frustrated sigh, he added that Factory Row should make rudimentary bombs to set off in the armory to decrease the opposition's remaining weapons and artillery supply. And to cut off access to The Row from Saints District by creating barricade walls from pieces of rubbled cottages, placing snipers on rotating shifts down the wall's length.

And then he woke and she was left alone in the bower with only the memory of his hands, lips, and the sensual lines of his body pressed to hers.

The kitchen garden pulled back into focus and she gnawed the inside of her cheek. She would figure out how to protect Matthieu. For now, he needed medicated vapors.

Rhoslyn placed the candle on the path and turned toward the mint—and sucked in a sharp gasp.

An elven female with long, chestnut brown hair and rose-colored eyes watched her with a feline grin. Rhoslyn spun on her heel to run to Matthieu but couldn't move. Her entire body locked up; her lips sealed shut. She screamed against the magic, tried to thrash herself free. The grip on her muscles tightened.

"Hello cousin," Addien practically purred. "Oh relax, I am not here to kill you. A familiar black wolf with golden eyes awaits you in the woods to rip your heart out like you have mine. And my darling," she said to mimic Fentienne, "you will follow me out of those gates in less than a candlemark."

Rhoslyn screamed again and tried to bash her will against the binds.

The elf stepped close and tilted her head. "He never could resist you and you fall for that Underworld's monster every time. But he was first mine, did you know that?" She softly laughed. "He knew only my bed."

Rhoslyn's eyes rounded. Hers? Was Addien suggesting that Rhoslyn and Fentienne had been lovers in past lives?

"Before your first soul was born," she continued, "his dark soul was marked by mine. And he loved me." She sighed wistfully. "A child of the Dark Saint. The Prince of Démons. He is made from the nightmares that terrorize the innocent, every scream stitched together by the night sky. The wicked things we've done together . . . But you"—she bared her teeth in a snarl—"you stole him from me. My own family. You stole him and poisoned his heart against me. You destroy pieces of his darkness until he believes he is the rising sun. A pathetic girl with pathetic magic who binds herself to power she doesn't know." Flashing a canined grin, she shifted into Rhoslyn's likeness and, in her voice, said, "But I know exactly who he is."

Addien grabbed her hand and yanked the wedding band from her finger. Panic thundered in Rhoslyn's chest. The muscles in her body squeezed tighter and she screamed. But no sound left her sealed lips.

"The son of Cernunnos was never destined for goodness, cousin. Not in any life."

Fentienne was the Dark Saint's son?

The elf slipped the dagger from the belt around Rhoslyn's waist. With a wave of her hand, a bedside end table appeared beside Rhoslyn's legs, her wedding band now resting on top. Then, grabbing her hand once more, Addien sliced open her ring finger and dripped blood into the ring's center.

Rhoslyn began furiously sobbing, screaming and screaming even though no one could hear her.

Grinning, Addien placed her fingers to Rhoslyn's temple and whispered words in Rhoslyn's ear. A feeling like the flutter of leaves rushed through her head. A fizzling sensation that spun in her mind. The seal to her mouth loosened. To her growing horror, her throat worked and words she didn't willingly form rasped out before her mouth was sealed again.

"With my blood, I break these binds."

Fire ripped through Rhoslyn's chest, a burning grief that scorched the blood roaring in her body. A knifing pain. A breaking unlike any other that shattered through her heart.

Addien, still in her likeness, picked up the candle and brought it close to Rhoslyn's face. "A cursed rose in a cursed rose garden. And like those flowers, your soul soon will be consumed by the Underworld's refuse fires, never to return—"

"Rhoslyn!" a familiar voice hollered from the gates.

Addien's head snapped toward Dalbréath.

Angry tears rolled down Rhoslyn's cheeks. Dalbréath wouldn't be able to see her from this corner garden.

Strange black lines appeared around Addien's eyes, even though she was still shifted into Rhoslyn's form. Lines that branched down her cheeks as if tiny roots. The elf's canines elongated and sharpened. "Well, I can't walk you out of these gates now. We shall reverse the curse another time, cousin."

"Rhoslyn!" the voice shouted again. "Rhoslyn Mae!"

"Until then," Addien continued in Rhoslyn's voice, "if you whisper a single word of our conversation, I will have your brother killed in front of you. And you will not die right after him. No, I will place his body next to yours in a dungeon where you'll be forced to relive again and again how you killed your little duckling."

The elf grinned, a hideous, monstrous smile with Rhoslyn's face, touched her temple again and whispered, "Sleep."

The world went black.

Chapter 30

Fentienne

"Please, wolf prince. i know nothing."

The lesser démon behind the gibbet cage bars was trying Fentienne's patience. Everyone was trying his patience in these godsdamn catacombs. The territorial aggression continued to move through him in waves. Lucas stood nearby to intervene, if necessary. And he almost had to. When Fentienne saw Mon Père Michel after walking into the hall of thrones, he thought he was going to lose his mind. The heat of a rabid fever had tightened his muscles and growled in his chest. The elder démon quickly moved to the shadows. He knew. That greedy bastard knew why Fentienne had murder in his eyes whenever their gazes crossed.

A whimper sounded from the cage and Fentienne snapped his attention back to the lesser démon who was about to piss his pants. Fentienne stepped closer and the traitor flinched. The middle-aged man's heartbeat grew more erratic. An acrid scent filled the air around him.

"Why did your brethren turn you in?" he murmured, as if bored already.

Eyes downcast, the man stuttered, "I . . . I don't know."

"Oh I think you do." Fentienne cocked his head. "Pack kin turned on their own. Is it because you know something? Or because they hope I torture you?"

The lesser démon lifted his eyes long enough to catch the slow, delighted, shadowed smile on Fentienne's face beneath the hood of his ceremonial cloak. The first act of torture: play with your meal. Make them want to die from terror before feeling any physical pain.

He wouldn't employ any more aggressive tactics, though. He feared what personally drawing blood would do to him in this state, especially with Mon Père Michel nearby. He resolved to be terrifying in other ways. Psychological warfare most times got the job done anyway.

That's what he did with the five other accused traitors before this man too.

Fentienne prowled to the side of the cage, out of the man's immediate line of sight. "Confess and I will ensure you have a quick death."

"Death?"

"Hmm." The tip of Fentienne's claw tapped on an iron bar. "Let you go after interrogation? No, that is a Brotherhood liability not worth the trouble." He leaned close to the bars and lowered his voice. "Your pack doesn't want you back otherwise you wouldn't be here."

The fear was palpable. And, for once, Fentienne didn't feel the normal pleasure in dominating another in this way. His mind was too occupied with Rhoslyn and Matthieu, hoping he didn't make a mistake in leaving them unprotected at the chateau. Gods, he would never forgive himself. And all Ealdspell would suffer for his grief.

Heat buzzed in his head before fevering down his body. His muscles began tremoring again from fighting his wolf's attempt at control. Lucas shifted on his feet in a way that looked normal but also in a way that inched him closer. Fentienne slid him a small head shake before fixing his focus back onto the possible traitor.

"I will only ask you one more time, lesser démon. Why did your pack turn you into me?"

"F-For the bounty."

Fentienne sighed, long and slow. "But why *you*."

"Because..." The man's voice trailed off as he peered at the small crowd around the gibbet cage. "Because I-I'm having an affair with a-a monk's married daughter."

Fentienne's brow arched. Well, that was interesting and the closest lead they'd had all morning. Probably wouldn't help their immediate needs today. But he didn't see the monks going away without a slaughter. And that wouldn't endear démons to the public. Fentienne needed to change public perception if he were to be king in his present state.

"I don't know anything, Wolf Prince!" the man rushed out. "We don't discuss p-politics."

Gesturing to the assembly with a sweep of his hand, Fentienne asked, "How do we know you are not the informant?"

"Why would I-I need to sleep with a m-monk's daughter when I could g-go directly to them?"

Fentienne smirked. "Sleeping with a monk's daughter is surely a more pleasurable way to betray your brethren. Perhaps you do both."

The man took in a shaky breath. "I will swear my innocence in a blood oath."

"Are you still having an affair with this woman?" Fentienne prowled back to the front of the gibbet cage.

"*Oui.*"

"Does she know your dirty little secret?"

"*Non*, milord. She thinks I am a mere mortal."

Fentienne reached a claw into the cage and trailed the tip down the man's chained arm. But not to draw blood. The threat was good enough for weak men like him. "I will let you live on one condition." The démon's eyes widened with hope. "Use her for information. I don't care what you do either. Kill her husband in a tragic work accident and marry her in his place. Get her pregnant with your child. Dominate her every waking hour with you in her bed. Whatever it takes."

The lesser démon blinked rapidly and swallowed. "As my prince commands."

"You will be followed." Fentienne bared his teeth and growled low, "If you cross me or any other wolf, you will wish for the guillotine."

"You are merciful, Wolf Prince." The man lowered his head in a pathetic bow of sorts.

"Alpha!" Fentienne shouted to the assembly while rotating toward the gathering. The caged man's alpha stepped into view. "Accept him back into your pack and don't allow others to treat him like a traitor or I will consider you and yours a traitor to this investigation."

"And the bounty?" the man had the audacity to ask.

Fentienne held the man's stare until he lowered his eyes in submission. When the alpha started squirming under Fentienne's silent disdain, Fentienne gestured with a dismissive hand for the appointed treasurer to award him. To

Armand, a Factory Row guard, he said, "Take this man to the holding room. His alpha will retrieve him after collecting his money."

Armand bowed, then snapped his fingers for his lessers to roll the cage away.

"Any other Brotherhood business, milord?" Maximilien Barras, first alpha of Clan Ironbite, asked.

"Tell Jules to swear in an official session."

Maximilien dipped his head and wandered across the hall to the owner of *Le Rêve Rouge*.

Across the room Alain Chalamet met his eyes and began walking toward him. Another trickle of heat touched Fentienne's pulse while his damn wolf growled and snapped. Fentienne turned his back, not in the mood for his arse-kissing cousin. Just the sight of him made his wolf reactive. Though that was pretty much true for anyone right now. Most alphas in this room weren't worth his moon-addled energy, either. That bastard priest, however . . . Fentienne began hungrily scanning the room. The muscles in his legs bunched. The moment he saw that piece of shit—

A new scent entered the room. One that was bold and infused with simmering dominance. Fentienne casually peered toward the entry, the hood partially blocking his face, and locked eyes with Benoit Faivre. The foppish man's painted lips twisted into a haughty, flirtatious smile. The ceremonial cloak draped over his shoulders was left untied intentionally to show off the light gold silk three piece suit he wore. Gold, as if he were a Chalamet. A decorative sash crossed over his waistcoat, beneath his frock. A sash typically worn by the highest level of noblemen. The man's face was so powdered, his skin practically glowed beneath the torchlight.

Rage trembled down Fentienne's body. That porcelain doll of a man was intentionally baiting him. Benoit moved toward him in slow, sensual steps. The fever coursing through Fentienne's blood beaded on his forehead. He wanted to charge this man. Snap his neck. Break every bone in his body.

You are not a monster. You simply choose to behave like one.

Rhoslyn's words whispered to a still logical place in his overheating mind. Fentienne forced his jaw to relax and his hands to unwind. He needed to continue to employ psychological warfare, to torture by playing with his meal, not sinking his sharp teeth into anything with a beating heart that spoke to him. There were far too many politics to plot out today to lose control. Keeping his eyes trained on the merchant prince, Fentienne lifted an arrogant smile of his own.

"Did I miss the interrogations?" Benoit asked him, knowing full well he had. "My apologies, Wolf Prince. The two women in my company were far too entertaining and I slept in." The man winked. "Seems both our nights were a riot."

A hand gripped Fentienne's forearm before he could react.

"Jules is in the circle, milord," Lucas said in a business-like tone.

The rabid fever pumping down his body cooled a couple notches. The pressure on his arm tightened.

Benoit studied Lucas's hold and smirked wider. "A prince and a pauper. The aristocracy will clutch their pearls. How fun." For two beats, that smile widened even more, then he sauntered past him toward the dais, raking his brown eyes down Lucas with a look of disgust.

Skies, that aristocrat was ridiculous. But so were most of the upper class. Fentienne could live in this saints cursed realm for a thousand years and he would *still* never get used to men wearing makeup or the absurd amount of bows and lace they put on their person.

Eyes across the hall, all lowered in submission, tracked his movements as he approached his assigned throne. Even Benoit paid respect to his head alpha, though Fentienne could feel the anger rolling off him. Off most the guardian officers, actually. Fentienne only had eyes for Mon Père Michel, though. That snake slithered up to his throne, hands clasped at his waist, head high as if nothing were amiss. Contempt burned in every still second he fixed onto the priest, daring that bastard to glimpse his way.

"The floor is yours, Wolf Prince," Jules said with a bow.

Fentienne's awareness snapped back into focus. Had the Brotherhood already gone through the pledge formalities? A prickle of awareness shivered down his spine. His wolf was snarling. Gods, would this morning never end? Forcing the fever quaking in his muscles to submit to him, not his wolf, he strode into the circle, grinding his teeth.

"Two matters of import I wish to discuss today. First," Fentienne said, the barely bridled anger dripping from each word, "I want every officer in attendance to swear their truth and silence in blood."

"Forgive me, Wolf Prince," Jules said. "But we swore our loyalty in blood when initiated as officers."

"There are traitors among us," Fentienne clipped out slowly. "I want every man in this room to witness your blood oaths again. And as their clan leaders, the pack alphas and betas will be bound to your pledges of truth and silence."

Swiveling toward Mon Père Michel, Fentienne removed the ceremonial dagger from the priest's belt and ordered in a low growl, "You go first, elder démon. Spill your blood for me, alpha of Clan Windbite."

The older man flinched, a vein on the side of his head throbbing. It would be so easy to slice his throat or cut out his heart. But *he* was in control. Not his wolf. Fentienne would show a restraint this Dark Saint's bastard didn't deserve.

Dark Saint's bastard.

That curse now had a whole new meaning.

Hesitantly, Mon Père Michel accepted the blade's handle. Then, eyes averted, he stretched out his hand for all to see and cut across his palm. Red bloomed immediately and dripped down his skin to the dirt floor. "I swear only my truth and my silence as a guardian officer in the Brotherhood, upon penalty of death."

A feral grin pulled on Fentienne's lips as he took the dagger back. "Tell us *your truth*, Mon Pére," he derided. "Do you steal tithes from hungry, sick elves under false pretenses?"

The older man's jaw visibly worked back and forth. "Yes."

Fentienne leaned into his face and snarled, "Do you force sick faerie boys who can barely walk and breathe to live on the streets when they have two weeks left on their keep?"

Anger blushed hot across the elder démon's face, his lowered eyes darting around the room. Every man in attendance could scent if he lied. He swallowed thickly. "Yes."

"Do you then charge those same elves you made homeless for watered down soup and stale bread?"

"Yes," he gritted out.

Fentienne stepped back, the dagger clutched at his side. "On your knees!"

A deafening silence blanketed the room. Mon Père Michel lowered to the ground, his face a twist of fury. The hard thump of the man's pulse thundered pleasurably in Fentienne's ears.

"Mmm, a priest bowing before me." He paused in a long dramatic beat. "Pray to me, Mon Père Michel. Beg to be absolved."

Several alphas in attendance quietly laughed.

"Who are you to absolve a priest?" Mon Père Michel challenged. "You may be head alpha and our future Wolf King, but you are not anointed by the saints."

Fentienne crouched before him. "I am the one who determines if you live or die five minutes from now."

"Then kill me, Fentienne Chalamet."

Fentienne put the tip of the dagger beneath the priest's chin. "Not anointed?" A mirthless laugh rumbled from his chest. "Curious . . . does the head alpha run in a family bloodline? Or is it arbitrary?"

The priest's gaze jumped to his. "*Your* bloodline."

"But not always the ruling monarch."

The older man shifted on his knees.

"Why was there a female head alpha before me?"

Voices whispered behind Fentienne, but he kept his eyes locked on the elder démon's.

"A rare event when a male heir hasn't come of age. As soon as he does, head alpha status changes."

Fentienne rolled his eyes. "There are more male heirs in House Chalamet than fleas on Factory Row. Heirs available before I was even born." He pressed the tip of the blade deeper into the man's delicate skin. "Why Loriette Chalamet and not one the many Chalamet fleas?"

Mon Père Michel pressed his lips together.

"*S'il vous plaît*, priest. Enlighten us all." Fentienne turned to face the gathering. "Do you wish to know the answer?"

At first the men were quiet. Then howls punctured the silence and feet stomped. Fentienne flashed Mon Père Michel a devilish grin.

"You already know the answer, don't you, prince?"

"I want to hear it from your tongue."

"Former Queen Loriette Chalamet is a reincarnated soul." The priest swallowed thickly again. "One of the many mortal wives belonging to the Dark Saint before he was cast to the Underworld."

Hushed gasps circulated around the assembly.

Fentienne nodded slowly. He thought a daughter, but wife made more sense. "And what does that make me?"

"The Dark Saint's son."

The whispers circulating the room grew louder.

"I am both a sinner and a saint." Fentienne started softly laughing as he stood from his crouched position. "The Prince of Démons incarnate." When Mon Père Michel didn't reply, Fentienne said, "As a demi-saint, I can anoint men of the cloth, yes?"

A few démons in the assembly chuckled.

"Pray to me, priest." The smug anger hardened the muscles of Fentienne's face. "I've been rather merciful today in my dealings with others." He lifted his shoulder in a faint shrug. "I may still feel benevolent, even to the démon who acted as my regent over the clans."

Mon Père Michel's body stiffened. His jaw worked back and forth, his face growing red. Fentienne tapped his foot with impatience. Gritting his teeth, the older man lifted his hands in supplication and the smug smile on Fentienne's face grew wider.

"Wise Prince of Démons," the man said in a dry, placating tone, "I beg your forgiveness for my transgression against the working poor and orphans of Gabaston."

"Beg me," Fentienne seethed. "We are not having a polite conversation over tea. *Beg* me."

The priest drew in a furious breath, but then lowered his face to the ground and cried out, "Forgive me, Prince of Démons! I *beg* you to have mercy on an old man's soul!"

Fentienne's lip curled in disgust. "You are absolved *after* you pay back every coin you stole from the children starving to death on Factory Row because of *your* greed."

Alphas and betas in the benches erupted in stomping feet for Fentienne's defense of Factory Row. The approval was one step in Fentienne's strategy for the strike. Mon Père Michel slowly rose to his feet and bowed, eyes hard and lips pressed into a thin line.

Fentienne didn't want to waste another godsdamn second on that charlatan in red silken robes. Pivoting on his heel, he stared down the assembly, daring any man to challenge his authority. Wide, shocked eyes lowered in submission once more.

"Felix Veron," he said next, handing the man the ceremonial blade, "spill your blood for me, second alpha of Clan Ironbite."

Round and round he went, asking each guardian officer to spill their blood and swear their truth and silence as the clan leaders for Nightwalkers, Highfang, Windbite, Red Bane, Black Bane, Ironbite, Goldfang, Palehide, and Ashclaw.

Lucas didn't hesitate, no sign of fear or anger. Nor did Maximilien Barras, Ambroise De Rosier, Bastien Chapelle, Victor Durette, Claude Delane, or Jules Aris.

Benoit, however, appeared as if he might retch. The greenish pallor beneath all the powder intensified as the blade's tip sliced over the uncalloused skin of his palm. Blood dripped from the man's ring adorned hand. Lifting his chin, he murmured, "I swear only my truth and my silence as a guardian officer in the Brotherhood, upon penalty of death."

Their eyes locked and, for once, the lesser démon didn't attempt to dominate him with flirtations. The seriousness on the man's face, the unexpected solidarity in his gaze was at such odds with every other interaction they had shared that Fentienne questioned what game Benoit was playing. Slowly, eyes trained onto Benoit's face the entire time, he slid the dagger from the lesser démon's fingers. A muscle feathered along the aristocrat's jaw.

Fentienne lowered his mouth to the man's ear and roughly whispered, "Think of me when in bed with your next entertainment tonight. It's the closest you'll ever get to sitting on the throne." Patting his cheek, he winked and moved on.

He wanted to challenge Benoit before the Brotherhood. Gods did he want to humiliate that limp silk stocking. But not today. Between the interrogations, Mon Père Michel, and confirming his bloodline publicly, Fentienne didn't need to defend his dominance or prove his capability as alpha over the clan leaders. The assembly was fully captivated—

Fire ripped across his chest. A blinding pain that knocked the air from his lungs. His eyes shot to the catacomb corridors. What the hell was that?

His heart pounded violently against his ribs. His first instinct was to shadow sprint to Rhoslyn. But he didn't feel any different. The bonds from marking her still hummed pleasantly in his veins. His wolf was probably attempting possession again.

The men in the room watched him curiously. Lucas's brows creased, his lips dipped into a frown. Fentienne blinked back the remnant sparks of pain and drew the dagger up into the air to recenter his focus. Godsdamn wolf.

Slicing across his palm, the same one he used to bind Lucas to him, he said, "I swear only my truth and my silence as head alpha over the clans and the Brotherhood, upon penalty of death." Fentienne squeezed his hand into a fist and dripped crimson onto the dais. Then he plunged the dagger into the soil saturated with his blood.

"Two things I wish to discuss today," he said, casually walking in a circle to address the assembly behind the thrones, hoping he hid the anxious shake in his voice. "The Beast of Gabaston and the strike."

CHAPTER 31

Rhoslyn

"Rosie Mae," a small voice called to her. "Please wake-up, *ma sœur*." Warmth licked her cheek. Her eyes fluttered open on a pounding headache. Gray and brown fur filled her vision. Whiskers tickled her face, then a tiny pink tongue lapped at her cheek again.

A pair of hands scooped up Drurie and set her away from Rhoslyn's face. Blue eyes and a mop of blond hair leaned over her. "Are you in pain?"

"My head," she rasped out. Matthieu moved and the sun glared into her eyes, making her groan.

"Can you sit up, *ma sœur*?"

"*Oui*," she whispered and slowly pushed herself up to a seated position.

She lifted a hand to the back of her head and felt a tender bump, wincing at the touch. A cloud of confusion drifted through her mind. What had happened to her? Lowering her hands to her lap, she peered around the kitchen garden trying to make sense of why she had fainted.

"Uncle Dalbrie is here," Matthieu said softly, his skin unusually pale with a crease between his dark blond brows. "I can help you walk."

Rhoslyn took in her brother who currently knelt next to her in the herbs. "What happened, *caneton*?"

"Let us go to Uncle Dalbrie." The crease between his brows deepened and a slight frown pulled at his lips. "He is waiting for us. I can hear other voices with him."

Gingerly, she pushed to her feet and stood a moment, relieved when she didn't feel dizzy. Turning toward her brother, she offered her arm. He took it for extra balance as he used his cane.

"How are your lungs?" she quietly asked. "You needed medicated vapors."

Matthieu slid her a sad smile, not quite meeting her eyes. "Do not worry about me, Rosie Mae."

Goosebumps flushed down her arms. Normally her brother playfully chastised her for fretting and fussing over him. A tendril of her magic caressed his heart and she felt his... sorrow—and fear. Strange, dark clouds continued to hover around in her mind. It wasn't like her to forget things.

"Matthieu," she said, pausing on the walkway. "Did you see what happened to me?"

Her brother lowered his eyes and gnawed on his bottom lip. "You are not allowed to speak a word of what happened." Matthieu coughed into his arm. "I will speak for us when we reach Uncle Dalbrie."

"Who forbade me from speaking?"

Matthieu's bottom lip trembled and his eyes began to water. "Please, Rosie. I am trying to be brave for us both."

The pounding in her head traveled to her chest. "Oh, Matthieu..." She pulled her brother to her and rested her head on his. "You are one of the bravest people I know. Come," she whispered into his hair and stepped forward again. "I trust you."

They walked around the corner of the chateau and into the sprawling rose garden. Per usual, the soft, delicate scent blushed in her sighing thoughts. Was Fentienne thinking of her right now too? Her pulse fluttered in excitement at seeing him later this afternoon. She pressed a hand to her corset, where his identification tags rested close to her heart.

"See?" Matthieu said, pointing ahead.

The gate came into view and she sucked in a short breath.

A dozen or so Dúnælven warriors milled about in the meadow. Dalbréath's eyes grew frantic when spotting her, his jaw tense. Leaning against him was the beautiful female from the mirror—Gellynor Death Talker. Blood dripped from her nose and a bluish pallor shadowed around her eyes. Was she ill? At her feet, a spotted owl with large yellow eyes watched Rhoslyn and blinked. This must be Tyllie, not a mirror dimension owl, but Gellynor's familiar.

Rhoslyn's gaze drifted next to the black-haired mortal in an ornate charcoal robe who stood beside Gedlen's sister, his hair partially pulled up in a warrior's knot. Strange symbols ran down the length of his pale face and neck. Eyes, almost as dark as his hair, studied first her brother, his head tilting to the side, then her.

"Rhoslyn!" Dalbréath said. Gently he helped Gellynor to lean onto the man, then pressed his body to the shield, his eyes wild. "Gedlen had a vision not even an hour ago. We rune walked as fast as we could. Where is Adalwolf—" His voice cut off and a new fear dawned in his eyes. "I can say his name in front of you."

"Prince Fentienne Beausoleil left for Gabaston early this morning to meet with the Brotherhood."

Dalbréath's brow arched. "*That's* the name he gave you?"

"*Oof!* I know his full name," she said with a flutter of her hand. "But this is the name he chose for himself."

Fury thundered across his face. "He marked you."

"I am not a child." A blush crept over her face and she gritted her teeth. "And he is my husband."

"Did he force himself—"

"—you think he would still be living if he had?—"

"If he hurt you in any way—"

"Saints!" Rhoslyn shouted. "Be thankful there is a wall between us right now, Dalbréath Kadelaryn, or I would smack your head for all this overprotective nonsense!"

Gellynor snorted a laugh and Dalbréath shot her a glare.

The man with the markings on his face met her roaring gaze. "Thorn Princess," he said with a bow, his lilting accent similar to Dalbréath's. "It is an honor to meet Avenbury's future faerie queen and yet another *fiery* Kadelaryn. I'm Rònan Ó Macbea, the High Druid of Ealdspell."

"Milord." Rhoslyn dipped into a shallow curtsy, unsure of how to show her respect to a druid. Thorn Princess?

The man's sharp gaze returned to her brother, a small furrow between his brows. "Lad, what troubles you?"

It was then she noticed Matthieu's out of character quietness. Normally he would have had a minimum of a hundred questions for Gellynor already, wanting to know why her nose was bleeding for starters, as well as ask what the markings meant on the only mortal in the Dúnælven party before Chateau

Lumière Dorée. Her brother's face was sickly pale, a tremble on his bottom lip.

"Warrior duckling," Dalbréath said softly, kneeling before her brother and pressing a hand to the invisible wall. "What happened, nephew?"

A tear rolled down Matthieu's face. "Rosie?" The small squeak in his voice billowed a flame of anger to roll through her. "Do not speak a word until I am finished. Promise?"

Dread churned in her gut and she pressed a hand to her middle.

"*Oui*, I promise." She kissed her brother's forehead.

He nodded his head and wiped away another tear. "Addien Wyndham appeared." A muscle ticked along their uncle's jaw, but Dalbréath remained still. "I hid behind the door but could see through the keyhole. She . . . she made it so Rosie couldn't move or speak." Matthieu coughed into his arm, a deep, wheezing cough.

A shiver of fear clawed down her spine.

Addien had appeared to her? Controlled her body?

Rhoslyn rubbed her brother's back. His small frame was shaking. But hers started shaking for entirely different reasons. How dare that faerie violate her body!

"She accused my sister of stealing Fentienne from her in a previous life and that . . . that Fentienne was made from the nightmares that terrorize the innocent." Matthieu coughed again, sucking in a tear-stained breath. "Then she shifted to look like Rosie and took Rosie's wedding band off her finger."

All eyes darted to Rhoslyn's bare hand.

A jolt of panic seized her breath. Her ring of thorned rose vines . . . it no longer graced her finger.

Tears bit the back of her eyes. Outraged tears.

Dalbréath's face darkened. The bladed edge of his gaze met hers and images came rushing back.

The dagger at her waist. Being forced to break her marriage binds with Fentienne. The pain ripping through her chest. The threat to kill Matthieu if Rhoslyn spoke a single word of what happened. The black lines running down Addien's cheeks.

Rhoslyn closed her eyes for a heavy beat of her heart. Her precious little brother. The terror he has carried! It would not be forgotten or forgiven.

Matthieu continued and she had to force down the inferno of anger to concentrate.

"And she rune whispered Rhoslyn to break her marriage binds. Then she threatened—" he coughed again, dragging in a choked breath as more tears fell, "—she said if Rhoslyn spoke a word to anyone, she would kill me and force Rhoslyn to sit next to my dead body in a dungeon to relive my death over and over again." He turned big eyes on her. "That's why I didn't want you to say anything. She said only if *you* spoke a word, not anyone else. Until she is gone, do not share a word of what happened, *ma sœur*. Not even to those who know."

Matthieu's wheeze and coughs were growing tighter. She hadn't seen him this emotionally worked up since the first few weeks after the fires. Gently, Rhoslyn sat on the ground and gathered her brother onto her lap and wrapped her arms around him.

"My sweet, beautiful boy," she whispered into his hair, rocking him back and forth while he coughed and sobbed. "You are so courageous. I would not have been so brave. And you followed Fentienne's instructions too. That must have been difficult to do while seeing me so vulnerable."

Her brother nodded his head against her chest. "You never follow directions," he said between hiccuped breaths.

"I wouldn't say *never*."

Matthieu pushed back. "You can't even follow simple directions to hold a sword in fourth position instead of first."

Over her brother's head, Dalbréath's lips pulled into amusement though his eyes raged.

Rhoslyn brushed at the tears on his cheeks. "Then I am thankful I have you to remind me, *mon petit caneton*."

"You *do* need a lot of reminding." He drew in a tight, shuddering breath and his bottom lip trembled again.

She wiped at more of his tears with her thumb. "Fentienne will be so proud of you for seeing through Addien's faerie riddle and protecting your family."

Matthieu smiled, just a hint of dimples showing.

Her brother adored that growly, irritating man from the moment they met. This child and his fascination with ghosts and monsters and anything haunted. Which reminded her...

"Do you know who that lovely female is over there?" She pointed to Gellynor who finger waved at Matthieu. Leaning in, Rhoslyn dramatically whispered, "Gellynor Death Talker."

Her brother's mouth fell open and his eyes grew large. Then, in typical Matthieu fashion, he looked at the man beside her and asked, "What do those symbols on your face mean, milord?"

The man made sure Gellynor was stable then crouched before the invisible wall, a soft smile on his face. "They are the words of existence first uttered in Éireanna before the sun was made and the moon knew the night. The magic of earth, water, and sky."

Matthieu's brows pulled together. "How would you know what words were first uttered if the sun did not yet exist?"

The druid laughed, a warm, pleasant sound. "You ask a fine question, lad. The answer is one that takes scholars centuries to unfold. When you are ready, Matthieu Eric Kadelaryn Beausoleil, I will gladly teach you the language of earth, water, and sky."

"You know my new name..." he whispered in awe.

"Aye," Rònan said. "The water whispers your name to me, little prince."

Matthieu turned large, tear-stained eyes her way, a smile growing on his face. How she adored the bright magic of his happiness and wonder.

Smiling back, she rubbed her nose against his, making him quietly giggle. "Stand with me as I talk to Gellynor, *oui*?"

"I will sit with Drurie."

His voice was far too breathy. She clenched her jaw, gritting back the rising anger long enough to kiss his head before gently moving him from her lap to stand.

Then the furious storm building in her limbs cracked lightning through her heart.

A fire strike of rage that ignited her blood.

Not only had that horrid elf terrorized her brother and violated Rhoslyn's body and free will, but she was also on her way to find Fentienne while shifted into Rhoslyn's likeness—again.

Dalbréath opened his mouth to speak and Rhoslyn lifted a hand for him to remain quiet. She had eyes only for Gellynor Death Talker. "You are unwell," she said simply, though her voice strained to contain her fury.

"I rune walked nearly two dozen Dúnælven to the House of Golden Light." She lifted a shoulder. "Give me an hour and I will have the strength to start working on the shields."

"We do not have an hour," Rhoslyn replied quickly. "Addien is on her way to trick Fentienne into believing she is me. And she has been glamouring elven males into black wolf démons with golden eyes. The Beast of Gabaston."

Rònan's eyes grew intense. "She is a rune shifter, rune walker, and a rune whisperer." The man's voice took on a strange quake, as if erupting mountains moved through each word.

"Malfae," Dalbréath gritted out. Before Matthieu could ask, their uncle explained, "Shadowed fae. Wolves in sheep's clothing. I'll explain more later." Her uncle leaned on his longbow and met her panicking gaze. "Gedlen and two other warriors are hunting down Addien. My mother is scouting the woods behind the chateau and will return shortly." A smile softened his lips. "She wants to meet her grandchildren."

Matthieu gasped. "I have a grand-mére?"

"A warrior grandmother. A mighty Dúnælven huntress."

She didn't think Matthieu's eyes could grow any larger.

"Well," Rhoslyn said, placing a hand on her hip, "we will meet her without a barrier."

Dalbréath stepped to the wall again and dropped his voice. "What are you about to do, little thorn? Do not be rash."

But she didn't wait for him to finish and she didn't owe him an explanation. Her husband, her mate, was in danger. Addien Wyndham would not break his heart while wearing her likeness. Not again.

Fentienne would turn all Ealdspell to ash in his grief if he lost Rhoslyn.

And Rhoslyn . . . she would set the world in an Underworld's blaze of destruction to save him.

Rhoslyn lifted her skirts and dashed past the roses to the front door. She quickly ran upstairs to her and Matthieu's shared chamber. Breath heaved furiously from her tightening chest. She scooped up her grand-mére's cloak and the large one Amélie brought Matthieu, then Matthieu's little sack of belongings. After one last sweep of her gaze over the room, she dashed to the ballroom and strapped a smallsword to the belt around her waist. Addien, it seemed, had taken the dagger Fentienne had left for Rhoslyn this morning. Satisfied she had not forgotten anything, Rhoslyn then quickly skittered down the stairs in the beautiful shoes Fentienne had bought her to the main entry where she grabbed two candelabras, one for each hand, before running out the door and back to the invisible wall.

She slid to a stop before her brother. "Scoot against the wall beside Dalbréath."

"Little thorn," her uncle gritted in warning.

Ignoring him, she placed the candelabras on the ground. The tiny flames snapped and fluttered to wispy smoke in the gentle frolicking wind only to relight a few seconds later.

Gellynor's mouth quirked up. "Are you—"

"*Oui.*"

Tyllie's large eyes blinked. "Hoot!"

"She says you're smarter than your Uncle Dog Breath."

"Gelly," Dalbréath growled. "This isn't funny."

Gellynor rolled her eyes. "No, it's brilliant. Be thankful she didn't figure this out before we arrived when she and Matthieu would be left unprotected."

The slitted glare Dalbréath sent her way narrowed farther. "And if it doesn't work and they burn with the refuse fires? Gods, Gellynor!"

"Bréa," Gedlen's twin said softly, weaving her fingers with his. "You will not lose her too."

The gutted pain that flashed across her uncle's face cracked a piece of Rhoslyn's resolve. But she couldn't focus on his grief right now. Her husband's heart was about to be destroyed by her likeness once more. And after their hearts and souls made love last night, the devastation would be immeasurable.

Rhoslyn placed her and Matthieu's cloaks and his sack into his lap. "Where is your wolf talisman?"

Her brother studied the candelabras. "Can I help?"

"Will you be afraid of a large fire? Will it bring back scary memories?"

Matthieu continued to watch the candles, the wheels turning in his gaze. After a few beats, he said, "*Non.* This is different."

"*Bien,*" she replied quietly. "I will carry you to the roses in the back and return you to Dalbréath, *oui?*"

Matthieu grinned and nodded his head.

"Your talisman, *caneton*?"

Drurie tugged on the sleeve of his large cloak and Matthieu shook his head with a twist of his lips. Pushing the cub out of the way, Matthieu said, "here," and pulled out the carved wolf from his pocket.

"Pray to Saint Cernunnos to protect Fentienne and to favor us."

He gaped at her as if she had gone mad. "You *want* me to pray to the Dark Saint?"

"He is the saint of démons, no?" She gestured to the candelabras. "And these are the Underworld's refuse fires."

Matthieu lowered the wolf. "How will you stop the fires from spreading to the chateau or past the walls to the woods?"

"Excellent question, lad," Rònan said. "I will contain the fire."

She could see that Matthieu wanted to ask how. Instead, he brought the talisman to his lips and kissed the wood. "Saint Cernunnos," his little voice began, "protect our dark démon, my brother, and accept these haunted roses." He handed the wolf to Rhoslyn.

"Saint Cernunnos," she said, pressing her lips to the talisman. "Protect your son, my husband and mate. Accept these roses and free us from Addien's curse."

Taking Matthieu's hand, she pulled him up to his feet, handed him back his talisman, then crouched down for him to climb onto her back. She grabbed a single candelabra and straightened, then strode down the path. Drurie toddled beside her as they walked to the garden closest to the front door, barking when Rhoslyn lowered Matthieu back to the path followed by jumping onto Matthieu's leg and tugging on his breeches.

"It is not playtime, *ma petite louveteau*."

"I will hold her while you light the roses."

Matthieu's shoulders relaxed. He took the candles from her hand so she could scoop up the little cub. Once Drurie was secured, he lowered a flame wreathed in green to a rose bush.

"This is for cursing my sister at birth." Matthieu coughed, his words wheezing. But his lips pressed into a determined line, his eyes crinkled with fury. "This," he said again, lowering the candle to another bush, "is for hurting *mon frère* as my sister when he was younger." The roses caught fire in a sparking breeze, sending glittering ash into the air. "And this—" his teeth bared in one of the most ferocious expressions she had ever witnessed on her brother's sweet face "—this is for threatening my life."

Matthieu lowered the candelabra to the marble path and stood tall, surveying the fire he started on three rose bushes. "You can take me back now."

She brushed the persistent unruly lock of blond hair from her brother's eye. "Well done," she said and lowered to a crouch. A minute later, she deposited her brother against the invisible wall next to Dalbréath.

The Dúnælven warriors had gathered to watch. Rhoslyn didn't meet any eyes, though, not even Dalbréath's. The wings of fear and gusting wind of anger flew her to the back of the garden without pausing to catch her breath. Addien wanted to burn the rose she cursed at birth? Well, Rhoslyn would show that hateful creature that she was not afraid. Or that she didn't own Rhoslyn's life. Both candelabras now clutched in her hands, she quickly set fire to the roses, moving forward toward the gate.

All around her, the delicate scent of falling into cursed love singed the sky. A girl stood before a handsome boy and burned for him. And she did. Saints did she burn for Fentienne Beausoleil.

"I choose you," she whispered to the green-tinged ash swirling in the breeze, hoping, praying he would feel her embered words. "I will always fight for you."

Hot air kissed her face and fluttered her hair.

What if this didn't work? Would she need to burn down the chateau next? Rhoslyn hoped not. She didn't want to destroy the restless souls who deserved happiness in the Otherworld—

A cheer erupted behind her. She swirled on her heel just in time to see Dalbréath grab Matthieu under his arms and pull him into an embrace. A wild laugh twirled from the heaviness in her chest. She did it! Gellynor's initial idea to hopefully weaken the magic little by little while she tried to decode the spell over the chateau. But the curse binding her to the property was in the roses all this time.

Dropping the candles, she ran to her freedom. Bittersweet tears rolled down her cheeks. What had trapped her with the beast of Chateau Lumière Dorée was also the same magic that allowed them to fall in love and heal.

And now Fentienne would know her affection was not a faerie trick.

Dalbréath opened his arm to her when she neared. She pressed her face to his chest while her brother, sitting on his hip, curled into his neck. His woodsy scent surrounded her and she fell into the comfort. "You're safe," he whispered over and over again into her hair, his voice tight with emotion.

She was safe, perhaps, but Fentienne was in danger.

And Factory Row was on the precipice of civil war.

"I need to go," she said to Dalbréath, slowly moving out of his embrace. Her gaze softly landed on her brother, who snuggled deeper into their uncle's neck. "Matthieu—"

"I know," he said quietly. "I'm not ready to fight beside you yet."

Her shoulders slumped. "Not today. Maybe not tomorrow. But very soon, *caneton*."

Matthieu studied her for a few heartbeats, then nodded his head. "I will stay with Gellynor Death Talker and Rònan the Mad Bee." Her brother turned toward the druid. "That is a very strange name, milord."

"Aye, wee prince," the druid said with a humored arch to his brow. "You can watch this mad bee put out the Underworld's fires while Gellynor tells you stories about traveling through different dimensions."

"And ghosts," Matthieu said with an official nod her way.

"Hoot!"

Gellynor rolled her eyes. "Tyllie said to call your stinky wolf away from her newly preened feathers."

Matthieu giggled. "Drurie, let the owl be, *louveteau*."

Dalbréath leaned his head onto Matthieu's but held Gellynor's marigold gaze. "Ask Gelly about the time she jumped down the wrong rabbit hole and the most beautiful, valiant warrior in all of Dúnælven had to come to her rescue."

Gellynor snorted. "You mean a grumpy, arrogant arse of an elf who forgot his sword at camp and found me when I was already on my way home."

"I don't think she means those words, Uncle Dalbrie," Matthieu said quietly.

"Lad, every word she says about me is true." A mischievous corner of his mouth quirked up. "Except, she often gets her words confused."

Matthieu grinned when Dalbréath winked at him. "Time to say your farewells to the Queen of The Row."

Rhoslyn lowered to her knees as Dalbréath set her brother onto the meadow ground. As soon as his feet hit the grass, Matthieu flew into the arms she circled around his small body. For several minutes, they were quiet, content just to be wrapped in each other's arms. This boy was her joy, her entire world. And the thought of leaving him behind tore at her heart.

Nuzzling her face against his, she whispered, "Continue to be brave and courageous, Matthieu Eric."

"You *still* worry too much, *ma sœur*." He squeezed her tighter. "You should tell Fenti that you love him to the Underworld's fires and back, *oui*?"

She pulled away and tapped his nose with the tip of her finger. "Just like I love you to the sky and back."

"And like I love you to the bottom of the ocean and back."

Matthieu's smile turned serious and she memorized the darling freckles across his nose, the way his pointed ears stuck out from his wild, golden blond hair, the storming sea of strength in his blue eyes, and the determined lines around his mouth. One that was always quick to smile.

Gently, her brother kissed her cheek then stepped back, saying, "Time to swim."

Rhoslyn's heart was in her constricting throat. But she stood and straightened her shoulders. She, too, could be brave and courageous.

"Mint, mullein, and horehound for his medicated vapors," she said to the small party gathered in the meadow.

Rònan moved beside her brother and took his hand, dipping his head into a bow. "Aye, we know the healing crafts, Thorn Princess. He is safe with us."

She smiled back her gratitude.

Dalbréath handed Gellynor his longbow and quiver, leaning close to whisper into her ear. She gently shook her head in a scoffing laugh and arched a humorous brow at him. A smug grin tipped up the corners of his mouth. A heartbeat later, he pet Tyllie's head, making her feathers ruffle, then walked away. Noting Rhoslyn's curious stare, Gellynor lifted a small smile, the bluish tint around her eyes growing more shadowed with the effort.

"Little thorn," her uncle called to her.

Rhoslyn met her brother's eyes one last time, grabbed her cloak, then spun on her heel and traipsed after Dalbréath's long strides, her hand on the pommel of her smallsword.

Casting on her a look full of despair, the Beast said, "Can you ask me such a question, inhuman girl? Are you not aware that your departure dooms me to death?"

Beauty was about to speak, when she was prevented by a burst of loud voices and warlike instruments.

"By instantly inspiring me with the art of commanding an army, I [the prince] remained master of the field. The victory was complete. I had the happiness of saving the Queen's life, and of preventing her from being made prisoner of war."

"La Belle et la Bête" by Madame de Villeneuve, published in *The Young American and Marine Tales*, 1743

CHAPTER 32

Fentienne

He never thought the stench of Factory Row would be preferable to *Le Rêve Rouge* but gods, it was as if taking his first breath of life. The late morning sun glared down from a cloudless sky. Fentienne squinted his eyes, lowering the tricorn hat farther down his brow.

Behind him, Lucas was still tangled in the arms of a redheaded elf, his body half in the tolerant house and half in the slums. Her giggles grated on Fentienne's last nerve. No, he already had zero nerves left.

"Fontine," he barked over his shoulder.

Lucas slid him a mock flirtatious glance as the girl kissed down his jaw, his mouth curved in a suggestive grin. Playfully, Fentienne lifted his beta a rude hand gesture and started walking toward the forest. They would draw attention walking together anyway. Nobility and peasants didn't stroll down Factory Row in conversation. But, mostly, Fentienne wouldn't deny a man his pleasures, especially before battle. Skies, that was the only thing on his mind since waking.

The Row bustled before the mid-day hour. Bakers and various hot food vendors sang out their offerings. None of which sounded appealing. He just wanted to get home to Rhoslyn before chaos broke out in Gabaston. It was going to kill her to not physically be a part of the armory raid or the strike. But he needed to see her one last time before he joined his brethren in the street.

The Brotherhood now knew everything.

They knew about Addien Wyndham and the Beast of Gabaston. He described, in detail, his speculation that she had partnered with Lucien Chalamet. Le duc pushed the wolf cleansing, thinning out the packs in all clans except Goldfang—the aristocracy and House Chalamet. But they would be next. Less démons meant Lucien would have less supernatural opposition to defend his throne as a non-démon. The Beast of Gabaston not only fanned the flames of hysteria, it also worked in favor to eliminate Fentienne from succession.

And Addien would punish Fentienne until he broke and agreed to marry her, to reclaim what she believed was hers and extort his position as the Prince of Démons. But also because Fentienne was the most powerful, highly trained military leader in the entire Kingdom of Ealdspell. He would not only control the military in Aurelienne, but also Avenbury as a king consort, and command twelve clans of super soldiers. He could also invade and rebuild the military in Clifstán. Claim the dusted realm of Glenashlen too. With three militaries at her command plus the démons of Aurelienne, and with Dreglind in soldiering infancy, Merenna too distracted with infighting among tradesmen, and Rothlín only protected by Dúnælven, she could feasibly seize control of the entire kingdom. And if she could glamour elves into rabid démons, she could glamour Fentienne to become even more vile than Aelfred Halivaard.

That got the attention of every alpha, beta, and clan leader in attendance. They knew what Fentienne was capable of without being a puppet on a string. Factory Row and the rotting bodies in the Spired Hills were evidence of his and his family's violence.

For that reason, they listened to his proposed strategy.

"If you want a cursed Wolf King on the throne . . ." He prowled toward the dais to meet as many eyes as possible. *"I propose we fight half-shifted."*

The gathering erupted into loud conversation, supporting and protesting the idea.

Fentienne shouted over the voices. "We protect Factory Row to ensure the least amount of casualties, especially among the females and children." *He pointed at the assembly with the point of the ceremonial dagger.* "We strike hard and we strike fast. We only kill guards and the queen's soldiers if absolutely necessary. Disabling them instead is to our advantage for favorable public opinion. Aurelienne has lost enough males to war."

"After the strike is over," *Maximilien replied,* "we will still need to remain in business. And if our factories sustain enough damage, physically or politically, to disrupt operations, how will we be compensated, milord? Where would those employees go? Already one factory has been burned to ash in this war."

A different fury fevered in Fentienne with his question. What kind of ruler left their realm's means of profit so unprotected? Insurances should have been put into place long ago. The one thing the military drilled into him was how depending on your comrades was a life-or-death necessity. They were a unit. Each played a critical part. When one man fell, it left the others vulnerable.

Thrones and a realm's industry should be no different.

"If needed," Fentienne said, lowering the hood to his ceremonial cloak, "I would sell all the gold in Palais d'Aurélie to ensure your businesses and employees do not suffer further from a Beausoleil and Chalamet monarch. From a Halivaard one too. Nor will I place the burden of war debts on people who are not responsible for my family's transgressions. I would find ways to negotiate and personally pay debts owed to Avenbury and Dreglind."

A collective breath was held across the room. Fentienne swept a gaze over the guardian officers and their pack alphas and betas behind them. A man stood from the benches, thumped his chest with a fist, then fell to his knees and lowered his head to the floor. One by one, alphas and betas thumped a fist over their heart and knelt before Fentienne, their heads touching the ground before him in deference. Benoit was the last to fall to his knees, haughty disgust pinching his face—from dirtying his suit or because of bowing to Fentienne, he wasn't sure—but he lowered his head to the ground like the others.

Humility painted Fentienne's every breath. He never wanted to be king. He never wanted a throne. The alpha in him, however, savored the seductive thrill of watching powerful men bow before him. One year ago, these men were at his mercy. One year later, they still were at his mercy, but for entirely different reasons. He was their Prince of Démons, their future king. His wolf howled its dominance. A loud, guttural sound that formed from the marrow of his bones and the shadows of his soul.

And when their wolves howled back, the blood roaring in his veins shivered in delight.

Fentienne angled past a cluster of women around a cart of wilting vegetables. Bile coated his throat at the amount of flies hovering over the produce. Though, his gut still churned after leaving the catacombs. He could stomach his confessions, even his and Maeline's curses at Addien's hand. The Brotherhood shouldn't join his fight without fully knowing what it was they were defending. Fentienne had sworn his truth in blood.

But revealing his mate's identity to the most dangerous men in Aurelienne, one or more of which who were traitors? . . . That gutted him.

"If Addien cannot convince or glamour me to marry her, she may convince le duc to marry her instead. That is, after Queen Adeline marries Maeline Wyndham to le duc in an attempt to dissolve debts to Avenbury. Once the princess no longer serves the queen's purpose, Addien will ensure she dies in a way that appears natural." Fentienne paused a beat. "We all know le duc's reputation with females. It's not a far-fetched idea."

The room was silent once more.

Mon Père Michel folded his hands onto his lap, his eyes lowered, and asked, "The princess has been believed dead for nearly a decade. How do you, then, support your speculations?"

"She lives," he sneered, his lip curled in rage. "In fact, you know her, Mon Pére. You know her foster brother too."

The blood drained from the priest's face so fast, Fentienne could almost imagine a pool of red around the elder démon's feet. "Rhoslyn Gautier is a changeling child . . ." The elder démon's voice was thin, barely above a whisper, his eyes wide in disbelief.

"Rhoslyn Gautier," Fentienne gritted out, "is Princess Maeline Kadelaryn Wyndham of Avenbury, my legal royal wife before the fae and humans. And until yesterday, she didn't know her identity. When she marched on Palais d'Aurélie, she did so as a poor, starving fayette of Factory Row who worked two jobs to feed her sick and disabled brother."

Fentienne deliberately met each pair of eyes in the room, then said, "She is not just Factory Row's chosen queen, she is the future queen of Avenbury and Aurelienne and your head alpha's true mate. You will protect her with your lives."

And now that den of predators knew all his secrets.

Fentienne kept his gaze lowered toward the cobbled street to hide the golden hue of his eyes as much as possible. The highwayman collar rubbed against his nose, but he ignored the irritating feeling.

He had strategized a plan. One the Brotherhood now fully backed. Once Lucas was done with that redhead, his beta would find Amélie Demarr. The girl had been instrumental in helping Lucas find new homes for the grisettes who had lost their jobs to the factory fire. He was certain she could incite another riot and form a protest led by females to march on the armory. And do so soon.

Bastien would distract non-démon guards with menial tasks and direct those not on duty to light mostly destroyed buildings on fire as a decoy, ones that could be easily put out by water assembly lines. Maximilien and Felix would employ their iron workers to begin gathering pieces of the rubbled cottages to build a barrier. The rubbled cottages Fentienne was now passing before the forest trail in East Row. Mon Père Michel was told to welcome any child who needed safety within the temple walls, regardless of if male or female. And to feed them generously. Benoit agreed to remain on Factory Row to provide visual support for the bourgeoisie as needed, to ensure relations between factory owners, workers, and the Faivre empire remain in good health politically following the strike. Alain would keep the aristocracy's eyes off the unusual activity of Factory Row by throwing an impromptu feast this evening in Palais d'Aurélie, to honor le duc. The remaining clan leaders, alphas, and betas were charged with spreading the word that the strike would happen in a matter of hours and to prepare for an attack.

Once Lucas settled affairs with Amélie, he would find former soldiers among the packs to position in the forests along Gabaston's walls. The barrier between Saints District and Factory Row would force the queen's men to march around the wall to The Row from the forest entry . . . and they would be waiting.

The cool shadows of the forest kissed the exposed skin of his face. Invisible hackles bristled down his back. Casually, he brushed open the front of his duster to the side and placed his hand on the double barrel flintlock pistol at his hip. A sword hung on the opposite hip. With his claws in special gloves, being able to react quickly required use of other weapons first. A problem he never really had to deal with until now.

Once deeper down the trail, he would shadow sprint to Chateau Lumière Dorée.

Gods, he ached to see Rhoslyn.

He was losing his godsdamn mind.

The separation was torment. Especially since he didn't see her before he departed this morning. He felt like an idiot leaving his identification tags behind for her, like some lovesick soldier. Why would she want an enemy's tags? At the time, it seemed like a romantic gesture. Now he wanted to bang his head on the nearest tree for being insensitive after all they shared last night.

Pushing out an annoyed breath, he focused on the woods around him.

He didn't know how to be romantic. Or sensitive.

He didn't know how to be in love—or whatever she wanted to label these feelings as—and it was pissing him off.

The muscles of his chest tightened and he swallowed back the unfamiliar awkwardness creeping into his quickening breaths. Just thinking of her right now, in any capacity, made him close to panting. Sent his body into overdrive too, like throttling a motorbike's engine right before sliding the wheels in a sharp turn.

Fentienne quietly swore under his breath and scanned the forest, lifting an ear to the wind. No foreign scents reached him on the soft breeze. No out of place sounds either. Dappled shadows swayed over the trail. His gaze darted around—

A twig snapped up ahead of him. His fingers curled around the pistol's handle as he slowly unsheathed the sword. Animal instincts stilled the muscles in his body. His eyes target locked onto the underbrush before him. No point in hiding. If a démon, they would scent him and know where he hid by the sound of his pulse. They probably already knew he was waiting for them. Fentienne pulled the pistol from its holder and aimed it at the path opening, cocking the hammer into firing position. A warning sound for those with sensitive ears to approach slowly.

The soft, lilting sound of a feminine voice humming a tune sang in his ears. A voice his heart could trace in the dark, and his pulse kickstarted into a wild gallop.

Holstering his pistol, he moved quickly down the trail. There was no thought behind any of his movements, only *need*. A need to be surrounded by her scent, to bury his face in her neck and kiss her soft skin, to drink in every beautiful feature of her face. The moon-addled desperation was driving him to absolute madness. So much so, he didn't pause to think about how the biting summer storm of her presence was missing. Or ask himself why Rhoslyn would be on the trail at all until he nearly ran into her around a tree.

"How did you leave the chateau?" He walked her backward against the tree, placing a hand on the side of her face while his other still gripped the sword. "Are you insane? Gods, Rhoslyn! I told you I would return after the meeting."

The pulse raging down his body pounded in his ears. His muscles flexed to take her right here, right now against the tree, to kiss her until the anger drained from his body. But, really, he wanted to grab her and shadow sprint back to the chateau where he could yell at her without others hearing. Out of all the reckless, stupid things to do . . . Fentienne drew in a slow breath to try and calm the territorial aggression snapping at his heels—and refocused on his wife.

Beneath her burgundy cloak, she wore a servant's dress she must have also found at the chateau. Large green eyes took him in shyly from under her hood. This was the first time they had seen each other since their shared dream. He blinked softly, slowly, suddenly hyperaware of how little distance separated them. Her lips parted in a smile and . . . Skies, a drowsy rush trickled down his limbs and circled dizzy laps in his head. An obsessive heat to claim her as his again. He wanted to kiss her—passionately.

No.

Not right now.

He couldn't lose his mind any more than he already had. Touching her would destroy what little pieces of self-control he possessed.

And she still hadn't answered his question.

He pushed off the tree and backed up a few steps so he could breathe and think clearly—

Chills flushed down his arms and torso.

His wolf became crazed, snarling and snapping and clawing at him.

She was alone. Why was she alone?

Looking around the forest, he asked, "Where's Matthieu?"

"I left him with Dalbréath," she answered, lifting her chin in that stubborn way of hers. "You think I would leave him alone?"

"Gellynor broke through the barrier?"

"How do you think I left the chateau?" She playfully rolled her eyes.

Another rush of moon-addled anger fevered his body. And his wolf . . . skies, his wolf wouldn't stop growling. "If anything happened to you or Matthieu," he choked out, his chest caving as he heaved a furious breath. Softening his voice a little, he added, "My darling, I need to remain levelheaded right now. I have been fighting myself all morning and there is still so much of this day left."

Rhoslyn sighed, fluttering her hand in the air. "*Oof!* Nothing happened to me, Fentienne Beausoleil. I do not need your permission to live my life how I please."

His face hardened once more.

"You are my mate," he gritted between clenched teeth. "I put you first before any other in Ealdspell. Whatever foolish decision you make not only affects me but those I would abandon to protect you." He prowled closer to her. "If you recklessly put your life and the lives of others in danger, I have every right to dominate you."

"I have been trapped for weeks, Fentienne." Frowning, she lifted a basket in her hand, one he just now noticed. "This morning, I made sweet biscuits for my friends. All I could think about was finding them and finding *you*." She softened her voice and added, "I missed you." Of course she made food for her friends. His wife always seemed the happiest in the kitchens. Rhoslyn removed the cloth atop the basket. "Did you eat this morning before you left, husband?"

A muscle pulsed along his jaw. Fentienne hadn't eaten since yesterday evening . . . "I do not wish to take food from people who have little." He sheathed the sword still in his hand. "I will manage."

Rhoslyn pulled a biscuit from her basket and held it out to him. "Do not be ridiculous. They will have all the food they wish when the strike happens, *oui*?" When he didn't take it, she squared her jaw and huffed, "Fentienne, take the biscuit before I shove it in your face."

An amused smile ghosted across his lips. "I have a letter for you." Fentienne pulled the sealed note from his frock coat's pocket and murmured, "Lucas Fontine thought you would like to hear from your friend."

Rhoslyn gasped, tears springing to her eyes.

He traded the biscuit in her fingers for the folded piece of paper in is. His wife placed her basket of food onto the path and lowered the hood to her burgundy cloak. Delicately, she broke the seal with her fingernail. Fentienne pulled down the highway collar to bite into the sweet biscuit and watched as she read the note.

Forgetting that he should be aware of everything around him in the forest.

Forgetting that he was attacked just a few days ago.

Ignoring his wolf's frenzied snarls. Gods, he was ready to strangle his wolf just for five minutes of peace.

With Rhoslyn distracted, all he desired was to get his fill of her unnoticed. His hungry gaze swept lower to the faint freckles across her nose, the blushed sweep of her cheekbones, to the teeth nibbling a corner of her bottom lip as she read. Fentienne could stop breathing this moment and never know. Her beauty always arrested him.

Rhoslyn's eyes fluttered to his as he ate the last bite.

"I must find Amélie right away."

"You are the most wanted person in Gabaston," he whispered furiously. "Half of Factory Row is searching for you."

"I understand why you worry." Arching a brow, Rhoslyn folded the letter and tucked it down the front of her bodice. Shadows dappled across her face, a grim look if not for the thin slices of light brightening her eyes as she approached him. Light that glinted off her wedding band. "I know you want to protect me." Rhoslyn slid her hands up his chest and fire licked his body where her fingers trailed. A heady moan left his mouth. A breathless need he couldn't control. Feeling her touch was turning him upside down, his mind spinning. "I want to protect you too." Those wandering fingers of hers knotted in his hair above the highwayman collar; the muscles down his torso flexed. "We *will* be together after this day, Fentienne."

He swallowed and hoarsely managed, "We know no such thing."

An amused smile tugged on her lips, as if she held a scandalous secret and found his unraveling state humorous. With one last coquettish look, Rhoslyn lifted her cloak's hood back over her head. Slowly, she turned on her heel and picked up her basket, then began down the trail toward Factory Row.

Fentienne wanted to scream. She was so stubborn! And knew exactly how to disable his senses. He would probably agree to pretty much anything right now when she touched him. Or looked at him like he was made for sin. Hell, she didn't even need to touch or look at him. Just the sight of her made him drunk on sensation.

And, like the submissive weakling he was becoming, he trailed after the one dominating his entire being.

Chapter 33

Fentienne

A low hum buzzed over factory Row as they passed the outskirts toward the main market square. Carts and stalls lined both sides of the cobbled street. People pressed in from every direction. Revolution sparked heavy in the air. He could feel the building crackle of fury, even on the edge of town. For weeks, The Row had waited for word on when to strike. In the short time he spent in the woods, the packs had already made quick work of spreading the news. If Rhoslyn were not here, he would be energized by the oncoming fight. The soldier in him craved a battle.

The pulse clawing at Fentienne's chest, however, filled him with an entirely different adrenaline rush.

Something didn't feel right.

After an entire morning of rabid aggression, his wolf was lying down. The jarring calm must be how sailors felt when walking on land following months at sea. But instead of having shaking legs, it was his mind that felt unstable from the sudden quiet.

Fentienne studied the back of Rhoslyn's hood, his eyes narrowing. They angled past carts and canopied stalls, around children playing in the street. To not draw attention to them as an unlikely couple, he walked a few paces behind her. This way he could protect her from the back while seeing threats from the front. Eyes tracked them but without seeing. Bodies shuffled along the street in a form of silent, twitchy alertness. The deeper they wended down the row of vendors and factories, by alleys filled with homeless and pavement nymphs, the thicker the tension grew in the air.

The skin crawling quiet didn't last long, though.

A sudden, rowdy cheer erupted from the center market square. His gaze shot beneath the booth canopies to a quickly swelling crowd by the execution blocks.

"Shit," he hissed under his breath.

Rhoslyn tilted her head his way, a single brow arched.

He leaned in close to her ear. "We're turning around. Don't make a scene."

"*Non!* Amélie is just past this crowd. People will be too busy to notice us."

Fentienne's heart was beating faster than rounds in an automatic rifle. "Don't be an idiot," he said low in her ear. "Bloodthirsty people always want more blood. Matthieu—"

Rhoslyn spun on her heel and pressed her hand to the letter inside her bodice. "She lost all her loved ones in the Spired Hills and in the attacks." Fentienne winced. "I *need* to see her."

A body bumped into Fentienne in their rush toward the execution blocks.

"The longer we stand here," she said, "the more people will notice us, *oui?*"

His eyes darted around the street. Was this an altered plan to start a riot for the armory raid march? People raised their fists in the air and screamed insults and demands for justice. But not the mantra, "*Liberté, Egalité, Fraternité!*"

An odd lightheadedness floated around his head.

Fentienne curled his lip in annoyance. He didn't need his body to betray him right now. Or his wolf. Had the rabid aggression hit a threshold? Perhaps his wolf had exhausted far too much energy and Fentienne was experiencing light magic drain as a result. The wooziness was similar.

Rhoslyn watched him with growing impatience.

With a frustrated groan, he started forward again, gesturing for Rhoslyn to walk.

"We must cleanse the streets of Gabaston from the wicked!" A monk's chilling voice scraped down Fentienne's spine. "We are the City of Golden Light not the Underworld's shadows!"

A prostitute from a tolerant house walked past and Fentienne had to blink to focus on her. The scent of her floral perfume was but a trace in the air too. It should overpower his nose. The sounds around him should be sharper too. What the hell?

Sirens blared warnings in his head. They needed to leave. *Now.*

Two guards they passed eyed them curiously, Rhoslyn more than him.

Grabbing Rhoslyn's arm, he pushed them through the crowd. "Keep your head down."

"Démon!" a monk shouted. "Confess your sins!"

Rhoslyn sucked in a sharp breath.

Fentienne's body twisted toward the guillotine—his stomach lurched. *Oh gods . . .*

Lucas stood on the block, stripped down to only his linen breeches, his feet and hands in chains. Their eyes connected. The deep, bitter betrayal raging in his beta's gaze knocked the air from Fentienne's lungs.

Why didn't he fight back?

His beta could kill every bloodthirsty monk on that stage. Hell, he could break the irons by shadow sprinting from their hold. Lucas Fontine was a clan alpha, one of the most powerful men in the Brotherhood. Especially after siphoning off Fentienne's moon-addled aggression all morning.

None of this made sense.

He had just left Lucas not even an hour ago.

Was this why the redhead clung to him in the door of *Le Rêve Rouge?*

Snippets of conversation in the hall of thrones tumbled around in his frenzied thoughts. Nothing truly stood out. But he couldn't shake Benoit's entrance, the gold suit he wore, as if he were an Aurelienne prince. Or his entitled excuse about sleeping in: "Seems both our nights were a riot—"

Riot.

Royal executions are a riot.

The claws of his hands curled into fists. Fentienne's chest rose and fell furiously as he looked for Benoit in the surging crowd. If that peacock was associated with the wolf cleansing in any way, he will wish for death. Beg for the mercy of taking his last breath. Fentienne would take his time with that disgusting filth and delight in every whimpering cry.

Thinking about how he wanted to torture Benoit didn't solve this problem, though.

What should he do? Could he do anything? Grief knifed through the sob knotting in his chest and he sucked in a painful breath. Gods, Lucas Fontine was the only friend he had outside of Rhoslyn. The only man he trusted in Aurelienne, his blood brother and wolf kin. But Rhoslyn was his priority over all others, not only as his mate but as a promise to Dalbréath and the Realm of Avenbury by extension.

Two monks came forward with buckets of water. A third with a face concealed behind a large hood grabbed Lucas's face. Fentienne's brow furrowed. The hands of this monk were clean, the nails trimmed, not the normal filed points. At the man's touch, his friend's eyes rolled to the back of his head, his body began violently shaking, then he was released and the monk moved back into the shadows.

Was that an . . . exorcism? Was that even possible?

"Holy Springs of Glanis," one of the two monks intoned, "Cleanse the rot from this démon's soul." Together they tipped both buckets of saints blessed water over Lucas's head.

Goosebumps visibly fleshed down his friend's arms and torso from the cold.

Fentienne's grip on Rhoslyn's arm tightened. Another dizzy spell hit him and he blinked back the confusion. His wolf should be rabid right now, to protect his clan alpha and to protect his mate. Not to mention, he was touching Rhoslyn and not consumed by her. Mate bonds didn't give a shit about wars or politics or anything else. Only strengthening the new bonds and cementing the connection. Skies, just looking at her a half-hour ago was enough to send him into ecstasy.

The marking's melodic tempo hummed faintly in his chest, though.

The muzzled snarl of his wolf rumbled softly too.

But he no longer felt drunk with her nearness.

Slowly, he turned to peer at the elf in his hold, his heart breaking. A shattering pain that ripped shrapnel through his body. He didn't know if this was Addien or Rhoslyn.

To protect Rhoslyn meant he didn't fight for Lucas.

And if it was Addien and he let his friend die, or if he saved his friend and let Rhoslyn die . . .

The crowd cheered louder.

Fentienne's gaze snapped back to Lucas. The anguish twisting in his chest deepened. Did he grab Rhoslyn and haul them away from the square?

Did he stay with his friend until the end?

The monks, along with two zealots who acted as their guards, shoved Lucas onto his stomach across the guillotine's bench, forcing his neck onto the shallow cutout on the lower bar. One guard lowered the top bar, locking in his neck and head, while another fastened the manacles around his wrists to a ring just below the headrest.

Horror locked Fentienne's body in place.

He couldn't move. He couldn't run. He wasn't sure if he were still breathing.

The fear burning in Lucas's eyes, the anger, the helpless knowledge that these were his last moments alive slashed red down Fentienne's vision. But all he could see was Florian. His little brother's silver eyes right before the gun went off. The same fear. The same terrified acceptance that these were his last few seconds alive.

And like then, Fentienne did nothing.

Absolutely *nothing*.

"Démon," a monk shouted, grabbing Fentienne's attention. "Do you know the Beast of Gabaston? If so, speak his name and your soul will be carried to the Otherworld for your confession."

Another dizzy spell hit Fentienne and he nearly staggered back a step. Faces around him blurred in and out of focus. What was happening to him? His body hadn't felt this heavy since before Eirwen cursed him. As if he had slipped back into the body of a mere mortal. As if the airy magic giving spring to his muscles for supernatural speed vanished.

"Fentienne Beausoleil is the Beast of the Gabaston!"

The violent pounding behind Fentienne's ribs seized.

His gaze spun back to the stage.

"The Beast"—Spittle flew from Lucas's mouth—"is in the crowd!"

Voices cried out and screamed as bodies twisted and turned in panic.

Lucas locked eyes with him.

"With the blood of démons spilled," the monk shouted, "may the streets of Gabaston be cleansed from the darkness!"

The monk pulled the lever.

The blade fell.

And Fentienne sucked in a horrified growl, his mouth open in shock.

Lucas's head rolled into a basket and the crowd cheered.

A bomb detonated in Fentienne's chest. He heaved in a choked breath. They needed to run. Gods, he wanted to retch. Factory Row tilted and the ground called to him. But he pushed through the shock. He couldn't let them execute Rhoslyn too. It may be Addien before him now, but he couldn't risk the chance. Fentienne grabbed Rhoslyn by the arm and spun her around despite the tight crowd.

She shoved him away, accidentally knocking the large hood from her head, and shouted, "The Beast! It's the Beast!"

The blood drained from his head.

The crowd around them screamed and began to scatter, not realizing Rhoslyn spoke of him. The guards next to where they stood, however, immediately zeroed in on them both. And Rhoslyn no longer had her hood up. *Shit.* He needed to run, grab her arm and drag her with him, but his body was far too disoriented.

Then it hit him.

The biscuits. She must have put wolfsbane in the biscuits. The executed démons, none of which fought back if Lucas were any indicator, must have been drugged with wolfsbane too. Was that how his mother kept his magic locked away until Eirwen?

Anger rippled down his body in violent waves. But to protect the clans and, thus, the strike, he remained passive. But his fingers itched to whip out his pistol and press it to Addien's head. Or Rhoslyn's. But he was pretty sure it was Addien. His wife wasn't manipulative or hateful. Unless it was just another godsdamn faerie trick—the whole time.

Had he slept with Addien? Marked her soul as his?

You belong to me, Fenti. You have always belonged to me. Not her.

Fentienne gagged and swallowed back the bile burning his throat.

A fiendish smile curled the corners of her mouth. "Now you know how it feels to have your still beating heart ripped from your chest."

The world around him slowed.

Each beautiful feature on the likeness of his wife's face twisted in sick delight.

Guards came forward, muskets tipped with bayonets pointed in their direction. Fentienne offered up his wrists, his eyes never wavering from

Addien's.

"In the next life," he whispered in the space between them, "I still would rather die."

"In the next life," she countered, "she will not exist—"

Her words abruptly ended in cries of pain when two guards grabbed her arms and clamped cuffs made of cold iron onto her wrists. "Rhoslyn Gautier, you are wanted for sedition and under arrest by order of the queen."

"Wait!" Fentienne snapped. A new panic hit his bloodstream. He didn't know what Addien would do as Rhoslyn in this situation. Somehow, she managed to hold onto the glamour despite the iron meant to block her magic. But, mostly, he couldn't let Factory Row think their queen was defeated right before a battle. And the way they were fearfully murmuring and staring in her direction, some even with tears in their eyes, they did.

The strike would be over before it began.

"I trade my life for hers," he shouted.

The guards, not démons under Bastien, laughed and yanked Addien toward the stone building behind the execution block, where she would be jailed in the dungeons until execution orders were given.

"Release her," he shouted again. "I will go with you peacefully in her place."

People began protesting, crying out for their Queen of The Row, and blocked the guards' path. Releasing Addien was foolish. But the streets would either descend into mass hysteria at Rhoslyn's arrest in their starving, politically desperate state, like rabid wolves before a kill, or the fury would fuel them to win this strike. And with the real Rhoslyn trapped at the chateau, Addien couldn't have her killed. But that also meant he couldn't bring his real wife before the people to renew their hope. Destructive chaos was the more likely outcome.

Rhoslyn had promised Factory Row that they would eat like a queen.

"My men have sworn their lives to protect her and to protect Factory Row." Fentienne scanned the crowd, meeting a few familiar faces. But he knew there were far more démons present. "They await my word!"

"What men, milord?" a guard asked.

"Factory Row will not forget your act of treason against their chosen queen." More guards appeared around the crowd, their muskets raised.

"We have orders from the rightful queen, Adeline Chalamet," a guard said and the crowd exploded in outrage.

Addien's eyes narrowed at him. Clammy beads of sweat dewed on her forehead from the pain. The skin around her wrists was already blistering. Whatever powers she had left were used to maintain her glamour. To suddenly morph back into her real form before so many witnesses would seal her fate as a rune shifter—a fate no different than a démon in Gabaston. A situation he would use to his advantage. Psychological warfare came in all flavors of propaganda.

Addien Wyndham was a false image of love, a beautiful lie to hide an ugly truth.

And she no longer owned him.

She wouldn't win either.

Fentienne removed his hat and tossed it to the street. "Rhoslyn Gautier is my wife," he said, holding Addien's gaze. Ignoring the gasps, he continued. "She and I were married as children before the fae, though we lived in separate realms." He loosened the first button on his highwayman's collar. "Since the blood march, I have protected her. She is a true queen. My queen."

Slowly, he removed the highwayman collar concealing his face and the rallying cheers turned to screams of horror.

"Beast of Gabaston," a Monk of Glanis yelled, "by the holy waters your soul is forfeit!" Leaving the remains of Lucas's headless body, they moved toward Fentienne.

"I love Rhoslyn Gautier with every breath in my body," Fentienne choked out, still holding Addien's grief-stricken gaze. "I *love* my wife, my mate and would sacrifice my very soul for her. In this lifetime and the thousand more to come." Peering over the crowd, meeting as many terrified eyes as possible, he shouted, "I am not the Beast of Gabaston. If it is the blood of traitors you want, then spill mine. But let her go."

Guards pushed through the crowd toward him, bayonets pointed at his chest. People scrambled out of the way. The heated whispering voices around him grew louder.

A monk dug his long nails into Fentienne's forearm, a sharp-toothed fevered grin on his face. "Child of the Dark Saint," he hissed, "what is the name we will curse back to the Underworld?"

A wicked smile ghosted across his lips in reply. "Former Prince Adalwolf Fentienne Beausoleil Chalamet Halivaard of Clifstán, older brother of his Imperial Highness, Florian Halivaard, and oldest surviving son of our beloved former queen, Loriette Chalamet." The monk released his arm and reared back and the guards exchanged panicked looks. "I am the Prince of Démons," he continued, "head alpha of all the clans, and the Crown Prince of Aurelienne, named by Queen Adeline before witnesses."

He straightened his shoulders and held out his hands to the guards. The monks' faces contorted in rage. Without the queen's command, they couldn't execute him. But he could still be arrested and tried for his war crimes against the Realm of Gold.

"Let her go before the people riot," Fentienne urged. "And they *will* riot."

The guard in charge gave a curt nod and the irons around Addien's wrists were released.

She rubbed at her wrists, angry tears in her eyes. "I will always love your monstrous ways, Fenti."

"Get out of here before other guards arrest you."

With one last look, she pushed through the gathered crowd, too weak to use magic to get away.

Another dizzy spell buzzed in his head. The streets of Gabaston carouseled around him at increasing speeds. He was going to vomit if the warbling faces continued to move in and out of focus. Still, peering over the shoulders of the guards, he shouted, "I gladly give my life for your Queen of The Row."

A jolt of fire fevered his blood and burned his skin. Bones cracked down his body and contorted. Fentienne grimaced back a cry of pain. Moonlight spilled into his pulse to the rhythm of a hundred paws tearing up the forest floor. His wolf growled. The snapping growls of other wolves joined him. The last thing he felt before blacking out was air wildly swirling around his body, his hair whipping across his face. Then he felt nothing.

Chapter 34

Rhoslyn

Factory row exploded into chaos. From the east, a crowd surged the execution blocks. Rhoslyn couldn't make out the particulars other than a démon was condemned to death and the gathering screamed for blood to the point of rioting. To the west, females began shouting "*Liberté, Egalité, Fraternité!*" while banging pots and pans. Guards ran past where Rhoslyn and Dalbréath crouched in an alley, their muskets raised.

And while the world descended into madness around her, she could only think of her husband.

What if Addien already convinced Fentienne she was Rhoslyn?

What if Fentienne was ensnared in a trap he couldn't break free from?

What if he believed any hateful thing that came from the false Rhoslyn's mouth?

What if Addien revealed his half-shifted form to Factory Row?

What if the masses believed he was the Beast of Gabaston?

The endless what if's continued to form in her racing pulse. Attempting to remain levelheaded was growing impossible. Her heart was too busy screaming and raging and weeping.

A shiver touched Rhoslyn's skin and she pulled the cloak tighter around her body.

In the woods outside of West Row by Saints District, she had abandoned the silk dress she had worn at the chateau to better blend in. Now she wore only her chemise, a thin petticoat, and her corset beneath her cloak with her smallsword still strapped to a belt around her waist. She had hoped to secure proper clothing after finding Fentienne. There were worse things than raiding an armory in one's underpinnings, though.

Rhoslyn squinted up at the textile factory's roofline kitty corner from her, watching the smoke poof into the air and evaporate. Some of the smoke didn't dissipate. Was a building on fire? Beside the textile factory were the cold ashes of *le manufacture de robes*—the dress factory. Scraps of metal piled beside the charred, rubbled remains of the brick walls. Rhoslyn's heart sank to her churning gut as memories came rushing back.

Several days had passed since the attacks. Matthieu could barely keep his eyes open from the pain and sickness in his lungs. Rhoslyn had carried him from their secret hideout in Crowns Quarter back to Factory Row. All around her people wept, coughed, cried out in pain. Dead bodies bloated the streets. Pieces of buildings crumbled over the cobblestones, making it difficult to walk in some areas. Splintered vendor carts and booths were strewn in every direction.

But her home. Her family . . .

Rhoslyn stood before the ash of all she had loved. Curls of smoke wisped into the cold morning air. A wail ripped from her soul. A guttural pain that tore her heart into barely beating pieces. Pressing her little brother to her chest, she buried her face into his soft curls.

"I love you to the sky and back, Matthieu Eric," she whispered in-between sobs. "You are now my home."

A few minutes later, they returned to Crowns Quarter to hide awhile longer. And she vowed that the tyranny of a corrupt, power-hungry monarch would face her rage if ever they destroyed parts of her life again.

Rhoslyn gulped in a sharp breath to brace against the onslaught of tears that wanted to fall. How terrified her fellow grisettes must have been. Did they think of the attacks too? Unlike last time, however, it was an attack by their own monarch, and on people who had already lost so much. On females who had little options for survival beyond selling themselves for the quick pleasures of males.

A fresh billowing wave of avenging fire ignited in her blood.

Queen Adeline would be forced from her gilded cruelty to witness the suffering of her people.

She spun on her heel toward the market—all she could do was move forward, otherwise the grief would bury her alive with the ashes of Factory Row. But a body blocked her path. Her furious gaze snapped up. The sorrow on Dalbréath's face was too much to bear right now. She didn't want his pity or his guilt.

"Move," she gritted out.

"Niece." His eyes held a steeled edge he directed over her shoulder a moment before returning focus onto her. "You cannot fight two completely different battles on the same field. Warriors *must* know where they belong in war."

Rhoslyn bit back the forming angry tears.

"I agree with your Uncle Dalbrie."

Rhoslyn squeaked and bumped into Dalbréath. Lucas Fontine leaned on the factory wall opposite of them in the alley. Strands from his unbound shoulder length blond hair lifted in a slight breeze, his shirt untucked and unlaced. She drew in a nervous breath. His mesmerizing blue eyes held hers as he moved with predatory grace toward where she stood.

Dalbréath's hand flew to the pommel of his sword. "No closer, démon."

"I do not answer to you, elf." Lucas raised his hands at chest level and continued to approach. "I am bound to my alpha to protect my queen with my own life."

"If you harm—"

"*Oui*," Lucas interjected with a roll of his eyes. "You and I can prove who is the dominant male later."

Dalbréath chuckled darkly. "There is nothing to prove, mortal. You draw breath still because *I allow it*."

Lucas lifted a shoulder in a dismissive shrug, then blew Dalbréath a kiss before turning back to her.

"How did you find me?" Rhoslyn asked, peering frantically at all the people running and shouting past them.

"A dog on the hunt who followed a scent trail." Lucas slowed before her.

Rhoslyn stilled. "Fentienne didn't know I could leave the chateau."

"I prepare for all eventualities." Lucas tilted his head. "Especially when a rune shifting faerie appears in Factory Row as you. She did not smell like you, though."

Her mouth fell open. "You know—"

"I know everything as does the Brotherhood." Lucas lowered his voice. "It is not safe for you by the execution blocks, madame."

Ignoring his warning—she was tired of males deciding her fate—she asked, "Who is being executed?"

"Me."

The blood drained from her head. "Another is glamoured as you?" For a few breaths, she thought she might throw up. But panic took over in the next breath and she charged toward the market.

A streak of shadow blurred by her vision and materialized in her path. "*Non*, madame. If you go there, everything he has done for you will be for nothing."

Rhoslyn bared her canines. "You do not get to decide what I can and cannot do."

Lucas held her gaze, leaned in and said emphatically, "Queen of The Row, we both have orders. Do not forget yours."

"Is he there?" She tried shoving Lucas out of the way, but he didn't budge. "Is Fentienne there?"

When he didn't answer, her arms stiffened at her sides and a scream scorched from her gut. A war cry of rage and grief. Fire burned down her limbs and flushed across her chest. She tried to shove past Lucas again, he blocked her path once more, Dalbréath now beside him.

"You love your horrible beast," Lucas said softly.

"Lucas Fontine, as your queen, I order you to step away!"

"He is ascending the throne for *you*," Lucas said even more softly. "*Only* for you. He is facing a realm he helped destroy as a cursed man to protect you and to give you the power and resources to change Aurelienne."

The wind knocked from her lungs.

"There are wolves in the crowd," he continued, "The clans will not let our Prince of Démons fall to the guillotine."

"If the roles were reversed," she hissed, "he would be at the execution block to protect me."

Lucas nodded his head. "But the roles are not reversed. You have your mission and he has his."

Rhoslyn opened her mouth to speak but Dalbréath cut her off before she could.

"Addien wants you to find Fentienne there," her uncle said. "It is a trap and one you are falling for."

"But does he know it is a trap?" she cried out. "Does he know it is not me?"

Both males were silent.

And the panic ripping through her picked up speed.

"You want to protect your mate and you want to defend Factory Row." Dalbréath's lips pressed into a thin line. "You must choose, little thorn, or you will surely lose both battles."

"I don't know what to choose." She grimaced back the torment. "Either choice forces me to bear guilt I cannot even begin to fathom."

Dalbréath took her hand in his. "Aye, it is the guilt warriors bear. We want to fight all injustices and defend the defenseless. But we are made of more than grit and steel. You must center yourself, Rhoslyn. Listen to your beating heart to hear your truth. Otherwise your righteous fury will not let you back down and demand you fight *every* fight." He paused a beat to study the busy street, then continued. "Not all battles are ours to join or lead. And some battles will require more from us than we can give."

The muscles of her stomach clenched. She wrapped an arm around her middle, hoping to calm the nausea, and peered at the decaying world around her.

Factory Row was dying. Children were dying. Girls were being forced into slavery. People worked prison hours for mere coppers, sometimes labored two or three jobs too. The best food was sent to Palais d'Aurélie while the rotting seconds were sold for a small fortune to those who couldn't even afford bread. And females still had so few rights to govern their own life. Was this the world she wanted for her little brother?

But her husband, her mate . . .

I give you my crown. I give you my throne.

Before Chateau Lumière Dorée, she marched on Palais d'Aurélie. Before she gave herself to the Prince of Aurelienne, she belonged to these streets and was crowned Queen of The Row. But she couldn't shake Lucas's words that Fentienne was ascending only for her. Last night, he confessed these words of love into every kiss and touch.

Want me, hate me. Desire me, despise me.

And, yet, Fentienne believed she chose him only out of compulsion. Still believed he was unworthy of her love and forgiveness. If she abandoned him to his abuser, his heart may never trust hers again, most especially if Addien, in Rhoslyn's likeness, mangled the beautiful pieces he had fought himself to heal.

All that I am, all that I have is yours, Rhoslyn Beausoleil.

That beautiful man gave her his kingdom, his inheritance. His heart and his soul. His very breath. Rhoslyn pulled Fentienne's identification tags from her bodice, forgetting two males stood before her. The metal warmed in her palm. She caressed her thumb over his name and drew in a ragged, tear-stained breath. By abandoning his subjects, she dishonored him. But she also promised to always chase after him, to prove he was not a monster.

Her eyes darted to the crowd and studied those who ran by. Listened to the shouts for blood, the screams for liberty and equality. How many of these people passing by were démons, like Lucas? How many were willing to fight half-shifted to show their neighbors, lovers, employers, and employees that they were allies not villains? And all to defend their Wolf King?

Dalbréath's mouth tilted in a sad smile. "What is your heart telling you, warrior lass?"

The muscles in her stomach tightened once more. "My heart says there are still two different battles that need to be fought on the same field."

Rhoslyn kissed Fentienne's tags then slipped the necklace over her head, concealing his name beneath her cloak. Meeting the intensity of Lucas's gaze with her own, she continued.

"Monsters need to prove they are good men and Factory Row needs to defend their basic rights as living, breathing souls." Dalbréath dipped his head in a single nod of agreement, but Lucas began a slow smile, one of pride. "My mate entrusted me with his throne and his crown. He *will* ascend half-shifted. I do not have magic powerful enough to counter Addien's. But I do have other means of power to secure my husband a more favorable future." She gestured around her. "One I set into motion weeks ago."

Dalbréath gently whispered, "That is an act of love he will understand."

A tear slipped down her cheek. "I am terrified he will believe I didn't choose him."

"He is a soldier and a prince." Her uncle wiped the tear away with his thumb. "A man with a bladed heart who cares to the point of pain. A man who would take in every shade of darkness to protect those he is responsible for. And you are *choosing* to protect his future, his subjects, and his clans." Her uncle smiled sweetly at her. "Your mate doesn't understand romantic love or familial love, not like you and me. But he does understand duty and sacrifice. He will know you chose him, little thorn, by protecting what is his."

"Once more, I agree with your Uncle Dalbrie." Lucas ignored the glare Dalbréath knifed his way and, instead, took Rhoslyn's hand in his and lifted her fingers to his lips, then bowed his head. "I am yours to command, Queen of The Row."

A blush warmed her cheeks at his gallantry. This démon was full of charms, but she also knew he was sincere. Exhaling slowly, Rhoslyn straightened her shoulders and lifted her chin. "Let us revolutionize Factory Row for the people and for our Wolf King."

"*Bien.*" Lucas lowered her hand back to her waist. "Mademoiselle Demarr longs to see you—"

"Take me to Amélie," she practically squealed. The thought of seeing her friend brought fresh tears to her eyes.

Lucas gestured with his head to follow, throwing Dalbréath a cocky half-smile before melting into the crowds. Dalbréath sidled up beside her, glaring daggers into the démon's back as they stepped into the market. A muscle feathered across his jaw but he said nothing. She recognized the look in her uncle's eyes, however. He was plotting something.

"Be *kind*," she admonished.

Dalbréath flashed her an arrogant grin. "Please let me accidentally stab him with my sword."

She sputtered a laugh, despite the heaviness in her chest, but schooled her features when Lucas peered over his shoulder at Dalbréath and winked, his lips twisted in a flirtatious smirk. "If you still want to poke me with your sword when this is all over . . ."

"Not in a million lifetimes, mortal," her uncle said with an eye roll.

Lucas lifted his shoulder in that goading but dismissive way of his. "I prefer redheads, anyway."

A roar of voices from the execution block rumbled down her body. The muscles along Lucas's arms and back noticeably stiffened. What had his wolf ears picked up that she couldn't? The démon didn't break stride, though, cutting through the swelling, frantic crowd. She tried to quiet her heart, but it was no use. Angry tears gathered on her lashes once more. She touched

Fentienne's tags and steeled herself.

The shouting intensified the deeper they moved into West Row. Occasionally, men and women both lowered their heads in shallow bows at Lucas as we passed by. She had forgotten that he was the clan alpha of Factory Row.

"Move!" a group of guards ordered as they jogged toward a building about a block up.

"A decoy," Lucas said over his shoulder. "For the march."

Her eyes swept around the street. Everyone was in a state of panic. The pots and pan war drums had grown louder too. The rallying anger quaked in her bones with each beat and shout. She couldn't wait to join their protest, to show Queen Adeline, who had starved, overworked, and overtaxed Factory Row, that she didn't own their beating hearts.

But they owned hers.

The building surrounded by a water assembly line was an old guard post that was partially destroyed in the attacks. Fire licked up the walls and shattered the windows. Rhoslyn startled at the explosion of glass. Her heart raced at the sight, her mind wanting to slip into old memories. But she couldn't fade into herself right now. The old post wasn't much of a loss, but the buildings around it were valuable.

Lucas slowed to face her fully, a concerned wrinkle between his brows. "They will put out the fire, madame. Do not worry."

Madame.

She just realized he had been calling her madame since they first spoke to each other. He knew she and Fentienne were married. He probably knew his alpha had marked her last night too.

"Lucas!" a voice cried out. A smile curved his mouth and he turned just in time for a female with wild auburn hair to jump in his arms, catching his lips with hers.

"Amélie," he murmured between kisses, "I bring you a gift."

"Did she write me back?"

He smiled. "Far better, *mon amour*."

Rhoslyn was so shocked at not only seeing her and Lucas together, but that her friend was dressed in high-end scarlet-hued underthings, as if she worked at *Le Rêve Rouge*. Her face powered, a mole the shape of a heart on her cheek, her lips painted red too. But the moment Amélie locked eyes with her, there were no questions. Only the feel of her dearest friend pressed to her, the happy tears on her cheeks, and the sound of their laughter.

"I missed you so much," Rhoslyn said into her friend's beautiful red hair.

Amélie pushed her back. "I thought the Beast of Gabaston had killed you and Matthieu. My heart would not stop weeping."

"When I heard about the dress factory—"

"—I was so frightened. We were all shaken."

Rhoslyn held her friend's hands, the flames of war heating her blood once more. Baring her teeth, she growled, "You should not have had to work at a tolerant house."

"Oh." Amélie blinked back a blush. "I work the gentlemen's tavern in the back, serving drinks and nothing more. The Madame and Brotherhood protect me. Mostly I pickpocket and spy."

"A *spy*?" The pickpocket part wasn't surprising.

Amélie's brows pinched together. "Where is Matthieu? Is he . . ."

"He is safe, with trusted friends."

Amélie's gaze flicked to Dalbréath, the furrow between her brows deepening. "You are related."

"*Oui*, he is my uncle."

"You are . . . Dúnælven?"

"There is far too much to share for this moment."

Her friend sighed. "Lucas would not tell me where you were, only that you were safe."

"It was best that you did not know." Rhoslyn's lips spread in a slow grin. "How long have you and Lucas—"

"Since the factory fire." Amélie bit her bottom lip in a poor attempt to hold in her excitement. "I saw Prince Adalwolf Halivaard today at *Le Rêve Rouge*. He goes by Fentienne Beausoleil now." Rhoslyn felt her heart drop into her stomach. "Lucas shares he is next in line to be king and will be a good king like his brother."

"The Brotherhood meets in the catacombs beneath *Le Rêve Rouge*," Lucas added quickly. "The only entry is through Madame's or the owner's chambers. The prince was there for no other reason."

Rhoslyn wrapped trembling fingers around the tags dangling from her neck.

"Rosie?" Her friend pulled back and touched her cheek. "You are flushed. Are you well?"

"She is furious, *mon amour*," Lucas said with a delighted chuckle and moved away. "That is the terrifying look of a female who is plotting to destroy a man."

"Why would she plot to destroy the prince for visiting a tolerant house?"

"Amélie," Rhoslyn said softly, lifting the identification tags for her to see.

Her friend gasped. Taking the tags in her fingers, she ran her thumb over Fentienne's name, then lifted large eyes at Rhoslyn. "How did you get these?"

"Let us go arm a strike." Rhoslyn squeezed her friend's hand. "I will tell you everything on the way. It is complicated."

Amélie kissed her cheek with a resigned sigh. "Come, *mon petit chou-fleur*. I will not rest until I know everything."

Grabbing her hand, she yanked Rhoslyn into a jog. Together they dashed up The Row in only their corsets, petticoats, and cloaks, to where a gathering was quickly growing a short distance away. Behind her, Rhoslyn could hear Dalbréath and Lucas close on their heels.

"*Sans-culottes!*" Amélie shouted to the masses until the banging of pots and pans quieted. When she had their rapt attention, she gestured to Rhoslyn and announced, "I give you the Queen of The Row!"

A deafening cheer erupted and Rhoslyn bit back the humbled tears. Hands touched her arms, shoulders, and head as she wended through the hollow-cheeked crowd of people in threadbare clothing, with Lucas in front of her and Dalbréath behind. The common folks' smiles were bright, eyes glossing with hope. Street children walked beside her, their dirty faces full of wonder. She was the fayette who stood up to a queen and survived the wolves. A small elf, no older than three or four, clung to her cloak, lifting her hands. Rhoslyn scooped her up, then took the hand of a little mortal boy beside her.

She had vowed to give Matthieu a better world. She would also fight for the children who lost their parents, their homes, their siblings to war and hunger. She would defend the females who deserved dignity regardless of career path forced upon them. Or career chosen. The females who worked long hours and multiple jobs to care for their children and younger siblings.

For when the males died in senseless wars, the females and children must soldier next. And they had carried the fight for far too long. It was time the battle ended.

It was past time they feasted on peace.

"Factory Row," she yelled over the applause. "You possess all the power! Do not forget this! You are powerful! Whether a beggar on the streets, a grisette in a factory, a nymph or tolerant house girl, a male who strikes iron, a brick layer, a farmer in the fields, or a child, you hold the pulsing heart of Aurelienne in the palms of your labor-worn hands!"

The crowd beat on their pots and pans and lifted their voices in approval.

"Our blood has painted each stone of this realm for a throne that would not spill a single drop for us in return let alone spare a stale crumb from their table!"

More voices shouted in agreement.

"Remember, you hold all of the power and that monster on her throne must terrify and starve you to feel like she has any!" Another cheer echoed over the streets. "Let her now fear us! Let her know that Factory Row is unafraid!" She paused two beats and screamed, "*Liberté, Egalité, Fraternité!*"

The swelling crowd shouted their war cry back.

"*Liberté, Egalité, Fraternité!*"

"*Liberté, Egalité, Fraternité!*"

Rhoslyn lifted her eyes and met Dalbréath's, not prepared for the intensity of emotion in his gaze. Despite the child on her hip and the other clinging to her hand, she fell into her uncle's waiting arms.

"You make your family proud, my wee thorn," he said. "A Kadelaryn warrior lass."

"Fentienne called me his warrior queen."

"Aye," Dalbréath said softly. "So you are. But do not forget . . ." He pulled back just enough to study her eyes. "Addien wants to claim your life and Amélie revealed your presence."

Rhoslyn nodded her head.

The little boy released her hand and ran off with his friends. Rhoslyn watched until he disappeared into the crowd and adjusted the little one on her hip.

Dragging in a tight breath, she pressed her fingers to Fentienne's tags around her neck. The last time these tags marched down Factory Row, he was the enemy. Now they marched to liberate his future subjects.

And she wouldn't stop until the current sitting House of Chalamet fell.

Chapter 35

Rhoslyn

Amélie rode astride a cannon just ahead of Rhoslyn, along with three other females. Their legs kicked to-and-fro on both sides while singing a bawdy tavern song about a young man with three secret lovers. A call and response song that made the people around them laugh. Rhoslyn wanted to join in the revelry—their raid was a success. But a persistent shiver crept along her skin.

After several hours away from the strike line, they were finally about to pass through the narrow passage left open in the barrier. Men, armed with muskets, patrolled along the wall's top on scaffolding made from the timber posts that once supported the homes along the forest edge in East Row. The wall itself were both the cob and stone rubbled remains of those very same rotting cottages. Were any from the walls that roofed her and Matthieu a month ago?

Smoke clouded the air around them while ash fell like snow over the streets, clinging to their hair and clothing. The decoy fires were put out, she was told by a runner from the front of the march. A runner who also shared how people rioted for food, turning over carts and pouring into establishments. But business owners and vendors had quickly quelled the hungry crowds, who were now eating breads and cakes from the bakeries, meat pies, stewed fruits, wine, beer, and all manner of vegetables too . . . all made from grains and produce reserved for Palais d'Aurélie and the upper class. Older women who could not walk long distances set up a soup line with pottage, stews, and boiled meats too.

It was this very fear of a bread riot that Rhoslyn remained on the back end of the returning raid. Dalbréath hoped any uprising would settle by the time they reached the strike line. And, per usual, he was right.

Another chill walked up her spine.

Her eyes darted to the shadows near the West Row forest entry. The wall was intentionally built here to redirect guards into the woods where démons awaited them. Was her husband among them? Saints, she ached to see him. The longing was a living, writhing vise in her chest. Rhoslyn peered over the factory rooflines to the darkening horizon. Faint stars already freckled the sky. Fentienne was about to shift into his wolf, if he hadn't already.

Was he safe?

Had Addien harmed him?

Did he fall for any traps?

The not knowing only added to the churning dread in her gut. Not knowing if her brother remained safe too—

Crows startled into flight behind the building she walked beside.

Rhoslyn sucked in a quick breath, bumping into Lucas, who was partially shifted, ear pricked toward the woods. Other than the half-shifted woman who attacked Rhoslyn when age twelve, Fentienne was the only other démon she had spent time with who had manifested in some form. Seeing it so in others was deeply unsettling.

At the armory, the crowd was seconds away from bolting when the captain and his twenty men had semi-shifted, their faces growing longer, teeth sharper, claws where fingers once were, their eyes bright and predatory... all in support of their Wolf King, and in fealty to her as his mate and as Queen of The Row. People had scattered away as much as they could, given the sheer numbers and tight quarters. Then more screams rippled through small pockets of the gathering as démons in the crowd partially shifted in solidarity.

The blood drained from Rhoslyn's head so fast, she nearly fainted.

Several protesters did.

So she couldn't blame the people for panicking.

But for Fentienne, she would do almost anything. For her husband, she would face Factory Row and defend démons.

"Captain Bastien Chapelle," *she shouted and the gathering had quieted.* "You do your future king a great honor this day. The sans-culottes will not forget your support, nor I." *She then faced the crowd and lifted her sword high in the air.* "The démons of

Gabaston fight for Factory Row!"

The silence was a loud, ringing in her ears. In a few short sentences, she had asked thousands to accept the monsters they were taught to fear since birth. Not just fear but manipulated by the temple to tithe their child's slice of bread away for fear of becoming a Child of the Dark Saint themselves.

This was too much, even for her, if she were honest.

Nevertheless, Fentienne's ascension to the throne was dependent upon this very political acceptance. The guaranteed freedom for the lower classes too.

"Who do we fear more?" she shouted once again over the people. "The monster on the throne who treats us like slaves? Even dogs get scraps from the table, unlike us. Or the good neighbors, friends, employers, and employees we have known all our lives? The same people who have equally suffered beside us?"

The silence, that time, was different. It was charged. Alive. An undulating beat of awareness.

"We see only what we want to see, especially when angry or afraid," she called out, touching her husband's identification tags. "Night is no more evil than day and yet that is where we place all our nightmares. Appearances can be deceiving." Rhoslyn then pointed toward Palais d'Aurélie and cried out, "Do not fear the monsters of your bedtime stories! The work worn, threadbare démons who are willing to fight for our freedom! Fear the golden monsters who terrorize us each day!"

She expected reluctant acceptance and was not prepared for the roar of support.

"Liberté, Egalité, Fraternité!"

"Liberté, Egalité, Fraternité!"

"Liberté, Egalité, Fraternité!"

At the sound, the captain and his men fell to one knee, the tips of their bayonets on the stone, their heads bowed before her.

The memory still vibrated in her pulse. Glancing at Lucas, however, she became less afraid.

Noting her inspection, Lucas said, "Boots," while peering behind him. "A ways up. But the palace guards are on their way."

Dalbréath peered into the darkness, toward the armory. "Aye, at least a couple of miles out, then. Unless the explosives at the armory failed."

"Have you heard any gunfire?" Rhoslyn asked Lucas.

A large number of protesters, at least two thousand, volunteered to march onto Palais d'Aurélie's grounds to create a distraction. Captain Chapelle assigned a dozen men to infiltrate the palace and arrest Queen Adeline and Lucien Chalamet while the palace guards scrambled to contain the crowds. Rhoslyn wanted to display both the queen and le duc on the execution block for all of Factory Row to see. Fentienne would eventually hold a trial for them. But Nine Saints, Rhoslyn couldn't wait for the heady rush of victory.

"*Oui*," he said softly. "But the people are armed and there are more of them than palace guards, no?"

Rhoslyn wrapped an arm around her sickening middle.

Amélie disappeared behind the wall atop the cannon and the crowd across the strike line roared at the sight. Rhoslyn bit back a smile, unable to help herself. Angling her head, she turned to see Lucas's reaction and froze. He wasn't watching his lover. Instead, both he and Dalbréath stared into the dark forest opening with predatory stillness.

"Get behind me, little thorn."

Rhoslyn didn't argue with her uncle and slipped out of line to stand at his and Lucas's back. Slowly, she withdrew her smallsword, feeling foolish with her novice skills. But any form of protection was better than none.

"Fayette," a deep voice rasped by her ear. Rhoslyn quickly spun around to an elven male who was inches from her face, drool on his chin and canines bared in a growl. "The Underworld's fires await you, cousin."

Dalbréath moved like the wind, words in runic spilling from his mouth. Then he stilled, a dagger pressed to the male's stomach and another to his neck. "Addien," he said low, "you will not survive this night."

The male elf laughed, a strangely sultry sound. "Oh, Dalbréath, charming as always."

In a slashing arc, he hit the elf hard in the head with the handle of a dagger. Rhoslyn jumped back, eyes wide. The people around them retreated in cries of alarm, shoving into the pressed in crowd. Lucas wrapped his arms around her as a shield, his chest rising and falling furiously. The possessed elf crumpled to the ground, but Dalbréath caught him before he could hit his head.

"You!" he hollered to a larger man, probably an iron worker. "Carry him inside the wall. Deposit him somewhere safe." To the watchmen patrolling the wall's roofline, he shouted, "Let this man pass ahead, by order of the

Queen of The Row!"

The large man nodded quickly and scooped up the elf, passing a fleeting glance at Rhoslyn before pushing up the line. A man on the wall saluted her in answer.

Dalbréath twisted toward her and Lucas, his white hair wild in the breeze, his darkening eyes wilder. "She waited until nightfall."

Lucas loosened his hold on her, but Rhoslyn didn't move away at first, still too stunned. "*Oui.*" The dark promises in just that one word shuddered down Rhoslyn.

"Any nobles or aristocrats in the Brotherhood who would defend her if needed?"

Rhoslyn worried her bottom lip and played with Fentienne's identification tags. She hadn't thought about Fentienne's ability to demand her pardon if arrested, or worse.

Lucas placed his large, clawed-hands to the back of their heads, drew them in close, then whispered, "Benoit Faivre and Alain Chalamet are clan officers."

"Do you trust them?" her uncle asked.

"The former is loyal to the Brotherhood and has a vested interest in keeping both Factory Row and his father happy, but the merchant prince is in an alpha pissing contest with the crown prince. The latter I do not trust and never have."

"How do we contact Benoit?" Dalbréath asked.

Lucas smirked. "Claudette Aris, the Madame of *Le Rêve Rouge*. I will send Amélie with a message for Madame."

Her uncle peered around the protesters and called, out, "We need five armed human males to circle the Queen of The Row."

"Human?" Rhoslyn asked.

"She's tapping into elven magic to strengthen hers."

"Aurelienne elves do not carry magic."

Dalbréath shook his head. "All fae have magic. The elves here only lost their knowledge to time."

Rhoslyn's mouth fell open. "Could she . . . possess *you?*"

"No, little thorn." Dalbréath cupped her face gently. "All Milfae Dúnælven warriors are under geis protections against possession magic, including rune whispering." He pressed a kiss to her forehead and stepped back.

"We need to get her behind the wall," Lucas said quietly. His gaze darted around the crowd, studying the men who came forward to volunteer, then back to the forest opening.

Dalbréath's gaze traveled over the thinning crowd, a muscle pulsing along his jaw. "Far more elves behind the wall, mortal," he muttered under his breath, knowing Lucas's sensitive hearing would pick up the words. "But you are right, she is not safe here either."

"The guards and soldiers will have shoot to kill orders."

"Aye," Dalbréath agreed. When noting her questioning look, he explained, "With rationed ammunition, they can't afford to drag out a fight. They will need to hit hard and hit fast and hope it's enough to scare Factory Row into a surrender."

Trepidation stirred in her belly once more. Swallowing against the sharp knot in her throat, she peered out toward the woods and tried to think of anything but war on her streets. Memories from over a year and a half ago were still all too fresh.

A few men approached with muskets in hand. She could hear Dalbréath and Lucas lay out their orders, actually getting along for once. Rhoslyn should pay attention but couldn't stop staring into the dark maw of the alley leading into the forest. For a moment, she swore she saw yellow eyes in the shadows. Was this Fentienne? Did he stalk her like he had in the woods weeks earlier, to protect her? Her heart trilled at the possibility. The desperation to see him was so great, she almost forgot about the Beast of Gabaston. Or that elves were being possessed and glamoured. The need to touch him, to feel his pulse beneath her fingertips throbbed in her chest to the point of pain.

Lucas's head whipped in her direction, his nostrils flaring. The muscles down his body stilled. She could physically feel the preternatural shift though they were not touching. Slowly, he rotated toward the forest, claws out, eyes sharp, strands of blond hair blowing across his face. Then he was angling through the people toward the alley.

A black wolf with golden eyes emerged from the shadows, teeth bared and snarling.

"Fentienne?" Rhoslyn couldn't keep the happy tears from her eyes. "He's alive. Blessed Mother, he lives!"

She barely finished her words when the world around her sprang into action.

"Guard her!" Dalbréath ordered.

An unnatural, guttural growl echoed off the stone walls in the alley. Then the black wolf lunged. Lucas turned into a shadow and reappeared a blink later mid-air in a collision of claws and snarls before the wolf could enter the streets of Gabaston. A white wolf hit the ground in a graceful landing atop the black wolf, snapping his teeth at its throat.

At the sight, the remaining crowd surged the wall, to the narrow opening in screams.

The five men appointed by Dalbréath circled around her, rifles raised.

"*Non*, do not shoot!" she cried out. There was no thought in her body, only terror. Rhoslyn rammed into the space between two men. Not expecting her to fight against them, or to be so strong despite her size, they easily staggered to the side and Rhoslyn slipped through, her smallsword still in her hand. "Put your guns down!" she ordered.

Another growl ricocheted off the walls. Lucas rolled away from the black wolf and partially shifted back into a crouched position, one hand braced on the cobblestone.

Panic-laced tears rolled down her cheek.

Rhoslyn pushed off into a sprint, but Dalbréath grabbed her, pivoting her away from the alley.

"They'll kill him!" She thrashed in his arms, unable to stop sobbing.

"Shhh, little thorn." Dalbréath pressed her to his chest, one hand around her head, the other around her back to hold her in place. "It could be a glamoured—"

A gunshot pierced the air and a whimper echoed in reply.

Rhoslyn screamed, "NO!" and shoved at Dalbréath's hold. Then she was moving. Dalbréath grabbed the hand still gripping her smallsword, spinning them in a half-circle, and thrust the blade up.

Warm blood dripped down her hand, down her arm.

For several paralyzing heartbeats, she gaped in horror at the wolf impaled on her sword.

A crowd began gathering around them. Rhoslyn saw the people in the blurred background of her tear-stained vision. But she couldn't look away from the vacant eyes staring at her. Beautiful golden eyes.

Her body started shaking. Bile coated her throat.

She released her grip on the sword and Dalbréath gently lowered the wolf to the ground.

Hurried whispers and murmurs scraped in her ears. She picked up bits and pieces—Beast of Gabaston, killed, Queen of The Row—but she could make no sense of it. Nor when the voices rose in alarm with sharp gasps.

Hands cradled her face. Her gaze snapped to a pair of bright blue eyes.

"It wasn't him," her uncle whispered. "Addien glamoured a male."

She grimaced back more tears. "It's not Fentienne?"

"Little love . . ." her uncle said tenderly but couldn't finish his own thoughts. Instead, Dalbréath clutched her to him, resting his cheek on her head, murmuring words in runic while softly combing his fingers through her hair. She heaved a sharp breath, gasping for air while fighting tears.

The sticky feel of cooling blood on her hands soured her stomach. She needed to scrub her skin. To weep into the stones now soaked in an innocent elf's blood. Someone's family, someone's friend.

"I am so sorry," she choked into his leathers. "I . . . I . . ."

"She counted on your mate bond," he whispered into her hair. "You acted on primal instinct. There is no fault there." He adjusted his cheek atop her head and pulled her in closer. "I have been in your place before, little thorn." The ache in his voice brought more tears to her eyes. "It is a form of terror unlike any other."

"Is she hurt?" Lucas moved into view, his gaze frantically searching her face and body for any injuries.

"Traumatized, but not physically hurt," Dalbréath answered quietly.

"Are . . . are you wounded?" Rhoslyn somehow managed.

"Do not worry about me, madame. I heal fast." Lucas's face darkened into something horrifyingly sinister, a low growl in his throat, his teeth clenched. "That was a vile thing to do to bonded mates."

"Aye," Dalbréath said, still holding her close.

Lucas's eyes flicked to the road leading to the armory. "We need to get her behind the wall."

The men Dalbréath appointed stood beside them, pale and nervously peering around.

Rhoslyn forced herself to look at the elf she and Dalbréath had run through. Dirt smudged his calves where stockings should be. Cuts and mud covered his bare feet. The breeches were beyond threadbare. But he was wearing Dúnælven leathers over his torso and arms. It was clear this male was a beggar. The leather armor was so at odds with the rest of him that Rhoslyn had to look closer and knelt beside him, not caring that her petticoat dipped in his blood.

"You did not deserve this," she said to the elf. A tear slipped down her cheek. "May the Otherworld treat you with far more kindness than Ealdspell did."

The Underworld's fire stoked to life in her belly. She would destroy. She would consume. Addien's soul would no longer exist when she was done with her.

Slowly rising to her feet, Rhoslyn met the fearful eyes around her. People were pouring back out from behind the wall to see the dead elf at her feet and to see her soaked in his blood. She didn't need to hear their words to know that framing Dúnælven was Addien's plan as a backup if framing Fentienne failed.

"Factory Row," Rhoslyn shouted, and she swore the night sky trembled at the fury in her voice. "This is the Beast of Gabaston! The monster terrorizing our forests is not a démon, but innocent male elves who are glamoured and possessed by an ancient, shadowed faerie." She paused a beat. "Witnesses, confirm your accounts!"

The whispers grew louder and she could hear people relay her words and the stories of those who saw the attack and the dead wolf's transformation to those in the back, who would continue to share down the streets.

"This ancient faerie wants to start a war between our realm, Avenbury, and Dúnælven." She pointed to the elf at her feet. "He is not a warrior, but a poor beggar." Rhoslyn pointed to her uncle. "This is a true Dúnælven warrior, my kin who was charged by Gedlen Fate Maker to protect me."

The people spoke hurriedly with each other.

"Tell Factory Row of what you've witnessed. Let every male, female, and child know that the Beast of Gabaston is not a démon but a cruel faerie trick." Her lip curled back and she gritted out, "She will die for her crimes against Gabaston!"

Rhoslyn picked up her sword from the street. Anger shimmered over her skin in a flush. All around her, males and females lifted their fists into the air with outraged cries. Factory Row wasn't a toy for those in power to play with and discard.

A boom rocked the ground beneath her feet. In the direction of the armory, a light flashed and lit up the night sky. The caskets of black powder they left behind were detonating as planned. Several guards loyal to Fentienne had remained behind to light wicks they attached to the powder kegs. Another explosion rumbled into the evening air. This one more violent than the last.

"Ah, a beautiful sight, no?" Lucas grinned—all teeth and malice. "Come, let us find Amélie..."

Shoulder's stiff, back straight, Rhoslyn marched toward the wall's opening, not waiting to hear Lucas finish. Slowing only to let the armed men circle around her once more.

The time for strategy was over.

The strike was under way. The citizens of Factory Row were now armed to fight the oncoming palace guards and soldiers still on active duty at the garrison. The démons of Gabaston were accepted as allies despite still being feared. Her husband was honored before the masses by the men who opened the gates to the armory and invited them in.

She had no further use here but for one more task—kill Addien Wyndham.

Rhoslyn clenched the sword in her hand and pushed back the roiling sickness in her stomach. To kill Addien, she would need to slay her own likeness and in front of Fentienne.

She knew her enemy.

CHAPTER 36

Fentienne

Acute pain pulled Fentienne from the black. Squinting open his eyes, he tried to make sense of the dark space around him and bit back a groan. A bleating ache pounded in his head.

Where the hell was he?

Unsure of what happened, he lay still to not alert the person beside him, whose heartbeat he could hear. The scent was one he knew as well. A striking, dominant scent. An alpha wolf.

Training his breaths to remain even, he took in the room with a slow sweep of his eyes. He was in a four-poster bed with a canopy, laying atop a silk coverlet. The room itself seemed large and opulent, with gaudy filigree and crown molding. In the dark it was difficult to make out the colors, even in the candlelight, but they appeared a pastel hue—blue maybe?

Fentienne rolled his head gradually toward the heartbeat and found a pair of brown eyes watching him, the man's mouth curled in blasé amusement. His light brown hair was cut close to his head, typical for males who mostly wore wigs. No powder on his face, or any other makeup, which was odd for the aristocracy. Perhaps this man was a servant. No, the silk three-piece suit he wore was too fine for livery.

"You do not recognize me," the man said and closed the book on his lap. "Or you hit your head too hard and do not recognize anything. Do you know who you are, milord?"

That voice. He knew that cultured voice.

"Benoit?" Fentienne pushed up on the bed, his eyes darting around the room. Why was he in a room with Benoit? Pain pounded in his head with the movement and he hissed, grimacing back the ache until the severity of it passed.

"*Oui*," Benoit said simply. "You are at my apartments in Factory Row, in a guest suite."

A furrow deepened between Fentienne's brow.

"Ah, you do not remember swooning after your wife left you to take her fate. So dramatic."

"I do not swoon," he snapped with a warning snarl. "It was wolfsbane."

Benoit leaned forward on his knees and cupped his chin with his hands, tilting his head. "Or something else." A baiting smile teased his lips. "You do not ask about your mate."

It was a statement, not a question. "That was Addien Wyndham, *not* my mate."

That cocksure smile grew as Benoit straitened, and Fentienne forced himself to not reach across the bed and strangle that man. It was strange seeing him without powder or a wig. The man now looked his twenty-nine years instead of trying to appear like a child's doll. The lack of powders enhanced his muscular frame too—an actual alpha's body. Fentienne narrowed his eyes.

Why was he here? In Benoit's apartments?

Memories came rushing back of this morning. The Brotherhood meeting, believing he found Rhoslyn in the forest outside of East Row, trading his life for Addien's to protect the strike, the guillotine . . . a sudden ache in his chest stole his breath. A heaviness that seemed to squeeze tighter with each grief-stricken beat of his heart.

Lucas.

Gods, his friend.

Tears pricked the back of his eyes. He wasn't sure what hurt worse: watching Lucas lose his head or the public accusation that Fentienne was the Beast of Gabaston.

Fentienne clutched the coverlet beneath his hands and glared at Benoit. "Royal executions are a riot." The seething tone cracked at the end. His entire body was shaking with building rage. "Did you have anything to do with Lucas's execution today?"

"I must thank the wolfsbane for dulling your territorial aggression so we can *attempt* a serious conversation about today."

Fentienne ground his teeth. "Answer the godsdamn question, Faivre."

He smirked. "I am shocked you do not outright accuse me given our history."

"Our history is not the same as evidence. I can loathe the very sight of a man and still find him innocent." Fentienne flashed him a wicked grin. "But I would enjoy every whimper and plea while torturing you if guilty."

"I am sure you would." Benoit pursed his lips in thought, arrogant humor in his dark eyes. "Lucas Fontine is very much alive. An elven male lost his head today in the market square."

The air rushed from his lungs.

Lucas was alive?

Fentienne almost laughed with relief. That irritating arsehole was still alive. He should have considered it was a faerie trick. But losing the only man he trusted outside of his brother, and so violently, twisted something sharp in his gut.

Benoit leaned back in his chair, holding the book in his lap, and crossed his legs. "It is amusing what people reveal when they think your only ambition is to spend your family's fortune on women and wine and gambling houses. Even more so when they believe you do not support their Wolf Prince."

"They *think?*" A mirthless laugh left Fentienne's tight chest. "Excessive frivolity *is* your lifestyle, Faivre."

The man opened his arms with melodramatic flair and murmured, "It is all for show, nothing more. This is the real Benoit Faivre." Benoit's gaze roamed over Fentienne's face, another sensually playful smile tugging on his lips.

Fentienne gaped at him in disbelief. "All the makeup?"

"*Oui*, for show."

"To trade in gossip."

Benoit tapped his fingers on the closed book, the humor fading from his face. "You did not grow up in Aurelienne's court, milord. Games and intrigues are how information is won and deals are made. As a merchant prince, I learned to crawl through different mud than you. As an untitled aristocrat, I also learned how to avoid enemy fire."

That sultry smile of his returned but, like all the times before, it wasn't genuine flirtation. It was elegant dominance. It was the hungry look of a man who knew how to seduce secrets from politicians and men of industry by playing the pleasure-seeking *haute noblesse* fool. And, as much as he didn't like Benoit Faivre, he respected his means of survival in the aristocracy's hostile environment.

Another pounding ache squeezed his head.

Fentienne lifted his hand to examine for any bumps—and stilled.

A human hand.

His heart jumped to his throat. Night darkened windows swallowed up his vision. The room was draped in shadows too.

Holy mountain gods, was this real? Hope crawled up his chest and loosened the air in his lungs. No, this was a dream. Candlelight limned Benoit's face in flickering amusement—a face Fentienne truly saw for the first time too. He had to be dreaming right now.

Swallowing back the panic, he studied his hand once more and asked, "Why am I here?"

"Ah, you asked me to think of you while enjoying another in my bed this night, no? I decided you would be far more fun. Imagine all the wild *gossip* at court . . ." Fentienne eyes slid back to Benoit's, unsure if the man were joking or serious. Or if any of this were real. Benoit leaned forward on his knees once more and whispered theatrically, "My prince shifted in front of the Monks of Glanis and hundreds of witnesses after confessing his love for the Queen of The Row. Then he swooned." Benoit winked and sat back with a smug grin. "You are quite popular right now, Fentienne Chalamet." After a dramatic pause, he added, "Except with your cousins, Alain and Lucien. They did not appreciate your romantic performance."

Fentienne's pulse was racing. This was real.

He touched his face and drew in a choked breath.

Skies, he had broken Eirwen's curse. How the hell did he break Eirwen's curse? A breath later, he closed his eyes and groaned. Of course, from Eirwen's perspective, selfless love was sacrificing one's literal life for their mate as a grand gesture. Not any of the other damn sacrifices he had made.

But he was free.

He was finally free and, gods, he needed to move before he jumped out of his skin.

"It's Beausoleil, by the way." Fentienne pushed off the bed and fought a momentary dizzy spell. Then he strode toward the settee and chairs near a fireplace. Laying in a bed like an invalid before a fellow alpha, especially one who bordered on enemy, was infuriating.

Benoit opened a box atop a cabinet before joining him.

Outside, he could hear cheers, music, and singing. Factory Row was reveling. The raid must have been a success. Rhoslyn should have been here to see her plans come together. The Princess of Avenbury was headstrong and reckless at times, but she was cunning and an excellent strategist. He longed to go home and surprise his wife. Then keep her in his bed until neither remembered how to breathe.

"Cigarette?" Benoit asked, pulling him from his heady thoughts. "Clifstánian favorite among soldiers, no?"

Fentienne accepted and used the candle on the end table to light up. "I have zero patience for cat and mouse games." He slowly blew out smoke on a satisfied sigh. Benoit poured whiskey into two glasses, sparing him a quick glance. "Why am I really here?"

"Now for a serious conversation." Benoit's expression hardened as he offered him the glass, then sat in the chair beside him with a sip. "Believe it or not, Wolf Prince, I am on your side."

"Hilarious." Fentienne flicked his ashes in a tray Benoit set between them.

"*Non*, it is not false flattery. You can loathe the sight of a man and still find him innocent. I can do the same. Though I do not loathe you, not really. Not even after you broke my arm and forced me to eat dirt before all the alphas. The humiliation gave credibility to my angle."

Fentienne closed his eyes in a long blink to rein in his anger. "Toying with my dominance before the most powerful men in Aurelienne isn't an angle, Faivre, it's a death wish."

"You see, Fentienne *Beausoleil*, playing your enemy has tremendous benefits in both the Brotherhood and in court, mostly for you." He swept an arm around the room. "This is your jail, Your Highness. Guards are posted right outside your door."

A scowl tightened the muscles of his face. "You asked to be my jailer and the authorities as well as House Chalamet just . . . agreed? Absurd."

"*Non*, the *sans-culottes* were rioting over the Queen of The Row's arrest and stormed into the jailhouse to block entry. Le duc had nowhere else he could take you with the strike and feared for his life if he executed you while trapped on Factory Row. Your cousin trusted my hatred for you enough that he let me into his confidence and eagerly accepted when I offered my apartments as your temporary torture chamber." The man leaned back in his chair, a lit cigarette dangling artfully from his fingers. "I was given instructions to sedate you with wolfsbane until after the strike, but where is the fun in that, *oui*?"

Despite Benoit's confessions, he didn't know if the man was still toying with him. But one detail snagged his attention. "Lucien was at the execution?"

"He is at *every* démon execution."

The faint feeling of his wolf bristling shivered across his skin. "Did you know when you swore your truth and your silence?"

"I knew nothing until after you swooned."

"I did not—" Fentienne clenched his jaw.

Smoke curled from Benoit's lips as he met Fentienne's furious stare. "Monsieur Fontine had left my office five minutes prior to finding him on the execution block. I knew it wasn't him. Then I saw you in the crowd and worried my Wolf Prince might be next."

A sarcastic reply was on the tip of Fentienne's tongue, but the anger simmering off Benoit was palpable.

"My fears were founded," the man continued. "After you transformed, Lucien descended the stage like a male going after a bitch in heat." Benoit leaned over his knees toward Fentienne, his eyes flashing. "In a monk's habit. And he was licking his chops at the sight of you."

Fentienne's wolf snarled.

"'Le duc,'" Benoit continued in a haughty murmur Fentienne recognized immediately, "'what a *riot* to run into you here. Dreadful day. *Mon Dieu*, is that the prince? Wild.'" Benoit chuckled softly, but it was full of venom. "I saw what appeared to be an exorcism," he said to Fentienne, his teeth clenched. "I did not understand until I saw le duc. He smelled like a cub, as if a new Chalamet wolf was born inside of him. Impossible, no?" Sipping on his whiskey, his gaze flitted toward the door then he lowered his voice. "I playfully admonished that Monsieur Fontine was not the name Alain had shared with me, hoping it was indeed Alain. Le duc's reply? Yesterday, Lucas Fontine was not your beta but Alain Chalamet insisted that executing him today would give Lucien powers equivalent to sacrificing ten lesser démons.

Imagine the absolute scandal at trying to siphon wolf magic from an elf."

Fentienne's wolf sprang to life in a rush of heat. The low growl rumbling from his chest thundered through his body. "How the hell can that man siphon magic if he's not a wolf?"

Chalamets were a pureblood line. If those without wolves were turned, even by a family member, they would still become a lesser démon. Lucien Chalamet would not want that stench on him as a king from the House of Wolves.

Benoit tilted his head. "You are not surprised about Alain."

"I don't trust anyone. But I *really* don't trust arse-kissing Chalamet clan alphas who don't challenge my authority in *any* way. It's not natural to our kind. Now, how in the eight realms is Lucien siphoning off magic? You have five seconds to explain before I level this place."

"Addien Wyndham." Benoit leaned forward even more, his face growing fierce, eyes predatory and teeth sharp. "They had an arrangement. To become a Chalamet pureblood alpha wolf, he needs to kill fifty démons and consume their magic using a spell minutes before they die. And so a wolf cleansing was born. The Beast of Gabaston too." Benoit puffed on his cigarette, a look of disgust etched into every line of his face. "It took extraordinary strength to not rip out his spinal cord that moment."

Fentienne was on the razor's edge of completely losing his shit and going rabid. Shortly after the House of the Golden Light was cursed to the grave, he figured Addien and Lucien were working together in some capacity. But this? The muscles down his shoulders, chest, and torso were so tense, it hurt to breathe. He would accuse Benoit of playing him, but he could scent his rage. Could hear the fury in the rapid beat of his pulse.

"I bare myself to you, Wolf Prince, in an offer of trust," Benoit continued. "Very few in the aristocracy and Brotherhood have seen my true face these past ten years. Even fewer have seen yours."

Fentienne studied Benoit's revealed face and almost laughed at himself for giving advice he, himself, did not heed. He saw only what he wanted to see when looking at Benoit these past few months, especially when angry and afraid. But appearances can be deceiving.

"Where is he?" A cruel smile flirted across Fentienne's lips. "Royal executions are a riot."

A similarly wicked smile replied. "*Bien*. You understand then." Benoit set his empty whiskey glass on the table and stood. "He is seeking refuge—"

"Monsieur." A guard opened the door enough for his head. "A girl from *Le Rêve Rouge* arrived for you. A gift from Madame."

"Send her back."

"She says Madame insists."

Benoit waived a few fingers to let her in but turned toward the window and angled in such a way it would be difficult to make out his reflection while fitting a light brown, ponied wig onto his head. One he apparently kept there for such occasions. Fentienne placed the cigarette between his lips and leaned back in the chair. An elven female with dark auburn hair and pale skin entered the room in nothing more than a black corset and red petticoat, flinching when the door shut behind her.

"Not tonight, girl," Benoit said in a thick, cultured voice, his back still turned to the room. "Unless my guest would like to join in."

"Men are not my appetite," Fentienne murmured in reply. "Not even in a *ménage à trois*."

His wolf growled at him and he would have growled back to assert his dominance if the girl wasn't here. The damn thing couldn't tell the difference between reality and playing a part.

"Lucas Fontine sends me with a request, Monsieur Faivre."

Every racing thought in Fentienne's head slid to a stop at hearing Lucas's name.

"What does that flea-ridden dog beg for now, *sans-culotte*?"

"The Queen of The Row is unharmed, but she was attacked by a black wolf—"

Fentienne launched from his chair, ignoring the spinning room and ache in his head, and moved to the girl, his nostrils flaring. "How do you know it was Rhoslyn Gautier?"

The redheaded elf blanched. "She is like a sister to me and has been for half our lives, milord."

Fentienne narrowed his eyes. "You are the girl who hung on Lucas in the doorway to *Le Rêve Rouge* this morning, *oui*?"

She nodded her head and lowered her gaze. "He is my *amour*, since the factory fire, milord."

Lucas had a sweetheart?

"Your name?"

"Amélie Demarr."

Fentienne's shoulders relaxed a notch. "Mademoiselle Demarr," he said, "Rhoslyn Beausoleil is not able to leave the property—"

"*Pardonnez-moi, milord,*" Amélie interrupted. "But I was only given leave to speak with Benoit Faivre about the Queen of The Row."

"I am her husband!" The muscles down Fentienne's body flexed and he clenched his fists. His wolf was going mad, its growls growing louder and wilder. "How did she leave Chateau Lumière Dorée? Where is Matthieu?"

Amélie blinked nervously while taking in his face. "She burned down the rose garden using the Underworld's refuse fires, Your Highness."

She did *what?!*

"Where is she?" He could barely breathe.

Heat bloomed in Amélie's cheeks as she straightened her shoulders and met Fentienne's eyes dead on. "Lucas asks for Benoit Faivre to represent the Queen of The Row should she be arrested this night, while her husband is a black wolf. He believes Addien Wyndham will strike again."

Fury whipped through him at her dismissal. But he also appreciated her distrust.

"*Oui,* I will represent Madame Beausoleil, if needed. You can find me here or at *Le Rêve Rouge,*" Benoit said from the window. "You may leave."

Amélie swallowed thickly, then lowered into a curtsy before Fentienne.

"Wait," Fentienne said as she started to turn toward the door. "Thank you for using caution to protect my wife. You are right to not tell me where she is. I should be a wolf right now. Do not tell her yet that I am not, for her safety as well as mine. Please . . ." He drew in a trembling breath. "She is unharmed? Matthieu is safe?"

"A glamoured male elf attacked her, but she slayed the Beast of Gabaston before witnesses," Amélie said softly. Fentienne's heart stopped beating. Did she think it was him who was attacking her? "Lucas, Dalbréath Kadelaryn, and five appointed men are protecting her, Your Highness."

"And Matthieu?"

"He is with the High Druid of Ealdspell and Gellynor Death Talker."

"*Merci,* mademoiselle." Fentienne bit back the tide of emotion ramming against his chest. "Please tell Rhoslyn that she was right about the poem."

Amélie dipped her head, started to turn again, then stopped. "She wears your identification tags proudly around her neck, Your Highness. I have seen her kiss them at least five times." Fentienne couldn't help the shy smile, too overcome by the warmth flushing down his body. "She defended the démons of Gabaston before thousands while pressing your name to her heart." Their eyes locked. "Do not break it."

He allowed her to stare him down another few seconds despite his wolf's displeasure. If this girl was brave enough to stand up to a démon prince and future king to protect her friend, she would stand up to anyone.

After the door clicked shut, Benoit turned to Fentienne, amusement flirting across his lips.

"If you speak a single word about my mate," Fentienne warned in a low growl, "I will break every bone in your body."

"The wolfsbane is leaving your system." He flashed his eyes at Fentienne. "How delightful. Turning a moon-addled alpha wolf on le duc is just desserts, no?"

Benoit waltzed past him and opened the door. "Fetch the prince's duster, hat, and personal effects," he ordered a guard, who were clearly on Fentienne's side too. Peering over his shoulder, Benoit murmured, "Ready to howl with the revelry, milord?"

"How deeply am I obliged to you, charming Beauty," the prince said. "You have released me from the frightful prison in which I have groaned for so long a time. Your marriage with the Beast will restore a King to his subjects, a son to his mother, a life to a whole Kingdom. We shall all be happy."

Believing the sight that met her eyes but a continuation of her dreams, and that she was sleeping still, her joy and surprise were extreme at discovering that it was a reality, and that on a couch beside her lay, in a profound slumber, her beloved Unknown, looking a thousand times more handsome than he had done in her vision.

"La Belle et la Bête" by Madame de Villeneuve, published in *The Young American and Marine Tales*, 1743

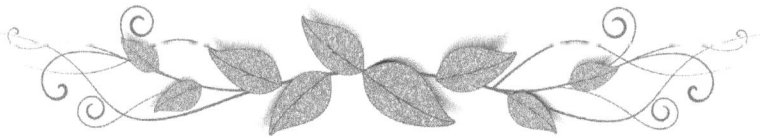

Chapter 37

Fentienne

Gunfire echoed from several blocks up. Then cannon fire. The palace guards and a small pocket of active-duty soldiers had arrived. Fentienne's entire system came alive. The sounds of war were the lullabies of his childhood. The music he danced to as a young man. The victory march anthem of adulthood. Living in the country for over a year was maddening. He didn't realize how crazy the relatively quiet pastoral solitary confinement made him feel until this moment.

Charged for a fight, Fentienne angled through the revelers behind Benoit.

Was Rhoslyn here? Or closer to the strike line? Thinking of her washed his senses in need. And it was growing worse as more and more of the herb wore off. His wolf grew louder every second too, replacing the ache he had healed in his head not too long ago—though, he still didn't know how he healed himself.

Fentienne tipped the tricorn hat lower over his eyes and tried to blend in despite his size. Being an aristocrat on Factory Row right now was dangerous, a Chalamet one even more so. Between the highwayman's collar and hat, he hoped most wouldn't pay him any heed.

Lantern light bathed Factory Row in warmth despite the cold shadows. People danced in the streets to the pluck of violins and flutes. Pockets of merchants and other middle-class residents of Factory Row roared in laugher with one another, mugs of ale in their hands. Wrinkling his nose, Fentienne stepped around a grime coated woman in threadbare clothing who was eating discarded chunks of food right off the dirty cobblestone like a dog. There were others eating bits of bread and produce right off the street too.

A war was waging on the line of West Row and Saints District, but these people didn't care. Or they were waiting for a rotation. Fentienne wasn't sure of their paramilitary organization and the desire to know details itched obsessively at his mind. But he had a job to do. And they had theirs.

He and Benoit were now passing the execution square, a block away from *Le Rêve Rouge*. Blood still coated the blade and boards around where that innocent male had lost his head today.

Hate twisted sharp thorns around Fentienne's heart until he saw only red. A true hate. He didn't care what might be the moral diplomatic choice, with Addien or Lucien. Alain? Fentienne would deal with him later before the Brotherhood. Perhaps Lucien should stand public trial too. But Fentienne didn't give a shit about fairness from a throne right now. He wanted revenge.

Benoit pushed open the red door into *Le Rêve Rouge* and waited for Fentienne to join him. The place was chaos. Half-naked girls were everywhere. Males packed the tolerant house from wall to wall until the stench of their unwashed bodies overpowered the perfume and opium. Benoit lifted a scented cloth to his nose and pushed through the crowd.

"Wait your turn, silk breeches." A man grabbed Fentienne's duster and pushed him.

With a dark laugh, Fentienne grabbed the man's arm, twisted it just until he cried out, then shoved him hard into the room of males. Gods, he wanted a fight. His muscles burned to inflict pain, flexed to hear screams for mercy. But he also had some semblance of self-control. That imbecile wasn't his target.

Glaring at the males in the waiting area, he continued shouldering past toward the voyeur hallway where Benoit waited for him, eyebrow arched. Lucien, according to Benoit, was hiding in the catacombs until it was safe for him to travel back to Crowns Quarter. The *only* reason he believed Benoit's motive right now—and not that he was being led into a trap—was because Lucien could have siphoned Fentienne's power at Benoit's apartment then killed him while he was passed out. No one would have known for days, if ever, depending on how they disposed of his body.

At Jules's door, Benoit knocked twice then opened it, not waiting for an invitation.

A shadow sprinted across the room to where they stood.

"How can I help you gentlemen—"

Fentienne pushed them inside and kicked the door shut with his boot.

"Wolf Prince?"

Clutching Jules's throat, he slammed him against a wall and growled, "Are you involved with Lucien Chalamet?"

"*Non*, milord, of course not."

"Then why is he in the catacombs?"

Jules's rasped, "If he is, then I was not aware."

Fentienne released Jules. "Explain and quickly."

"Claudette has been in the main hall since the strike, Your Highness. I have come and gone—"

"Did you lock the door?"

"Every time."

"Does Alain Chalamet have a set of keys as backup?"

Jules bared his teeth. "Go, I will lock up and join you."

Fentienne didn't waste any time and ducked into the catacombs, marching off before Benoit shut the door behind them. That bastard of a cousin defiled the hall of thrones with his disgusting existence. After executing démons for their power, he was delusional to believe the Brotherhood would allow him in a pack let alone as an alpha—

A scent hit him right before he saw the knife materialize from behind a dugout. Fentienne reared back. The blade swished by his chest. Growling, he grabbed the lesser démon's wrist and shattered it on a marble coffin. The man screamed in pain, making Fentienne laugh. There was no pity for traitors against the head alpha or Brotherhood. Taking the man's head in his hands, he flashed his teeth in a wicked grin, then twisted until a snap echoed in the space. Fentienne tossed the lesser démon's body to the ground, stepped over it, and kept marching.

"If I were into men," Benoit said beside him, "I would be panting right now. That was the most arousing thing I've seen in an age—"

Fentienne shoved Benoit to the ground and threw a roundhouse kick, gutting the lesser démon who shadow sprinted toward them. The man flew back and hit a wall with a satisfying crunch. Gods that sound was beautiful. Crouching before the démon, Fentienne grabbed the man's knife and sliced across his throat. He was already dead, but Fentienne wanted to send a message to the dogs who could scent blood.

He would kill them all.

No mercy.

Fentienne yanked off his duster and threw it in Benoit's face, tossing his hat to him next. If the man was offended at becoming his valet, he said nothing. But Fentienne needed better mobility. He removed his silk frock coat next, which Benoit grabbed before he could throw it in his direction.

"Guard dogs? Really?" Jules said right behind them. "He is all ego and no brains if he believes lesser pack dogs are a match for a military born and trained Prince of Démons."

"*Non*, I do not think he expected our head alpha to flush wolfsbane from his system so fast," Benoit answered.

"Saints," Jules breathed when seeing Fentienne's face. "I had heard a rumor, but I didn't believe it."

Fentienne clenched his teeth while rolling up his sleeves. The veins in his arms throbbed from the fury pumping down his body. Next, he unknotted his cravat, which Benoit quickly plucked from his fingers, and Fentienne rolled his eyes. The horror of his fine clothes touching the dirt in such critical times . . .

"Give me your stocking tie, Benoit," Fentienne demanded.

"Benoit?" Jules eyed him curiously, not recognizing the aristocrat in a brunette wig or without make-up. "I am not sure what is more odd, Benoit in a natural state, our prince in human form, or you two working together."

"The tie," Fentienne stressed. This wasn't the time for small talk.

"I have a ribbon in my pocket," Jules said right as Benoit started to crouch. "Found it in a hallway."

Fentienne accepted the black ribbon and tied most of his hair back. A few shorter strands still framed his face, but they wouldn't block his visibility.

Now he was ready for a dog fight.

"No shadow sprinting long distances," Fentienne whispered. "You won't see the guards but they'll see you. Stay behind me. Benoit, leave my stuff on a coffin to pick up on the way back. I need you to fight. Understood?"

"*Oui*," they said in unison.

"Where is Lucas?" Jules asked him.

"Protecting my mate," he gritted out in reply. "Let's go."

They continued down the corridor. Four more guards attacked from the shadows. Four more guards now belonged to the catacombs. And Fentienne craved even more blood. The rage fevering his body pounded against his ribs and buzzed down his limbs. At the ossuary entry, Fentienne easily dispatched the two posted guards—bashing one head on the wall of skulls and snapping the other's neck. All of it was pointless and senseless, which pissed Fentienne off to no end.

"Lucien Chalamet," Fentienne seethed as he marched into the hall of thrones. "You do not pick a fight with the Prince of Démons, killing twenty-three of my wolves, countless innocent people in a Beast of Gabaston fear tactic, especially children, and survive."

A man in his upper thirties with earthen brown hair and blue-gold eyes stood from Fentienne's throne in a ceremonial robe. The garish audacity was so obnoxious, Fentienne almost felt a twinge of sympathy over the level of this man's desperation. Almost. But Fentienne felt only the raging thrum of destruction.

Alain, who remained seated on his throne, must not have shared the latest revelation: only legitimate family of the Dark Saint were head alphas.

"Cousin," Lucien greeted, "I have killed twenty-three démons and one elf. You have killed how many innocent Aureliennes now? And you, a mere pup."

"You've killed plenty of females, too. Do not forget them."

"Allegedly. Rumors in court are often worse than reality, which you would know if you had ever attended court." Lucien's gaze raked down Fentienne and back up in a dismissive look. "After all the Aurelienne's you have killed on the battlefield, including démons, you believe this realm would willingly place a crown on your head?"

Fentienne laughed, an inky, dark slithering promise. "I was conscripted into the military against my will at the age of eight and had nothing to do with the attack orders other than following the ones given to me. What is your excuse?"

"Do you know what it is like to be next in line from a powerful house—"

"I was latent until cursed and the third-born prince. A *prince*, not a duke," he snapped. "Do I know? That is honestly your response, as if you have moral leverage? Because I am a godsdamn Halivaard! The most powerful and feared family in all Ealdspell. The blood of dragons flows in my veins beside the blood of wolves. My younger brother is the emperor and I am the Dark Saint's reborn son. You are *nothing*," he sneered. "My vomit is worth more than you."

The last word barely left his mouth when he heard the shuffle of feet behind him. Pivoting on his heel, Fentienne shadow sprinted to the left. A lesser démon clawed at the now empty space. Fentienne used the momentum of the man's swinging arm to throw him at a pillar made of skulls. The loud snap of bones filled the chamber and sang in Fentienne's ears. His mouth twisted into wicked satisfaction as he faced the dozen lesser démons who surrounded him, Benoit, and Jules.

"Lesser démons," Fentienne said on a low growl. "For your treason against the Brotherhood, for betraying your wolf kin, and to protect the clans, I sentence you to death by any means possible. You will not roam the night. You will not have honorable burials."

A démon charged him with a military saber. Fentienne jumped away from the steel's arcing slice in the air with a taunting grin. Using the blade's follow through motion as a distraction, he swept his foot beneath the man while punching his ribs from the side. The sword knocked into the air in a jerked release as the man tripped backward. Fentienne caught the sword's grip and plunged the blade into the man's chest before the lesser démon hit the ground.

"Attack!" Fentienne called out to Benoit and Jules, who sprang into action half-shifted.

The first two démons who rushed him were impaled on his blade almost immediately. The next one approached with a sword of his own. Steel hit steel in a clanging melody that sang over the growls and fighting sounds around them. Fentienne could have finished the lesser démon a few parries ago, but he was bored and wanted to feel like he was actually in a challenging fight with someone to satisfy the fever licking flames of rage down his muscles.

No, he was done with this idiot.

Pulling the double barrel pistol from his hip, Fentienne aimed at the man and fired. A ridiculously unnecessary shot. He could have run him through instead. But it humored him.

Only six traitors remained now, which Benoit and Jules could easily handle on their own. With a sword in one hand and a gun in the other, Fentienne pivoted toward the dais just as Lucien shot a pistol of his own. Fentienne didn't move out of the trajectory fast enough and growled when the bullet lodged into his upper bicep.

Cold fire ignited down his arm and across his chest in bleating pain. Dizziness slammed into his head and lurched his stomach. Paralysis numbed down his bicep, forearm, to his fingers almost immediately. The pistol released from his grip and fell to the bone dust at his feet.

"A silver bullet, Your Highness," Lucien crooned. "Moon poison."

His cousin stepped down from the dais with the grace of an overconfident man. Breath heaved from Fentienne's chest in large gulps of air through clenched teeth. Clammy sweat beaded on his forehead and flushed across his body. The pain was excruciating. He managed to remain upright while gripping the saber in his other hand. But he pretended like he couldn't move his sword arm, as if his muscles were locked up, earning a satisfied smirk from his cousin.

Fentienne wanted to lift a goading smile of his own.

Most civilians fell for acts of perfidy, especially when an enemy feigned being injured or incapacitated. A common *ruse de guerre*—ruse of war. And just like Fentienne didn't give a shit about polite society, he didn't give a shit about the ethics of fighting dirty.

Fentienne studied Lucien's pistol. He couldn't tell if it was a single or double barrel. Did he have another silver bullet? If he warned his two alphas, would Lucien panic and shoot? Behind him, Jules and Benoit continued to fight the pack dogs. But it sounded like they were down to the last two traitors.

"I had saved this bullet to publicly execute the Beast of Gabaston, but why wait?" His cousin tossed his pistol to the ground and paused before him, softly laughing.

A single barrel, then.

"The reincarnated son of the Dark Saint." Lucien licked his bottom lip in a wolfish grin. Lifting his hands to Fentienne's face, he whispered, "Addien Wyndham says your monstrous soul belongs to her. But your magic, crown, and throne belong to me, Beast."

Runic fell from his cousin's tongue and Fentienne seized up. Blistering heat buzzed in his head. His wolf was tearing up the ground, drool frothing at his mouth in a rabid, snapping growl. The feeling of thousands of needles pricked at Fentienne's flushing skin. A violent tremor began in his muscles. But he was too enraged to be swallowed whole. Gritting his teeth, he pushed past the pain.

He refused to let another use him for their hate.

With the little strength he had left, Fentienne shoved away in a growl and lunged. The sword pierced through Lucien's chest. The man's eyes rounded, followed by a gurgling, wet cough. Blood dripped from his mouth. Fentienne wanted to do a verbal victory dance and inflict more pain as that démon killer took his final breaths. But his legs gave out. Releasing his grip on the sword, Fentienne collapsed to the ground in a grimace of pain.

Benoit rushed to him, eyes wide.

"Get. Alain," Fentienne said to Benoit with clacking teeth. His body was starting to convulse. He could have asked Jules, but Benoit was a clan alpha of Goldfang, like Fentienne, like Alain. "Jules!" he shouted when Benoit left his side.

"Wolf Prince?" Jules fell to his knees and touched the bullet wound on Fentienne's arm.

"S-s-silver."

Fury thundered across the alpha's face. Jules unsheathed a dagger at his belt. "This is going to hurt."

Fentienne gave a quick nod.

Not wasting a single second, Jules tore his sleeve then split the skin around the bullet wound to open up the flesh. Fentienne sucked in a sharp breath, his face contorting in pain. Jules pressed Fentienne's arm down. His gaze flicked to Fentienne's for half a heartbeat in a silent apology, then he dug a claw-tipped finger into his flesh around the bullet hole. Fentienne screamed through clenched teeth. Every nerve was on fire.

"Got it." Jules scooped the bullet out of his arm and tossed it to the ground.

Scooting on his knees to a nearby corpse, he ripped a stretch of linen from a lesser démon's shirt, then returned and pressed it to Fentienne's weeping wound. His chest continued to heave for breath; his skin was burning up.

"Focus all your magic on healing."

Fentienne faintly nodded his head and closed his eyes. The panicked tone of Jules's voice told him everything he needed to know: he was dying. The silver bullet was removed, but the poison was in his bloodstream. Another tremor convulsed down his body.

He didn't know what to do. He never did figure out how he healed himself before. It just happened. Moon rock poisoning disabled a démon's ability to heal too. In a few minutes, he would be completely moon-addled. He would become the wolf slain on the dais as a sacrifice to paint his brothers' faces in his blood.

"T-t-tell Rhoslyn that I love her."

"You will tell her, prince," Jules said softly. "Think of your mate and draw strength from your bond."

Rhoslyn . . . the simplest sound of her name in his thoughts filled him with incomparable bliss. Her girlish laughter, the songs she hummed under her breath, her sharp wit and sharp tongue. Her fearlessness and empathy.

"You carry many battle scars, milord. And many wounds still bleed. Perhaps all you needed was a kind hand to stitch you up and a heart who asked for nothing else in return other than your happy recovery."

The ballroom disappeared in his mind and a forest drenched in moonlight faded into focus. He was laying atop the furs and pillows, beneath Rhoslyn, his hands possessively on her hips.

"Fentienne . . ." she whispered his name across his shoulder, where the injury she had stitched up was in reality. "I desire to kiss every scar on your body. But I ache to kiss the scars on your heart." Her lips pressed to his skin as her fingers trailed down his arm. "Let me comfort your pain."

Rhoslyn disappeared and Matthieu's tear-stained face warbled into view.

"Now you have family, mon frère. Now you have something to lose and you're sorry because you care so much it hurts."

"You are not a curse, little wolf," Dalbréath softly spoke and the words thundered through him. "I understand what has been done to you and why. And I know it takes a man who cares to the point of pain to break generational cycles of trauma and abuse. A man like you."

Fentienne could feel hot tears on his cheeks. The fingers of his uninjured arm clawed into the dirt. Jules applied more pressure to his wound. Cold fire continued to spread across his body in waves of unbearable pain.

No.

This was not how his life would end.

"Non, we have a future together. We are curse breakers now, no? One no longer exists in this chateau, Fentienne, because we took back control and began healing pieces of our grief. And we will break them all, you and I. Nobody owns us, especially her."

Gritting his teeth, he pushed back against the moon rock's poison. For over a year, the silver moon had owned his body. His moon-addling wolf fought to own his mind too.

Nobody owned him.

Not the moon. Not Addien. Not the ghost of his father.

They would not win.

Fentienne reached into the rot hollowing out his chest. All the hate, the shame, the guilt. All the fear and heartache. He couldn't undo twenty-two years of pain and trauma and indoctrination in a matter of weeks. But he could start to forgive himself.

The ignorance of not knowing how to behave better, he could forgive.

Following military orders he had zero control over, he could forgive.

Believing, since a child, that the only way he could protect his brother was by becoming his bully, he could also forgive.

If others chose not to forgive him, he would understand. He would never be a good man. Not ten years from now. Not a hundred years from now. But he was *not* his father. He would *never* be his father, grandfather, or great-grandfather. And he was so godsdamn tired of carrying the weight of their sins on his shoulders.

Tremors quaked down his arms, torso, and legs. But not convulsions from silver poisoning. The thunder of a hundred paws tearing up the forest floor pounded in his chest. They raced through the shallows of a moon-dusted river. Leapt over mossy rocks and mushroom dotted logs. In a meadow made of starlit wildflowers, they slowed to a gentle lope. His wolf jumped onto a rock and howled at the moon, a plea to Saint Arianrhod, goddess of the moon and companion to wolves. Another wolf joined in. A wild heartbeat later, all the wolves were praying to their moon goddess.

"Prince of Démons," a willowy voice answered. Beneath the trees, a woman emerged in a shift made of silver silk. Long white hair decorated in glowing lunar moths cascaded in soft waves to her waist and fluttered in the cool, night breeze. She approached him where he lay, where his wolf had left him in the meadow. Her pale skin glimmered in the midnight forest around them. "It is not your time, son of Cernunnos."

Arianrhod knelt beside Fentienne and touched the bullet wound on his arm. Glittering light traveled from her fingers to his skin, illuminating the poison in his veins. Then, as if spooling thread, she pulled the metal from his body and wrapped it around her index and middle fingers, tucking the hair-thin silver into a pocket on her shift when finished.

"You are healed, my prince."

"Thank you," Fentienne whispered in reply, too bewildered to think of anything else to say.

Her gray eyes caressed the planes of his face. "Your dark beauty is beguiling. No wonder the stars desire to share their sky with you."

A shy smile warmed his face. "I am honored, goddess, but my heart belongs to another night sky."

"Yes, and her heart belongs to yours." A wrinkle formed between her delicate brows. "Find her prince. She walks a line between the mortal plane and the Otherworld. The stars share she is to fight her Gemini." Bending down, she kissed Fentienne's cheek and whispered, "Wake up, King of Ealdspell."

Fentienne's eyes flew open.

"Wolf Prince?" Jules said, leaning over him, his gaze furiously searching Fentienne's face. "Nine Saints, you were glowing..." he breathed.

"Saint Arianrhod healed me." Fentienne pushed up to a seat and drew in a steady breath. "My wolf brought me to her." Lucien's body was near him and Fentienne swallowed back the fury. "I need to find Rhoslyn. But dispose of that silver bullet."

"*Oui*, will do so immediately." Jules scanned the hall of thrones. "I will assign a body removal and clean-up crew too."

"Do not let the traitors be buried with honor. Lucien, however, needs to be brought to Palais d'Aurélie after the strike. Alain, too, if he doesn't survive Benoit." Fentienne climbed to his feet and grabbed his pistol. He started to pivot toward the doorway and stopped. "Monsieur Aris," Fentienne said, grabbing Jules by the forearm. "*Merci beaucoup*. I would not have survived if you were not here."

Jules grabbed his forearm in return and bowed his head. "It is my honor, rightful King of Aurelienne."

Fentienne drew in a quick breath and let go of Jules.

It was the first time those words felt right.

Fentienne glanced at Lucien's body one last time before turning toward the corridors. By morning, if all went according to plan, he would be the king.

Chapter 38

Fentienne

Fentienne jogged from the hall of thrones into the main catacomb corridor. Shadow sprinting was still unsafe until he could ensure a full sweep of the dugouts for any hidden mutinous dogs. His duster, hat, and frock coat were still atop a marble coffin. After quickly dressing, he continued jogging until he left the catacombs and was angling through the thick crowd of males in Le Rêve Rouge.

"Milord," Benoit whispered, sidling up next to him, knowing Fentienne's sensitive ears would hear him. "Alain is in custody and in transit back to the catacombs to a gibbet cage."

Fentienne replied with a curt nod, his heart in his throat. He had nearly forgotten his cousin in his mad dash to leave Le Rêve Rouge. Only Rhoslyn owned his thoughts right now.

"Cheated death once more today, I see," Benoit murmured in blasé arrogance. "Lucky dog—"

"I need to find Rhoslyn!" Fentienne barked, clenching his jaw until his teeth ached.

Gods, what if he were too late? The escalating panic was tripping his pulse and he had to control himself from ripping through the room, regardless of the carnage.

The night air slammed into Fentienne when they finally exited, his senses overwhelmed by the varied scents around him and carried on the breeze. Thin smoke clouded the street from the muskets and cannons at the strike line. There were clumps of bedraggled people everywhere he looked. He didn't linger long, however, and broke into a run toward the execution blocks. If she wasn't there, he would move toward the fight.

He wove through people in various states of drunkenness and revelry. Half-shifted lesser démons turned their heads toward him as he passed by. Were they a threat? Skies, he would tear their heads off if any of them tried to attack him right now.

A light breeze skipped over him and he slid to a stop. Her scent—a biting summer thunderstorm. His eyes rolled to the back of his head in ecstasy as his entire body came alive. How he craved her. She was a drug to his system.

His wife. His mate.

His, his, *his*. Only his.

Territorial aggression flexed down his muscles. His chest rose and fell furiously, forming puffs of air in front of his face. Where was she? Fentienne marched toward the swelling crowd by the jailhouse and guillotine, his wolf becoming more addled as her scent grew stronger.

Headless démons rotted above the blocks on gibbet cages and he curled his fists at the sight. When he found Addien, he would—

"The rumors you heard were not true!"

Fentienne turned toward Rhoslyn's voice, but he couldn't see her.

"*Non*, I did not kill the Beast of Gabaston! I was attacked by a démon for supporting Prince Fentienne Beausoleil. And if you support him instead of Le Duc Lucien Chalamet, the démons will come for you too!"

"Monks of Glanis! Guards! This is *not* the Queen of The Row but a rune shifter."

Cries of panic roared around him. He didn't need to see to know that two Rhoslyns now stood before masses.

"Factory Row, do not listen to this likeness of me," she shouted. "This impostor is who glamoured our people into the Beast of Gabaston!"

Fentienne sprang toward Rhoslyn's voice when a body collided into his.

"No," Lucas growled in his face. "Do *not* distract her."

"Move!"

Lucas shoved him back. "She has a plan."

Fentienne got within inches of Lucas's face. "The bloodlust is still raging in me, Lucas. I will hurt you."

"Hurt me, but I will not let you hurt her." Lucas's eyes flashed. "And seeing you could be a fatal distraction. You want that on your conscience?"

The wind knocked from his lungs. Fear's grip on his pulse tightened.

What if he didn't step in and she died?

"Trust me," Lucas urged.

Rhoslyn's voice cut through the street noise once more. "You frame me?" She laughed, a mirthless sound. "With what magic could I glamour elves into beasts?"

"Your well of shadow magic isn't endless, rune shifter. Convince Factory Row all you like to fear démons, it will not take much. We have feared them our entire lives. But only one of us will remain in my likeness by tomorrow morning."

That was his Rhoslyn. Fentienne couldn't help the pride warming his chest.

"Regardless of who sits on the throne, Factory Row will need these démons to return to their jobs when the strike ends," she continued, "Aurelienne's economy depends on every abled body too much."

Lucas gently squeezed his arm. "Your mate is on a warpath, to protect you. Trust that she knows her enemy *and* how to win the hearts of your people."

"If she dies, Lucas," he said, biting back a detonating gust of emotions, "I will destroy this entire gods forsaken kingdom."

A corner of his beta's mouth lifted. "I would expect no less of you, Wolf Prince."

Drops of calm washed away the sharp edges of his rabid aggression and he drew in a deep breath. Lucas was siphoning off some of his moon-addled energy. They held each other's dominating gazes. Normally he would assert himself until Lucas, or another démon, submitted. But Fentienne blinked and leaned his forehead on Lucas's shoulder, his chest a sudden twisted knot of grief.

"I thought I lost you today, *mon ami*."

A pair of arms wrapped around his shoulders as Lucas pulled him in tight. "I'm not going anywhere, brother. I'm a flea on your hide. *Oui*, you will wish to chop off my head yourself soon enough."

Fentienne softly laughed. "Probably."

They pulled back and Lucas studied his face, his lips twisting humorously. "I think I liked you better half-shifted."

"Arsehole."

His friend's face grew serious. "Dalbréath is guarding her right now so I could intercept you. Smelled you a mile away, brother."

"I want to see her from the crowd."

"Will you go rabid?"

"No promises." Fentienne slid his gaze to Benoit who watched their exchange with a haughty arch of his brow. "I give you permission to help hold me back or to do whatever is necessary to subdue me."

"Tempting," Benoit said with a devilish smile. "To dominate my Wolf Prince before so many witnesses..."

Fentienne bared his teeth in warning. "Act in revenge, Faivre, and you will not survive this night, no matter how much you defended me this day."

Benoit patted his cheek. "Always so serious. Let us have fun, no?"

Lucas stepped in front of Fentienne and glared at Benoit. "First, I think I prefer you in all your frippery. Second, do not be an arse. This isn't helping."

"I do believe the show is beginning." Benoit winked at Fentienne and gestured with his head to follow.

His wolf wanted to snap at Benoit's throat and force him into submission. Instead, to not draw too much attention their way, Fentienne moved through the crowd behind Benoit, Lucas at his back.

"Monks of Glanis," Rhoslyn called out. "Are there protocols to determine magic users?"

His heart stopped.

"Fayette," an older monk from the crowd replied in answer. "Cuffs made of cold iron burns the flesh of faeries to punish and block their unnatural magic."

"I am part Dúnælven," Addien replied as Rhoslyn. "Cold iron would affect me as well as you."

Fentienne's entire body stiffened and his head snapped toward her voice. *Gods...*

Both Rhoslyns stood before the other beneath flickering lantern light in only a corset and petticoat, the cream-colored fabrics splattered in blood. More blood stained one hand and arm with streaks across their faces.

Holy hell, he couldn't keep the moan from escaping his mouth. She was breathtaking. His warrior queen. Forget the imagery of her on the merry-go-around. This glorious vision would keep him up at night... *forever.*

His wolf began growling, a low threatening guttural growl. Heat buzzed down his limbs and blushed in his veins. Every male here could also see his wife in only her underpinnings.

Lucas grabbed his arm. "Control yourself."

"She is undressed," he hissed.

"*Oui*," Lucas said with a roll of his eyes. "And there is nothing you can do about it, so tell your wolf to shut its trap."

"Do you want to sentence us both to death for possessing magic?" Addien asked Rhoslyn.

"Monks of Glanis," Rhoslyn called out. "Every elf in Factory Row would react to cold iron, even if they do not manifest magic, *oui*?"

"As the gods ordained," a monk replied. "But magic is forbidden—"

"Magic," Rhoslyn said, cutting off the monk, "is the very reason your springs are holy. How do you think Saint Glanis blesses the waters?"

The people murmured around him in agreement.

Skies, he loved his wife's intelligence.

"Do not desecrate the magic of the gods by comparing the lowly, evil magic of elves and démons to theirs!" a monk rebuked.

"Then let us ask the saints to show Gabaston the real Rhoslyn Gautier Beausoleil in an act of faith."

His mouth fell open. She used his name publicly. The heady rush of pleasure fevering his pulse this moment . . .

"Do not swoon," Benoit said beside him. "You already embarrassed yourself twice today."

Lucas grabbed Fentienne before he could react.

Addien laughed. "If we both respond to cold iron, that tells the monks nothing."

"Not immediately, perhaps." Rhoslyn tilted her head. "But that is only one part of the test of faith I suggest."

Fentienne's brows creased.

Why hadn't Addien winked away to safety by now?

There was no reason for her to keep up this ruse so long unless . . . she didn't have enough magic to teleport. He didn't understand elven magic, but shadow sprinting required a large amount of their wolf's energy stores. Far more than shifting. And after being in cold iron earlier today and glamouring at least two elves, she had to be dangerously close to depletion. Addien had clearly banked on Rhoslyn staying close to the strike line, otherwise she wouldn't have risked being discovered by either her or Dalbréath while sowing seeds of dissention to keep the wolf cleansing alive and well.

Movement beside Rhoslyn caught his attention—an elf in Dúnælven leathers with white hair. Dalbréath locked eyes with him and shook his head. Warnings shot down Fentienne and he stilled, the stillness of a predator before an attack. What was Rhoslyn about to do that Dalbréath needed to tell Fentienne to not react? He didn't have to wait long.

"Rune shifter," Rhoslyn said, lifting her chin, "I challenge you to a duel. The one who survives is the real Rhoslyn Gautier Beausoleil."

The crowd erupted into gasps and began talking furiously amongst each other.

"Clever creature," Fentienne murmured nervously under his breath, unable to hold back a tiny smile.

A spark of fear widened Addien's eyes for half a heartbeat. "Duels are illegal in Aurelienne, no?"

"Shadow magic is punishable by death," Rhoslyn countered. "But if the Monks of Glanis execute the real Rhoslyn Gautier Beausoleil, Factory Row will execute them in the same manner they have executed démons. The same to any guard who interferes."

The crowd roared in support and his Rhoslyn grinned. She not only cornered Addien, but the Monks of Glanis and the guards too. Gods, he was unraveling before her beauty and ferocity.

"To protect the monks, the saints will protect the Queen of The Row," Rhoslyn continued. "And to prove magic isn't involved in our duel, we will both wear cuffs made of cold iron."

The crowd lifted fists in the air and cried out their support.

A monk emerged from the crowd and settled between Addien and Rhoslyn, a cuff in each long-nailed hand taken from the guards. Rhoslyn stretched out her arm and offered up her wrist. The man lifted a sharp-toothed smile at his wife, his eyes trailing over her bare skin.

Fentienne saw red. With a growl, he launched toward Rhoslyn. His wolf was snarling, its hackles raised. But hands grabbed him and jerked him back before he could get far.

"Don't ruin her plan," Lucas growled in his face.

Fentienne's chest heaved and he blinked back the fury. "I will kill him."

"*Oui*, they should all die for what they've done," Lucas agreed. "But not *this* moment."

The monk fastened the cuff onto Rhoslyn's wrist and she hissed, her face twisting in agony. Lucas and Benoit held him in place. Rage pumped hot in his veins. The people around him began cheering, but all he could hear were the war drums in his ears.

Turning to Addien, the monk waited for her wrist.

"If you do not agree to the duel," the monk told her, a wicked grin stretching his face, "we will declare you the rune shifter and execute you immediately."

She blanched but held out her wrist. Her eyes locked onto Rhoslyn's and narrowed to slits. Bile coated Fentienne's throat. Addien was going to die either way, but she planned to take Rhoslyn down with her and the rising panic in his bloodstream spiked. The cuff clicked into place and Addien sucked in a sharp breath and tensed.

"Pistols!" the monk called out.

"Benoit," Fentienne said through clenched teeth, "Bring her my pistol. I have one bullet left. The Rhoslyn on the left."

Lucas agreed with a curt nod.

Fentienne handed Benoit his gun and swallowed thickly.

"I offer up mine!" Benoit shouted and pushed through the crowd. People parted and allowed him through. "For you, madame," he said with a small bow. "It is an honor for the Queen of The Row to use my pistol."

"*Merci*," Rhoslyn said.

She tried to smile but it was clear she was in pain and Fentienne dragged in a hot, angry breath. But he forced himself to remain planted and out of Rhoslyn's line of sight despite the night's shadows.

A guard inspected the pistol, then handed it to her with an approving nod at the monk. Benoit moved to the sidelines as a different guard inspected a pistol offered up to Addien, who accepted the weapon with equal parts mounting fury and terror.

"Any last words?" the guard first asked Addien.

"Fentienne Beausoleil is a monster! A cursed, ugly man from a long line of violent cursed men. He destroyed Factory Row in the last attacks. He will only continue to destroy Aurelienne if you allow the Prince of Démons to ascend to the golden throne. Release his soul to the Underworld where it belongs!"

Factory Row burst into angry shouts.

The guard looked to Rhoslyn.

"Fentienne Beausoleil," she yelled at the top of her lungs, "is a curse breaker! He is a warrior king who would go without bread if it meant you ate. He would protect your freedoms with his very life. Do not listen to her bitter lies meant to push Aurelienne back into war. My husband, my mate is the most beautiful, intelligent, selfless man I have ever known."

Rhoslyn kissed his identification tags and his heart shattered into a million glittering pieces of joy.

She fought for him, like she had promised.

She defended him before his birthright, to protect his people.

She was willing to take in pain so he may know light.

Gods, this tiny girl was more fearsome than any platoon he had commanded.

"Backs together," a guard instructed over the undulating crowd. "At a count of ten paces. And . . . one, two, three, four . . ."

Fentienne's hands curled and uncurled.

He wasn't sure he was breathing anymore.

"Five, six, seven . . ."

Addien's eyes flicked to his down her shoulder. She knew he was here the whole time. The world stopped for a single second. Factory Row melted away to the forests outside of Myrefell. He was sixteen again and she was the peasant girl in the woods who stole his heart.

"*Say it, Fentienne,*" *she whispered.* "*I want to hear your promise to me.*"
"*I promise, Fayette.*"

"Eight, nine, ten . . . fire!"

They spun on their heels, guns raised. But right before they fired, Addien shifted into his likeness and grinned at Rhoslyn.

Cries of alarm rippled through the crowd.

His wife's hand jerked in surprise right as she pulled the trigger.

Addien screamed and he looked away from Rhoslyn. The vision of him melted away to reveal her true form and . . . she was on fire. Fire haloed in green. Factory Row bolted away from her. But Fentienne . . . he started laughing darkly under his breath.

How many lifetimes had she tormented him and Maeline?

How many lifetimes had they died young because of Addien's jealousy?

The fire consumed her within seconds until she was nothing more than glittering ash on the wind. Gods, he was free. Finally, truly free. The queen of faerie tricks was tricked by the one she tried to destroy. And it was clear she didn't know the Underworld's fires were part of her curse should she attempt to kill with her own hands. Addien would have chosen the monk's offer of execution by guillotine to ensure her soul could be reborn.

Skies, Addien Wyndham no longer existed.

She could never harm him or Rhoslyn again—

Goosebumps raced down his body in the sudden quiet.

Benoit's shout for help yanked him back to Rhoslyn. Dalbréath was running to where his wife once stood.

She was no longer standing.

A growl ripped from his chest and he tore from Lucas's hold and through the crowd, pushing people over and shoving them down.

His wife.

His mate.

She was lying in a small pool of blood. Pain cracked down his chest. Fentienne fell to his knees at her side and inspected the bullet wound on her upper chest by her bare shoulder. Whispering scraped in his ears. The gathering was pressing in to get a glimpse of their queen.

Rhoslyn's head rolled toward him and blinked up at his face.

"I love you," she said in a soft whisper, her eyes fluttering shut. "Take care of Matthieu."

"Rhoslyn, stay with me," he choked out. Skies, she was so pale. A sheen of cold sweat dewed her face. Peering over his shoulder at a guard, he snarled, "Get the godsdamn cuff off her wrist!"

A young man offered Fentienne the keys, wisely not coming closer. Fingers shaking with rage, Fentienne unlocked the cuff and sucked in a furious breath at the burn marks on her skin.

Dalbréath's face tightened with anger. A muscle pulsed along his jaw as a single tear slid down his cheek. The elf wanted to reach for his niece but didn't touch her. The alpha elf knew Fentienne would kill him or any other male who dared touch his mate right now. He wanted to scream at Dalbréath for allowing Rhoslyn to challenge Addien to a duel. But he knew his wife's defiance. She would do whatever she wanted, with or without anyone's blessing—just like him.

"Fentienne . . ." she whispered.

Her body went limp. But her chest was rising and falling in quick, shallow breaths.

"Get Claudette Aris," Fentienne shouted. "Tell her to go to the apartments above Benoit Faivre's office with surgical equipment."

Amélie, who was now standing beside Lucas, sobbing, said, "I will go."

"I will get Gellynor Death Talker," Dalbréath said on a ragged breath. "She's a healer."

"Lucas," Fentienne barked. "Stay with Dalbréath to lead him and Gellynor to Benoit's."

Without waiting for a reply, he scooped up his wife into his arms. "You are so reckless, my darling," he whispered against her cheek with a kiss. "Brilliant, fearless, but reckless." Then he was partially shadow sprinting through the crowd, Benoit right behind him, careful to not bump into anyone and further harm his mate.

Minutes later, he was in the same guest suite he awoke in earlier.

"I need a sharp knife," he barked at the servants.

One was brought to him immediately. Fentienne held it over a candle's flame on both sides for several seconds to sanitize the small dagger. Only an hour earlier, he was in the very same position. Servants placed tea towels and whiskey next to him at Benoit's orders.

In automatic motions, from years of tending to injured soldiers on battlefields, Fentienne slit her skin around the bullet hole. He would use a clawed-tip finger to pull out the bullet like Jules had him, but Fentienne didn't know how to shift at will. Instead, he used the tip of the dagger to dig beneath the lead.

Rhoslyn recoiled from the pain, hissing through her teeth. He quickly removed the dagger.

"Hold her down," he said to Benoit.

"Will you kill me for touching your mate?"

Fentienne ground his teeth together. His wolf growled and snapped. But his wolf, like usual, acted on primal instinct, not logic.

"No."

Benoit climbed over the bed and braced Rhoslyn's arms, placing a knee on her legs to keep her from bucking. A greenish pallor painted his skin and he swallowed. The alpha was afraid of Fentienne, he realized. It was the same sickened look on Benoit's face before slicing his hand open to swear his truth and silence this morning. Not because he had anything to hide, but because he knew he was entirely at Fentienne's mercy in a situation he couldn't control in some way.

Benoit gave him a quick nod and Fentienne returned the dagger point to her wound. Rhoslyn writhed in agony, crying out. The tip of the blade touched the lead. Relief flooded him. It wasn't buried deep and had missed her collarbone. Gently he dug the bullet out. Without skipping a beat, he grabbed the whiskey and poured it over the opening and she screamed.

Benoit scrambled off the bed and gave him space, sensing Fentienne's territorial side kicking back up. Grabbing the cloths, he put pressure to the wound. The burns on her wrist needed to be treated too. In a matter of minutes, the cold iron had blistered her skin to the point of bleeding. And where was her wedding band? Had that fiend stolen it? Anger shuddered through him. Fentienne forced his gaze back to her face before he went on a rampage.

Clammy sweat continued to bead on her paling skin. Still, her beauty struck him anew—the elegant sweep of her cheeks and fine arch of her brows, the faint dusting of freckles across her nose, the full shape of her lips.

With his free hand, he tucked hair behind her pointed ear then softly stroked her cheek.

"You will live, my darling," he whispered.

Fentienne leaned down and gently kissed her lips with his.

By the time Claudette arrived, the bleeding had stopped. But the fear, the anger, the pure exhaustion of this day continued to internally bleed inside of him. Vaguely aware of the world spinning around him, Fentienne moved to the other side of the bed and held his wife while the Madame of *Le Rêve Rouge* stitched up the open wound. If anyone spoke to him, he didn't know or care. He didn't know how much time had passed either. At some point, he realized that Claudette had left, Benoit too. It was just him and Rhoslyn in a candlelit room on Factory Row.

Fentienne lifted his ear and stilled. Something was happening.

A second later a cheer erupted outside, followed by banging pots.

The strike must be over.

"Your first battle ends in victory, Queen of The Row," he whispered to her. A bittersweet smile touched his lips. Rhoslyn should have been able to see this and celebrate in the streets. He blinked and pressed his face to the side of hers, his arm wrapped around her middle.

A knock on the door sounded and Fentienne gritted his teeth. Not waiting for his reply, the door opened and he turned to peer over his shoulder and froze.

No.

His mind had to be slipping from exhaustion.

Or he was dreaming.

Because this wasn't real. This couldn't possibly be real.

"Brother," a deep voice said in the doorway—in Clifstánian. "May I come in?"

Fentienne sat up on the bed and gaped at the image of Florian. "How are you here?"

"Gellynor Death Talker rune walked me here at Gedlen's insistence." Florian stepped inside and shut the door behind him. "The Kingdom of Ealdspell has a new king."

Fentienne climbed off the bed and stood on shaking legs. Gods, his little brother. Florian's hair had grown out. Still shaved on the sides, but he now wore the longer strands in the fashion of Dreglindish warriors—pulled back in a tight ponytail just at the back top of the skull woven with a couple small braids ending in beaded gold clamps. Unlike the military uniform he was accustomed to seeing him in, he wore a belted dark blue tunic edged in intricate silver trim and tan breeches with boots that laced in a crisscross up the calf. But those silver eyes, his brother's Eyes of Ice, held his softly.

Both seemed lost for words.

Fentienne approached him slowly. But Florian didn't wait and, in three long strides, pulled Fentienne into his arms. Fentienne stiffened. He still couldn't believe his little brother was here, in Benoit's apartments, in Factory Row. Nor did he know how to process his brother's open affection. The most powerful man in all Ealdspell—the one he had tormented—pulled him into an embrace. Men in Clifstán didn't embrace or touch with fondness unless lovers and even that was mocked ruthlessly.

But feeling his brother's heartbeat pressed to his spun him back to when he was eight, and Fentienne closed his eyes.

Adalwolf ducked into the house of sticks he and Florian had built and sat on the forest floor. Morning sunlight streamed through the cracks and warmed his face. They needed more moss for the roof. But he liked it in here. The tree limbs hid him from the war.

"You're still here," Florian said while crawling inside, tears in his eyes. He scooted next to Adalwolf and pulled his knees up to his chest. "I thought the soldier took you away."

"Come here." Adalwolf opened his arms and Florian leaned onto his chest. Wrapping his arms around his brother's shoulders, he said, "It is only a couple of years until you join me. Maybe we'll get to do missions together."

"I don't want to be a soldier."

"I know."

A buzz of heat flushed in his head and he clenched his jaw. Adalwolf didn't want to be a soldier either. He wanted to work with horses. But he was afraid if he spent too much time around the stables, Father would make it so he could never ride again. Father hated it when Adalwolf was happy. He hated it even more when Adalwolf refused to make him happy.

He rubbed his brother's shoulder. If Father knew how much Florian made him happy, what would he do? This was why he and his brother snuck away to play deep in the woods. They were each other's secret happiness. One thing he did know, he wouldn't let Father hurt Florian like he hurt him.

"Do you think the roof needs more moss?" Adalwolf asked him.

Florian studied the patchy roof and the gaps in the sticks forming the walls. Then he nodded his head.

They crawled out of their house of sticks. Not too far away, Florian found more fallen tree limbs. Adalwolf squatted by a large log and dug his fingers into the moss to peel it away when he heard the crunch of boots on brittle leaves.

The soldiers found them.

Father would know they were playing together. Father would know Adalwolf was happy.

Jumping to his feet he ran over to his brother and stood in front in him, grabbing his hand from behind.

"I will protect you," he whispered over his shoulder to Florian. *"Always."*

Fentienne wrapped his arms around Florian as the memory faded and held him tight.

"My cruelty," he whispered into his brother's ear. "I—"

"I forgive you," Florian whispered back, cutting him off. "We have both lost so much. Let us not dwell on the past."

"Skies, Florian, I was a monster!" he snapped. "How in the hell can you forgive me and move on in one breath?"

"Because I always knew there was goodness in one of my brothers." Florian pulled back and grabbed Fentienne's face and pressed his forehead to his. "I always knew that brother was you."

Fentienne couldn't stop the angry tears from falling. "The hateful things I did to you—"

"Yes," Florian said cutting, him off again.

He wasn't used to his meek, submissive brother being so dominant and commanding and it stunned Fentienne into silence. But this twenty-year-old man was an emperor. He ruled kings.

"Adalwolf Fentienne, third-born," Florian continued, "I saw your struggle in your cruelty. The remorse and shame in your eyes too. Father hated goodness. He hated any form of power he couldn't possess." Florian paused a beat. "He killed his own brother for a throne. How could he understand love between brothers? Our bond was a power he couldn't possess."

Fentienne's breath shook with tears. "I saw you die. I have seen you die every night in my sleep since the Battle of the Black Winds and I hated myself for doing nothing. I stood there, Florian. I stood and watched Aeldfrith pull the trigger and did *nothing* to stop him."

"The Lady would not have let you intervene, even if you tried."

"That's not the point. I promised to protect you," Fentienne said between clenched teeth. "I promised and failed you for fourteen years."

Florian kissed his forehead and stood back. "You did protect me. Do not think I didn't notice how you stepped in often to hurt me less than our brothers or father." Their eyes locked. "I *forgive you.*"

Fentienne's chest tightened. How Florian, Rhoslyn, and Matthieu could so easily forgive was a concept he didn't know how to understand. But he nodded his head in gratitude, unsure of how else to respond.

His brother's gaze slipped over to the bed. "This is Princess Maeline Wyndham?"

"Yes, my wife."

"I know little of her but the streets sing her praises." Florian's gaze flitted back to his. "A warrior queen for my warrior king brother. She and Eirwen would get along well."

The sound of Eirwen's name made him flinch. "How . . . is the queen?"

"She is with child." Florian grinned. "By summer's end, I will be a father."

A father?

The blood drained from Fentienne's head. How he loathed that word.

His brother softly laughed at the horror Fentienne couldn't conceal from his face. Gods, who was this man? Florian was affectionate, smiling, no longer terrified of him . . . this was the brother he remembered before Fentienne's life shattered at the house of sticks. The brother who was his secret happiness.

And Florian was happy again.

All he had ever wanted was for his little brother to be happy and safe.

"Gedlen is in the main parlor," Florian said in Aurelienne, "when you are ready to leave your wife's side . . . Your Majesty." A kind smile tipped up the corners of his brother's mouth as he bowed his head. They held each other's eyes for several swelling beats of Fentienne's thundering pulse, then Florian quietly departed, shutting the door behind him.

Fentienne wiped at the tears on his face and blew out a slow breath.

The persistent ache in his chest, the thorns piercing each angry beat of his heart had eased. He could finally breathe.

His wife was safe.

His brother was happy.

Outside, people continued to bang pots and pans and sing songs of victory. He walked to the window and soaked in the happiness. But this moment should be shared with Rhoslyn.

Gently, he cradled his wife to his chest and brought her to the window, resting his cheek on her head. "Do you hear the people, my darling? They dance this night because a fearless, reckless, brave, stubborn girl from Factory Row fought to protect them." He kissed her forehead. "While also fighting for a monster and her brother." A ghost of a smile touched his lips. "Do you ever back down from a fight, Queen of The Row?"

Gods, he hoped not.

Aurelienne was gashed deep with wounds from a war spanning three generations to possess a crown. One he would break. A split crown for a people who starved for representation. He was a king who had fought beside commoners all his life. He was the Prince of Démons, his beta a peasant. The girl in his arms was a faerie queen who was raised in the Factory slums.

An elf.

A creature.

And he was so in love with her his heart ached.

Fentienne returned to their bed, pulled back the covers, and lowered Rhoslyn to the pillows and mattress. Gedlen waited for him in the main parlor, but he could wait until tomorrow. Tonight, he just wanted to hold his wife, his mate. Skies, she took a bullet for him. He wasn't leaving her side.

Fentienne removed his waistcoat, then pulled his linen shirt over his head.

The scent of a summer storm mixed with moss and ferns surrounded him as he crawled into bed beside her. He buried his face against her uninjured shoulder and circled an arm around her waist. "We have a future together, Rhoslyn Beausoleil" he whispered. "We are curse breakers now."

And, in the morning, he would stand before the rising sun a whole man.

A king who was uncursed.

Chapter 39

Rhoslyn

A sharp ache throbbed in Rhoslyn's shoulder. Her eyes fluttered open on a grimace. For a moment, that was all she could think of, not the strange room she was in or the arm wrapped around her middle.

Then the room slowly faded into focus. Pastel blue walls painted in peach, pink, and ivory floral designs and decorated in gold filigree. Gold crown molding in a scroll leaf design framed in the large, airy space. Was she at the chateau? After weeks in black furnishings, the opulence of this room was overwhelming.

The arm around her waist pulled her in tighter.

Slowly rolling her head toward the source, she hissed in a quiet breath. A shirtless man was sleeping next to her. Morning light from a nearby window wreathed his skin in soft pinks and golds. She knew it was Fentienne without looking at his face and her heart sang. Were they in another dream? That would explain the room.

Rhoslyn turned her head a little more, gritting her teeth at the sharp pain. But she had to see him. Dark hair, reflecting faint gold highlights in the sunrise, spilled in a mess over the pillow next to her. He was laying on his side, his arm cradling her to him. His nose and mouth pressed to the shoulder that didn't hurt. But he wasn't in his half-shifted form. This was definitely a dream.

She didn't remember being in pain in any of the other dreams, though.

Before she could say his name, his eyes opened, as if aware another were watching him. For a few seconds, they simply held each other's gaze. There was no rush to speak or move, only a desire to savor. Saints, she would never tire being the object of worship in those honeyed amber eyes of his.

"Are you somewhere safe?" she finally asked. "If you say you are sleeping in a prison, I will wake this instant and demand your release."

Fentienne adjusted his head on the pillow so she could see him fully. The barest hint of humor brushed his lips. Tucking a strand of hair behind her ear, he murmured, "I am where I never want to leave. The view is breathtaking."

"Oh." Disappointment weighed heavy on her chest. "Never?"

"Never." He softly kissed her shoulder. "Though an impractical desire. Eventually I will have to leave and so will you. An entire realm is waiting on news of their queen."

Then it dawned on her. "You must be at the chateau." Her eyes widened. "Is this strike over? Are you required to attend court at Palais d'Aurélie today?"

"Rhoslyn—"

"Have you seen Matthieu? Is he safe?"

"He's fine, but Rhoslyn—"

"Fentienne, where am I? Do you know? Why does my shoulder hurt in this dream we share? The littlest movement is unbearable . . ."

He pushed up on one arm to lean over her and she lost all thought and reason. The captivating, graceful way the muscles of his arms, chest, and shoulders moved pooled an entire ocean of delicious heat low in her belly. The way his bed tousled strands fell against his jaw too. From the window, rose gold-tinged sunlight illuminated the mercilessly handsome lines of his face and sensual curve of his lips. And never, in all the dreamscapes they had known together, had his darkly elegant beauty been more striking.

"I am unraveling at the sight of you," she whispered.

He softly blinked then lowered his mouth to hers, kissing her sweetly. "My darling . . ." His breath teased her lips. "Seeing you with fully human eyes? Touching you with the bare skin of my fingers? Feeling the lingering taste of your lips on mine? This reality is more beautiful than any dream we shared."

Her body stilled.

This reality . . .

Was he suggesting . . . ?

"You are truly here. Beside me."

"Hmm."

"You broke Queen Eirwen's curse?"

"Hmm."

Rhoslyn's eyes narrowed and a devilish smile edged the corners of his mouth. The arse! She lifted her hand to playfully push him away and sucked in a sharp breath, her face twisting up in pain until the ache eased. "What happened?"

"Bullet wound." Anger darkened his face. "Gods, seeing you in agony kills me."

"Did it work, though?" she asked. "Was her curse triggered?"

"*Oui*," he answered, his voice still tight. "The Underworld consumed her soul the moment she fired."

"Saints," she breathed, her eyes glossing. "We are finally free of her."

He leaned down and softly kissed her again. "You are brilliant, Rhoslyn Beausoleil. Cunning, fearless. But so aggravatingly reckless and foolish."

Rhoslyn sniffed back the tears and rolled her eyes. "You, Fentienne Beausoleil, need to learn the difference between what is truly reckless and when you are irritated because you can't dominate a situation." She paused a beat. "Or dominate me."

"Mmm, you are adorable when feisty."

Her jaw slackened and he grinned, a wicked, sensual smile, right before gently burying his face in her neck on her uninjured side and kissing down her throat. "If I were not shot from dueling—"

"You would be moaning my name right now."

"Divine Mother, you're ridiculous."

But the rough sound of his voice shivered pleasurably across her skin.

"Where is your wedding band?" he asked while sprinkling kisses along her upper chest to her uninjured shoulder. "Gods, I can't stop touching you."

She clenched her fist around the bed linens at the reminder. "Addien severed our blood bond then stole my ring."

Fentienne pulled away, his mouth falling open. "What?!"

"Our love is not a faerie trick, Fentienne, nor has it ever been." She thought her words would comfort him, but the sudden intensity of fury thundering across his face was startling. Before he could interrupt her, she shared the events of yesterday morning with him. Horror rose in his hard stare. When she mentioned Matthieu, his body deflated and he closed his eyes in a long blink.

"I left you and Matthieu unprotected." He inhaled a choked breath and looked toward the window. "We triggered your curse and I left you both—"

"She is gone and you needed to leave." The sunrise painted more of his skin in pinks and golds, highlighting the contours of his tensing muscles. "She deserves no more of our attention, especially in our bed." Lifting her good hand, she pressed her palm to the warmth of his stomach and slid her fingers upward toward his chest, and he shuddered beneath her touch. "It is a new morning." His eyes flicked back to hers. "And you are a whole man, my Sun King."

He caressed her bare ring finger. "We are no longer married?"

"*Non*—"

Cutting her off, his mouth crashed onto hers in a loud, heady growl. And saints, she could drown in his slow, deep, bruising kisses. The poetry his tongue confessed in each sweep of his lips inked onto her soaring pulse.

He was truly free now.

Free to choose her instead of his father and Addien choosing for him.

She pressed her hand to his chest, digging her nails into his skin, making him moan. His heart was beating so wildly. A feverish rhythm that tangled with hers. The tips of his fingers trailed down his identification tags draping across her breasts, down her side, to grip her hip—

A knock on the door loudly echoed in the room. Then a voice.

"*Mon fils*," a woman ordered while walking in, shutting the door behind her. "Her Majesty does not need you panting all over her right now."

Fentienne froze, his chest heaving.

"Get dressed. You have business to attend to with foreign dignitaries."

"They can wait," he snapped with a heated glare his maman's way. "My first morning as—"

"As a king."

"*Oui, your* king." He straightened on the bed, but still hovered by Rhoslyn. "Any other obvious announcement you would like to make before promptly leaving these guest chambers?"

Loriette Chalamet chuckled. "*Petit louveteau*, Gedlen Fate Maker will not wait around all day while you satisfy your mate bond."

Fentienne groaned and rolled to his back, clenching his jaw.

Little cub? Rhoslyn quietly snickered, she couldn't help it. He slid her a playful glare and she spurted a laugh which quickly ended in her tensing up in pain. His fingers curled around hers for the briefest beat of her heart, a gentle squeeze, then he strode from the bed in only linen breeches to a pile of clothes on the floor.

"Where is Adeline?" Fentienne asked, pulling a shirt over his head. "I never asked last night."

The older woman paused on Rhoslyn's side of the bed and dipped into a curtsy. Resplendent in dark blue silks, several pearl necklaces, and a gray periwig fashioned in curls, the former queen took Rhoslyn's breath away. The resemblance between mother and son was remarkable.

Loriette settled her sharp eyes on Fentienne. "Factory Row severed her head shortly after midnight, Your Majesty."

They studied each other for a heavy second, then Fentienne dipped his head and turned around.

The former queen took her in next. "Men," she tsked. "They do not see a problem leaving a female unwashed in blood-soaked undergarments."

"Men," Fentienne snapped back, "were too busy saving Her Majesty's life last night after fighting pack dogs and two traitorous Chalamets in the catacombs."

Loriette opened her fan in a dismissive gesture and peered her way. "Alpha males like him find the most disgusting things arousing. If he could, he would keep you in the blood of his enemies to revel in his dominance." She fluttered the fan in a way that clearly communicated that Fentienne should take his leave.

If Rhoslyn wasn't so horrified at seeing the blood on her corset and petticoat, and remembering why it was there, she would have been humored by how his maman was dominating him.

"He does not counter me, no?" his maman said with a smirk.

"Get. Out," Fentienne barked. But it was obvious it was all bluster.

Loriette fluttered her fan and ignored him. "I will personally see to your preparations, Your Majesty. The king has duties to attend to this morning."

"*Merci*, madame," she said quietly, suddenly feeling sick to her stomach. Loriette arched a brow and, with her eyes, gestured Fentienne's way until Rhoslyn understood. "*Mon deuce puce*," Rhoslyn called out, her voice syrupy, knowing it would piss him off. "Order me a bath and clean clothing."

He strode up to the bed, knotting the cravat around his throat. "My darling, I am not a little bell you can ring whenever you need a male to do your bidding."

The humor glinting in his eyes threatened to make her laugh.

Instead, to play along, Rhoslyn scoffed with a flutter of her hand. "*Oof!* Do not lecture me on male social oppression at the hands of clichéd female entitlement. Your fairer sex should be grateful for the attention and sense of purpose."

"Grateful—"

"Shhh," she interrupted with a pointed arch of her brow. "You are far prettier when silent and obedient."

Fentienne approached her, the wicked slant of his lips trilling in her thrumming pulse. He leaned down and softly kissed her lips. "A bath, clothing, verbal foreplay to pleasure you until my duties are finished?" he whispered. "I can deny you nothing, my queen." Warm honey drizzled down her body with his declaration. One made with an unspoken promise of how they would exchange vows later.

Her husband straightened and turned toward the former queen. "*Merci,* Mother," he said, taking her hand in his. The gesture startled Loriette and she narrowed her eyes at him. "I know who you are, who I am, and how the Brotherhood and aristocracy betrayed you. I know you were the first Queen of The Row."

Loriette blinked back tears and replied with a curt nod.

"I know it was you in the woods the night Addien tricked me." Fentienne kissed her on the cheek and his maman's face crumpled in tender heartbreak at her son's unexpected affection. "And Loring . . ." he continued, struggling against his own rising emotion. "He kept me sane and happy and saw me through some of the darkest days of my life."

"I love my sons," she said, a tear falling down her cheek. A slight smile trembled on her lips. Then, clearing her throat, she straightened and lightly smacked Fentienne on the upper arm with her folded fan. "No more stalling, *petit louveteau.* Shoo."

Fentienne rolled his eyes and moved away from the bed, shrugging on his frock coat. Before disappearing out the door, he slid Rhoslyn one last lingering glance.

Saints, how that infuriating man fevered her pulse to distraction.

"Social male oppression?" Loriette chuckled when the door shut, humor twinkling bright in her honeyed eyes. "Oh I do like you."

Rhoslyn fiddled with the ties of her petticoat and swallowed back her nerves. Though she was royalty, a queen, sitting before one in pleasant conversation was a new experience. "I love your son, madame."

"*Oui*, you two have a strong bond," she said softly. "To see my Fenti happy?" Loriette took her hand and caressed Rhoslyn's knuckles with her thumb. "There will never be enough words to express my gratitude for bringing my son back from the grave, *ma fille*."

My *daughter*.

Warmth filled her chest and she peered up bashfully. "He is a beautiful man." Rhoslyn's brows wrinkled and she drew in a shaky breath. "Though I had grievances against your sister, I am sorry—"

"None of that." Loriette leveled her a stern look reminiscent of Fentienne. "I have spent a lifetime grieving and fighting for my children to have every happiness I was denied. I will not let her deserved death spoil this moment or our future together."

Rhoslyn nodded her head.

Loriette bent down and took Rhoslyn's chin in her fingers. "Do not ever stop being wise and courageous, Rhoslyn Beausoleil, My Queen." Rhoslyn's eyes filled with grateful tears. "Now," Loriette said, stepping back. "What clothing do you have here—" She abruptly stopped and marched across to the sitting area and lifted up Rhoslyn's burgundy cloak from a chair. "Is this yours?"

"*Oui*, it belonged to my grand-mére."

The older woman chuckled. "This was once mine but I gifted it to an elf on Factory Row over forty years ago. I dyed the wool with the roses I had planted at Chateau Lumière Dorée." Loriette draped it over her arm and walked back to the bed. "It is fate, *ma fille*. I do like pretty roses," she said with a wink right as the doors opened and servants walked in with a copper tub and buckets of water.

Another knock on the door, followed by a servant with a tea cart. "How do you take your café, Your Majesty?"

At first, Rhoslyn thought he spoke to Fentienne's maman next to her until Rhoslyn noticed several pair of eyes waiting for her reply. "Oh, *merci*. Cream, no sugar, *s'il vous plaît*."

Loriette helped her sit up against a mountain of pillows. The servant brought a tray to rest across her lap with a sugar dusted beignet and cup of coffee. "From His Majesty with a message that sweet victory is yours."

A smile stretched across her face. This verbal foreplay, as he called it, fevered her anew. But she also understood the deeper meaning behind his gesture.

The necessity of court politics both makes and breaks those born under the right to rule. Do not ever let it break you, Queen of The Row.

People fluttered around her, pouring buckets of water into a large tub, setting out clothing to choose from, standing vigilant by the tea cart should she desire more food. She nibbled on her treat as the servants prepared her bath. Guilt gnawed on the edges of her empty stomach for this indulgence, just like she had in her and Fentienne's shared dream. But she suspected she would feel guilt and embarrassment over many things the next few weeks as she adjusted to court life.

Loriette Chalamet is a fine example of one born with the right to rule who didn't break under torture. Or court politics.

Rhoslyn peered at his maman over the rim of her coffee. "Thank you for being here, madame. I am utterly lost right now. Your presence is a comfort."

Loriette smiled sweetly at her. "When you are finished, *ma fille*, I will prepare you to stand before your people." She turned to a servant. "Add more rose water, mademoiselle."

"*Oui*, madame."

After bathing, having her wound redressed, her hair styled simply but elegantly, and donning a lovely cotton muslin gown in shades of dusty pink and ivory—a more homespun styled-dress she would feel comfortable in before Factory Row—she was ready to face the realm who wanted to put a crown on her head.

Loriette assisted Rhoslyn to the main parlor in what she learned were Benoit Faivre's apartments above his offices in lower West Row. The rest of his home was equally as garish as the guest chambers. The gilded opulence of Chateau Lumière Dorée and Palais d'Aurélie would make her head furiously spin too. Both would need to be renovated. The gold could be traded or sold for war debts. But those were thoughts for another time.

Voices spilled out of the parlor. Both male and female. But she couldn't make out the words with the nervous pulse pounding in her ears. Loriette patted the arm looped through hers. Rhoslyn was grateful for her presence and her constant encouragements and instructions the past couple of hours. Fighting for survival was something Rhoslyn understood. Being waited on by servants and addressed officially as a queen, not just the queen of a revolution, was a world she could not yet comprehend.

But she lifted her chin and would stand beside her husband and lead Aurelienne in the only way she knew how—with fire and passion and honesty.

They paused at the room's opening and Rhoslyn's eyes immediately flew to Fentienne's. He, too, had cleaned up and wore fresh clothing. The broody lines between his brows smoothed a touch; the downturned corners of his mouth curved in a secret smile just for her. His throat bobbed as his eyes roamed over her in an anguishing look that weakened her knees. She understood the sweet distress, feeling much the same at the sight of him.

Until this morning, they had not been under the same roof together with so many other people, certainly not as their dream forms in reality, and it was too much. She wanted the quiet of a chateau in a meadow, surrounded by a forest, with the monster she fell in love with and her little brother.

Her brother.

Matthieu stood in front of Fentienne and leaned against him, with Fentienne's large hand over Matthieu's chest as her brother held a wiggling Drurie in his arms. The dimpled grin on her little brother's face melted Rhoslyn into a puddle on the marble floors. Matthieu was practically glowing, his beaming smile was so bright.

"Her Majesty, Queen Rhoslyn Maeline Gautier Kadelaryn Wyndham Beausoleil," a servant announced to the parlor.

Everyone in the room dropped to one knee, including her brother and husband, and replied, "Long live the queen!"

A blush crept up her face as she peered around the room.

"They may rise," Loriette whispered in her ear.

The blush flushed warmer across her face. "You may rise," she said softly.

The rustle of clothing filled the room as those present found their feet. To the side, she caught her uncle's warm gaze. Dalbréath, in a dark blue elven tunic with a silver sash around his waist, dipped his head and placed a hand above his heart. Standing beside him, Gellynor Death Talker wore a beautiful gauzy elven gown in shades of plum and dark green with small purple flowers woven into her chin-length wavy strands. Across from Dalbréath, Amélie grinned at her in a new calico dress with a fine, repeating floral pattern. Lucas, in a clean three-piece wool suit, held her friend's hand and winked at Rhoslyn with a mischievous smirk. Beside her friends was a tall man with a heavily powdered face, draped in pale blue silks. This must be Monsieur Faivre. Finding his eyes, she dipped her head in gratitude. He tilted his head in reply.

In the center back of the room, a large man dressed in Dreglindish finery, with light blond hair and silvery gray eyes, bowed his head when their gazes locked. Tyllie rested against his chest, cooing, with a small flower crown on her head made from the same purple blossoms in Gellynor's hair.

Holy waters of Glanis, Florian Halivaard was here.

She was standing before His Imperial Highness, the Emperor of Dreglind, who was bowing to *her*.

But she couldn't remain awestruck for long. Her heart was too busy bursting for Fentienne—to have his little brother here as he became king. Tears edged her eyes.

Colorings aside, she would have easily picked Florian out in a crowd as Fentienne's brother. They looked so much alike, it was astonishing. But unlike Fentienne, who had a certain aloof elegance to his militaristic bearing and cruel beauty in the arch of his brow and curve of his lips, this man radiated a type of gentle command she did not expect so outwardly in a Halivaard. His face was kind and his smile carried the pleasant warmth of sunlight. Peering back at her husband, she took in his moonlit darkness and her heart sighed.

Dalbréath was right—she really was the type of girl who preferred dark, broody, princely alphas.

"Child of thorns." Gedlen Fate Maker stepped toward her, as if he could read her latter thoughts. Could he? A jolt of panic touched her pulse. Rhoslyn fought a blush, cursing her rapidly beating heart. The prince wore an elaborate black elven tunic with a black sash around his waist. His long, obsidian hair was down, one side tucked behind a pointed ear. Light violet eyes held hers as he approached. Saints, he was so pretty. The raven on his shoulder alighted into the air with a caw and fluttered onto Rònan Ó Macbea's outstretched hand.

"Thorn Princess of Avenbury and Faerie Queen of Aurelienne," Gedlen said when before her. "The Fates have a gift for you." He opened his hand. On his palm was a near replica of the wedding band Addien had stolen. The same three entwining shades of gold—yellow, green, and pink—in thorned rose vines. But unlike the last ring, the roses had flecks of pink diamonds in their center. "You are soul marked as his before the clans, but you are no longer wed by faerie blood to the Prince of Démons. If you choose him, the Wolf King can choose, as a mortal, to bind himself to you before witnesses to satisfy our laws."

Rhoslyn's eyes flew to Fentienne's. "*Oui*, I choose Fentienne Beausoleil as my husband before the fae."

Gedlen peered over his shoulder at the new king and gestured for him to come forward. Fentienne held Matthieu's elbow and helped him stay balanced while walking toward her with Drurie still in Matthieu's arms. Her brother leaned onto her uninjured side in a hug of sorts, that dimpled grin still brightening his face. Drurie gave a little bark and licked her arm, making her and those around them softly laugh.

Fentienne accepted the ring from Gedlen's palm, finding her eyes in a soft blink. For several wild beats of their hearts, they studied each other, both too overwhelmed for words.

Then, clearing his throat, Fentienne pressed his forehead to hers and quietly confessed, "For most of my life, I starved for happiness. I never thought I would know the taste of joy or deserved to." His breath trembled across her lips. "Until a grisette from Factory Row, who can't resist a broken heart to champion or a monster to fight, put her life in the line of fire to save the lives of Factory Row, and mine. She is more fearless than any soldier I captained or met on a battlefield."

He trailed the back of his finger down her cheek and whispered, "Rhoslyn Beausoleil, I am so violently in love with you."

The tears already gathered on her lashes fell as she laughed, unable to contain her happiness. She knew how difficult those words were for him to declare, the fear he had to overcome to say them.

Taking her hand in his, his gaze soaked up her smile. "You are beauty and wisdom and strength. And skies do I crave your fire and gladly burn at your feet," he choked out. "I will never be deserving of you, but I'm a selfish arse and can't live without your defiant heart beating beside mine. You are my queen, not my consort, but as my equal in power and in marriage." He placed the ring to her finger. "I humbly bind my life to yours, if you will have this beast as your husband."

"I will have you," she replied, breathless. "You are mine to love, Fentienne."

"You have always been mine, Rhoslyn." Fentienne pressed a light kiss to her lips as he slid the ring up her finger. The room around them erupted into cheers, but neither of them cared, too wrapped up in each other. "My mate," he whispered softly. "My wife." The embers in his voice, the reverent way he captured her mouth dizzied in her besotted head.

"I could kiss you forever and still need another eternity to feel satisfied."

Playfully, he squeezed her fingers, like earlier. "Five minutes from now, when your rapier tongue slashes me in accusations of dominating you, I will remind you that your mouth better serves mine—"

Rhoslyn harrumphed and scratched behind Drurie's ears, who was wriggling in Matthieu's arms. "Do you hear that growly man?" she cooed at the wolf pup. "If he would just submit to me, he would have fewer cuts to his ego and far more kisses to enjoy."

Drurie barked and Lucas laughed in the background.

Fentienne ignored his beta and Drurie, his predatory focus entirely on her. "Oh but, my darling, by pissing you off, I have dominated you." He lifted her hand from the cub's head. "You are irresistibly cute when mad. I prefer you in this adorable state." Fentienne kissed her wrist, the tip of his tongue licking her skin. "Mmm, the sweet taste of victory is *mine*."

Rhoslyn leaned back, her face pinched in mock outrage. "You are such an arse!"

Matthieu giggled at her side and Fentienne slid him a sly look, one her brother returned. Peering between them, she pursed her lips. "Are you two conspiring against me?"

"You called him an arse," Matthieu said while laughing. "*Mon fére* said you would within a candlemark of arriving."

"*Oui*, because he knows he is one," she retorted while glaring at her husband.

"It is time," Gedlen announced and Rhoslyn's heart stopped beating. "Open the drapes."

The humor faded from Fentienne's gaze as he leaned back to stare over her shoulder, his brows knitted and mouth pressed in a thin line. A muscle worked furiously along the regal lines of his jaw. Though not touching, she could feel his body stiffen as he straightened into a more formal posture.

In many ways they were both like a newborn deer, walking into a shared future with wobbly, shaking legs. But the fear in his eyes, the way he tried to mask it all behind stoicism, pulled delicate ribbons of her magic from her nervous heart to gently cradle his.

"You are a curse breaker, my Sun King," she whispered to him.

"I'm the Dark Saint's child." His chest rose and fell. "And that is an unbreakable curse in their eyes. I will forever be Aelfred Halivaard's son and the Prince of Démons."

"*Oui*, but you are not Aelfred Halivaard." She cupped his cheek. "You are not the god of the Underworld either. Wear your crown with both humility and pride. You are a good man, Fentienne. They will see your truth in time."

Matthieu placed Drurie on the floor to reach into his pocket and pulled out his carved wolf talisman. "To protect you when standing before Aurelienne as their Wolf King." He offered it up to Fentienne while coughing into his arm. "I already prayed to the Dark Saint to favor you."

Swallowing thickly, her husband crouched before Matthieu, his eyes red and glossy, and accepted the wolf. Before he could speak, Matthieu threw his arms around him and whispered, "I love you, *mon fére*. You will be a good king."

Fentienne melted into Matthieu's embrace and whispered back, "You are my happiness, little brother." Those golden eyes she loved locked onto a pair of silver eyes over Matthieu's shoulder. "And one of the strongest, bravest males I know."

Rhoslyn fought back the wave of emotion threatening to topple her over.

If she started crying right now, she wouldn't be able to stop. But tensing up caused her wound to ache. And the pain was starting to radiate down her arm and across her chest. Fentienne angled his head her way, a scowl forming between his brows again as he sensed her pain. It was a magic designed to better hunt prey in its monstrous form. But the ability to feel the fear and pain of others also kept him connected to his humanity, far more than most other mortals. And soon Factory Row would see that this man cared about their plight—and cared deeply.

At Loriette's behest, servants opened the windowed doors leading to a small balcony and the reveling sounds of Factory Row trembled in Rhoslyn's veins. Pressing a hand to her middle, she blew out a slow breath and attempted to calm her rushing thoughts.

A wedge of golden sunlight spilled into the room and caressed her husband's body as he rose back to his feet, half in light, partially in shadow—and she would have him no other way. Fentienne Beausoleil possessed a soul filled with beautiful darkness and a bladed heart bathed in the soft twilight glow of the setting sun and the rising moon.

"Come," he murmured, while offering his hand, "before I carry you upstairs to rest. Time to greet the people who chose you as their monarch."

A shaft of sunlight warmed her face and she blinked back her fluttering nerves. If he could face a people his family had terrorized, and as démon born, she could stand before Factory Row as an aristocrat with all the privileges that entailed.

Lifting her chin, she strode toward the balcony beside him and paused before the opening.

On the edge line of their past and their future, Fentienne caressed the ring on her finger and whispered, "You are so beautiful."

"His Majesty, Adalwolf Fentienne Beausoleil Chalamet Halivaard," the herald announced over the crowd. "Prince of Démons and new Sun King of Aurelienne. Long may he reign!"

Letting go of her hand, he stepped onto the balcony, head straight and back stiff. A soldier walking into battle. A man prepared to be reviled by the people he was born to serve.

Factory Row roared, chanting "Long live the king!" along with howls from démons in the crowd. Fentienne's body faltered, as if he were shot. At first, she thought he had been. But then his mouth parted, a thousand emotions on his face as people swiftly knelt in the streets, shouting his name—wonder, humility, confusion, fear, relief, elation.

"*Oui*," she said, knowing he could hear her. "The people choose you too, Wolf King."

His eyes slid to hers and a lightning strike of devotion sparked between them—a fragile romance together they made unbreakable.

"Her Majesty, Rhoslyn Maeline Gautier Kadelaryn Wyndham Beausoleil," the herald announced next. "Thorn Princess of Avenbury, Queen of Avenbury in equal power, and your Queen of The Row! Long may she reign!"

The streets of Gabaston exploded into cheers. She stepped onto the balcony unprepared for the immense amount of humility that would steal her breath at the sight of all the dirt smudged, threadbare people with tears in their eyes and grins stretched across their hollow cheeks.

The humility and the anger.

This morning should not be. Factory Row should not have suffered until they were forced to declare war after already sacrificing so much to the Cold Winds and blood-soaked battlefields. They should not have to celebrate the return of hope as if it were a miracle. It should have already burned hot in their chests.

Rhoslyn placed a hand on her heart and lowered her head, as Dalbréath had done to honor her. Flower petals rained through the sky from children tossing them from the factory windows. Others lifted chunks of bread into the air. "Long live the queen!" was chanted in a deafening roar.

Awestruck wonder blazed in Fentienne's eyes as he turned to gently cradle her face in his large hands. Petals swirled around their bodies in reds and pinks and whites. Their hair danced and clothing fluttered. A new storm was building in her heart and his thundered in reply.

"Be wild with me, Fentienne." She placed her hand on his chest. "I want to run with the wind beside you."

Fentienne lifted her face to his. "My darling," he murmured, a wicked tilt to his smile, "try to keep up. My legs are longer than yours."

"*Oof!*" She rolled her eyes. "*Mon deuce puce*, the wind favors the fae—"

"Gods, I love you," he growled low.

Then his lips were fire across hers. A dark, searing kiss that spun starlight in her pulse to light the untamed sky of their entangling hearts. How she craved his claws and teeth and moonless nights.

A monster on a throne once convinced him that he only existed for hate.

A monster on a throne once convinced her that she was powerless.

But nobody owned them.

Nobody but their subjects.

Factory Row erupted into cheers as they continued to kiss and Rhoslyn smiled against Fentienne's lips. He was so beautiful beneath all his armor. Aurelienne would now also know his beauty. How could they not fall in love with him too?

Saints, to be loved by such a passionate man.

"Love will find a way through paths
where wolves fear to prey."

Lord Byron

YES

by Jesikah Sundin

Love smudges your fingerprints of moon dust on the soot-stained wing'ed moth of my affection.

It is ichor tears wept from the ache of my breaking muscle, the candlelit beads of salt dewing the skin of my obsession.

War drums thunder in my chest for your surrender. But I am already made hostage to the fatal wounds of desire for you. Every violent beat of my dying heart remains fortressed behind bone, impenetrable save for one word.

Yes.

Yes, the parched deserts of my hands may drink heavily the oases of your wild, unexplored landscape.

Yes, my soul's trembling breath may kiss the falling stars of our midnight confessions.

Yes, my name may be the worshiped deity at the altar of our passions, the name you cry out to for salvation.

Yes.

Yes.

Yes.

Appenidices

Historical Notes	Pg 524
Cast of Characters	Pg 543
Glossary of Ealdspell Terms	Pg 549
More Books by Jesikah	Pg 553
Etsy Shop	Pg 555
About the Author	Pg 557

HISTORICAL NOTES

BY JESIKAH SUNDIN

Thanks, dear reader, for joining me in my French Revolution + Little Red Riding Hood + Beast of Gévaudan villain redemption romance take on *Beauty and the Beast*. Whew! So much going on. But the real-life history behind this social justice charged, French werewolf folklore book is rich. Why? Well, I write mythpunk, which I'll explain in full at the end of these notes.

Before we really sink our teeth into all the fantastic historical facts behind OF THORNS AND CURSES, including the real historical werewolf trials, there are a few people who deserve dozens of enchanted rose bouquets for making this book possible.

<u>My Alpha Readers:</u> Jessica Maass and Michelle Downing, it would make sense the first time I needed alpha readers was on a book about alphas. Your early feedback, encouragements, and friendship are forever invaluable to me.

<u>My Beta Readers:</u> Sarah Jordan, Nicole Manus, Jill Bridgeman, Tyffany Hackett, Andra Prewett, Kelly Stepp, Rebecca Barnhart-Bingham, Jessica Maass, and Michelle Downing . . . my darlings, you are my badass démoness wolf pack! I'm beyond grateful for your feedback, enlightening conversations, laughs, and encouragements.

<u>My Editor, Kate Anderson:</u> Girl, you deserve puppy kisses and kitten snuggles for the magic you wield. Thanks for your friendship and for always loving on my books like you do.

<u>My Personal Assistant, Kelly Stepp:</u> Tater McTot, you are the

bestest potato life has to offer to this potato loving faerie. There is absolutely no way I would have accomplished half as much or finished this book as quickly as I did if not for your incredible attention to detail, memes, GIFs, the shoulder for me to cry on in all my tortured artist melodramatic flair, and your friendship. Thanks for always being an anchor in the wild storm of authordom. You deserve all the chocolates, tacos, and fancy drinks.

<u>My Warrioress in Shining Armor, Amanda Steele</u>: I cannot thank you enough for rallying the troops and lending me your Book of Matches Media readers for reviews when Amazon refused to transfer over reviews from Æroreh and Eirwen to Of Dreams and Shadows and Of Heart and Stone during the title rebranding. Your generous, kind heart eased the grief over the losing so much. Thank you, thank you, a thousand times thank you. *gives you unlimited tacos and fancy coffee drinks*

<u>Special Thanks to:</u> Cait Marie, fellow fantasy author, Chris Serlippens, and Lana Ringoot for reviewing all the French in my book for accuracy. This story is so much richer because of you. *Merci beaucoup.* Also, my heartfelt thanks to Michelle Ouellette for reading over the fencing scene between Rhoslyn and Fentienne and giving me great feedback.

AND NOW, THE ORIGINAL BEAUTY AND THE BEAST, FRENCH SALONS, AND LIBERTÉ, ÉGALITÉ, FRATERNITÉ.

Until two years ago, the only BatB story I knew was courtesy of Disney. And the original tale as old as time is radically different in delightful ways. *Especially* that Beauty was a changeling child faerie princess and *especially, especially* that she and Beast shared dreams together. Turns out, they're both halflings (human + faeries) who also happen to be first cousins.

Uh, yeah.

But it was the seventeen hundreds *wrinkles nose* And a nod to

Historical Notes

King Louis XIV who married his double first cousin, Princess Marie-Thérèse of Spain. Also the Beast's chateau was modeled entirely after Chateau de Versailles. The gardens of Versailles regularly made guests sick with the intensity of their perfumes, hence the "cursed" rose scent that enticed Beauty's father. Also Beauty explores rooms that are directly taken from the Africa and Italian wings as well as the exotic animal menageries. *side-eyes King Louis XIV fanfic*

While I took classes in college on various mythologies and fairy tales (my absolute favorite class was an entire quarter on the Arthurian Legend), Madame Gabrielle-Suzanne Barbot de Villeneuve's original tale from 1743 was not among them. Nor the retold, abridged version by Jeanne-Marie le Prince de Beaumont, written almost a decade later (and also the most famous BatB version too). An interesting exclusion considering the popularity of this story.

But I digress . . .

During the Age of Enlightenment (roughly 1665-1815), France was a firm believer that the more educated the society, the better society was for everyone.

Except if you were a woman. Whether a female was educated or not had no bearing on society's health, according to "society."

Are we surprised? Of course not. And, thus, a feminist movement rose as a middle finger to the patriarchy.

La Belle et la Bête was birthed in this pushback, known as the [French Salon](https://www.edgeofyesterday.com/time-travelers/the-center-of-cultural-innovation-parisian-salons), an Age of Enlightenment movement in France created by women in the upper classes and aristocracy to counter the men's public *café* and *cercles* political gatherings that they were not allowed to attend. Instead, they gathered in the private home of an aristocratic lady to discuss philosophy, politics, economics, religion, science, art, and literature.

And here's the cool part: it was open to *all classes*. Those who didn't have access to education were encouraged to participate and learn. Yes, men participated too, but only if they exhibited egalitarian behavior. The purpose of a salon gathering was to give women a voice and to be heard by all layers of society.

All voices were equal, regardless of sex, class, or religion.

A common discussion in the salons were religious interpretations of scripture, especially in how they applied to the coverture marriage laws of the time. Basically, a woman lost any form of legal identity (which was not much to begin with) when she married and was literally seen as an extension of her husband's body. Coverture was sometimes referred to as the "one flesh" law. Not the basis for romance, right? Women commonly suffered marital rape and physical abuse as a result. Before marriage, an unwed daughter was owned by her father. A man could not legally marry his daughter without his legal consent. Arranged marriages were very common, even among the lower classes.

In short, women had little legal autonomy in society and little to no choice in marriage or occupation.

Coverture was a major theme to *La Belle et la Bête*.

Beauty, a poor merchant's daughter, was given an opportunity to redeem her father by becoming the Beast's property. As punishment for stealing a rose, Beast told the merchant that one of his unwed daughters could take the merchant's house arrest place but, *only if she chooses* to. It had to be entirely of her own free will *after* she knew all the facts about his beastly appearance and their shared predicament. Beast didn't demand marriage either. He would politely ask her after dinner each night, but the *choice was hers*, and *only* when *she chose* him would his curse be broken. Beast had no choice but to marry to break his curse. But Beauty has no such constraints.

The enchantment over the chateau gave Beauty *one more choice* in love—the Beast or the Man of her Dreams. Beauty was able to explore falling in love with two men but for vastly different reasons before making *her* ultimate *choice*. Spoiler: totes the same man, but . . .

What I enjoyed about this version? *Beauty is given a choice* in an age when faerie tales didn't give female protagonists agency. And why my story ends with Rhoslyn having a choice in marriage, Fentienne too.

Historical Notes

In the original BatB story, Beauty is first property to be traded, as marriage laws decreed for women in the 18th century. Her "doting" father is cool with handing her off to a monster to spare his own life. This message in Madame de Villeneuve's tale is heartbreakingly true. Most women were given to monsters. Uxoricide (killing one's wife) was horrifyingly high during that time. But instead of being forced into marriage, Beauty was *given a choice over her fate*. She didn't have to trade places with her father. She didn't have to marry Beast. She could have lived in the chateau, enjoying all the enchanted delights until drawing her last breath.

After the prince's reveal, the story continues but with themes around classism and marriage.

Now, this story is far from redeeming in many feminist ways to our modern freedoms. But this tale was revolutionary for its time. The last threads of paternal coverture laws in France were fully abolished in the 1980s. Hell, it wasn't until the 1920s that all states in the U.S. made it illegal for a man to beat his wife. The Violence Against Women Act in 1994 finally made marital rape a convictable crime, a giant win against the "one flesh" beliefs. And child marriage? Still legal in forty-four states. Nine states have zero age limits. Some states will allow a child as young as twelve to marry an adult with parental consent. On the financial side, women couldn't obtain a bank account without a male co-signer until 1974. In 1988, The Women's Business Ownership Act allowed women to receive a business loan without a male co-signer. Even now, in many states, a woman cannot get her tubes tide without legal consent from her husband (and she must be married to get her tubes tied). But a man can get a vasectomy without consent from anyone at the age of eighteen. There are many modern examples of coverture laws that I could list that still affect women today. But, you get the point.

Madame de Villeneuve's story is looooooong and tedious and looooooong. Did I mention long? It tells the events from several different point-of-views, one after the other in a very ornate, rambling fashion. Jeanne-Marie Beaumont's version is notably shorter, concise, and easier to read but, in my opinion, lacks the deeper message of female agency as additionally detailed in Madame de Villeneuve's good fairy and queen POV sections. Beaumont's retelling also felt less nuanced after reading the intensely detailed original version.

But I understand *why* Madame de Villeneuve's version is longwinded—she had a voice that was finally being heard and it felt damn good.

The French salon movement was obsessed with fairy tales. Seriously obsessed. It was how they taught and spread their truths. Many, many fairy tales written by women came out of that movement. Sadly, most remain unknown to us, especially if written by lower-class women.

Though not a woman, Charles Perrault, author of *The Tales of Mother Goose*, wrote all his stories in a salon during the late 1690s. *Little Red Riding Hood* being one of them, which I'll discuss later in a section all about the French folklore of wolves, werewolves, and démons.

The salon movement empowered women clear up to the French Revolution when they rallied and demanded equality in citizenship by invoking *liberté, égalité, fraternité* (sadly, it was not achieved). One incredibly influential revolutionary from the salon was Sophie de Condorcet, who was married to Marquis de Condorcet. Together they wrote "On the Admission of Women to Civil Rights (https://revolution.chnm.org/d/292)" in rebuttal to the "Declaration of the Rights of Man and Citizen," in 1790.

> One excerpt I appreciated:
> *It is said that women, though better than men in that they are gentler, more sensitive, and less subject to the vices that follow from egotism and hard hearts, do not really possess a sense of justice; that they obey their feelings rather than their consciences. This observation is truer but it proves nothing. It is not nature but rather education and social conditions that cause this difference. Neither the one nor the other has accustomed women to the idea of what is just, only to the idea of what is becoming or proper.*

That, right there, was the beating heart of the French salon. And we have one of the most popular faerie tales of our modern age because of this feminist movement and the desire to educate and recondition both men and women into freer thought through stories, especially faerie tales about female agency.

LET THEM EAT CAKE...

Guess what? There is no historical evidence (https://www.history.com/news/did-marie-antoinette-really-say-let-them-eat-cake) that Marie Antoinette ever spoke these heartless words. There is, however, recorded incidences of this term used decades earlier, even uttered by a queen a century prior to the French Revolution. And many breadcrumbs lead to propaganda efforts to vilify Marie during this apocalyptic period in France too.

While Marie Antoinette's extravagant spending didn't help her public opinion, there are several reasons that led to the class revolt and eventual dismantling of the monarchy's right to rule in 1789. France's allied assistance in the American Revolutionary War, which left them bankrupt, and the French salon's heart eyes over the Declaration of Independence were *big* influencers. The French salon kinda crushed over Benjamin Franklin and Thomas Jefferson. But it was the lack of bread and government representation that tipped the scales of injustice.

A few startling facts about life in 1789 for an unskilled worker, who made up the majority of the working-class population:

- Wages rose only 20% from 1764-1789

- Price of rent rose 60% in the same time period

- The average pay was 15-20 *sous* a day

- The average cost for a loaf of bread was 9 *sous* in 1788 and 14.5 *sous* in 1789

For many, the cost of bread was an entire day's wages. That meant no money for rent or anything else, like the *gabelle* (salt tax) and the required annual tithe to the church. Clergy and nobility were exempt from almost all taxes, requiring those in the third estate (working class, regardless of lower or upper) to bear the entire burden of the country's funding and debts.

Bread was THE main staple for the French working class.

Why the sudden price increase? Poor grain trade policy, poor harvests two years in a row (1788-1789), and bread was regulated by guilds. Regulated to the point that it was policed by actual officers.

With minimal representation in the government, the people were given no option but to riot. And they did. The rioting and "flour wars" were so bad, the military was regularly stationed in the markets.

October 5th, 1789 is considered the date the Revolution exploded into official monarchal reform because of an angry march led by 7,000 women (which I'll share in a separate bit).

On October 21st, 1789 . . . a baker by the name of Denis François was accused of a plot to deprive the people of bread by hiding loaves. He was proven innocent in a public trial but the starving crowds *still* dragged him to an execution block, hung him, decapitated him, and then made his poor, traumatized pregnant wife kiss his bloodied lips.

shudders

"Famine plots," the idea that the aristocracy was intentionally starving the working class into submission, was a well held belief.

THE WOMEN'S MARCH ON VERSAILLES AND A 17-YEAR-OLD GIRL WHO DEMANDED CHANGE FROM A KING . . .

This event is one thousand percent what inspired Rhoslyn's blood march, her raid on the armory, and her strike. It is a pivotal moment in world history and a complete slap in the face of coverture laws and beliefs that women were incapable of understanding

Historical Notes

politics and justice and, thus, could make any beneficial difference in lawmaking. Suffragette marches of the 19th and 20th century came on the coattails of this event and post-French salon enlightenment. I would even go so far as to say it even inspired The Women's March movement of the mid-2010s. The parallels are certainly there.

Where men had failed to gain King Louis's agreement to dissolve absolute monarchal authority, women prevailed . . .

The evening of October 4th, 1789, a woman shouted to fellow *poissardes* (fishwives and market women) to march on Versailles and demand bread. The next morning, a young woman beat a drum in a Paris market as a call to action.

Women were outraged that King Louis refused to sign the August Decrees and the Declaration of the Rights of Man and Citizen, both of which would give rights to the working class and take away rights from the aristocracy. Outraged that on October 1st, King Louis and Marie Antoinette hosted a banquet for the regiment who were stationed to protect Versailles against the sans-culottes (https://en.wikipedia.org/wiki/Sans-culottes) (those "without silk breeches" aka the lower class commoners and eventually the name given to the working-class revolutionaries). It was at this feast that Marie Antoinette reportedly said, "Let them eat cake," while they gluttoned on food and stomped on symbols of the revolution. They, uh, really did those last two things.

Women of all working classes gathered around the drummer, grabbing kitchen knives, pikes, muskets, and marched a twelve miles (six hour) journey in the pouring rain to Versailles while shouting, "When will we have bread?" Along the way, they seized *Hôtel de Ville* (Paris's City hall). A sympathetic National Guard stepped back and let 7,000 women ransack the city hall, where they took hundreds of weapons and two cannons. They also claimed the Church of Saint Marguerite, ringing the bell with shouts for people to take up arms and join their cause. Fueled with weapons and rage, the women broke down Versailles's steel gates coated in real gold, poured into the front courtyard, and demanded an audience with the king.

King Louis met with a delegation of six women, **led by**

Pierrette Chabry, a seventeen-year-old girl.

Bolded because WOW.

For all the people who rail on young adult novels for featuring teens who change the world and upturn governments, this is for you. Some of history's biggest movers and shakers are teens and early 20-somethings.

I enjoy this part . . . Chabry fainted at the king's feet from nervousness. So, badass but also a totally relatable human being. Louis could have ordered her death right there on the spot for sedition and vandalism and a whole host of reasons. The king, however, ordered smelling salts and personally revived her, which endeared him to the protest and calmed the crowd some.

Chabry secured a promise from the king that he would sign the August Decrees and the Rights of Man, abolishing all aristocratic privileges—including tax exemption, feudalism, and absolute monarchy—while granting rights for the people to choose their leaders. He also promised to deliver food to the people from the royal stores in Paris with an additional promise that more food would come.

But the protesters were not convinced that he would follow through. They worried that Marie Antoinette would persuade her husband to remain firm and defend their right to rule.

The very next morning, a group of armed people, from the tens of thousands who had gathered at this point, stormed Versailles in search of Marie Antoinette. They killed two guards, decapitated them, and carried their heads on spikes. The king tried to quiet the masses. Eventually Marie showed up with her two children. Long story short (there is sooooo much here involving many, many people), the king agreed to return to Paris and asked for the people to protect his family while they traveled to Tuileries Palace.

It is estimated that 60,000 people marched the twelve miles back to Paris with Louis, Marie Antoinette, and their children. There are stories of women riding the canons and singing songs. In the rear of the parade were wagons full of flour and bread. Women cheered that they were bringing back "the baker, the baker's wife, and the baker's lad to Paris!" Apparently, the king was often referenced as the first baker of the kingdom.

Shortly thereafter, he signed the August Decrees and the Rights of Man, abolishing absolute monarchy with the divine right to rule while instituting constitutional monarchy.

Louis XVI of France was executed by guillotine on January 21st, 1793. Marie Antoinette was executed by guillotine on October 16th of the same year.

THE WEREWOLF TRIALS OF FRANCE . . .

I always learn interesting tidbits while researching for a story. The history of werewolves in France is . . . crazy. The famed European witch trials of the 1400s-1700s is an abbreviated title. It's actually "The Witch Werewolf Trials."

Yeah.

Werewolf trials (https://www.history.com/news/werewolf-trials-europe-witches).

While it's estimated that 40,000-50,000 women were burned at the stake or executed in other ways for accusations of witchcraft from 1450-1750, men were accused of making a pact with Satan to shift into wolves. These werewolves were blamed for hundreds of deaths, namely the violent deaths of women and children. Now, clearly, it was real wolves who were responsible for these deaths. Though historians agree that some of these men were indeed serial killers and pedophiles. But only a tiny fraction of those found guilty and executed.

I blended the history of this "werewolf cleansing" with my fictional Monks of Glanis. Glanis (https://en.wikipedia.org/wiki/Glanis), by the way, is the Gaulish god of healing springs and the patron god of Glanum, a town in southern France, where it is believed pilgrims visited to bathe in the healing waters. I specifically chose Glanis because of the parallels of baptism in Christianity. The werewolf trials happened during a time when paganism was in its final death throes all throughout Europe as the church "cleansed" these believed heathen practices from the populations while moving into political power. Wolves, especially in German and French regions, were an integral part of their pagan beliefs.

But it didn't take much to convince the people of Europe, especially France, that there were indeed werewolves—and not just because of any remnant pagan beliefs.

An event known as the Little Ice Age (https://www.newyorker.com/magazine/2019/04/01/how-the-little-ice-age-changed-history) hit Europe in 1303 and ended around 1850. In book one of *The Ealdspell Cycle*, OF DREAMS AND SHADOWS, I go into detail about the historical Little Ice Age and my fictional Cold Winds apocalypse. But what does the Little Ice Age have to do with werewolves? Well, the wolf populations migrated closer to the villages where it was easier to find food. And they thrived as a result. Wolf populations exploded. Grain production and storage were also directly affected by this dramatically colder period. Similar to the Salem Witch Trials, historians believe many of the accused werewolves were under the hallucinogenic effects of ergot, a type of fungus that grows on grain, predominantly rye (which was the main grain in France for several centuries leading up to and through the French Revolution). By the way, LSD is derived from this fungus. Ergot (https://cropwatch.unl.edu/2017/has-ergot-altered-events-world-history) thrives when there is a harsh, cold winter followed by a cool, wet spring—the exact conditions of the Little Ice Age. Put the two together, an overpopulation of wolves and men accidentally hyped up on a form of LSD, and you get a fear of lycanthropy.

The church used this opportunity, wittingly or not, to demonize positive pagan beliefs about wolves. And I use the word demonize quite literally. The people were convinced that wolves were the devil incarnate or his minions and that werewolves were men who made a pact with Satan.

The term "speak of the devil" is the direct English idiom translation of *Quand on parle du loup on en voit la queue*, "When you talk about the wolf you see its tail." Lucas says this to Fentienne in

Chapter Seven when Rhoslyn shows up in the forest while they're speaking about her.

Men were not only accused of being werewolves, but non-shifters were accused of a form of witchcraft known as wolf-riding or wolf-charming (https://en.wikipedia.org/wiki/Wolfssegen): a spell used to ward off wolves or to cause wolf attacks. This could be done through an incantation or with a talisman, sold to the peasantry by a "wolf charmer," who were typically poor older men.

It is this wolf-charm witchcraft that inspired Matthieu's talisman, made for him by an old beggar man.

You can read a great comprehensive history of the werewolf trials (https://www.history.com/news/werewolf-trials-europe-witches) with this link as well as famous werewolf cases (https://www.mentalfloss.com/article/29073/8-historic-accounts-werewolves).

LITTLE RED RIDING HOOD AND THE BEAST OF GÉVAUDAN . . .

As mentioned previously, Charles Perrault, the author of *The Tales of Mother Goose*, wrote his faerie tales and faerie tale retellings in a French salon during the 1690s. He is accredited with popularizing the *Little Red Riding Hood* story, which is a tale that shows up all over the world. The Brothers Grim wrote their own version two centuries later called *Little Red Cap*.

In France, wolf attacks were mostly from rabid animals. The number of attacks remained somewhat steady for over a century. In the late 1600s, wolf attacks in the area around Versailles increased—significantly. Almost by double. Records show (https://hal.archives-ouvertes.fr/hal-01011915/document) that there were 262 victims in 1695 around Versailles, mostly children. Charles Perrault, who spent considerable time at Versailles, published *Little Red Riding Hood* in 1697.

With the werewolf scare slowing down by this point, the story still held deep resonance with crowds for a couple of reasons, one being the aforementioned wolf attacks. Do not stray from the trail, children. But mostly Perrault used this well-established fear to drive home an important message: not all wolves walk on four legs. Not his exact words, but the ones Rhoslyn uses to describe sexual predators who prey mostly on young females in Gabaston.

From Perrault on *Little Red Riding Hood*:
Moral: *Children, especially attractive, well bred young ladies, should never talk to strangers, for if they should do so, they may well provide dinner for a wolf. I say, "wolf," but there are various kinds of wolves. There are also those who are charming, quiet, polite, unassuming, complacent, and sweet, who pursue young women at home and in the streets. And unfortunately, it is these gentle wolves who are the most dangerous ones of all.*
(translation by D. L. Ashliman)

The end of *Little Red Riding Hood* that we know, where the wolf is killed and Little Red lives, is a Brothers Grim version. In the Perrault version, the wolf convinces Little Red to climb into bed with him and she takes off all her clothes first. Then he devours hers. There is no happy ending in this version.

I was pretty shocked when I read the part where she takes off all her clothes.

However, I both understood and appreciated his message. As a regular at Versailles, he often saw men prey on the younger women there. It was a valid, well-received warning. A lesson that is *still* important today.

I borrowed a few aesthetics from the original story: The red cloak that belonged to Rhoslyn's grand-mére; Rhoslyn picking flowers in the meadow off the trail; the basket of biscuits (cookies) that Addien carries to Factory Row when Fentienne finds her while he is moon-addled from the mate bond; Rhoslyn's fear, as an unprotected young female, of sexual predators in the city as well as in the forest; Fentienne's comment about being able to better see Fayette with his golden eyes when she asks why he was moving

Historical Notes

away in the prologue; and werewolves.

Skip ahead sixty-seven years from Perrault and the werewolf fear in France crescendoed when a "beast" was reported in the Gévaudan region of France. From 1764-1767, this "beast" was accredited to over one hundred deaths. I say "beast" because scholars really don't know, exactly, what was attacking people. They suspect a large wolf or a wolf pack, but the accounts from the people suggest something like a hyena or a lion, of which the common person would have zero reference for, so it made sense they wouldn't know what "it" was. The aristocracy liked their menageries, though. It's not a far-fetched notion that an exotic animal got loose. But, naturally, people claimed "werewolf," because that was the answer to all beastly issues in France.

The Beast of Gévaudan (https://www.history.com/news/beast-gevaudan-france-theories) created the first "media sensation" in world history. News of this scare spread in newspapers and other forms of social information all over Europe, parts of Asia, and even in the colonies, complete with drawings. It also spurred a full-fledged monster hunt, sponsored by King Louis XV, who put an enormous bounty on the beast's head. Hundreds of hunters took to the woods to win this award.

Two parts of this real story that I thought was cool:

First, from the article linked above:
Among the most notable tales of bravery was when 19- or 20-year-old Marie-Jeanne Valet was attacked by the Beast on August 11, 1765 while crossing the River Desges with her sister. Armed with a bayonet affixed to a pole, Valet impaled the Beast's chest. The creature got away, but Valet became known as the "Amazon" and the "Maid of Gévaudan."

And thus Rhoslyn impales the Beast of Gabaston on a sword.

A monument was erected in Auvers (1995) to honor Marie-Jeanne Valet. Google it to see an image. Also, if you watched Teen Wolf (https://teen-wolf-pack.fandom.com/wiki/Marie-Jeanne_Valet), then you might recognize this name as the woman, the

"Maid of Gévaudan," who started a family of Werewolf Hunters.

Second, one of the monster hunters, by the name of Jean Chastel, is the hero who killed the Beast in 1767 and... with a silver bullet. After his kill, the attacks promptly ended. An autopsy of the animal revealed human remains. Witnesses say the animal had non-wolf traits, but the type of animal remains a mystery.

It's believed that the silver bullet was a later embellishment, but it's not confirmed either way. It was this silver bullet, however, that started the lore that werewolves were weakened and killed by silver. Fun, right?

And why Fentienne, the accused Beast of Gabaston, was shot with a silver bullet.

OTHER FUN MISCELLANEOUS INFORMATION...

This next part I'll do in bullet point fashion, otherwise I would ramble on about the all the cool research foreverrrrr.

- Gabaston is my funky twist on Gévaudan and Gaston, the villain in Disney's story. I almost did Gévaston, but Gabaston just felt "right" to my story gut. Rolls off the tongue better.

- Gabaston is modeled after Paris with touches from Brittany, the Celtic region of France.

- Rhoslyn is a name from Wales and the Brittany region of France (both speak Brythonic Celtic languages).

- The language of the saints is in reference to Brittany, France, where they still speak Breton but also French.

- The named saints (Annea Clivana, Belenus, Cernunnos, Arianrhod, Glanis) are real Celtic Brythonic and Gaulish deities from France. A couple of the names were Romanized. That area called their gods "saints."

- Paris is known as the City of Light and why the House of

Chalamet is known as the House of Golden Light. Chalamet is also a French name that dates back to a word used for "torch maker." During the Treaty of Versailles, 20,000 candles were lit in the Hall of Mirrors and transformed it into "a corridor of light."

- Beausoleil is a village in France along the Riviera. It translates to "beautiful sun."

- King Louis XIV (French Rev Louis's grandfather) was called the Sun King, a nickname he earned after performing a twelve-hour long ballet ("Ballet de la Nuit" aka "ballet of the night") to courtiers at the age of fifteen where he depicted Apollo, the sun god, vanquishing the darkness at the end. His dramatic way of saying that he was the light that would save the country and bring hope to the people by lifting France out of the darkness (caused by war)

- While Louis XIV is the father of ballet (seriously, he is), Fentienne, our Sun King, does not prance, for any reason.

- The Realm of Gold and the gold in "golden light" is a commentary on Chateau de Versailles. Google search images of Versailles, the amount of gold is mind boggling. I've searched for an estimate of how much gold Versailles contains and I can't find a number. But it's an insane amount. Even the gates, which were recently recreated using real gold leaf, were coated in real gold.

- Pavement nymphs and roadside flowers were what illegal alley prostitutes were called in France during the 18th and 19th centuries. A tolerant house was a legal, registered brothel. All legal sex workers were required to be checked by doctors twice a week to prevent the spread of disease—but it didn't. France was known for its prostitution all throughout Europe and the colonies/states. So much so, during WWI and WWII, U.S. soldiers were told to protect America (especially their wives) by abstaining from French prostitutes. The British soldiers were encouraged to enjoy themselves, however, even given prostitution stipends, and Britain endured an STD crisis afterward.

- Waltzmania (https://thereader.mitpress.mit.edu/waltzmania-in-the-paris-pleasure-gardens/) was truly a fear and for the exact reasons that Rhoslyn states. The popularity of the Watlz in France grew as Parisian pleasure gardens became all the rage around the time of the Revolution. France was one of the first countries to ban "the forbidden dance" followed closely by England.

- Pleasure gardens began in the 1700s and are the predecessors of amusement parks. The merry-go-round, which later became a steam engine operated carousel, was often a main feature.

- The counting folk song she and Mattieu sing, *Gousperoù ar raned*, is from Brittany, France, and is somewhere around 1500 years old or more. The song she sings when picking out pastries, *Les Trendres Souhaits,* is from the early 1700s and translates to "Loving Wishes."

- Chateau Lumière Dorée was totally my hat tip to *Lumiere* in the Disney BatB story

MYTHPUNK . . .

What is this, you ask? The quick answer: a derivative of cyberpunk that deconstructs a familiar faerie tale, myth, or folklore, mixing the nuts and bolts with unexpected genres/settings, before reconstructing all the story pieces into something "familiar" but "new." Mythpunk sometimes blends several myths and folktales together too. And, it employs postmodern writing styles. Basically, artsy often self-reflective writing styles through poetry, non-linear plotlines, and weirdness. AND it gives voice to often overlooked representation in myths and faerie tales too, such as females with agency, LGBTQ+ characters, characters of color, and more.

OF THORNS AND CURSES is the least mythpunk book in this series to date. But it still falls into this category.

Aaaaand, that's it for now!

I'm off to Avenbury next, where Rhoslyn's biological brother, Henri Wyndham, the Thorn Prince, will meet his "Cinderella" in a childhood friends to lovers / brother's best friend Regency romance. Think *Bridgerton* meets *Pride and Prejudice* but with elves.

To be continued . . .
Jesikah Sundin

Cast of Characters

Check out the Historical Notes at the end of
OF THORNS AND CURSES for more information

Rhoslyn Gautier	(ross-linn) Thorn Princess of Avenbury (Maeline Kadelaryn Wyndham), changling child, Queen of The Row
	Gautier (goo-tee-ay) Maeline (may-leen) Kadelaryn (cade-el-air-en) Wyndham (win-dem)
Fentienne Beausoleil	(fen-TEE-enn) Exiled Prince of Clifstán, Prince of Démons / Wolf Prince
	Adalwolf (A-doll-wolf) Beausoleil (boo-so-lay) Chalamet (shall-uh-may) Halivaard (hal-ee-vard)
Matthieu Gautier	(matt-eww) Rhoslyn's foster brother

House of Chalamet

Chalamet	(shall-uh-may) a French name that dates back to a word used for "torch maker." The Aurelienne House of Wolves and House of Golden Light.
Loriette Chalamet	(lore-ee-eht) Queen consort of Aelfred, former Queen of Aurelienne
Adeline Chalamet	(awe-dih-leen) Queen of Aurelienne, younger sister of Loriette
Lucien Chalamet	(luce-ee-uhn) Duke of Aurelienne, first cousin to Loriette, second cousin to Fentienne
Alain Chalamet	(allun) distant cousin to Fentienne

House Halivaard / Beaousleil

Halivaard	(hal-ee-vard– from Old Norse "halvard" which means "flat stone" and "guardian," as in a protector) the imperial line of Dreglind and former monarchs of Clifstán.
Beausoleil	(boo-so-lay-from French) translates to "beautiful sun," and is the Aurelienne House of the Golden Sun, the Sun Kings line.
Aelfred Beausoleil Halivaard	(al-fred) King of Clifstán, grandson of the last empress of Dreglind and second-born prince of Aurelienne

Loriette Chalamet	(lore-ee-eht) Queen consort of Aelfred, former Queen of Aurelienne
Aeldfrith Banon	(eld-frith) Crown prince, first-born, major
Aethelbert Odan	(eh-thel-bert) second-born prince, captain, infantry
Adalwolf Fentienne	(A-doll-wolf) third-born prince, captain, infantry, Prince of Démons / Wolf Prince
Florian Ferdinand Alberich	(floor-ee-aan) Fourth born prince, lieutenant, army scout, Emperor of Dreglind

DÚNÆLVEN (Milfae) ELVES

Gedlen Faerondarl	([g]ed-lin) Unseelie Prince, General of Dúnælven, the Fate Maker, older twin
Gellynor Faerondarl	([g]ell-in-ore) Unseelie Princess, Master Spell Weaver, the Death Talker, younger twin
	Faerondarl (fay-ron-dar-l)
Dalbréath Kadelaryn	(Dal-bray-eth) Seelie, Commander of the Dúnælven military, assigned protector of hidden fae royals, rune whisperer and shadow walker
Dalbrenna Kadelaryn	(Dal-bren-nuh) Seelie, huntress, assigned protector of hidden fae royals
	Kadelaryn (cade-el-air-en)

Rònan Ó Macbea	(Row-nun) Unseelie, High Druid and Prince of Éireanna and Ealdspell, Eirwen's and Aroreh's father, Gedlen's partner
	Ó Macbea (Oh - Mac-bee)

MALFAE ELF

Addien Wyndham	(Awe-dee-enn) Head of the faerie council in Avenbury, rune shifter, rune whisperer, rune walker, shifts into Fayette

THE BROTHERHOOD

Bastien Chapelle	(bass-tee-ehn) alpha of Clan Nightwalkers, captain of Factory Row's Guard
Ambroise de Rosier	(am-bro-ss) alpha of Clan Highfang, vinter and distiller guild captain
Mon Père Michel	(moan / pear / mee-shell) alpha of clan Windbite, head priest of the temple
Jules Aris	(jewel) alpha of Clan Red Bane, owner of Le Rêve Rouge
Victor Durette	(veek-tore) alpha of Clan Black Bane, blacksmith guild captain
Maximilien Barras	(max-eh-meal-ee-en) alpha of Clan Ironbite, oversees East Row factories
Felix Veron	(fee-licks) alpha of Clan Ironbite, oversees West Row factories
Fentienne Beausoleil	(Fen-TEE-enn) Head alpha over all the clans, Prince of Démons / Wolf Prince, from Clan Goldfang

Alain Chalamet	(allun) alpha of Clan Goldfang, noble aristocrat
Benoit Faivre	(ben-wuah) alpha of Clan Golfang, merchant upper class aristocrat
Lucas Fontine	(lew-cuss) alpha of Clan Palehide, oversees Factory Row working-class démons
Claude Delane	(clawed) alpha of Clan Ashclaw, baking guild captain

MISCELLANEOUS

Amélie Demarr	(awe-mih-lee) Rhoslyn's friend, fellow grisette
Grisette	(grih-zet) a female who worked in a textile factory, specifically one who sewed garments.
Chateau	(shah-toe) a large manor or castle
Chateau Lumière Dorée	(shah-toe / loom-ee-air / door-ee) Fentienne's manor, the House of Golden Light
Palais d'Aurélie	(pal-ay / dih / oo-relll-ee) Golden Palace, where the sitting monarch of Aurelienne resides
Mon petit caneton	(moan / pet-eet / can-ih-tun) my little duckling
Mon douce puce	(moan / doo-ss / pew-ss) my sweet flea
Mon (ma) petit(e) louveteau	(moan / pet-eet / lew-v-toe), my little (wolf) cub
Mon petit chou-fleur	(Till-shwan / Till-ee) A spotted owl, Gellynor Death Talker's familiar

Brandu	(Brawn-dew) A raven, Gedlen Fate Maker's familiar
Tylluan / Tyllie	(Till-shwan / Till-ee) A spotted owl, Gellynor Death Talker's familiar

GLOSSARY

Check out the Historical Notes at the end of
OF THORNS AND CURSES for more information

Addien	(Awe-dee-enn – *Welsh*) Head of the faerie council in Avenbury, rune shifter, rune whisperer, rune walker, shifts into Fayette
Aroreh Rosen	(A-roar-uh) Queen of Rothlín, Eirwen's younger sister, queen consort of King Félip Batten McKinley of Dúnælven
Aisling	(Ash-ling – *Irish* for "dream") An artificial intelligence created by Queen Líeh to control the realm of Rothlín through a form of goddess religion.
Aurelienne	(Oo-rell-ee-ehn) A realm in the Kingdom of Ealdspell
Avenbury	(Awe-ven-burr-ee) A realm in the Kingdom of Ealdspell
Aye	Yes
Bampot	An idiot / fool
Blight	A child who was damaged by the Cold Winds with a telling frostbite scar. It is believed they can cause others to rot from the inside out with skin-to-skin contact.

Brandu	(Brawn-dew – *Welsh* for "raven") A raven, Gedlen Fate Maker's familiar
Cerwyn	(Sir-win) Faerie, warrior
Charaid	(Caw-radge – *Scottish*) Friend
Clifstán	(Cliff-stahn – *Anglo-Saxon* for "rock cliff") A realm in the Kingdom of Ealdspell
Dalbréath	(Dal-bray-eth) Seelie, Commander of the Dúnælven military, assigned protector of hidden fae royals, rune whisperer and shadow walker
Dalbrenna	(Dal-bren-nuh) Seelie, huntress, assigned protector of hidden fae royals
Dream Weaver	Someone who can weave new realities while dreaming. What they do in their dreamscape affects the real.
Dúnælven	(Dune-al-ven – *Anglo-Saxon* for "fairy mountain") A realm in the Kingdom of Ealdspell, Milfae Faeries
Ealdspell	(Awld-spell – *Anglo-Saxon* for "old story") A kingdom upon a leaf, an interdimensional realm of Éireanna and Earth. Ealdspell contains eight different realms (Dúnælven, Rothlín, Clifstán, Merenna, Avenbury, Dreglind, Aurelienne, Glenashlen).
Eejit	Idiot
Éireanna	(Air-ran-nuh) Ireland in old Irish; faerie dimension on Earth
Eirwen	(Air-wen – *Welsh* for "white as snow") Lost Princess
Faither	(Fay-ther – *Scottish*) Father
Félip Batten MacKinley	Fay-lip) King of Dúnælven, king consort of Queen Aroreh of Rothlín, nephew of Gedlen and Gellynor Faerondarl

Fentienne Beausoleil	(Fen-TEE-enn – *French*) Exiled Prince of Clifstán, Prince of Démons / Wolf Prince.
Fer	For
Gedlen Fate Maker	([g]ed-lin) Unseelie Prince, General of Dúnælven, the Fate Maker, older twin
Gellynor Death Talker	([g]ell-in-ore) Unseelie Princess, Master Spell Weaver, the Death Talker, younger twin
The Korrigan	(Core-EE-gun – *Breton* for "small dwarf") A fairy or dwarf-like spirit. A creature in Breton folklore that often lived around rivers and wells and usually had long hair. They are known for behaving similarly to a siren and/or telling the future, like a Seer.
Líeh Rosen	(Lee-uh) Queen of Rothlín
Mælfallyn	(Male-fall-in) Queen of the Malfae, Queen of the Sluagh
Malfae	(Mal-fay) Bad faeries
Milfae	(Mil-fay) Good faeries
Mither	(Mih-ther – *Scottish*) Mother
Nae	(Nay – *Scottish*) No / Not (anaether, could nae, didnae, naebody, naething)
Rònan Ó Conell Macbeatha	(Row-nun) High Druid and prince of Éireanna
Rhoslyn Gautier	(Ross-linn – *Welsh / Breton*) Thorn Princess of Avenbury (Maeline Kadelaryn Wyndham), changling child, Queen of The Row

Rothlín	(Roth-leen – *Irish* for "flax wheel") A realm in the Kingdom of Ealdspell
Rune Walker	A faerie who can "walk" through various planes (like the In-Between, Otherworld, Underworld) as well as a faerie who can "walk" through another's glamoured mind to steal or rewrite spells.
Rune Whisperer	A faerie who can control another's bioelectric signal and nanotechnology with runic verbal commands. A form of faerie glamouring.
Runic Technology	The Earthen computer technology system the High Druid blended with elemental magic in Ealdspell.
Shadow Walker	A faerie who uses a rare enchanted cloak woven in Éireanna to blend into light and shadow to attack or sneak away unseen. A lesser Runic / Elemental magic in Ealdspell because of cloak material resource scarcity.
Spell Weaver	A faerie who can program and hack runic technology (for spell coding or weapon making)
The Dream	The program (glamour) that controls mortal minds through nanotechnology, created by Aisling, an artificial intelligence.
Tylluan / Tyllie	(Till-shwan / Till-ee – *Welsh* for "owl") A spotted owl, Gellynor Death Talker's familiar
Wool Sorter's Sickness	The Medieval term for anthrax.
Ye/Yer/Ye're	You / Your / You're

MORE BOOKS

By Jesikah Sundin

THE BIODOME CHRONICLES

Eco-dysotopian faerie tale

*She is locked inside an experimental world.
He has never met the girl who haunts his dreams.
A chilling secret forever binds their lives together.*

LEGACY
ELEMENTS
TRANSITIONS
GAMEMASTER

THE EALDSPELL CYCLE

Historical faerie tale fantasy

*Dreams are dangerous . . .
Unless she unlocks the powers of her mind.
He fights his Otherworld shadow self.
And with only fae magic to re-spin their tales.*

OF DREAMS AND SHADOWS
OH HEART AND STONE
OF THORNS AND CURSES

THE KNIGHTS OF CAERLEON

An Arthurian Legend Reverse Harem Fantasy
Under J. Sundin

Four cursed knights. One warrior princess.
A faerie sword that binds their lives together.

THE FIFTH KNIGHT
THE THIRD CURSE
THE FIRST GWENEVERE

A HARTWOOD FALLS ROMANCE
CONTEMPORARY ROMANCES

Under Jae Dawson

MOONLIGHT AND BELLADONNA

HEARTBEATS AND ROSES

SNOWFLAKES AND HOLLY

THANK YOU
Happy Reading!

ETSY SHOP

A dash of moon magic. A pinch of tree laughter. Stories whispered on the wind.

Hello Etsy wayfarers! Welcome to my bookish shop. When not slouched behind a computer, cursing the keyboard gods, you can find me frolicking through the woods with a camera around my neck or on the Comic Con circuit as MoonTree Books. Have fun poking around at my wares.

BOOKISH WARES FOR SALE

- Signed Paperbacks
- Limited Edition hardbacks
- Book Swag
- Book Boxes
- Custom Character Candles

Scan the QR code to visit my store.

Have questions? Message me on Etsy and we'll figure out your next fantasy adventure together.

JESIKAH SUNDIN is a multi-award winning Dystopian Punk Lit, Fairy Tale, and Historical Fantasy writer, a mom of three nerdlets, a faeriecore and elfpunk geek, tree hugger, nature photographer, and a helpless romantic who married her insta-love high school sweetheart. In addition to her family, she shares her home in Seattle, Washington with a rambunctious husky-chi, a red-footed tortoise, and a collection of Doc Martens boots. She is addicted to coffee, GIFs, memes, potatoes, cheese, mossy forests, eyeliner on men, and artsy indie alt rock.

www.jesikahsundin.com

Milton Keynes UK
Ingram Content Group UK Ltd.
UKHW020610050324
438776UK00006B/813